THE
PUSHCART PRIZE, V:
BEST OF THE
SMALL PRESSES

1980-81 *Edition*

✹ ✹ ✹ THE PUSHCART PRIZE, V:

An annual small press reader. Founding Editors Anaïs Nin (1903–1977), Buckminster Fuller, Charles Newman, Daniel Halpern, Gordon Lish, Harry Smith, H. L. Van Brunt, Hugh Fox, Ishmael Reed, Joyce Carol Oates, Len Fulton, Leonard Randolph, Leslie Fiedler, Nona Balakian, Paul Bowles, Paul Engle, Ralph Ellison, Reynolds Price, Rhoda Schwartz, Richard Morris, Ted Wilentz, Tom Montag, William Phillips. Assembled with the assistance of 136 staff and Special Contributing Editors for this edition, and with the cooperation of the many outstanding small presses whose names follow . . .

BEST OF THE SMALL PRESSES

BEST OF THE SMALL PRESSES

...WITH AN INDEX TO THE FIRST FIVE VOLUMES

EDITED BY BILL HENDERSON

published by THE PUSHCART PRESS
1980–81 Edition

THE PUSHCART PRIZE, V: 🔥 🔥 🔥

Library of Congress Card Number: 76-58675
ISBN: 0-916366-10-3
ISSN: 0149-7863

First printing, April, 1980

Manufactured in The United States of America
by RAY FREIMAN and COMPANY, Stamford, Connecticut

ACKNOWLEDGEMENTS

The following works are reprinted by permission of the publishers and authors:

"A Suitcase Strapped With A Rope" © 1979 *Durak: An International Magazine of Poetry*
"Trinc: Praises II" © 1979 *The Ark*
"Stones" © 1979 The Washington Writers Publishing House, reprinted from *The Poet Upstairs*
"Story" © 1979 *The Ohio Review*
"Heart of the Garfish" © 1979 *The Iowa Review*
"Blue Wine" © 1979 *The Kenyon Review*
"Levitation" © 1979 *The Partisan Review*
"Two Lives" © 1979 *The Kansas Quarterly*
"Jean Rhys: A Remembrance" © 1979 *The Paris Review*
"Column Beda" © 1979 Inwood Press
"Amsterdam Street Scene, 1972" © 1979 *Open Places*
"Melancholy Divorcée" © 1979 The Modern Poetry Association, reprinted by permission of the Editor of *Poetry*
"Faith" © 1979 *Virginia Quarterly Review*
"Pretend Dinners" © 1979 *Crazy Horse*
"Showdown" © 1979 *Shenandoah: The Washington and Lee University Review*
"Some Food We Could Not Eat: Gift Exchange and The Imagination" © 1979 *The Kenyon Review*
"Young Women At Chartres" © 1979 *The Georgia Review* and James Wright
"The Tortoise" © 1979 Canto Inc.
"Wrapped Minds" © 1979 *The Chouteau Review*
"Idolatry" © 1979 *American Poetry Review*
"Portrait of the Artist With Li Po" © 1979 *Durak: An International Magazine of Poetry*
"The Cold in Middle Latitudes" © 1979 *The Black Warrior Review*
"The Literature of Awe" © 1979 The Antioch Review Inc.
"Codex White Blizzard © 1979 *Montemora*
"The Carribbean Writer and Exile" © 1979 *Caliban: A Journal of New World Thought and Writing*
"Eiron *Eyes*" © 1979 *Parnassus: Poetry In Review*
"On The Big Wind" © 1979 *New Letters* (University of Missouri-Kansas City), edited by David Ray
"Tranquillity Base" © 1979 *Fiction International*
"Institutional Control of Interpretation" © 1979 *Salmagundi*
"from The Death of Love: A Satanic Essay In Möbius Form" © 1979 *The Georgia Review*
"Wish Book" © 1979 *Chicago Review*
"For Johannes Bobrowski" © 1979 *Chicago Review*
"Breath" © 1979 *Aspen Anthology*
"Of Living Belfry and Rampart: On American Literary Magazines Since 1950 © 1979 *TriQuarterly*
"The Girl Who Loved Horses" © 1979 *The Ontario Review*
"I Was Taught Three" © 1979 Ploughshares Inc.
"The Shark and The Bureaucrat" © 1979 Cross-Cultural Communications
"The Air Between Two Deserts" © 1979 *Cincinnati Poetry Review*
"I Remember Gallileo" © 1979 The Modern Poetry Association, reprinted by permission of the Editor of *Poetry*
"The Pears" © 1979 L'Epervier Press
selections by Andrei Codrescu and Marvin Bell from *The Poets' Encyclopedia* © 1979 Unmuzzled Ox Foundation Ltd.
"By The Pool" © 1979 *The Paris Review*
"The Infinite Passion of Expectation" © 1979 Ploughshare Inc.
"Giant Steps" © 1979 *Chicago Review*
"Temple Near Quang Tri, Not on The Map" © 1979 Bruce Weigl and *New England Review*
"Scenes from the Homefront" © 1979 Sara Vogan and *Antaeus*
"The Students of Snow" © 1979 *Chowder Review*
"Sweet Talk" © 1979 Stephanie Vaughn and *Antaeus*
"Farming" © 1979 Joseph Bruchac from *The Good Message of Handsome Lake* (Unicorn Press)
"Out And Down Pattern" © Holy Cow ! Press and *The Spirit That Moves Us*
"My Vegetable Love" © 1979 *The Paris Review*
"How St. Peter Got Bald" © 1979 *St Andrews Review*
"Josefka Kankovska" © 1979 13th Moon, Inc.
"Whisper Song" © 1979 *The Montana Review*
"One Spring" © 1979 *THIS*
"Mennonite Farm Wife" © 1979 *Mississippi Review*
"Marathon of Marmalade" © 1979 George Hitchcock and *Linguis*
"Song: So Often, So Long I Have Thought" © 1979 *The Oconee Review*
"The Chicago Odyssey" © 1979 *Shantih*
"The Only Poem © 1979 Robert Penn Warren and *American Poetry Review*
"The Otter" © 1976. 1979 Seamus Heaney, reprinted by permission of Farrar, Straus and Giroux, Faber and Faber Ltd.
     and *Antaeus*. Originally appeared in *Field Work*.
"Michael At Sixteen Months" © 1979 *Y'Bird* and Al Young

This Book Is For
Sam Vaughan

🔥 🔥 🔥

INTRODUCTION:

About Pushcart Prize V

IN FIVE YEARS I have seen about 20,000 nominations for this series. Never has the quality, the variety or the inspiration of the nominations surpassed those for *Pushcart Prize V*.

As we assembled this volume from work published in independent literary presses last year, the praises for those presses continued to arrive from grateful readers.

For the first time in the thirty-seven year history of *Publishers Weekly's* Carey-Thomas Award it was presented exclusively to a small press project—The Pushcart Prize—and symbolically to every press that has supported this series.

Also, as this vast, geographically scattered and diverse group of authors and editors contributed to our fifth anniversary volume, *The New York Times Book Review* named *Pushcart Prize IV* one of the "Outstanding Books of the Year." This was the fourth year in a row that this series has received that honor.

The Books Across the Sea Program of The English Speaking Union selected *Pushcart Prize IV* as one of the dozen most important titles of the year and dubbed it an "Ambassador Book."

Finally, perhaps the most startling tribute to small presses of all, from Founding Editor Paul Engle and Peking's Chinese Writers Association word arrived as we went to press that all five Pushcart Prize volumes are to be considered for translation and distribution in The People's Republic of China, where freer literary expression is being reestablished. More on this in next year's introduction.

In *Pushcart Prize V* we are proud to include seventeen fictions, thirty-three poems, and twelve non-fiction works from fifty presses, plus hundreds more titles in the "Outstanding Writers" section. Also, this edition contains an Index to the 337 selections from 325 writers and 197 presses in the first five collections.

As usual almost all of the writers in PPV are new to the series, and most of the presses appear here for the first time in the series. We welcome *Antioch Review, The Ark, Aspen Anthology, Beloit Poetry Review, Black Warrior Review, Caliban, Canto, Cincinnati Poetry Review, Chowder Review,* Copper Canyon Press, *Crazy Horse,* Cross Cultural Communications, *Durak: An International Magazine of Poetry,* Holy Cow!, Inwood Press, L'Epervier Press, *Linguis, Montana Review, Montemora, Mississippi Review, New England Review, Oconee Review, Shantih, The Spirit That Moves Us, 13th Moon, THIS, Unmuzzled Ox,* and Washington Writers Workshop.

To single out any particular story, essay or poem is practically impossible in such quality. But a few notes might be appropriate. Gerard Shyne, author of "Column Beda" (Inwood Press) is perhaps the most original black voice to arrive in years. His bio blurb on the back of the Inwood Press book says: "Served in Engineers during WWII, North Africa and Italy. Attended Columbia School of General Studies on G.I. Bill. B.A. in English . . . Custodian at Post Office for 25 years. Now a widower. Three children. Writes sitting up in bed with a pad and pencil. Also likes to write in Central Park after he leaves work in the morning (works night shift)—pencil and pad there too."

The Lamport Foundation Award for an outstanding work in our annual volumes goes to David Plante's essay "Jean Rhys: A Remembrance" *(Paris Review),* Seamus Heaney's poem, "The Otter" *(Antaeus),* and Cynthia Ozick's story, "Levitation" *(Partisan Review).*

Other than these notes I won't attempt further description of this varied volume. *Pushcart Prize V* is our anniversary present to all the reviewers who have given their critical attention to this series; to Walter Meade, publisher of Avon Books, and to the entire staff at Avon who have made this a popular trade paperback (and the most widely distributed annual literary anthology by far); to Poetry Editors Jon Galassi and Grace Schulman; to the Special

Contributing Editors and Staff Editors; to our Founding Editors; and to the thousands of small press editors and authors who think and care about literature.

Happy fifth anniversary Pushcart Prize to all of you.

And to you too, honored reader.

Bill Henderson

Note: nominations for this series are invited from any small, independent, literary book press or magazine in the world. Up to six nominations—tear sheets or copies selected from work published in that calendar year—are accepted by our October 15 deadline each year. Write to Pushcart Press, P.O. Box 845, Yonkers NY 10701 if you need more information.

THE

PEOPLE WHO HELPED

FOUNDING EDITORS—*Anaïs Nin (1903–1977), Buckminster Fuller, Charles Newman, Daniel Halpern, Gordon Lish, Harry Smith, Hugh Fox, Ishmael Reed, Joyce Carol Oates, Len Fulton, Leonard Randolph, Leslie Fiedler, Nona Balakian, Paul Bowles, Paul Engle, Ralph Ellison, Reynolds Price, Rhoda Schwartz, Richard Morris, Ted Wilentz, Tom Montag, William Phillips. Poetry editor: H.L. Van Brunt.*

EDITORS—*Walter Abish, Elliott Anderson, John Ashbery, Robert Boyers, Harold Brodkey, Wesley Brown, Hayden Carruth, Raymond Carver, Malcolm Cowley, Paula Deitz, Steve Dixon, Mort Elevitch, Loris Essary, Raymond Federman, Ellen Ferber, Carolyn Forché, Stuart Friebert, Tess Gallagher, Louis Gallo, John Gardner, George Garrett, David Godine, Barbara Grossman, Harold Hayes, DeWitt Henry, J.R. Humphreys, John Irving, June Jordan, Karen Kennerly, Mary Kinzie, Jerzy Kosinski, Richard Kostelanetz, Seymour Krim, Maxine Kumin, Seymour Lawrence, Naomi Lazard, Herb Leibowitz, Stanley Lindberg, Mary MacArthur, Frederick Morgan, Howard Moss, Cynthia Ozick, George Plimpton, Eugene Redmond, Teo Savory, Harvey Shapiro, Bill and Pat Strachan, Ron Sukenick, Anne Tyler, Sam Vaughan, David Wilk, Yvonne, Bill Zavatsky, Max Zimmer*

SPECIAL CONTRIBUTING EDITORS FOR THIS EDITION—
Kristine Batey, Robert Bringhurst, Lorna Dee Cervantes, Thadious Davis, R.C. Day, Susan Strayer Deal, Vine Deloria Jr., M.R. Doty, Daniel Mark Epstein, Ellen Gilchrist, Gerald Graff,

James B. Hall, Michael Harper, Brenda Hillman, Judith Hoover, Shirley Kaufman, Margaret Kent, Carolyn Kizer, Stanley Kunitz, James Laughlin, Barbara Lefcowitz, Larry Levis, John Love, Barbara Lovell, Cleopatra Mathis, Paul Metcalf, Charles Molesworth, Barbara Myerhoff, Susan Schaefer Neville, Mary Oliver, Alicia Ostriker, Lon Otto, Jayne Anne Phillips, Robert Phillips, Stanley Plumly, Joe Ashby Porter, Manuel Puig, Gary Reilly, William Rueckert, Margaret Ryan, Max Schott, Christine Schutt, Constance Sharp, Ron Silliman, Jane Smiley, Dave Smith, Gjertrud S. Smyth, William Stafford, David St. John, Shirley Ann Taggart, John Updike, Mona Van Duyn, George Venn, Jeff Weinstein, Dallas Wiebe, John Willson

DESIGN AND PRODUCTION—*Ray Freiman*

EUROPEAN EDITORS—*Kirby and Liz Williams, Gene D. Chipps*

AUSTRALIAN EDITORS—*Tom and Wendy Whitton*

JACKET DESIGN—*Barbara Lish*

POETRY EDITORS FOR THIS EDITION—*Jon Galassi and Grace Schulman*

EDITOR AND PUBLISHER—*Bill Henderson*

🔥 🔥 🔥

PRESSES FEATURED IN THE FIRST FIVE *PUSHCART PRIZE* EDITIONS

Agni Review
Ahsahta Press
Ailanthus Press
Alcheringa/Ethnopoetics
Alice James Books
American Literature
American Pen
American Poetry Review
Amnesty International
Anaesthesia Review
Antaeus
Antioch Review
Apalachee Quarterly
Aphra
The Ark
Assembling
Aspen Leaves
Aspen Poetry Anthology
Barlenmir House
Beliot Poetry Review
Bilingual Review
Bits Press

Black American Literature Forum
Black Rooster
Black Sparrow
Black Warrior Review
Blue Cloud Quarterly
Blue Wind Press
Boxspring
Caliban
California Quarterly
Canto
Capra Press
Cedar Rock
Center
Chariton Review
Chicago Review
Chouteau Review
Chowder Review
Cimarron Review
Cincinnati Poetry Review
City Lights Books
Clown War
CoEvolution Quarterly
Cold Mountain Press
Columbia: A Magazine of Poetry and Prose
Confluence Press
Confrontation
Copper Canyon Press
Cosmic Information Agency
Crazy Horse
Cross Cultural Communication
Cross Currents
Curbstone Press
Dacotah Territory
Decatur House
December
Dryad Press
Duck Down Press
Durak
East River Anthology
Fiction

Fiction Collective
Fiction International
Field
Firelands Arts Review
Five Trees Press
Gallimaufry
Georgia Review
Ghost Dance
Goddard Journal
The Godine Press
Graham House Press
Graywolf Press
Greensboro Review
Greenfield Review
Hard Pressed
Hills
Holmgangers Press
Holy Cow!
Hudson Review
Icarus
Indiana Writes
Inwood Press
Intermedia
Intro
Invisible City
Iowa Review
The Kanchenjunga Press
Kansas Quarterly
Kayak
Kenyon Review
Latitudes Press
L'Epervier Press
Liberation
Linquis
The Little Magazine
Living Hand Press
Living Poets Press
Lowlands Review
Lucille
Lynx House Press

Manroot
Magic Circle Press
Malahat Review
Massachusetts Review
Milk Quarterly
Montana Gothic
Montana Review
Missouri Review
Mississippi Review
Montemora
Mulch Press
Nada Press
New America
New England Review
New Letters
North American Review
North Atlantic Books
Northwest Review
Obsidian
Oconee Review
Ohio Review
Ontario Review
Open Places
Oyez Press
Painted Bride Quarterly
Paris Review
Parnassus: Poetry In Review
Partisan Review
Penca Books
Penumbra Press
Pentagram
Persea: An International Review
Pequod
Pitcairn Press
Ploughshares
Poetry
Poetry Northwest
Poetry Now
Prairie Schooner
Prescott Street Press

Promise of Learnings
Quarry West
Quarterly West
Raincrow Press
Red Cedar Review
Red Clay Books
Red Earth Press
Release Press
Russian *Samizdat*
Salmagundi
San Marcos Press
Seamark Press
Second Coming Press
The Seventies Press
Shantih
Shenandoah
A Shout In The Street
Sibyl-Child Press
Small Moon
The Smith
The Spirit That Moves Us
Southern Poetry Review
Some
Southern Review
Spectrum
St. Andrews Press
Story Quarterly
Sun&Moon
Sun Press
Sunstone
Telephone Books
Texas Slough
THIS
13th Moon
Transatlantic Review
Three Rivers Press
Thorp Springs Press
Toothpaste Press
TriQuarterly
Truck Press

Tuumba Press
Undine
Unicorn Press
Unmuzzled Ox
Unspeakable Visions of the Individual
Vagabond
Virginia Quarterly
Washington Writers Workshop
Western Humanities Review
Westigan Review
Willmore City
Word-Smith
Xanadu
Yardbird Reader
Y'Bird

CONTENTS

INTRODUCTION: ABOUT PUSHCART PRIZE V   11

LEVITATION   29
     by Cynthia Ozick

JEAN RHYS: A REMEMBRANCE   43
     by David Plante

THE OTTER   84
     by Seamus Heaney

MELANCHOLY DIVORCÉE   86
     by Sherod Santos

I REMEMBER GALILEO   88
     by Gerald Stern

COLUMN BEDA   89
     by Gerard Shyne

INSTITUTIONAL CONTROL OF INTERPRETATION   107
     by Frank Kermode

WISH BOOK   124
     by Bo Ball

YOUNG WOMEN AT CHARTRES   136
     by James Wright

OF LIVING BELFRY AND RAMPART: ON AMERICAN
LITERARY MAGAZINES SINCE 1950   138
     by Michael Anania

MARATHON OF MARMALADE   154
    by George Hitchcock

MENNONITE FARM WIFE   155
    by Janet Kauffman

ONE SPRING   156
    by David Bromige

SOME FOOD WE COULD NOT EAT: GIFT EXCHANGE AND
THE IMAGINATION   165
    by Lewis Hyde

A SUITCASE STRAPPED WITH A ROPE   198
    by Charles Simic

TEMPLE NEAR QUANG TRI, NOT ON THE MAP   199
    by Bruce Weigl

SWEET TALK   201
    by Stephanie Vaughn

WRAPPED MINDS   212
    by David Perkins

HEART OF THE GARFISH   219
    by Kathy Callaway

BY THE POOL   221
    by Allen Grossman

BLUE WINE   222
    by John Hollander

TRANQUILLITY BASE   227
    by Asa Baber

THE LITERATURE OF AWE   244
    by David Bosworth

TRINC: PRAISES II   268
    by Thomas McGrath

FAITH   275
    by Ellen Wilbur

THE CARIBBEAN WRITER AND EXILE   287
    by Jan Carew

PORTRAIT OF THE ARTIST WITH LI PO   315
    by Charles Wright

I WAS TAUGHT THREE   316
    by Jorie Graham

AMSTERDAM STREET SCENE, 1972 318
    by Raphael Rudnik

THE GIRL WHO LOVED HORSES 320
    by Elizabeth Spencer

CODEX WHITE BLIZZARD 338
    by Ed Sanders

BREATH 342
    by Heather McHugh

GIANT STEPS 343
    by John Taggart

MICHAEL AT SIXTEEN MONTHS 346
    by Al Young

MY VEGETABLE LOVE 347
    by Barbara Grossman

THE SHARK AND THE BUREAUCRAT 356
    by Vlada Bulatovic-Vib

STONES 358
    by Michael Blumenthal

THE INFINITE PASSION OF EXPECTATION 360
    by Gina Berriault

HOW ST. PETER GOT BALD 368
    by Romulus Linney

THE CHICAGO ODYSSEY 374
    by Jim Barnes

THE TORTOISE 376
    by Irving Feldman

ON THE BIG WIND 377
    by David Madden

SONG: SO OFTEN, SO LONG I HAVE THOUGHT 397
    by Hayden Carruth

STORY 399
    by Patricia Zelver

JOSEFA KANKOVSKA 403
    by Barbara Watkins

from THE DEATH OF LOVE: A SATANIC ESSAY IN
MÖBIUS FORM 405
    by Richard Vine

IDOLATRY   422
    by Carol Muske

PRETEND DINNERS   424
    by W.P. Kinsella

selections from THE POETS' ENCYCLOPEDIA   432
    by Andrei Codrescu and Marvin Bell

THE PEARS   435
    by Pamela Stewart

SCENES FROM THE HOMEFRONT   437
    by Sara Vogan

FOR JOHANNES BOBROWSKI   456
    by Sandra McPherson

SHOWDOWN   458
    by Michael Brondoli

FARMING   499
    by Handsome Lake, transcribed by Joseph Bruchac

OUT-AND-DOWN PATTERN   501
    by William Kloefkorn

EIRON *EYES*   503
    by William Harmon

WHISPER SONG   523
    by David Wagoner

TWO LIVES   524
    by H.E. Francis

THE AIR BETWEEN TWO DESERTS   545
    by Marea Gordett

THE STUDENTS OF SNOW   546
    by Jane Flanders

THE ONLY POEM   548
    by Robert Penn Warren

THE COLD IN MIDDLE LATITUDES   550
    by John Engels

CONTRIBUTORS NOTES   555

OUTSTANDING WRITERS   561

OUTSTANDING SMALL PRESSES   571

INDEX TO THE FIRST FIVE PUSHCART PRIZE VOLUMES   591

THE
PUSHCART PRIZE, V:
BEST OF THE
SMALL PRESSES

1980-81 Edition

𝄞 𝄞 𝄞

LEVITATION

fiction by CYNTHIA OZICK

from PARTISAN REVIEW

nominated by PARTISAN REVIEW, *Nona Balakian, Robert Boyers, Gordon Lish and Joyce Carol Oates*

A PAIR OF NOVELISTS, husband and wife, gave a party. The husband was also an editor; he made his living at it. But really he was a novelist. His manner was powerless; he did not seem like an editor at all. He had a nice plain pale face, likable. His name was Feingold.

For love, and also because he had always known he did not want a Jewish wife, he married a minister's daughter. Lucy too had hoped to marry out of her tradition. (These words were hers. "Out of my tradition," she said. The idea fevered him.) At the age of twelve she felt herself to belong to the people of the Bible. ("A

Hebrew," she said. His heart lurched, joy rocked him.) One night
from the pulpit her father read a Psalm; all at once she saw how the
Psalmist meant *her*; then and there she became an Ancient Hebrew.

She had huge, intent, sliding eyes, disconcertingly luminous,
and copper hair, and a grave and timid way of saying honest things.

They were shy people, and rarely gave parties.

Each had published one novel. Hers was about domestic life; he
wrote about Jews.

All the roil about the State of the Novel had passed them by. In
the evening after the children had been put to bed, while the
portable dishwasher rattled out its smell of burning motor oil, they
sat down, she at her desk, he at his, and began to write. They wrote
not without puzzlements and travail; nevertheless as naturally as
birds. They were devoted to accuracy, psychological realism, and
earnest truthfulness; also to virtue, and even to wit. Neither one
was troubled by what had happened to the novel: all those declarations about the end of Character and Story. They were serene.
Sometimes, closing up their notebooks for the night, it seemed to
them that they were literary friends and lovers, like George Eliot
and George Henry Lewes.

In bed they would revel in quantity and murmur distrustingly of
theory. "Seven pages so far this week." "Nine-and-a-half, but I had
to throw out four. A wrong tack." "Because you're doing first
person. First person strangles. You can't get out of their skin." And
so on. The one principle they agreed on was the importance of
never writing about writers. Your protagonist always has to be
someone *real,* with real work-in-the-world—a bureaucrat, a
banker, an architect (ah, they envied Conrad his shipmasters!)—
otherwise you fall into solipsism, narcissism, tedium, lack of
appeal-to-the-common-reader; who knew what other perils.

This difficulty—seizing on a concrete subject—was mainly
Lucy's. Feingold's novel—the one he was writing now—was about
Menachem ben Zerach, survivor of a massacre of Jews in the town
of Estella in Spain in 1328. From morning to midnight he hid
under a pile of corpses, until a "compassionate knight" (this was the
language of the history Feingold relied on) plucked him out and
took him home to tend his wounds. Menachem was then twenty;
his father and mother and four younger brothers had been cut
down in the terror. Six thousand Jews died in a single day in

March. Feingold wrote well about how the mild winds carried the salty fragrance of fresh blood, together with the ashes of Jewish houses, into the faces of the marauders. It was nevertheless a triumphant story: at the end Menachem ben Zerach becomes a renowned scholar.

"If you're going to tell about how after he gets to be a scholar he just sits there and *writes*," Lucy protested, "then you're doing the Forbidden Thing." But Feingold said he meant to concentrate on the massacre, and especially on the life of the "compassionate knight." What had brought him to this compassion? What sort of education? What did he read? Feingold would invent a journal for the compassionate knight, and quote from it. Into this journal the compassionate knight would direct all his gifts, passions, and private opinions.

"Solipsism," Lucy said. "Your compassionate knight is only another writer. Narcissism. Tedium."

They talked often about the Forbidden Thing. After a while they began to call it the Forbidden City, because not only were they (but Lucy especially) tempted to write—solipsistically, narcissistically, tediously, and without common appeal—about writers, but, more narrowly yet, about writers in New York.

"The compassionate knight," Lucy said, "lived on the Upper West Side of Estella. He lived on the Riverside Drive, the West End Avenue, of Estella. He lived in Estella on Central Park West."

The Feingolds lived on Central Park West.

In her novel—the published one, not the one she was writing now—Lucy had described, in the first person, where they lived:

By now I have seen quite a few of those West Side apartments. They have mysterious layouts. Rooms with doors that go nowhere—turn the knob, open: a wall. Someone is snoring behind it, in another apartment. They have made two and three or even four and five flats out of these palaces. The toilet bowls have antique cracks that shimmer with moisture like old green rivers. Fluted columns and fireplaces. Artur Rubinstein once paid rent here. On a gilt piano he raced a sonata by Beethoven. The sounds went spinning like mercury. Brea-things all lettered now. Editors. Critics. Books, old, old books, heavy as centuries. Shelves built into the cold fire-place; Freud on the grate, Marx on the hearth, Melville, Hawthorne, Emerson. Oh God, the weight, the weight.

Lucy felt herself to be a stylist; Feingold did not. He believed in putting one sentence after another. In his publishing house he had no influence. He was nervous about his decisions. He rejected most manuscripts because he was afraid of mistakes; every mistake lost money. It was a small house panting after profits; Feingold told Lucy that the only books his firm respected belonged to the accountants. Now and then he tried to smuggle in a novel after his own taste, and then he would be brutal to the writer. He knocked the paragraphs about until they were as sparse as his own. "God knows what you would do to mine," Lucy said; "bald man, bald prose." The horizon of Feingold's head shone. She never showed him her work. But they understood they were lucky in each other. They pitied every writer who was not married to a writer. Lucy said: "At least we have the same premises."

Volumes of Jewish history ran up and down their walls; they belonged to Feingold. Lucy read only one book—it was *Emma*— over and over again. Feingold did not have a "philosophical" mind. What he liked was event. Lucy liked to speculate and ruminate. She was slightly more intelligent than Feingold. To strangers he seemed very mild. Lucy, when silent, was a tall copper statue.

They were both devoted to omniscience, but they were not acute enough to see what they meant by it. They thought of themselves as children with a puppet theater: they could make anything at all happen, speak all the lines, with gloved hands bring all the characters to shudders or leaps. They fancied themselves in love with what they called "imagination." It was not true. What they were addicted to was counterfeit pity, and this was because they were absorbed by power, and were powerless.

They lived on pity, and therefore on gossip: who had been childless for ten years, who had lost three successive jobs, who was in danger of being fired, which agent's prestige had fallen, who could not get his second novel published, who was *persona non grata* at this or that magazine, who was drinking seriously, who was a likely suicide, who was dreaming of divorce, who was secretly or flamboyantly sleeping with whom, who was being snubbed, who counted or did not count; and toward everyone in the least way victimized they appeared to feel the most immoderate tenderness. They were, besides, extremely "psychological": kind listeners, helpful, lifting hot palms they would gladly put to anyone's anguished temples. They were attracted to bitter lives.

About their own lives they had a joke: they were "secondary-level" people. Feingold had a secondary-level job with a secondary-level house. Lucy's own publisher was secondary-level; even the address was Second Avenue. The reviews of their books had been written by secondary-level reviewers. All their friends were secondary-level: not the presidents or partners of the respected firms, but copy editors and production assistants; not the glittering eagles of the intellectual organs, but the wearisome hacks of small Jewish journals; not the fiercely cold-hearted literary critics, but those wan and chattering daily reviewers of film. If they knew a playwright, he was off-off-Broadway in ambition and had not yet been produced. If they knew a painter, he lived in a loft and had exhibited only once, against a wire fence in the outdoor show at Washington Square in the spring. And this struck them as mean and unfair; they liked their friends, but other people—why not they?—were drawn into the deeper caverns of New York, among the lions.

New York! They risked their necks if they ventured out to Broadway for a loaf of bread after dark; muggers hid behind the seesaws in the playgrounds, junkies with knives hung upside down in the jungle gym. Every apartment a lit fortress; you admired the lamps and the locks, the triple locks on the caged-in windows, the double locks and the police rods on the doors, the lamps with timers set to make burglars think you were always at home. Footsteps in the corridor, the elevator's midnight grind; caution's muffled gasps. Their parents lived in Cleveland and St. Paul, and hardly ever dared to visit. All of this: grit and unsuitability (they might have owned a snowy lawn somewhere else); and no one said their names, no one had any curiosity about them, no one ever asked whether they were working on anything new. After half a year their books were remaindered for eighty-nine cents each. Anonymous mediocrities. They could not call themselves forgotten because they had never been noticed.

Lucy had a diagnosis: they were, both of them, sunk in a ghetto. Feingold persisted in his morbid investigations into Inquisitional autos-de-fé in this and that Iberian marketplace. She herself had supposed the inner life of a housebound woman—she cited *Emma*—to contain as much comedy as the cosmos. Jews and women! They were both beside the point. It was necessary to put aside pity; to look to the center; to abandon selflessness; to study power.

They drew up a list of luminaries. They invited Irving Howe,

Susan Sontag, Alfred Kazin, and Leslie Fiedler. They invited
Norman Podhoretz and Elizabeth Hardwick. They invited Philip
Roth and Joyce Carol Oates and Norman Mailer and William
Styron and Donald Barthelme and Jerzy Kosinski and Truman
Capote. None of these came; all of them had unlisted numbers, or
else machines that answered the telephone, or else were in Prague
or Paris or out of town. Nevertheless the apartment filled up. It
was a Saturday night in a chill November. Taxis whirled on patches
of sleet. On the inside of the apartment door a mound of rainboots
grew taller and taller. Two closets were packed tight with rain coats
and fur coats; a heap of coats smelling of skunk and lamb fell
tangled off a bed.

The party washed and turned like a sluggish tub; it lapped at all
the walls of all the rooms. Lucy wore a long skirt, violet-colored,
Feingold a lemon shirt and no tie. He looked paler than ever. The
apartment had a wide center hall, itself the breadth of a room; the
dining room opened off it to the left, the living room to the right.
The three party-rooms shone like a triptych: it was as if you could
fold them up and enclose everyone into darkness. The guests were
free-standing figures in the niches of a cathedral; or else dressed-up
cardboard dolls, with their drinks, and their costumes all meticul-
ously hung with sashes and draped collars and little capes, the
women's hair variously bound, the men's sprouting and spilling:
fashion stalked, Feingold moped. He took in how it all flashed,
manhattans and martinis, earrings and shoe-tips—he marveled,
but knew it was a falsehood, even a figment. The great world was
somewhere else. The conversation could fool you: how these
people talked! From the conversation itself—grains of it, carried
off, swallowed by new eddyings, swirl devouring swirl, every
moment a permutation in the tableau of those free-standing figures
or dolls, all of them afloat in a tub—from this or that hint or syllable
you could imagine the whole universe in the process of ultimate
comprehension. Human nature, the stars, history—the voices
drummed and strummed. Lucy swam by blank-eyed, pushing a
platter of mottled cheeses. Feingold seized her: "It's a waste!" She
gazed back. He said, "No one's here!" Mournfully she rocked a
stump of cheese; then he lost her.

He went into the living room: it was mainly empty, a few lumps
on the sofa. The lumps wore business suits. The dining room was
better. Something in formation: something around the big table:

coffee cups shimmering to the brim, cake cut onto plates (the mock-Victorian rosebud plates from Boots' drug store in London: the year before their first boy was born Lucy and Feingold saw the Brontës' moors; Coleridge's house in Highgate; Lamb House, Rye, where Edith Wharton had tea with Henry James; Bloomsbury; the Cambridge stairs Forster had lived at the top of)—it seemed about to become a regular visit, with points of view, opinions; a discussion. The voices began to stumble; Feingold liked that, it was nearly human. But then, serving round the forks and paper napkins, he noticed the awful vivacity of their falsetto phrases: actors, theater chatter, who was directing whom, what was opening where; he hated actors. Shrill puppets. Brainless. A double row of faces around the table; gurgles of fools.

The center hall—swept clean. No one there but Lucy, lingering.

"Theater in the dining room," he said. "Junk."

"Film. I heard film."

"Film too," he conceded. "Junk. It's mobbed in there."

"Because they've got the cake. They've got all the food. The living room's got nothing."

"My God," he said, like a man choking, "do you realize *no one came?*"

The living room had—had once had—potato chips. The chips were gone, the carrot sticks eaten, of the celery sticks nothing left but threads. One olive in a dish; Feingold chopped it in two with vicious teeth. The business suits had disappeared. "It's awfully early," Lucy said; "a lot of people had to leave." "It's a cocktail party, that's what happens," Feingold said. "It isn't *exactly* a cocktail party," Lucy said. They sat down on the carpet in front of the fireless grate. "Is that a real fireplace?" someone inquired. "We never light it," Lucy said. "Do you light those candlesticks ever?" "They belonged to Jimmy's grandmother," Lucy said, "we never light them."

She crossed no-man's-land to the dining room. They were serious in there now. The subject was Chaplin's gestures.

In the living room Feingold despaired; no one asked him, he began to tell about the compassionate knight. A problem of ego, he said: compassion being super-consciousness of one's own pride. Not that he believed this; he only thought it provocative to say something original, even if a little muddled. But no one responded. Feingold looked up. "Can't you light that fire?" said a man. "All right," Feingold said. He rolled a paper log made of last Sunday's *Times* and laid a match on it. A flame as clear as a streetlight whitened the faces of the sofa-sitters. He recognized a friend of his from the Seminary—he had what Lucy called "theological" friends—and then and there, really very suddenly, Feingold wanted to talk about God. Or, if not God, then certain historical atrocities, abominations: to wit, the crime of the French nobleman Draconet, a proud Crusader, who in the spring of the year 1247 arrested all the Jews of the province of Vienne, castrated the men, and tore off the breasts of the women; some he did not mutilate, and only cut in two. It interested Feingold that Magna Carta and the Jewish badge of shame were issued in the same year, and that less than a century afterward all the Jews were driven out of England, even families who had been settled there seven or eight generations. He had a soft spot for Pope Clement IV, who absolved the Jews from responsibility for the Black Death. "The plague takes the Jews themselves," the Pope said. Feingold knew innumerable stories about forced conversions, he felt at home with these thoughts, comfortable, the chairs seemed dense with family. He wondered whether it would be appropriate—at a cocktail party, after all!—to inquire after the status of the Seminary friend's agnosticism: was it merely that God had stepped out of history, left the room for a moment, so to speak, without a pass, or was there no Creator to begin with, nothing had been created, the world was a chimera, a solipsist's delusion?

Lucy was uneasy with the friend from the Seminary; he was the one who had administered her conversion, and every encounter was like a new stage in a perpetual examination. She was glad there was no Jewish catechism. Was she a backslider? Anyhow she felt tested. Sometimes she spoke of Jesus to the children. She looked around—her great eyes wheeled—and saw that everyone in the living room was a Jew.

There were Jews in the dining room too, but the unruffled, devil-may-care kind: the humorists, the painters, film reviewers who went off to studio showings of "Screw on Screen" on the eve of the Day of Atonement. Mostly there were Gentiles in the dining room. Nearly the whole cake was gone. She took the last piece, cubed it on a paper plate, and carried it back to the living room. She blamed Feingold, he was having one of his spasms of fanaticism. Everyone normal, everyone with sense—the humanists and humorists, for instance—would want to keep away. What was he now, after all, but one of those boring autodidacts who spew out everything they read? He was doing it for spite, because no one had come. There he was, telling about the blood-libel. Little Hugh of Lincoln. How in London, in 1279, Jews were torn to pieces by horses, on a charge of having crucified a Christian child. How in 1285, in Munich, a mob burned down a synagogue on the same pretext. At Eastertime in Mainz two years earlier. Three centuries of beatified child martyrs, some of them figments, all called "Little Saints." The Holy Niño of LaGuardia. Feingold was crazed by these tales, he drank them like a vampire. Lucy stuck a square of chocolate cake in his mouth to shut him up. Feingold was waiting for a voice. The friend from the Seminary, pragmatic, licked off his bit of cake hungrily. It was a cake sent from home, packed by his wife in a plastic bag, to make sure there was something to eat. It was a guaranteed nolard cake. They were all ravenous. The fire crumpled out in big paper cinders.

The friend from the Seminary had brought a friend. Lucy examined him: she knew how to give catechisms of her own, she was not a novelist for nothing. She catechized and catalogued: a refugee. Fingers like long wax candles, snuffed at the nails. Black sockets: was he blind? It was hard to tell where the eyes were under that ledge of skull. Skull for a head, but such a cushioned mouth, such lips, such orderly expressive teeth. Such a bone in such a dry wrist. A nose like a saint's. The face of Jesus. He whispered. Everyone leaned over to hear. He was Feingold's voice: the voice Feingold was waiting for.

"Come to modern times," the voice urged. "Come to yesterday." Lucy was right: she could tell a refugee in an instant, even before she heard any accent. They all reminded her of her father. She put away this insight (the resemblance of Presbyterian ministers to Hitler refugees) to talk over with Feingold later: it was nicely analytical, it had enough mystery to satisfy. "Yesterday," the refugee said, "the eyes of God were shut." And Lucy saw him shut his hidden eyes in their tunnels. "Shut," he said, "like iron doors"—a voice of such nobility that Lucy thought immediately of that eerie passage in Genesis where the voice of the Lord God walks in the Garden in the cool of the day and calls to Adam, "Where are you?"

They all listened with a terrible intensity. Again Lucy looked

around. It pained her how intense Jews could be, though she too
was intense. But she was intense because her brain was roiling with
ardor, she wooed mind-pictures, she was a novelist. *They* were
intense all the time; she supposed the grocers among them were as
intense as any novelist; was it because they had been Chosen, was
it because they pitied themselves every breathing moment?

Pity and shock stood in all their faces.

The refugee was telling a story. "I witnessed it," he said. "I am
the witness." Horror; sadism; corpses. As if—Lucy took the image
from the elusive wind that was his voice in its whisper—as if
hundreds and hundreds of Crucifixions were all happening at
once. She visualized a hillside with multitudes of crosses, and
bodies dropping down from big bloody nails. Every Jew was Jesus.
That was the only way Lucy could get hold of it: otherwise it was
only a movie. She had seen all the movies, the truth was she could
feel nothing. That same bulldozer shoveling those same sticks of
skeletons, that same little boy in a cap with twisted mouth and his
hands in the air—if there had been a camera at the Crucifixion
Christianity would collapse, no one would ever feel anything about
it. Cruelty came out of the imagination, and had to be witnessed by
the imagination.

All the same, she listened. What he told was exactly like the
movies. A gray scene, a scubby hill, a ravine. Germans in helmets,
with shining tar-black belts, wearing gloves. A ragged bundle of
Jews at the lip of the ravine—an old grandmother, a child or two, a
couple in their forties. All the faces stained with grayness, the
stubble of the ground stained gray, the clothes on them limp as
shrouds but immobile, as if they were already under the dirt, shut
off from breezes, as if they were already stone. The refugee's
whisper carved them like sculptures—there they stood, a shadowy
stone asterisk of Jews, you could see their nostrils, open as skulls,
the stony round ears of the children, the grandmother's awful twig
of a neck, the father and mother grasping the children but strangers to each other, not a touch between them, the grandmother
cast out, claiming no one and not claimed, all prayerless stone
gums. There they stood. For a long while the refugee's voice
pinched them and held them, so that you had to look. His voice
made Lucy look and look. He pierced the figures through with his
whisper. Then he let the shots come. The figures never teetered
never shook: the stoniness broke all at once and they fell cleanly,

like sacks, into the ravine. Immediately they were in a heap, with random limbs all tangled together. The refugee's voice like a camera brought a German boot to the edge of the ravine. The boot kicked sand. It kicked and kicked, the sand poured over the family of sacks.

Then Lucy saw the fingers of the listeners—all their fingers were stretched out.

The room began to lift. It ascended. It rose like an ark on waters. Lucy said inside her mind, "This chamber of Jews." It seemed to her that the room was levitating on the little grains of the refugee's whisper. She felt herself alone at the bottom, below the floorboards, while the room floated upward, carrying Jews. Why did it not take her too? Only Jesus could take her. They were being kidnapped, these Jews, by a messenger from the land of the dead. The man had a power. Already he was in the shadow of another tale: she promised herself she would not listen, only Jesus could make her listen. The room was ascending. Above her head it grew smaller and smaller, more and more remote, it fled deeper and deeper into upwardness.

She craned after it. Wouldn't it bump into the apartment upstairs? It was like watching the underside of an elevator, all dirty and hairy, with dust-roots wagging. The black floor moved higher and higher. It was getting free of her, into loftiness, lifting Jews.

The glory of their martyrdom.

Under the rising eave Lucy had an illumination: she saw herself with the children in a little city park. A Sunday afternoon early in May. Feingold has stayed home to nap, and Lucy and the children find seats on a bench and wait for the unusual music to begin. The room is still levitating, but inside Lucy's illumination the boys are chasing birds. They run away from Lucy, they return, they leave. They surround a pigeon. They do not touch the pigeon; Lucy has forbidden it. She has read that city pigeons carry meningitis. A little boy in Red Bank, New Jersey, contracted sleeping sickness from touching a pigeon; after six years, he is still asleep. In his sleep he has grown from a child to an adolescent; puberty has come on him in his sleep, his testicles have dropped down, a benign blond beard glints mildly on his cheeks. His parents weep and weep. He is still asleep. No instruments or players are visible. A woman steps out onto a platform. She is an anthropologist from the Smithsonian Institute in Washington, D.C. She explains that there

will be no "entertainment" in the usual sense; there will be no
"entertainers." The players will not be artists; they will be "real
peasants." They have been brought over from Messina, from
Calabria. They are shepherds, goatherds. They will sing and dance
and play just as they do when they come down from the hills to
while away the evenings in the taverns. They will play the instruments that scare away the wolves from the flock. They will sing the
songs that celebrate the Madonna of Love. A dozen men file onto
the platform. They have heavy faces that do not smile. They have
heavy dark skins, cratered and leathery. They have ears and noses
that look like dried twisted clay. They have gold teeth. They have no
teeth. Some are young; most are in their middle years. One is very
old; he wears bells on his fingers. One has an instrument like a
butter churn: he shoves a stick in and out of a hole in a wooden tub
held under his arm, and a rattling screech spurts out of it. One
blows on two slender pipes simultaneously. One has a long strap,
which he rubs. One has a frame of bicycle bells; a descendant of the
bells the priests used to beat in the temple of Minerva.

The anthropologist is still explaining everything. She explains
the "male" instrument: three wooden knockers; the innermost one
lunges up and down between the other two. The songs, she
explains, are mainly erotic. The dances are suggestive.

The unusual music commences. The park has filled with
Italians—greenhorns from Sicily, settled New Yorkers from
Naples. An ancient people. They clap. The old man with the bells
on his fingers points his dusty shoe-toes and slowly follows a circle
of his own. His eyes are in trance, he squats, he ascends. The
anthropologist explains that up-and-down dancing can also be
found in parts of Africa. The singers wail like Arabs; the anthropologist notes that the Arab conquest covered the south-
ernmost portion of the Italian boot for two hundred years. The
whole chorus of peasants sings in a dialect of archaic Greek; the
language has survived in the old songs, the anthropologist explains.
The crowd is laughing and stamping. They click their fingers and
sway. Lucy's boys are bored. They watch the man with the
finger-bells; they watch the wooden male pump up and down.
Everyone is clapping, stamping, clicking, swaying, thumping. The
wailing goes on and on, faster and faster. The singers are dancers,
the dancers are singers, they turn and turn, they are smiling the
drugged smiles of dervishes. At home they grow flowers. They

follow the sheep into the deep grass. They drink wine in the taverns at night. Calabria and Sicily in New York, sans wives, in sweat-blotched shirts and wrinkled dusty pants, gasping before strangers who have never smelled the sweetness of their village grasses!

Now the anthropologist from the Smithsonian has vanished out of Lucy's illumination. A pair of dancers seize each other. Leg winds over leg, belly into belly, each man hopping on a single free leg. Intertwined, they squat and rise, squat and rise. Old Hellenic syllables fly from them. They send out high elastic cries. They celebrate the Madonna, giver of fertility and fecundity. Lucy is glorified. She is exalted. She comprehends. Not that the musicians are peasants, not that their faces and feet and necks and wrists are blown grass and red earth. An enlightenment comes on her: she sees what is eternal: before the Madonna there was Venus; before Venus, Aphrodite; before Aphrodite, Astarte. Her womb is garden, lamb, and babe. She is the river and the waterfall. She causes grave men of business—goatherds are men of business—to cavort and to flash their gold teeth. She induces them to blow, beat, rub, shake and scrape objects so that music will drop out of them.

Inside Lucy's illumination the dancers are seething. They are writhing. For the sake of the goddess, for the sake of the womb of the goddess, they are turning into serpents. When they grow still they are earth. They are from always to always. Nature is their pulse. Lucy sees: she understands: the gods are God. How terrible to have given up Jesus, a man like these made of earth like these, with a pulse like these, God entering nature to become god! Jesus, no more miraculous than an ordinary goatherd; is a goatherd miracle? Is a leaf? A nut, a pit, a core, a seed, a stone? Everything is miracle! Lucy sees how she has abandoned nature, how she has lost true religion on account of the God of the Jews. The boys are on their bellies on the ground, digging it up with sticks. They dig and dig: little holes with mounds beside them. They fill them with peach pits, cherry pits, cantaloupe rinds. The Sicilians and Neapolitans pick up their baskets and purses and shopping bags and leave. The benches smell of eaten fruit, running juices, insect-mobbed. The stage is clean.

The living room has escaped altogether. It is very high and extremely small, no wider than the moon on Lucy's thumbnail. It is still sailing upward, and the voices of those on board are so faint that

Lucy almost loses them. But she knows which word it is they mainly use. How long can they go on about it? How long? A morbid cud-chewing. Death and death and death. The word is less a human word than an animal's cry; a crow's. Caw caw. It belongs to storms, floods, avalanches. Acts of God. "Holocaust," someone caws dimly from above; she knows it must be Feingold. He always says this word over and over and over. History is bad for him: how little it makes him seem! Lucy decides it is possible to become jaded by atrocity. She is bored by the shootings and the gas and the camps, she is not ashamed to admit this. They are as tiresome as prayer. Repetition diminishes conviction; she is thinking of her father leading the same hymns week after week. If you said the same prayer over and over again, wouldn't your brain turn out to be no better than a prayer wheel?

In the dining room all the springs were running down. It was stale in there, a failed party. They were drinking beer or Coke or whiskey-and-water and playing with the cake crumbs on the table-cloth. There was still some cheese left on a plate, and half a bowl of salted peanuts. "The impact of Romantic Individualism," one of the humanists objected. "At the Frick?" "I never saw that." "They certainly are deliberate, you have to say that for them." Lucy, leaning abandoned against the door, tried to tune in. The relief of hearing atheists. A jacket designer who worked in Feingold's art department came in carrying a coat. Feingold had invited her because she was newly divorced; she was afraid to live alone. She was afraid of being ambushed in her basement while doing laundry. "Where's Jimmy?" the jacket designer asked. "In the other room." "Say goodbye for me, will you?" "Goodbye," Lucy said. The humanists—Lucy saw how they were all compassionate knights—stood up. A puddle from an overturned saucer was leaking onto the floor. "Oh, I'll get that," Lucy told the knights, "don't think another thought about it."

Overhead Feingold and the refugee are riding the living room. Their words are specks. All the Jews are in the air.

JEAN RHYS:
A REMEMBRANCE

by DAVID PLANTE

from THE PARIS REVIEW

nominated by THE PARIS REVIEW *and Robert Phillips*

I ASKED AT RECEPTION for Mrs. Hamer. It always gave me pleasure to use her married name, not the name she was known by. She once told me some of the names she had used in her life to keep her life secret, and I forgot them. To refer to her as Mrs. Hamer, which was a private name, and not Jean Rhys, meant, I suppose, I was a part of her private world, the world she wanted to remain forever her world. I wondered why I should want to be a part of it. The receptionist, an old woman with lank hair, looked at the register. Behind her was a mirror and, on either side of the mirror, were white glass shells with lights inside. She said, "I don't think we have a Mrs. Hamer." I said, "Jean Rhys." "Yes," she said, "she's waiting in the pink lounge."

I was carrying a bottle of wine. The carpet of the pink lounge was patterned with large soft pink roses on a grey background. The wallpaper was pink. The floor lamps, lit, had great dark pink shades. Jean was sitting at the corner of a red sofa, under a lamp; she wore a wide-brimmed pink hat. Her head was lowered, her fist up to her chin, and she was staring at the floor, her blue eyes bulging a little. She did not look up as I approached.

I said, "Jean."

With a sudden jolt of her small, hunched body, as if I had frightened her, she dropped her hand and raised her head to look at me. "Oh David," she said, "I can't tell you how happy I am to see you."

I put the bottle of wine on the little table before the sofa and kissed her. "You're looking marvelous," I said.

"Don't lie to me," she said. "I'm dying."

I sat on the couch by her.

"Can I ask you something?" she said. "Will you go buy me a bottle of sweet vermouth? They don't have any in this hotel." She laughed, a small *ha*, that lifted her shoulders. "It's that kind of hotel." She looked about, as with sudden suspicion, and gave another small shrugging laugh. "A big dreary hotel in South Kensington filled with old people whom they won't allow to drink sweet vermouth."

On another red sofa across the room, and in big red armchairs, were old people, men and women, their canes held along side them or between their legs; none were talking, and some were asleep.

When I went out quickly to an off license it occurred to me the day was bright, and I was very aware, when I came back to the hotel, of the grey interior, and all the lights lit with dim bulbs. I ordered glasses and ice from a waiter with satin lapels and a crooked black bow tie.

As I poured out the drinks on a table before us, Jean sat back and crossed her legs; she had to grab one leg and heft it across the other, and, once crossed, you thought she could never uncross them. I gave her a drink and she smiled. As she drank she pulled at the brim of her hat.

This was December, 1975. I hadn't seen her in a year, since the last time she had been up to London for a few weeks.

"Now," she said, "give me your news. I hope it's cheerful."

I tried to make my news entertaining; she listened, drinking and pulling at her hat, her large blue eyes staring attentively at me. Sometimes she laughed.

"Now," she said, "I'll tell you my news."

She prepared herself by taking a drink.

"Well," she said, "I got a letter from the tax people. They said I hadn't paid my taxes. I got very upset. I thought I had. I'd sent everything off to my accountant, as he'd told me to. But a tax man came to the house and said I had to pay my taxes. I said I'd written to my accountant, but he said that didn't matter, I had to pay. I said I couldn't. He said, "I'm only here on orders." I said, "That's what the fascists used to say." He left angry. The next day I got a letter saying if I didn't pay my taxes they'd take my house away from me. I rang up my accountant. He said, "Oh, they're always threatening to do things like that." But I was worried. I was so worried, I fell. I've been dying ever since."

"I hate tax people," I said.

She bared her teeth. "Hate them," she said. "I know what they do. I know." She snorted. "Fascists!" Her drink splashed over her glass. "They take what I have and put it in their pockets." I wondered if she were joking, and I laughed; but her face twisted a little, and she bared her teeth again and said, "They've taken over the world." Then she looked at her drink. "Well, I'll be dead soon. They won't be able to get anything more from me." She drank.

I said, "The fact is I don't understand much about taxes and—"

She giggled. "Neither do I. I never did. I never understood anything that had to do with mathematics and machines, so I never understood more than half of what goes on in the world."

A thin young woman with black hair and dressed in black came into the pink lounge. She went to a window and drew closed the grey drapes over the net curtains, making the lounge dimmer. At her appearance, a number of old people, grabbing their canes for support, began to rise.

Jean said, "That's the manageress. When she appears, everyone rises."

"Why?"

"She doesn't exactly announce it, but they know that when she comes in lunch is being served.

I sat with Jean as the old people followed the manageress out of the lounge into the dining room.

She said, "All those old people, all alone."

I looked at them.

Jean said, "This is a horrible hotel."

"It is a bit grim."

"Well," she said, "we'd better go in. The manageress will be annoyed if we're late. Will you give me my stick?"

I gave her first her purse, then her silver-topped stick, which she used to steady herself as I helped her up with my hand under her arm. She was surprisingly heavy, and dropped back. I got her to her feet, held her arm, picked up the bottle of wine from the table, and supported her as we walked slowly to the dining room.

She said, "Let's pretend you're my son. That'll cheer me up."

A waiter opened the bottle of wine while Jean and I studied the menus. She was wearing her glasses, got from her purse; the lenses were so smeared I wondered how she saw through them. We both ordered curried eggs. She put the glasses back in her purse. The waiter poured out the wine.

There was a smell of mould in the dining room. My napkin was almost wet.

With one glass of wine Jean began to giggle as she talked. I could only get words, as she held her hands, sometimes her napkin, to her mouth while she talked. Whenever she giggled I smiled. Her hands were as if disjointed at the knuckles.

With more wine she ceased giggling. I still didn't understand most of what she said, which, spoken in a soft grave voice, seemed to me jumbled. She tugged more and more at her brim, pulled her hair, and rubbed her forehead, and I understood that what she was talking about was making her somewhat frantic. I heard: "The world . . . awful it is . . . gone *phut* . . . want out, that's all . . . taken over . . . not understanding, anyone . . ." she held out her glass to be refilled.

We had baked apples for pudding, but she left most of hers. She said, throwing her napkin down, "Thank God that's over. Now we can go up to my room for a drink."

Getting Jean up to her room was difficult. She leaned on me so heavily I at times lost balance. We lurched from piece of furniture to piece of furniture, wall to wall, she with her hand extended to lean for a moment before we continued. Sometimes her cane got caught between her legs. Getting her into the lift I had to twist my body, it seemed, in many directions at the same time. I could not imagine how she had got down to the lounge from her room. She leaned her small hunched back against the passage wall and sighed as I opened the door to her room with her key.

The room was all pink. There were two beds; a lamp, with a big pink shade, was on a table between the beds. Jean, in her pink hat, sat on a red armchair before a window with net curtains and red-brown drapes. She threw her cane down and closed her eyes; after a moment she opened her eyes wide, shook her head, and said, "Never mind."

"Never mind what?" I asked.

She laughed. "Let's have a drink," she said.

"What do you want?"

"Rum."

I went to the desk where the drinks, bottles and glasses were on a tray.

"The manageress won't let us have ice," she said.

"That's ridiculous. Of course we'll have ice." I rang.

She did not seem impressed or in any way proved wrong when the ice came; she might have thought the ice came because I was a man.

I said, "Jean, there's no rum here."

"No rum? Did you want rum?"

"No. You asked for it."

"Did I?" She passed her hand over her forehead. "That's strange, I must have thought I was in Dominica, where of course you'd have rum. But it's so long since I've been in Dominica. I'll have a gin and vermouth. And please don't put too much ice in. *They* fill the glass with ice so I won't drink too much. Well, why shouldn't I?"

I thought: yes, why shouldn't she? I gave her a big drink. I took a smaller one, lit a light in the dim room, and sat on a chair near hers.

"When were you last in Dominica?" I asked.

"Oh years and years ago, on a visit. But I left when I was sixteen to come to England, and the visit later made me see that I could never go back to the island I knew as a girl. It was beautiful. It *was* so beautiful. When I went back I found all the rivers—you know. there are 365 rivers on Dominica, one for every day of the year—all were polluted. I used to drink from them when I was a girl. Gone, all gone. And who's responsible? Who?" She crossed her legs. "I know, I know." She snorted a little. "Yeah. I know."

I didn't know, and I didn't know if I should ask her. I said, "Who?"

She stared at me. "You're liberal, aren't you? I'm surrounded by liberals. You don't understand what's happening. *They're* taking over. Yeah. I know. I used to be liberal. No more."

I said, "I thought you told me you were once a communist."

She laughed; her thin yellow teeth showed. "I was a G.K. Chesterton sort of socialist, a cow and an acre of land for every man, that kind of thing. No." She threw up a hand; the other held the glass. "Anyway, honey, I'll be dead before they take over."

I said, "We'll fight them together."

"Will we?"

She pulled her brim and leaned forward. She said, "I'm going to tell you something."

I smiled at her.

"I'm going to tell you how I started to write."

I kept my smile, a smile, I recognize now, I always kept when she told me something that interested me very much, but which I did not want her to think I had in any way solicited from her. Perhaps one of the reasons I was with her was to hear how she started to write; but the moment she was about to tell me, I wasn't sure I wanted to hear, or wasn't sure I wanted her to think I did.

"Do you want to hear?" she asked.

"Of course I do."

"Maybe," she said, "you'll write it down. I can't now. I can't write. It'll never be written. I'll tell you, and you write it down."

"All right."

"Give me another drink first, honey."

I put a lot of ice in the drink and very little gin in the vermouth.

She raised her glass to me. "Here's to you."

"Here's to you," I said and raised my glass.

"No, not me. I don't matter. I never did, much. I don't now."

"That's not true."

"It is. It is true. I don't matter, and I want out." She looked at her drink as she brought it to her mouth. She said, "You put a lot of ice in this."

"It'll melt," I said.

"That's what they all say," she said.

Startling me, she suddenly stuck out her thin neck and shouted, "Oh what a Goddam shitty business we've taken on, being writers! Oh what shit! What shit!" She shook her head, with its hat, whenever she said "shit," as if to shake the word out with physical disgust. I had never heard her use the word before. "I'm over eighty." She had never revealed her age before. "Look at me. And what have I done? Nothing! Nothing! Mediocrity. Mediocre, that's what my work is. And these stories they want me to publish. Not good. I don't want to publish them. I've wasted two and a half years on them. I wanted to write about my life. I wanted to write my autobiography, because everything they say about me is wrong. I want to tell the truth. I want to tell the truth, too, about Dominica. No, it's not true we treated the black people badly. We didn't, we didn't. Now they say we did. No, no. I'm becoming a fascist. They won't listen. No one listens."

"I'm listening," I said.

"Oh yes, you," she said, as though I *would* listen. "I remember a black man in Dominica walking through the yard. My father and I were on the back steps of the house. My father made me give loaves of French bread—Dominica was once French and the bread was still in long loaves—and six-pence to poor black men who came to us. No women ever came. I recall this black man walking away from us, the loaf under his arm, and his dignity. His dignity and his unconquerable mind. Do you believe it?"

I asked, "What's that Jean?" I was suddenly speaking, it seemed to me, from a great remoteness.

"You don't know?"

"No."

"Live and take comfort . . . thou has great allies; thy friends are exultations, agonies, and love, and man's unconquerable mind."

"I don't recognize it," I said.

"Fancy you don't know it. That's maybe because you're American. Americans are so stupid. They don't know anything, only their own literature, which isn't much. We're all friends, aren't we? You've got to forget about all past American writers. You've got to forget about Henry James. You've got to forget about America. Live and take comfort . . . thou has great allies; thy friends are exultations, agonies, and man's unconquerable mind—" She put her glass down, her hands to her face; when she took her hands away her face was wet and twisted with weeping. "—and man's unconquerable mind." She raised her hands. "Oh, to die like a tree falling. Oh, to be big, to be large, to be huge. That's what you have to be. To be big. There are no big people in the world now. You must be big." She picked up her drink, paused, then whispered in sing-song, "Oh England, my England, what can I do for you? No, that's wrong. What can I do for you, oh England, my England?" Her face tersed. She spat. "It's shit. It's shit, England." Her face became smooth, her eyes went out of focus. "And yet, and yet. Nelson, he was big. There were big people in England. He was like a Caesar. Kiss me, Hardy. He wasn't homosexual, I don't believe it. He was bisexual, as we all are. He was big, was great, was huge. He died for England. England? What can I do for you, oh England, my England? I came here when I was sixteen, to this cold dark country, where I was never warm." Her upper lip rose and she again spit. "Shit!" Immediately, her face relaxed again, became, it seemed, as soft and vague as her eyes. "And yet, I do know it has a certain gentleness, an honesty. Gone, all gone. In the West Country, there you can still find people who are like trees, and when they die they die like huge trees falling over. People close to the land. I'll never, never forget the dignity of that black man walking through the yard with his sixpence and the loaf of bread under his arm. And it's all gone, all gone. They've destroyed it themselves. Are there any men now like that black man? We didn't treat them badly, we didn't. They say we did. It's all gone, the dignity, and I want out. There are no big men left. It's all gone. I wanted to tell you how I started to write. I'm telling you. I'll never write it now that I'm telling you. Will you write it? If you don't, it doesn't matter. Nothing matters, nothing matters. It's all shit." She laughed. "I'm a slut without a penny." Her face twisted and she wept. "Nothing matters. Nothing." She laughed again, with a shrug of her body, and, in a very quiet voice, sang:

If you want to be happy,
Like a child with a toy balloon,
Turn your money over in your pocket
In the light of a full moon

She shook her head and drank. "Man's unconquerable mind. Fancy you don't know that. Upon this bank and shoal of time, I'll leap to time to come. Do you know that?"

I half frowned, half smiled. "Let me think—"

"You don't know. It's because you're American, and Americans are stupid. You should know. You should know it all. You should know all the big writers, the big big writers." She raised her hand. "You have to be big." She lowered her hand. "And yet, and yet, I'm so small. I'm nothing."

"Jean," I said, "please—" I did not know how to respond to her. When she laughed, I smiled; when she wept, I stared sadly at her. Sometimes, because her feelings changed so quickly, I stared when she laughed, and smiled when she wept.

She said, "Listen to me. I want to tell you something very important. All of writing is a huge lake. There are great rivers that feed the lake, like Tolstoy and Dostoyevsky. And there are trickles, like Jean Rhys. All that matters is feeding the lake. I don't matter. The lake matters. You must keep feeding the lake. It is very important. Nothing else is important."

Tears came to my eyes.

"Do you believe that?" she asked.

"Yes."

"But you now should be taking from the lake before you can think of feeding it. You must dip your bucket in very deep."

I blinked to rid my eyes of tears.

"Oh David, oh, what one could do, what one could do! Not I. I can't do anything. I don't matter. What matters is the lake. And man's unconquerable mind."

I reached out and held her wrist for a moment.

Jean's upper lip drew up as if she'd tasted something very sour, and she began to cry; the tears ran down her nose and cheeks, and when she wiped them away with the sides of her crooked hands, her make-up smeared. She looked at me, weeping and, I thought, pleading with me. I said, "I'll get you a tissue." I went into the bathroom and brought back a bit of toilet tissue for her. She put her drink down, wiped her eyes, blew her nose. She sat still.

Suddenly she shouted, "I hate. I hate. Do they understand? No. Does anyone understand? I hate. I hate them. We didn't treat them badly. We didn't. I hate them." She put her hand to her chin and looked down. "And yet I was kissed once by a Nigerian, in a cafe in Paris, and I understood, a little. I understand why they are attractive. It goes very deep. They dance, danced in the sunlight, and how I envied them."

She stopped, appeared to collapse inwardly, her drink resting on her crossed leg; then she seemed to suddenly rouse herself internally.

Again she shouted, "Oh David, I'm unhappy. You be happy. I'm so unhappy, all my life I've been so unhappy. It's unfair. I'm dying. I want to die. It's unfair. I'm dying, my body's dying, and inside I think: it's unfair, it's unfair, I've never lived, I've never lived."

She sank back and finished her drink.

"But I don't care any more. I'm not even interested in make-up any more. I'm going to give up on my life. I'm indifferent, even to passion. I'll wear red slacks, a shabby silk blouse, and a red wig.

"Give me another drink, will you, honey? And put only one cube in it."

I did. I took another for myself; but, attentive and in my attention frightened of Jean, I didn't get drunk.

She said, "I wanted to tell you how I started to write. I was living in Holborn. I hated it, the bed sitting room. A girl friend came. No, she wasn't a girl friend. We were in a movie together. I can't remember her name. She said, "Move to Chelsea. You'll have a good time in Chelsea. You'll get over him there." I moved, not to Chelsea, but to Fulham, into a room that was exactly like the one I left, I was going to my room one day and I saw in a shop window some quills, red and green and blue, and I thought, how pretty, I'll buy some quill pens to liven up my grim little room. I went into the shop. I didn't know why, but I bought a copy book, too, a thick copy book with shiny black covers and a red edge. I bought, too, nibs, a blotter, ink. When I got back to my room I put everything on a table. I swear, I swear I didn't know what I was about to do until the palms of my hands began to tingle and I knew, all at once, that I was going to write. I was going to write in the copy book everything that had happened to me, and I started then. I wrote for days.

"I filled out the copy book and I put it under my underclothes in the back of a drawer. When I went to Holland to marry Jean I packed it. I packed it, over and over, every time we moved, and we moved about a lot. Anyway—" She closed her eyes slowly, as if she were very tired.

I said, "Would you like to rest now, Jean?"

She opened her eyes, as if surprised. "Don't go now, honey. Stay. But maybe you want to go."

"No," I said, "I want to stay."

"How can you like listening to me talk on and on?"

I said, "I used to listen to my mother—"

The corner of her upper lip rose and her face took on the hardness of an old whore who, her eyes red with having wept for so long, suddenly decides to be hard. "Your mother?" she snapped. "I don't want to hear about your mother!"

I shut up. I thought: what am I doing here, listening to her? Is it because she is a writer? I am not sure I have read all her books, not even sure I admire her very greatly as a novelist. Is it because I want to know her well enough that I will know her better than anyone else, or know at least secrets she has kept from everyone else, which I will always keep to myself? If so, why?

She said, pulling the brim of her soft wide hat so it now hung unevenly about her head, "Jean and I lived in Paris. We lived in a hotel. We didn't have any money. I suggest to Jean that he write some articles and I would translate them. I remembered meeting Mrs. Adam in London, through Rebecca West. Mrs. Adam was the Paris correspondent for the *Daily Mirror*. I took the articles to her. She said she couldn't use them. Then, I suppose when she saw the desperation on my face, she asked me if I wrote anything. I said, at first, no. But, I don't know why, I remembered the copy book I had filled up with writing years before. I told her about it. She said she wanted to see it. I went home, I wrapped it in newspaper, and left it with her concierge, and I thought, well, that's the last of that. She got in touch with me. She asked me if she could type it out and alter it, and I said yes. I didn't know what she saw in it. She called it a *Triple Sec*. She asked me if she could send it to Ford Madox Ford. I didn't know who he was. She said, 'He runs a review, the *Transatlantic Review*, and he's very famous for spotting good young writers and helping them.' Well she sent it." Jean raised her arm and let her hand fall into her lap. "And that's how I got to know Ford."

With the mention of his name, I became more attentive, and more, I think, frightened. Here Jean was talking to me about this most private episode, the episode about which, she had said in her only references to it, so many people had told lies, lies, lies. It was as if she suddenly opened the door to the closed center of her life, a café in Paris in the twenties, and in the café were Jean and Ford and his wife Stella at one table, and at other tables were Hemingway, Gertrude Stein and Alice B. Toklas, and half-blind James

Joyce. I thought, staring at her: you are attentive to her, not as Mrs. Hamer, but Jean Rhys; you are not really interested in the private life of Mrs. Hamer, but very much in that of Jean Rhys. It is because she is a writer that you see her, sit with her, listen to her; your interest in her is literary. Her head was tilted and she was looking at me. You want to know her secrets because they have to do with Jean Rhys, the writer.

I said, "Jean, I think I should go."

She said, wistfully, her eyes large, "Do you, honey?"

"I should."

She smiled. Her eyes went out of focus. She said, "You've cheered me up."

"I'm glad."

"One more," I said.

"I promise I won't bore you."

"You don't bore me."

I gave her another drink. She reached for it with both hands. Her make-up had streaked down her face with her crying, and her hair, which she had been pulling at, stuck out stiffly under the warped brim. Her eyes and nose were red.

She said. "Tell me about yourself."

"I'd much rather hear about you."

"You would say that."

I laughed. I asked, "Quote me some more line of poetry."

She laughed, too. "You like that?"

"Yes."

She rubbed her forehead. ". . .man's unconquerable mind," she said.

"Because I'm an American and inveterately stupid," I said, "tell me who wrote that."

She frowned a little, as if it were an embarrassment to say something so obvious. "Wordsworth."

"Which bit?"

"To Toussaint l'Ouverture, the black man who governed St. Domingo and led the free slaves—"

"I see," I said.

When she drank, the drink spilled down the side of her chin onto her dress; she did not seem aware. It was as if she had to look all over the room to find me before she could stare at me and say, "I'll die soon." Her eyes narrowed on me. "I'll die without having lived." A sneer came over her face, and I had the uncomfortable feeling that she was sneering at me. She said, with the sneer, "Upon this blank and shoal of time, I'll leap to time to come." Her head wobbled. "Yes, yes, I'll leap. I want out." She leaned towards me. "You don't understand. You never understood. I want out. I never wanted to be a writer. Never. I couldn't help it. All I wanted was to be happy."

I put my glass down on the table between us. I said, "Jean, excuse me."

She slumped back.

I got up, went, moving carefully about the furniture, to the bathroom just off her room. I peed, washed my face. I looked at myself in the mirror above the wash basin. When I came out, I thought Jean had died: slumped, she was utterly motionless, her eyes wide open and blank. I stood over her, said, "Jean," and her body, it appeared, was shocked into attention to me; she looked up at me, and after a while, in a slurred voice, said, "I know, you've got to go." "I really have got to," I said.

"Before you go," she said, "help me to the toilet."

It took a lot of maneuvering to get her up and into the bathroom; I left her, her hat still on, holding to the wash basin. In her room, I walked about. There were vases of flowers on the bureau, with cards. I thought: she's been in there a long time. I heard: "Oh, my God!," and it occurred to me that she had seen her face in the mirror. I waited more, a longer while. I heard her say, "David, David." I went to the bathroom door, leaned close to it, and called, "Jean." there was no response. "Jean," I called. She said, in a weak voice, "Help me." I thought: but I can't go in. What does she want me for in there? "Help me," she said. I opened the door a little, imagining, perhaps, that if I opened it only a little only a little would have happened. I saw Jean, her head with the battered hat leaning far to the side, her feet, with knickers about her ankles, just off the floor, stuck in the toilet. I had, I immediately realized, forgotten to lower the seat after I had peed. Jean said, with a kind of moan, "Help me." Her eyes were huge. She was clasping her raised knees. I put my arms around her, and lifted her. I held her, but I was frightened to hold her too closely because she felt so frail, and I thought I might hurt her. Her body shook as she sobbed. The brim of her hat was under my chin; with one hand I took off her hat, put it on the washbasin, and, holding Jean, kissed her on her forehead. I held her till she stopped sobbing.

I said, "Shall I try to carry you to the bed or can you walk?"

"I'll try to walk," she said.

But she was hobbled by her knickers. I leaned her against a wall, bent down, asked her to lift one foot then the other, and took off her sopping knickers. We walked small step by small step to the bed. I turned her round so she could sit on the foot and she dropped backwards. She couldn't raise herself to lie full length. I drew her up by holding her under her arms and pulling slowly, but she was very heavy; the bedspread rucked under her. I finally got her full length. She was shivering. She said, "I'm so cold." I took a blanket from the second bed and covered her. She rolled her head back and forth against the pillow, and, weeping, said, "It doesn't matter. It doesn't matter. Nothing matters." Tears came from her nose as from her eyes; she tried to sniff them back. Her entire face, swollen and red, was wet. She wailed, "Nothing matters. Nothing matters."

I thought: what shall I do?

I said, "Jean, I must go out for a moment. I'll be back, I promise."

She didn't answer.

In the hotel lobby, my hand shaking, I rang the only person I knew of who could help, Sonia Orwell. She had first introduced me to Jean some years before. She had helped Jean by getting her to London, entertaining her, taking her to the doctor's and dentist's, doing her laundry and ironing, shopping for her, and seeing her every day. I said to Sonia, "She seems to be having an attack." She said she would come in fifteen minutes. I went back to Jean, who was still quitely moaning, "It doesn't matter."

Sonia came; she said severely, "For God's sake, David, don't you know when someone's drunk too much?"

She told me to leave Jean to her now.

The next morning I rang Sonia. I said, "I want Jean to know I wasn't embarrassed and I hope she wasn't."

Sonia laughed. She said, "I'm putting Jean in another hotel. Give her a day or two to recover, then visit her. But, please, remember to close the toilet seat next time."

She was staying now in a suite in a lovely small hotel off Portobello Road. The windows at the back gave out to a garden with big bare trees. Jean, wearing a long blue dressing gown, was sitting in a beautiful chair in the middle of the sitting room.

She said, "Now, David, if that ever happens to you with a lady again, don't get into a panic. You put the lady on her bed, cover her, put a glass of water and a sleeping pill on the bedside table, turn the light down very low, adjust your tie before you leave so you'll look smart, say at reception that the lady is resting, and when you tell the story after, make it funny."

I ordered glasses and ice. A young man with a long gold earring, white hair, and a suit that looked as though made of black plastic, came in with a tray; he placed the tray on a low table by Jean and kissed her, said, "Darling, blue has to be your favorite colour, it suits you so," and Jean, giggling, said, "I never wear green, that's an unlucky colour for me." The young man made the drinks for us.

Jean raised her glass to me and smiled; I raised mine to her.

She was, I realized, happy: she was wearing a pretty dressing gown in a pretty room. One of the signs of Jean's happiness, I came to realize, was her sadness, as though her happiness allowed her to deny the happiness, and be, at least a little, sad. When she was really unhappy, she was angry. She had been unhappy at the hotel in Kensington; however, instead of taking a practical step to change the hotel, even to asking for another to be found for her, she simply raged, as though nothing could be done and all she could do was rage. Now, in the hotel off Portobello, she smiled a little sadly when I told her she was looking beautiful.

She said, "Wouldn't what happened to us make a funny story? We should write it."

I was somewhat amazed that she should so quickly think of turning the episode of falling into the toilet bowl into a story: but I was excited, too. "Yes, let's," I said. Then an uncomfortable feeling came over me which I then didn't recognize, but which I now do: a feeling as of stealing manuscripts or letters from Jean, though she was allowing me to steal them, a feeling of some presumption, because *of course* I would be tempted to steal manuscripts and letters, *of course* I would want to write a short story with Jean. Again, I wondered if my deepest interest in her was as a writer I could take advantage of. I did not like this feeling. Though I

wanted to start writing the story immediately, I let it drop; I
wanted her to realize the idea came from her, not me, and it was up
to her to act on it. But, too, I wanted to let her know I was
interested; she very quickly imagined no one was interested at all.

She said, "What names shall we use for the old woman and the
young man?"

"I'll get some paper," I said.

"Yes, do."

I visited Jean often, and each time we worked a little on the
story. I wrote bits of it at home and read them out to her; she
corrected. The manuscript became very messy. One of Jean's
notes, dictated, was: "Cut down on her drink. Only two goes of
malt whiskey." Jean was responsible for most of the dialogue, I for
the descriptions. She gave the story its name: 'Shades of Pink'.
After a couple of weeks, as I became more interested in finishing
the story, Jean seemed to me to become less. She finally said, "You
keep it now and do what you want with it. It's a gift." At home, I
cut it down to a few pages, following the advice she said Ford had
given her: "When in doubt, cut." I put it in a bottom drawer.

Jean stayed on in the hotel over the winter. She was correcting
the proofs of a collection of short stories, *Sleep it Off, Lady*. She
once asked me to read out the story "Rapunzel, Rapunzel." She
asked me to cut a sentence, then said, "It's a bad story. They're all
bad stories. Mediocre. Worse than bad, What can I do? The
reviews, quite rightly, will be condemning. I shouldn't have
allowed them to be published. But it's done, they'll be published,
and maybe it won't matter. What I wanted to do was to write my
autobiography, but no one seems interested in that. I can't do it
myself. No one can help me."

From her letters, I knew that Jean could write with only great
difficulty, her words large and shaky. I had also seen her sign books
for visitors, holding the pen clutched between her thumb and
middle finger and jabbing at the paper.

I said, "Look, Jean, if it's a question of your needing someone to
write down what you want to dictate, I'd be happy to do that."

She looked at me; she appeared doubtful. "Would you?"

The uncomfortable feeling came over me. "Of course I would."

"You see," she said, "I just wanted to get down a few facts to
correct the lies that have been said. I want to do that before I die."

We started, I think, the next day, after lunch. She sat in a chair
with a big pillow behind her, and she had one drink to get her

going. She dictated a passage which, in connection with her fiction, followed on directly from *Voyage in the Dark;* the heroine of that novel, who lived in Langham Street, might have written the opening sentences of Jean's dictation; recalling her recovery from her "illegal operation": "After I got better, I stayed on in the flat in Langham Street. I didn't suffer from remorse or guilt. I didn't think at all like women are supposed to think, but I was very tired. My predominant feeling was one of intense relief. I was not at all unhappy. It was like a pause in my life, a very peaceful time. I didn't see him, but he sent me a big rose plant in a pot and a very beautiful kitten."

After a few pages of dictation, she fell back on the cushion and closed her eyes; she suddenly opened them, shook her head, and said, "Never mind. Let's have a drink now."

We sat drinking, and she, lounging back on her pillow, told me stories from her life. We were very easy with one another, and in the easy way she talked about her life, I talked about mine. We were spirited. But it was when we talked about writing that we got excited. Her excitement was in her eyes.

She said, "I think and think for a sentence, and every sentence I think for is wrong, I know it. Then, all at once, the illuminating sentence comes to me. Everything clicks into place."

What had happened to us in the bathroom was not more personal than our talk about writing; if we could talk about what had happened, we could talk about writing in the most open and vulnerable ways, which, perhaps, we would not want anyone else to hear.

I felt I could ask her anything. I said, "Do you ever think of the meaning of what you write?"

"No. No." She raised a hand. "You, see, I'm a pen. I'm nothing but a pen."

"And do you imagine yourself in someone's hand?"

Tears came to her eyes. "Of course. Of course. It's only then that I know I'm writing well. It's only then that I know my writing is true. Not really true, not as fact. But true as writing. That's why I know the Bible is true. I know it's a translation of a translation of a translation, thousands of years old, but the writing is true, it *reads* true. Oh to be able to write like that! But you can't do it. It's not up to you. You're picked up like a pen, and when you're used up you're thrown away, ruthlessly, and someone else is picked up. You can be sure of that: someone else will be picked up."

I went to Jean, week after week, three or four days a week. Sometimes she was too tired to dictate, having been out to lunch or to shop the day before. We talked. I half imagined she told me a lot about her life hoping I would write down what she had told me the past day, that I had been listening to Jean for the sake of writing down what she had said, I wrote down, not what she said, but my reactions; this, too, I felt was using my interest in, my love for Jean, to simply write.

I was reminded of Pascal: *"Curiosité n' est que vanité; on ne voyage sur la mer que pour en parler—"*

One grey day in late March, after she had dictated from previous visits a number of disconnected bits about her life, we tried to organize them chronologically. She found this very difficult, as she couldn't recall the sequence of events of so many years before. I had been careful not to interfere in what she dictated; I told her I was the one machine she could use. (She had never learned to type because she couldn't understand machines. She refused to speak into a tape recorder because it was an incomprehensible machine. It took me three visits to teach her how to open a compact she was given as a gift.) But, now I began to help her to sort out the months and years of her life: 1917, 1918, 1919. She often passed her hand over her face in her attempts to remember, and when she slumped back on her pillow, as if, suddenly, uninterested, I said, "Come on, Jean, when did you and your husband stay at Knoeck-sur-Mer and for how long?" She raised herself from the pillow and tried to concentrate. She said, "All I can remember is the sea, cold and green." "Try," I said. "1923, I think," she said, "and we stayed for two weeks. It was cheap. We bathed. We recovered." I stayed with her a long time, till long past her supper. As we got into the chronology, we were uncertain about the dates.

1913—Jean's sad Christmas

1914—Moved to Fulham, wrote "diary," moved back to Holborn, which was more familiar. Met a journalist, who took her to the Crabtree Club every night. The club was CLOSED FOR THE DURATION, as a sign on the door said, in August, 1914. Survived on money from "him."

1915—Worked in a canteen for soldiers

1916—

1917—Met Jean Lenglais, to whom she became engaged.

1918—Jean L. went to Holland. Jean was to follow after Armistice, but there were no boats to Holland.

1919—Early in year, Jean sent a letter to "him" to tell him she would no longer need his money, and went to Holland to marry Jean L. They stayed in the Hague briefly, which Jean didn't like, and in the autumn they went to Paris and lived in a hotel. Jean got a job teaching English to the children of a French Jewish family, the Richelots, who became helpful friends. A son was born and died.

1920—Early in year, Jean L., somehow in connection with the Inter Allied Commission, went to Vienna. After a few months, Jean went to Vienna to join him.

1921—Vienna. Jean L. had Japanese friends with whom he did business in exchanging money, shillings and yen. Lovely summer.

1922—Commission went to Budapest, Jean L. too. With a Japanese passport. Jean went to London. "They stopped me, they said, 'You don't look Japanese.' " She stayed at the Berkeley Hotel, where she discovered she was to have a child. She was happy. This was the only time she liked London. She returned to Budapest to join her husband, but found that "everything had gone wrong," and they had to run away. They got as far as Brussels. In May, a daughter was born. As soon as she was able, Jean left her daughter in a clinic and went to London to raise money "from the only person who, as usual, would give it." Her husband stayed in Brussels—or perhaps went to Amsterdam, where he always went when he didn't have a job, didn't know what to do. Jean met him at Ostende and they went to Knoeck-sur-Mer. Their daughter remained in the clinic; they had very little money, some of which they sent to the clinic to keep their daughter a while longer. Jean and her husband went to Paris. Jean suggested to her husband, who was, among other things, a journalist, that he write some articles in French, and she would translate them. She took them to Mrs. Adam, who worked on the *Daily Mirror*, and whom she knew from London. Mrs. Adam turned down the articles, but asked Jean if she herself wrote. "Well, you know the rest of this bit."

1923/24—Jean L. went to Amsterdam ("Can't recall why, maybe because his mysterious job took him there.") and Jean stayed with Mrs. Adam. She went to Brussels, all in one day, to take her daughter from the clinic ("She had grown and was heavy.") and returned to Mrs. Adam. When her husband came back to Paris, they all lived in a hotel near the Gare Montparnasse. Jean got back one day to find her husband gone. The landlady said, "He was arrested." The Richelots found a place for her daughter. Ford and Stella wrote to her to ask her to have dinner with them. They knew her husband had been arrested, and during dinner they asked her to stay with them.

Stella was patronizing; she gave Jean yellow lunch tickets for meals at a cheap restaurant, and when they were all in a taxi she made Jean sit on the *strapontain.* Ford was a liar, he lied about being in a terrible storm crossing the channel, but he didn't lie about his youth, which he talked about mostly. Ford and Stella were both snobs. Ford was a romantic snob; his great ambition was to be like an Englishman, but a certain kind of Englishman, strong and silent, and sometimes he succeeded. Stella was a down to earth, business-like snob, grimly determined to get on. She found out about people in Montparnasse. All the time Jean knew her, she never knew her to read. She said she detested books and got all her pleasure visually from pictures. She was quite a good painter. Ford knew such a lot and took such a lot of care over Jean's writing. He was kind. He took her to the Cluny museum to see the tapestries, and took her to meet people: Hemingway, and Gertrude Stein (Jean talked with Alice), and once, going to a party, they shared the lift with James Joyce, who stood behind Jean and told her the back of her dress was undone, and he tried to hook it up. (But Jean is not interested in putting these names in her autobiography.) Ford, reading aloud from her writing, would exclaim, *"Cliché! Cliché!"* If he liked what he read, he put on a special solemn voice. He read in the presence of Stella, the three of them together. He got Jonathan Cape to publish her first book of stories, *Left Bank*, in 1927.

Ford found Jean a job in the South of France. He knew an American woman, a Mrs. H——, who believed she was, among other reincarnations, the reincarnation of Madame du Barry. She believed that if you could remember the civilizations you had lived in and dressed and furnished your house according to your recollections this would make you happy. Mrs. H——'s former selves came from different periods of civilization: Egypt, Persia, Gothic, Directoire, English 18th, French 18th. Greece and Rome were skipped. She needed a ghost writer to help her with her work: she wanted to write a book about decorating. Ford sent her an article on English 18th Century furniture and a fairy story called "The Tale of Dusham, a Serbian Tale," which he had written but said Jean had written. Mrs. H——engaged Jean.

1925—Jean went to Juan les Pins, rather glad to get away from the Fords. The H——s, wife and husband, lived in the Chateau Juan les Pins, which had been built by a Russian before the revolution who shot himself after gambling his fortune away. Jean found a flat, thought of staying and having her daughter come down. Mrs. H—— said she knew several people who wanted books ghosted. Mrs. H—— wore a simple black dress outside the house (she disapproved of short skirts) and in the house wore long gowns. She had one that was pink with long sleeves and green lining which you saw when she raised an arm. She disapproved of Mr. H——'s gambling, and gave him only a certain amount. Jean went out once with him to Monte Carlo to gamble, which she quite liked. Mr. H—— said that every night at the casino someone committed suicide, and they quickly put the body in the piano to hide it. He made scent. He had a little room with all the essential oils. He said you could only get the essential oils in France, not in England or America, where essential oils are heavily taxed and because of that scents made in America and England use artificial essential oils. He had a pile of linen handkerchiefs on his desk and a yellow rose. He put some scent on the handkerchief and had you smell the rose, then the scent, to compare. Once, on the way back from the casino, he tried to kiss her in the back seat of the car. The chauffeur must have seen, and said something. Jean took dictation from Mrs.

H——, who wanted to describe a room decorated in the Egyptian style. She said, "The piano must have an Egyptian sound." She left Jean to describe a banquet, and Jean thought there should be skulls on the table. They were, Mr. and Mrs. H——, really quite nice.

Then Ford sent a letter to Mrs. H——. It was rude. He accused Mrs. H—— of paying Jean less than a house maid in New York—" 'exploiting her shamelessly'—no, not shamelessly, that's not a Ford word—'exploiting her disgracefully.' " Mrs. H—— came to Jean with the letter, not smiling. She thought Jean had written to Ford. There was now no question of Jean's staying on. And as for Jean's work, Mrs. H—— said, "It's in long hand. I can't accept what you've done in long hand. It has to be typed before I pay you." Jean went to Nice and in a street near the Negresco found the office of an American newspaper, where a girl typed the pages for nothing. Mrs. H—— said she was going to Paris and Jean could travel with her. She was affable on the trip, and they dined together. In the Gare de Lyons, Ford met them, smiling, his hand out, and Mrs. H—— walked past with her porter wheeling the luggage, her head in the air, without speaking to Ford or saying goodbye to Jean. She was meeting her daughter, Natasha, who was the wife of Rudolf Valentino. But later Mrs. H—— visited Jean in her hotel with her peke. She said her daughter had asked, first thing, "Have you got any hooch?"

Ford found a room for Jean in the Hotel de la Rive, near the Gare Montparnasse. At drinks before lunch, Jean tried to get from him why he had sent the letter to Mrs. H——. He said, "She was exploiting you disgracefully, wasn't paying you as much as a house maid in New York." But he never really explained.

All of this Jean left out of the novel *Quartet* because it did not fit into the novel's shape.

Jean was disappointed. She was at loose ends. Ford seemed her only friend. She fell for him. She thought she fell for him. Stella was completely hostile.

Jean used a lot of the money she had made in the South of France to buy her daughter a pretty blue dress. Her husband had got out of prison, could stay in Paris only a few days before he had to leave for Amsterdam. Ford said Jean mustn't have anything to do with him. He himself couldn't have anything to do with him, as he was sure to come back and be arrested again. "I can't get mixed up in a thing like that," Ford said. But he and Stella said they did want to meet him, and Jean was taken by them to meet her husband at a café, La Taverne Panthéon. She went to stay with her husband for the few days he was allowed to remain in Paris. Ford and Stella were angry. Ford took Jean's going back to her husband as the end of everything. He couldn't have anything to do with her. When her husband left for Holland he took their daughter with him; she was wearing the expensive pretty blue dress.

Jean stayed in another hotel, depressing, in the rue Vavin, off the Boulevard Montparnasse. She collapsed, but, collapsed, nevertheless started *Quartet*.

Ford and Stella lent her money to return to the South of France. She stayed in l'Hotel les Oliviers, Crûs-de-Caigns. She met Paul Nash. Ford paid for the hotel.

Jean felt depressed, in a rage. She felt that all Ford had said about her writing, his concern for it, was false. That was what hurt most: she had imagined she had been a bit in love with Ford, but she wasn't, and she didn't think he was ever in love with her, but only in her writing, and he was, finally, false to that, because she couldn't believe he could behave as he had and still be sincere about her work.

Her husband sent her a letter in the South of France from Amsterdam saying he would return to Paris, though he had no passport. He knew he could stay there with someone without the police knowing. Jean went straight to Paris. And because she didn't know what else to do, didn't want to stay in Paris, hated Ford, she accepted her husband's offer to go to Amsterdam, though he was angry about what had happened between his wife and Ford, whom he hated, too. He never forgave Jean for Ford. They went almost immediately, and left their daughter in Paris at the place the Richelots had found there.

Ford got Jean a job translating *Perversité*, by Francis Carco. The slang was difficult, and her husband had to help. When the book was published, Ford was credited with being the translator. Ford said it was Covici, the Chicago publisher, who used his name instead of Jean's because it had more drawing power. Jean didn't care or think about it much at the time. The book was banned.

In Amsterdam, Jean finished *Quartet*. ("Now I am confusing the novel and what actually happened.")

Her husband went to Paris to take their daughter back to Holland. People had been wanting to adopt her. Jean refused, her husband had thought it a good thing.

When the novel was finished, Jean went to London to try to sell it, though she hated it. She was ill. Her husband persuaded her to go. Through Ford, Jean had an agent in London, Leslie————. He had written Ford asking him if Ford wanted an agent, and Ford had replied that he himself didn't, but he knew of a writer who could use an agent, Jean. Leslie ———— gave the book to Edward Garnett, a kind comfortable man, an influential publisher's reader. He said that Cape, who had published *Left Bank,* didn't want to publish *Quartet* because of libel, but Chatto would. They all had tea. Jean and Leslie had a fifty-fifty affair. The book was sold in America, from which Jean got enough money to go to Paris, alone.

Though Jean did not stay long in Paris, she wrote half of *After Leaving Mr. Mackenzie.* She returned to Leslie in London.

1937—By now, Jean's husband was very distant. When he found out about Leslie, he asked for a divorce. He asked, too, for possession of their daughter. He wrote Jean a nice letter: they couldn't go on as they were, he wanted their daughter to be educated in Holland, but she could visit on holidays. Jean agreed.

1938—Jean and Leslie eventually married. Jean wrote *Voyage in the Dark,* which was based on the original exercise books Ford had insisted she keep. "You'll want to use them."

Leslie died, and Jean married his cousin, Max Hamer, and started work on her last novel, *The Wide Sargasso Sea*—

Jean said, "I can't go on, David, I can't. This isn't the way I work." We never again attempted to make a chronology.

In November, Jean came back to London. She was put into a small flat in Chelsea, just across the Thames from where I lived in Battersea. She had a young woman help her with her baths and dressing, and her friends to prepare lunches and dinners, and to entertain her. She didn't like the flat. The walls of the sitting room were green. Bad luck. She was quite sure it was a mistake to have come up to London, but she so hated Devon in the winter; maybe, though, she would return to her cottage when she recovered a little from her trip.

She had, over the summer, dictated more of her autobiography to a young writer who lived near her in Devon, Michael Schowb. This more consisted of memories of her early life on the West Indian island of Dominica, where she was born. It would make up the first part of her autobiography. She asked if I would continue to help her if she stayed in London. I was writing myself, but I said, "Yes, of course."

Often, crossing Chelsea bridge on my way to her, I would think: You don't want to go to Jean's, you want to say home to do your own writing. Also, I had very little money, and thought I should use the time I was with Jean to do a translation job, or write blurbs or book reports for a publisher.

Helping her became difficult. She needed a drink to start, a drink to continue, and yet another, and after two hours she was muddled, couldn't remember what she'd been saying, and she'd repeat, over and over, that, say, Victorian knife sharpeners were terribly good, you just stuck the knife in and turned the handle and the knife came out sharp and clean, so you didn't have to clean them on wood, and they were much better than stainless steel knives—which showed that in many ways the Victorians were very clever, not what people think now. But people don't understand. No one understands. No one! I was never quite sure what she wanted to go into the autobiography and what she was simply talking drunkenly about. I put in everything I thought interesting by condensing it often to a sentence fragment to insert somewhere later: the Victorian knife sharpener her father brought from England so the help wouldn't have to sharpen the knives on wood. A flash of anger would sometimes pass through her eyes when I'd read a passage to her to make sure I'd got it right, and she'd say, "No, that's not right."

In a little black briefcase that opened into a file, she kept the many bits and pieces of the autobiography, plus earlier writing on yellowing, torn paper. I wanted to go through them and sort them out, but I couldn't presume; they seemed in the file to be very private. The time came in our work, however, to organize the autobiographical pieces. Versions of the same section, or detached paragraphs, confused her; she would ask me to read the different versions, she would choose what she thought the best, and then tell me to tear up the others. I tore up wastepaper baskets full. She seemed to get satisfaction from this, as if getting rid of something was a great clarification. (And, in fact, she told me that to her writing was a way of getting rid of something, something unpleasant especially. She asked me once to write down for her a short poem that was going round and round her head. "Two hells have I/Dark Devon and Grey London—/One purgatory: the past—" And after I wrote it down she said, "Thank God, now I can forget that.") After as much clarification by tearing up what could be done, there still remained a mass of bits. Jean often talked of the "shape" of her books: she imagined a shape, and everything that fit into the shape she put in, everything that didn't she left out, and she had left out a lot. She could not see the shape yet of the autobiography. Some chapters were together, some were in fragments, and she wasn't at all sure of the order of the chapters, much less the fragments in the chapters. We spent days trying, in our minds, trying to fit together pieces, which, to remember, we gave names. Jean would often say, "It can't be done. It's too jumbled." I might say, "Well, Jean, this bit about your mother, don't you think it should go into the Mother chapter?" She'd become enthusiastic. "Good. We'll do that."

One evening, as I was sitting with her while she ate her soup, I said, "Jean, why don't I do a paste-up of what's already been done of the autobiography?"

"A paste up?"

I tried to explain, but it was like trying to explain a computer system to her.

She said, "If you think so."

"I'll do it tonight. You'll see, it'll help us."

She said, "Please put it all in chronological order and cut out all the repetitions."

I took the entire autobiography with me. Crossing Chelsea Bridge, the feeling came over me, as it often comes over me to jump when I am at a height, to throw the folder into the river. In my small study, before the gas fire, I spread pages and parts of pages on the floor. I cut out paragraphs which Jean had wanted to save from what she wanted to throw out. I cut in half a section called the Zouaves. I pasted the pages and paragraphs and sometimes single sentences in what I thought the right order on large sheets.

The next day I brought the paste-up to Jean and read the whole thing straight through. She said nothing. As I read, I saw her, her head tilted to the side, glance sideways from time to time at the page.

I asked, hoarsely, "What do you think?"

"Fine," she said weakly.

"Now," I said, "I'll take it home and type it all up."

I left when her editor came to help her to bed.

In the morning her editor rang me. She said that Jean had gone into a frightful state after I left, so frightful the editor hoped she would never have to see anyone in such a state again. She was drunk and swearing and thought I had destroyed her book; she thought, too, I would lose it. She was particularly upset that I had cut in half a section called "The Zouaves." She said, "It's David's book now, not mine." Her editor asked if we could have lunch the following day.

I spent all that day and the next morning typing out the paste-up. I put the two halves of "The Zouaves" together. Before I went to lunch, I stopped by Jean's and left the new typescript off.

I said, "Jean, this is *your* book, not mine or anyone else's."

She said, "Of course it is, and if I don't like it I'll tear it up and throw it away."

"Good," I said.

I decided on my way to lunch that I would have nothing more to do with it. I thought Jean might have instructed her editor to say as much; but, in her office, she gave me a cheque for £500. Later, I found out that in fact it came from Jean, who had instructed her editor to tell me it came from the house.

I did not mention the autobiography again to Jean. I saw her often, as it was the holiday season. On New Year's there was a champagne party in her flat. She, sitting in the midst, raised her glass and said, sadly, "Oh well, another year." She was wearing a long silver dress. All her close friends were about her.

Shortly after, when I went to give Jean her evening soup, I found her very close friend the literary critic Francis Wyndham with her in a haze of smoke. We all talked for a while, then Francis left. Jean asked me, timidly, if I could continue to help her. I was reassured, and thought: well, I wasn't paid off. I wondered if she had been discussing it with Francis.

I said, "I'm very happy."

"Why?" she asked.

"Well, three reasons. My agent likes my new book."

Jean clapped her hands and laughed and said, "Hurrah."

"Then," I said, "I dropped a glass on the kitchen floor and it didn't break."

"Oh that's great luck," she said.

"And because I'm here."

She said, "That's very tactful."

We sat with drinks.

She raised hers to me. "You know, you're going to write what you want to write. I know it."

Whenever she said this, the implication was: not now, in time, in time.

I said, "Ah Jean—"

"Now don't disappoint me, honey."

We talked about writing in a very simplistic way.

I asked, "Have you ever thought about your readers?"

She shook her head. "No, never. They're sheep. Sweet. I appreciate them. But they're sheep, they follow after. And I never thought about money or fame. You mustn't ever think of money or fame. The voices go if you do. I don't think about anything but my writing."

"You don't think about yourself?"

She laughed. "I always thought I was different. I always thought I was a freak, that I felt things they didn't feel."

"Who?"

She shrugged. "They."

I laughed. "The ones who don't understand?"

"Yes, all of them. I've always felt best when I was alone, felt most real. People have always been shadows to me, and are more and more. I'm not curious about other people—not about what they do, a little about what they think—and the more dependent I become on people, as I must, the more I shy away from them. I don't know other people. I never have known other people. I have only ever written about myself."

"Yes," I said. "But doesn't that make you selfish?"

"Very," she said. "You have to be selfish to be a writer."

"Monstrously selfish?"

"Monstrously selfish," she said. "But you've also got to realize that if you're going to be that selfish you can't expect anything from anyone."

"And you're upset that you're so dependent now on others?"

She spoke in a flat, tired voice. "I'm a prisoner. I can't go out to shop, I can't prepare my own food, can't bathe alone, or make my bed. I worry that people resent my depending on them. And they do, of course they do."

"But do you in any way feel justified in accepting help because you're writing?"

She raised her hands and dropped them. "Oh that: writing. No, nothing ever justifies what you have to do to write, to go on writing. But you do, you must, go on. You hear a voice that says, 'Write this,' and you must write it to stop the voice. I don't hear any voices any more. My last collection of stories was no good, no good, magazine stories. I wasted two and a half years on that book. Not good. Oh, the reviews say it's good. But you know when you've done something good, and those stories are no good. I can't do it any more."

She said it in such a sober, straight way I almost said, "Yes."

She said, "Let's have more drinks, honey. I know I'm not supposed to, but—the sins of the flesh and drink are very minor sins, aren't they?"

There was very little drink left. I had to run out to buy another bottle of gin and of sweet vermouth.

She was sitting in the middle of the couch. She said, when I sat on my chair, "David, what will I do with my life?"

"What would you like to do?"

"I want to go away, I want to do something really wild, really really wild. What shall I do? I'm a prisoner."

Her small body appeared to me more hunched and twisted than ever, and looked in that position, so when she moved even her head her entire body, rigid, moved too, in jerks.

"I once tried to commit suicide," she said, "a long time ago. I cut my wrists. The doctor when I got to him sewed me up as if he'd done it six times before that same evening. I thought he'd be angry with me, send me to an asylum, but he didn't say anything to me."

I said, "Jean, would you like to hear some music?"

"Yes," she said, "the Polovtsian Dances. I saw Prince Igor once in Nice."

I put the record on, just at the part I knew she liked; the music was filled with the crackling and popping of scratches. She raised her thin gaunt arms high as the music pounded, and seemed to be punching the air above her head with her fists, her head lifted to look up, tears pouring down her cheeks, and she said, "It's so alive! It's so marvellous!"

The moment the particular dance she liked ended, she lowered her arms, wiped her eyes with her hands, and said, "That's enough of that."

When I next went to work with her, I found her, on the divan, surrounded by cosmetics: compacts, lipsticks, creams. She was rubbing colors from a little flat box of many different shades of eye make-up onto the back of her hand. She was excited. "Look at this," she said, "someone sent me all this. It'll keep me happy for weeks." I asked her who had sent it all, but she couldn't remember. I sat next to her, and we discussed the shades of make-up that might best suit her. She took out her compact to look in the mirror and try a shade; I was worried that with her shaking hands she'd get it in her eyes. She smeared some on a temple. Looking at herself in the little round mirror, she raised her upper lip as in a sneer. She dropped her hand.

"You know," she said, "being attractive is alien to women, so when they try the strain shows."

I didn't know what she meant, and I didn't ask her.

She asked me, before we got to work on her autobiography, if I would help her with some correspondence. I helped her to a chair by the desk and I opened a drawer to a heap of torn, open letters. She put on her spectacles, and reached out for a letter from the heap, examined it closely without, I thought, reading it, and handed it to me. Some letters were from acquaintances. We discussed if she should answer them, but as all the letters said the senders would be in touch again, Jean asked me to tear them up. When we came across statements from publishers or letters from her accountant, she would put her hands over her eyes and say, "I can't, I can't." She never knew who her foreign publishers were or what, exactly, was happening to her books; and she never knew, no matter how often she was told, how much money she had, except, she was sure, that it was very little. Letters from fans she asked me to read out to her and as I did she looked wistfully sad. If the letters included reviews, she asked for the title and the first line, then said, "Tear it up." When the title was "The Dark Underworld of Women" or "The Woes of Women" or had "women" in it in any way, she'd grab the review from me and tear it up herself and throw it in the basket, laughing, and say, "No, I've had enough of *that!*"

It is impossible to say what Jean's attitude was towards any subject. She seemed to have little interest in reactions to her work from serious readers, and, I think, she found it improbable that any opinion of hers should be taken seriously in the world; and yet she raged that no one paid any attention to her, no one at all. I wrote down some of the things she said about women: "I'm not at all for women's lib. I don't dislike women exactly, but I don't trust them. You can never tell them what you really think, because if they know what you think they'll do you down. I'm not, I've never been intimate with them. It's not worth it. Sometimes I think I'm not like other women, that I lack feminine qualities. I'm not, and I have never been jealous, for example, never, and women are very jealous of one another." And: "Don't tell anyone this. Women are kind, but they do for you what *they* want to do, not what *you* want to do. They can't imagine that you may want something quite different to what they want. Men at least try to do for you what *you* want." And when women who were not close friends spoke to her, she looked at them with a superior and wounded tolerance as she listened, and said in answer, simply, "Perhaps." To have argued with Jean about her opinions would have been mad: she simply would not have understood if one had said, "But, Jean, don't you wonder *why* you say that about women?" Self-conscious Jean—that is, the Jean who thought she knew—was bigoted; she became this way when she was drunk. When sober, the unself-conscious Jean—the Jean who knew she knew very little—emerged, and in her writing that Jean of course took over. As she herself said, her novels had no meaning, and any meaning imposed on them was ridiculous. Whatever attitude she had towards women (and blacks and liberals and any suppressed group struggling for equality), it was not in her self-conscious opinions, but in the unself-conscious writing, where, because she wrote about herself as she was, she had no set attitudes. In terms of psychology (she said she had never read Adler, Jung or Freud, didn't know what they were about, and didn't want to know) or social studies (she wouldn't have understood what a social study was), she never asked why her main female characters acted as they did: they just did, as she did. There is about them a great dark space in which they do not ask themselves, removing themselves from themselves to see themselves in the world in which they lived: why do I suffer? When Jean said she delved and delved into herself, I didn't understand; it was certainly not to question her happiness, or, more, unhappiness, in terms of the world she lived in, and certainly not her prejudices. These prejudices were many, and sometimes odd: Protestants, Elizabethans—

When the time came for dictating, she put her glass down. "All right," she said, "I'm ready to do some work on the autobiography."

Quickly, and it seemed to me without thinking, she dictated this paragraph:

"Below the lonely house was the distant sea and Roseau Bay, and in the bay there was sometimes a strange ship flying the yellow flag, and we knew there was contagion on board. Rising up behind the house was untouched forest and, further up, a range of mountains, Morne Anglais, Morne Colle Anglais, Morne Bruce, Morne Diabletin. Morne Diabletin was the highest, and covered in mist. It had never been climbed because the summit was rock, and round the summit flew large black birds called devil birds. We could see the rain coming over the mountains and ran for shelter before it fell on us. There were a great many storms with forked lightening and thunder and great wind and heavy showers of rain, after which it cleared instantly, and the sky was blue again. When it was clear, the smell was fresh and sweet, and the sea below and the mountains above were bright."

I thought: this is beautiful, and it is because of this that I am working with her.

But the paragraph went under many different changes. She kept saying, "It should be vague, more vaguely remembered." After a while, I was writing it with her, and she seemed to like the collaboration.

She said, after the paper and pencil were put away, "You know, what I'm trying to write about, my life in Dominica happened almost a century ago. I remember songs my great aunt taught me

which her mother had taught her. It all goes such a long way back."
With another drink, she said, "And what is Dominica like now?
They say there are no roses in Dominica now. There were, I
remember them. They gave such a scent to the air." She suddenly
shouted, "Lies! Lies!" She bared her teeth. "A pack of lies. and
who cares? Who does anything? Terrible things people do. Getting
rid of the roses in Dominica. I hate the word 'people.'" She spit
the word out. "People! I hate people! I hate everyone. I think
they're all enemies. Terrible. No roses in Dominica. Who got rid of
them? I know. I know. Up the Dreads. Yeah, the Dreads. They're
in London, too, and they wear dark glasses. In Dominica they live
in the forests. They're taking over. And who cares? Who gives a
damn? Who? *No one* understands! Well, so what? I'll be dead
soon."

I let her rage. Often she would open her compact, always with
difficulty, and I'd watch her look in the little round mirror to
powder her nose and cheeks and pull and push the hair around her
face, her lips pursed with bitterness.

She suddenly stopped talking and looked at me for a moment in
silence, blurry eyed, then asked, "Why do you come to see me?"

I smiled.

She said, "I feel I can say anything to you, that you do understand, a little, just a little. Why do you come? Is it curiosity?"

I kept my smile. "A little."

"And what else?"

I didn't know what to say. I said, "For some mad reason, I love
you."

"You're not pretending that?"

"I said it was mad. Could madness be a pretense?"

"No, it couldn't. I do trust you."

I thought: why do I love her?

We didn't work the next time I saw her. Diana Melly, the writer
and one of Jean's close friends, helped me to take her to a beauty
clinic. She had been saying that no one understood how her morale
depended on make-up and pretty clothes. She wanted her face
done up and her lashes dyed black. The clinic was at the top of a
very long flight of stairs, which we took one at a time, pausing at
each step. In the rather severe grey waiting room, Jean said, "This
looks serious." A young woman came for her, and I helped her up
another flight of stairs into an alcove with green velvet curtains,

then left to do shopping, and came back after an hour. She looked exactly as I had left her. In the car back to the flat, she said, "I'm a fool." Then she giggled and said, "Well, I'll never go back *there* again."

I stayed with her for a few hours. We didn't work. I said, "Do you consider yourself a West Indian?"

She shrugged. "It was such a long time ago when I left."

"So you don't think of yourself as a West Indian Writer?"

Again, she shrugged, but said nothing.

"What about English? Do you consider yourself an English writer?"

"No! I'm not! I'm not! I'm not even English."

"What about a French writer?" I asked.

Again, she shrugged and said nothing.

"You have no desire to go back to Dominica?"

"Sometimes," she said. She remembered something. "Honey, will you get from the top of the desk a piece of folded paper?"

I did, and gave it to her; she unfolded the paper to reveal three dried black leaves.

She said, "They're voodoo. Someone, I can't remember who, gave them to me. They're from Haiti. You put them under your pillow and you dream the solution to your problem. You can't drink too much and you can't take sleeping pills. I must try it tonight. I won't say I believe, and I won't say I don't believe."

She had the solution to her problem when I saw her again. She would do something really wild and go to Venice. Diana Melly and Jo Batterham would go with her. She asked me to come next time with two huge manila envelopes and a stick of sealing wax. We put the unfinished autobiography into the envelopes, sealed them with melted wax, and I wrote on each TO BE DESTROYED UN-OPENED IF ANYTHING SHOULD HAPPEN TO ME, and she signed, with both Jean Rhys and E. G. Hamer. The envelopes were to be given to her accountant.

She said, "My work is ephemeral."

The work put aside, my following visits with Jean were chatty, and when I asked her about her life it was simply to get her to chat, and she did, with ease. I did not write anything down after in my diary, except this: "Jean told me she remembered seeing Sarah Bernhardt on the stage, in the last act of *La Dame Aux Camélias*. It was after her leg had been amputated, and she did the whole thing in a chaise lounge. Jean recalled her saying, *"Je ne veux pas mourir, je ne veux pas mourir,"* and a man in the seat next to Jean, tears streaming down his face, said, 'But she's just an old woman with one leg.' Jean herself began to weep; she took a handkerchief from her purse and wiped her eyes and said, laughing, 'I'll bet my tears are 90% gin.' I felt close to her."

Sometimes we talked about writers, and she admitted, with no sign of great regret, that she hadn't read Balzac, Proust, Fielding, Trollope, George Eliot, James, Conrad, Joyce. She couldn't read Austen, she had tried. She had read a lot of Dickens. She had read, and remembered in great patches, the English Romantic poets, and Shakespeare. Her favorite writer, she said, was Richard Hitchens, who wrote turn of the century melodramas; she said his books took her away, especially *The Garden of Allah.* But when friends brought her from used book shops his novels she left them in a pile. She read, instead, thrillers, and in her late life she read almost nothing else but. In Chelsea, she read, over and over, a novel called *The Other Side of Midnight,* and she said, "It's trash, perfect trash, but it takes you away," and made a sign as of going away, far off, with her hand. She said it was very important for a writer to have read a great deal at some time in his life. I presumed this was when she was a girl in Dominica, when she read books from her father's library and from the public library, where she sat on a veranda to read, with a view of the sea. While she was on tour in music hall the girls read *The Forest Lovers,* and Jean read it too. It was about a couple in the middle ages who ran away into the forest because everyone disapproved of their love, but they always slept with a sword between them. The sword, Jean said, was an endless topic of conversation. ("What a soppy idea. What'd they do that for? I wouldn't care about an old sword, would you?") *The Forest Lovers* was the only book Jean read for years. She must have read when she started to write, though I am not sure what. She spoke very highly of Hemingway, and she at least knew many modern writers enough to comment on them. About Beckett, she said, "I read a book by him. It seemed to me too set up, too studied."

Shortly before she was to leave for Venice, amidst all the organization, she developed a slight cold. She thought she shouldn't go. The doctor said she could. On my last visit before she left, she was wrapped in a quilt, and had a silk scarf tied as a turban around her head. Her cold, she said, was worse. She really thought she couldn't go to Venice. She said she'd been reading a guide book about that city which said it was full of rats. She looked at me as if she had found out something everyone had deliberately kept from her to give her a false impression, and she had now found out the truth for herself. I said, "But there are a lot of cats." She raised her eyebrows.

I fantasized this when I left her, telling myself I shouldn't: that Jean would die in Venice, the typescript of the unfinished autobiography would be destroyed, and I would alone be left with the hand written pages of dictation, I, alone, would have Jean Rhys's secrets.

This was in late February, 1977. In November of the same year Jean returned to London for the last time. She stayed for months in the house of Diana and George Melly, where she had a bedroom and sitting room with pink floors. Diana helped her buy new dresses, and in her new dresses she sat in the sitting room off her bedroom and received visitors. But she would say, "I don't want to see anyone," and, then minutes later, "No one ever comes to see me."

We resumed work on the autobiography. She had done very little on it over the summer and autumn, but she had made a mess of it. I sorted it out. Each time I came back it was messed up again. I would put it in order, with clips; she would ask to see it, the whole thing would fall apart in her lap and to the floor, and she would say, "I don't know if this will ever be finished, it's in such a mess." Finally, I put each section, or chapter, in a different colored folder, wrote in big letters the name of the sections on the folders, and numbered them. If, however, there was more than one version of the section in the folder, she would become confused; I had to make sure there was only one copy, and the previous work copies I tore up and threw away in Jean's presence. This tearing up and throwing away satisfied her for a time.

The days were dark grey and rainy; we had to light the lamps shortly after lunch, when we began the work. I read, countless times, the sections she wanted to hear again, and at the end she always said, "That needs more work," but she never got around to doing the work unless I said, "All right, let's do it now." As often as I read certain passages to her, she always wept at some and laughed at others; she might have been hearing them for the first time. I thought: yes, she's right, it will never be done. Many days, she couldn't work. There was no inspiration. She quickly became drunk. I became drunk with her. The work sessions degenerated into her shouting, "Lies! Lies!" And she would look at me, her face hard, and say, "You don't understand."

Once, angry, I said, "I do understand."

She immediately sat back, her face softened, and she said, softly, "I don't mean you."

I gathered, then, that when she said "you" she meant a very general "you": people.

When she said, "You know what you must do. Do you? You must know, and you *must* do it," I wasn't sure if she meant what I or people must do. "You know what you must do in your writing," she said. I became reassured: she was going to say that I must in my writing save all civilization. But she stared keenly at me, expecting me to reply to her repeated, "Don't you know?" I smiled. She said, "You must tell the truth about them." She slammed her hand down on the arm of the chair. "You must tell the truth against their lies." My anger gave way to sudden sadness.

She must have seen the sadness in my eyes. She said, "When I was a little girl I was always saying, 'That's not fair, that's not fair,' and I was known as Socialist Gwen. I was on the side of the Negroes, the workers. Now I say, 'It's not fair, it's not fair,' about the other side, because I think they *aren't* treated fairly."

I simply looked at her.

Her face, it seemed to me, became that of a little girl. She looked at the floor. She said, "I don't know. I don't know any more."

She continued to stare at the floor, her head tilted. She said, "Maybe I do have black blood in me. I think my great grandmother was colored, the Cuban. What else would I get my love for pretty clothes?" She looked up at me and smiled. "And oh how I envied them in their clothes, dancing in the street."

But the autobiography was coming together in a rough way. The first part, which dealt with her life in Dominica, was at least in a completed draft. The second part, her life in England and France, had big holes. I took the sections home to work on them; she knew this, and approved at least to the extent that, when I read them with her on my next visit, she said, "That's all right."

In the black file which Jean had with her were yellow scraps of earlier stories; we went through them, and some of these, because they were her life, we transferred to the second part of the autobiography. Among the scraps was an old brown-covered notebook, half the pages torn out. Jean took it out.

"I don't know," she said, "if this should go in. I wrote it, a kind of diary, a long time ago, when I was living in a room above a pub called the Ropemakers' Arms in Maidstone."

"Why were you living in a room above a pub in Maidstone?"

She made a face. "My third husband, Max, was in Maidstone prison. I have always been attracted, I suppose, to thieves and saints, not that they were thieves exactly, and they weren't saints. I didn't know, and I don't know now, why my first and third husbands were sent to prison. I don't know much about my husbands, and I don't know much about my parents. Perhaps I wasn't curious. My daughter once told me my first husband, Jean, was in the Deuxième. I didn't know. Max was married before, but whether he had any children or not I don't know—perhaps a boy or girl. Men used to come to the house. I didn't like them, especially one. I didn't know what Max did with them. He went to prison. Enough. I have enough letters with the heading HMS PRISON. I visited him. One prisoner said to me, "It's all right for people like me, we should be here, but not for people like him." The warder with the one leg was nice. Max got a bit of money in prison and he saved it to buy me chocolates. The whole thing was so beastly I try not to think about it. I know the real villain, that one man I especially couldn't stand, went free. Max never recovered. When he got out, we moved to Bute, had a little house at the end of a row of houses, just at the edge of the downs, where we'd go walking. He began to fall. He fell on one of the walks. He began to fall as I've begun to fall. He died soon after he was released." She held the notebook out to me. "Anyway, I wrote this in my room. I called it 'Death Before the Fact.' Do you know that? It's from St. Theresa. In my room were two black elephants with long curving tusks on the mantle, and from the window I saw laundry and cabbage stumps. Will you read it to me? You'll see how long ago I wrote it, because the handwriting is clear."

I read, and tears came to my eyes, Jean had put herself on trial. She saw herself, defenseless, answering the questions of a judge who condemned her to a simple fate: to be unhappy, to write, and to die.

She asked me if I would take the notebook home and type it out. I did.

At the back of the notebook were the ragged margins of a number of torn out pages, and in the margins were words. I was not sure what had been written in the torn out pages, but I imagined drafts of letters. These words I typed out too, though I decided I would not tell her I had.

"My dear . . . I've just . . . worrying . . . to help . . . a little . . . to me . . . know . . . Leslie . . . called . . . Edward . . . with . . . why they . . . took such . . . will be free . . . We are supposed . . . London . . . money . . . that I . . . lives . . . for a little . . . I can't . . . them . . . me . . . all . . . I didn't want . . . went . . . because . . . down . . . hell . . . I do . . . place . . . the . . . tell . . . was . . . just before Max . . . approached by . . . a radio play . . . and I would . . . from . . . I can't . . . well . . . going . . . here . . . person . . . But I fear . . . hopeless . . . do so . . . looking . . . live . . . My Dear Edward . . . The enclosed . . . Will you . . . I have . . . you please . . . is likely . . . careful . . . but . . . I . . . you . . . allowance . . . I gave . . . worried . . . living . . . where . . . I get 36/6 a . . . Admiralty . . . from the P . . . from . . . that is . . . but . . . for the . . . 30/ . . . as . . . by . . . I . . . by . . . out . . . So I'm going to . . . I married . . . know because . . . Brenda . . . to be . . . to get . . . it . . . died I . . . sincerely wish I . . . So I'll . . . oh how I wish . . . of waiting . . . I . . . I . . . been . . . stresses . . . to see . . . and leave . . . approve of them . . . safeguards . . . that my . . . only be . . . think . . . I'm afraid the . . . gone on . . . I . . . after . . . kind things . . . so badly . . . to feel . . . else . . . has . . . dread . . . year . . . looking . . . be fair . . . you'd paid . . . lasted . . . friendly . . . after hearing . . . still . . . Strauss . . . As for the other . . . home that . . . a looney-bin . . . that at all . . . Brenda and . . . you must . . . necessary . . . You . . . who . . . I . . . myself . . . do . . . myself . . . after . . . A . . . only . . . he . . . them . . . Did you, either of you . . ."

When I came back and read the typed-out diary to her, she thought she wouldn't include it in the autobiography. I insisted she must. She said, "All right, if you cut certain passages." I cut them, but include here only this:

"Do you wish to write about what has been happening to you?"
"No, not yet."

"You realise that you must?"

"I doubt whether it is as important as all that. Still I will write it, but not today."

"Softly, softly, cathee monkey."

I asked, guiltily, I suppose, as I had not only written about her in my diary, I had now stolen from her, "Do you mind people writing about you?"

"Yes," she said. "And I know people will try to uncover everything about me after I die to write it all down."

"Well," I said, "you won't know."

"Perhaps," she said.

The February days continued the January days of dark grey. Jean was not well. She didn't know what to do. Perhaps she should return to her cottage in Devon where a nurse would take care of her, as she was utterly incapable of taking care of herself. The first part of the autobiography was completed, the second part scrappy towards the end. I promised I would go down to Devon in the Spring to help her; she smiled at me as she might smile distantly on all promises.

On my last visit, Jean was in bed. She had a plaster on her forehead covering a bruise she'd got from falling. She looked frail.

She said, "I want to tell you about an experience I had once." It was as if she had been thinking of it for a long time and had finally decided to tell me.

I asked, "Do you want me to write it down?"

"No," she said.

She said, "I've tried to write it, but have never been able to. It shows how inadequate words are. In Paris, my close friends the Richelots suggested and paid for a holiday for me in the South of France. I went with another girl. This was in the 30's. We went to Theoule, near Cannes. One day, alone, I had a bath in the sea, then lunch. As I knew the bus to Cannes, where I wanted to go to shop, was leaving soon, I ate my lunch quickly, and I didn't have any wine. But I missed the bus, and thought, oh well, I'll walk, it isn't a long way. At La Napoule I felt tired and left the road to sit by the sea. You could do that in those days. I can't describe what happened. No words, no words, there are not words for it, except, perhaps, in a still unknown language. I felt a *certainty* of joy, and terrific, terrific happiness, not only for me, but for everyone. I knew that the end would be joy. I felt, too, a part of the sea, the sun, the wind. I don't know how long I was there, but after a while I got up, went back to the coast road, and walked to Cannes. I went to a café for coffee. There was a big tree outside the café. I sat and I looked about and I thought: why do I hate people? They're not hateful. When I got back to Theoule I of course said nothing to my friend, but my feeling for the happiness for everyone lasted, lasted, perhaps, three or four days."

I picked up my pencil and paper.

"Are you going to write it down?" she asked.

"Only if you want me to," I said.

"If you want to," she said, and she repeated it again as I wrote. After, she looked out the dark window on which rain was falling, and she said, "Is there anything else I have to tell you? No, I don't think so. Anyway, none of the rest matters."

I stared at her.

She said, suddenly, "David, I think you've just seen my ghost."

I asked, "Do you believe in a life after death?"

She smiled. "Well, how can one be sure unless one has died? But I think there must be something after. You see, we have such longings, such great longings, they can't be for nothing."

"But you don't have any definite faith?"

"Oh, whatever faith I have I find expressed in man-made things, and to me the greatest expressions of faith I've ever seen are Botticelli's *The Birth of Venus* and *The Winged Victory of Samothrace.*"

"Do you see your books as an expression of faith?"

"My books aren't important," she said. "Writing is. But my books aren't."

Before I left, she said, "Give me the file, will you, honey?"

I put it on the bed beside her and with her spectacles she looked through the few scraps of old paper left in it. She took out a sheet.

"This is what I want to give you," she said and handed me the sheet. "It's the outline of a novel I wanted to write called *Wedding in the Carib Quarter*. I won't write it. Maybe you will."

I asked, "Will you sign it?"

She wrote on it, in large shaky letters that looked like Arabic script the message: "Think about it. It is very important." Then she handed it over to me.

THE OTTER

by SEAMUS HEANEY

from ANTAEUS

nominated by Tess Gallagher and Grace Schulman

When you plunged
The light of Tuscany wavered
And swung through the pool
From top to bottom.

I loved your wet head and smashing crawl,
Your fine swimmer's back and shoulders
Surfacing and surfacing again
This year and every year since.

I sat dry-throated on the warm stones.
You were beyond me.
The mellowed clarities, the grape-deep air
Thinned and disappointed.

Thank God for the slow loadening.
When I hold you now
We are close and deep
As the atmosphere on water.

My two hands are plumbed water.
You are my palpable, lithe
Otter of memory
In the pool of the moment,

Turning to swim on your back,
Each silent, thigh-shaking kick
Re-tilting the light,
Heaving the cool at your neck.

And suddenly you're out,
Back again, intent as ever,
Heavy and frisky in your freshened pelt,
Printing the stones.

MELANCHOLY DIVORCÉE

by SHEROD SANTOS

from POETRY

nominated by POETRY *and Dave Smith*

If you find yourself burning only now for a clumsiness
you have always possessed, for the way your coat hangs
   askew
on your shoulders, and the methodical, unthinking manner
in which you cross and uncross your legs in public,
then you will lie down in your bed at night
like a white and spotted thing
lying down in the moonlight of an open field;

and if you desire something out of place to disappear
from your breakfast table,
and the polished spoons and buttons and clean saucers
to carry their secret lives no longer
into the proud metaphor at the center of your sorrow,
then you desire no more than the eucalyptus leaves
thrashing the air at the beginning of October;

and if you discover the words *cacophony* and *colloquy* and
   calumny
recurring obsessively in the crossword puzzles,
and yourself expecting the windows of your neighbor's
   house
to stay lit much later than they do, and when they do
you worry, then you are beginning to understand and
   forgive

the Hungarian woman next door
for burning leaves all day in a blowing drizzle;

and if you learn to stop hating the grocery clerk
for counting your change out loud,
for the tattooed name on his wrist and the ugly way
the bills fall apart in your hands,
then you will grow to love the company
of the blue and nameless flowers
that pepper the earth around the olive trees each Spring;

and if looking out your window you see the blue shirts
of the workmen moving up Highland Street to begin
    their day,
and if you catch yourself falling as easily as they
into the smell of coffee and the empty dream of the
    afternoon,
then you will stop turning to Browning and Chopin
to explain how you feel, and you will speak
in the anger and conspiracy of your own dark eyes;

and if walking downtown one blazing afternoon it
    occurs to you
that people have always said too much, that you have
    gone there
to hear their voices, and to watch your own image
    floating
with theirs through department store windows, then you
    are learning
the luxury of the warm earth floating beneath your feet,
and of the black waters at the mouth of the Corbuscu
    River
voluptuously reclaiming their silted shores.

I REMEMBER GALILEO

by GERALD STERN

from POETRY

nominated by POETRY, *Alicia Ostriker and Rhoda Schwartz*

I remember Galileo describing the mind
as a piece of paper blown around by the wind
and I loved the sight of it sticking to a tree
or jumping into the back seat of a car,
and for years I watched paper leap through my cities;
but yesterday I saw the mind was a squirrel caught
    crossing
route 80 between the wheels of a giant truck,
dancing back and forth like a thin leaf,
or a frightened string, for only two seconds living
on the white concrete before he got away,
his life shortened by all that terror, his head
jerking, his yellow teeth ground down to dust.

It was the speed of the squirrel and his lowness to the
    ground,
his great purpose and the alertness of his dancing,
that showed me the difference between him and paper.
Paper will do in theory, when there is time
to sit back in a metal chair and study shadows;
but for this life I need a squirrel,
his clawed feet spread, his whole soul quivering,
the hot wind rushing through his hair,
the loud noise shaking him from head to tail.
    O philosophical mind, O mind of paper, I need a squirrel
finishing his wild dash across the highway,
rushing up his green ungoverned hillside.

COLUMN BEDA

fiction by GERARD SHYNE

from UNDER THE INFLUENCE OF MAE (Inwood press)

nominated by INWOOD PRESS, *Raymond Federman, J. R. Humphreys*

and QUARTO

ONE OF THE MANY STORIES I heard in Mae's Friday night kitchen—which was a very special kitchen because of its storytelling—was Ralph Herkimer's account of Column Beda, the black giant of Pag-Paw, Georgia.

Column Beda was seven feet tall, weighed over three hundred pounds, and back in 1918 was the biggest nigger, Herkimer said, Pag-Paw, Georgia, had ever seen. He wasn't ugly, but he wasn't good-looking either. He wasn't light-skinned nor was he coal-black complexioned. Still, he was referred to as that big-black nigger. He was a giant really. He could not be that big and be anything else but. And truly, we were to believe, he was a splendid specimen of manhood to behold, much over-muscled but strong as an elephant and dexterous as a tiger. None could get around him. He'd beat you at any game—yours or his—in his gentle way, and when you got rough, he could still handle you without hurting you.

"How can you hate him?" said one, Danny Folger. "He's bitch without malice."

The game of life was fun to Column Beda. Three to four days out of a week he worked picking cotton; the other times he gambled, shot pool, and pranked on everyone, black and white.

He played a borderline game of jail and the chain-gang with laughter at the end of everything he did. He lived dangerously really, because "Crackers" only play so much and then they say, and mean it: "Cut it out, nigger!"

And after the white sportsmen's club had a night of drinking, they couldn't get out of the hall. A hugh tree trunk under the porch, limbs in the yard, was blocking the front door.

"Column Beda did it," someone said.

"He did it," said Flagg Gray.

"Not necessarily," said Sheriff Alms.

"Always defending him, huh?" said Steve Hows. "You like that big nigger, don't you?"

"I want him arrested!" said Jason Dex. He was the president of the club. "Suppose the place had caught on fire?"

"Let's see if he did it first," said Sheriff Alms.

Column Beda wasn't home that night. They looked everywhere without finding him. Even on Sly Street where the blacks hung out, he was not to be found.

"Looks like he mightn't have done it since he's not around," said Sheriff Alms.

"Oh, he did it," said Jason Dex. "I know his style."

Later on they met Column Beda's friend, Luke Hackey. "He's visiting with old Widow Marview in the Pageman Hotel."

"See," said Sheriff Alms, "he's been busy."

They went over to the Pageman Hotel and found Column sitting with the old widow. "He's been here for four hours," said the widow.

"How come?" asked the sheriff.

"We talk a lot sometime. You know his mother worked for me. I was there when he was born."

"Rubbish, I'd say," said Jason Dex. "You're covering for him because you figure he's done something."

"You're calling me a liar," snapped the scrawny, sharp-eyed old woman.

The men all left.

"What'd you do, Column?" asked the Widow Marview.

"Just a tree in front of the sports club door, Miss Marview. Them sportsmen given us niggers a tough time all week."

"Suppose a fire started?"

"They got the back door," said Column.

The next day there was betting to see if anyone could move the tree. No one could. As the strong men of the town, black and white, failed, they heard the laughter of Column Beda.

"Can't budge it! You can't budge it!" roared Column. He was shaking with laughter.

"Son of a bitch!" yelled Shawl Hawkins, one of the bigger white men trying. He punched Column Beda in the body, which did nothing at all to end his laughter.

Then the others joined in, punching and kicking. Column took and handled it all like it was nothing, still laughing.

"Stop it!" ordered Sheriff Alms. And they did.

"If you don't move that tree out of there, Column," said the sheriff, "you'll be working at my house again this weekend."

Column Beda stopped laughing. He didn't like working the weekend at Sheriff Alms' big spread. Not for the working so much, but because it was so confining and so lonely. And he hated being alone.

"All right, I'll move it," he said, and tried but couldn't.

There was Column Beda straining and grimacing, grunting like he would die, but to no avail. The tree wouldn't budge. All seven feet and over three hundred pounds of him looked dejected. And more people gathered to see him fail.

"Oh, hell!" said Sheriff Alms. "I still say he can do it!"

"He's your nigger," said one.

"And Widow Marview's 'boy,' " said another. "But that's not helping him."

"He can do it, and I'm betting he can," said Sheriff Alms. "That is, if I can find a bettor."

"You've got one," said Rene Baines, the town's newest banker and a former wrestler.

"It's a trick!" said Barbara Bedden, the mayor's buxom daughter and a housewife. "He put it there! I never saw him fail in a feat of strength yet when there was money involved."

"Who cares?" said a townsman. "I'll bet he can."

"I'll bet he can't," said another.

And there were many bettors, because many, having seen Column Beda fail in his first effort, felt he couldn't do it.

Up to the huge tree, with a fond pat from Sheriff Alms, went giant Column Beda for a second time. He wrapped his arms around the big trunk and began to strain, grunt and grimace, his great strength and enormous size, wrestler's muscles, fighter's muscles, worker's sinews all rippling and bulging as his powerful frame strove and strove, poured in all his over three hundred pounds until: There it was! The tree was superhumanly moved! Gigantically pulled from the door, off the porch, and down the street, dragged to even the losers' cheers.

About a week later, the small Ted Benner Circus came to town with its two elephants and their feats of strength. One elephant could pull two railway cars. The other could raise a set of train wheels.

That's something for Column Beda, thought Barbara Bedden, and she got Sheriff Alms interested.

"You really hate that boy!" said Sheriff Alms. "What's he ever done to you?"

"Done to me? He better never try!" said Barbara Bedden.

"I've done that before, in New Bedford, Sheriff," said Column. "But that's not what Miss Barbara has in mind. If I press that weight, which I'm sure she figures I will, then she has in mind those two railway cars the elephant moves."

"What?"

"Sheriff, Miss Barbara means to break me. All us niggers know she hates me cause I'm strong and black!"

"Well, goddamn, Column! You know how the white race is! That is, many of them," said Sheriff Alms.

"It's not the same thing. It's different—stronger white hate," said Column Beda. "My people say they feel sorry for Miss Barbara. Hate is eating her up."

Sheriff Alms looked bewildered. "Column, I never heard you talk like this before. People in Pag-Paw love all you niggers."

"Miss Barbara ain't people in Pag-Paw, Sheriff," said Column Beda.

"She's one of us, Column," said the sheriff. "Her father is Mayor Cardy Reedy."

"You'll see, Sheriff," said Column Beda.

Word got around and the issue was pushed to its happening. Pag-Paw wanted to see this. And so it came down to the wire.

"You know I'm betting on you, Column," said Sheriff Alms.

And so were many others.

Column bent over the thick bar that held the huge wheels, took a deep breath and paused. Barbara Bedden smiled. There was tenseness!

A gigantic effort cleared the wheels up to his shoulders, an even more gigantic effort jerked them, and they were overhead. High to the sky. Cheers broke out, cloud-jarring.

Ted Benner offered Column a chance to be in his show. Said he could make a lot of money and travel and have girls everywhere.

"I don't know," said Column. "I just like it here where I am."

"No future here," said Ted Benner. "You can make some money though," he argued. "And girls? Loads of them!"

Column Beda didn't look impressed or enthused at all.

"Girls!" said Danny Pitter. "I wish I had that chance. Forget about the motherfucken money! Get that pussy!"

But Column Beda wasn't moved.

"That's strange," said Danny Pitter to friend-buddy Monkey-Gland Bates. "But come to think of it, I've never seen Column with. . .or make much talk about girls as girls."

"What's strange about that?" said Monkey-Gland.

"He's a man, and a man's man," said Danny Pitter. "But when does he fuck?"

"Man, what hoar can take Column Beda's three hundred pound dick?" said Monkey-Gland.

"You got a point there," laughed Danny.

"Goddamn right!" said Monkey-Gland. "That motherfucker's a cuntsplitter or there ain't none!"

"Goddamn, it must be big!"

"Nothing like it when it swells!" said Monkey-Gland. "Have the hoars in panic-run to save themselves!"

And both men laughed heartily.

But just as Column expected, Barbara Bedden had another challenge: moving, like the other elephant, two railway cars.

The word spread, so that Quester County got the news of what Pag-Paw was talking about. And it grew so that Quester County began saying it couldn't be done, and Pag-Paw said it could.

"It would be the biggest feat of strength this county ever saw," said Rene Baines.

"If Column could do it," said Barbara Bedden. "But he can't."

"You really want to break him, huh?" said Sheriff Alms.

"Like he was all wishbone!" said Barbara Bedden.

What Sheriff Alms thought Barbara Bedden really felt about Column Beda he could never say in the South or admit to himself.

The interest grew, the doubt grew, the controversy expanded, bearing down heavily to a sure head: Column Beda would have to attempt those cars. In Pag-Paw and in Quester County there were sporadic fights and donnybrooks about the issue. Even Column Beda was cornered in anger by crowds demanding, "Attempt those cars. Strain those cars."

The handwriting was on the wall. Barbara Bedden had got it there. Now it was up to Column Beda.

The day came. Column Beda breathed heavily, sighed heavily, and felt doubt for the first time. For the first time in Pag-Paw's history, Pag-Paw encouraged a nigger not to work but rest before an ordeal, even bringing him some of their best pots and dishes to give his body all the possible strength it could get. This was a transcending time, color didn't matter. Hero worship was the order of the day. They would show Quester County and all doubters their strongest man could do the impossible.

It was a big day when it came. A carnival day. Even bigger than the circus that stood by—a show dwarfed down to its two elephants. Column Beda, his size and strength, were bigger— bigger than anything, anything that the two counties had ever seen. A man—a giant—doing what an elephant had done: move two railroad cars.

They used the same harness and cables and padded their hero in the body where the skin could tear and cut from the strain and poundage it would be exposed to. On his feet they placed tough leather shoes with rubber bottoms that could hold and stand the abuse and mistreatment they would encounter. All was in readiness down to unlocking the brakes of the huge cars.

And as Column Beda walked up to the harness and it was placed upon him, Barbara Bedden was human bundled glee. Column Beda stood against the sky as one who was from it; and the struggle began.

Column Beda was on the tracks, a grimace on his face from the first tug. He strained backwards, he tried forwards—no avail! He settled down. His effort showed in the veins of his massive and African face. His huge muscles danced, rippled, and leaped into view like boiling quicksand and wave-controlled water. His heart was unrestrained frenzy, beating like the drums of his ancestral land. He strained, pulled, man-mountain tugged at, myth-Hercules labored at, God-anointed Samson battled with, before cheers, encouragements and urgings. And the cables taut and strained, straight as the lines in a painted picture, seemed forever in pose and posture, a stance in power for all time displayed. The portrait in human endeavor was still, the power all inside—nothing visible in movement, but the strain was so absolute, the picture finally moved; and the trains rolled down the tracks. An elephantine man had moved them!

Such cheers as the skies of Pag-Paw and Quester County had never felt shifted the sky as they exploded from human jubilation—great Column Beda had done it. Moved a mountain. Elephantized himself. What a man!

But a tragedy loomed suddenly. The train kept moving after the brakes had been slammed—like they couldn't hold. And they weren't holding. Column Beda, seeing what happened, took to running to save himself. A slight decline now came up on the rails to give the cars dangerous momentum. The brakes, the decline, the momentum. And Column trapped in his harness was struggling to free himself, and running. It was a terrible moment and a terrible change of events. Crowds of people, mostly men, ran behind and at the sides of the train as the cars sped on with Column Beda in full sprint in front of them.

Column Beda thought if he fell down on the tracks, the train passing over the cables might cut them and free him before he was mashed and mangled in a hodgepodge of steel, rail-ties, and butchered flesh. And down went Column Beda with a flash prayer. The wheels went over his cables and snapped them in two, derailing the first car. The second car went up into the air before crashing, too, with him rolling out of the way—just in the nick of miraculous time.

From where many stood, Column Beda had been destroyed. But, lo, there he stood, safe and unmarked. Miracle of miracles and another miracle to that.

Into the town they marched him to a big feast on a transcending day, when color didn't count—only being a hero mattered.

Sheriff Alms' new deputy was Laid Bodram, a man who had served in many counties. He didn't stay in a county very long, in fact, before the central office moved him off somewhere else. He was not very likable, was too stern and too odious. Nevertheless, he was a lawman.

"This is a quiet county," Sheriff Alms told him. "People here are very law abiding."

"They better be," said Laid Bodram, a big man, a wide man, and a strong man.

"We'll tour together most of the time," Sheriff Alms said.

On one occasion, touring together, Laid Bodram said to Sheriff Alms, "What are all these niggers doing sitting around in the streets? Isn't there a law against loitering?"

Before Sheriff Alms could act to stop him, he was out of the car barking commands. "If I catch you sitting around on the streets like this again, I'll lock your asses up."

"You acted too rashly," said Sheriff Alms when Bodram came back to the car.

"You may think I did, but if you don't keep a nigger down all the time, he'll be in trouble."

It saddened Sheriff Alms afterwards to see the empty benches, vacant and hardly frequented. Even some of the townsfolk were unhappy about it. They said, "Our niggers are no longer sitting around. What's happening to our town? It's that new lawman. He says it's in the books—no loitering. He means to change a lot of things. He's mean, too. Ever see how he looks at you? Like just break the law and in you go. I don't like him. I wish he'd go from

here. Where'd the fucker come from? From hell I guess. He looks
like the devil! Even Column Beda with all his bigness doesn't look
as frightening as him. We'd see the tail if he didn't wear pants.
Cocksucker!"

"I know they don't like me," said Laid Bodram to Sheriff Alms,
"but I don't give a fuck! I enforce the law; people don't like the law
because it won't let them do like they want."

But for all Laid Bodram's cruelty, there was one in town who
strongly agreed with everything he did, and told him so.

"Oh, I'm right on them, Mrs. Bedden," he said. "A nigger
breathes heavy and I got him. Maybe the chain gang for him."

"Maybe the chain gang for him?" said Barbara Bedden.

"Oh, yeah," laughed Laid Bodram. "The chain gang for just
breathing heavy. Even if he don't do it in my presence. If I just
hear about it: A nigger's breathing heavy!"

"In jail he goes, huh?" roared Barbara Bedden.

"For life!" roared Laid Bodram. "Send a black motherfucker to
jail for life just because he breathed heavy!"

They both laughed so hard they could hardly stand up and tears
from laughter were in their evil eyes.

They met many times thereafter, and talked and laughed many
times thereafter, Barbara Bedden and Laid Bodram did. And one
time when they were laughing together, Laid Bodram pressed real
close and Barbara Bedden felt his hardness and looked up and saw
his broad shoulders and passion-ridden eyes and face, knew he
needed to go under her dress, and when he fiercely kissed her, she
felt her own fires light, too, and became uncontrolled and all
submissive and couldn't stop him and didn't want to try, and he
pressed further and straight out fucked her! Did it to her
thoroughly! One fierce fuck like she had never known before in all
her young and quiet life; and they became lovers, with her a
respectable married woman.

Column Beda had been away on a delivery trip to upper
Tennessee and returned on the occasion of the opening of the first
theatre Pag-Paw had ever had. A theatre called the Paw-Pag, a
reversal of the town's name, and a beautiful edifice, built just
recently and owned by a Northerner, Tracy Lundrich, a gentleman
of a man, who said he would abide with the Southern tradition of
Negroes at the back of the theatre, upstairs in the balcony.

And so waves of laughter prevailed throughout the place as Column Beda squeezed his big self into the small seat in the small upstairs area.

"It's just too big for you, Column," quipped Danny Pitter. "They should have made you smaller."

Column Beda laughed his jarring laughter and made everybody else laugh, too, before the show amusement.

It was 1918 and the pictures starred William S. Hart in a Western, and Theda Bara in a tragedy of gold-rush days. The comedy starred Buster Keaton. And Column's jarring laughter caused even extra laughter from the packed audience.

After the show, when everybody was leaving the theatre, Column Beda was for the first time seen by Laid Bodram.

"What the hell is that?" said Laid Bodram, startled at the size and height of towering Column Beda.

"That's our Column Beda," said Sheriff Alms, proudly.

"Oh, so that's him," said Laid Bodram reflectively. "Yes, I've heard of him and all his feats." And Laid Bodram frowned and darkened like an extra midnight had settled on him. Yes, he thought, I hate him even more when I see him than I hated him before.

"He's just too popular," said Barbara Bedden. "I can't stand it!"

"I know," said Laid Bodram. "But it won't be for long. I've got a plan."

"A good one?"

"The oldest in the South," said Laid Bodram. "I'm bringing over an old girl friend of mine to set it up. There used to be something between us," he said, seeing the agony he wrought in his love at the mention of another woman. "Her name is Romanza Shellis. She's a looker and in Buckettown I had her claim a nigger raped her.

"His name was Chatham There-ee, the blackest motherfucker in all Georgia, and he made two mistakes. The first was when she showed it to him in the woods, all her under charms, the pinkness and everything, and he went for it, hook, line and sinker, crying like a newborn baby all the while, before it gets its first bottle and is starving to paining. Oh, he fucked her! But he shouldn't have. The law of the South—nix white. But how could he help it? She showed him the gash and he was pink-pussy conquered. Immediately he poured his liquid-pits into her, she jumped up

screaming and running wild-hoar into town before he could stop
her, hollering that a black motherfucker had just raped her. Tore
her open with his big kidney-cadenza. Said she didn't have a
chance against his brute strength, but fought hard to protect
Southern womanhood and lost, as he savagely ripped her like her
cunt was side-gutter garbage!

"The rage of the populace rose and burst like a giant bomb, with
dynamite-people screaming one thing as they tore out of the town
and into the woods where they knew for sure Chatham There-ee
would run. And run he did, and that was his second mistake. He
was guilty, he had fucked a white woman, and he ran. But how
could he help it?

" 'Run, nigger, run!' they screamed. 'We'll get you, nigger! You
fucked her! We'll get you!'

"Chatham ran. Oh my god, how he ran. All speed and getaway.
All moves forward. Tearing. Tearing. Leaves, woods, greenery—
self. Getaway was everything!

"Then he heard the barking, which when you hear it, you know
that the two legs you have will not carry you faster than theirs: the
four-legged dogs!

"When the voices were on him, he knew it was hopeless, but he
tried.

" 'There he goes! Get him! Run, nigger! Run, nigger! Oh, run,
nigger!!'

"About him! Near him! On him! They had him! A shivering black
jelly!

" 'Please boss! Oh my god, boss! Please, boss!'

"They seized him though, so jelly trembling they could hardly
hold him—but they did.

"The rope was stiff and unbending. It looked like a stick as they
tightened it around his black neck—kicking, punching, beating,
stomping, and clubbing his submissive jelly-hide all the time.

" 'I didn't do it, boss!'

" 'You didn't, nigger?'

" 'Yes, I did it, boss! Don't kill me, boss! Mercy, boss!'

" 'Did you show mercy, nigger? Mongrel-dog!'

"They tied him up tightly, and just before they took him up, I
pulled out my knife and ripped open his trousers.

" 'Not that, boss! Not my dick, boss! Kill me first, boss! Not that,
please, boss! Not that!'

"I grabbed his dick and slashed at it as violently as I could. Three strokes cleaned it from his stomach, shattering screams from him all the while.

"Then they yanked him high, bleeding heavily from his underbelly I threw his dick into the bushes, balls and all!"

"Balls and all?" laughed Barbara Bedden.

"Balls and all!" laughed Laid Bodram.

They both laughed heartily.

"And I thought as I looked at him hanging there: He is neither a man or a woman now, just a dead un-nigger bleeding."

"That's the most beautiful story I ever heard," said Barbara Bedden. "And now I want you to stone-fuck me like just before your dick was going to be cut off."

And Laid Bodram stone-fucked, gun-fucked, savage-fucked, butcher-fucked Barbara Bedden until she went into convulsions and was paralyzed with passion and overwrought emotions when he squirted his built-up, seemingly screaming liquid-pits into her wide open, accepting and spasmodic cunt, in a superhuman come on both sides that near wrung the lives out of the two of them.

"The house is all ready, Widow Marview," said Column Beda. "Want me to drive you out, Ma'am?"

"Please do, Column," said the old Widow Marview. "It'll be a pleasure to get away from this hotel awhile. It's been so noisy lately since the soldiers arrived, especially on the weekends."

The town populace watched as the Widow Marview's boy, the Widow Marview's big, towering boy, Column Beda, drove her out of town in her own private horse-drawn coach.

From the moment Romanza Shellis arrived in town and checked in at the Stairs Hotel, all eyes were upon her, men and women.

What was she doing here? That beauty. Just passing through? Wish she'd leave! She looks like trouble! Too stunning!

And Romanza Shellis strolled her stunning self out on the streets of Pag-Paw for all eyes to eat in her compelling beauty. And Barbara Bedden wondered greatly about this woman—this fascinating woman, and hated her.

"She'll do the trick," said Laid.

"Be sure you don't," said Barbara.

"You want another exhaustion?" asked Laid.

And Barbara Bedden got all weak again but collected herself because this was not the time or place.

When Romanza Shellis saw Column Beda for the first time upon his return from the Widow Marview's house, she was amazed at so huge and mountainous a man. How could she take all him? He must be ripping! But Laid had said he wanted it in for sperm and bleeding and whatnot. And Laid had been and still could be her man. So, she'd hoar for him. After all, a nigger was in truth a man, too—only black!

Romanza Shellis carefully followed Column Beda everywhere he went outside of town. And one day, a good ways from town, she presented herself and got a surprise.

"I know you've been following me," said Column Beda.

"I want you," said Romanza right off. She raised her skirt to show Column the whole of her under theatre.

"Put it down," said Column. "I'm not moved."

"What, nigger?" blasted Romanza, angry and hurt.

"That's right," said Column Beda, and he walked away.

"You goddamn black bitch! Don't you turn your back on my beautiful cunt!" screamed Romanza.

But Column never turned, and, towering, he walked on.

"You goddamn, you goddamn double nigger!" screamed Romanza, frustrated and bitter as brine and three sixes. "I'll get you yet!"

"He turned me down, Laid," she told Bodram afterwards when they met alone and not too far from town.

"Huh?" said Laid. "That big nigger didn't fuck you?"

"Never flinched, Laid. And I showed him all my theatre-pussy!" said Romanza Shellis.

"Showed a nigger all your theatre-pussy and he never flinched?" screamed Laid. "Then show it to me!" And he threw Romanza down, punched her in the face, ripped half her clothing off and fucked her hard as his body could, and she loved it!

Then he ripped her clothes even more, scratched her about the body, and told her to run screaming into town that Column Beda had fucked her like a dog in the woods! Raped her brutally!

And that is what Romanza Shellis did, with Laid Bodram staying behind to rip up her panties and fling them on the ground.

It was 1918, and the town of Pag-Paw went wild hearing the

dreadful news. Some had seen Romanza running into town, naked but for her half-off dress, every treasure of sex she ever owned seen by any eye that wanted to see it. And sight it was.

"How could Column? But he has. He's niggered. He's done it. They all do. Treat them right and they nigger. Rape your women. We gotta get him. Our own Column!"

The whole town and community ran then. Into the woods to get Column Beda, and Sheriff Alms, who wouldn't believe it, had to go along.

"Column didn't," he insisted.

"He did! He did!" shouted Laid Bodram. "And we've got to get him!" And he with the populace hit the woods so hard the trees shook.

"There he is! There's Column! Get him! Get Fubber! Get motherfucker!"

And they leaped on the astonished Column Beda, because astonished he was at seeing all the people he knew so well coming at him so furiously.

"What is it? What is it?" he yelled, his great strength and adroitness fending them off. And try though they did, they couldn't get at him good.

"Rapist! Rapist!" they screamed.

"Rape who!" yelled Column. "Who? I'm no rapist."

"Liar!" they screamed. "Liar!" coming at him full force now with clubs and stones and bricks.

Sheriff Alms wouldn't shoot or allow Laid Bodram to shoot, but some shotguns that missed everything went off.

"Order! Order! Shut up!" Column Beda was told by the sheriff to put out his hands, but he wouldn't, even when the sheriff drew his gun. He would not be handcuffed if they killed him.

"I didn't do anything to be handcuffed or beaten for, and that's that," shouted Column Beda. "Go ahead and kill me!"

"You've got to go in for questioning," said Sheriff Alms.

"O.K.," said Column, "but not in cuffs!" And he got his way as he marched to jail, his head and shoulders high above an angry Southern crowd.

"I believed in you, Column," said Rene Baines.

"I didn't rape anyone," said Column Beda.

"You're lying!" yelled Jason Dex. "You big bitch, you!"

"No, I'm not," yelled Column Beda. "I'm no rapist!"

"You are, you are!" yelled Barbara Bedden, and all the women of Pag-Paw were behind her.

Once he was in jail, things got quieter, but crowds outside never left, even when it was dark.

Sheriff Alms thought he'd have to take Column to the penitentiary for his own safety because the medical report showed blood and sperm. A new rage swept the town, and a lynching seemed certain.

Everything black in Pag-Paw was ready to head for a night in the deepest woods; that was the only safe place with Column Beda caught.

"I don't believe Column did it," said Flu Gratta. "He's not girl crazy."

"Me neither," said Look Down. "Who was raped?"

"That new bitch in town claims she was," said Danny Pitter. "I'm going to town to tell them all I know about her."

"You know about her?" asked Flu.

"All about her," said Danny. "And Laid, too."

"Danny," said Look Down, "they'll cut your cock off as sure as your name is Pitter."

"Column's my friend," said Danny. "I've got to tell the truth, come what may. He's not afraid, and neither the fuck am I!"

"You're so small, Danny," said Flu. "Like a fucken ant."

"An ant's a tough bitch!" said Danny.

"It's him! Oh, it's him!" said Romanza Shellis when brought face to face with Column Beda in his cell.

"You're lying, woman," thundered Column. "I wouldn't even look at you. You know this. Who told you to lie?"

"Bodram!" yelled little Danny Pitter. "They both did this to Chatham There-ee over in Buckettown!"

But he couldn't say more before Laid Bodram knocked him near senseless.

"It's true," he muttered, bloody.

"Is it, Bodram?" demanded Sheriff Alms.

"Hell, no! I never saw this woman before in my life," said Laid Bodram.

"The devil lying!" yelled Danny Pitter, on his feet now. "You know he did, Miss Shellis," said Danny. "You're lovers and you know it!"

"What?" said Sheriff Alms, but it didn't matter. The crowd outside broke in and overpowered all deputization and went for the cell.

But the keys were useless. Somehow Column Beda had got hold of a cable and wrapped it around the grating so it couldn't be opened and attached the cable to a pipe in the corner and braced himself. It was immovable.

"Open up, Beda! Open up!" they shouted, "or we'll shoot!"

"You won't shoot," said Column. "You want to lynch me. You won't shoot!"

It was too much for Romanza Shellis. "He didn't do it! He didn't do it!" she recanted.

"Miss, you're trying to save him now?" asked Jason Dex.

"That's right," said Sheriff Alms. "Turn him loose."

"Shut up, Sheriff! You're going soft," said Barbara Bedden, the only other woman with the jail mob. "Not standing up for Southern womanhood anymore, huh?"

"You don't understand," shouted Sheriff Alms.

The mob didn't hear him though, and maybe not Barbara Bedden either.

"Open it up! Drag him out! Drag that nigger out!"

"He didn't do it!" pleaded Romanza Shellis, recanting again. But she was beyond being heard now.

"We're going to shoot, Column!"

"Go ahead and shoot!" yelled Column.

But they didn't.

"Drag Pitter over!" ordered Barbara Bedden. "And bring a rope."

They dragged up little Danny Pitter, threw a rope over one of the overhead pipes and placed the other end around his neck.

"Now, will you let go, Beda?" demanded Barbara Bedden. "Look, we're going to hang your friend right before you."

"Hang away!" yelled Danny Pitter. "You dirty bitch, you!"

Barbara Bedden spit in his face, and two of the men punched him down. They were going to hang him.

"Wait!" said Column. "I'll open."

When he did, they rushed in and seized and bound his hands behind him.

"Where'll we take him?"

"The big tree," said Jason Dex.

"Yeah, the house tree," said Barbara Bedden.

"You're making a mistake," warned Rene Baines.

Loaded into cars, wagons, trucks and coaches, they traveled in the darkness, the Pag-Pawians, Sheriff Alms' helpers, Laid Bodram, Barbara Bedden, Romanza Shellis, and even Danny Pitter.

While this was happening, Flu Gratta and Look Down rode out to the Widow Marview's place to see what she could do to save Column Beda.

After she got the news the Widow Marview said nothing, just told Look Down to drive them to town as fast as hell and haste could take them.

The house tree reared its big self in the ominous darkness of the night. A circus shout went up from the lynch-prone mob.

It was a huge, tall tree, with a trunk as wide as a house, its branches so high they were lost in the height overhead. Over one of these they threw a thick rope. Torch-lit, they were ready to hang him.

It was hard to lynch Column Beda, but it was going to have to be done.

Column Beda stood on a horse-drawn wagon, bound tightly, a rope around his neck for the hanging. Column Beda couldn't move, he was so trussed up. But no one would whip the horses. No one, not even Jason Dex.

"Why, why? The girl's denying it now."

"She's gotten soft though. She's lying."

"Did he rape you, hussy?"

"No."

"But there was evidence!!"

And Romanza Shellis couldn't tell on her lover, Laid Bodram, now a silent dog.

"It's got to be done!" said Barbara Bedden.

"Does it?" said Rene Baines.

"If no one will, I will!" said Barbara Bedden, taking up the whip.

"Think, Barbara," said Sheriff Alms.

The mob had tied the sheriff up.

"Miserable bitch, now murderess!" said Danny Pitter.

"She really is!" It was the old Widow Marview, coming up fast from nowhere. "A married woman, and the lover of Deputy Bodram. Right, Flu?" She stood fierce and straight in the torch light.

"I've seen them," said Flu.

"Column Beda didn't do it," said the energetic old lady. "I can prove it." And she climbed up on the wagon with Column.

The Widow Marview took the thick rope from around Column's neck. The crowd with torches watched in silence. Then she did a strange thing for a woman of her station and standing in the world. The crowd gasped. She reached down and unbuckled the belt of the tied captive so his trousers could fall, and his trousers fell revealing all that he had in all his life held sacred.

"It'll clear your name for all time," she shouted. And she stepped back out of the way so the torches and eyes of the people could find what they now sought around that area between his legs. She was pointing—and they saw!

"My god! Heaven help us! He has been saved! Amen!"

And there it was, what all the talk of the black stud is all about, all the horror and fear and tales and sometimes lies, lies, the one and only, strong, gigantic, tall and towering Column Beda was as infantile as infant could be.

"You can't see it! It's so small!"

And the lights and eyes pressed closer to see the strange sight.

"A baby there! He never grew!"

"God has been cruel!"

"Couldn't have ever done it—not rape!"

Column Beda was cut free, with apologies and pardons, to which he never answered. He marched without a word straight off toward the north woods and to where? They knew! To the swamp to take his life!

"Please don't, Column, please! We didn't know! We were tricked!"

But they couldn't stop him. Couldn't touch him further. He had been touched beyond anymore touching and could not be stopped by the power of strong words and fierce, soul-weighted pleas.

The torches burned their lights on him as long as they could, until the thick foliage swallowed towering him up, and he disappeared into the heavy growth like Moses, Jesus, and Francois Villon, never to be seen again.

"To clear his name," said Danny Pitter, "they had to expose his only shame—infantile dick!"

"Life is really all dick," said Flu Gratta.

INSTITUTIONAL CONTROL
OF INTERPRETATION

by FRANK KERMODE

from SALMAGUNDI

nominated by SALMAGUNDI

A VERY LARGE NUMBER of people, of whom I am one, conceive of themselves as interpreters of texts. Whoever expounds a text (no matter at what level) and whoever castigates a text, is an interpreter. And no such person can go about the work of interpretation without some awareness of forces which limit, or try to limit, what he may say, and the ways in which he may say it. They may originate in the past, but will usually be felt as sanctions operated by one's contemporaries (this will be true whether or not one opposes and resents them). There is an organisation of opinion which may either facilitate or inhibit the individual's manner of doing interpretation, which will prescribe what may legitimately

be subjected to intensive interpretative scrutiny, and determine
whether a particular act of interpretation will be regarded as a
success or a failure, be taken into account in licit future interpretation or not. The medium of these pressures and interventions is the
institution.

In practice, the institution with which we have to deal is the
professional community which interprets secular literature and
teaches others to do so. There are better-defined and more
despotic institutions, but their existence does not invalidate the
present use of the expression. If we wanted to describe its actual
social existence we should get involved in a complex account of its
concrete manifestations in universities, colleges, associations of
higher learning; and if we wanted to define its authority we should
have to consider not only its statutory right to confer degrees and
the like, but also the subtler forms of authority acquired and
exercised by its senior and more gifted members. But we need not
at present bother with these details. It can surely be agreed that we
are talking about something quite easily identified: a professional
community which has authority (not undisputed) to define (or
indicate the limits of) a subject; to impose valuations and validate
interpretations. Such are its characteristics. It has complex relations with other institutions. In so far as it has, undeniably, a
political aspect, it trespasses on the world of power; but of itself, we
will agree, it has little power, if by that one means power to bind
and loose, to enforce compliance and anathematize deviation.
Compared with other institutions, that is, the one we are talking
about is a rather weak one. But it has none the less a family
resemblance to the others.

Such a community may be described as a self-perpetuating,
sempiternal corporation. It is, however unemphatically, however
modestly, hierarchical in structure, because its continuance depends on the right of the old to instruct the young; the young
submit because there is no other way to the succession. The old, or
senior, apply at their discretion certain checks on the competence
of those who seek to join, and eventually replace them. Their right
to do this is accompanied by an assumption that they possess a
degree of competence, partly tacit, partly a matter of techniques
which may be examined and learnt; that one has acquired these
latter is of course a claim that can be straightforwardly tested, but

the possession of interpretative power, power of divination, is tested only by reference to the tacit knowledge of the seniors, who nevertheless claim, tacitly as a rule, that they can select candidates capable of acquiring these skills, and have the right to certify that they have achieved them. I am describing the world as it is or as we all know it, and am doing so only because its familiarity may have come to conceal from us its mode of operation.

The texts on which members of this institution practice their trade are not secret (though some of them are in practice inaccessible to the uninitiated) and the laity has, in principle, full access to them. But although the laity may, unaided or helped only by secondary or sub-institutional instruction (radio talks, Sunday newspapers, reading groups or literary clubs) acquire what in some circumstances might pass for competence, there is a necessary difference between them and persons whom we may think of as licensed practitioners. It is as if the latter were "in orders". Their right to practice is indicated by arbitrary signs, not only certificates, robes and titles, but also professional jargons. The activities of such persons, whether diagnostic or exegetical, are privileged, and they have access to senses that do not declare themselves to the laity. Moreover they are subject, in professional matters, to no censure but that of other licensed practitioners acting as a body; the opinion of the laity is of no consequence whatever, a state of affairs which did not exist before the institution now under consideration firmly established itself—as anyone may see by looking with a layman's eye on the prose its members habitually write, and comparing it with the prose of critics who still thought of themselves as writing for an educated general public, for *la cour et la ville*.

However, my concern here is to explore a little further the means by which the institution controls the exegetical activities of its members. Though it does so in part by fairly obvious means— for example, it controls the formation and the subsequent career of its members (who decides whether one is to have one's Ph. D?)—it has subtler resources, such as *canonical* and *hermeneutic* restrictions, and these are more interesting. By the first of these expressions I mean the determination of what may or ought to be interpreted, and by the second the decision as to whether a particular means of doing so is permissible. Of course canons change, especially in a "weak" institution; and so do styles of interpretation. How these changes occur is another part of my subject, and a subdivision of that part is the question of heresy.

I first considered these matters in a very brief essay written in 1974,[1] and I must ask leave to give a summary of what I said. The question was, how do we know an interpretation is wrong? We claim this knowledge, obviously; if a student in reading "my love is fair/ As any she belied with false compare" construes "she" as a personal pronoun and not as a noun we have no compunction about saying he is wrong; though if William Empson said the "wrong" sense was present, as an instance of one or other (fourth to seventh) type of ambiguity (a "verbal nuance. . .which gives room for alternative reactions to the same piece of language") most of us would be less ready with our pencils. I. A. Richards, who did so much to encourage liberty of interpretation, has always been exercised as to the moment when this liberty becomes license; he deplores people who have no sense "of what is and is not admissible in interpretation," and sees in some of Roman Jakobson's work means by which poetry may be defended against such "omnipossibilists". Yet it seems clear that the necessary decisions are rarely if ever arrived at methodically. What happens is rather that the institution requires interpretations to satisfy its tacit knowledge of the permitted range of sense; the requirement operates very simply when the disputed interpretation is the work of a novice, and may be harder or even, in the long run impossible, to apply if the author is known to be competent—one reason why the institutional consensus changes. But there clearly is a sense in which a professional body *knows;* how it does so was a preoccupation of Michael Polanyi's. There is an institutionalised competence, and what it finds unacceptable is incompetent. It does not, as a rule, have to think hard about individual cases—Polanyi gives amusing examples of the application of this tacit knowledge to scientific contributions which have every appearance of soundness but arrive at conclusions *known* to be impossible. Of course there is no guarantee that this tacit knowledge is infallible; it is founded on the set of assumptions currently available—the paradigm, if you like, or, if you like, the *epistème,* and a revolution may change everything. Mendel is a famous instance; but such instances may be harder to come by outside the physical sciences. I cited Walter Whiter, and some lesser Shakespearian examples. But the im-

mediate point is simply that it is upon the basis of a corpus of tacit
knowledge, shared—with whatever qualifications—by the senior
ranks of the hierarchy, that we allow or disallow an interpretation.

There is nothing astonishing about this conclusion, which might
even be regarded as trite by members of other institutions no less
quarrelsome though possibly more self-conscious than our own. In
the psychoanalytic community, we are told, "the experience of
insight results from the construction of a perspective most satisfying to the present communal initiative".[2] That is, what is found is
the sort of thing it is agreed we ought to be looking for. True
interpretation is, in fact, what Jürgen Habermas calls it: "a consensus among partners."[3] How else shall we judge its truth? Yet we
should not altogether omit to mention that the institution also
values originality; if there is agreement that some contribution has
the force to modify or even transform what was formerly agreed,
then that contribution is honored and may become the staple of a
new pattern of consensus. Yet even such rare and revolutionary
departures depend upon the consent of the hierarchy.

Of institutions having a primary duty to interpret texts, and to
nominate a certain body of texts as deserving or requiring repeated
exegesis (interminable exegesis, indeed) the Church is the most
exemplary. Self-perpetuating, hierarchical, authoritative, much
concerned with questions of canon, and wont, as we are, to
distinguish sharply between initiate and uninitiate readings, it is a
model we would do well to consider as we attempt to understand
our own practice.

It is, of course, difficult to make such brief generalizations stick,
and the Church has been prone to fission on precisely the issues I
am discussing: authority, hierarchy, canon, initiation, and differ-
ential readings. But if it has something to teach us we must do what
we can to overcome this difficulty. Let us first consider the canon.
The word means "rod" or "rule" or "measure" and we all know,
roughly, how it applies to the Old and New Testaments, or to
Shakespeare: *Hamlet* belongs to the canon, *The Yorkshire Tragedy*
to the Apocrypha, *Two Noble Kinsmen* is still among the latter, but
many think it should belong to the former. Apocrypha meant
"hidden ones", but came to mean "spurious ones", and now just
means "uncanonical ones". The canon possess an authenticity
which the Apocrypha lack. But to say in what that authenticity
resided or resides is a very complicated matter.

The canon seems to have begun to crystallize in reaction against an heretical attempt to impose a rigorously restricted list of sacred books on the church of the mid-second century. Marcion rejected the whole of the Old Testament, accepted one gospel (Luke, much reduced) and added ten purged versions of Pauline letters to complete the canon. Marcion's canon may remind us at once of some rigoristic attempts (Leavis, Winters) to purge our own. He certainly knew what he wanted. In abolishing the Old Testament he was acting on a belief that its types and prophecies were false. This was a bold way of solving a difficulty of the early church. The establishment of a narrow canon eliminated, among other awkwardness, the problem of the status of the Old Testament. The first Christians had no scripture except the Old Testament, but as the Law ceased to be of prime importance to them their relation to it grew problematical; rejecting the agnostic rejection, they instituted a new way of reading it, as a repertory of types prefiguring Christianity. In so doing they virtually destroyed its value as history or as law; it became a set of scattered indications of events it did not itself report. But the correspondences between what was to be the New Testament and the Old were very important, since they were held to validate the Christian version. Marcion thought the Old Testament wrong and wicked, and he accepted the conclusion that Christianity up to his time had been erroneous, the true words of the founder adulterated[4]

Marcion was certain that he knew what the original tradition was in its purity; he is the first in a long line of protestant reformers who enjoyed the same assurance. The magnitude of the crisis he brought upon the church is well described by Von Campenhausen. And he was for a time very successful. His was the first canon. The counter-offensive had to include the provision of a canon more acceptable to the consensus of the church. There is much dispute about the criteria employed. The Old Testament was defended, and out of a mass of gospels four were chosen as "authentic" (the rejected included of course Marcion's). All this took time; and the idea of closing the canon took more time, and was prompted by the threat of another heresy, namely Montanism, which used innumerable apocalyptic books. Thus was the canon achieved; and eventually the habit grew of thinking of it as two books, or two parts of one total, comprehensive book.

Later came further benefits. For at various moments the institu-

tion, protecting its text, conferred upon it the virtues of apostolic-
ity, infallibility, inexhaustibility and inspiration. Indeed, it took
centuries of scholarly research and dispute to reach the point
where the text was believed to possess all these qualities; the canon
was not finally closed, even for Roman Catholics, till the Council of
Trent, in 1546, when it was also pronounced equally authoritative
in all its parts. The Lutheran tradition opposes this doctrine still. It
is among Protestant theologians that one notes a tendency at
present to re-open the canon—and perhaps admit the Gospel of St.
Thomas, discovered at Nag Hammadi in 1945.[5]

This brief allusion to the history of the canon is meant simply to
demonstrate the nature of the operations conducted by the institution which formulates and protects it, and the close relation
between the character of an institution and the needs it satisfies by
validating texts and interpretations of them. The desire to have a
canon, more or less unchanging, and to protect it against charges of
inauthenticity or low value (as the Church protected Hebrews, for
example, against Luther) is an aspect of the necessary conservatism
of a learned institution. An interesting example of this conservatism
is the history of Erasmus' edition of the Greek New Testament,
which was for three centuries the *textus receptus*. Erasmus hardly
began the editorial job, even in terms of the manuscripts and
editorial techniques then available; for some parts of the book he
had no Greek text at all, and himself translated it from the Latin.
His errors were obvious enough, but his successors dared not alter
his text, reprinting the mistakes and putting the better readings in
the notes. So it remained until Lachmann; and the vast editorial
effort which he began still goes on. The institution had its own
sources of truth, and purposes best served by claims of inerrancy,
even in a text that could not (like vernacular translation) seduce the
unlearned, or free interpretation from the control of Tradition held
to be more authoritative even than the text itself.

It is obvious that control of interpretation is intimately connected with the valuations set upon texts. The decision as to
canonicity depends upon a consensus that a book has the requisite
qualities, the determination of which is, in part, a work of interpretation. And once a work becomes canonical the work of the
interpreter begins again. For example, so long as the institution,
assuming inerrancy, desires to minimize the contradictions and
redundancies of the gospels, a main object of interpretation must

be the achievement of harmony—"the concord of the canonical scriptures," as Augustine proclaims it in *The City of God*. There is a very long lapse of time between the first known "harmony" and the first known "synopsis," made in the nineteenth century under a new impulse to explain rather than explain away the discrepancies. They had been noted from the earliest times, and either elided (as in the *Diatessaron* of Tatian) or discounted (as by Origen and Augustine). Scrutiny of the gospels never ceased to be intense; but the attention they got was controlled by the desire of the institution to justify them as they were and find them harmonious; until, in the long course of time and under the pressure of changes in the general culture, a more secular form of attention prevailed.

The acceptance within the institution of the position that there is no separate discipline of sacred hermeneutics was very slow and is still incomplete. But one thing is true, whatever the measure of secularization achieved: at all stages the interpretation of the scriptures is primarily the task of professionals. The position that they are openly available to all men, yet in an important sense closed to everybody except approved institutional interpreters has been maintained from the beginning (in Mark, 4: 11) and is far from fully eroded. The work of the early interpreters was intended not only to establish harmonies between canonised texts, but also to elicit senses not available to persons of ordinary perceptions. Interpretation of the Old Testament was required to deal with its peculiar relation to the new established faith, to make it part, as Clement said, of the "symphony of senses".[6] Whatever seemed not to suit the institution's requirements had to be glossed into conformity. Gaps which opened between the apparent literal sense and the sense acceptable to doctrine or later-established custom had to be filled by interpretations, usually typological or allegorical. And always there were the secret senses, protected by the institution itself. At first these were oral, part of a tradition for which the institution was responsible; later there might be two texts, one generally available, the other reserved for initiates. And even of the public text there might be private interpretations. The Roman Catholic Church preserved at Trent (and I suppose in theory continues to preserve, though restrictions on Catholic exegetes have been much reduced) the position that it alone has the right, in the light of tradition, to determine interpretation. It was at Trent—in violent reaction against the enemy's

bibliocentrism—that the inutility of scripture was seriously proposed; for since scripture was always subject to the superior traditional knowledge of the Church, it could be called redundant and,
in the hands of ignorant outsiders, a source of error.

Yet, despite the success of protestants in contesting this institutional position, and despite the availability of the texts to a laity of
much increased literacy, the interpretation of the works of the
canon continued to be the duty of the clergy. Between the layman
reading his bible and the modern exegete disintegrating the
Pauline epistles or performing newly-validated hermeneutic
operations—form-criticism, redaction-criticism, structuralist
criticism—on the texts, there is as great a gulf as ever. The extent
of it can be judged by anybody who looks at a modern gospel
commentary written for professionals with one written for laymen—say, the Cambridge commentaries on the Greek New Testament, and the Cambridge commentaries on the New English
Bible. The difference is astonishing, and cannot be explained in
terms of the relative inaccessibility of the Greek text; the nature
of the discussion is wholly altered.

It is clear, then, that there is, in the canonical texts, a reserve of
privileged senses which are accessible only to people who in some
measure have the kind of training, and are supported by the
authority, of the learned institution to which they belong. And
even in the most disinterested forms of interpretation—those
which depend on historical enquiry or editorial techniques—there
is, practically always, some effect from a prior doctrinal commitment. The practitioners believe, that is, in the religion whose
doctors have instructed them in scholarship. This is not in the least
surprising, but its obviousness ought not to prevent our taking it
into account. It is a very important aspect of the sociology of
interpretation. There are senses beyond the literal; but to divine
them one needs to know where they are, how they relate to
doctrine more broadly defined, and how it is permissible to attain
them. Changes occur, certainly; a very radical change began in the
late eighteenth century, and we have still not seen the last effects
of it. For though they occur, they are slow and complicated; and
they are attended by comparable changes in the institution itself,
some of them signalled by public announcement and demonstration, as in Vatican II, some of them less obvious. A neat instance of
the relation between the desires of the institution and the kinds of

interpretation undertaken is this: after Leo XIII proposed the philosophy of St. Thomas Aquinas as a subject of neglected importance, there was a neo-scholastic revival. After Vatican II Catholic scholars acquired a new freedom in exegesis; disciplinary threats removed or diminished, they were able to do the kind of speculative research and commentary that had been largely forbidden them, so that modern biblical scholarship had been overwhelmingly non-Catholic. Of course we should remember that changes in different parts of the institution occur at very different speeds; the new liberty of Catholic scholarship is one thing; the fact that there are in the modern world many fundamentalisms, some merely popular but others belonging to highly organised institutions with control over interpretation, is another.

To labour the matter no further, let me turn to the literary institution and its canon. The points of comparison are that like its senior, though much less effectively, it controls the choice of canonical texts, limits their interpretation, and attends to the training of those who will inherit the presumption of institutional competence by which these sanctions are applied.

Can one really speak of a canon of literary-academic studies? It has perhaps grown a little more difficult to do so, but I think the answer is still yes. The only serious attempt at a description of its formation is, so far as I know, the sixteen-page essay by E. R. Curtius in his *European Literature in the Latin Middle Ages*.[7] Curtius shows that the ecclesiastical canon grew in importance, not only as a measure of the sacred writings, but also in the liturgical and juristic activities of the institution. So there was a canon of Fathers, a canon of Doctors; the notion that there was a set scheme for everything took hold. The medieval schools evolved a blend of pagan and Christian authors which also became canonical. It changed between the Middle Ages and the Renaissance, and it has changed again since then. The Renaissance also saw the first vernacular canon, which was Italian; other vernaculars followed suit, the French in the seventeenth, the English in the eighteenth centuries. I suppose we could say that the American canon is a formation of the present century. Curtius is somewhat impatient with these nationalistic canon-formations, and wants a canon of world literature which will put an end to such local conceptions.

The formation of a secular world canon is, however, outside the scope of existing institutions; the success of "comparative literature" in the academic world has been real but limited, partly because it does not work easily within the bureaucratic systems that give force to institutional decisions. The interest of Curtius' valuable and learned but inconclusive essay lies in his understanding of the fact that the relation between a canon and the historical situation of the institution which establishes it is close and complex; and he gives some support to the view that the formation and control of the secular canon we are now considering are historically related as well as analogous to those of the Church.

Of course we must not look, in an institution which lacks formal creeds and has no conceivable right to discipline a laity, for anything resembling that ecclesiastical rigor of which Trent is the image. The canon we are now discussing will necessarily be a more shadowy affair, even more subject to dispute than the ecclesiastic. The contenders for inclusion, and the apocrypha, will be more numerous, and it is impossible for us to settle the question by burning either the books or those who support their claim to inclusion.

Our institution is relatively new, and it is not so long since the question of the canon was simpler. It was defined, in a manner familiar to us from ecclesiastical history, by attacks upon it, which usually included moves to replace some member of the canon with another brought in from outside it. When did Donne become canonical? With Grierson's edition? Not quite; probably only with Eliot's essay of 1921, or even later, when that essay (itself a very late move in a campaign which had been going on intermittently for the best part of a century) gained academic support. Eliot was very much a canonist; the argument of "Tradition and the Individual Talent" presupposes a canon, though one to which works can be added in a timeless mix, the new affecting the sense of the old, much as the New Testament altered the sense of the Old.

As everybody knows, the accession of Donne was the cause of major alterations in the canon, or at any rate of attempts to change it radically. For example, the doctrinal changes which enabled that accession also implied a new valuation or even the extrusion of Milton, not to speak of the rewriting of the history of poetry in accordance with the law of the Dissociation of Sensibility. I myself was taught by enthusiasts who believed that Milton had been "dislodged," to use Dr. Leavis's celebrated word for it. The Chinese Wall had been outflanked. This movement began outside

the academy, but was taken up within it. In the long run Milton
stayed in; but great changes in the method of interpreting his texts
became necessary, as anybody can see who compares the Mil-
tonists of the early part of the century with those now dominant—
say M. Y. Hughes with Stanley Fish, or Walter Raleigh with
Christopher Ricks, whose book on Milton is indeed a splendid
example of the ways in which a need to defend a canonical author
may call forth new critical and exegetical resources. Meanwhile the
motives of the antiMiltonists were scrutinized with hostility.

Sociologists of religion tell us that institutions react, broadly, in
two ways to threats from outside. Either they "legitimate" the new
doctrine or text (the reception of Donne) or they "nihilate" it (the
defeat of the attempt to dislodge Milton). In our institution the first
of these is the more usual course, partly because of a relative lack of
power, partly because of a looseness of organization, and partly
because the tradition in which we work is predominantly Protestant. There is a measure of tolerance in all that we do. What we
value most in work submitted to us by those who would like to join
us is an originality that remains close to the consensual norms.
Moreover we are, in general, inclined to pluralism and none too
systematic, as scholars who take method seriously are often willing
to tell us. And yet there is some rigor somewhere in the institution.

If you look at any M.L.A. December program you will see what
looks like total license in regard to canon, or, to put that more
liberally, an openness to innovation, a willingness to respond to
legitimate pressures from the (political) world outside. There are
sessions on Black literature, on neglected women writers, and the
like; there are also discussions of relatively avant-garde critical and
theoretical movements which have certainly not won their appeal
to the senior consensus. On the other hand, the M.L.A. Bibliography shows a solid concentration of interpretative effort on the
canonical figures. One concludes that here, as with the national
and regional variations of canon that everybody is aware of, we
have evidence of the ability of the institution to control marginal
innovation and unrest. A few years ago the M.L.A. suffered
something that looked for a moment like a revolution; but it was
only a saturnalian interlude (appropriate to the season of their
meeting), an episode of Misrule, tolerated because in the end
reinforcing the stability of the institution. The boy bishops had
their day, and the more usual, more authentically prelatical figures

have resumed their places. We can tolerate even those who believe the institution should be destroyed. As Thoreau remarked, "They speak of moving society but have no resting place without it."

I have digressed from the question of our canon to speak of the forces within the institution which operate to change it, usually slowly. Over a period we can see marked differences. When I was a student nobody taught Dickens; we can trace his acceptance (in England, anyway) by the stages of Dr. Leavis's slow change of mind (he is the Marcion of the canon, unless that role is reserved for Yvor Winters). Few of my teachers even mentioned George Eliot. Blake hovered on the canonical margin, Joyce was still an outsider, though we read him. At Oxford all these problems were simplified somewhat by the decree that studiable, judgeable literature came to an end in 1830; nothing after that was licensed for exegesis.

How do changes in the canon occur? They usually depend on the penetration of the academy by enthusiastic movements from without. This is not always so; for example, there seems to be in progress at the moment an academic evaluation of early American literature; Cotton Mather is suddenly full of interest, Charles Brockden Brown is readable and capable of interpretation. But however the changes originate, there seems to be a law which says that the institution must validate texts before they are licensed for professional exegesis. After that there seems to be no limit, the exegetical progress is interminable. *Ulysses* is a good instance of this; a more remarkable one is Melville, ignored for sixty years or more and now fully canonical and endlessly explicated. George Eliot is another interesting case. The laity had probably gone on reading her, as it went on reading Dickens; but only lately, in my own time, has she become the subject of an apparently infinite series of interpretations, which are of quite a different kind from those which for years served as standard, say those of Leslie Stephen and Henry James.

Licensed for exegesis: such is the seal we place upon our canonical works. How do we license the exegesis itself? The intrusion of new work into the canon usually involves some change in the common wisdom of the institution as to permissible hermeneutic procedures. Thus the admission to American faculties of New Critics from outside the academy was a complex phenomenon, involving a quasi-political victory over the older philologists, a change in the canon (acceptance of Donne, Eliot, etc.) and a new hermeneutic, popularised by Brooks and Warren, and formalised by Wimsatt. The more evangelical success of Leavis resulted in the penetration of the English system of literary education by his followers; at the pastoral level they are still, probably, the most powerful teachers of reading in the country, and their moralistic contempt for non-believers—the unargued certitudes of the conventicle, the easy sneers of the epigoni—still makes its lamentable contribution to the tone of English literary debate. They hold to a rigorous canon (the line of wit, the great tradition, the wheelwright's shop) into which, from time to time, there are furtive insertions (Dickens, Tolstoi), uneasy candidatures (Emily Brontë), apocryphal appendices (L. H. Myers, Ronald Bottrall, Hawthorne).

From the institutional point of view the New Criticism and *Scrutiny* were (and still are) pretty successful heresies. They revised the canon and they changed the methods. The people initiated into reading by the institution began to read differently. Other attempts to alter canon and doctrine—those of Winters, Pound, James Reeves—had markedly less success. But we are now observing the progress of what may be more radical heresy. Unlike the theologians, we are not good at finding distinctive names for hermeneutic fashions; this is another New Criticism, or *nouvelle critique*, though it has moved a long way on from the French innovations of the sixties. The revival of Russian Formalism, the development of a new semiology, a new Marxism, a new psychoanalysis, a new post-Heideggerian anti-metaphysics, with new forms of cultural history—all the developments we associate with such names as Barthes, Lacan, Derrida, Foucault—have had some success within the institution, and may have more. A certain ideological fervour accompanies these manifestations, and they undoubtedly alter the shape of institutional interests in interpretation. Indeed they are avowedly subversive. They alter the limits of the subject, propose new views of history, institutions and meaning. This is not the place to enter into discussion of the validity of such new doctrine; I should, to keep within the boundaries of my topic, merely ask how we may expect the institution to contain or control it.

The fact that interpretation, under these new auspices, has a different sociology is not, in the end, subversive at all; it was probably necessary to move away from the aesthetic or iconic mode in which we spent a generation, and to view literary texts as texts among texts, all perhaps requiring "deconstructive" interpretation to give them another span of life. Certain kinds of literature, what the Germans call *kleinliteratur,* or "trivial literature," and also film, are accommodated in a sort of deuterocanonical sense. The institution, by hierarchical consensus, will try to protect itself against barbarism, but it will do so by control of appointments and promotions more than by working on the canon. For there is a risk that new hermeneutic procedures can be taken up by people interested only in new procedures, methodological mimics whose gestures seem empty, and who care nothing for any canon. They will have to be controlled in some other way. The new modes of interpretation, seriously practiced, are in themselves much less of a problem because of the underlying continuity between them and the traditional modes.

I hope that if I manage to explain what I mean by this I can justify the whole strategy of speaking about the institution of literary and critical scholarship as if it had some analogy with ecclesiastical and other institutions. First let us ask what kind of thing such institutions find on the whole to be acceptable as changes. The flatly unacceptable (a demonstration that the average gestation period of mammals is an integer multiple of the number II) is not even examined, and regarded as a joke. (But this example comes from the annals of an institution far more sure of itself than ours, or even the church, which, in its present uncertainties, lets all manner of things through the gate that would have been kept out even twenty years ago. In short, we must see that control over interpretation may vary with the social stability of the institution.) On the other hand thousands of relatively unimportant findings, made within the confines of "normal" science, are tested and approved but not greatly applauded. In between are the works, very few of them, which, in Polanyi's words, "sharply modify accepted views" yet are themselves accepted; to them the authorities "pay their highest homage".[8] The authors of such contributions—Einstein, Dirac, Godel—have a security of fame within their institutions which is beyond the dreams of all others. In short, the institution does not resist, rather encourages change; but it monitors change with very sophisticated machinery.

Our practices, though less decisive, are analogous, and their traditional justification is much older. When we teach we do so (unless we are very dishonest) on the assumption that what we do is something that can be learned. This can be a worrying assumption; for example, it was by asking discriminating questions about it that Northrop Frye arrived at his negative theory of value, his view that what can be taught is literary taxonomy. But most of us suppose that we are doing more than that (if indeed we are doing that at all). And in practice we do more than that. We wean candidates from the habit of literal reading. Like the masters who reserved secret senses in the second century, we are in the business of conducting readers out of the sphere of the manifest. Our institutional readings are not those of the outsiders, so much is self-evident; though it is only when we see some intelligent non-professional confronted by a critical essay from our side of the fence that we see how esoteric we are. And in this respect we have to think of ourselves as exponents of various kinds of secondary interpretation—spiritual understandings, as it were, compared with carnal, and available only to those who, in second-century terms, have circumcized ears, that is, are trained by us.

And here we may reflect on the resemblance between ours and the psychoanalytical practice. Our concern, when we depart from the merely descriptive, is with latent sense. We learn, and teach others, to be alert to condensation and displacement in the text; we develop a strong taste for, and a power to divine, overdeterminations. That is why my reading of a Conrad novel, say, is different from an undergraduate's, though his will grow more like mine; and even more different from a layman's. The layman, we like to think, sees without perceiving, hears without understanding. He who has ears to hear, let him hear.

The continuity of the newest criticism with the early forms of interpretation licensed by the establishment is in the perpetuity of such assumptions. Poets may have a third eye, analysts a third ear, exegetes a circumcized ear; these additional or purified organs are figures for the divinatory skills acquired within institutions. The deconstruction of a text is a bold figure for what exegetes *de métier* have always claimed the right to do. In the early enthusiastic stage the techniques employed may seem overbold, and attract the censure of the hierarchy—this is what happened to Empson, and to the anti-historical element of the New Criticism. But in the end the fate, so much dreaded by the newest critics, who are conscious enough of history and of the cultural forces of inertia, will overtake the enthusiasts; they will be "recuperated" or, if they are not, they will be nihilated. I do not offer an opinion as to whether this is right or just, but merely argue that when the charismatic becomes institutional some "routinization" is bound to occur; and if it does not become institutional it falls into neglect. As it has, in not too fanciful a sense, been institutional all along, and as nobody outside the institution has much chance of understanding it, I do not think there is much doubt about the outcome. How the experience will alter the future "tacit knowledge" of the institution it is impossible to guess.

I wonder whether some among my hearers, the younger perhaps, may not find what I have said a little cynical and gloomy. I believe that institutions confer value and privilege upon texts, and license modes of interpretation; and that qualification for senior membership of such institutions implies acceptance, not total of course, of this state of affairs. And I suppose one might well look upon this as an unhappy situation. Such institutions as ours do reflect the larger society which they somehow serve, and it may be an unjust society. But how else shall we protect the latent sense? The mysteries, said Clement, were not proclaimed openly, "in such a way that any listener could understand them"; they were spoken in parables, riddles, requiring exegesis.[9] And exegesis has its rules, on the foundation of which has been built the whole structure of modern hermeneutics. It is by recognizing the tacit authority of the institution that we achieve the measure of liberty we have in interpreting. It is a price to pay, but it purchases an incalculable boon; and for my own part I cannot bring myself to say that my conclusions concerning the power of the institution to validate texts and control interpretation are sad ones. They might even be a reason for moderate rejoicing.

[1]*Art, Politics and Will: Essays in Honor of Lionel Trilling*, ed. Q. Anderson, S. Donadio and S. Marcus (New York, 1977), pp. 159-172.

[2]David Bleich, "The Logic of Interpretation," *Genre* 10 (Fall, 1977), p. 384.

[3]*Knowledge and Human Interests.*

[4]See Hans von Campenhausen, *The Formation of the Christian Bible*, trans. J. A. Baker (Philadelphia 1977 (1972)), pp. 147 ff.

[5]See David L. Dungan, "The New Testament Canon in Recent Study," *Interpretation*, 29 (1975), pp. 339-51; Albert C. Sundberg, "The Bible Canon and the Christian Doctrine of Inspiration," *Interpretation* 29 (1975), pp. 352-71.

[6]Quoted by Von Campenhausen, p. 304.

[7]translated by Willard R. Trask, 1963 [1953], pp. 256 ff.

[8]Michael Polanyi, *The Tacit Dimension*, 1967, p. 68. The paper on gestation periods is also from Polanyi, p. 64.

[9]Von Campenhausen, p. 303.

🔥 🔥 🔥

WISH BOOK

fiction by BO BALL

from CHICAGO REVIEW

nominated by CHICAGO REVIEW

Brownie's LAZIEST BARK always announced her, with Buck in her arms, and two skinny dogs and a sore-eyed cat following. She never knocked, but we could hear the bones of her dogs find scratching space on the kitchen porch.

If Daddy was home, he rose from the table to go sit by his silent radio in the big room. But Mama never turned anyone away. And Maudie didn't beg. She just stood on the porch till Mama fanned the screen door to say, "Come eat with us."

"I ain't a bit hongry," she'd say. But she came inside to sit by the cookstove to watch us eat.

"Give Buck some bread," Mama would say.

Maudie chewed and then slipped little wads past the sores on Buck's lips. If there was any left, she would hide it in the pocket of her chop-sack dress that spelled COW CHOW, PIG STARTER. She couldn't spare for bleach, and the many boilings in her iron pot had taken only the bolder blacks.

When we had work, Maudie tried to help.

If it rained, we played Wish Book. Or Fortune.

Mama liked Fortune.

She took her limber Bible from the mantel in the big room. We gathered in a circle on the floor. One at a time, we closed our eyes and parted the Bible. We let a finger touch a verse which told us what the present was and what eternity would be.

If "it shall come to pass" or "it shall be" hid on the page, the Fortune was twice as strong. Mama, going on her fifth reading, knew which books of the Bible made things happen. And she interpreted the hardest ones for us. I got a string of "verily-verilies" and Mohab howling after Mohab.

When Jo fingered plagues and pestilence, she laughed and refingered for the coming of bridegrooms, for deer stags who could leap across green meadows.

Maudie never asked for seconds. While Jo read for her what her fingers found, Maudie's blue eyes rounded in wonder.

Once she got a verse that said that the bitter was sweet to the soul that hungered.

I thought it meant the wild flowers Maudie knew to eat— redbuds, sour grass, locust blooms—or the clay she let me help her nibble when nobody watched.

A better game was Wish Book. Each player repeated, blind, the Bible moves, but in a catalogue. The reward was what the pointed finger cleared closest to. We had the three catalogues Sears Roebuck gave—Fall-Winter, Spring-Summer, and the smaller Christmas Special. We wore the pages wrinkled playing Wish Book.

Mama turned up harness, seeds, plowshares.

Jo fingered thin for frocks.

I got to play twice—for me and for Buck whose fingers were too curled for pointing. For myself, I knew the general location of the coloring books, of crayons with rainbows more than eight. For Buck my fingers found toys enough to fill three mail trucks.

Maudie's hands had not learned where the good things were. She usually got nails. Ax handles. Bedpans.

A tally was kept of prizes and their prices. At the end of five, or ten, whatever times the players agreed on, the winner would be added.

Tractors and hardware brought bigger numbers, but everybody won. Then hands that had idled turned to hoes for the corn that Mama raised.

"Youens come see me," Maudie said.

"We will, and you come," Mama said.

Maudie waited by the door for a piece of wheat bread on good days, cornbread on the average. Her blue eyes kept her bare feet company while she backed out the door.

Sometimes we watched her from the big room window. If Roland was in the fields, her path was never straight. She held Buck tight to her bosom while she parted barbed wire to hand her gift away.

Daddy said they were hungry because Roland was too sorry to work in the mines. But Roland was scared of the dark.

Their land had been worn out before they came to it, and they could not afford fertilizer. In spring and summer they made do, but in the best of years their potatoes never lasted beyond Christmas. Their corn never planted a second spring.

Maudie's rocky garden didn't yield right. And she had no jars to pickle summer in.

They had one skinny pig and some banty chickens that laid eggs no bigger than a thumbnail.

Roland wouldn't hire out. But when they needed winter food, he came unasked to chop our wood or mend our fences.

"The Lord will provide," he said to Daddy.

"Hear that, Lord?" Daddy said to Mama.

Mama gave double to get even for blasphemy.

In the early winter of my eighth year, Buck and Maudie came each weekday to play with me. I was sick with the lungs. Mama's daddy was even sicker. After I had thrown the fever, Mama went to care for him.

The mines had laid Daddy off. But he wouldn't sit in the house. He counted trees all day or went to his brother Jaspar's to judge the bead on moonshine.

I boasted I could stay alone, but I was afraid of Raw Bones and Bloody Skull, of Haskew Fletcher who bit the nubs off little boys.

Before Jo left for school, Brownie announced Maudie carrying Buck, and the two skinny dogs and a sore-eyed cat following. Rags were tied around her feet. She had no shoes and she ran fast to beat frostbite. She wore an old Army coat and, underneath, the same dress as summer's.

Jo would point out the day's pintos, already simmering on the stove, and a fritter left especially from breakfast.

As soon as Jo's song rounded the curve, Maudie got the fritter from the iron skillet. She nibbled while I measured Captain Midnight's tail or recounted the calendar's five Dionnes. She chewed some of the bread for Buck and hid the rest in her pocket.

Then I would bring out the catalogues and we would move to the big room to play. We didn't keep tally. I didn't know double-line addition. But we pointed out and talked about our prizes.

"Pretty as a pup," Maudie said to my red wagon.

"Pretty as a pup," I said to her gray flannel.

"What on God's green earth is 'at?" she said to my crank Victrola.

"What on God's green earth is 'at?" I said to the bones of her corset.

We made up some new games. We counted how many times the same head peeped up from the necks of dresses, coats, robes.

"Red Head is twelve," I said from one Sears.

"Same as Raven Hair," she said from a second.

We searched to see if we could find somebody who didn't have a smile on. There were no frowning children, no sad women, though some men in mackinaws beaded mean into the sights of rifles.

I wondered why underwear had no heads or feet, just the middle.

"Mortify their faces if a Kodak cought 'em naked," Maudie said.

We exchanged Wish Books so I could feel all the crayons and she could touch all the baby clothes.

We chose and hunted our colors. Hers was blue. Mine the green and red of Christmas.

We liked to smell the slick pages—a crisp odor hinting of new linoleum.

Once she said to a full spread of apple trees, "Smells good 'nuff t'eat."

"Let's try it," I said.

We tore the page from the catalogue and divided it up three ways.

Buck spat his out. We laughed and almost choked, but I followed Maudie's swallow.

"Ever eat starch?" she asked.

I found Mama's Niagara, and Maudie and I pretended we were dipping snuff.

From last year's Wish Books, we cut off the heads, past necks, of entire families and then headless outfits for every day and Sunday. When we put tops on bottoms, the heads were sometimes too small, sometimes too large, for the clothed bodies under the necks. A face with color might have a black-and-white trunk, but we weren't particular. We put them all through frets and fevers.

For a change, Maudie took down Mama's Bible and looked at the glossies. I knew them by heart, and I told her about Joseph's coat of striped candy, of good Sammy and the beggarman, of Jesus going hunting for spring lambs.

She also liked to hear Mama's glow-in-the-dark signs that decorated the walls of all three rooms. I played I was reading them.

"Be Sure Yore Sins Will You Find Out."

"Ask and You Shall Get It."

"Knock and Doors Will Open."

"Suffer Little Children."

"John: 3.16."

"What's 'at mean?" she asked.

"Three dollars and sixteen cents," I said.

Maudie stopped all games at 10:30. We moved back to the kitchen where I nussed Buck and she mixed cornbread and peeled taters to go with the beans that needed more cooking than she could wait for. The taters she sliced into thin quarter moons. She added circles of onion. While the lard was frying one side, she sprinkled corn meal on top. She turned them once. They were white, moist, seasoned in their own iodine.

Roland brought to the table the scent of the sap of roots that his mattock had wakened.

At their house, his voice could make muscles in the next room jerk, but he didn't talk in Mama's kitchen. He sat opposite me at the table. We tried not to eye each other.

Maudie sat by the cookstove and fed Buck.

As soon as Roland finished eating, he rose, silent, and went back to grubbing ground.

Maudie moved to the table. She used Roland's plate. She rolled the half-raw beans into cornbread, one at a time, and ate them, fast.

"Hoover's little hunger pills," she said.

If anything was left, I divided it for Brownie and her dogs, for Captain Midnight and her cat. The Bible told Roland not to cast his bread unto dogs. Maudie liked to see them eat.

"Swaller 'at thang," she said to whichever nosed the scraps in my palm. "Swaller 'at thang."

Maudie washed the dishes. I dried. Then we had three more hours to play.

If the blue veins of Buck's belly tightened him into sleep, I brought out my coloring book I got for being sick. (Buck ate the crayons when he was awake.)

Maudie and I lay down on the linoleum in front of the fireplace. She took one page, I the other.

Maudie laughed at all the animals dressed up like Christians. She could not color right. While I turned the yard of the Old Lady's shoe into a brag farm, she colored blue the gaping beak of Henny Penny. The face and lamb of her Little Bo Peep were purple. She couldn't even keep inside the lines. And she licked the crayons. But her eyes rounded blue and she laughed so hard I didn't have the heart to tell her what she was doing wrong.

When her teeth hurt she didn't laugh. She didn't play. She chewed tobacco and held the juice on the pain.

I chewed some too. It was bitter to the taste.

Once her pain was so hard she held Mama's iodine in her mouth, though cross-bones and a skull spelled out death.

I sinned when she cried. I turned Daddy's radio on. The batteries were for Roosevelt or Amos 'n Andy on a week night, for an hour of fiddles in the dark of Saturdays. Maudie was never around then. Roland didn't nightwalk, and Daddy didn't like strange ears eavesdropping in on his Philco anyhow.

I fingerprinted where the dials had been and turned them for Bessie up in heaven or hoecakes brown on earth. The music helped the pain go away.

"Can they hear us, ye reckon?" she asked.

Late November added Christmas to our Wish Book.

Maudie liked the pages of wavy chocolate candy, of oranges from afar, of fruit cakes that twinkled jewels. But when we made out our lists of presents—not in pencil, but in talk—she chose for Buck a jumpsuit with a hood as blue as his eyes. For Roland, a flashlight long as an arm. For herself, a pair of shoes that nurses wore. A sheep-skin coat for my lungs.

I picked out ten colored frocks for her, the same ones as for Mama. Buck I gave a train that crossed two pages. A hope chest for Jo, and falsies and a cameo. My list was longer, for I also had Daddy, all of Mama's people, Daddy's.

She didn't have kin. And she wouldn't order Roland's people anything.

Before we could wish away all of December, Mama told her daddy to take up his bed and walk. He did. She came home to put her hand on the forehead and to rule that my lungs had dried.

I went back to school for my second year in the first grade, where the teacher let us trace pictures or help her make the hook rugs she sold for a bonus.

Mama didn't have time for games. She and daddy hauled manure for the fields. Persuaded Nell the mare to yank boulders from the ground.

Maudie and Buck stayed home. But I had time with them. Every day.

The teacher let the low grades out early. I didn't wait for Jo. I built Maudie and me a collection of Wish Books so we could make longer our Christmas lists.

I knew which toilets had last year's catalogues. I slipped in and out of the Wamplers' for *Montgomery Ward*, the Comptons' for *Alden's*, the Perrys' for *Spiegel's*, Fletchers' for *Walter Fields*, Nuckols' for *National Bellas Hess*.

I stole one a day until we had a full set. I put it in the belly of my overalls and held my hands in my front pockets to keep it in place. "Be sure yore sins will you find out" rang in my ears as I sneaked from the toilets and, once on the road, outran the posse from Revelations.

When I puffed steam through Maudie's door, she'd say, "Lord God-a-mighty, where's ye get it at?"

"You go first," I said.

She closed her eyes and let her hands travel through new territory.

When we heard Jo argue with herself for Ray Colley's eyes, we put the Wish Books into a nest under the bed, and I went on home.

Christmas came too late. The Company Store cut Daddy off on the twenty-third.

But Jo and I got a candy bar in the toe of our stockings.

Maudie never said what she got.

She came rag-shod in the snow to watch us eat our Christmas. Daddy got mad and kicked the dogs off the porch on his way out to Jaspar's.

Maudie took her chair by the stove and pulled out a dry breast for Buck to butt on.

She gave no milk. Mama said that was why we had to make sure that Buck got something.

"Sure you can't eat a bite?" Mama asked.

"Ain't a bit hongry," she said. She pushed back the strings of her hair and watched Buck practice his first teeth on her nipple.

"Give Buck some," Mama said.

Maudie put her breast back in her dress. She made Buck his wads of bread.

We played one game of Fortune from the New Testament, where Jesus lived.

Mama got shepherds. I got Herod. Jo got babies on the third try. Maudie found rocks and mountains falling on her.

Mama tied ribbons around three half-gallon jars of pickled beets and gave them to Maudie for a merry Christmas.

The next day I went down to her house to play. The skinny pig from its pen by the garden smiled red bruises at me. In the yard, their last two banties pecked after a stray ball of wineness.

The dogs that usually slurked their dead ribbons between their haunches now wagged them and smiled bleeding mouths for the palm of my hand. Even the cat had red whiskers.

Maudie's mouth and Buck's were ringed with the same red.

Three empty jars were on the table.

"We's had us a bait," she said. She rubbed her belly and laughed deep from her bosom, as if the vinegar had made her drunk.

We played one fast game of New Year's Wish Book, three prizes each, before we heard Roland bellow the dogs from his path.

Maudie held Buck tight to her breast and hummed a sound I didn't know.

I hid the catalogue before Roland's feet found the steps.

I ran home.

The next day Maudie wouldn't play. Black circled her eyes and she had lost two teeth.

"Slipped on a patch of ice an' fell," she said.

I traced a train for Buck. He cried when I showed it.

The Dionne quintuplets stretched their growth on a new calendar. School started up again.

I brought my tracings home to show Maudie.

Her blue eyes looked at my Pocahontas bending her neck for the settler's ax, at my men in buckskin cupping hands over brows to help them see Kentucky. But her throat hummed the strange noise and her shoulders rocked wherever she sat.

The tails of the dogs weakened.

The cat forgot to purr when I scratched its ribs.

We ran out of corn.

Daddy sold the cow.

Roland started a rock fence around Mama's garden. It already had slats no chicken could crawl through.

Mama shook her head in wonder when she counted our empty jars.

Daddy cussed and went to Jaspar's.

Maudie dug deep into the frozen ground for Jerusalem artichokes.

She parted snow to look for buckberries.

Mama saved our tater peelings.

"Ask Maudie can she use these," she told me.

Maudie chewed them raw. She gave Buck the pulp. It soured his stomach.

A false thaw came in early March. Maudie tied Buck to her back and climbed Cherry Mountain in search of greens.

A freeze took back the heady shoots of wild mustard, dock.

Her dogs licked Buck's used diapers.

The cat lifted a weak paw toward robins.

The pig hid in its cornshuck bed and refused the warm water she fed it.

Before it could die, Roland sold it and the two banties to his daddy.

$3.00.

He bought corn.

On my way to school, I helped Maudie, barefoot and coatless, build a fire under her iron pot. She was going to bypass the mill, which took one-third, and turn the corn into hominy.

Mama lent her the lye.

That day I stole a live catalogue from the Wamplers' mail box. It had an Easter woman on the cover, with daffodils, biddies, dyed eggs.

Maudie didn't thumb it once. She peered wild-eyed into the pot and stirred the rising husks with the broken handle of a hoe.

"How long's it take?" I asked. I was hungry. We had cut out all mid-day food.

"Be soon," she said.

Her blue feet tapped out hoedown.

The dogs and cat waited on the road bank where they sniffed the steam that went uphill.

"Be good," she said.

Jo came to nudge me home before Maudie could start the nine rinsings.

"Youens come," she said. "Be plenty."

That night, after Roosevelt told us spring had come, we went to bed.

But not to sleep.

Roland came in the dark to get Mama to help Buck and Maudie die.

Daddy unbanked the fire. He turned the radio on.

Then he left to help Mama.

We sat silent till only static played.

Daylight drew Mama's face for us.

"Too late," she said. "She couldn't wait. She picked at the hominy before it was rinsed."

"Buck too," she said.

She hugged me hard and then passed the circle of her arms on to Jo.

Daddy stayed to help Roland bury the dogs who also hadn't waited. Then he went to find a casket on his credit.

Jo gave her blue nightgown she was saving for the bridegroom. She sent Buck her Shirley Temple comb. Mama gave my baby blanket she had hidden for a keepsake.

I had nothing to give, except my crayons and our Wish Books still hidden in their nest.

"Just you remember her like she was," Mama said.

That night she warned us, but I went with her to the wake.

The cat, with scabs for eyes, came out from under the porch to sniff my empty hands.

Maudie's table was heavy laden with sugar cakes, store bread, jars of peaches from some forgotten summer.

In the other room, women sang of heaven's open door and Preacher Singleton Bible-drilled for Fortune and found a price that was above rubies.

Then the crowd parted enough for the forming of a line past the casket.

It wasn't Maudie. Nor Buck, cradled awkward on a stiff bent arm. The mouths were masked by gauze. The necks scarfed in bandages. Cheekbones blushed blue through rouge. Four nickels bought eyelids a costly sleep.

Mama petted the hands that lye had scaled. Then she stared straight into the humps of buffalo and cried for picnics in the sky.

I pushed through the growth that the tips of toes had given legs, unlocked the bones of mothers' hands that pulled their children's arms into the rigid gawk of May I.

My blurred eyes found the table. It didn't miss the loaf of light bread which I took to the cat in its hiding place under the porch. Once I jerked quiet, I counted the cat's ribs till its belly swelled them from my fingers, till purrs trembled the chill from my hands.

I didn't go back the next day for the burying, but from the big room window I could hear them sing of blind wretches and grace that amazed them.

I got my picture tablet and lay down in front of the fireplace and tried to draw Maudie and Buck, without anything to trace them on.

I wasted paper. Their heads were white circles with blue lining the blanks.

I closed my eyes in daydream to dig up the way she laughed at the blue-beaked Henny Penny who cackled that the sky would surely fall. Her smile at the white bones of corsets. The lick of her finger as it chased a colony of cats that followed Dick Whittington around the curve of the next page.

At night real sleep took all ruffles, all the lace. The popcorn eyes of banties flecked purple blood. Dogs grinned gums jeweled with maggots. The eyes of the cat dripped pus.

And Maudie, draped in chop-sack, lay heavy with her hunger. The head of Buck stretched for the perch of a shoulder blade. From under the gauze flowed the red wine of beets, its furrows following the blue ropes of veins that curved inward for the necks.

I waited for eye sockets to spit out their plugs to dance the blue of robin eggs that have been abandoned for the rain to cry on.

But the night could not afford the hue.

YOUNG WOMEN AT CHARTRES

by JAMES WRIGHT

from THE GEORGIA REVIEW

nominated by THE GEORGIA REVIEW, *Robert Boyers and Tess Gallagher*

(in memory of Jean Garrigue)

> ". . . like a thief I followed her
> Though my heart was so alive
> I thought it equal to that beauty."
> ("The Stranger")

one

Halfway through morning
Lisa, herself blossoming, strolls
Lazily beneath the eastern roses
In the shadow of Chartres.
She does not know
She is visible.
As she lifts her face
Toward the northwest,
Mothwings fall down and rest on her hair.
She darkens
Without knowing it, as the wind blows on down toward the river
Where the cathedral, last night,
Sank among the reeds.

two

Fog
Rinses away for a little while the cold
Christs with their suffering faces.
Mist
Leaves to us solitary friends of the rain
The happy secret angel
On the north corner.

three

You lived so abounding with mist and wild strawberries,
So faithful with the angel in the rain,
You kept faith to a stranger.
Now, Jean, your musical name poises in the webs
Of wheatfield and mist,
And beneath the molded shadow of the local stones,
I hear you again, singing beneath the northwest
Angel who holds in her arms
Sunlight on sunlight.
She is equal
To you, to her own happy face, she is holding
A sundial in her arms. No wonder Christ was happy
Among women's faces.

ᛒ ᛒ ᛒ

OF LIVING BELFRY
AND RAMPART:
ON AMERICAN LITERARY
MAGAZINES SINCE 1950

by MICHAEL ANANIA

from TRIQUARTERLY

nominated by TRIQUARTERLY

1

A number of years ago the editor of *Young Guard,* the principal
literary magazine for Soviet writers under forty, visited my office in
Chicago. He and several companions were touring the United
States west to east—Hollywood, Disneyland, the Grand Canyon, a
Kansas wheatfield, an Iowa cornfield, Chicago's Michigan Avenue,
and, by sheer social accident, the Swallow Press: a dusty, chaotic
loft, half a block from police headquarters, south of the Loop in the
natural habitat of marginal commerce and the half-pint bottle. We
drank coffee, exchanged cigarettes, and through a translator talked

about literature and publishing. We toured the offices and the warehouse. It must have been a strange experience for the Soviet editor—that gaping old structure, with wooden beams exposed above pallets of unsold poetry books, the busy disarray of the offices, the blare of WVON Soul Radio from the packing table in the back room, classical FM in stereo from atop the file cabinets in the office space in front, the regular thud of falling objects in the Senior Citizens' Workshop one floor up. State Department tours do not, as a matter of course, feature sight-seeing at the raffish edges of capitalism. I couldn't tell whether he thought we were dilettantes or lunatics, but it was clear that our experience had very little in common with his. Back in my office, he browsed through the shelves of literary magazines on the wall beside my desk. "What are these things?" he asked, holding an early copy of *Toothpick, Lisbon and the Orcas Islands* until the translator finished the question in English.

"Literary magazines."

The answer made its way to him in Russian. He glanced at the shelves again, then at his companion, an agricultural economist in amber-tinted glasses, and asked that the answer be repeated. The shelves held three or four years' worth of fifty or so literary magazines. "How can there be so many?" I explained that what I had was barely a sample of the number of magazines being produced across the country. Again he questioned the translator about my answer. "And do they all have many readers?" I told him that some had very few readers. "How many?" He was doing arithmetic in his head, trying to figure the enormity of a literature that could sustain all this, I suppose. His magazine in Russia had a circulation of more than 200,000, with regional and ethnic supplements. It was the point of entry for most young writers into the writers' union, and so was essential to employment. It was also the key to publication by the magazine's book publishing affiliate.

"A few—just two or three—have circulations of about 10,000," I said. "Most are printed in runs of less than 2,000 copies, and many have fewer than a hundred readers." The translation reached him like a cool breeze, and he relaxed a bit. If this was to be the day on which the literature gap was discovered, at least he would be on the high side. He was still puzzled. What was the point of having so many magazines with so few readers? Wouldn't it be better to have just a few magazines that everyone interested in literature could read?

He pulled more magazines down from the shelf: an *Antioch Review*, thick as an anthropology textbook in paperback; *Kayak*, bantamweight in rough paper with untrimmed edges, on the cover an old engraving demonstrating the use of an antique prosthetic device; a yellowed *Floating Bear* in uncertain mimeograph; *Extensions*, deliberately international and tidy as a French suitcoat; a more ample *Chicago Review* with a busy post-psychedelic drawing of a tree on the cover; *Goliards* in high-gloss newsstand format and disjointed graphics, like a top hat decked out with fishing flies and campaign buttons; *Poetry*, as thin, sedate, and costly as a dowager empress. There was a last question—unasked, perhaps unformulated. He shuffled through the pile of magazines he had moved to my desk, confused and a little embarrassed. I tried hard to explain the kind of diversity the magazines represented and said something, oft-repeated during years of fund-raising, about their place in the history of modern literature. The translator worked away at this like a tireless journeyman with a bad set of blueprints and knotted lumber. The Russian listened, trying to arrange the magazines at hand into a pile that would not fall over. I wanted to convey something of the romance of little magazines, their individuality and the deep personal commitments that sustain them— something, that is, of my own attachment to them. My interrogator nodded at the translator's version of my flourish, but without conviction. He was acquiescing, not agreeing.

I consoled myself with the notion that in riffling through those magazines in a disheveled Chicago editorial office he had seen more of American literary publishing than most literary visitors, and I confess to a certain perverse pride in the irregularity of it all—the odd idiosyncrasies of magazines so intent on individuality that they refuse to share a format that will make a neat stack or an orderly shelf. But where I saw freedom (or, at least, license), he saw ineffectual diffusion, yet another Disneyland where the illusion of choice is the disguise of limitation and fidgeting activity replaces movement. His questions were clearly rooted in Soviet literary and political bureaucracy, but they are not easily dismissed. *Why are there so many magazines? Who reads them, anyway? Wouldn't it be better to have fewer magazines with larger resources and more readers?* I have heard the same questions asked by U.S. government officials, foundation executives, and little magazine editors.

> *Go in for scribenery with a*
> *satiety of arthurs . . .*
> *malady of milady made*
> *melodi of malodi.*
> —James Joyce

2

In the introduction to *The Little Magazines: A History and a Bibliography,* authors Hoffman, Allen, and Ulrich estimated that six hundred little magazines had been published in English between 1912 and 1946. Informed guesswork—not much else is possible—suggests that at least fifteen hundred such magazines are being published in the United States right now. The figure is approximate because so many magazines exist so briefly. The Coordinating Council of Literary Magazines, a nonprofit organization that distributes state, federal, and private funds to magazines nationwide, has a current membership of over six hundred publications, and the organization requires that each member magazine must have published three issues and have existed for at least a year before applying for membership or financial support. *The Directory of Little Magazines and Small Presses* poses neither of these restrictions and offers a longer list, nearly a thousand; and it has to be assumed that magazines are published that do not find their way onto either list. A great number of magazines die before the appearance of a second issue. Three issues, the CCLM requirement, is a tough distance for most beginners. A modest first issue is likely to consume all the ready cash its editors can muster; with luck and a fair-sized circle of friends, donations and subscriptions can support a second number; but the third issue has no natural resources. It is the one that naive editors suppose will be supported by sales, but it is a rule of literary magazine publishing that there are no sales, certainly none sufficient to sustain publication. Each year hundreds of magazines are born and die with one or two issues that never find their way onto lists or into copyright registry.

So the numbers are conjectural but extremely high—twice as many magazines in print at any moment in the mid-seventies as existed altogether in the first thirty-five years of little-magazine history. An explosion in little-magazine publication occurred in the late sixties and continues. It is supported in part by the availability of grants—from CCLM, state arts councils, and the National Endowment for the Arts—but depends, as well, on a growing population of writers and on access to various kinds of printing technology. Nearly 67 percent of the magazines in CCLM's most recent catalogue (May 1977) have come into existence since 1970; less than 9 percent existed before 1960; and only eight magazines from Hoffman, Allen, and Ulrich's extensive bibliography survive. The world of little magazines is characterized not only by growth but by incessant change. Magazines die, not only because they lack funds but because their editors, often quite deliberately, allow them to die—sometimes out of frustration or exhaustion and sometimes because they feel that the task of the magazine has been accomplished. This last is especially true for magazines with a closely defined literary point of view and a tightly knit group of writers.

Little magazines have always functioned primarily for writers. Readers are desirable, sometimes even actively sought out, but the impulse behind most magazines is the writer-editor's conviction that there are writers who are not being served by existing publications. At their best, little magazines draw together groups of writers and, however marginally, find them an audience, in contrast, commerical magazines find audiences and financial support and then, almost incidentally, find their writers. Because of their attention to writers the little magazines register, in their numbers and shifting variety, the literary activity in the country. The modern quarterly emerged from a period of intense interest in criticism in the late thirties and forties and seemed to dominate the literary scene well into the fifties. Yet we see the fifties in retrospect as an intense period of activity, particularly in poetry supported by a number of remarkable small magazines—*Ark, Contact, Folder, Circle, Measure, Poetry New York, Big Table*, the *Black Mountain Review*, and others—that deliberately set themselves against the larger magazines' reliance on criticism. More important, they had an entirely new group of writers to publish, among them Creeley, Duncan, Ginsberg, Merton, Olson, Levertov, Merwin, O'Hara, and Snyder. None of these magazines survive; of the "Chief Periodicals" listed by Donald Allen in *The New American Poetry, 1945–1960,* only two magazines are still publishing: *Poetry* and *Chicago Review.* The interplay between eclectic quarterlies and highly individualistic smaller magazines continued into the sixties; but the sharp line between critically buttressed work in quarterlies (once called *academic*) and newer work faded quickly as the numbers increased and as writers of all kinds found their way into expanded versions of academe.

In the sixties and seventies, the audience for serious literature has not grown nearly as fast as the number of writers. Some have claimed that the actual number of readers has diminished. Nonetheless, writers' workshops proliferate in colleges and universities (the final redoubts of failing English departments), and poets and fiction writers in increasing numbers enter the world in search of publication. For the first time in history, we may have more writers than readers. Editorial offices of established magazines are drifted over with manuscripts, and new magazines are born to meet the writers' needs for print. Increasingly, magazines seem to reflect a sociological circumstance as much as an aesthetic one.

Aesthetically most new magazines declare themselves to be avant-garde. Very few are. The declaration is ritualistic, a part of the magazine's acknowledgment of its lineage among the magazines of the first part of the century. Many of the recent magazines are really involved in the eccentric use of literary precedents—a useful procedure, but one that is more cautious and traditional than most editors would like to admit. Typically, a magazine will be generated out of a sense of common interest— even of immediate community—among writers. The editors write to one or two prominent figures they admire, asking for contributions. Sometimes, in less coherent groups, all that is being sought is a little authority with which to launch the project, that and some validation of the less notable writers the magazine will include. In more carefully organized groups, the figureheads define the magazine's aesthetic precedent. Thus the magazine's orbit is in perigee around its most notable contributor. Usually the writers chosen for these roles are not broadly accepted national figures— never a Lowell or a Berryman, Roth or Cheever—but are the distinguished vestiges of previous new waves. Modern American literature has seen a succession of avant-gardes; very few have captured an enduring authority. For all the ballyhoo, the center of American letters has remained fairly conservative since the 1930s.

An example of a magazine that started in this way is *Milk Quarterly*, a Chicago publication that emerged from a group of writers which met regularly. The magazine began as a forum for writing done by members of the group, but declared at the outset an allegiance to the New York School with regular appearances by Ted Berrigan. Berrigan gave precedent to much of what appeared in the magazine, though very little of what was published was directly generated from Berrigan's work. This kind of situation can be seen in magazines with precedent-figures as different as Thomas McGrath, Thomas Lux, Charles Bukowski, Harold Norse, and Ed Dorn. In the almost totally decentralized literature of the late sixties and early seventies, these associations are measures of what was once called influence. Magazines of this sort can be seen as developmental. What's going on is an experiment with the possibilities of a fairly well-articulated aesthetic; the play is outward from, then back to, a source, like a game of hide-and-seek—furtive, sometimes daring, but always in sight of home base. When the exploration of possibilities is especially thorough or eccentric, the magazine can be very exciting.

In their attachment to the very recent past (the day before yesterday, in some cases), many magazines reflect a general trend in the society; in America, after all, nostalgia has replaced history. The association of literary movements with precedents is obviously not new. The magazines that presented the "new poetry" of the 1950s all exhibited strong ties to the modernists, to Pound and Williams most firmly; they looked to a tradition of experimentation in the twenties and before, and beyond that to Whitman. What is peculiar to the contemporary use of literary precedent is that it is willing to take its masters from so close at hand. With few exceptions, history, at least literary history, is largely absent from newer magazines. In addition to their role as adversaries to popular literary trends, the magazines of the early part of the century exhibited a number of broad historical and critical concerns. In *The Little Review, Dial,* and *Hound and Horn* there appeared regularly essays by modern writers that treated historical figures—

reclamation, even conscription for the movement of Dante, Homer, Blake, Shelley, the Elizabethans, the Metaphysicals, the French. Ezra Pound's brief essay, "The Tradition," first appeared in *Poetry* (III, 3, December 1913); essential essays by Eliot and Joyce first appeared in *The Little Review* and *The Dial*, along with essays by Santayana and Bertrand Russell. If the modern movement was intent on reinventing the past to suit its own purposes, contemporary writing seems preoccupied with knitting up the tattered edges of the present. Few contemporary magazines take a critical stand; essays, even book reviews and correspondence, are less and less common, especially in newer magazines. Perhaps the weight of criticism that filled the quarterlies is still being counteracted, or it may be that the excesses of academic, scholarly criticism are now too apparent. There are exceptions. *Io*, which is involved primarily in myth and cosmology, is full of prose discourse by poets, but by design none of it is what would traditionally be called critical. At the other end of the scale is *Parnassus*, a magazine composed entirely of critical reviews of books of poetry. Some quarterlies still attempt a traditional balance of fiction, poetry, and criticism, but few of these have much critical authority among writers. *Partisan Review* sustains itself but with far less of the political and cultural focus it once had. *American Poetry Review* includes a great deal of commentary through a number of regular columns, and *Salmagundi* and *Massachusetts Review* are noteworthy for the consistently high quality of their critical essays. There are also some notable smaller magazines that have reserved space for closely focused commentary. *Kayak*, an exemplary smaller magazine in a number of ways, still includes letters and comments that have a clear relationship to the concerns of the magazine. Robert Bly's magazines (*The Fifties, The Sixties*, and *The Seventies*) have been models for idiosyncratic editing and highly personal critical commentary. Somewhere between the larger magazines with balanced content and these smaller, more personal publications is *Field*, a magazine with particular interests in translation and in surrealism, which has engaged a number of important writers in important theoretical discussion.

There are broad literary differences among the magazines of the last three decades: university-based reviews with eclectic interests; quarterlies with distinct critical frameworks; independent eclectic

magazines that have invariably served the centrist literature nobly
and well (*Poetry Northwest* and *Beloit Poetry Journal* are just two
examples of this type of magazine); and adversary magazines, those
quicksilver enterprises that hold much of the romance of the little
magazines in their invariable insistence that everybody in print is
wrong about nearly everything literary and cultural except the few
people published in their thirty-two saddle-stitched, untrimmed
pages. Distinctions among very recent magazines—the 69 percent
founded since 1970—are less easily drawn. Obviously, the field is
too big and too crowded. Differences are also confused by quarrels
about size and funding. In the clamor for grants and the squabbling
that has ensued, literary matters have been entangled with financial statements. "Hard-pressed" has been taken to include experimental; "independently owned" in some circles is synonymous
with avant-garde. Except for the activities of a few publications
involved with conceptual art, like *Vile* or *Northwest Mounted
Valise*, most experimentation in magazines seems internecine or
elaborately involved with the play of precedents discussed earlier.
Concretism came into American magazines late and was introduced here by a university magazine *(Chicago Review)*. As far as I
know, there was never a magazine in this country comparable to
Ian Hamilton Finlay's *Poor. Old. Tired. Horse.* or a publishing
program like Agenzia in France. The most intense literary experimentation in the last decade has been in fiction, and the
economics of magazine publication kept most of the little
magazines out of the center of these activities. There was also an
area of conflict between the new fiction and small pressmanship. In
addition to demanding increased expenditures for typesetting and
paper, the new fiction's antirealism became the focus for charges of
social elitism that poetry—its mantle of sentimental individualism
and licensed narcissism still intact—was spared. Fiction, it seems,
invokes a politics from which (sadly) poetry has been excused.
When I was a director of CCLM, I was accused in public of being
antirealist, and therefore elitist, by a small-magazine editor who in
the previous breath had proclaimed himself a member of the
avant-garde and one of the few true heirs of the modern magazine
tradition. If the new fiction wanted magazines, it would have to
make its own.

In the 1960s little-magazine publishing, like much of the rest of the culture, was suffused in politics. Poets who would never have spoken to one another on literary grounds were allied in reading against the war in Vietnam, and there was a companion solidarity among magazines. As in the general culture also, there remains in the magazine world a residual leftism, focused occasionally on conservation or on a particular struggle, which surfaces in literary discussion here and there. Institutions are still distrusted. A populism never required of poetry is frequently demanded of fiction, and experimental fiction is seen as dangerously self-involved. The editor's inherent interest in production and distribution veers dangerously close to capitalism. With all the cosmological froufrou of the Whole Earth Movement, do-it-yourself printing and binding is often raised from its place as economic necessity to a level of singular and unassailable virtue. As I suggested before, the magazine boom requires sociology as much as it does criticism or literary history. There are basic contradictions between the obvious goals of most magazines and the political sentiments that seem native to meetings of little-magazine editors, and are part of the relationship of literature to the society as a whole. Magazine editors, as much as any group, are concerned about the dangers of growth. There is a sense among them that whatever it is that makes literature most valuable and vital cannot survive corporate climates and the manipulations of large amounts of money and resources. The problems are quite real, but the emotional recoil from them frequently results in limits set so close at hand that they make any development impossible. I have attended meetings at which any editor who talked about professionalized production or energetic distribution was hooted down as a sellout.

> *Where there are angels,*
> *there are wrangles, where*
> *there are editors, there are*
> *creditors . . . it is as simple*
> *as that.*
> —Cyril Connolly (1964)

3

Literary magazines are all failing business propositions. That any survive at all is a tribute to editors skilled at everything from typesetting to down-home flimflam. Traditionally, magazines were supposed to be supported by angels, creatures as implausible in contemporary literature as they are in modern theology. There are some magazines that still have benefactors left over from the fall of the patronage class. Some rely on university support—a financial base that has grown less dependable as universities themselves have lost much of their financial stability. It was once assumed that a university-based editor was on easy street; now he has to be seen as someone deftly juggling a small morsel above a tank of piranha. The majority of contemporary magazines are supported almost entirely by their editors—in cash and labor. Even with the infusion of editorial labor, most magazines have fairly high unit costs; magazines with cover prices of a dollar to a dollar and a half frequently cost two or three dollars to produce and distribute. Some larger magazines can manage better cost figures because of larger print runs, but distribution barriers seem to exist that keep them from taking advantage of favorable numbers. Simply put, all magazines need money, and money for literature is hard to get. Foundation support for literature nationally is less than 1 percent of all grants made, and the National Endowment manages less than 2 percent. Literature is altogether too private, both in its production and consumption, to gather the support given to operas, orchestras, theater companies, and ballets. There are no opera house overheads, no unions, no guarantees, no advance ticket sales, and, finally, no grand openings to ooze social prominence and drip jewelry.

Since 1967 the Coordinating Council of Literary Magazines has served as a grant-giving agency for literary magazines, distributing funds from the Endowment and a few private sources. Because the organization deals in funding magazines and has a large membership, it is a good context in which to test the possibility of cooperation suggested by my friend the Russian editor. If the total consolidation of production, distribution, and editorial judgment he had in mind are both impractical and undesirable in our situation, some sense of common purpose once seemed possible through CCLM. The grants program brought the magazines together, however churlishly. The initial notion was to fund quality magazines according to their needs. The idea never sat well with the small-magazine editors, who argued that because of large costs of big magazines, they would get all the money. Figures sailed back and forth between CCLM and COSMEP, a coalition of small magazine and small-press editors, with attendant accusations. Grants committees were elected from among the editors and writers involved with the magazines, but since the amount of money available in grants was never large enough, no one was ever really satisfied. No big magazine could ever hope to get a grant that would make a useful dent in its deficit; the smaller magazines were never persuaded that deficits were anything more than the numerical record of the capitalistic vices of larger magazines.

The fracture between large and small, in many ways unjustifiable on hard evidence, was fairly permanent. Also, the Endowment seemed eager to be swayed by the quarreling that went on, largely because the CCLM grant represented a large portion of Literature Panel funds that had gone out of the Panel's control. The arena for charges, accusations, and threats simply expanded. Eventually the Endowment established two grants programs for magazines independent of the CCLM program.

The future of CCLM in the midst of such fractured funding is uncertain. Certainly the sort of magazine unity I had once thought possible has been foreclosed. The grants procedure has always posed a threat to the independence of the magazines, though it was hopelessly exaggerated by all the quarreling. If judgments were made on the basis of quality, then marginally, at least, the organization was monitoring the editorial content of the magazines. It was presumed that the elected grants committees would disarm this concern. They did not. The degree of distrust was so high that everyone involved was suspect. The final stage in the grants committee system was reached in 1977, when an elected committee decided that it would not make qualitative judgments of any kind. The funds were simply divided equally among all the applicants, giving each a grant of about $900. In this gesture some of the grantees received more than a year's total budget; others were stuck with far less than a meaningful sum of money. The organization, which had spent years building assurances of noninterference into the rules governing committee procedures, was forced to sit by and watch its basic assumptions about magazine funding fall victim to a single committee. Unity had come to mean equity, and equity finally became equivalency.

Quite apart from issues of literary quality, but in keeping with populist attitudes within the organization, CCLM has undergone another set of strains on its potential unity. Along with the society as a whole, the organization has been forced into an awareness of minority needs. A program was established to bring minority magazines into the grants procedure early by waiving the three-issue rule. Affirmative action resolutions were passed. The scenario is a familiar one, but CCLM, more than most institutions, is ill suited to the situation. Its history has been completely involved with independent, highly individualistic operations, the literary equivalent of Jefferson's American frontiersman, nervous when anyone else has settled within ten miles. For political and social reasons, minority magazines tended to be the work of coalitions. A very nearly atomized pluralism that had just been served by replacing judgment with long division was being asked to deal with a series of collectivist groups. Although the goals of ethnic literary magazines were acceptable, the nature of their demands was dangerously close in dollars to the amounts requested by larger magazines, but in this instance accusing the magazines of rampant capitalism seemed implausible.

Because CCLM had been involved primarily with editors and their magazines, their needs came to overshadow the concern with writers and their work. Magazines can easily become their editors' primary form of self-realization—peculiar monads of intense self-reflexivity. The tendency is probably endemic and not altogether bad, for it carries some of the essential brave lunacy that keeps editors and magazines going. Still, it is hardly conducive to organizational strength. When self-realization is a primary goal, then one self-realization is as good as any other; the more liberal sanctity a demand has, the less likely it is to be treated in any sort of measured way. The alternatives are simply capitulation or self-serving retreat.

Like the welfare system, CCLM has identified a community it has neither the resources nor the will to serve. It has made enough effective grants at lower levels to insure the marginal survival of much of its burgeoning population, but in the process has generated a new range of expectations that it cannot fulfill. All this could be an incentive to positive action if some sense of common purpose could be agreed upon. A Disneyland without Disney's resources, my Russian friend might argue—a system of illusions at the point of collapse, praising its own tatters as signs of virtue.

> *Nothing much then in the way of sights for sore eyes. But who can be sure who has not been there, has not lived there, they call that living, for them the spark is present, ready to burst into flame, all it needs is preaching on, to become a living torch, screams included.*
> —Samuel Beckett

4

The questions posed by my Russian friend—*Why are there so many magazines? Who reads them? Why aren't there fewer magazines with more readers?*—are troublesome because they sit so readily among the anxieties I have had about them as a writer, editor, and . . . what's a good term for a CCLM director? . . . strategist (perhaps). They also play evil tricks with the deformations of my own nostalgias. I have a fondness for the magazines of the first half of the century. I keep them around—not a collection, nothing so orderly as that, just a scattering of things: a few *Poetrys* from 1913, a *Horizon* from 1944, some early *Partisan Reviews*, some few *Botteghe Oscures*, a *Dial* from 1929. What I do have in sequence begins in the 1950s when I started subscribing. The earlier things are talismans, magical remnants of a world made orderly, even heroic, in retrospect. The great magazines of that era seem so singular that, taken one by one, they suggest an overall clarity of literary purpose that could never have existed.

Of course, the Russian did not understand the import of that stack of magazines he could not keep upright. How could he? Their significance so easily eludes *us*. The answers to his questions are altogether too simple to give us much comfort. *Why are there so many?* Because that's how it is for a literature committed to change. Literary magazines today fill the same functions they filled at the beginning of the century. They give a place to writing for which no other place has been made. Criticism is slow and cautious; popular taste, as important as it is in other contexts, has nothing to do with the development of writing; commerce is too cautiously trying to pace a slow criticism to quixotic popularities. The world of literary magazines is raffish and irregular because nothing else will do in a setting in which the best hope of every serious writer is to undermine every notion of what makes a piece of writing good and durable.

Of course there are too many magazines. The genius that magazines have shown for graceful dying has not been entirely lost, and it should be cultivated. Yet the magazine explosion, finally, is not the fault of editors or national endowments but of writers. More and more we have drawn the magazines to our various isolations, instead of moving on, as we should, into riskier associations. If the magazine community is past fragmentation and nearer atomization, so are its writers. The magazines have always moved with writers. In our fear of any authority we have accepted a certain protective diffusion, and the magazines have responded by replicating and amplifying that diffusion in ways which make authority nearly impossible. In a symbiosis refined to neural complementarity, they serve our fears as well as our more cogent desires.

Who reads magazines, anyway? Again the answer is too simple. Editors and writers, mostly, and a few stray fans. Some of the larger magazines have enormous impact. Most small magazines are communications among contributors. In a CCLM survey of magazine subscribers, we found the readers are largely writers, then teachers, followed by librarians and students. Most are highly educated and underpaid, not the sort of community that would make for a good advertising sales campaign. Perhaps magazines that have very small readerships are occasionally read by editors of magazines with larger readerships; it's hard to know. In some instances, magazines serve largely as the medium through which writers give their work its public gesture—that crucial, if phantom, reader out there who is often important chiefly as a hypothesis.

The Russian's last question is the one I have spent the most time puzzling over, here and elsewhere. I became involved with CCLM in the conviction that some unity among magazines could be fashioned which could be a service to them without getting in their way. Obviously, we cannot have a *Young Guard* taking the place of our fifteen hundred magazines. Throughout the century, American literature has taken its vitality from its own extreme edges, since its center is too often lifeless and boring. This last is not only a corollary of the tradition of the new; it has to do, as well, with the desperation with which status is held onto in a society that claims not to value status. Without the graduated steps of a writers' union and an official publishing bureaucracy, we cling to our little tracts of notoriety with all the tenacity and imagination of suburbanites. American letters can survive only by confronting change, and the magazines serve as both belfry and rampart in this essential confrontation.

MARATHON OF MARMALADE

by GEORGE HITCHCOCK

From LINGUIS

nominated by Hayden Carruth

deliver me please from
    the glass of dust in its tattooed cage
    the decorative cigar quacking like a duck
    the shaved Tyrolean piano
    the rubber armpit
    and the embroidered eyes of wax marigolds

bring me then if you will
    the osprey in its taffeta kaftan
    the safety-match dancing in the cathedral
    moons which sweat kerosene
    elephant salt
    and the ventilated shriek

let me go gazing at
    monuments and diplomats leaping alike
    from prehistoric windows
    antelope grazing on the tenniscourt
    the railroads of the inner ear
    wrinkled wine
    and the solar batteries of your smile

MENNONITE FARM WIFE

by JANET KAUFFMAN

from MISSISSIPPI REVIEW and BELOIT POETRY JOURNAL

nominated by Gordon Lish

She hung her laundry in the morning
before light and often in winter
by sunrise the sheets were ice.
They swung all day on the line,
creaking, never a flutter.
At dusk I'd watch her lift each one
like a field, the stretches of white
she carried easily as dream
to the house where she bent and folded
and stacked the flat squares.
I never doubted they thawed
perfectly dry, crisp,
the corners like thorn.

🔥 🔥 🔥

ONE SPRING
by DAVID BROMIGE
from THIS

nominated by THIS *and Ron Silliman*

IT HAILED. 0.06 inches were precipitated where the instruments are kept. At least one driver found his windshield wipers clogging. High winds drove the hail into the orchards of apple, pear & prune. It hailed on the new Vacu-Dry plant, an independent, publicly-owned corporation, making instant apple-sauce for the government. During the following night, thieves walked off with the bus-bench.

Next day samples were brought to the inspector. The leaves were shattered & the fruit already indented. Though the sun shone bright, some wisps of high cirrus appeared shortly after midday.

Next day dawned clear & bright, & by the middle of the afternoon the thermometer registered 73 degrees Fahrenheit. That night the valley-bottoms were free from frost. Next day began well also, the sky a clear deepening blue, the light flickering off the eucalyptus leaves.

At Goat Rock State Park, a man sat in a car, inhaling carbon monoxide. Sunset occurred at 6:35. The weather continued fine & warm for the remainder of the week. Some black lambs were gambolling in one green dell. Their dams had recently been shorn. The fence looked very old.

It had been built by coolies in the last century. That night, a ring-tail cat showed up in a passing pair of headlights. The driver thought it was a raccoon. The ring-tail cat is neither cat nor raccoon, but more closely allied to the bear. It dropped to 44 that night; next day, it rose to 86.

The blue sky was no longer a strip, & beneath it in the earth had risen grandly into hills—clean, bare buttresses, trees in their folds, & meadows & clear pools at their feet.

But the hills were not high, & there was in the landscape a sense of human occupation—so that one might have called it a park, or garden, if the words did not imply a certain triviality & constraint.

A person shopping at the market paid 89¢ for a pound of ribroast, 17 cents for a pound of cantaloupe. Corn cost the shopping person 49 cents for 5 ears; tomatoes were 2 for a quarter. Edward Bartlett, who had been a ranger with the State Beach Parks Service for about 12 years, reported Monday to be Maintenance Co-ordinator for the River area of the State Park System.

This was a promotional transfer & he would be working with rangers along the coast also. There had been two suicides in the park last week, one at Goat Rock & one at Blind Beach.

All the new restrooms were in & the old ones were being removed. The warm weather had brought large crowds to the area over the weekend. It had been foggy Saturday & Sunday mornings but the ocean was fairly calm & boats were able to bring in good catches. Elsewhere, low tides two feet below the lowest on record concerned farmers, who feared a rise in salt-content of that water they employ in irrigation. "The tide is out," said Farmer Warren Tallman, "and as far as I can see, it'll never come back." This day the stock market finished lower, partly in reaction to the President's foreign policy message & partly the result of normal pre-weekend evening-up of pressures.

In late trading Burroughs, Walt Disney & Corning Glass were up a point or so apiece. The following morning was clear & sunny, with the fresh warmth of a full-summer day; the flowers were blossoming profusely & the grass was richly green. A student was arrested early in the day after the car he was driving struck the State College Library.

A man who was stealing $250 from a service station made up a story: he worked there, & would say that he passed out after two gunmen forced him to take some capsules & beer. When he woke up, they had rifled the place.

He would be due for sentencing within three weeks, having entered guilty pleas to charges of filing a false felony report, & petty theft. Days passed, & a 31-y-o-woman stabbed her sister-in-law to death in a bar on Tuesday evening.

Wind again last weekend & our hills were beginning to look brown. The grass had had a much shorter season—less feed for the sheep & an earlier fire hazard. The first began at 2 p.m. at the home of C. Hodges. Hodges was pouring gasoline into the carburetor when the fuel ignited. All the electrical wiring was destroyed in the '58 Olds. 15 firemen responded to the fire which was extinguished within 10 minutes.

At 8:45 p.m. a '65 Olds caught fire at the Phillips 66 station. The ignition had been left on while the car was being worked on. The wiring under the dash & the hood was destroyed. This fire was out within 10 minutes also.

Between 11:15 a.m. & 3:15 p.m., a human being entered a

residential structure, pried open another human being's dresser drawer & a tin box inside that drawer, & removed $8,800 in cash.

Taxpayers had not built a school, staffed & maintained it in order that children should echo the revolutionary clatter from the state colleges.

Fog came in sometime Saturday night & hung on all day Sunday but it was very warm & pleasant for gardening. As soon as it got warm in the valley one noticed an increased interest in real estate at the coast. Walter Brain, recently hospitalized, returned home, able to get about again. The day dawned bright.

The pre-dawn light was green, a function perhaps of dust or even smog, over the valley eastward. Then bright orange, & then the rim of the sun appeared behind the mountain range that forms the eastern edge of the valley. Some people boating, swimming or fishing or otherwise visiting the river & perhaps also some other large creeks could have been startled to see a gigantic & nightmarish rat, as the animal is fully as large as a raccoon, brown like a rat with a long scaly tail, over two-thirds of its body & head-length. It has very glossy yellowish-brown to dark-brown fur, which is actually a silk-like & water-proof under-fur, & which is covered on the outside by colorless guard-hairs, that you do not see.

The enormous hind feet, about 6 inches long, are heavily clawed & widely webbed. After the first shock of seeing it wears off & you begin to realize that even large as it is it is still hardly large enough to attack & eat a man, the observer is inclined to say, "O well, just another animal!"

But it is not just another animal, creeping silently inland & tearing up whole plants.

That afternoon, a skindiver fell off a rock & stabbed himself in the side with a fish spear. It was a relief that the wound proved not fatal. County Coroner Andrew Johansen had his work cut out for him. He continued to investigate a blaze that claimed the life of two men early Tuesday.

Killed in a cabin fire on the Johnson Ranch were Charles Simons, 26, & Gerry Dee Stone, 38.

Johansen said the pair had apparently driven another couple from the cabin on the Johnson Ranch earlier that night. The fire broke out around 4:30 a.m. The weather for the weekend was overcast but quiet. They had been using a kerosene lamp.

Sunday the wind came up & blew the fog away for a while. Tress Aiken reported the lupine at Duncan's Landing was beautiful this year. Her friend, Georgia Herring, answered that we were fortunate along the coast that we had wild flowers from early spring through summer. The rose cactus in the gardens were blooming this year with their tall stalks of small, starry, yellow blooms. At grange last week Mrs. Aiken had used these blooms with some nasturtiums & an orange cactus blossom to make decorations for the hall.

The seasons must be changing. Here it was June & we were having a very heavy mist called rain. While it would do some "rejuvenating" of the springs from which our drinking water comes, it would also damage some of the fruit crops. So it was a bright day for the wedding. The home was decorated for the occasion with spring bouquets. That afternoon the couple carved their initials in the family birch tree.

It was the bright day they had hoped it would be, had feared it would not be, those performing in the school auditorium: Russell Beach with a yo-yo demonstration; Fred Wilkoff, Kathy Collins, & Dan Elder, vocal trio; Jack Gerboth, acting out a memory skit; Mrs. Schlobohm presenting a driver-training monolog; & Loren Wilbur's class, performing their skit, Watermelons for Aquarius. More performances were being planned.

Elsewhere, students paid tribute to police officers. The Student Body President said, "We know the police are getting a pretty raw deal at Berkeley & other state colleges. If it wasn't for their courage & dedication we might not have a college to attend when we graduate from high school." Two sounds rent the peace of the day.

According to Highway Patrol reports, the car, westbound, went out of control & hit a mailbox. The other was a shot of some light-bore gun. A 14-y-o boy had accidentally shot a younger boy in the foot with a BB gun. The wound in the bottom of the foot was not deep, Jimmy's mother later reported. But she was frightened that next time he might be hit in the eye.

Young Eric told police that the wound was unintentional. The shot may have ricocheted. Police took Eric's BB gun & gave him a lecture. It is illegal to discharge firearms within city limits.

A teacher named Ward had informed the board in an acid letter that his free time & energy, which the board's administration had so graciously donated to the outdoor education project without asking Ward, consulting him, or offering him any type of extra compensations other than a few cents for gas mileage, was no longer at their disposal. To work beyond his contract, Ward continued, would require the board pay him time & a half above his hourly rate for time exceeding his contract time, & double time on Sundays & other holidays. "This is after all no more than a plumber asks," Ward went on. "Board member Jim Bryant, who voted for my ouster, is a plumber."

Night fell & nocturnal animals left their burrows & nests, some for the last time. Some motorists slowed at the sign "Deer Crossing," others paid it no attention. In those areas the fog reached in to this night, it gathered in the stands of eucalyptus & Monterey cypress & dropped like rain. From Washington, where it was already tomorrow, word came of the first major contract to be awarded on the $80 million dam project. Work was to begin almost immediately.

The next day I woke very early. The sun had only just risen; there wasn't a single cloud in the sky; everything around shone with a double brilliance—the brightness of the fresh morning rays & of yesterday's precipitation. I went for a stroll about a small orchard, now neglected & run wild, which enclosed the little lodge on all sides with its fragrant, sappy growth. On the slope of a shallow ravine, close to the hedge, could be seen a beehive; a narrow track

led to it, winding like a snake between dense walls of high grass &
nettles, above which struggled up, God knows whence brought,
the pointed stalks of dark-green hemp.

Those of us who remembered the May 5 stabbing at Skip's Bar
noted that Margie Denise Doneza, 31, was pleading innocent to
murder. Susan Myrtle Bogue, 30, died in the hospital with a 9-inch
butcher knife in her back. It was stuffy in the courtroom. The heart
of the city had been rendered barren by a recent earthquake. We
were glad to be home.

Walter Brain's daughter visited Sunday at the Brain home. A week
before, Mrs. Walter Brain & daughter, Mrs. Dorothy Robinson,
met two women friends from Colorado, & all four drove to Lake
Tahoe for the remainder of the week. Mrs. Brain returned home
Friday evening. They chatted persistently in familiar tones. Few
realize that their life, the very essence of their character, their
capabilities & their audacities, are only the expression of their
belief in the safety of their surroundings. The courage, the compo-
sure, the confidence; the emotions & principles; every great &
every insignificant thought belongs not to the individual but to the
crowd: to the crowd that believes blindly in the irresistible force of
its institutions & of its morals, in the power of its police & of its
opinion.

After a few drizzly days the wind came up Saturday night, &
Saturday turned out to be a howler of a day with lots of whitecaps
on a rough ocean. The Barbara Jean, a fishing boat owned &
operated by Anthony Cabral of Pacific Grove, burned in the
channel Tuesday morning.

It was a fairly calm morning & the smoke could be seen for quite a
distance, so those coming down the coast early that morning knew
something was wrong before they reached the bay. An electrical
plug apparently ignited the boat's gasoline engine.

With the white cardboard boxes held high above her head, & with
her robe open, flapping behind her, a young woman leaped high &
for a moment seemed to float above the top strands. She landed
running. Pieces of her white robe adhered to the wire barbs.

Along the side of the country lane, back where her car was parked, a county employee was mowing the wildoat grass. He was turning over in his mind a report he'd read that morning at breakfast. Narcotics & drugs was the health topic of greatest concern to local residents. "How to understand the Bible" had been the most often checked Bible topic in the survey conducted by the Christian Brotherhood Church. 23.7% had checked that one.

21.5% had checked "Why so many churches?"; 17.5% had checked "What does God expect?"; 15.7% had checked "Life after Death"; 15% "How to pray"; 15% "What is Faith?"; 13.6% wanted to know about "Money & the Church"; 12.5% were curious as to "World situation & prophecy"; 12.5% also wondered, "Is the Devil real?"

The other Health topics had been, & in this order of concern: Prevention of heart attacks, What can be done about cancer, Help for arthritis, Tips on gardens, Weight control, Mental health, Nervous breakdown, Help for smokers, Emergency first aid, Physical fitness, Ulcers. Sweat ran into his eyes.

Concentration was required, to keep the blade from shattering on a concealed roadside rock. He was allergic to pollens, & wore a kerchief across mouth & nose, like a bandit. Across a small flat meadow some careful rancher had tied strips of white cloth to his barbwire fence, to prevent people from walking into it in the dark. A Volvo was abandoned directly in his path.

Raising the blade, he drove around the foreign body, then, lowering his instrument, resumed cutting. The kingfisher spies a fish or frog in the water or on the bank & dives down to seize it. He will often fly straight down into the water like a flying spear.

The dipper, on the contrary, either walks about over the rocks in a shallow part of the stream, picking up with his bill the insects he finds, or may calmly dive down into a pool & walk along the bottom & over the rocks picking up insects & eating them right there, not later. Such soft greens & grays, after the hot white days! It's a strange thing that when the fog comes in it seems to deaden all the normal sounds except the bird calls. His & los for this week: 52/100-57/104-58/106-55/93-49/81-47/79-47/76 (Wednesday thru Tuesday). It is worth noting that the weather records for the City of Sebastopol are actually kept by a person who lives on Green Valley Lane, 4 miles outside city limits, & where the range in temperature tends to be greater than in our town. The end of Main Street is looking good.

Superior French Laundry folks painted their building. Safeway is always super clean & probably one of their finer stores. Goodsports & Ernie's Liquors reflect modern merchandising techniques, & so does Robbie's Grill. All doubtless show significant growth in revenues. Owners keep their store areas clean & neat. Who wants to wade through litter & debris to enter a store?

Pretty Karen Gerboth, 14, the daughter of Mr. & Mrs. John Gerboth, is examining a basket of plump, ripe raspberries at the Handsome Goatz Ranch on Green Hill Road.

🔥 🔥 🔥

SOME FOOD
WE COULD NOT EAT:
GIFT EXCHANGE
AND THE IMAGINATION

by LEWIS HYDE

from THE KENYON REVIEW

nominated by THE KENYON REVIEW

I WOULD like to write an economy of the imagination. I assume any "property system" expresses our own spirit—or rather, one of our spirits, for there are many ways to be human and many economies. As we all know, capitalism brings to life and rewards its own particular spirits (aggression, frugality, independence, and so on). My question is, what would be the form of an economy that took the imagination as its model, that was an emanation of the creative spirit?

The approach I have taken to this question might best be introduced by telling how I came to it in the first place. Some years ago I sat in a coffeehouse listening to someone read an exceptionally boring poem. In trying to imagine how or why the poem had come into existence, the phrase "commodity poem" came to mind—as if I had heard the language equivalent to a new Chevrolet. Even at that early point I meant "commodity" as opposed to "gift," for my own experience of poetry (both of reading and of writing) had been in the nature of a gift: something had come to me unbidden, had altered my life, and left me with a sense of gratitude—a form of "exchange," if you will, clearly unlike what happens to most of us in the marketplace.

I am obviously speaking of gifts in a spiritual sense at this point, but I do not mean to exclude material gifts. For spirits take on bodies and it is in that mixture that we find human liveliness and attraction. Both economic and erotic life bring with them a mixture of excitement, frustration, fascination, and confusion because they must occur where body and spirit mingle, and it is in that union we discover the fullness of the world, or find it missing.

I should add that on a more mundane level my topic has found a source of energy in the situation of my own life. For some years now I have tried to make my way as a poet and a sort of "scholar without institution." Inevitably the money question comes up. You have to pay the rent. All artists, once they have passed their thirtieth birthday, begin to wonder how it is that a man or woman who wishes to live by his gifts is to survive in a land where everything is bought and sold.

These beginnings—the money question for myself and a sense of art as an "exchange" different from the market—became focused for me only after some friends had introduced me to the work that has been done in anthropology on gift exchange as a form of property.[1] In many tribal groups a large portion of the material wealth circulates as gift and, not surprisingly, such exchange is attended by certain "fruits": people live differently who treat a portion of their wealth as gift. As I read through the ethnography I realized that in describing gift exchange as an economy I might be able to develop the language I needed in order to address the situation of the artist living in a land where market value is *the* value. At about the same time I began to read all the fairy tales I could find with gifts in them, because the image of what a gift is and does is the same in these tales as it is in the ethnography, but fairy tales tell of gifts in a manner closer to my final concern, the fate of the imagination.

I will not be able to fully describe what I mean by "gift" in the space of one essay. I want, therefore, to remark on two or three characteristics of a gift which shall not be addressed here.

One is that gifts mark or act as agents of individual transformation. Gift exchange institutions cluster around times of change: birth, puberty, marriage, sickness, parting, arrival, and death. Sometimes the gift itself actually brings about the change, as if it could pass through a person's body and leave it altered. The best examples are true teachings—times when some person changes our life either directly or through the power of example. Such teachings are not like schoolbook lessons; they move the soul and we feel gratitude. I think of gratitude as a labor the soul undertakes to effect the transformation after a gift has been received. We work, sometimes for years, until the gift has truly ripened inside of us and can be passed along. (Note that gratitude is not the "obligation" we feel when we accept a gift we don't really want.)

Second, when you give someone a gift, a feeling-bond is set up between the two of you. The sale of commodities leaves no necessary link. Walking into a hardware store and buying a pound of nails doesn't connect you to the clerk in any way—you don't even need to talk to him if you don't want to (which is why commodities are associated with both freedom and alienation). But a gift makes a connection. With many gift exchange situations, the bond is clearly the point—with marriage gifts and with gifts used as peace overtures, for example.

Finally it must be said that gift exchange has its negative aspects. Given their bonding power, "poisonous" gifts and gifts from evil people must be refused. In a fairy tale, the hero is in trouble if he eats the meal given to him by a witch. More generally, anyone who is supposed to stay "detached" (a judge, for example) shouldn't accept gifts. It is also true that the bonds set up by gift exchange limit our freedom of motion. If a young person wants to leave his or her parents, it's best to stop accepting their gifts because they will only maintain the parent-child connection. As gifts are associated with being connected to a community, so commodities are associated with both freedom and rootlessness.

In part because of these restrictions, I do not feel that gift exchange is, in the end, the exclusive "economy of the imagination." But it is a necessary part of that economy; the imagination will never come to its full power until we are at home with the gifts of both the inner and the outer world. An elaboration of the nature of gift exchange must, therefore, precede any more precise qualifying remarks, and it is this elaboration which I begin here.

I

When the Puritans first landed in Massachusetts they discovered an Indian custom so curious they felt called upon to find a name for it. In 1767, when Thomas Hutchinson wrote his history of the colony, the term was already an old saying: "An Indian gift," he told his readers, "is a proverbial expression signifying a present for which an equivalent return is expected."[2] We still use this, of course, and in an even broader sense. If I am so uncivilized as to ask for the return of a gift I have given, they call me an "Indian giver."

Imagine a scene. The Englishman comes into the Indian lodge. He falls to admiring a clay pipe with feathers tied to the stem. The tribe passes this pipe around among themselves as a ritual gift. It stays with a family for awhile, but sooner or later it is always given away again. So the Indian, as is only polite among his people, responds to the white man's interest by saying, "That's just some stuff we don't need. Please take it. It's a gift." The Englishman is tickled pink. What a nice thing to send back to the British Museum! He takes the pipe home and sets it on the mantelpiece. The next day another Indian happens to visit him and sees the gift which was due to come into his lodge soon. He too is delighted. "Ah!" he says, "the Gift!" and he sticks it in his pouch. In consternation the Englishman invents the phrase "Indian giver" to describe these people with such a low sense of private property. The opposite of this term would be something like "white-man-keeper," or, as we say nowadays, "capitalist," that is, a person whose first reaction to property is to take it out of circulation, to put it in a warehouse or museum, or—more to the point for capitalism—to lay it aside to be used for production.

The Indian giver (the original ones, at any rate) understood a cardinal property of the gift: whatever we are given should be given away again, not kept. Or, if it is kept, something of similar value should move on in its stead, the way a billiard ball may stop when it sends another scurrying across the felt, the momentum transferred. You may hold on to a Christmas gift, but it will cease to be a gift in the true sense unless you have given something else away. When it is passed along, the gift may be given back to the original donor, but this is not essential. In fact, it is better if the gift is not returned, but is given instead to some new, third party. The only essential is this: *the gift must always move.* There are other forms of property that stand still, that mark the place or hold back water, but the gift keeps going. Like a bird that rests on the rising air near cliffs, or water at the lip of the falls, standing still is its restlessness and the ease of the gift is in its motion.

Tribal peoples usually distinguish between two sorts of property, gifts and capital. Commonly they have a law which repeats the sensibility implicit in the idea of an Indian Gift. "One man's gift," they say, "must not be another man's capital." Wendy James, a British social anthropologist, tells us that among the Uduk in northeast Africa, "any wealth transferred from one subclan to another, whether animals, grain or money, is in the nature of a gift, and should be consumed, and not invested for growth. If such transferred wealth is added to the subclan's capital [cattle in this case] and kept for growth and investment, the subclan is regarded as being in an immoral relation of debt to the donors of the original gift."[3] If a pair of goats received as a gift from another subclan is kept to breed or to buy cattle, "there will be general complaint that the so-and-so's are getting rich at someone else's expense, behaving immorally by hoarding and investing gifts, and therefore being in a state of severe debt. It will be expected that they will soon suffer storm damage. . . ."

The goats in this example move from one clan to another just as the pipe moved from person to person in my fantasy. And what happens then? If the object is a gift, it keeps moving, which, in this case, means that the man who received the goats throws a big party and everyone gets fed. The goats needn't be given back but they surely can't be set aside to produce milk or more goats. And a new note has been added—the feeling that if a gift were not treated as such, if one form of property were to be converted to another, something horrible might happen. In folk tales the person who tries to hold on to a gift usually dies; in this anecdote the risk is "storm damage." (What happens in fact to most tribal groups is worse than storm damage—foreigners show up and convert gift to capital, universally the tribal group is destroyed as a group.)

If we turn now to a folk tale we will be able to see all of this from a different angle. Folk tales are like the soul's morality plays—they address the gift as an image in the psyche. They are told at the boundary between our inner feelings about property and the ways in which we handle it in fact. The first tale I have chosen comes from Scotland. It may seem a bit long so early in our discourse, but almost everything in it will be of use. The tale is called "The Girl and the Dead Man."[4] I have put a few obscurities into modern speech, but other than that, this is how the story was told by a Scottish woman in the mid-19th century:

There was before now a poor woman, and she had a leash of daughters. Said the eldest one of them to her mother, "I had better go and seek for fortune." "I had better," said the mother, "bake a loaf of bread for thee." When the bread was done, her mother said to her, "Which wouldst thou like best, a little bit and my blessing or the big bit and my curse?" "I would rather," said she, "the big bit and thy curse."

She went on her way and when the night was wreathing around her she sat at the foot of a wall to eat the bread. There gathered the ground quail and her twelve puppies, and the little birds of the air about her, for a part of the bread. "Wilt thou give us a part of the bread?" said they. "I won't give it, you ugly brutes; I have not much for myself." "My curse will be thine, and the curse of my twelve birds; and thy mother's curse is worst of all." She rose and went away, and the bit of bread had not been half enough.

She saw a little house a long way from her; and if a long way from her, she was not long reaching it. She knocked at the door. "Who's there?" "A good maid seeking a master." "We want that," said they, and they let her in.

Her task was to stay awake every night and watch a dead man, the brother of the housewife, whose corpse was restless. She was to have a peck of gold and a peck of silver. Besides this she had, of nuts as she broke, of needles as she lost, of thimbles as she pierced, of thread as she used, of candles as she burned, a bed of green silk over her, a bed of green silk under her, sleeping by day and watching by night. The first night when she was watching she fell asleep; the mistress came in, struck her with a magic club and she fell down dead. She threw her out back in the garbage heap.

Said the middle daughter to her mother, "I had better go seek fortune and follow my sister." Her mother baked her a loaf of bread; and she chose the big half and her mother's curse, as her elder sister did, and it happened to her as it happened to her sister.

Said the youngest daughter to her mother, "I had better go myself and seek fortune too, and follow my sisters." "I had better bake a loaf of bread," said her mother. "Which wouldst thou rather, a little bit and my blessing or the big bit and my curse?" "I would rather the little bit and your blessing."

She went on her way and when the night was wreathing round her she sat at the foot of a wall to eat the bread. There gathered the ground quail and her twelve puppies, and the little birds of the air about her. "Wilt thou give us some of that?" "I will give, you pretty creatures, if you will keep me company." She gave them some of the bread; they ate and they had plenty, and she had enough. They clapped their wings about her till she was snug with the warmth. She went, she saw a little house a long way from her . . . [here the task and the wages are repeated].

She sat to watch the dead man, and she was sewing; in the middle of the night he rose up and screwed up a grin. "If thou dost not lie down properly, I will give thee the one leathering with a stick." He lay down. After a while he rose on one elbow and screwed up a grin; and a third time he rose up and screwed up a grin.

When he rose the third time she walloped him with the stick. The stick stuck to the dead man and her hand stuck to the stick and off they went! They went forward till they were going through a wood; when it was low for her it was high for him; and when it was high for him it was low for her. The nuts were knocking their eyes out and the wild plums taking their ears off, till they got through the wood. Then they returned home. She got a peck of gold and a peck of silver and the vessel of cordial. She rubbed the vessel of cordial on her two sisters and brought them alive. They left me sitting here, and if they were well, 'tis well; and if they were not, let them be.

There are at least four gifts in this story. The first, of course, is the bread which the mother gives to her daughters as a going away present. This becomes the second gift when the youngest daughter shares her bread with the birds. She keeps the gift in motion, the moral point of the tale. Several things, in addition to her survival, come to her as a result of treating the gift correctly. These are the fruits of the gift. First, she and the birds are relieved of their hunger. Second, the birds befriend her. And third, she's able to stay awake all night and get the job done. (As we shall see by the end of the essay, these are not accidental results, they are typical fruits of the gift.)

In the morning the third gift appears, the vessel of cordial. It is a healing liquid, not unlike the "water of life" that appears in folk tales from all over the world. It has power: with it she is able to bring her sisters back to life. This liquid is thrown in as a gift for her successful completion of the task. It's a bonus, nowhere mentioned in the wonderful litany of wages offered to each daughter. We will leave for later the question of where it comes from; for now we are looking at what happens to the gift after it is given, and again we find that this girl is no dummy—she moves it right along, giving it to her sisters to bring them back to life. That is the fourth and last gift in the tale.[5]

This story also gives us a chance to see what happens if the gift is not allowed to move on. Just as milk will sour in the jug, a gift that is kept still will lose its gift properties. The traditional belief in Wales is that when the fairies give gifts of bread to the poor, the loaves must be eaten that same day or they will turn into toadstools.[6] Some things go rotten when they are no longer treated as a gift.

We may think of the gift as a river and the girl in the tale who treats it correctly does so by allowing herself to be a channel for its current. If we try to dam up the river, one of two things will happen: it will either fill us until we burst or it will seek out another path and stop flowing through us. In this folk tale it is not just the mother's curse that gets the first two girls. The night birds give them a second chance and one imagines they would not have repeated the curse had they met with generosity. But instead the girls try to dam of the flow, thinking that what counts is ownership and size. The effect is clear: by keeping the gift they get no more. They are no longer vehicles for the stream and they no longer enjoy its fruits, one of which seems to be their own lives, for they end up dead. Their mother's bread has turned to toadstools inside of them.

Another way to describe the motion of the gift is to say that a gift must always be used up, consumed, and eaten. *The gift is property that perishes.* Food is one of the most common images for the gift because it is so clear that it is consumed. Even when the gift is not food, when it is something we would think of as durable goods, it is often referred to as a thing to be eaten. Shell necklaces and armbands are the ritual gifts in the Trobriand Islands and, when they are passed from one group to the next, protocol demands that the man who gives them away toss them on the ground and say, "Here, some food we could no eat." Or, again, a man in a different tribe that Wendy James has studied speaks of the money he was given at the marriage of his daughter saying that he will pass it on rather than spend it on himself. Only he puts it this way: ". . . If I receive money for the children God has given me, I cannot eat it. I must give it to others."[7]

To say that the gift is used up, consumed, and eaten sometimes means that it is truly destroyed as with food, but more simply and accurately it means that the gift perishes *for the person who gives it away*. In gift exchange the transaction itself consumes the object. This is why durable goods are given in a manner that emphasizes their loss (the Trobriand Islander throws the shells on the ground). A perishable good is a special case and a surer gift because it is sure to be lost.

Now it is true that something often comes back when a gift is given, but if this were made an explicit condition of the exchange it wouldn't be a gift. If the girl in our story had offered to sell the bread to the birds the whole tone would have been different. Instead she sacrifices it—her mother's gift is dead and gone when it leaves her hand. She no longer controls it, nor has she any contract about repayment. For her, the gift has perished. This then is how I use "consume" to speak of a gift—a gift is consumed when it moves from one hand to another with no assurance of anything in return. There is little difference, therefore, between its consumption and its motion. A market exchange has an equilibrium, or stasis: you pay in order to balance the scale. But when you give a gift there is momentum and the weight shifts from body to body.

I must add one more word on what it is to "consume" because the Western industrial world is known for its "consumer goods" and they are not at all what I mean. Again, the difference is in the form of the exchange, a thing we can feel most concretely in the form of the goods themselves. I remember the time I went to my first rare book fair and saw how the first editions of Thoreau and Whitman and Crane had been carefully packaged in heat-shrunk plastic with the price tags on the inside. Somehow the simple addition of airtight plastic sacs had transformed the books from vehicles of liveliness into commodities, like bread made with chemicals to keep it from perishing. In commodity exchange it's as if the buyer and the seller are both in plastic bags; there's none of the contact of a gift exchange. There is neither motion nor emotion because the whole point is to keep the balance, to make sure the exchange itself doesn't consume anything or involve one person with another. "Consumer goods" are a privatized consuming, not a banquet.

The desire to consume is a kind of lust. We long to have the world flow through us like air or food. We are thirsty and hungry for something that can only be carried inside of bodies. We need it. We want it. But "consumer goods" just bait this lust, they do not satisfy it. They can never, as the gift can, raise lust into a kind of love, an emotional discourse. Love may always grow from lust, but not in the stillness of commodity exchange. The consumer of commodities is invited to a meal without passion, a consumption with neither satiation nor fire. Like a guest seduced into feeding on the drippings of someone else's capital without benefit of its inner nourishment, he is always hungry at the end of the meal, depressed and weary as we all feel when lust has dragged us from the house and led us to nothing.

Gift exchange has many fruits and to the degree that the fruits of the gift can satisfy our needs there will always be pressure for property to be treated as a gift. This pressure, in a sense, is what keeps the gift in motion. When the Udak warn that a storm will ruin the crops if someone tries to stop the gift from moving, it is really their desire for its motion that will bring the storm. A restless hunger springs up when the gift is not being eaten. The Grimm brothers found a short tale they called "The Ungrateful Son":[8]

> Once a man and his wife were sitting outside the front door with a roast chicken before them which they were going to eat between them. Then the man saw his old father coming along and quickly took the chicken and hid it, for he begrudged him any of it. The old man came, had a drink, and went away.
> Now the son was about to put the roast chicken back on the table, but when he reached for it, it had turned into a big toad that jumped in his face and stayed there and didn't go away again.
> And if anybody tried to take it away, it would give them a

poisonous look, as if about to jump in their faces, so that no one dared to touch it. And the ungrateful son had to feed the toad every day, otherwise it would eat part of his face. And thus he went ceaselessly hither and yon about in the world.

This toad is the hunger that appears when the gift stops moving, whenever one man's gift becomes another man's capital. To the degree that we desire the fruits of the gift, teeth will appear when it is hidden away. When property is hoarded, thieves and beggars begin to be born to rich men's wives. A story like this says that there is a force seeking to keep the gift in motion. Some property must perish, its preservation is beyond us. We have no choice, or rather, our choice is whether to keep the gift moving or to be eaten with it. We choose between the toad's dumb-lust and that other, graceful perishing in which the gift is eaten with a passion not unlike love.

II

The gift is to the giver, and comes back most to him—it cannot fail. . . .

WALT WHITMAN

A Song of the Rolling Earth

A bit of a mystery still remains in the Scottish tale "The Girl and the Dead Man": Where did the "vessel of cordial" come from? My guess is that it comes from the mother, or from her spirit, at least. The gift not only moves, it moves in a circle. In this tale it circles through the mother and her daughter. The mother gives the bread and the girl gives it in return to the birds whom I place in the realm of the mother, not only because it is a mother bird who addresses her but also because there is a verbal link (the mother has a "leash of daughters," the mother bird has her "puppies"). The vessel of cordial is in the realm of the mother as well (the original Gaelic word means "teat of ichor" or "teat of health": it is a fluid that comes from the breast). The level changes, to be sure—it is a different sort of mother whose breasts hold the blood of the gods—but it is still in the maternal sphere. Structurally, then, the gift moves mother → daughter → mother → daughter. In circling twice in this way the gift itself increases from bread to the water of life, from carnal food to a spiritual food. At that point the circle expands as the girl gives the gift to her sisters to bring them back to life.

The figure of the circle in which the gift moves can be seen more clearly if we turn to a story from ethnography. Gift institutions seem to have been universal among tribal peoples; the few we know the most about are the ones that Western ethnographers studied around the turn of the century. One of these is the Kula, the ceremonial gift exchange of the Massim tribes, peoples who occupy the South Sea Islands off the eastern tip of New Guinea.[9]

There are a dozen or more groups of islands in the Kula archipelago. They are quite far apart—a circle enclosing the whole group would have a diameter of almost 300 miles. The Kula is (or was sixty years ago) a highly developed gift system conducted throughout the islands. At its heart lies the exchange of two ceremonial gifts, armshells and necklaces. These are passed from household to household, staying with each for a time. So long as one of the gifts is residing in a man's house, Bronislaw Malinowski tells us, the man is able "to draw a great deal of renown, to exhibit this article, to tell how he obtained it, and to plan to whom he is going to give it. And all this forms one of the favourite subjects of tribal conversation and gossip. . . ." Armshells and necklaces are talked about, touched, and used to ward off disease. Like heirlooms, they are pools where feeling and power and history have collected. They are brought out and palavered over just as we might do if we had, say, some fine old carpenter's tools that had been used by our own grandfather, or a pocket watch brought from the old country.

Malinowski calls the Kula articles "ceremonial gifts" because their social use far exceeds their practical use. A friend of mine tells me that the gang he ran with in college continually passed around a deflated basketball. The joke was to get it mysteriously deposited in someone else's room. It seems that the clear uselessness of such objects makes it easier for them to be vehicles for the spirit of a group. My father says that when he was a boy his parents and some good friends passed back and forth, again as a joke, a huge open-ended wrench that had apparently been custom cast to repair a steam shovel. The two families found it one day on a picnic and for years thereafter it showed up in first one house and then the other, under the Christmas tree or in the umbrella stand, appearing one year fully bronzed and gift-wrapped. If you have not yourself been a part of such an exchange you will easily turn up a story like this by asking around, for these spontaneous exchanges of "useless" gifts are fairly common, though hardly ever developed to the depth and elegance that Malinowski found among the Massim.

The Kula gifts, the armshells and necklaces, move continually around a wide ring of islands in the archipelago. Each travels in a circle, the red shell necklaces moving clockwise and the armshells moving counterclockwise.

A man who participates in the Kula has gift partners in neighboring tribes. If we imagine him facing the center of the circle with partners on his left and right, he will always be receiving armshells from his partner to the left and giving them to the man on his right. The necklaces flow the other way. Of course these things are not actually passed hand over hand; they are carried by canoe from island to island in journeys that require great preparation and cover hundreds of miles.

The two Kula gifts are exchanged for each other. If a man brings me a necklace, I will give him in return some armshells of equivalent value. I may do this right away or I may wait as long as a year (though if I wait that long I will give him a few smaller gifts in the interim to show my good faith). When I have received a gift, I can keep it for a time before I pass it on and initiate a new exchange. As a rule it takes between two and ten years for each article in the Kula to make a full round of the islands.

Because these gifts are exchanged for each other it seems we have already broken the rule against equilibrium that I set out in the first section. But let us look more closely. We should first note that the Kula articles are kept in motion, though this does not necessarily mean there is no equilibrium. Each gift stays with a man for awhile, but if he keeps it too long he will begin to have a reputation for being "slow" and "hard" in the Kula. The gifts "never stop," writes Malinowski. "It seems almost incredible at first, . . . but it is the fact, nevertheless, that no one ever keeps any of the Kula valuables for any length of time. . . . 'Ownership,' therefore, in Kula, is quite a special economic relation. A man who is in the Kula never keeps any article for longer than, say, a year or two. "The Trobriand Islanders know what it is to own property, but their sense of possession is wholly different from the European. The social code . . . lays down that to possess is to be great, and that wealth is the indispensable appanage of social rank and attribute of personal virtue. But the important point is that with them *to possess is to give* [my emphasis]—and here the natives differ from us notably. A man who owns a thing is naturally expected to share it, to distribute it, to be its trustee and dispenser."

The motion of the Kula gifts does not by itself assure that there will be no equilibrium, for, as we have seen, they move but they are also exchanged. Two ethics, however, govern this exchange and both of them insure that, while there may be a macroscopic equilibrium, at the level of each man there will be the sense of imbalance, of shifting weight, that always marks a gift exchange. The first of these ethics prohibits discussion: " . . . the Kula, " writes Malinowski, "consists in the bestowing of a ceremonial gift, which has to be repaid by an equivalent counter-gift after a lapse of time. . . . But [and this is the point], it can never be exchanged from hand to hand, with the equivalence between the two objects discussed, bargained about and computed." A man may wonder what will come in return for his gift, but he is not supposed to bring it up. In barter you talk and talk until you strike a bargain, but the gift is given in silence.

A second important ethic, Malinowski goes on, "is that the equivalence of the counter-gift is left to the giver, and it cannot be enforced by any kind of coercion." If a man gives some crummy necklace in return for a fine set of armshells, people may talk, but there's nothing you can do about it. When we barter we make deals and when someone defaults we go after him, but the gift must be a gift. It is as if you give a part of your substance to your gift partner and then wait in silence until he gives you a part of his. You put your self in his hands. These rules—and they are typical of gift institutions—preserve the sense of motion despite the exchange involved. There is a trade, but these are not commodities.

We commonly think of the gifts as being exchanged between two people and of gratitude as being directed back to the actual donor. "Reciprocity," the standard social science term for the return gift, has this sense of going to and fro between people (the roots are *re* and *pro*, back and forth, like a reciprocating engine). The gift in the Scottish tale is given reciprocally, going back and forth between the mother and her daughter (until the very end).

Reciprocal giving is a form of gift exchange, but it is the simplest. The gift moves in a circle and two people don't make much of a circle. Two points establish a line but a circle has to be drawn on a plane and a plane needs at least three points. This is why most stories of gift exchange have a minimum of three people. I have introduced the Kula circuit here because it is such a fine example. For the Kula gifts to move, each man must have at least two gift partners. In this case the circle is larger than that, of course, but three is its lower limit.

Circular giving differs from reciprocal giving in several ways. The most obvious is this: when the gift moves in a circle no one ever receives it from the same person he gives it to. I continually give armshells to my partner to the west but, unlike a two-person give and take, he never gives me armshells in return. The whole mood is different. The circle is the structural equivalent of the prohibition on discussion. When I give to someone from whom I do not receive (and yet I do receive elsewhere) it is as if the gift goes around a corner before it comes back. I have to give blindly. And I will feel a sort of blind gratitude, as well. The smaller the circle is—and particularly if it is just two people—the more you can keep your eye on things and the more likely it is you'll start to think like a salesman. But so long as the gift passes out of sight it cannot be manipulated by one man or one pair of gift partners. When the gift moves in a circle its motion is beyond the control of the personal ego and so each bearer must be a part of the group and each donation is an act of social faith.

What size is the circle? In addressing this question I have come to think of the circle, the container in which the gift moves, as its "Body" or "ego." Some psychologists speak of the ego as a "complex" like any other: the Mother, the Father, the Me—all of these are important places in the field of the psyche where images and energy cluster as we grow, like stars in a constellation. The ego complex takes on shape and size as the Me, that part of the psyche which takes everything personally, retains our private history, how others have treated us, how we look and feel and so on.

I find it useful to think of the ego complex as a thing which keeps expanding, not as something to be overcome or done away with.

An ego has formed and hardened by the time most of us reach adolescence, but it is small, an ego-of-one. Then if we fall in love, for example, the constellation of identity expands and the ego-of-one becomes an ego-of-two. The young lover, often to his own amazement, finds himself saying "we" instead of "me". Each of us identifies with a wide and wider community as we mature. We come to think and act with a group-ego (or, in most of these gift stories, a tribal-ego), which speaks with the "we" of kings and wise old people. Of course the larger it becomes the less it feels like what we usually mean by ego. Not entirely, though: whether an adolescent is thinking of himself or a nation of itself, it still feels like egotism to anyone on the outside. There is still a boundary.

If the ego were to widen still farther, however, it really would change its nature and become something we would no longer call ego. There is a consciousness in which we act as part of things larger even than the race. When I picture this I always think of the end of "Song of Myself" where Whitman dissolves into the air:

I effuse my flesh in eddies, and drift it in lacy jags.
I bequeath myself to the dirt and grow from the grass I love,
If you want me again look for me under your boot-soles.

Now the part that says "me" is scattered. There is no boundary to be outside of, unless the universe itself is bounded.

In all of this we could substitute "body" for "ego." Aborigines commonly refer to their own clan as "my body," just as our marriage ceremony speaks of becoming "one flesh." Again, the body in this sense enlarges beyond our own skin and in its final expansion there is no body at all. We love to feel the body open outward when we are in the spirit of the gift. The ego's firmness has its virtues, but in the end we seek the slow dilation, to use another of Whitman's words, in which the self enjoys a widening give-and-take with the world and is finally lost in ripeness.

The gift can circulate at every level of the ego. In the ego-of-one we speak of self-gratification and, whether it's forced or chosen, a virtue or a vice, the mark of self-gratification is its isolation. Reciprocal giving, the ego-of-two, is a little more social. We think mostly of lovers. Each of these circles is exhilarating as it expands and the little gifts that pass between lovers touch us because each is stepping into a larger circuit. But when it goes on and on to the exclusion of others it stops expanding and goes stale. D H Lawrence spoke of the "egoisme à deux" of so many married couples, people who get just so far in the expansion of the self and then close down for a lifetime, opening up for neither children nor the gods. A folk tale from Kashmir tells of two Brahmin women who tried to dispense with their alms-giving duties by simply giving alms back and forth to each other.[10] They didn't quite have the spirit of the thing. When they died they returned to the earth as two wells so poisoned that no one could take water from them. No one else can drink from the ego-of-two. It has its time in our maturation, but it is an infant form of the gift circle and does not endure.

In the Kula we have already seen a fine example of the larger circle. The Maori, the native tribes of New Zealand, provide another, similar in some ways to the Kula, but offering new detail and a hint of how gift exchange feels if the circle expands beyond the body of the tribe.[11] The Maori have a word, *hau* which translates as "spirit," particularly the spirit of the gift and the spirit of the forest which gives food. In these tribes when hunters return from the forest with birds they have killed they give a portion of the kill to the priests who, in turn, cook them at a sacred fire. The priests eat a few of the birds and then prepare a sort of talisman, the *mauri*, which is the physical embodiment of the forest *hau*. This *mauri* is a gift that the priests give back to the forest where it causes the birds to be abundant so that they may again be slain and taken by hunters.

There are three gifts in this hunting ritual; the forest gives to the hunters, the hunters to the priests, and the priests to the forest. At the end, the gift moves from the third party back to the first. The ceremony that the priests perform is called *whangai hau* which means "nourishing *hau*," that is, feeding the spirit. To give such a name to the priests' activity says that the addition of the third party keeps the gift in motion, keeps it lively. Put conversely, without the priests there is a danger that the motion of the gift will be lost. It seems to be too much to ask of the hunters to both kill the game and return a gift to the forest. As we said in speaking of the Kula, gift exchange is more likely to turn into barter when it falls into the ego-of-two. With a simple give-and-take, the hunters may begin to think of the forest as a place to turn a profit. But with the priests present, the gift must leave the hunters' sight before it returns to the woods. The priests take on or incarnate the position of the third thing to avoid the binary relation of the hunters and forest which by itself would not be abundant. The priests, by their presence alone, feed the spirit.

Every gift calls for a return gift, and so, by placing the gift back in the forest, the priests treat the birds as a gift of nature. We now understand that this is ecological. Ecology as a science began toward the end of the nineteenth century, an offshoot of all the interest in evolution. It was originally the study of how animals live in their environments and one of its first lessons was that, beneath all the change in nature, there are steady states characterized by cycles. Every participant in the cycle literally lives off of the others with only the energy source, the sun, being transcendent. Widening this study to include man meant to look at ourselves as a part of nature again, not its Lord. When we see that we are actors in natural cycles then we understand that what nature gives to us is influenced by what we give to nature. So the circle is a sign of ecological wisdom as much as of gift. We come to feel ourselves as one part of a large self-regulating system. The return gift, the "nourishing *hau*," is literally feedback, as they say in cybernetics. Without it, that is to say, with any greed or arrogance of will, the whole cycle gets out of whack. We all know that it isn't "really" the *mauri* placed in the forest that "causes" the birds to be abundant, and yet now we see that on a different level it is: the circle of gifts replicates and harmonizes with the cycles of nature and in so doing manages not to interrupt them and not to put man on the outside. The forest's abundance is in fact a consequence of our treating its wealth as a gift. We shall see as we go along that there is always this link between gift and abundance, as there is always a link between commodities and scarcity.[12]

The Maori hunting ritual enlarges the circle within which the gift moves in two ways. First, it includes nature. Second and more importantly, it includes the gods. The priests act out a gift relationship with the deities, giving thanks and sacrificing gifts to them in return for what they give the tribe. A story from the Old Testament shows us the same thing in a tradition with which we are more familiar. The structure is identical.

In the Penateuch the first fruits always belong to the Lord. In Exodus the Lord tells Moses: "Consecrate to me all the first-born: whatever is the first to open the womb among the people of Israel, both of man and of beast, is mine." The Lord gives the tribe its wealth and the germ of that wealth is then given back to the Lord. Fertility is a gift from God and in order for it to continue, its first fruits must be returned to Him as gift. In pagan times this had included sacrificing the first-born son. The Israelites had early been allowed to substitute an animal for the first-born son, as in the story of Abraham and Isaac. Likewise a lamb was substituted for the first-born of any unclean animal. The Lord says to Moses:

All that opens the womb is mine, all your male cattle, the firstlings of cow and sheep. The firstling of an ass you shall redeem with a lamb, or if you will not redeem it you shall break its neck. All the first-born of your sons you shall redeem.

In a different chapter the Lord explains to Aaron what is to be done with the first-borns. Aaron and his sons are responsible for the priesthood and they minister at the alter. The lambs, calves, and kids are to be sacrificed: "You shall sprinkle their blood upon the altar, and shall burn their fat as an offering by fire, a pleasing odor to the Lord; but their flesh shall be yours. . . ." As in the Maori story, the priests eat a portion of the gift. But its essence is burned and returned to the Lord in smoke.

This gift cycle has three stations and more—the flocks, the tribe, the priests, and the Lord. The inclusion of the Lord in the circle—and this is the point I began to make above—changes the ego in which the gift moves in a way unlike any other addition. It is enlarged beyond the tribal ego and beyond nature. Now, as I said when I first introduced the image, we would no longer call it "ego" at all. The gift leaves all boundary and circles into mystery.

The passage into mystery always refreshes. We lie on the grass and stare at the stars in their blackness and our heaviness falls away. If, when we work, we can look on the face of mystery just once a day, then all our labor satisfies, and if we cannot we become willful and topheavy. We are lightened when our gifts rise from pools we cannot fathom. Then they are not all ego and then they are inexhaustible. Anything that is contained contains as well its own exhaustion. The most perfectly balanced gyroscope slowly wears down. But we are enlivened when the gift passes into the heart of light or of darkness and then returns. This is as true of property as it is of those gifts we cannot touch. It is when the world of objects burns a bit in our peripheral vision that it gives us jubilation and not depression. We stand before a bonfire or even a burning house and feel the odd release it brings. It is as if the trees were able to give the sun return for what enters them through the leaf. Objects pull us down into their bones unless their fat is singed occasionally. When all property is held still then the Pharoah himself is plagued with hungry toads. When we cannot be moved to move the gift then a sword appears to seek out the first-born sons. But that Pharaoh was dead long before his first-born was taken, for we are only alive to the degree that we can feel the call for motion. In the living body that calls is no stranger, it is a part of the soul. When the gift circles into mystery then the liveliness stays and the mood is the same as in those lines of Whitman. It is "a pleasing odor to the Lord" when the first fruits are effused in eddies and drifted in lacy jags above the flame.

We described the motion of the gift earlier in this essay by saying that gifts are always used, consumed, or eaten. Now that we have seen the figure of the circle we can understand what seems at first to be a paradox of gift exchange: when the gift is used it is not used up. Quite the opposite in fact: the gift that is not used is lost while the one that is passed along remains abundant. In the Scottish tale the girls who hoard their bread are fed only while they eat. The meal finishes in hunger though they took the larger piece. The girl who shares her bread is satisfied. What is given away feeds again and again while what is kept feeds only once and leaves us hungry.

The tale is a parable, but in the Kula ring we saw the same as a social fact. The necklaces and armshells are not diminished by their use, but satisfy faithfully. It is only when a foreigner intervenes to buy a few for the museum that they are "used up" by a transaction. The Maori hunting tale showed us that not just food in parables but food in nature remains abundant when it is treated as gift, when we participate in the moving circle and do not stand aside as hunter or exploiter. Gifts form a class of property whose value is only in their use and which literally cease to exist if they are not constantly consumed.[13] When gifts are sold they change their nature as much as water changes when it freezes and no rationalist telling of the constant elemental structure can replace the feeling that is lost.

In E M Forster's novel *A Passage to India*, Dr Ariz, the Moslem, and Fielding, the Englishman have a brief dialogue, a typical debate between gift and commodity.[14] Fielding says:

"Your emotions never seem in proportion to their objects, Aziz."

"Is emotion a sack of potatoes, so much to the pound, to be measured out? Am I a machine? I shall be told I can use up my emotions by using them, next."

"I should have thought you would. It sounds common sense. You can't eat your cake and have it, even in the world of the spirit."

"If you are right, there is no point in any friendship; it all comes down to give and take, or give and return, which is disgusting, and we had better all leap over this parapet and kill ourselves."

In the world of gift, as in the Scottish tale, you not only can have your cake and eat it too, you can't have cake *unless* you eat it. It is the same with feeling. Our emotions are not used in use. They may rise and fall, certainly, but they become strong and sure as we use them and only die away when we try to keep the lid on.

Gift and feeling are alike in this regard. Though once that is said we must qualify it, for the gift does not imitate all emotion, it imitates the emotions of relationship. As I mentioned in my introductory remarks, the gift joins people together. It doesn't just carry feeling, it carries attachment or love. The gift is an emanation of Eros. The forms of gift exchange spring from erotic life and gifts are its vehicles. In speaking of "use," then, we see that the gift displays a natural fact: libido is not lost when it is given away. Eros never wastes his lovers. When we give ourselves to that god he does not leave off his attentions; it is only when we fall to calculation that he remains hidden and no body will satisfy. Satisfaction comes not merely from being filled but from being filled with a current that will not cease. With the gift, as in love, our satisfaction sets us at ease because we know that somehow its use at once assures its plenty.

Scarcity and abundance have more to do with the form of exchange than with how much stuff is at hand. Scarcity appears when wealth cannot flow. Elsewhere in *A Passage to India*, Dr. Aziz says, "If money goes, money comes. If money stays, death comes. Did you ever hear that useful Urdu proverb?" and Fielding replies, "My proverbs are: a penny saved is a penny earned; A stitch in time saves nine; Look before you leap; and the British Empire rests on them." He's right. An empire does need its clerks with their ledgers and their clocks, saving pennies in time. The problem is that wealth ceases to move freely when all things are counted and carry a price. It may accumulate in great heaps but fewer and fewer people can afford to enjoy it. After the war in Bangladesh, thousands of tons of donated rice rotted in warehouses because the market was the only known mode of distribution and the poor, naturally, couldn't afford to buy. Marshall Sahlins, an anthropologist who has done some of the best work on gift exchange, begins a comment on modern scarcity with the paradoxical contention that hunters and gatherers "have affluent economies, their absolute poverty notwithstanding."[15] He writes:

> Modern capitalist societies, however richly endowed, dedicate themselves to the proposition of scarcity. [Both Samuelson and Friedman begin their economies with "The Law of Scarcity"; it's all over by the end of chapter one.] Inadequacy of economic means is the first principle of the world's wealthiest peoples. The apparent material status of the economy seems to be no clue to its accomplishments; something has to be said for the mode of economic organization.
>
> The market-industrial system institutes scarcity, in a manner completely unparalleled and to a degree nowhere else approximated. Where production and distribution are arranged through the behavior of prices, and all livelihoods depend on getting and spending, insufficiency of material means becomes the explicit, calculable starting point of all economic activity. The entrepreneur is confronted with alternative investments of a finite capital, the worker (hopefully) with alternative choices of remunerative employ. . . . Consumption is a double tragedy: what begins in inadequacy will end in deprivation. Bringing together an international division of labor, the market makes available a dazzling array of products: all these Good Things within a man's reach—but never all within his grasp. Worse, in this game of consumer free choice, every acquisition is simultaneously a deprivation, for every purchase of something is a foregoing of something else, in general only marginally less desirable. . . .

Scarcity appears when there is a boundary. If there is plenty of blood in the system but something blocks its passage to the brain, the brain does well to complain of scarcity. The assumptions of market exchange may not necessarily lead to the emergence of boundaries, but they do in practice. When trade is "clean" and leaves people unconnected, when the merchant is free to sell when and where he will, when the market moves mostly for profit and the dominant myth is not "to possess is to give" but "the fittest survive," then wealth will lose its motion and gather in isolated pools. Under the assumptions of trade, property is plagued by entropy and wealth becomes scarce even as it increases.

A commodity is *truly* "used up" when it is sold because nothing about the exchange assures its return. A visiting sea captain may pay handsomely for some Kula necklaces, but because their sale removes them from the circle it wastes them, no matter the price. Gifts that remain gifts can support an affluence of satisfaction, even without numerical abundance. The mythology of the rich in the over-producing nations that the poor are in on some secret about satisfaction—black "soul," gypsy *duende*, the noble savage, the simple farmer, the virile gamekeeper—obscures the harshness of modern capitalist poverty, but it does have a basis, for people who live in voluntary poverty or who are not capital-intensive do have more ready access to "erotic" forms of exchange that are neither exhausting nor exhaustible and whose use assures their plenty.

If the commodity moves to turn a profit, where does the gift move? The gift in all its realms, from the soul to the kitchen, moves toward the empty place. As it turns in its circle it always comes to him who has been empty-handed the longest, and if someone appears elsewhere whose need is greater it will leave its old channel and move to him. Our generosity may leave us empty, but our emptiness then pulls gently at the whole until the thing in motion returns to fill us again. Social nature abhors a vaccum. The gift finds us attractive when we stand with a bowl that is unowned and empty. As Meister Eckhart says, "Let us borrow empty vessels."

The begging bowl of the Buddha, Thomas Merton has said, "represents the ultimate theological root of the belief, not just in a right to beg, but in openness to the gifts of all beings as an expression of the interdependence of all beings. . . . When the monk begs from the layman and receives a gift from the layman, it is not as a selfish person getting something from somebody else.

He is simply opening himself in this interdependence. . . ."[16] The wandering mendicant takes it as his task to carry what is empty from door to door. There is no profit; he merely stays alive if the gift moves toward him. He makes its spirit visible to us. His well-being, then, is a sign of its well-being, as his starvation would be a sign of its withdrawal. Our English word "beggar" comes from the Beghards, a brotherhood of mendicant friars that grew up in the thirteenth century in Flanders. There are still some places in the East, I gather, where wandering mendicants live from the begging bowl. In Europe they died out at the close of the Middle Ages.

As the bearer of the empty place the holy mendicant has an active duty beyond his supplication. He is the vehicle of that fluidity which is abundance. The wealth of the group touches his bowl at all sides, as if it were the center of a wheel where the spokes meet. The gift gathers there and the mendicant gives it away again when he meets someone who is empty. In European folk tales the beggar often turns out to be Wotan, the true "owner" of the land, who asks for charity though it is his own wealth he moves within and who then responds to neediness by filling it with gift. He is godfather to the poor.

Folk tales commonly open with a beggar motif. In a tale from Bengal, the king has two queens, both of whom are childless.[17] A faquir, a wandering mendicant, comes to the palace gate to ask for alms. One of the queens walks down to give him a handful of rice. When he finds that she is childless, however, he says that he cannot accept the rice but has a gift for her instead, a potion that will remove her barrenness. If she drinks his nostrum with the juice of the pomegranate flower, he tells her, in due time she will bear a son whom she should then call the Pomegranate Boy. All this comes to pass and the tale proceeds.

Such stories say that the gift always moves in its circle from plenty to emptiness. The gift seeks the barren and the arid and the stuck and the poor.[18] A commodity stays where it is and says "I am," but the gift says "I am not" and longs to be consumed. A guest in any home, it has no home of its own but moves on, leaving early in the morning before the rest of us have risen. The Lord says "all that opens the womb is mine" for it is He who filled the empty womb, having earlier stood as a beggar by the sacrificial fire or at the gates of the palace.

III

THE gift the beggar gives to the queen in this last folk tale brings the queen her fertility and she bears a child. Fertility and growth are common fruits of gift exchange. Think back on all we have seen so far—the Gaelic tale, the Kula ring, the rites of the first-born, feeding the forest *hau*, and so on—fertility is often a concern and invariably either the bearers of the gift or the gift itself grows as a result of its circulation.

If the gift is alive, like a bird or a cornstalk, then it really grows, of course. But even inert gifts, such as the Kula articles, are *felt* to increase in worth as they move from hand to hand. The distinction—alive/inert—is not finally very useful, therefore, because if the gift is not alive it is nonetheless treated as if it were and whatever we treat as living begins to take on life. Moreover, gifts that take on life will in turn bestow life. The final gift in the Gaelic tale is used to revive the dead sisters. Even if such miracles are rare, it is still a fact of the soul that depression—or any heavy, dead feeling—will lift away when a gift comes toward us. Gifts not only move us, they enliven us.

The gift is a servant to forces which pull things together and lift them up. There are other forces in the world that break things down into smaller and smaller bits, that find the fissures in stones and split them apart or enter a marriage and leave it lifeless at the core. In living organisms, the atomizing forces are associated with decay and death, while the cohering forces, the ones that wrap the morning-glory around a fence post or cover the ashy slopes of a new volcano with little pine trees, these are associated with life. Gift property serves an upward force. On one level it reflects and carries the form of organic growth, but above that, at the level of society and spirit, the gift carries our own liveliness. We spiral upward with the gift, or at least it holds us upright against the forces that split us apart and pull us down.

To speak in this manner risks confusing biological "life" with cultural and spiritual "life"—a confusion I would like to avoid for the two are not always the same. They are linked, but there is also a gap. In addressing the question of increase let us therefore take a gift at the level of culture—something inorganic and inedible in fact—and see how far we can go toward explaining its *felt* increase without recourse to the natural analogy.

The North Pacific tribes of the American Indians (the Kwakiutl, Tlingit, Haida, and others) exchanged as ceremonial gifts large decorated copper plaques.[19] These coppers were always associated with the property given away at a potlatch—a ceremony that marked important events such as a marriage or, more commonly, the assumption of rank by a member of a tribe. The word "potlach" means simply "giving."[20]

Coppers increased in worth as they circulated. At the time when Franz Boas witnessed the exchange of a copper in the 1890s, their worth was reckoned in terms of woolen Hudson Bay Company trade blankets. To tell the story briefly and in terms of the increase involved, one of the Tribes in Boas's report has a copper to give away; they invite a neighboring tribe to a feast and offer them the gift.[21] The second tribe accepts, putting themselves under the obligation to make a return gift. The transaction takes place the next day on a beach. The first tribe brings the copper and the leader of the second tribe lays down 1,000 trade blankets as a return gift.

Then things get interesting. The chiefs who are giving the copper away don't accept the return gift. Instead they slowly replay the entire history of this copper's previous passages, first one man saying that just 200 more blankets will be fine and then another saying that really an additional 800 will be needed to make everyone feel right, while the recipient of the copper responds saying either "What you say is good, it pleases my heart," or else begging for mercy as he brings out more and more blankets. Five times the chiefs ask for more blankets and five times they are brought out until 3,700 are stacked up in a long row on the beach.

When the copper's entire history has been acted out, the talk stops. Now comes the true return gift, these formalities having merely raised the exchange into the general area of this copper's worth. Now the receiving chief, on his own, announces he would like to "adorn" his guests. He brings out 200 more blankets and gives them individually to the visitors. Then he adds still another 200, saying, "you must think poorly of me," and telling about his forefathers.

These 400 blankets are given without any of the dialogue that marked the first part of the ceremony. It is here that the recipient of the copper shows his generosity and it is here that the copper increases in worth. The next time it is given away, people will remember how it grew by 400 blankets in its last passage.

To return to the question of increase at the level of culture, there is a particular kind of investment in the exchange of copper. Each time the copper passes from one group to another, more blankets are heaped into it, so to speak. The source of increase is clear: each man really adds to its worth as the copper comes toward him. But it is important to remember that the investment is itself a gift, so the increase is both concrete (blankets) and emotional (the spirit of generosity). At each transaction the concrete increase (the "adornment") is a witness to the increase in feeling. In this way, though people may remember it in terms of blankets, the copper becomes enriched with feeling. And not all feelings, either, but those of generosity, liberality, good will—feelings that draw people together.

Coppers make a good example here because there is concrete increase to manifest the feeling, but that is not necessary. The mere passage of the gift, the act of donation, contains the feeling and therefore the passage alone is the investment. The gift is a pool or reservoir in which the sentiments of its exchange accumulate so that the more often it is given away the more feeling it carries, like an heirloom that has been passed down for generations. The gift gets steeped in the fluids of its own passage. In folk tales the gift is often something seemingly worthless—ashes or coals or leaves or straw—but when the puzzled recipient carries it to his doorstep he finds it turned to gold. In such tales the mere motion of the gift across the boundary from the world of the donor (usually a spirit) to the doorsill of the recipient is sufficient to transmute it from dross to gold.[22]

Typically the increase inheres in the gift only so long as it is treated as such—as soon as the happy mortal starts to count it or grabs his wheelbarrow and heads back for more, the gold reverts to straw. The growth is in the sentiment and cannot be put on the scale.

The potlatch can rightly be spoken of as a good will ceremony. One of the men giving the feast in the potlatch Boas witnessed says as the meal begins: "This food here is the good will of our forefathers. It is all given away." The act of donation is an affirmation of good will. When someone in one of these tribes is mistakenly insulted, his response, rather than turning to a libel lawyer, is to give a gift to the man who insulted him, and if indeed the insult was mistaken, the man gives a gift in return, adding a little extra to demonstrate his good will, a sequence which has the same structure (back and forth with increase) as the potlatch itself. When a gift passes from hand to hand in this spirit—and here we have come back to the question of increase—it becomes the binder of many wills. What gathers in it is not only the sentiment of generosity but the affirmation of individual good will, making of those separate parts a *spiritus mundi,* a unanimous heart, a band whose wills are focused through the lens of the gift. In this way, the gift is an agent of social cohesion and this banding function again leads to the feeling that a gift grows through its circulation. The whole really is greater than the sum of its parts. If it brings the group together, the gift increases in worth immediately upon its first circulation, and then, like a faithful lover, continues to grow through constancey.

I do not mean to imply that gifts such as these coppers are felt to grow merely because the group projects its own life onto them, for that would imply that the group's liveliness can be separated from the gift, and it can't. If the copper is taken away, so is the life. When a song moves us we don't say we've projected our feeling onto the melody, nor do we say a woman projects the other sex onto her lover. Equally the gift and the group are two separate things and there is nothing to be withdrawn. We could say, however, that a copper is an image for the life of the group, for a true image has a life of its own. All mystery needs its image. It needs these two, the ear and the song, the he and the she, the soul and the word. The tribe and its gift are separate but they are also the same—there is a little gap between them so they may breathe into each other, and yet there is no gap at all for they share one breath, one meal for the two of them. People with a sense of the gift not only speak of it as food to eat, they also feed it (as the Maori ceremony "feeds" the forest *hau*). The nourishment flows both ways. When we have fed the gift with our labor and generosity, it grows and feeds us in return. The gift and its bearers share a spirit which is kept alive by its motion among them and from that the life emerges, willy-nilly. Still, the spirit of the gift is alive only when the gift is being passed from hand to hand. When Black Elk, an Oglala Sioux holy man, told the history of the Sioux "sacred pipe" to Joseph Epes Brown, he explained that at the time the pipe had first been given to him, his elders had told him that its history must always be passed down, "for as long as it is known, and for as long as the pipe is used, [the] people will live; but as soon as it has been forgotten, the people will be without a center and they will perish."[23]

The increase is the core of the gift, the kernel. In this essay I use the term "gift" for both the object and its increase, but at times it seems more accurate to speak of the increase alone as the gift and to treat the object involved more modestly as its vehicle or vessel. Certainly it makes sense to say that the increase is the real gift in those cases where the gift-object is sacrificed, for the increase continues despite (even because of) that loss; it is the constant in the cycle, not consumed in use. A Maori elder who told of the forest *hau* distinguished in this way between object and increase, the *mauri* set in the forest and its *hau* which causes the game to abound. In that cycle the *hau* is nourished and passed along while the gift-objects (birds, *mauri*) disappear.

Marshall Sahlins, when he commented on the Maori gift stories, asked that we "observe just where the term *hau* enters into the discussion. Not with the initial transfer from the first to the second party, as well it could if the *hau* were the spirit in the gift, but upon the exchange between the second and third parties, as logically it would if [the *hau*] were the yield on the gift. The term 'profit' is economically and historically inappropriate to the Maori, but it would have been a better translation than 'spirit' for the *hau* in question."

Sahlins's gloss highlights something which has been implicit in our discussion, though not yet stated directly—the increase comes to a gift as it moves from second to third party, not in the simpler passage from first to second. It begins when the gift has passed through someone, when the circle appears. But, as Sahlins senses, "profit" is not the right word. Capital earns profit and the sale of a commodity turns a profit, but gifts that remain gifts do not *earn* profit, the *give* increase. The distinction lies in what we might call the vector of the increase: in gift exchange it stays in motion and follows the object, while in commodity exchange it stays behind (as profit).

With this in mind, we may return to a dictum laid out early in the essay: one man's gift must not be another man's capital. A corollary may not be developed, saying: the increase which comes of gift exchange must remain a gift and not be converted to capital. St Ambrose of Milan states it directly in a commentary on Deuteronomy: ". . . God has excluded in general all increase of capital."[24] This is an ethic in a gift society. Just as one may choose to treat the gift as gift or to take it out of circulation, so the increase may either be passed along or laid aside as capital.

I have chosen not to allow this essay to wander very far into the labyrinths of capitalism, so I shall only sketch this choice in its broadest terms. Capital is wealth taken out of circulation and laid aside to produce more wealth. Cattle devoured at a feast are gift, but cattle set aside to produce calves or milk are capital. All peoples have both and need both. A question arises, however, whenever there's a surplus. If you have more than you need, what do you do with it? What happens to the gravy? Capitalism as an ideology addresses itself to this choice and at every turn applauds the move away from gift and calls that sensible ("a penny saved . . .").[25]

Here it becomes necessary to differentiate two forms of growth, for the growth of capital is not the increase of the gift. Nor are their fruits the same. The gift grows more lively but capital grows in a lump—more cows, more factories . . . When all surplus is turned to capital, the stock increases but not the liveliness, and there is busyness without elevation, increase without feeling, a growth more sedimentary than organic, the conglomeration of stones rather than the flourishing of trees.

The accumulation of capital has its own benefits—security and material comfort being the most obvious and appealing—but the point here is that whatever those benefits, if they flow from the conversion of gifts to capital then the fruits of the gift are lost. At that point property becomes correctly associated with the suppression of liveliness, fertility, and emotion. To recall our earlier tales, when a goat given from one tribe to another is not treated as a gift, or when any gift is hoarded and counted and kept for the self, then death appears, or a hungry toad, or storm damage. Capitalism as a system has the same problems on a larger scale. Somewhere property must be truly consumed. The capitalist, busy turning all his homemade gravy back to capital, must seek out foreigners to consume the goods (though as before they get only the dumb consumption of commodities). And what was a toad in the psyche or storm damage in the tribe now becomes alienation at home or war and exploitation abroad, those shades who follow capital whenever it feeds on the gift.

The gift remains a gift only so long as its increase remains a gift. Those people, therefore, who prohibit "in general all increase on capital," as St Ambrose has it, those who insist that any conversion of property from one form to another must be in the direction of the gift, who love the increase more than its vehicles and feel their worth in liveliness, for such people the increase of gifts is not lost and the circle in which they move becomes an upward spiral.

[1]The classic work is Marcel Mauss's 1924 "Essai sur le don," now published in English as *The Gift*, trans Ian Cunnison (New York: Norton, 1967).

[2]Thomas Hutchinson, *The History of the Colony of Massachusetts-Bay,* vol 1. (Boston: Thomas & John Fleet, 1764; reprint ed. New York: Arno Press, 1972), p 469n.

[3]Wendy R. James, "Why the Uduk Won't Pay Bridewealth," *Sudan Notes and Records,* vol 51 (1970), pp 75-84.

[4]John Francis Campbell, "The Girl and the Dead Man," in *Popular Tales of the West Highlands,* vol 1 (Paisley: Alexander Gardner, 1890: reprint ed Detroit: The Singing Tree Press, 1969), pp 220-25.

[5]This story illustrates almost all the main characteristics of a gift and so I shall be referring back to it throughout the essay. As an aside, therefore, I want to take a stab at its meaning. It says, I think, that if a girl without a father is going to get along in the world, she'd better have a good connection to her mother. The birds are the mother's spirit, what we'd now call the girl's psychological mother. The girl who gives the gift back to the spirit-mother has, as a result, her mother-wits about her for the rest of the tale.

Nothing in the tale links the dead man with the girls' father, but the mother seems to be a widow or at any rate the absence of a father at the start of the story is a hint that the problem may have to do with men. It's not clear, but when the first man the daughters meet is not only dead but hard to deal with we are permitted to raise our eyebrows.

The man is dead, but not dead enough. When she hits him with the stick we see that she is in fact attached to him. So here's the issue: when a fatherless woman leaves home she'll have to deal with the fact that she stuck on a dead man. It's a risky situation—the two elder daughters end up dead.

Not much happens in the wild run through the forest, except that everyone gets bruised. The girl manages to stay awake the whole time, however. This is a power she probably got from the birds, for they are night birds. The connection to the mother cannot spare her the ordeal, but it allows her to survive. When it's all over she's unstuck and we may assume that the problem won't come up again.

Though the dilemma of the story is not related to gift, all the psychological work is accomplished through gift exchange.

[6]Wirt Sikes, *British Goblins* (London: Sampson Low et al, 1880), p 119.

[7]Wendy R James, "Sister-Exchange Marriage," *Scientific American,* vol 233, no 6 (December 1975), pp 84-94.

[8]In *The Grimms' German Folk Tales,* Francis P Magoun, Jr and Alexander H Krappe, trans, tale no 145 (Carbondale: Southern Illinois University Press, 1960), p 507.

[9]Bronislaw Malinowski lived on these islands during the first world war. Most of my material on Kula comes from his book, *Argonauts of the Western Pacific* (London: George Routledge and Sons, Ltd. 1922; reprint ed New York: E P Dutton, 1961) chapter 3, pp 81-104.

[10]W Norman Brown, "Tawi Tales" (Unpublished manuscript in the Indiana University Library).

[11]Elsdon Best, "Maori Forest Lore . . . . , Part III," in *Transactions of the New Zealand Institute* 42 (1909), pp 433-81, especially p 439. From Marshall Sahlins, *Stone Age Economics* (New York: Aldine-Atherton, Inc. 1972) pp 152 and 158.

[12]When things run in a self-regulating cycle, we speak of time and cause and value in a different way. Time is not linear (its either "momentary" or "eternal") and one event doesn't "cause" another, they are all of a piece. In addition, one part is no more valuable than another. When we speak of value we assume we can set things side by side and weigh them and compare. But in a self-regulating cycle no part can be taken out, they are all one. Which is more valuable to you, your heart or your brain? The value, like the time, is not comparative, it is either "priceless" or "worthless."

We say these things about gifts as well. It's almost a matter of definition, of course, that gifts cannot be sold, but here we see their pricelessness as a characteristic that goes with the circle. Likewise gifts have no cause. One doesn't say "I got this gift because I gave him one." Or rather, one can, but if he does he's out of the circle looking in, that is to say, he's begun to barter. In barter the sale causes the return: but gifts just move, that's all. When a wheel spins we don't say that the top of it "Causes" the bottom to move around. That's silly. We just say, "the wheel spins," as we say, "the gift moves in a circle." Likewise, the sense of time is different. In exchange trade we know when the debt is due. In gift we do not speak, we turn back to our own labor in silence.

[13]They call this "use-value" in economics. I am not fond of the term. It usually shows up at the borrom oline, a passing admission that at the boundary of exchange calculus there are folks who really use property to live.

[14]E M Forster, *A Passage to India* (New York: Harcourt Brace and World, Inc., 1924), pp 160 and 254.

[15]Sahlins, *Stone Age Economics*, pp 3-4.

[16]N Burton et al. ed, *The Asian Journal of Thomas Merton* (New York: New Directions, 1973), pp 341-42.

[17]L B Day (Lalavihari De), "Life's Secret," in *Folk-Tales of Bengal* (London: Macmillan, 1883).

[18]Folk tales are the only "proof" I can offer here. The point is more spiritual than social in the spirit world, new life comes to us when we "give up."

[19]Philip Drucker, *Cultures of the North Pacific* (Scranton, Pa: Chandler Publishing Co. 1965).

[20]I cannot here tell the story of potlatch in its full detail, but I should note that two of its better known characteristics in the popular literature—the usurious nature of loans and the rivalry or "fighting with property"—while based on traceable aboriginal motifs, are really post-European elaborations. The tribes had known a century of European trade before Boas arrived. When Marcel Mauss read through Boas's material he declared potlatch "the monster child of the gift system." So it was. As first studied, potlatch was the progeny of a "civilized" commodity trade mated to an aboriginal gift economy: some of the results were freakish.

[21]Franz Boas, "The Social Organization and the Secret Societies of the Kwakiutl Indians," *U S National Museum, Annual Report, 1894-1895* (Washington, 1897), pp 311-738. Part 3 of this work is on the potlatch, pp 341-58.

[22]Here is a typical tale from Russia: a woman walking in the woods found a baby wood-demon "lying naked on the ground and crying bitterly. So she covered it up with her

cloak, and after a time came her mother, a female wood-demon, and rewarded the woman with a potful of burning coals, which afterwards turned into bright golden ducats."

The woman doesn't cover the baby because she wants to get paid, she does it because she's moved to: then the gift comes to her. It increases solely by its passage from the realm of wood-demons to her cottage.

[23]Joseph Epes Brown, *The Sacred Pipe* (Norman: The University of Oklahoma Press, 1953), p xii.

[24]St Ambrose (S Ambrossi), *De Tobias*, a commentary, trans Lois M Zucker (Washington, D C: The Catholic University of America, 1933), p 67.

[25]To move away from capitalism is not to change the form of ownership from the few to the many, though that may be a necessary step, but to cease turning so much surplus into capital, that is, to treat most increase (even if it comes from labor) as a gift. It is quite possible to have the state own everything and still convert all gifts to capital, as Stalin demonstrated. When he decided in favor of the "production mode" he acted as a capitalist, the locus of ownership having nothing to do with it.

🔥 🔥 🔥

A SUITCASE STRAPPED WITH A ROPE

by CHARLES SIMIC

from DURAK: AN INTERNATIONAL MAGAZINE OF POETRY

nominated by DURAK: AN INTERNATIONAL MAGAZINE OF POETRY

They made themselves so small
They could all fit in a suitcase.
The suitcase they kept under the bed,
And the bed near the open window.

They just huddled there in the dark
While the mother called out the names
To make sure no one was missing.
Her voice made them so warm, made them so sleepy.

He wanted to go out and play.
He even said so once or twice.
They told him to be quiet.
Just now the suitcase was moving.

Soon the border guards were going
To open it up,
Unless of course it was a thief
And he had a long way to go.

TEMPLE NEAR QUANG TRI, NOT ON THE MAP

by BRUCE WEIGL

from NEW ENGLAND REVIEW

nominated by NEW ENGLAND REVIEW *and Stuart Friebert*

Dusk, the ivy thick with sparrows
Squawking for more room
Is all we hear, we see
Birds move on the walls of the temple
Shaping their calligraphy of wings.
Ivy is thick in the grottos,
On the moon-watching platform,
And keeps the door from closing fully.

The point man leads us and we are
Inside, lifting
The white wash bowl, the smaller bowl
For rice, the stone lanterns

And carved stone heads that open
Above the carved face for incense.
But even the bamboo sleeping mat
Rolled in the corner, even the place of prayer
Is clean. Also, a small man

Sits legs askew in the shadow
The farthest wall casts halfway
Across the room.
He is bent over, his head
Rests on the floor, and he is speaking
Something as though to us, and not to us.
The CO wants to ignore him,
He locks and loads and fires
A clip into the walls
Which are not packed with rice this time
And tells us to move out.

But one of us moves to the man,
Curious about what he is saying.
We bend him to sit up straight
And when he is where we want him,
Nearly peaked at the top of his slow uncurling
His face becomes visible, his eyes
Roll down to the charge
Wired between his chin and the floor.
The sparrows
Burst off the walls into the jungle.

𝖓 𝖓 𝖓

SWEET TALK

fiction by STEPHANIE VAUGHN

from ANTAEUS

nominated by Ellen Gilchrist and Pat Strachan

Sometimes sam and I loved each other more when we were angry. "Day," I called him, using the surname instead of Sam. "Day, Day, Day!" It drummed against the walls of the apartment like a distress signal.

"Ah, my beautiful lovebird," he said. "My sugar sweet bride."

For weeks I had been going through the trash trying to find out whether he had other women. Once I found half a ham sandwich with red marks that could have been lipstick. Or maybe catsup. This time I found five slender cigarette butts.

"Who smokes floral-embossed cigarettes?" I said. He had just come out of the shower, and droplets of water gleamed among the black hairs of his chest like tiny knife points. "Who's the heart-attack candidate you invite over when I'm out?" I held the butts beneath his nose like a small bouquet. He slapped them to the floor and we stopped speaking for three days. We moved through the apartment without touching, lay stiffly in separate furrows of the bed, desire blooming and withering between us like the invisible petals of a night-blooming cereus.

We finally made up while watching a chess tournament on television. Even though we wouldn't speak or make eye contact, we were sitting in front of the sofa moving pieces around a chess board as an announcer explained World Championship strategy to the viewing audience. Our shoulders touched but we pretended not to notice. Our knees touched, and our elbows. Then we both reached for the black bishop and our hands touched. We made love on the carpet and kept our eyes open so that we could look at each other defiantly.

We were living in California and had six university degrees between us and no employment. We lived on food stamps, job interviews and games.

"How many children did George Washington, the father of our country, have?"

"No white ones but lots of black ones."

"How much did he make when he was Commander of the Revolutionary Army?"

"He made a big to-do about refusing a salary but later presented the first Congress with a bill for a half million dollars."

"Who was the last slave-owning president?"

"Ulysses S. Grant."

We had always been good students.

It was a smoggy summer. I spent long hours in air-conditioned supermarkets, touching the cool cans, feeling the cold plastic stretched across packages of meat. Sam left the apartment for whole afternoons and evenings. He was in his car somewhere, opening it up on the freeway, or maybe just spending time with someone I didn't know. We were mysterious with each other about our absences. In August we decided to move east, where a friend said he could get us both jobs at an unaccredited community college. In the meantime, I had invented a lover. He was rich and wanted to take me to an Alpine hotel, where mauve flowers cascaded over the stone walls of a terrace. Sometimes we drank white wine and watched the icy peaks of mountains shimmer gold in the sunset. Sometimes we returned to our room carrying tiny ceramic mugs of schnapps which had been given to us, in the German fashion, as we paid for an expensive meal.

In the second week of August, I found a pair of red lace panties at the bottom of the kitchen trash.

I decided to tell Sam I had a lover. I made my lover into a tall, blue-eyed blond, a tennis player on the circuit, a Phi Beta Kappa from Stanford who had offers from the movies. It was the tall blond part that needled Sam, who was dark and stocky.

"Did you pick him up at the beach?" Sam said.

"Stop it," I said, knowing that it was a sure way to get him to ask more questions.

"Did you have your diaphragm in your purse?"

We were wrapping cups and saucers in newspaper and nesting them in the slots of packing boxes. "He was taller than you," I said, "but not as handsome."

Sam held a blue and white Dresden cup, my favorite wedding present, in front of my eyes. "You slut," he said, and let the cup drop to the floor.

"Very articulate," I said. "Some professor. The man of reason gets into an argument and he talks with broken cups. Thank you Alexander Dope."

That afternoon I failed the California drivers' test again. I made four right turns and drove over three of the four curbs. The highway patrolman pointed out that if I made one more mistake I was finished. I drove through a red light.

On the way back to the apartment complex, Sam squinted into the flatness of the expressway and would not talk to me. I put my blue-eyed lover behind the wheel. He rested a hand on my knee and smiled as he drove. He was driving me west, away from the Vista View Apartments, across the thin spine of mountains which separated our suburb from the sea. At the shore there would be seals frolicking among the rocks and starfish resting in tidal pools.

"How come you never take me to the ocean?" I said. "How come every time I want to go to the beach I have to call up a woman friend?"

"If you think you're going to Virginia with me," he said, "you're dreaming." He eased the car into our numbered space and put his head against the wheel. "Why did you have to do it?"

"I do not like cars," I said. "You know I have always been afraid of cars."

"Why did you have to sleep with that fag tennis player?" His head was still against the wheel. I moved closer and put my arm around his shoulders.

"Sam, I didn't. I made it up."

"Don't try to get out of it."

"I didn't, Sam. I made it up." I tried to kiss him. He let me put my mouth against his, but his lips were unyielding. They felt like the skin of an orange. "I didn't, Sam. I made it up to hurt you." I kissed him again and his mouth warmed against mine. "I love you, Sam. Please let me go to Virginia."

"George Donner," I read from the guidebook, "was sixty-one years old and rich when he packed up his family and left Illinois to cross the Great Plains, the desert, and the mountains into California." We were driving through the Sierras, past steep slopes and the deep shade of an evergreen forest, toward the Donner Pass, where in 1846 the Donner family had been trapped by an early snowfall. Some of them died and the rest ate the corpses of their relatives and their Indian guides to survive.

"Where are the bones?" Sam said, as we strolled past glass cases at the Donner Pass Museum. The cases were full of wagon wheels and harnesses. Above us a recorded voice described the courageous and enterprising spirit of American pioneers. A man standing nearby with a young boy turned to scowl at Sam. Sam looked at him and said loudly, "Where are the bones of the people they ate?" The man took the boy by the hand and started for the door. Sam said, "You call this American history?" and the man turned and said, "Listen, mister, I can get your license number." We laughed about that as we descended into the plain of the Great Basin desert in Nevada. Every few miles one of us would say the line and the other one would chuckle, and I felt as if we had been married fifty years instead of five, and that everything had turned out okay.

Ten miles east of Reno I began to sneeze. My nose ran and my eyes watered, and I had to stop reading the guidebook.

"I can't do this anymore. I think I've got an allergy."

"You never had an allergy in your life." Sam's tone implied that I had purposefully got the allergy so that I could not read the guidebook. We were riding in a second-hand van, a lusterless, black shoebox of a vehicle, which Sam had bought for the trip with the money he got from the stereo, the TV, and his own beautifully overhauled and rebuilt little sports car.

"Turn on the radio," I said.

"The radio is broken."

It was a hot day, dry and gritty. On either side of the freeway, a sagebrush desert stretched toward the hunched profiles of brown mountains. The mountains were so far away—the only landmarks within three hundred miles—that they did not whap by the windows like signposts, they floated above the plain of dusty sage and gave us the sense that we were not going anywhere.

"Are you trying to kill us?" I said when the speedometer slid past ninety.

"Sam looked at the dash surprised and, I think, a little pleased that the van could do that much. "I'm getting hypnotized," he said. He thought about it for another mile and said, "If you had managed to get your license, you could do something on this trip besides blow snot into your hand."

"Don't you think we should call ahead to Elko for a motel room?"

"I might not want to stop at Elko."

"Sam, look at the map. You'll be tired when we get to Elko."

"I'll let you know when I'm tired."

We reached Elko at sundown, and Sam was tired. In the office of the Shangrila Motor Lodge we watched another couple get the last room. "I suppose you're going to be mad because I was right," I said.

"Just get in the van." We bought a sack of hamburgers and set out for Utah. Ahead of us a full moon rose, flat and yellow like a fifty-dollar gold piece, then lost its color as it rose higher. We entered the Utah salt flats, the dead floor of a dead ocean. The salt crystals glittered like snow under the white moon. My nose stopped running, and I felt suddenly lucid and calm.

"Has he been in any movies?" Sam said.

"Has who been in any movies?"

"The fag tennis player."

I had to think a moment before I recalled my phantom lover.

"He's not a fag."

"I thought you made him up."

"I did make him up but I didn't make up any fag."

A few minutes later he said, "You might at least sing something. You might at least try to keep me awake." I sang a few Beatles tunes, then Simon and Garfunkel, the Everly Brothers, and Elvis Presley. I worked my way back through my youth to a Girl Scout song I remembered as "Eye, Eye, Eye, Icky, Eye, Kai, A-nah." It was supposed to be sung around a campfire to remind the girls of their Indian heritage and the pleasures of surviving in the wilderness. "Ah woo, ah woo. Ah woo knee key chee," I sang. "I am now five years old," I said, and then I sang, "Home, Home on the Range," the song I remembered singing when I was a child going cross-country with my parents to visit some relatives. The only thing I remembered about that trip besides a lot of going to the bathroom in gas stations was that there were rules which made the traveling life simple. One was: do not hang over the edge of the front seat to talk to your mother or father. The other was: if you have to throw up, do it in the blue coffee can, the red one is full of cookies.

"It's just the jobs and money," I said. "It isn't us, is it?"

"I don't know," he said.

A day and a half later we crossed from Wyoming into Nebraska, the western edge of the Louisiana Purchase, which Thomas Jefferson had made so that we could all live in white, classical houses, and be farmers. Fifty miles later the corn began, hundreds of miles of it, singing green from horizon to horizon. We began to relax and I had the feeling that we had survived the test of American geography. I put away our guidebooks and took out the dictionary. Matachin, mastigophobia, matutolypea. I tried to find words Sam didn't know. He guessed all the definitions and was smug and happy behind the wheel. I reached over and put a hand on his knee. He looked at me and smiled. "Ah, my little buttercup," he said. "My sweet cream pie." I thought of my Alpine lover for the first time in a long while, and he was nothing more than mist over a distant mountain.

In a motel lobby near Omaha, we had to wait in line for twenty minutes behind three families. Sam put his arm around me and pulled a tennis ball out of his jacket. He bounced it on the thin carpet, tentatively, and when he saw it had enough spring, he dropped into an exaggerated basketball player's crouch and ran across the lobby. He whirled in front of the cigarette machine and passed the ball to me. I laughed and threw it back. Several people had turned to stare at us. Sam winked at them and dunked the ball through an imaginary net by the wall clock, then passed the ball back to me. I dribbled around a stack of suitcases and went for a lay-up by a hanging fern. I misjudged and knocked the plant to the floor. What surprised me was that the fronds were plastic but the dirt was real. There was a huge mound of it on the carpet. At the registration desk, the clerk told us the motel was already full and that he could not find our name on the advance reservation list.

"Nebraska sucks eggs," Sam said loudly as we carried our luggage to the door. We spent the night curled up on the hard front seat of the van like boulders. The bony parts of our bodies kept bumping as we turned and rolled to avoid the steering wheel and dash. In the morning, my knees and elbows felt worn away, like the peaks of old mountains. We hadn't touched each other sexually since California.

"So she had big ta-ta's," I said. "She had huge ta-ta's and a bad-breath problem." We had pushed on through the corn, across Iowa, Illinois and Indiana, and the old arguments rattled along with us, like the pots and pans in the back of the van.

"She was a model," he said. He was describing the proprietress of the slender cigarettes and red panties.

"In a couple of years she'll have gum disease," I said.

"She was a model and she had a degree in literature from Oxford."

I didn't believe him, of course, but I felt the sting of his intention to hurt. "By the time she's forty she'll have emphysema."

"What would this trip be like without the melody of your voice," he said. It was dark, and taillights glowed on the road ahead of us like flecks of burning iron. I remembered how, when we were undergraduates attending different colleges, he used to write me letters which said keep your skirts down and your knees together, don't let anyone get near your crunch. We always amused each other with our language.

"I want a divorce," I said in a motel room in Columbus, Ohio. We were propped against pillows on separate double beds watching a local program on Woody Hayes, the Ohio State football coach. The announcer was saying, "And here in front of the locker room is the blue and gold mat that every player must step on as he goes to and from the field. Those numbers are the score of last year's loss to Michigan." And I was saying, "Are you listening? I said I want a divorce when we get to Virginia."

"I'm listening."

"Don't you want to know why I want a divorce?"

"No."

"Well, do you think it's a good idea or a bad idea?"

"I think it's a good idea."

"You do?"

"Yes."

The announcer said, "And that is why the night before the big game Woody will be showing his boys reruns of the films *Patton* and *Bullitt*."

That night someone broke into the van and stole everything we owned except the suitcases we had with us in the motel room. They even stole the broken radio. We stood in front of the empty van and looked up and down the row of parked cars as if we expected to see another black van parked there, one with two pairs of skis and two tennis rackets slipped into the spaces between the boxes and the windows.

"I suppose you're going to say I'm the one who left the door unlocked," I said.

Sam sat on the curb. He sat on the curb and put his head into hands. "No," he said. "It was probably me."

The policeman who filled out the report tried to write "Miscellaneous Household Goods" on the clipboarded form, but I made him list everything I could remember, as the three of us sat on the curb—the skis and rackets, the chess set, a baseball bat, twelve boxes of books, two rugs which I had braided, an oak bed frame Sam had refinished. I inventoried the kitchen items: two bread cans, two cake pans, three skillets. I mentioned every fork and every measuring cup and every piece of bric-a-brac I could recall—the trash of our life, suddenly made valuable by the theft. When the policeman had left without giving us any hope of ever recovering our things, I told Sam I was going to pack and shower. A half hour later when I came out with the suitcases, he was still on the curb, sitting in the full sun, his cotton shirt beginning to stain in wing shapes across his shoulder blades. I reached down to touch him and he flinched. It was a shock—feeling the tremble of his flesh, the vulnerability of it, and for the first time since California I tried to imagine what it was like driving with a woman who said she didn't want him, in a van he didn't like but had to buy in order to travel to a possible job on the other side of the continent, which might not be worth reaching.

On the last leg of the trip, Sam was agreeable and compliant. If I wanted to stop for coffee, he stopped immediately. If I wanted him to go slower in thick traffic, he eased his foot off the pedal without a look of regret or annoyance. I got out the dictionary. Operose, ophelimity, ophryitis. He said he'd never heard of any of those words. Which president died in a bathtub? He couldn't remember. I tried to sing to keep him company. He told me it wasn't necessary. I played a few tunes on a comb. He gazed pleasantly at the freeway, so pleasantly that I could have made him up. I could have invented him and put him on a mountainside terrace and set him going. "Sammy," I said, "that stuff wasn't much. I won't miss it."

"Good," he said.

About three a.m. green exit signs began to appear announcing the past and the future: Colonial Williamsburg, Jamestown, Yorktown, Patrick Henry Airport. "Let's go to the beach," I said. "Let's just go all the way to the edge of the continent." It was a ludicrous idea.

"Sure. Why not."

He drove on past Newport News and over an arching bridge towards Virginia Beach. We arrived there just at dawn and found our way into a residential neighborhood full of small pastel houses and sandy lawns. "Could we just stop right here?" I said. I had an idea. I had a plan. He shrugged as if to say what the heck, I don't care and if you want to drive into the ocean that will be fine, too.

We were parked on a street that ran due east towards the water—I could see just a glimmer of ocean between two hotels about a mile away. "All right," I said, with the forced, brusque cheerfulness of a high school coach. "Let's get out and do some stretching exercises." Sam sat behind the wheel and watched me touch my toes. "Come on, Sammy. Let's get loose. We haven't done anything with our bodies since California." He yawned, got out of the van, and did a few arm rolls and toe touches. "All right now," I said. "Do you think a two-block handicap is about right?" He had always given me a two-block advantage during our foot races in California. He yawned again. "How about a one-and-a-half-block lead, then?" He crossed his arms and leaned against the van, watching me. I couldn't tell whether he had nodded, but I said anyway, "I'll give you a wave when I'm ready." I walked down the middle of the street past houses which had towels hanging over porch rails and toys lying on front walks. Even a mile from the water, I smelled the salt and seaweed in the air. It made me feel light-headed and for a moment I tried to picture Sam and myself in one of those houses with tricycles and toilet trainers and small latched gates. We had never discussed having a child. When I turned to wave, he was still leaning against the van.

I started out in a jog, then picked up the pace, and hit what seemed to be about the quarter-mile mark doing a fast easy run. Ahead of me the square of water between the two hotels was undulating with gold. I listened for the sound of Sam's footsteps but heard only the soft taps of my own tennis shoes. The square spread into a rectangle and the sky above it fanned out in ribs of orange and purple silk. I was afraid to look back. I was afraid that if I turned to see him, Sam might recede irretrievably into the merciless gray of the western sky. I slowed down in case I had gone too fast and he wanted to catch up. I concentrated on the water and listened to the still, heavy air. By the time I reached the three-quarters mark, I realized that I was probably running alone.

I hadn't wanted to lose him.

I wondered whether he had waited by the van or was already headed for Newport News. I imagined him at a phone booth calling another woman collect in California, and then I realized that I didn't actually know whether there was another woman or not, but I hoped there was and that she was rich and would send him money. I had caught my second wind and was breathing easily. I looked towards the shore without seeing it and was sorry I hadn't measured the distance and thought to clock it, since now I was running against time and myself, and then I heard him—the unmistakable sound of a sprint and the heavy, whooping intake of his breath. He passed me just as we crossed the main street in front of the hotels, and he reached the water twenty feet ahead of me.

"Goddammit, Day," I said. "You were on the grass, weren't you?" We were walking along the hard, wet edge of the beach, breathing hard. "You were sneaking across those lawns. That's a form of cheating." I drummed his arm lightly with my fists pretending to beat him up. "I slowed down because I thought you weren't there." We leaned over from the waist, hands on our hips, breathing towards the sand. The water rolled up the berm near our feet and flickered like topaz.

"You were always a lousy loser," he said.

And I said, "You should talk."

WRAPPED MINDS

by DAVID PERKINS

from CHOUTEAU REVIEW

nominated by Stephen Dixon

The ignorance of the unlettered takes no scrutiny to establish. What we need to plumb is the ignorance of the educated and the anti-intellectualism of the intellectual. What matters to a nation is whether the best product, or in certain cases the high average, which prides itself on excellence, deserve its reputation.

—*Jacques Barzun*
The House of Intellect

EDITOR'S NOTE: This essay was occasioned by the installation of a construction—a covered walkway— by the artist Christo in Loose Park, Kansas City. The entire walkway system of the Park was covered with a golden fabric. The event was highly publicized and the artist was feted in Kansas City "society."

We need more to be reminded than to be informed.

—*Samuel Johnson*

Christo's Wrapped Walkways has the importance of all public incidents: it gives us the opportunity to sharpen our own identities. That this opportunity is not always welcomed is evidenced by the response to what was probably the most important incident in our recent history—the prosecution of the war in Vietnam. It is clear now, if it wasn't at the time, that much of the resistance to comprehending that war owed much to our resistance to comprehending ourselves. The Christo incident is minor indeed compared with the war, and involves only a certain public, not the public at large. Nonetheless, it offers the same opportunity to test what we think, to test what we can say; the use of words in such matters reflects not only the limits of our intelligence, but of our characters. A failure to respond is more "playing possum," more "don't look at me." It more than bodes the same psychological failure for the "high average" we witnessed with the war; it represents it.

*   *   *

Vivien Raynor, in a *Horizon* review of a photography show at MOMA, writes, "Szarkowski's new monograph follows an old pattern in art writing of being more challenging and profound than the work it explains." This is certainly true of anything serious one might wish to say about Wrapped Walkways, but why? One thinks of the enormous hype, the great commotion, surrounding recent blockbuster movies such as *Close Encounters,* and of the banality of the movies themselves. Perhaps it is the very vacuousness of the Christo project which allows our response to rush in. It is like the emptiness of certain personal close encounters we are desperate to fill with speech, as there is nothing else for them.

Eudora Welty remarked that most writing is bad because it is not serious and it is not the truth. This is certainly as true for the visual arts—which we still stupidly call art—even though they are often by self-definition less serious (that is, merely decorative). It is also true that it is easier to appreciate what is good than to understand what is bad. The latter is insidious. Applying critical analysis here is as difficult, and nearly as hopeless, as driving away fog with hand grenades. What we are analyzing finally is absence.

*   *   *

The local critical response to Christo—in the *Star* (except for Mr. Hoffman), *City* magazine, and the Kansas City Artist Coalition *Forum*—has been interesting. It has been to forgo criticism. Ms. Melcher's reviews were flat-out society page writing. The reports in the *Forum*—including a wide-eyed interview—were those of fans, enthusiasts. One reads them as one would watch a TV report on a Donny and Marie concert. Perhaps these volunteer workers saw themselves in a great tradition—Raphael's assistants preparing the walls, waiting for the Master to sweep in, mount the ladder, and apply the master stroke. But I think the spirit of the operation owes more to a recent antecedent—the Schlitz "gusto" television commercials. However, The *City* reviewer's remarks were more interesting, and more incredible, because of the writer's connection with the Kansas City Art Institute. The failure here is not merely personal, but institutional, and it is against these remarks that much of what follows should be set.

*   *   *

To whom is it a comfort to read that "we can take the project any way we like and it doesn't matter?" Hannah Arendt has written of the "systematic banalization of the world," of the drive, for repressive political purpose, to drain the content from what had formerly been of consequence in the public word. It was Arendt, too, who defined the successful propagandist not as one who persuades us to believe some transparent nonsense, but as one who dulls our capacity for receiving the truth from any source. It is startling to see this campaign of banalization taken up by the learned, and their institutions, as if its repressive implications had never occurred to them.

The idea that we are extending the frontiers of art by including "what cannot be called anything else" betrays not so much an elevation of values as a decline in the job market. *There simply are too many people who are not required.* The drift quite naturally into the new art world, where process has replaced product, and sloth masquerades as philanthropy. What is being maintained here is not only America's tradition of the new, but her more venerable tradition of anti-intellectualism. In fact, a recent Channel 19 show featuring leaders of the Art Institute was a virtual archetype for that heritage. Art was everywhere. Art was for everyone. Who was to say what art was, anyway? It was all a Nieman-Marcus catalogue of world-class thought-cliches, and it appeared we were not listening to representatives of an institution of higher learning, but of vocational rehabilitation. One wondered, then ceased to wonder, whether this betrayal of standards was going on so much in the interest of opening the game to the dull, as it was in selling the game to the dull rich.

Art and politics are the principal phenomena of the public world, and they are both essentially matters of taste. How can it have escaped us that the motivation of the populist artist, his alignment with the "little people," is likely as tainted as that of the populist politician? His ambition, after all, is only to dissolve his own mediocrity, by bathing it in ours.

*   *   *

Although columnist James Kilpatrick's continuing attacks on Federal funding for the arts are wrong on a technicality—his failure to distinguish between art and culture—he is right to imagine that much of what passes for contemporary art is inane, incompetent, and high tomfoolery. These aspects appear independently, however, and it is art featuring the first two aspects with which we are most familiar. The country is literally awash with nice people trying to be artists—their works, and we with them, drip with sweat. It is not enough that we must search this work for something to like: we must scour it for something to *dislike*. And so what a relief, what fun, to pass to the work of the con-artist, to breathe, in the company of various contemporary art societies, the heady air of dimestore decadence, anti-bourgeois pretension, and big bucks chicanery. Here we must take no pains for the sensitive feelings of the hapless amateur; we can critique the stuntman-artist with innocent, gleeful savagery.

And "stuntman" is certainly no careless appellation for Christo. For that is what his art reduces to—a stunt—and that is why his admirers—bloodless thrillseekers—flock to him. (This is aside from the obvious attraction of someone who, as Freud said of Adler, has a flair for the ordinary.) So why is art brought into it at all? Because Christo is not a very good stuntman. If what he had done in Loose Park were half as interesting as Evel Knievel's leap across the Grand Canyon in a jetmobile, he wouldn't need to trade on all our internalized approval for "art" to support it. But, imagine the reverse—not Christo as a stuntman, but Evel Knievel passing himself off as an artist. How similar the language would be, how readily we could expect Knievel to "liberate our conception of art," "make art fun," "leap the ineffable," "take art to the people," "involve ordinary people in my struggle against the institutional and gravitational restraints of the past." Without a doubt, we would have on our hands the *new, improved* project for the Contemporary Arts Society. (I wonder who else is reminded by the name of this ponderously ordinary organization of Gibbon's remark about the Holy Roman Empire—that it was neither holy, nor Roman, nor an empire?)

*   *   *

Wrapped Walkways is another of those not uncommon cases where the will to be charmed has replaced the urge to see. The uncritical response to the work is similar to the response Eliot found to *Hamlet*: more people find it a work of art because it is interesting, than find it interesting because it is a work of art. And the enthusiasm for it recalls another Eliot response to the popular thought-cliche, "Man craves an enthusiasm that will lift him out of his merely rational self." Eliot wrote, "It would be nice if we could infect a few people with an enthusiasm for getting up to the level of their rational selves."

With few exceptions, the verbalized enthusiasm for this work— praise, description, explanation—even from Christo himself, has been strikingly inane. (It's reminiscent of the language of transactional banalysis, and not surprisingly, comes from the same people.) The work is beyond description, liberated from explanation (grounded, as this is, in the past). The enthusiast's difficulty with expressing his soulful response reminds me of the student writers who are inclined to say, when discussing one of their own confusing passages, "I guess I'm not really saying what I mean; I'm not expressing myself very well." But the fact is they are expressing themselves *perfectly*. Their writing is clumsy and confused because their thought is. And their writing improves, becomes "better expression," when they themselves improve.

We are all aware of the satisfactions of naming things tragic when they are merely horrible, horrible when they are merely unpleasant, art when it is merely entertainment, entertainment when it is merely diversion. It seems more *interesting* to be wrong. Bewitchment, intoxication, is our everyday pursuit, and we are probably never more in possession of it than when we least know it, when, as Wittgenstein says, our intelligence is bewitched by our language.

*   *   *

Wrapped Walkways, and much work like it, is the beneficiary of the prejudice of touch. And this is what the Christo enthusiasts appeal to. But this puts them in an interesting double bind. Easily enough the enthusiasts desert the field of critical standards, and understandably enough, too. Since any response in the viewer is acceptable, nothing in particular can be demanded of the work. Since it is relation-less, it cannot be found inadequate. Since it holds out no promise, it cannot be charged with reneging.

But when the enthusiasts move from the field of sense, as it were, to the field of sensation, they have hardly done themselves a service. If anything, they have only entered the work into a stiffer competition. For if we are dealing now with naturalistic effects, rather than with linguistic and/or logical constructions, the work must be compared against—whatever. Moonlight on a lake, a sunset, a volcanic eruption, *a supernova.* Now, more quickly than before, the significance of the work, its aesthetic value, falls nearly to zero. Even compared to the indirect effects of technicism, (the view of New York City at night, approaching La Guardia) this *striving* for effect is simply embarrassing. These artists, who are unable to make any cognizable statement with their work, and who then try to take sides with nature, remind me of that stock film character, the traitor. This sniveler betrays his good friends to the crooks, expecting to be made part of the gang; instead, he finds himself cleaning out the spittoons, or worse, wearing concrete shoes.

But this betrayal is real. When the emphasis on art process was not so common, it was a relatively harmless fraud. But so many artists are engaging in it now that it has become a real threat to the enjoyment of life processes. When spontaneity becomes an art market product, we can no longer enjoy it as a personal freedom. This enlargement of the province of art is no longer creation; it is theft, theft from life. Our life processes, our work experiences, become self-conscious, lose their vitality, when they become the property and the plaything of aesthetes. Nature can overcome this comic presumption on their part, but we cannot. To paraphrase Ortega y Gasset, in the forest one can be artistic with impunity. In the garden, we must be careful how much we yank up and call "Still Life."

*   *   *

The words here, strung end to end, would probably make the circuit of the Loose Park walkway several times, which is more than I have ever done personally, but I think it is worth it. In a vital society one must be defined by one's enemies. Friends cannot do it because they are with us at the center—it is the enemy at our limits. I hope I have been successful here in defining my enemy, and it is certainly not the man Christo. It is not a person at all, really, nor even an idea. It is simply a question: What does it matter?

And our purpose *against* that question need not be grand to be important. It was enough for Locke to define himself, seriously, as a custodian. And it was enough for Freud to maintain that the purpose of analysis was to "transform hysterical misery into everyday unhappiness." And it is enough here not to have answered that nihilistic question (and its fraternal twin, Who cares?) even with Louis Armstrong's famous remark about jazz. It's enough to have reduced, by a few, the number of people who are inclined to ask it.

HEART OF THE GARFISH

by KATHY CALLAWAY

from THE IOWA REVIEW

nominated by Tess Gallagher and Grace Schulman

One thing you don't talk about in Minnesota
is the meaning of water. You can say
what a lake did to you, or
what you got away with in spite of it,
solving that equation where one whole side
equals zero. It's done over beers, at night,
safe from the gravity that keeps us
stupefied and turning during the day.
A lake's the lowest thing around,
filling up all the best hiding places.

Our houses keep their backs to it.
We drift down anyway, push out in our
thin ribbed boats, oars beating away
at the surface. We know that underneath is
freedom from the body. It's why we're here.
We push bait on like penitents for the garfish,
because they never die, because we're
full of love. The shoreline turns hourly—
our local zodiac, shapes we live by
when we're out of this.

So when someone goes under we can guess
what he's got: the bottoms of our boats
and things overboard, shouts and blear faces,

innertubes, apologies, all we have. He'll have
the lifesaver of the sun wholly dissolving,
and years of regrets, like two stones tapping
under water. We'll wrap him in white, for everyone.
He's everybody's. That's why we're back the next day
rocking over water, jamming worms on hooks *kyrie eleison,*
pulling the living teeth out of the lake.

BY THE POOL

by ALLEN GROSSMAN

from THE PARIS REVIEW

nominated by DeWitt Henry

Every dwelling is a desolate hill.
Every hill is a desolate dwelling.

The trees toss their branches in the dark air,
Each tree after its kind, and each kind after
Its own way. The wind tosses the branches
Of the trees in the dark air. The swimming
Pool is troubled by the wind, and the swimmers.

Even though this is not a tower, this is
Also a tower.

             Even though you are not
A watchman, you are also a watchman.

Even though the night has not yet come,
The night has come.

BLUE WINE

by JOHN HOLLANDER

from THE KENYON REVIEW

nominated by Walter Abish and Robert Phillips

for Saul Steinberg

1

The winemaker worries over his casks, as the dark juice
Inside them broods on its own sleep, its ferment of dreaming
Which will turn out to have been a slow waking after all,
All that time. This would be true of the red wine or the white,
But a look inside these barrels of the azure would show
Nothing. They would be as if filled with what the sky looks like.

2

Three wise old wine people were called in once to consider
The blueness of the wine. One said: "It is 'actually' not
Blue; it is a profound red in the cask, but reads as blue
In the only kind of light that we have to see it by."
Another said: "The taste is irrelevant—whatever
Its unique blend of aromas, bouquets, vinosities
And so forth, the color would make it quite undrinkable."
A third said nothing: he was lost in a blue study while
His eyes drank deeply and his wisdom shuddered, that the wine
Of generality could be so strong and so heady.

3

There are those who will maintain that all this is a matter
Of water—hopeful water, joyful water got into
Cool bottles at the right instant of light, the organized
Reflective blue of its body remembered once the sky
Was gone, an answer outlasting its forgotten question.
Or: that the water, colorless at first, collapsed in glass
Into a blue swoon from which it never need awaken;
Or: that the water colored in a blush of consciousness
(Not shame) when it first found that it could see out of itself
On all sides roundly, save through the dark moon of cork above
Or through the bottom over which it made its mild surmise.
There are those who maintain this, they who remain happier
With transformations than with immensities like blue wine.

4

He pushed back his chair and squinted through the sunlight
   across
At the shadowy, distant hills; crickets sang in the sun;
His mind sang quietly to itself in the breeze, until
He returned to his cool task of translating the newly
Discovered fragments of Plutarch's lost essay "On Blue Wine."
Then the heavy leaves of the rhododendrons scratched against
Gray shingles outside, not for admittance, but in order
To echo his pen sighing over filled, quickening leaves.

5

"For External Use Only"? Nothing says exactly that,
But there are possibilities—a new kind of bluing
That does not whiten, but intensifies the color of,
All that it washes. Or used in a puzzle-game: "Is blue
Wine derived from red or white? emerging from blood-colored
Dungeons into high freedom? or shivering in the silk
Robe it wrapped about itself because of a pale yellow chill?"
One drink of course would put an end to all such questioning.

6

". . .and when he passed it over to me in the dim firelight,
I could tell from the feel of the bottle what it was: the
Marques de Tontada's own, *El Corazón Azul.* I had
Been given it once in my life before, long ago, and
I tell you, Dan, I will never forget the moment when
It became clear, before those embers, that the famous blue
Color of the stuff could come to mean so little, could change
The contingent hue of its significance: the truer
To its blue the wine remained, the less it seemed to matter.
I think, Dan, that was what we had been made to learn that
  night."

7

This happened once: Our master, weary of our quarreling,
Laughed at the barrel, then motioned toward us for a drink; and
Lo, out of the sullen wooden spigot came the blue wine!

8

And all that long morning the fair wind that had carried them
From isle to isle—past the gnashing rocks to leeward and around
The dark vortex that had been known to display in its whorls
Parts, not of ships nor men, but of what it could never have
Swallowed down from above—the fair wind blew them closer to
The last island of all, upon the westernmost side of
Which high cliffs led up to a great place of shining columns
That reddened in the sunset when clouds gathered there. They
  sailed
Neither toward this, nor toward the eastern cape, darkened by
  low
Rocks marching out from the land in raging battle with the
Water; they sail'd around a point extending toward them, through
A narrow bay, and landed at a very ancient place.

Here widely-scattered low trees were watching them from the
   hills.
In huge casks half-buried there lay aging the wine of the
Island and, weary half to madness, they paused there to drink.
This was the spot where, ages before even their time, Bhel
Blazed out in all his various radiances, before
The jealousy of Kel led to his being smashed, as all
The old tales tell, and to the hiding and the parcelling
Out of all the pieces of Bhel's shining. Brightness of flame,
Of blinding bleakness, of flavescent gold, of deepening
Blush-color, of the shining black of obsidian that
Is all of surface, all a memory of unified
Light—all these were seeded far about. There only remained
The constant fraction, which, even after every sky
Had been drenched in its color, never wandered from this spot.
And thus it was: they poured the slow wine out unmingled with
Water and saw, startled, sloshing up against the insides
Of their gold cups, sparkling, almost salty, the sea-bright wine. . .

9

It would soon be sundown and a shawl of purple shadow
Fell over the muttering shoulders of the old land, fair
Hills and foul dales alike, singing of noon grass or Spanish
Matters. The wooden farmhouses grew grayer and the one
We finally stopped at, darker than the others, opened its
Shutters and the light outside poured over the patio.
Voices and chairs clattered; we were welcomed and the youngest
Child came forth holding with both hands a jug of the local wine.
It was blue: reality is so Californian.

10

Under the Old Law it was seldom permitted to drink
Blue wine, and then only on the Eight Firmamental
Days; and we who no longer kept commandments of that sort
Still liked to remember that for so long it mattered so
Much that they were kept. And thus the domestic reticence

In my family about breaking it out too often:
We waited for when there was an embargo on the red,
Say, or when the white had failed because of undue rain.
Then Father would come up from the cellar with an abashed
Smile, in itself a kind of label for the dark bottle.
At four years old I hid my gaze one night when it was poured.

11

Perhaps this is all some kind of figure—the thing contained
For the container—and it is these green bottles themselves,
Resembling ordinary ones, that are remarkable
In that their shapes create the new wines—*Dus Rheinblau,
    Château
La Tour d' Eau, Romanée Cerulée,* even the funny old
Half-forgotten *Vin Albastru.* And the common inks of
Day and night that we color the water with a drop of
Or use for parodies of the famous labels: these as
Well become part of the figuring by which one has put
Blue wine in bold bottles and lined them up against the light
There in a window. When some unexpected visitor
Drops in and sees these bottles of blue wine, and does not ask
At the time what they mean, he may take some drops home with
    him
In the clear cup of his own eye, to see what he will see.

🔥 🔥 🔥

TRANQUILLITY BASE

fiction by ASA BABER

from FICTION INTERNATIONAL

nominated by FICTION INTERNATIONAL

U NION STATION, CHICAGO, after five in the afternoon. What a day, what a day, with the heat in the streets. But Avery is happy after work and he hums to himself as he walks down the steep incline towards the concourse. He has his light tan suit coat thrown recklessly over his shoulder: his forefinger tugs the minor weight and that gesture flexes his bicep. He has his sleeves rolled a bit too high, but all the better to show his new vacation tan.

Once into the cavernous station with its cathedral light, with its steady stream of visitors and its strangely muffled echoes at this hour—only the shuffling sound of thousands of shoes crossing the floor—Avery buys his paper at the candy counter and moves into the flow that leads to the Burlington line. If there is an eternal special moment to his days, it is this time when he senses the sleek silver tube waiting for him in double-deckered air-conditioned comfort. Oh how he longs for the silence and focus of that ride to Highlands. No one bothers him, yet he recognizes many of the faces, conductors and commuters, all brothers and sisters in this journey westward that leads out of the city and its grit.

Avery is getting himself ready, sorting out the signals, smelling as he passes through steam from the airbrakes that faint tinge of uric acid that lies in the railroad bed. His ears hear the hiss and groan from the undercarriage. Somewhere far off two flatcars jolt together.

He calibrates the distance to the middle of his train. He will walk two cars past that. It is his guessing game with the engineer, for when the train stops at Highlands there is only one exit that crosses the tracks. If Avery winds up ahead of that magic point he will have to tramp through milkweed and cinders to get back to the spot. If he is too cautious he will have to wait in line while others more lucky pass across. But there are times when Avery is winner, when he is *there*. That makes his day, and he trots down the cement stairs in first place, and his children cheer him from the station wagon, and Ellen beams at his little triumph.

Today he feels no special ease, not even knowing that things have gone well for him (for the world, really—for the Universe). Yes, he hums, and as much as he can, he struts. He is conscious of that secret roll of fat that suitcoats usually hide. He hums to blot out his habit (especially when he is tired) of talking to himself. Only last week Collins—who rides the same train, but never with Avery—had confronted him at the office and asked Avery if he was all right; it seems he had seen Avery mumbling to himself as he boarded the train. Avery laughed it off very heartily, but he knew he would have to watch his public image.

Looking at him walking towards you on the platform, you would find him easy to like or ignore. Of average height and average weight for a man of thirty-five; hair a little thinning with silver streaks in the brown crewcut; jowls a bit flabby, and two worrylines that crease his forehead vertically and come to rest under the sinuses; a face eager to please, tired, wary, probably proud.

The headlines all say the same thing. The world is going home tonight for a special extravaganza and the newspapers cater to it.

There are transcripts, feature articles, biographies, pictures, quotations from leaders and confidants, best wishes even in advertisements. There is the feeling that one has been included, that each and every one is part of the venture.

As he passes the middle of the train, Avery hears a sharp whistle. It pierces his ears and makes him wince. He looks around, but no one else seems to have heard it. Avery walks again—whistle again. He turns; nothing. He shakes his head and nods to a conductor who has been watching him. He continues on his way.

Then it comes, a fierce slap on the back, and a greeting shouted in his ear, "Brooks, you son of a bitch!"

Avery checks his happy reaction of surprise that someone knows him, for he turns and looks up into a fat face that he does not recognize. But he keeps his grin on and his hand out; he doesn't want to muff it. "Whatdeyuh say!"

"Brooks, you bastard!" Affection again from this unplaceable.

Avery searches his memory hard. He runs through old school yearbooks and company rosters. He still has to fake it. "Yep. It's me, all right."

"Brooks Avery on the five-twenty! You live out this way?"

"Sure do. We moved here last year." Avery searches wildly: no special insignias on the lapel of the seersucker; a raincoat thrown over the arm that carries the briefcase—there's a clue, a big D in Gothic print on the light clear skin of the case, a skin so lucid at this angle that it appears almost phosphorescent. In his fast associations Avery assumes that the material was stripped from some exotic animal in Argentina or Peru. Smart shoes of the same mysterious hide (more nearly boots than shoes), a straw hat with a paisley band.

"Goddamn, Brooksy, it's been fifteen great years, hasn't it?"

Avery smiles and nods. There is a hint, and he works on it; fifteen years ago means college; still nothing.

The Anonymous reaches out and pats Avery's waistline. "Looks like you've put on a little too, baby! A pound a year, I always say." He laughs and Avery laughs with him. As usual when standing beside someone taller, Avery pulls in his backbone and shifts his weight to his toes. "Come on, let's hit the bar car and I'll buy you a drink."

Avery feels like a dude and apologizes. "Look, I'm sorry, but we don't have bar cars."

"The hell you say! No bar car for me and my buddy?" He flips a big arm around Avery's shoulders and they begin to walk again towards the head of the train. "You ought to see the bar car on the Orient Express—until it hits Yugoslavia, of course, and then they take it off."

"Really?" Avery says; he is damned if he is going to make countryboy comments such as "You sure have been around."

"Yes, really, by Christ! I've never seen anything like it. There you are whizzing along the Adriatic, coming into Trieste eating grapes and drinking wine, and zip boom bah they switch a few railroad cars and you're in Starvationville. I mean it. STAR-VATIONVILLE! Nothing to eat until you hit the Turkish border. And then it's goat's cheese and bread. My god I thought I was going to die."

Avery stops, uncertain, and holds out his hand. "This is where I get on."

But the arm does not leave the shoulders and the hand is ignored. They simply climb through the double doors together. "Let's hit the smoking car. OK?" the man says. "I've still got to have my coffin nails."

"Yeah, me too," snickers Avery. They file into the aisle. "You want to sit upstairs? Only single seats—" he gets rather desperate "—but we could read the paper."

"Sure, sure." The guy is all amenable. "Got to read up for the Big Happening."

"Yep," says Avery as he slides into the narrow seat. "It's really incredible, isn't it?"

"I'll say it is. Makes you wonder, doesn't it?" says his amigo as he sits in the seat behind him.

"Sure does. I wish them luck."

"Sure as hell do. They'll need more than that, a lot more."

"Skill," nods Avery. He holds the front page section over his shoulder. "Here you go."

"Naww, that's OK. Give me the Sports."

"No, go ahead, take it."

They settle back in silence. Avery lights a cigarette and takes that first delicious puff. The air conditioning and nicotine work on him, comfort him, and for a moment he does not care who the man is. Avery has had a long day.

He can see himself in the window. He brushes his palms across

his temples. He checks his wristwatch and precisely to the minute
he feels the sudden small jolt as the train pulls out. He catches a
hard tap on the shoulder and he turns. The face is almost touching
his and it blows smoke at him as it says: "Liftoff!" Then the face
laughs loudly at its own joke.

Avery plays the game. "Roger. The clock is started."

They seem to have exhausted that lingo so they settle back again
and read. Now out of the station, the sunlight pours on his forearm
and Avery lowers the shade only to find it raised again by his
copilot. That might be a pugnacious gesture and Avery checks
behind him to see what this is all about. He gets a friendly wink:
"Got to see the city too. May buy a house out this way and I want to
see what I'll be riding through."

"You don't live out here?" Avery asks.

"Yes I do," says the face with a confirming nod.

Avery cannot cope with that paradox so he ignores it. He looks
out over the dreary familiar scene: rickety back porch stairs that
climb three and four stories, crawling up the grimy apartment walls
as if they are separate stilts leaning for rest on the dark bricks; old
refrigerators tied closed with ropes; cinders and innertubes; the
sparkle of glass from a thousand facets of backyard earth, glittering
as if this was a moon's surface; rotting wooden fences and, enclosing the properties of factories and stores, rusted mesh fences with
barbed wire crowning their fringes; junked cars and twisted rails;
steel structures on the skyline; children swinging on clotheslines or
running through alleys or staring out of windows; all the old and
clearly known elements of this part of town.

"How's Ellen?" comes the voice after long silence.

Tone and content frighten Avery. Just how much did this
interrogator know? "She's fine, just fine."

"Fourteen years is a long time."

That remark floats for a moment, and Avery is about to turn and
say "Look, who are you?" but the voice leans into his ear and
whispers, "Don't tell old Dave that fourteen years isn't a long
time." And he nudges Avery's shoulder. "Huh? Isn't it true?
Fourteen-year itch twice what the seven-year itch is, huh?"

Avery has to laugh. It comes out modest but knowing. "There's
an itch sometimes, all right." And there is relief in his laugh too, for
now he has a name to work with. He uses it immediately. "Yes sir,
Dave, there is an itch. I guess you know, huh?"

"Don't look at me, Brooksy, I never did the deed. I spend my time wandering, baby." Great guffaws. "I figured . . . I figured if a man gets married, he's stuck in earth orbit, you know?" He laughs with tears in his eyes now. "No apogee, no perigee!" His large hands make crude circles in the air.

Avery has to laugh with him. "I guess you broke out of that."

"Out with the pulsars, Brooks, out of sight!"

Their laughter dies down slowly and they return to their reading, shaking their heads at their good time and understanding, flipping the newspapers occasionally with their wrists.

Once past the tight homes of Cicero, the scene outside the windows begins to change towards greenery. The yellow heavy sky slowly lifts and by the time they hit Cissna Park there is a sense of clean air and trees.

Avery makes his preparations for descent. He tightens his tie and rolls down his sleeves. The air conditioning has made him feel spruce again and he wants to greet his family in full dress. He stubs out his last cigarette and puts on a false friendly air. "Well, Dave, it's been great."

"Ohhoho" comes a deep rumbling laugh from the huge frame. "How about a drink on me, Brooksy? You aren't going to run out on me, are you?"

Avery shrugs uneasily. "Next stop is my stop, Dave. Got to meet the wife and kids."

"All the better. Buy them all a drink!"

"Well, the kids don't drink, Dave. I don't want to put you to any trouble."

"No trouble! No trouble, kid!" He chucks Avery not too gently under the chin. They are moving down the stairs before Avery knows it. "I mean, how often do we get together? Every fifteen years? You think I don't have time to drink with a buddy I haven't seen for fifteen years?"

Avery pulls the sliding doors open and stands in the vestibule of the car. Out here it is hotter. He nods at the conductor. "You see, Dave, Ellen and the kids . . . you know . . . this is their worst hour . . . it's chaos at home, really."

"No trouble! Chance to meet your kids. How are they? Nice bunch?"

"Oh, they're great, Dave, really great. Beautiful."

The train crosses the tollway bridge. The arm comes back over

Avery's shoulder and a sigh leads into a statement: "One thing I regret, Brooks, about not getting married. No kids of my own. I love the little bastards." The arm gestures and chokes Avery slightly. "What do we build roads like that for if it's not for our children? Huh?"

"That's a great road, Dave. Goes up to Milwaukee."

"Kids—the only reason to get married as I see it."

"It's one of the main ones, that's for sure."

"You bet your sweet ass it is. Something to lead your life for." He points at the headlines of the folded paper. "Something to run risks for, by God."

Avery tries to think through the moments ahead. His wife will be waiting in the parking lot. How will she handle this one? She is good at picking up his signals and if he plays it right she will not ask too many questions or make it embarrassing for him. But it is going to take some diplomacy on his part. He hates days like this when the obligations never end and rest never comes.

Off the train at almost the right point, across the tracks, Avery pounds rapidly down the steps hoping to have time to warn his wife. But there is no shaking the big lug at his side. Avery watches Ellen's face through the tinted windshield. He sees the children asking questions of her. He comes up to the driver's side and she opens the window.

"Honey, you remember Dave?"

Only the slightest pause on her part, only the hitch of an eyebrow and lip before she comes through, that beauty: "Dave! How are you? Nice to see you."

Avery is brushed aside and he hears a kiss as Dave leans in the window. "Ellen, I'll be damned if you've changed a bit."

Very cautious this time: "Same to you, Dave," and a frantic look at Avery, who shrugs his shoulders and gives her a reassuring wink.

Avery opens the door and Ellen starts to get out of the front seat, but she is pushed back by the large hand that flips the bucket and paws its way into the back with the children. Avery clears his throat and makes the introductions rapidly. "Kids, this is an old friend of mine. His name is Dave, kids. Dave, this is Tony and Mark."

"Dave who?" asks Tony.

Oh you wise ass punk, thinks Avery, but his embarrassment is covered by guffaws from Dave. "Dave who? Dave whoever, that's who!" says the voice in the back seat.

"That's a weird name," says Mark. "Dave Whoever."

Avery turns the air conditioner to maximum. He wants to cover the drive home with chatter. "Tony's eleven and Mark's six."

Ellen picks up his frantic mood and fills in too. "They're both very excited about tonight, Brooks, and I promised them they could stay up if they were good boys. They can watch until one of them misbehaves. When one goes to bed, the other goes."

Avery wants to ramble on; he has a speech already outlined, but the voice interrupts. "These are great kids, just great. I should have known, though. Good breeding! Good stock!"

Ellen blushes. "Dave, really, I—"

"Don't be silly! Good stock, by God. Plump and healthy. Prime! Prime!" He cups Tony's head as if he is palming a basketball. "I just love kids, I tell you." The children move away from him.

"What are you doing with yourself these days, Dave?" Ellen asks. She is still uneasy and her voice cracks.

"Oh, stuff and things, here and there." A silence. "Finance, mostly, international finance. Sales. A little lobbying on the side."

"Dave really gets around, honey," says Avery. "He was telling me about Turkey."

"How interesting!" Ellen turns so that she can watch the children. "How long were you there?"

"Oh, I'm there almost every year. I make a run out to the Mideast every six months or so. Good pickings out there."

Avery laughs. "I'll bet you do a hell of a business anywhere you go."

"That's about right," Dave answers seriously.

Avery turns off County Line Road and heads for Oak Street. "You know, it's nice to see some of my classmates really make it big," he says.

Dave shrugs and ruffles Tony's hair, pinches Mark's cheeks. "You hear that, boys? Your old man is trying to make himself modest. He lives out here in a damn fine spread, good wife, luscious children, and he tries to build me up. What do you think of that, guys?" The children simply stare at him.

"Come on, Dave, you've probably stashed away your first million by now."

Dave laughs and rubs his stomach. "Well, I knew I was fat, but not that fat! No sir, I didn't know it showed."

Avery pounds the steering wheel in his discovery and chuckles. "There, you see, Ellen? A real go-getter!"

Ellen shifts in her seat. "Well I think Dave is right, Brooks. You shouldn't run yourself down in front of the boys." She turns again towards the back seat. "Brooks is doing very well."

"Aww, cut it, Ellen."

"Of course I shouldn't tell you this, Dave, but Brooks is going to be managing the Central Bank Card."

"Ellen, this is still confidential." He looks at his guest in the mirror. "Don't listen to her, Dave, she's biased."

Ellen slaps his forearm. "I'm proud of you but not biased. Sometimes you think I'm—"

"—my own severest critic . . . I know, honey. Let's just cut the shoptalk."

Dave pulls Mark onto his knees and leans forward. "Come on, Ellen, tell me what Brooks is doing."

"I just did. The Central Bank Card? For the whole Midwest? You know?"

"Do I know?" And then to Mark. "Do we know?" Mark giggles. "You bet your skin we know! The charge card to end all charge cards!"

Avery shakes his head. "End a few careers too. You ought to see the people who apply. You would not believe it. In debt, prison records, divorced and paying too much alimony, people right out of the ghettos. . . . They have no money sense, none at all."

Dave punches Mark's stomach with his forefinger. "Your dad will sort them out, huh boy?" Mark giggles again.

Avery wheels into the driveway. In the full summer, wet and rich, the oaks and elms seem to drip sap and the lilac bush still holds its bloom and roses droop. The garage door opens with a signal from somewhere inside the car. They pull in next to the Volkswagen. The garage door shuts and lights come on. As he exits into the livingroom, Avery smells the odor of thick grass freshly cut mingling with traces of gasoline. "Tony! How many times have I told you to wash the lawn mower after you're done!"

But Avery does not have it in him to be a stern father tonight. For one thing, he has a policy of not scolding the children in front of guests. For another, he wants to watch television. He picks up the automatic tuner and presses the button.

The rest of the crew have followed him in. They all stand while the set warms up and flashes into color. They see an animated film describing what will be happening. "They're landing!" screams Tony.

Dave pulls the boy against him and rubs his shoulders. "Not yet, champ. This is just a cartoon, sort of."

Tony does not pull away immediately and Mark sidles up to get attention too. Dave notices this and holds the shorter boy's head against his hip. "You guys are OK in my book."

Both Avery and Ellen beam. Avery rubs his hands together as if he is washing them. "How about a little drink, Dave?"

"Whatever you've got, old buddy."

"Bourbon? Scotch?"

Dave walks to the kitchen with him. "I'll tell you what I really like—maybe you've got it, maybe you haven't."

"Name your poison."

"Well, the last time I was in Bangkok I had a banana liqueur. . . ."

Avery stumbles on his words. "I'm afraid we don't—"

"It was sweet as mother's milk."

"Dave, we haven't got—"

"That's OK. Just give me a tequila sour . . . and if you haven't got that, a little bourbon is OK by me."

Avery sighs fast. "A black label Daniels coming right up!"

Dave leaves for the livingroom again. Ellen enters fast to corner Avery. "Who *is* he?"

"Ellen, why isn't the ice maker working?"

"There's ice in the bucket, Brooks. Who is he?"

"He's who he says he is. He's Dave. He's a classmate."

"Was he in your fraternity?"

"Don't think so, Ellen. Hand me the jigger."

She stamps her foot. "I'm trying to talk to you, Brooks Avery! I don't have anything to feed that man. I don't like him just barging in here."

"Shhh! Now settle yourself down and feed him whatever you were going to feed us and act like the nice girl you usually are. Let's watch the tube and enjoy life, OK?"

"What made you bring him home? Why didn't you call?"

"Ellen, this is not the first time I've brought someone home with me. He is an old friend and he is a wealthy friend. All right? In my business you do not kick people of substance out your door. Now let's go."

The issue is closed. They come smiling back into the livingroom. They find Dave leading the boys in a poem he has taught them. They are trying to recite it while he pinches and tickles them:

> Oh I'm being eaten by a boa constrictor
> a boa constrictor a boa constrictor
> Oh I'm being eaten by a boa constrictor
> and I think that I shall die—
>
> Oh no, it's eating my toe
>
> Oh sin, it's up to my shin!
> Oh me, it's up to my knee!

"Drink, Dave?" Avery tries to hand the glass over in the wiggling crowd.

"Not yet, thanks. Set it over there. We're busy here." The face is red and happy.

> Oh my, it's up to my thigh!
> Oh fiddle, it's up to my middle!

There are great howls of laughter here, for Dave is prodding both their stomachs.

> Oh mess, it's up to my chest!
> Oh heck, it's up to my neck!
> Oh dear, it's up to my ear!

And then the three clowns collapse with muted sounds of suffocation:

> Glub, glub, glub!

Avery gets the children calmed down and seated in front of the TV. "Now you guys watch, because this is *history*. Man's first landing on the moon." But in fact there is not much to see except long shots of the Control Room. The boys wander in and out while

Avery tries to play host. He raises his glass. "A little sentiment, Dave. Luck to those guys tonight."

"I'll drink to that. And to the machine that brought them there and has to get them back."

"Yes sir, to that too."

"You think there isn't money riding on this shot?" Dave asks this almost meanly.

"No sir! I know there is. I know that."

"Listen, some of the people I represent have got their hearts in their throats right now."

"The banks aren't *un*involved, you know," says Avery with some pride.

"People have got to dream, Brooks. We need this thing. It's going to open our eyes."

"Right, Dave; dream the impossible dream." Now with the good smoky scotch in his gullet Avery feels expansive and aware. Ellen comes and sits beside him. They drink and small-talk.

Dinner comes and goes, a meal unnoticed in the excitement of the time: food eaten without being seen, TV tables nearly toppled as hands search vaguely across the surfaces for crackers, herring, ham, cheese, wine, all the time the eyes and ears strain to be sociable and yet not miss the moments of black and white wonder. The boys are frozen without motion.

"Good picture—great picture—fantastic! Jesus, all those miles!" Dave roars his approval. His face is swelling as he drinks.

Ellen brings in strawberry shortcake and a cannister of whipped cream. There is coffee too but the men go back to whiskey. After the two-hour show the screen fills with color and commentators again. Ellen pushes the children out of the room, but not before Avery gets his hugs from them and Dave gets the same.

The room is gently spinning for Avery in that familiar soft first-edge of a high. Things have gone so well! He cannot keep all compliments back. "Dave, you are great with kids. Just great."

Dave spreads his hands in a gesture of humility. "Like I said, Brooksy, they're my life."

"You should get married, Dave. I mean it. Have kids of your own."

"Oh. I do OK."

Avery takes this as studsmanship and he leers. "Lots of war stories, huh? I'll bet you do OK." But that buddy-buddy locker-room approach does not spur reaction. Avery is slightly embarrassed at his own crudity and he regroups with a serious topic. "How about some words of wisdom, Mister Financier? A little shoptalk before we get too blotto."

Spread hands again. "You name it."

"Dave. Dave." Avery mutters affectionately, "I'm small potatoes. I'm not in your league. Just pick up your briefcase there and tell me what will make my million for me." The briefcase goes to the lap and again Avery is fascinated by the object. It seems to pick up the colors from the TV and melt them into a magic palette of patterns and moving structures. "Dave, that is the goddamdest hunk of leather I ever saw. What the hell is it?"

A private laugh. "If I told you, you wouldn't believe it."

"I would, I would. Cross my heart."

But he is leafing through papers and does not answer. Avery does not pursue the subject because there might be a hot tip coming up. Finally, Dave throws his hands up in despair. "Christ, Brooks, I don't know where to begin. We're spread out all over the place, you know? I could talk about teak from Cambodia or oil from South Africa or munitions from here. We are so damned diversified!"

"Boy," says Avery into the echo chamber of his glass, "I'll bet you really get around."

The conversation goes on in counterpart with the TV. Avery cannot remember all that is being said. His eyes cross lightly once or twice. He notices Ellen come into the room and turn down the volume on the set. And he sees two towheads peeking around the corner from the stairs. "Get back in bed!" he yells once.

Then a silly mood hits him. The TV picture with all its flip-flopping challenges Avery. He stands and sprays whipped cream on the TV screen. It is a delightful feeling, a sort of freedom that surges over him in a flash. Ellen grabs futilely for the can and catches an eyeful of the stuff and runs crying from the room. Avery paints a cream mustache on the tempered glass, two fat dots for eyes, a jiggly hairline, a sloppy mouth.

And of course the regrets come on as fast as the urge did. Something snaps inside his head and he realizes his absurdity. He stands there with the can dripping. Avery tries a laugh. Nothing. He walks carefully across the carpet. "It wasn't just the liquor," he says. "I'm not that drunk." He turns and sees his wife cleaning the

TV with a paper towel. She is crying. "Ellen, honey, it was just a joke."

"How do you expect the boys to get to sleep? As if they haven't had enough excitement! Listen to them up there bouncing on their beds."

"So they'll make good astronauts," Avery ad-libs. "So they'll go to Mars and Venus and Saturn."

"Not Saturn," says Dave with a smile and a nudge in Avery's side.

Avery smiles back and plays straight man. "Why not Saturn?"

Dave starts to laugh, and it rolls from somewhere in his gut and infects the room, and tears come into his eyes as he tries to push the answer out. Even Ellen laughs.

"Why not Saturn?" Avery asks again, prompting.

"Because—" handkerchief goes to eyes "—because she eats her children!" And if the line is not that funny, so what, because the sight of that huge man doubled up and gasping for breath is riotous, and Ellen and Avery join him in a release of nerves. It is a special happy thing like a roller-coaster ride, and they hit the highs and lows at different times so that when one stops laughing another begins again, and the children know from the sounds that something is going on, and they run down the stairs again into the middle of the helpless hystericals, and they are hugged.

"What's so funny?" asks Mark uneasily after a time; this triggers another wave of amusement, but not for too long.

"It is your bedtime for the last time!" says Ellen severely.

Dave crosses and takes each boy by the hand. He is serious and dignified. "Let me do the honors, Ellen."

She gasps and pretends embarrassment. "Why I'll do no such thing! You're a guest in this house—"

Avery holds up his hands. "Ellen! Ellen. Here is a man who loves children, and he doesn't get this kind of chance very often. Just stop being the careful mother."

But it is really out of both their hands. Dave is leading the kids up the stairs in a cute hippety-hop dance that synchronizes with the poem they are chanting again.

The door shuts at the top of the stairs and Avery hugs his wife warmly. "Your bedtime too, sweet."

"But I've got to clean up, Brooks."

"Can't you ever accept a favor? I'll scrape the dishes and load the washer. Dave will put the kids to sleep. Now take advantage of our hospitality before it melts."

She yawns widely, grins sweetly. "Dave will have to sleep—"

"—in the hide-a-bed in the playroom. I know."

She climbs the stairs slowly, already unzipping her dress. "The sheets are in—"

"Ellen, I *know*."

"Kiss the boys for me," is her last reminder as she rounds the corner.

Avery pours himself another scotch, light this time with water. There is still a wrap-up of the day and night beaming out of the TV. Avery laughs at his own idiocy with the whipped cream. He can still see white streaks of the stuff in the corners of the picture tube. He sits and stares dully, hardly listening to the low voices coming from the set.

How much time passes he cannot guess. He awakens to the sound of footsteps coming down the stairs. He turns to the TV and hears the anthem, sees the flag, and then the picture cuts to garbled haze.

Dave walks slowly into the room, straightening his tie. Avery hops up with the sleep still in his eyes. He punches the set off. "How about a nightcap, buddy?"

"No thanks," says Dave in a quiet voice. "I'm full."

Avery scratches the back of his neck and yawns. "No offense, Dave, no offense. It's just been a long day. You won't mind sleeping in the basement, will you? We've got it all fixed up; it's dry and there's a couch down there and—" Avery watches as Dave picks up his briefcase, puts on his raincoat and hat. He is non-plussed only for a moment. "Great idea, Dave. Walk will do us good." He starts to get his windbreaker but is stopped by Dave's outstretched hand.

"Been nice seeing you, Brooks."

Avery won't take the shake. He doesn't understand. "Hey, wait a minute, guy, you can't leave now. It's after one in the morning! This isn't New York, you know. We don't have cabs cruising right down the middle of Oak Street at this hour. Come on, Dave, this is crazy."

"Sorry, Brooksy, I've got to move along. Don't worry about me."

"Well I by Christ am going to worry about you." Avery is getting a little angry. "There's no reason for you to go storming off."

The big hand grasps his shoulder and Avery has to admit that it transmits comfort and power to him. "Brooks, who's storming? I've got to be in Atlanta by noon today." Avery sulks. "Brooks, I am not afraid of the dark."

Avery sees he has lost. "At least let me drive you to the cabstand in LaGrange."

"Wouldn't hear of it, Brooksy. Wouldn't want to waste your time."

"Dave, this is crazy!"

The big face laughs and pats him again. "Maybe I'll see you in another fifteen years, huh?"

"Maybe," says Avery halfheartedly.

"Tell Ellen goodbye for me. And thank her for the food." He rubs his stomach. "It was great."

"Nothing to it, Dave." They shake hands firmly. "And listen, listen . . ." Avery slows because he is choked up about this. "I just want to say that you were great with the kids."

Dave punches him on the bicep. "Take it from me, Brooks, those are delectable children. Some of the best."

"Anytime you're in this part of the world, Dave . . ."

"You bet, Brooks." He is already out the door and down the flagstones. "Goodnight!"

Avery watches the large white back disappear into the shadows. He closes the door softly and stands there a minute nodding affectionately. Then he sweeps his eyes around the room and flips the switches.

The moon lights his way up the stairs. He is a little dizzy at the top and he goes straight to the bathroom, takes two bicarbonate tablets, brushes his teeth, makes himself drink a glass of water.

He opens his bedroom door and hears the spasmodic snore of his wife over the rumble of the air conditioner. He laughs to himself and thinks that sometime he will tape her nightsounds.

He goes down the hallway and carefully twists the boys' doorknob. He imagines himself sly as a snake or burglar as he opens the door without a squeak.

His first thought is: What a great trick! But that does not last more than a millisecond, for there is something final and real and infinite about the two skeletons on the beds, something the moonlight cannot hide. These are the bones of his children, disjointed but arranged properly, like rifles field-stripped for inspection. There is no pose to them. They lie stiff as exhibits, picked clean to the slivers.

In the midst of his nausea and disbelief Avery starts to scream for his wife. But he controls that impulse and tries to think, fights to keep from fainting. He shuts the door and stumbles down the stairs, slams open the front door and runs into the yard. All his instincts cannot keep him from trembling wildly. He falls shaking on the sidewalk and his heart races. He screams for help and screams again, waits for his echoes to simmer, waits for lights to turn on in the houses across the way. No response, so he screams again and again in a high cracking falsetto that astounds him. His voice meets nothing but the trimmed tropic beauty of the summer suburb and the full moon.

♨ ♨ ♨

THE LITERATURE
OF AWE

by DAVID BOSWORTH

from THE ANTIOCH REVIEW

nominated by THE ANTIOCH REVIEW, *Ellen Ferber and Mary Oliver*

Art and Life.   The territory of fiction is that boundary, pressed on both sides, between the senses and the sensible world—not just the outside event or that event's human witness, but the witnessing itself, the marriage of observer and evidence, the act of experience. Art *is* experience: experience human-crafted, experience stopped and translated; in short, experience imitated. And because art is human-crafted and therefore limited, it is experience reduced. The extent to which an author reduces experience (tames, trims, reorders, deflates it) is no inconsequential matter. To bear witness, to be an author, to make art, is a profound act; there is no work more serious or demanding or finally audacious.

And no work more liable to failure. For businessmen and farmers make products, and doctors and politicians provide services which sustain life, but authors dare to aspire to life's re-creation—they dare to show us what and how life actually is.

To discuss serious fiction, then, is to discuss life. Elegant exchanges addressed in the specialized vocabularies of critical canon are irrelevant here. What matters is life, what it is and how it is lived and the function art serves in the living of it. Fictional techniques are not important in themselves but because they imply the most basic truths; narrative strategies matter because they imply world views. Plot, style, point-of-view, the stuff whereof a story is made, reflect the stuff whereof life is made and how life is ordered. Plotted fiction implies a plotted universe; the plotless fiction of some modern authors (or as in Pynchon's case, the subversion of plot) evokes a very different kind of world. When in "Fizzle 3" Samuel Beckett eschews traditional punctuation, using only commas to separate phrases, the effect is profound, presenting a reality stripped of hierarchical order, a reality dramatically different from that of, say, *Daisy Miller* or *Absalom, Absalom.* Debates over style, when viewed in this light, take on a relevance and gravity beyond the rationale for English department symposia. In bearing witness to the act of experience, an author, whether consciously or not, makes judgments about the very nature of existence and what it means to be human; and the crafted experience he offers can challenge the most fundamental common-sense notions of what reality is.

That different views of reality exist at all, of course, reveals in itself something basic about the human condition and about an art that tries to re-create that condition. We are born to a fundamental uncertainty. We are sentient, thinking creatures but our sense and reason have their limits. We are bound by space and bound by time, held separate from the outside world, from the past and from the future. We can glimpse past these boundaries, we can compose a detailed reality from the data received, but that reality is still second-hand and incomplete, and even this second-hand reality is far too complex, astonishing, and immense for our reasoning minds to comprehend fully. And we *know* that we do not comprehend. To know is to know that we do not know enough; to bear witness to the universe is to be shown how small we are (in space, in time) compared to that universe and how little we are able to control it.

The price of consciousness, then, is the uncertainty caused by its incompleteness. And since the more "conscious" we are, the more we are aware of that incompleteness, I would argue that this essential uncertainty, this *felt* discrepancy between what actually exists and what we rationally can know of existence, between the infinity "out there" and the finiteness of "me," is the most profound and honest reaction of a man to this world. Further, I would call that reaction "awe" and expect that fiction aspiring to art would make awe its special province.

The awe I am speaking of is not simply intellectual or emotional or aesthetic, but all of these and all at once. The awe I am speaking of is best measured by its intensity; for it is, above all, an extremity of experience, the gift of consciousness stretched to its outermost limits, one man pressed right up against that boundary which separates him from the outside world. This communion-confrontation between the individual and creation, although potentially exhilarating, can terrify too. The balance is tipped from wonder to dread; the scope of our vision suddenly seemed minacious and intimidating. Because the world *is* so immense and complex, because we *are* so small in comparison to it, because we *do* have so little control, and, finally, because our truest moments impress us so vividly with these our natural limitations, we tend to retreat from those moments; we shy away from the experience of awe. And yet we have eyes and must see, have ears and must hear; we are, all of us, witnesses to creation, spectators by virtue of our very natures as sentient creatures to an awesome world. To deny awe, we must deny that world; we invent safer spectacles to play witness to, artificial doll-house realities, built of ideologies and easy isms, of rigid rituals and eviscerating theories. And we worship these self-made realities fanatically, bow before these clinquant idols, the false gods of our false security.

The problem is as old as civilized man. Much of the Old Testament, that primal record of Western history, is laced with condemnations of idolatry, and Isaiah's three-thousand-year-old, outraged lament that men were "bowing down to the work of their hands" seems just as relevant today as then. For the Hebraic obsession with banning idols from worship was based on a fundamentally wise understanding of human nature. They realized that it was too easy to mistake an image of God for his actual presence; that a God reduced to human dimensions was a God robbed of his vital essence, which was beyond measurement and comprehension; that an image molded by human hands implied a God that men could manipulate. They, the ancient Israeli prophets, wanted instead to worship the less concrete but authentic God of the burning bush, the am-who-am, the swirling cloud in the Sinai Desert; they wanted their people to approach this irreducible God whose powerful presence evoked the experience of awe. But many Jews, as the prophets' own lamentations testify, were tempted by an easier path, bowing to Baal instead of Jehovah.

And modern men are similarly tempted. The idols are different, of course, ranging from Sports Cars to Education, from the Bible itself to Revolution, but their nature is still the same, just as debilitating, just as profane—and just as false. Every ideology clung to tightly is idolatrous; every intellectual system—whether aesthetic, economic, or mathematical in nature—if assumed to be Truth rather than a convenient strategy for approaching truth, is idolatrous. They are idolatrous because they set up in place of an awesome reality (call it God or Truth, the am-who-am or the is-what-is) paler, surer playpen worlds whose contingencies are predictable but which only occasionally and accidentally match our experience. That we must try to understand our experience seems inevitable; that we must fail to understand our experience seems just as inevitable. Our idols serve to fill that gap between our drive to comprehend and our destiny to fall short of total comprehension. And to a degree, the degree to which we must have a tentative theory to test for truth at all, they are necessary. But when hubris or panic sets in and we begin to accept these man-made images for Truth itself, then we bow to the work of our own hands and further estrange ourselves from the world as it really is.

A fiction aspiring to art aspires to show us that world and must, therefore, ever be about the business of destroying the false gods that would hide it from us, ever challenge and subvert the current manifestations of that same age-old reductionist idolatry that shields us from the truth. An author aspiring to be an artist aspires in this sense, then, to the role of prophet, dismantling through the power of his words the Temple to Baal we all carry within us, for beyond those temples lie the vast, vast horizon, the illimitable expanse of creation—the experience of awe. This is why the work of the artist is so difficult and important, so frequently unpopular and occasionally dangerous; it's his business to shatter the pet illusions of his audience, those fashionable idols that so many hold so dear. This, too, is why the artist and the tyrant are always at odds, for absolute power requires an absolute reality to rationalize its existence, and so the tyrant must reduce the world to an idolatrous cartoon of perfect heroes and irredeemable foes, of ironclad moral certainties. But the artist, by the very nature of his work, reveals the flagrant falsehood of that counterfeit reality; he presents the world as it is, and the world as it is is never so simple nor so certain as the tyrant must make it appear to be.

Must is the salient word here, with a twofold, intensified meaning; for in the tyrant, political necessity and psychic compulsion begin to merge, the tyrant-state a cancerous reification of a private insanity. Stalin, for example—the murderer of Mandlestam, the imprisoner of Solzhenitsyn, and harrasser of Pasternak—was in a curious way as much victim as benefactor of his imposed world view, scarcely freer of his own tyranny than those he ruled. Towards the end, he had reduced his environment to one basic room, a self-sufficient womb he rarely left, a womb he had re-created in all the cities he commonly visited so that no matter where he went, he always appeared to be in the exact same place. The same dimensions, the same furnishings in the same positions, day after day after day; no matter where he was, the same four walls greeted him; his own Temple to Baal; his own gulag cell, if you will; his own sentence of imprisonment. The special and monstrous evil of Stalin, of course, was that he imposed this madness on the Soviet people; private compulsion became public policy as he tried to squeeze an entire country into one spare, unchanging room. And those like Mandlestam who resisted him, who refused to accept his cartoon reality, he imprisoned or killed.

The lesson here goes beyond its obvious historical importance, for the classic confrontation between the artist and the dictator recapitulates on a larger scale each man's solitary struggle for truth and sanity, and it reminds us that we are all vulnerable to a fear-tempted tyrant who lurks in our psyches. Few of us possess the rampant megalomania of a Stalin, of course, but we all to some degree condemn ourselves as he did to a prison-cell world. We hide within our habits, within our inflexible moralities and acquired prejudices, wrap ourselves in a perceptual cocoon that blinds us from a reality we find too awesome to confront. We are, in short, afraid. And we are afraid because to catch a glimpse of the world as it actually exists is to sense, if only fleetingly, the powerlessness of our condition here. It is to sense, too, though, a world dazzling in its intricacy, beauty, and scope, a world whose colors, shapes, and sounds delight and astound. And that range of response from dread to wonder, when pressed right up against the boundary between oneself and creation, encompasses the most basic decision of all in life: brought to the top of the mountain, we either turn away and shrink our world or expand ourselves to embrace the view; we either bow to Baal or worship Jehovah, choose either the antiseptic room of Josef Stalin or the vast and vivid landscape of *Doctor Zhivago*.

And the right choice is not the easy one. Our fear is so primal, our instinct for self-protection so powerful, our reasoning minds so given to the production of intellectual idols, that only in rare moments do we transcend the tyranny within and choose to bear witness to the whole truth. Instead, to anesthetize our fear, we perjure ourselves, and the price exacted for this temporary relief is dear indeed. Our sedations kill the pleasure with the pain; we turn numb, wonderless, unaware. Condemned to a chrysalis of self-woven illusions, we are not prepared, our only defense against danger the sorry pretense that it isn't there. And when danger comes, as it inevitably must, when suffering invades and through the rent holes in our flimsy cocoons the world of awe is suddenly made visible, then our eyes, too long accustomed to the dark, ache all the more painfully in the light of the truth.

It is the necessary and special function of the best literature to intervene in this struggle on the side of truth, to light candles in our self-imposed darkness and illuminate the real world. It is the function of the best fiction to save us from ourselves, from our own illusions, from our idols and ideologies—from our pretense of control. But to understand the importance of literature is first to admit its fallibility. Fiction, too, is reductionist; like all human striving after truth, it is but a pale approximation of life. It is a special kind of approximation, however, in that it engages us, as does reality itself, through the senses, in that it aims to re-create the experience of life rather than just to abstract life's meaning. Thus, although fiction, because it is human, must reduce, its uniquely imitative nature makes it among our least reductionist ways of knowing: *Anna Karenina,* while not equal to the experience of love, comes far closer to evoking that experience than some

psychological treatise on the subject or a physiological description
of dilating pupils and palpitating hearts. This mimetic quality of
fiction, which is both its most obvious and definitive feature, places
the author in a tenuous position. He finds himself straddling two
ever-divided ledges; the precarious paradox that best describes his
difficult mission: he aims for the whole truth, trying to show reality
as it actually is, while forced to reduce that truth, so awesome in
scope, to human dimensions. His is the nearly impossible goal of
condensing reality without changing its essense.

Given the difficulty of the task, failures clearly outnumber
successes; and, of course, some "literature" never even attempts to
sustain the necessary balance between verisimilitude and artifice.
Propaganda and most genre fiction, to take obvious examples,
imitate not life but models previously abstracted from life (political
doctrine and esthetic convention), and by enshrining those cultural
idols in place of reality, they confirm or institute our perceptual
prejudices. The heroic worker who always conquers in the end, the
wily detective who in the final scene always solves the mystery at
hand—these, it seems almost redundant to say, are not metaphors
of the life we share; the world we live in is not nearly so sure, so
circumscribed by comprehensible rules, so adamantly resolved.
Genre literature is not a mirror to life as it is, but to life as we wish
it to be, as it never can be, and we enter the radically idealized
world of certain books just as we enter a sports coliseum—not to
discover truth but to escape it, to find an hour's respite from the
real and anxious uncertainties of everyday life.

Of course entertainment is to be valued in its own right. *Of
course* some genre fiction surpasses its own limitations while much
"arty" fiction can't even succeed as simple diversion. *Of course*
there is no absolute line separating popular literature from art, and
any one work can have both sublime and inept moments in varying
proportions. Great works of art *can* be popular; detective novels
can illuminate the truth, and to believe otherwise is to make the
kind of blind prejudgment that constitutes the very idolatry I am
warning against. But even as we recognize the possibility of any
piece of fiction ascending to art, we must continue to distinguish
exceptions from rules. Entertainment passes time; art confronts it.
Propaganda perpetuates idols; art destroys them. Serious art and
popular literature, if not mutually exclusive, are not the same, and

it serves no good end, aesthetic or political, to pretend that they are.

And yet, that very equation is being made today, certain "egalitarian" critics insisting on the superiority of popular forms. The danger these critics represent, however, lies not in the literature they choose to support— popular fiction, serving its own and often legitimate purposes, will, after all, always have a following—but in the enervating cynicism that would equate those purposes with art. And that cynicism is not limited to a few radical professors or to any set number of issues or arguments; rather, it constitutes a tone, a pervasive and sinister modern attitude which, infecting our spirit and corrupting our thought, has led us to overvalue a kind of "serious" literature that has failed to achieve art's highest ends. This failure, it should be stressed, is by no means solely a literary event, but a cultural phenomenon in the widest sense. The literature of despair that has flourished in the mid-twentieth century, as typified by such authors as Beckett and Kosinski, has its philosophical counterpart in nearly every aspect of Western society: Behaviorism in psychology, the International Style of architecture, Minimalism in the visual arts, and a certain social-engineering approach to government. What these apparently dissimilar movements share, I would argue, to the detriment of the people they serve, is a reductionist view of human nature, a view which, engrained in our culture, is the product of a long, complex historical process. And if we are to grasp why that view is mistaken, if we are to understand exactly how the literature of despair has failed us, it is to that process we first must turn, to the intellectual tradition of the Western world.

For most of recorded time, mankind's basic model or metaphor of reality was anthropomorphic; the physical world was explained in human terms, physical events given human motivations. But in the seventeenth century, with the advent of classical mechanics and the scientific method, a pronounced change began to take place. Aiming for a simple, objective description of reality, thinkers began to disassociate themselves from certain traditional preoccupations of natural philosophy. Purpose, meaning, the why of existence were left to the church, the unified if flawed approach to knowledge that had predominated since ancient times, abandoned for a more specialized study. The goal then bacame *what* not *why*, and the assumption was that the answer could be found by an ever finer dissection of reality, a paring away of illusory qualities that would eventually reveal some elementary, unchangable particle of truth. Measurement became the method, numbers the language; subjective human experience, so complex and chaotic, so dependent on the senses, was generally dismissed as unreliable. And the final result was a model that confidently reduced reality, despite all its apparent diversity, to just two fundamental concepts: there was matter and there was motion. Reality consisted of so many identical, indivisible atoms which, existing in a vacuum, were caught up in a chain reaction of cause-and-effect movements.

This dehumanization of the world picture, this shift in metaphors from organism to mechanism, had a profound effect on Western culture. For what began primarily as a way of describing the stars gradually became a way of describing everyday life, until, by the early twentieth century, an ironic reversal had taken place. Whereas in the beginning man saw the physical world as an extension of himself to be described in human terms, man now saw himself as an extension of the physical world to be described in physical terms. At first this shift in self-image, as articulated in the newborn "social" sciences (sociology, psychology, Darwinian biology), aroused a surge of optimist. There was the hope, even the expectation, that mankind's happiness could be engineered by a studied application of those same principles that first had been applied to the distant stars.

But almost immediately problems arose. That radically abstracted metaphor of so many atoms bouncing in a void, which even physical science was forced to amend, proved especially incompatible with human experience. It spoke a language—mathematics—so severely abstracted that most of daily life was lost in translation, all the diversity and splendor, all the emotive content of man's sensual existence, dismissed by implication as illusory or irrelevant. Its reductionist assumption that the whole was equal to the simple sum of its atomistic parts ignored the organizational complexity of living things. And finally, not only did it fail as an accurate and practical description of man, it never addressed man's basic need for meaning and purpose. This last failing, of course, was hardly the fault of classical science; born in an age when the church utterly controlled metaphysical speculation, it had never aimed to answer those larger questions. But by the twentieth century, when the church had lost most of its authority, science was more and more dominating man's common-sense way of understanding the world; and what had begun three hundred years before as an honest attempt to limit goals was then being perceived as an actual limit on reality itself. The failure to ask the question began to assume the shape of an answer; a description of a reality that ignored meaning implied a reality that was in fact meaningless.

If atoms, the primary particles of matter, move only from external causes, and if man is made of matter, then aren't all human actions caused externally as well? Isn't all human behavior a mere link in a complex causal chain, free will, morality, justice merely subjective, therefore irrelevant notions which hide the true "objective" reality of particles of matter bouncing in a vacuum? The implications were as ironic as they were dispiriting; even as man was achieving his most impressive physical feats—controlling the environment, curing disease—he was falling victim to self-doubt and despair. He had reduced the world in order to get better control, but in the process he had reduced himself. Once again means had been mistaken for ends; once again man had mistaken an idea of reality for reality itself, "bowing down to the work of [his own] hands." The tyrant-within had won, declaring himself absolute ruler of the realm; but the realm was an abstraction, a two-dimensional, colorless map, his power an illusion sustained at the expense of his basic nature.

This process of self-abstraction, this denial of the subjective side to human nature, can be traced in almost every field of thought through the twentieth century. In psychology, interest in states of consciousness (James) gave way to the early experimentalists (Watson), who excluded consciousness from study because it couldn't be observed or measured in the laboratory, and then to the prue Behaviorists (Skinner), who took that exclusion one step further by denying that consciousness existed at all. In visual arts, representational works gave way first to more abstracted renderings of recognizable forms (Cubism, for example), then to work without any recognizable forms (Abstract Expressionism), and finally, to conceptual art, where the "idea" and the work were one and the same, a typed proposal replacing a canvas. *A psychology that denies consciousness? an art that has no visual existence?*—these oxymorons are the result of reductionism gone berserk, of abstraction carried to its furthest limits, the complete conquest of theory over sense, of concept over experience, and they typify a dominant intellectual imbalance, which has drastically debased man's perception of himself.

If we return to fiction, the relevance of this detour into the history of ideas now becomes apparent; for literature, which is always both mirror to and product of its surrounding culture, could no more escape the misperceptions of its age than could psychology or painting. Fiction, too, succumbed to the prevailing reductionism, to an eviscerating impoverishment of man's self-image. If we take the basic model from classical physics of so many identical atoms bouncing off each other in an infinite vacuum and translate it to social reality, where an individual man, not much different from those around him and lacking an effective "inner self," is pushed and prodded by forces beyond his control and comprehension, the result is an eerily accurate paradigm of the modern anti-heroic novel. The landscape barren, the language stripped, the pervasive tone of despair leavened only by a desperate wit, the characters too existentially inept to control themselves, their fate, their environment; behind it all the sure belief that life is irredeemably meaningless—we've all experienced this fictional world in the works of Vonnegut, Beckett, Kosinski, and others. That it expresses an attitude prevalent in modern Western culture is beyond dispute, but the question remains whether that attitude is correct or desirable. Does this fictional world meet the high standards of art? Does it bear witness to the whole truth by re-creating the experience of reality as it actually is? Are its authors modern-day prophets, warning us against our intellectual idols, or are they unwitting servants to Baal, themselves victims of the age's illusions?

The Literature of Despair.   Kurt Vonnegut, Jr., succinctly sums up his own world view in the opening chapter of *The Sirens of Titan* when the narrator, a voice set in the far future, describes our present age as a time when men discovered in space "what had already been found in abundance on Earth—a nightmare of meaninglessness without end . . . empty heroics, low comedy, and pointless death." A witness to one of World War II's worst massacres, the Allied fire-bombing of Dresden, Vonnegut expresses a relentlessly pessimistic vision of man, a pessimism far surpassing the cynic's belief in the eventual victory of evil or the fundamentalist's version of a fall from grace. For there can be no victory without a battle and no fall if one from the start is inescapably mired at the bottom of the pit. The moral drama between right and wrong loses all meaning if men are not free to choose and competent to act, and Vonnegut sees man as neither competent nor free. In his fictional world, there are no villains and, as well, no heroes to oppose them; both good and evil are beyond man's grasp. When he writes in the introduction to *Slaughterhouse-Five* that he learned in college "there was absolutely no difference between anybody," the ironic tone does not belie the accuracy of the words. Vonnegut does believe that all men are the same, and to read his fiction is to meet a cast of characters who are uniformly pathetic, helpless victims of a random, incoherent, meaningless existence, and whose suffering, unmitigated by any true higher purpose, is distinguished only by the self-delusions embraced to relieve it.

It is precisely this unrelievedly debased view of man that cripples Vonnegut's fiction and undermines his effectiveness as a moral critic. Caught in a conflict between what he wishes and what he believes, between what he wants for mankind and what he thinks mankind is fated to have, his fiction constantly exposes folly only to submit to inevitability. In Vonnegut's books, anger—which is, after all, a kind of hope—is always defeated by resignation, his criticism of society always emasculated by his final belief that man can do no better. *The Player Piano*, Vonnegut's first novel, reveals most clearly this sad process of self-defeat. Its plot set at some future date when a fully automated America is being run by an oligarchy of technocrats, the book has as its satiric target the same mechanization of society discussed in this essay. At the outset, the main character, Dr. Paul Proteus, whose late father was a founder of the technocracy, is himself on the verge of ascending to the highest levels of authority within the organization. But just as he had a difficult relationship with his father, Proteus has a difficult time adjusting to the society his father helped engineer. He lacks ambition, he finds himself attracted to that society's outcasts and critics, and eventually he is persuaded by a charismatic preacher called Lasher to lend his prestigious name to an organized rebellion against the state.

At this point in the narrative, Vonnegut seems to be flirting with transforming Proteus into a realistic hero, a character who has overcome his weakness by choosing a moral and courageous course of action. But an habitual debunker, Vonnegut must debunk his own spokesman as well; a despairing egalitarian, he mustn't allow one character to surpass the others in moral stature. Proteus is captured, put on trial, and then, just as he seems to be reaching heroic proportions, expressing Vonnegut's own arguments against an automated society, he is abruptly reduced to the level of his enemies. As he testifies, Proteus is strapped to a lie detector which finally "reveals" that his "true" motivation for joining the revolt was a subconscious hatred of his father and not some elevated moral ideal. The nobility of his sacrifice (and by implication his argument) undermined, Proteus can't deny the results; he admits that the accusation is probably true, adding that "sordid things, for the most part, are what make human beings . . . move." He tries, though, to insist that the revolt can be "right" no matter what his motivation for joining it; but the only image he can summon to convince his courtroom audience is that "some of the most beautiful peonies" he has ever seen were grown in "pure cat excrement."

One can sense in these final words, this strained metaphor, Vonnegut himself struggling through Proteus for some satisfactory answer, and when rebels burst into the courtroom, ending the scene, it is the author as much as his character who is being rescued, saved from the contradictions inherent in his point of view. He wants to criticize the mechanization of society for making life meaningless, but he himself believes life to be fundamentally meaningless. He wants to support Proteus over his enemies, but he himself believes that "there is absolutely no difference between anybody," that we are all "moved" by "sordid things." *Vonnegut's problem, you see, is that although he abhors our mechanized culture, he believes the world view upon which it is based;* his vision of mankind—so many like individuals pushed by forces beyond their control—is really the same, nothing more than that same mechanistic metaphor misapplied again. And the result of that misapplication is always the same: pessimism, cynicism, resignation, despair. At the novel's end, the rebellion is easily crushed and the futility of the enterprise emphasized when Vonnegut has Lasher, his most competent character, admit that their revolt had been doomed from the start, that it had been merely "for the record," a symbolic gesture, a fist shaken against an onrushing tank.

There will be no more serious rebellions in Vonnegut's fiction and no more flirtations with realistic heroism; there will be no more waiting till the end of the book to point out the futility of symbolic gestures. The implications of his thinking now clear, his subsequent novels will begin where *The Player Piano* ends, with characters trapped in a fate they can neither change nor escape, doomed to a nightmare existence of "low comedy and pointless death." But Vonnegut is, above all else, a compassionate man; he may not respect his characters, but he does care about them, is driven by an urge to ease their suffering. Given the pessimism of his outlook, however, all he can offer is the very solution he so often mocks: illusion, fantasy, the "harmless untruths" of Bokonism, of Tralfamadorian metaphysics, the soothing escapism of Billy Pilgrim's time-travel. As his recurring character, Eliot Rosewater, says to a psychiatrist in *Slaughterhouse-Five,* "I think you guys are going to have to come up with a lot of wonderful *new* lies, or people just aren't going to want to go on living." And there it is again, the same basic conflict resurfacing—between thought and feeling, between the artist and the humanitarian. Vonnegut wants to tell us the truth and at the same time spare us from it; he wants to ease our pain and at the same time show us that only "lies" can achieve that end. To comfort, he must lie; to tell the truth, he must hurt; for in the world as Kurt Vonnegut, Jr., sees it, happiness is utterly incompatible with truth. What he believes is what he hates; the peonies are still there, but now they are fake, manufactured illusions to ease our pain—now only the excrement real.

But as bleak as the fictional world of *Slaughterhouse-Five* seems to be, there is another that is bleaker still. The loneliness, the despair, the suffering beyond hope of redemption, the disgust and self-disgust, the rank and relentless debasement of mankind, in short, that "nightmare" version of existence that has so affected the sensibility of the age, is etched in its most resolute purity in the fictional works of Samuel Beckett. Beckett is the extreme, the quintessence, the soul of modernist writing stripped of all obscuring flesh: its philosopher; and because he dares to draw out every hidden assumption to its ultimate conclusion, he is the clearest example of why reductionist fiction fails. For Beckett, existence is, as the first-person narrator of *Molloy* says, "senseless, speechless, issueless misery," his typical character (and there *is* a typical Beckett character; again the atomistic vision, again the reduction to a sorry sameness) even more pathetic than Billy Pilgrim. Molloy, Moran, Malone are all trapped in the same state of inescapable ignorance; for them "all grows dim," their "sight and hearing are very bad," their memories almost nonexistent; their first-person narrations are jeremiads of epistemological doubt, littered with "I don't know's," "I wasn't sure's," "I can't remember's"—every statement qualified by a subsequent uncertainty. Molloy, at various points in his narration, can't remember his name, the name of his mother, which of his legs is lame, whether he has a son and by whom he had one, and he is forced to absorb what little information he receives "through that mist . . . which rises in me every day and veils the world from me and veils me from myself." Isolated in this impoverished world of dim shapes and obscure sounds, of unreliable information, unable to retrieve the past or apprehend the present, Molloy, Moran, Malone are brought to the ultimate uncertainty best expressed by Malone's resigned statement: "I shall go on doing as I have always done, not knowing what it is I do, nor who I am, nor where I am, nor if I am." The metaphysical ignorance emphasized by Vonnegut has been taken one step further here. Doubt has corrupted the very process of knowing, rendering all the world unintelligible. Vonnegut's characters cannot know why they live, but Beckett's cannot know even *if* they live, cannot confirm even the most mundane facts of their existence.

Such an inherent and therefore inescapable ignorance implies, of course, an incompetence too—if man cannot know, what can he do?—an incompetence that in Beckett's fiction is immediate and physical. The disgust of the human body, seen in mild degrees in Vonnegut (Billy Pilgrim's orgasmic moan is described as sounding like a "small, rusty hinge"), is further exaggerated in Beckett's prose, for he, like his character Moran, finds "a horror of the body and its functions" "the most fruitful of dispositions." Once again Beckett, the extremist, extends mankind's reductionist debasement. Bodies rot, stink, vomit, slobber, their decay detailed with a graphic obsession; sex is portrayed as a tiresome coupling of hobbled animals, a lowly comic act. Good for only pain, the body gives no pleasure and is impotent to perform even the simplest functions. Not only are Molloy and Moran nearly deaf and blind, but they are lame as well, and Malone, poor Malone, cannot move from his bed. This physical impotence is complementary to and symbolic of a larger impotence as well; when Malone says, "I could die to-day, if I wished, merely by making a little effort," he has to add the obliterating qualifiers, "if I could wish, if I could make an effort." Man's incompetence has reached its ultimate culmination; in Vonnegut's world, despair was based on the discrepancy between wishes and facts; in Beckett's world, even wishing is beyond man's grasp.

This existential ignorance and impotence insure a condition of loneliness too; unable to see or hear, unable to move, and thus, like Molloy's deaf and dumb mother, almost completely cut off from the outside world, Beckett's characters are being apart. This isolation is at its most superficial a social and physical fact—Malone and Molloy are locked up in their rooms, the Murphy of "Fizzle 1" trapped in the wet-stone gloom of an underground labyrinth, each man an individual, an integer, alike but apart and cut off from those who surround him. But in Beckett the atomistic reduction is further extended, the integer itself split asunder, the estrangement becoming a self-estrangement, an apartness from self. That "mist," after all, "veils" not only the world from Molloy, but Molloy from himself, the mind, or perhaps more accurately the voice, severed from the body and, to an extent, from the emotions as well. The room within which the voice is trapped has become the body within which the voice is trapped, an existential prison. "You may say that it is all in my head," Malone asserts, "and indeed sometimes it seems to me I am in a head. . . . But thence to conclude the head is mind, no, never."

By condition ignorant, by condition impotent, by condition alone; an obsessive voice, "crying out more or less piercingly," unable to escape a decaying body, a suffering self—that is Beckett's vision of man, a vision that, embraced with a curious enthusiasm, admits of no qualifying alternatives. There is, in fact, in both authors discussed above, a similar relentlessness, not only an accord on the general meanness and meaningless of existence, but a similarly obsessive repetition of the evidence. Like Moran, who has "an extremely sensitive ear" yet "no ear for music," they play the same dissonant note again and again, until the reader begins to understand that to hear that note is to hear the score, that the "whole" in the anti-heroic novel tends to be equal to merely one of its parts. Vonnegut's books, for example, usually consist of many, short, generically identical passages, passages anecdotal in nature and ironic in tone and whose punchline conclusions always serve to evoke the pathetic qualities of the characters described: section after section of sadly comic put-downs.

And Beckett, as would be expected, extends this approach to its furthest limits; for when Molloy says, "You would do better, at least no worse, to obliterate texts than to blacken margins, to fill in the holes of words till all is blank and flat and the whole ghastly business looks like what is, senseless, speechless, issueless misery," he is in effect describing Beckett's own fictional style. Beckett writes his words, but then fills them in; he makes a statement, then denies its truth; he creates characters only to reduce them in stature; he floats dim hopes only to obliterate them. And this strategy of relentless negation eventually infiltrates the narrative itself. After all, if Molloy, Moran, Malone are incompetent and ignorant, can their first-person narrations be at all reliable? If every fact reported is called into question, can any of the story be accepted as true? The answer to a purist like Beckett is an obvious no; even the doubts must be called into doubt, the text "obliterated" along with the story it tells, and thus Moran is made to undermine the credibility of his entire narrative by using his last words to deny his first: "I . . . wrote, 'It is midnight. The rain is beating on the windows.' It was not midnight. It was not raining." [Internal quotes mine.]

Beyond these stylistic similarities, though, the most significant aspect shared by all the books discussed above is their drastically diminished view of man. Men shit and piss and pick their noses, brutalize each other and themselves, but they never dance with grace, never experience beauty, love, satisfaction, are never shown achieving or creating or conquering a problem. Now men do shit and piss and pick their noses, they do brutalize each other and themselves, but that is not all they do; and what are we to say about a literature that limits itself to only those aspects of existence that denies either overtly or by implication any positive quality in human nature? Are we to praise it, as has been the case so often in modern criticism, for its honesty and courage, for what A. Alvarez calls Beckett's "remorseless stripping away of superfluities"? But are love, compassion, wonder, courage really "superfluities"? Are they really irrelevant to the human condition? And is this "stripping away"—so analogous to the stripping away of consciousness from the study of mind in Behaviorism, and of the actual object from the act of creation in conceptual art—really a method that will unveil the truth, or is it, in fact, a method that obscures the truth by denying its complexity?

The problem, then, we begin to see, is not the reductionist author's pessimism per se, but his failure to "earn" his pessimism on the printed page, his stripping away essentials as well as superfluities in presenting his case. Instead of tracing love's defeat, he pretends that love isn't there, that it doesn't exist; instead of creating a world, complex and ambiguous, within which to explore man's ultimate failure, he invents another world, flat and barren, within which failure is prescribed from the start. No one can deny Kurt Vonnegut's right to despair after his experience as a prisoner of war, but if he expects us to accept that view as fundamentally true, his fiction will have to account for more of the evidence, just as even a history of the Holocaust must include and consider the men and women who hid Jews in their homes at the risk of death. But instead we are given a pre-molded, idolatrous fiction, wherein the immeasurable has been reduced to the definite, the complex to the simple, mankind to Billy Pilgrim, reality to Samuel Beckett's exitless room: a fiction which seems to stack the evidence, insisting always on the same final answer.

That this "answer" given by the literature of despair is that there is no answer does not mitigate the charge; the ubiquitous uncertainty promoted by Beckett, after all, is itself a kind of deluding certainty, the same reply again and again to every—*to every*— aspect of existence. And this relentless naysaying is no closer to the truth of things than a relentless yeasaying, Beckett's constant pessimism no less deluding than a Pollyanna optimism; they are, in fact, mirror images of the same perceptual fanaticism, which "strips away" ambiguity at the expense of truth. And it is essential in an age so susceptible to cynicism and despair to grasp this parallel, to understand that a "blackwash" of reality is no truer, no more courageous or honest, than a "whitewash," that both are "cover-ups," that both hide a complex, multiform, and multi-colored canvas and as such constitute a kind of surrender, a forfeiture of the artist's high responsibility to bear witness to an infinite and ambiguous world.

The corrupting consequence of this philosophical surrender
eventually appears in the books themselves, the limit they place on
man ironically invoking a limit on their craft, the resulting repeti-
tiveness of both message and technique diminishing their ability to
elicit a response. As funny and touching as these authors sometimes can be, the longer one reads them, the less effective they
seem to become. Just as Malone, "cowering deep down among [his
sufferings feels] nothing," the reader, immured in Beckett's relentless pessimism, begins to feel nothing. That "piercing" cry, so
rarely relieved by a whisper or a sigh, assaults the ear till the ear
grows deaf, till, in a revealing example of the imitative fallacy, a
literature describing men who are incapable of emotion becomes
itself incapable of evoking emotion—a lifeless text. This connection
between man as failure and an art that fails, between a message of
failure and a failure of effect, has a certain philosophical inevitability. Since fiction is itself a man-made product, any fiction espousing
man's essential incompetence must, if it is at all honest, eventually
espouse its own incompetence. Thence the post-World War II cry,
"The novel is dead!"—for how can any literature exist if man is, in
fact, too existentially ignorant to know his world?

The trap, then, is set and sadly inescapable, the anti-heroic
author a victim of his own premises: a fiction that loses faith in man
must eventually lose faith in itself; a literature of defeat must
eventually become self-defeating and deny its own validity. On the
first page of *Molloy*, the narrative voice admits, "I don't know. The
truth is I don't know much." On page 17 of *Slaughterhouse-Five*, a
two-hundred-page book about a massacre, we read that "there's
nothing intelligent to say about a massacre." The former book ends
with one of the narrators denying the credibility of all he has said;
the latter ends with "all there is to say about a massacre": a bird's
meaningless chirp. The circle, we see, is now complete, the
connection to a pancultural reductionism now drawn clearer; for
the anti-heroic novel provides us with the perfect oxymoronic
analogue to a psychology that denies consciousness and to an art
that has no visual existence: a literature that has nothing to say.

Beyond Despair. The works of Vonnegut and Beckett are just
two examples of an entire body of literature whose basic perspective is one of despair. And the reason for this literature's existence
rests not solely on the traumatic events of our past half century (the

modern age, after all, is hardly unique in its violent history) but also on the acceptance of certain crucial ideas, a mode of thinking, that when made manifest in the very fabric of society, transformed man's view of himself and his world. We can point out the limited value of this reductionist view, how it distorts and deflates human experience, but we can hardly ignore its influence on the modern sensibility. Despair, in this sense, is real. Although a fashion, it is not merely fashionable, not just a quick and inconsequential fad; rather, arising from our most basic assumptions about reality, it lies at the center of our culture, symptomatic of a flaw in our view of the world.

And it is in this sense, too, of course, that the literature of despair *does* (despite its own pose that nothing can be said) have something to say to us. Vonnegut's often hilarious, sad-edged irony, Beckett's suffocating immersion into a traumatized psyche do reflect a real aspect of modern life and have a value we should recognize. But the severe limits of these authors should be recognized as well, limits that too far surpass the inescapable limitations placed on all artists by the nature of their craft. No novel, no fiction writer's oeuvre, can be equal to life, but the literature of despair, in an important way, fails even to approximate life. Just as a series of magnified photos of acne scars tells us too little about a human face, the incredible obsessiveness with which Beckett depicts just one possible state of mind, while admirable perhaps in its clinical accuracy, in the end tells us too little about human experience. One might argue, of course, that a larger metaphor was never intended, but to believe this and at the same time to accept Beckett as a great artist seems an overvaluation of a limited accomplishment and a sad diminution of the potential of art. Our best authors—Melville, Conrad, Faulkner (none of whom could be described as cheery optimists)—have always given us more: more of the whole face of human experience, not just one of its parts.

The literature of despair fails us, then, because, like Behaviorism, its metaphorical world is too specialized and reduced, too abstracted to capture that whole, "felt" truth that the best fiction has always rediscovered for us. By presenting some small truths to the exclusion of all others, by stripping them of any complicating context, it is too much the captive of its own conclusions about reality. The difficult question remains, though, why anyone would choose to champion those conclusions, why despair

is not only reluctantly accepted as in Vonnegut, but enthusiasti-
cally embraced as in Samuel Beckett. Why, at least for a time, did
the violent ending replace the happy ending as the clichéd convention of popular entertainment? Why is it so frequently the case in
this modern age that we, as Molloy, don't "like [the] gloom to
lighten," finding instead something "nourishing" in the "murk"
that surrounds us? Despair, it seems, has its own peculiar consola-
tions and the literature of despair its own peculiar attractiveness to
something basic in human nature. The tyrant-within craves his
cartoon reality, the secret idolater his hand-sized god; fearful and
anxious, we beg for simple and predictable answers, a resolution of
the tension that is the enduring cost of the gift of consciousness. It
is a measure of our essential insecurity that we are tempted to
accept even the blackest world view if it simultaneously succeeds
in simplifying reality; and it is exactly this form of *perceptual*
security, this reduction to certainty, that despair and its literature
offer us: the hand-sized god, the cartoon realm, Stalin's unchanging
room where all things sit in their appointed place.

That this god may be defined as malevolent, that life in Stalin's
cell may prove utterly barren, seems, to some, less important than
an end to the anxiety that inevitably comes from trying to judge an
ambiguous world. Like Murphy in "Fizzle 1," who shuts his eyes
rather than stare into the gloom to search for light, the man of
despair also closes his eyes and, by prejudging his world black,
spares himself the potential disappointment of a continued search.
And here we begin to see the special temptation of a bleak world
view, what "blind" despair offers that "blind" faith can't. Bad news,
after all, is less traumatic if expected, and for those unable to
tolerate anxiety, hope is, as Moran calls it, a "hellish" experience.
Thus, like a julted lover who chooses to assume that all women are
liars in order to spare himself the chance of being hurt again, the
despairing man chooses to assume that all life is miserable in order
to spare himself those traumatic disappointments he fears. Despair, then, in a world of uncertain rewards and punishments, is
embraced by the fearful as a defense against pain; but it is a
desperate and self-deluding defense that accepts a dull imprisonment, a shutdown of the senses, as a hedge against emotional
collapse. For just as a society unable to cope with uncertainty
surrenders itself to the rule of a tyrant, so does a man unable to cope

with anxiety surrender himself to the tyrant-within. Malone's room mirrors Stalin's room mirrors Stalin's reign.

It is to this same impoverished room that the anti-heroic authors condemn us—to a stripped and barren cell of their own invention, a cell which, they imply, is an apt metaphor for the larger reality we share. But in the end, despite occasional flashes of recognition, that metaphor is more alien than familiar—alien because it is too simple and sure, because instead of staring out, its authors seem to write as Murphy lives, with their eyes closed, advocates ahead of time of a point of view. Theirs is a self-confirming, stereotyped world, an abstracted world of limited options, of final answers; as such, it constitutes a kind of philosophical propaganda and becomes, in the end, too much a form of genre literature—the genre of despair.

But we do not need more genre literature or more propagandist art; we do not need a fiction that eviscerates truth by making it simply equivalent to unhappiness. Living in a complex and confusing world, we are already too vulnerable to simpleminded solutions, to strategies of comprehension that mill down all the diverse data of life into neatly categorized, homogenous pellets—the computer's binomial zero and one, the paranoid's capitalized Us and Them—reductions which, if pleasing in their simplicity, violate the nature of our experience, implying a "flatter" reality than actually exists. What we *do* need, and what, in fact, great literature provides, is a counteracting force, an antidote to the very reductionism that so dominates our everyday lives. In a world raucous with solutions, we don't need more answers but a restoration of life's raw data, an act of perception that, exposing our idols as pale simulacra, evokes the primary experience of existence in all its fullness. It is experience, not abstraction, that great art offers, and although the great author, in fact, may have a philosophical perspective, it is not his "message" that makes him special but his mimetic talent, his ability to see and make us see the experience of life as it actually is—less reduced than whole, less explained than felt: the *subjective* truth of the world we share. And he reminds us, by recapturing the wholeness of that subjective truth, that life is always more than our "ideas" about it, always much more than any final meaning we choose to assign it.

"Know the truth," Jesus said to the men who questioned him,

"and the truth will make you free"; but to know the truth in a world so wonderous, so frightening, so uncertain and varied, so immense and pulsing with intensity is no simple matter of answers or beliefs. Reality will never be as safe or certain as we wish it to be, as we pretend it to be; and if we are not the "slaves to sin" whom Jesus described, we are—all of us at times—slaves to our insecurity. To be free, to know the truth, we must somehow escape the idolatrous illusions we invent for ourselves; to be wise and to be good, to act truly and to act well, we must first see the world as it actually is, make that difficult search for the reality of things. The special gift and moral significance of serious fiction rest in its ability to enact that search, to seduce us, through its evocative depiction of other men and women, into an expanded view of that larger world which lurks beyond the habit-shrunk borders of our everyday lives. Good fiction forces us to be more than ourselves, makes us a little less finite in this infinite universe, and is, therefore, like evolution itself, an expression of life's highest aspirations. The literature of despair, however, insists on the futility of those aspirations, on restricting that search; it insists on making us *less* than we are: will-less Billy Pilgrims, impotent Malones, faint stick figures in a cartoon void. It preaches the simplest answer of all: that there is no answer and therefore no reason to hope.

Times change, of course, and with them fashions; the bleak vision of life that peaked in the sixties already is losing its popularity. A simple reflexive reaction, however, a mirror-image swing of fashion's pendulum, is not a sufficient response to the challenges posed by the literature of despair. The goal is not to replace a bleak formula with a benign one, but a fiction without formulas. The goal is not to overthrow a grim-visaged idol for a smiling one, but an idol-less literature. For as plants reach out to colonize the open spaces, as all life reaches out in time and space to invade the unknown, so must our best fiction dare to extend itself in its exploration for the truth. And this exploration demands flexibility; it demands, above all else, a refusal to preclude any possibility, the artist pressed right up against that permeable border between himself and creation, eyes open all the time. The compass of awe includes both terror and joy and the palpable uncertainty which will occur; the literature of awe, like all true explorations, is a mapless journey whose end is obscure. But if we are to rescue ourselves from the tyrant-within, from the perceptual idols we ceaselessly invent, it is a journey we must have the courage to make. Whether we are left with the secure apathy of Beckett's room or the uncertain hopes of an infinite world, whether we are left with a fiction of negation which must eventually deny even its own validity or a fiction of creation which, risking failure, insists on becoming more than its words, depends on us—and there is no escaping our responsibility. As writers, as readers, as heirs and witnesses to the human condition, we must, by default or volition, choose an attitude to the life we've been given: the surrender of despair or the ambition of art, a literature of idols or a literature of awe.

🔥 🔥 🔥

TRINC: PRAISES II

by THOMAS McGRATH

from THE ARK and COPPER CANYON PRESS

nominated by THE ARK

for Tomasito

Once, when the grand nudes, golden as fields of grain—
But touched with a rose flush like homeric cliches of dawn!—
Dreamed in prudential calm above the parochial lightning
Of bad whiskey;
   and when the contentious and turbulent General,
Handcrafted of fringed buckskin, legend, aromatic gunsmoke,
On the Greasygrass Little Bighorn lay down his long blond hair
At last at peace
   in his quiet kingdom:
      over the back-bar:
Then: the myth of Beer was born and the continental thirst!

O Beer we praise thee and honor thy apostalic ways!
Primero: for the glory of thy simple and earthy ancestors! As:
Instance: the noble Barley, its hairy and patriarchal
Vigor: golden
   in the windy lagers of manfarmed machine-framed fields;
Or in shocks or stooks
    tented
      like Biblical tribes
       bearded

(But without the badrap of their barbaric god) gay,
Insouciant as encampments of the old Oglalla Sioux
Where each lodge opens eastward to the Land of the Morning
   Sun!

Praise for:
            segundo: the lacy and feminine elegance of the hops
Raising into the sun their herbal essence, medicinal,
Of the scent of the righttime rain fallen on rich earth.
They lift their tiny skirts—of Linnean Latin made!
Like those great nudes of the barrooms: souls of the newborn
   beer!

And we praise also Yeast: the tireless marine motors
Of its enigmatic enzymes, and its esters: like the submarine stars
Of astral rivers and horoscopic estuaries shining.

And we praise, last, the secret virtue of pure water,
A high lord among the Five Elements, gift of the heavens,
Its mineral integrity and the savor of secret iron!
Guitars are distilled from wine: from the politics of moonlight,
From the disasters of tequila and the edible worm in the deep
   well
Of mescal.
            But from beer come banjos and jazz bands ecstatic
Trumpets midnight Chicago early thirties Bix.

It was Beer that invented Sunday from the long and salty days
Of the workday week:
                  that from the fast beer on horseback or the warm
Beer of the burning fields of the harvest, when the barley comes
   in,
Fermented the Sabbatarian leisure;
                     that, in the eye of the workstorm,
For the assemblyline robotniki and the miner who all week long
Must cool his thirst at the root of the dark flower of the coal
Offered reprieve;
                  and for slow men on tractors (overalled
And perpetually horny) turned off their motors for the Sabbath
   calm.

It is farther from Sunday to Monday than to any other day of the
   week.
And Monday begins farther from home than a month of Sundays.
It begins in a deeper darkness than other days, and comes
From farther away, but swifter, to the sound of alarums and
   whistles.
Six hours ahead of the sun it appears: first in dreams
Where we shudder, smelling the strength of sweat from the
   earlier east,
(Already at hard labor) and our sleep is filling with fireflies
From ancient forges, the hot sparks flying; then
It appears as grief for a lost world: that round song and commune
When work was a handclasp—before it built fences around us.
Monday is a thief: it carries in its weak and tiny fist,
A wilted flower wrenched from our Sunday garden . . . still blue
With hope: but fast fading in the heat of his metal grasp.

Tuesday is born and borne like an old horse, coming
Home to the stall from the salt of the harvest fields, where,
   hitched
To sun and stubble, flyplagued and harness galled, sweatcrusted,
(The lather from under his collar whitening the martingales)
Teamed up he lugged the stammering machines through the
   twenty one-mile rounds
On the slowly narrowing field . . .
                         Tuesday comes without flowers—
Neither Queen Anne's lace nor even Yarrow or Golden Rod—
(Most colorless of all the days of our week and work)
                         without thunder,
(Like the old horse too tired to roll in the dust)
                         without even
The anguish of Monday exile. It follows us home from our work.

Wednesday is born in the midweek waste like the High Sierra
Rising out of the desert, Continental Divide
In the long division of the septimal and sennight thirst;
                         from where,
At Bridger's Pass or near Pike's Peak, at the last pine,
Cold, in the Wednesday snow, we halt for a moment and see:
Faraway, shining, the saltwhite glow of that Promised Land:

The Coast of Sunday—
               gold and maltgold—
                      beyond Thursday's Mohave heat.

But Thursday is born in that mid-point halt at the hinge of the
    week
Where we seem too tired to push open the ancient five-barred
    gate
That lets on flowery holts and heaths and the faraway antic hay
Where leisure sprawls and dances in the fair of work-free fun . . .
Here thirst compounds his salty rectitudes: in Skinny Thursday:
That midweek Dog Day curse in Monday's cast-off shoes!

Friday is born in desperation, in the shadow of parables,
In the tent of Surplus Value, in the hot breath of Profit.
Yet it cometh forth as a fawn, yea as a young lamb
It danceth on prophetic mountains whose feet the Jordan laves!
Here is the time of the Dream Drinking, where our loves and
    needs
Come under the same roof-tree.
                 Evening of hope.
                 Freer
Than manic Saturday and more adventurous than Sunday's calm.
Now we cast lots for our workweek clouts or put them in pawn!
And the night opens its enormous book wherein we invent our
    lives . . .
 Saturday's children had far to go. We arrive as strangers
Entering the Indian Nation in the paycheck's prairie schooner,
Homesteaders in the last free land of the West . . .
                 Already
The Sooners, those Johnny-Come-Earlies and claim jumpers
On the choicest barstools assert their squatter's rights . . .
They claim (these Dream Drinkers)—40 acres and a mule
Or a King Ranch bigger than all of Texas!
                 It is Time they would
Reclaim from the burntout wagon train of the workweek waste.
Here each is Prince in his Castle Keep, but, outside, Time
Elaborates warp and woof and the ancient Enemies gather . . .
O blessed Beer, old Equalizer—doom for Comanches:
Shot down on Saturday's mesa in the flash of a 6 pack of Schlitz!

Deadflower, harness, halt-in-the-snow, dogday, holy hour!
By these five signs and passages we knew the laboring week
As we travelled and travailled toward Castle Keep, Companyeros
    Trabajeros!
And now, where Sundays buzz like flies caught in a web,
Drained of their workday strength, the golden spirit of Beer
Comes by to lead us out of the net, if only a moment,
To where Possibility rolls out its secret roads
To picnic places where Potato Salad and the Olive and the Onion
And Ham-and-Cheese sandwiches position the kids on the grass;
Or to lazy creeks or lakes where the lunkers lounge and lunge,
Guides us;
            or into the popcorn smell and afternoon rituals
Of baseball fields shills us
                  where forever the high homer,
Smoking, of the great stars, writes their names on the sky. . .
And later, the firefly-lighted evenings, on back porches—
The vegetable lightning of those small stars caught in the
    grass. . .

Beer, birra, la biere, tiswin, pivo, cerveza—
In all its names and forms, like a polymorphic god praise!
As, among Mexican stars and guitars: *Cresta Blanca*
And *Cuautemoc*: to be drunk under Popocatepetl
And Xochimilco;
        and *Fix*
(named for Fuchs) in Greece,
Either in Aumonia Square where the poor go or in Syntagma
Where the umbrellas gather the bourgeoisie in their shade;
And *San Miguel* where the Philippines offer expendable chickens;
And *Heinekin* cold as the Hans Brinker canals where the Dutch
Are skating around on tulips and wooden shoes; and *Pilsener*
Resurrected from Nazi and allied bombings, old-world gold,
Of the Czechs and Slavs;
               and all the melodious beers of Spain;
And of England, land of the mild and bitter: *O'Keefe's* and
    Watney's Ales;
And, of Ireland, *Guinness Stout* with its arms of turf and gunfire;
And Australia's *Melbourne Bitter* from way down under!

Beer which passes through vats like the multiple stomachs of
    ruminants
To be lagered in sunken cloisters in monkish gloom till the day
When, on the brewery dray, it is ceremonially borne
Through the sunny morning towns by those great and noble
    beasts
Those horses with necks of thunder and fetlocks like hairy paint
    brushes.

Beer of Milwaukee! Beer of St. Louis! Where Lewis and Clark
Passed in the days of the furtrade and the wide ranging
    voyageurs.
And pass still, like ghosts, day after day, unseen
And forgotten: still hunting that West that was lost as soon as
    found—
Legends in search of a legend:
                    As the new beers of the West
Lucky and *Lone Star, Olympia, Grain Belt, Coors*
Seek the phantom perfection of the mythic beers of the past!
Beer, not to be sipped but lifted against the palate—
Like the mystical cargo of argosies: lofted into the holds
Where the hideaway ports of the Spanish Main set their
    top-gallants
To drag their island-anchors into the New World!

Comestible beer that puts the hop in the Welsh Rabbit!
Beer-soup-du-jour that causes the cheese to sing!
Beer that transmogrifies the evening's peasant pot roast!
That metamorphizes the onion in the Sunday carbonnade!

Praise, then, for *pulque* and *kvass*, for *chang*, for *weissbier*
For *suk* and *sonshu*, for *bousa* and all the hand-me-down
Home brews!
            No firewater, aqua forte, blast-head or forty-rod
But heart medicine: made for Fast Days or fiesta:
For the worker in his vestments of salt at the end of our laboring
    days,
Or for corroboree and ceilidh where the poem sings and says:
Praise for the golden liquor of Wakan Tanka or god!

Praise for its holy office—O offer hosanna and laud!
By sip, by sup, by tot, by tipple, by chuglug—*all* ways:
Hallelujah! For the People's Beer! And for all His comrades:
    praise!

FAITH

fiction by ELLEN WILBUR

from THE VIRGINIA QUARTERLY REVIEW

nominated by Joyce Carol Oates

I WAS CHRISTENED Faith Marie after my mother's favorite sister, who died of Parkinson's disease the week before her 18th birthday, and whose memory has been preserved with stories of her courage and kindness that always inspired me as a girl. "The good die young," my mother used to sigh, whenever she mentioned Auntie Fay, and the saying always worried me. I wanted to be good. It was the one success I could imagine. While I was young, I tried to be as good as I could be, and for as long as my father lived, I gave him little trouble. I was his pride, my mother used to say. If he hadn't died of a stroke in his sleep that Sunday afternoon ten years ago, my life would never have taken the turn it did.

Were father and mother alive today, I know we'd be living just the same as always. We'd be rising at six and retiring at eleven seven days a week. Father would be winning at checkers, gin rummy, and hearts, and mother and I would still be trying to beat him. On Thursday nights we'd eat out at one of the same three restaurants we always went to, and father would be manager of Loudon Bank and Trust, where he hardly missed a day for 30 years. Wherever he went, he'd be making a grand impression with the profound conviction of his voice and the power of his penetrating eyes, which could see right into a man. And all the anger in him, which he rarely expressed, would still be stored at the back of his eyes or in the edge of his voice, so that even when he laughed you'd know he wasn't relaxed. He never was relaxed, no matter how he tried. I know I'd be dressed like a proper school girl, conservative and neat in cotton or wool dresses, never pants, my long hair pinned at the sides and rippling down my back or tied up in a braid for church or holidays or dinners out, but never short and boyish the way I wear it now. I'd be odorless and immaculate as ever, without an inkling of a body. And people would still be saying what a graceful girl I was. The way I moved was more like floating. The way I'd walk across our lawn, carrying a frosted glass of mother's minted tea out to the hammock where father read his evening paper in the summer before dinner. Sipping his drink and surveying the mowed yard and trimmed bushes and ever blooming flowers (which were my mother's work), he'd tousle my hair and sigh, "Now this is the life," as if he nearly believed it. Listening to him, I know I'd be as pale as ever with the face of a girl who lives as much in books as in the world. And I'd feel as far removed from father and that yard as if each page of history or poetry I'd ever read were another mile I'd walked away from home, and each word I learned another door that closed behind me. Though I'd know, no matter what I read, that my mind would never countermand my conscience or overrule my heart. Looking at me, my father's eyes would turn as warm as ever, the way they only seemed to do when he looked at me. Not even at my mother, whose whole mind and heart had been amended, geared to please him, would he ever look that way without a trace of anger or suspicion. But when he'd look at me I'd see the love he'd never put in words and the faith I'd never disappoint him. I hoped I never would. To keep the peace, his, my mother's and my own, was such a need I had that had they lived I'm sure the three of us would have passed from Christmas to Christmas, through the dips and peaks of every year, like a ship that's traveling the same circle where the view is always familiar.

I remember one Sunday father and I were walking home from church all finely dressed and fit to impress whomever we passed. We crossed the green at the center of town and were approached by a pretty girl no more than 20, who was singing at the top of her voice. She smiled at us as she went by, leaving a strong soprano trill in our ears. I wasn't surprised when father turned to look at her, outraged. "Now that's the kind of bitch I'd like to see run out of town," he said. I knew he'd say the same to mother or me if we ever crossed or disappointed him. Because he couldn't tolerate the slightest deviation from his rules. He loved me with all of his heart on the condition that I please him.

Poor mother couldn't live without father. He'd been the center of her life for 30 years. Unlike father, whose beliefs were sacred to him, she had no strong opinions of her own. When he died, she wept with fear as much as grief, as if his death had been a shattering explosion that left our house and town in ruins. She sat all day in his easy chair and couldn't be moved, as if all of her habits as well as her heart were permanently broken. My words and tears never touched her. Exactly like the garden flowers she used to cut to decorate the house, she faded a little more each day. And it was only two months after father was gone that she was laid beside him. She was buried in June, the week before our high school graduation.

Compton people who wouldn't speak to me today were concerned and kind when mother died. There were several families that offered me a home. But I was 18, old enough to be on my own, and more at ease in the drawing rooms of novels than I'd ever be in any Compton house. Today there are many in town who believe it was a great mistake, letting me live alone. But I was adamant about it, and I appeared to be as responsible and as mature as any valedictorian of her class is expected to be.

I was as shaken by my parents' death as if the colors of the world had all been changed. Having adjusted myself to my father's wishes for so many years, I had no other inclination. After he was gone, I continued to live exactly as he would have liked me to. If anything, I was more careful not to hurt him than before, as if in death his feelings had become more sensitive than ever and the burden of his happiness was entirely left to me. After mother's death and the end of school, I took the first available job in town at Compton library. I was grateful that the work suited me, because I would have taken any job to keep me busy.

Our town of Compton is a tourist town. For three months out of every year the population triples, and Decatur street is a slow parade of bodies and cars that doesn't end for 90 days. At the end of June, the summer people come. In their enormous yachts and their flashy cars, they arrive. Every year it is a relief to see them come and then a relief to see them go. They are so different from us.

Compton people are short on words. Even in private with their closest kin, the talk is sparse and actions have more meaning. Whenever father was troubled, mother made him a squash pie or one of his other favorites to indicate her sympathy or support. She never asked him to explain. If a man in Compton is well-liked, he'll never have to buy himself a drink at the taverns. By the little favors, by the number of nods he receives on the street, or by the way he is ignored as much as if he were dead, he'll know exactly what his measure is with people. And by the silences, by whether there is comfort or communion in the long pauses between sentences, he'll know exactly how close he is to an acquaintance. I've always known that Compton people were unique. Our women never chattered the way the summer women do, as if there were no end to what they'd say. I've seen the summer people's children awed and muted by the grave reserve and the repressed emotion of a Compton child. And I've seen the staring fascination of all Compton with the open manner of the summer people, who wander through the streets at noon, baring their wrinkled thighs, their cleavage and their bulges to the sun for everyone to see—a people whose feelings flash across their faces as obvious and naked as if they had no secrets. As a child, I used to wander down to watch them at the docks. They seemed as alien and entertaining as a circus troupe. At five o'clock, from boat to boat, there was the sound of ice and glasses, the smell of tonic water, shaving lotion, lipstick, and perfume. For evening the women dressed in shocking pink and turquoise, colors bright enough to make a Compton woman blush. There was always laughter interwoven with their conversation, and the liquor made the laughter louder and the talk still freer until the people were leaning into each other's faces or

falling into embraces with little cries of "darling" or "my dear."
And as I watched them, the gaiety, the confidence, and the warmth
of these people always inspired me with affection and yearning for
the closeness and the freedom that they knew. It wasn't till I was
older I realized that all of their words and embraces brought them
no closer to each other than Compton people are—that the distances between them were just as painful and exactly as vast, in
spite of the happy illusion they created.

The summer mother died, I walked to work through the crowds
to the rhythm of the cash registers, which never stopped ringing
till ten o'clock at night in the restaurants and gift shops all along
Decatur Street. And all summer the library, which is a busy place
in winter, was nearly empty. I sat at the front desk in the still, dark
room, listening to the commotion of cars and voices in the streets.
And through the windows I could tell the weather in the patch of
sky above the heavy laden elms whose leaves were never still, but
trembled, bobbed, and shuddered to every slightest nuance of the
air. And seemed to capture and proclaim the whole vitality of every
day more truly and completely than any self-afflicted human soul
could ever hope to render it. I have no other memory of that
summer, which disappeared as quickly as it came. But the end of
every Compton summer is the same. Even the most greedy
merchants are frazzled and fatigued by the daily noise and the
rising exuberance of the tourists passing down the coast to home.
By then, the beaches and the streets are strewn with cans and
papers, as if the town had been a carnival or a zoo, and Compton is
glad to see the last of the crowd, whose refuse is only further
evidence of the corruption of their pleasure-happy souls.

My first winter alone there were many nights when I cried
myself to sleep. I missed my mother's quiet presence in the house,
and the smells which always rose from the warm, little kitchen
where she baked or washed or sat across from me on winter
afternoons when I came in from school. Even for a Compton
woman she was more than usually quiet, so shy that she had no
friends. She went to church on Sunday but the rest of the week she
hardly left the yard. My father shopped for all of our food to save
her the pain of going out in public. If she'd had her way, she'd
never have eaten out with us on Thursday nights. But father
insisted on it. "She needs the change," he used to say.

I don't remember mother ever raising her voice to me in anger.

All discipline was left to father. She didn't often kiss or hug me either. But she used to brush my hair one hundred strokes a night, and I remember the gentle touch of her hands. There were times when her shyness made her seem as self-effacing as a nun, and times when I thought I must be living with a saint, the way she read her Bible daily and seemed to have no selfish desires or worldly needs. She dressed in greys and browns, and her dresses hung loose on her bony frame. Though her face was usually serious if not sad, I always believed she was happy in her life with father and me. She couldn't do enough for us, particularly father. About her past I only knew that she was born of alcoholic parents who were now both dead, that she'd worshipped her sister, Faith, and that she never corresponded with her other sister, Mary, who lived in California and was also alcoholic. Most often mother didn't like to reminisce. If I asked her a question she didn't like, she didn't answer it. There were some weeks when she spoke so little that if she hadn't read aloud to me, I hardly would have heard her voice. It was her reading aloud at night that I missed the most after she was gone. It was a habit we kept from before I could read to myself, when to hear her speak page after page was a luxury as soothing and as riveting as any mystery unravelling itself to revelation. It was through the sound of her voice speaking someone else's words that I knew my mother best.

Many nights I cried with all the fear and passion of the child I was and would ever have remained had I been given a choice. And, with a child's love, I saw the images of my father and mother rise up in the dark above my bed as clear and painfully defined as the impression they had left upon my heart. For the simplicity of my old life, I also cried. The simple life of a child who wants to please. For I recognized myself among the spinster women of our town, of whom there are many. Women who never leave the houses of their stern fathers and their silent, sacrificing mothers, houses of a kind so prevalent in Compton. Daughters with all of the rebellion driven out of them at an early age, all of the rudeness skimmed away, severely lashed and molded by the father's anger and the mother's fear of all the changing values in the sinful world. Many of our Compton spinsters are sensitive, high strung. You can see they were the children who avoided pain, preferred endearments and affection. They rarely gossip the way the married women do. To their mothers and their fathers they are faithful and devoted to the end, loyal to the present and the past, forgetful of the future. So much I see about them now that I didn't know when I counted myself one of them.

I had one friend from childhood, Mary Everly, who was studying to be a nurse in a city 50 miles away. Though she sometimes wrote to me, she never came home, finding Compton a "stifling" place. I was close to no one else in town. A few months after mother died, the invitations to supper and the concerned calls from neighbors stopped. Like my mother, I was shy. I had no skill at small talk and was relieved to be left in peace. But I analyzed myself the way a lonely person wonders why he is not loved. And I studied my life until I was as far removed from it as if I had been carved and lifted out of Compton and left to hover like a stranger over everything familiar.

Two times I went to visit Father Ardley in his blue-walled office at the vestry, and twice the touch of his thumb on my forehead, where he signed the cross, brought me to tears. I was drawn to the love of the church. I had an unexamined faith in God, but a fear that His demands would be crushing, were I to take them to heart. It was an irrational fear I tried to explain to Father Ardley, whose eyes were as cold as a winter sky while his voice was like the sun warming it. "You are still in mourning Faith," he said to me. "Such a loss as you've suffered can't be gotten over quickly. You must pray to God and keep yourself busy, child," he said, though I had never been idle in my life, not ever then or now.

For seven years I was as busy as I could be. My conscience kept me well supplied with tasks, and there is no end to what a person ought to do. I worked at the library. I lived in my father's house. I baked for the church bazaars. I visited Father Ardley. The summer people came and left as regular as the tides. I had as many warm acquaintances as ever, and I had no close friends. I still wrote letters to Mary Everly, who was now a nurse, married, and living in Cincinnati with her second baby on the way. Though the memory of my parents' love sustained me, and my father's wishes continued to guide me, time diluted their power to comfort me. Some mornings, walking through the sunny streets to work, the thought of death would take me by surprise, and I knew that mine would mean no more to anyone in town than the sudden disappearance of a picket fence on Elm street or a missing bed of flowers in Gilbey Park.

I never went out with men. Not that I wasn't attractive. My father used to tell me I was pretty, and Mrs. Beggin at the library said I was a "lovely looking girl" and she couldn't see why I wasn't married yet. But Compton men knew different. Something they saw behind my shyness frightened them away. Something my mother and father had never seen. For beneath it all I wasn't a normal Compton woman, not typical no matter how I tried to be. Whether it was the influence of the summer people or the hours I had escaped in books, I was always "different" as far as Compton men could see, and they were just as strange to me.

It was the eighth summer after mother's death that I met Billy Tober. I was just 26. William Tober IV, his family had named him. He was a summer boy, four years younger than I, a college student, though his eyes were the shallow blue of a flier or a sailor. I noticed him before he ever noticed me. I'd always see him with a different girl with the same smile on his lips. He began to come to the library many afternoons. He liked poetry and novels, and he'd ask me for suggestions. I was surprised when he began to appear at the end of the day to walk me home. It wasn't long before we began to meet in the evenings too.

I wish I could say that I remember Billy well, and I wish that I could describe him clearly. But I can't remember much that he ever said and barely how he looked. I only remember the effect he had upon me. As if I knew how it would end, I never invited him to my house, and I'd only allow him to walk me halfway home, which made him laugh at first. In the evening, I'd meet him at Gilbey Park, which is just outside the center of Compton. It is a pretty hill of bushes, trees, and flowers which overlooks the harbor. On a hidden bench we sat and sipped the wine that Billy always brought. Though I'd never tasted liquor or sat and talked with a young man, I was completely at ease. The wine and dusky out-of-doors loosened my tongue until my hidden thoughts rose up as urgently as if my life depended on telling them. It often surprised me what I said, because whenever I was with Billy I was a different woman, so unlike my usual self I'm sure no one in Compton would have recognized me. It was as natural as breathing, the way I'd change into a giddy girl whenever I was with him. I fed on his flattery and couldn't get enough of it. "Where did you ever get such hair?" he asked about the curls my mother never let me cut. After that, it was my eyes he noticed. My neck was regal as a queen's, he said. And there was pride as well as grace in the way I walked. My hands, the smallness of my waist, my legs, my voice he also praised. I couldn't hear enough. For the month of July, we saw each other every night. At home, I'd often stare for an hour at the stranger in the mirror, this woman with a body that a man desired.

Whatever it is that attracts a man to a woman I've too little experience to know. But I believe that for Billy every woman was a challenge. To win her heart as well as her body was his goal. He was as restless and driven a person as I've known. Obsession with a woman must have soothed him. He used to tell me that he loved me, but I'm sure that if he'd heard the same from me, his feelings would have died. If I had loved him, I would have told him. He begged me often enough to say it. But I never was able to. "We're too different," I insisted. "I'm not myself when I'm with you." But I gloried in the power he'd given me. I was in love with his desire, which singled me out from all the world and made the world a painless kingdom where I ruled the more he wanted me. We met most nights in August. We drove out to Haskall Beach to a private place I knew. By then we hardly spoke, and there were times, with his breath hot on my face and his voice crying my name, I felt I'd be more comforted and serene if I were sitting there alone and free of all the yearning human arms can cause.

All those nights we spent together, I never took precautions. "Is it safe?" he asked me many times. But I ignored the question, as if it would have been the crowning sin if I'd been careful to prevent any meaning or possibility of love to come out of the fire of vanity and ignited pride which burned between us. Driving back to town, the silence in the car was so oppressive that it taunted us.

The day that Billy left, I felt relieved, and in the weeks that followed, I didn't miss him once, which surprised me. We wrote no letters to each other. Life went back to normal, and the longer he was gone the more I began to hope I'd never see him again.

When doctor Filser told me I was pregnant, I could see he was surprised the way all Compton would be. I saw the way he looked at me with new, appraising eyes, and I burned to think of all the other eyes that would be privy to scenes of Billy and me on

Haskall Beach. For I knew they'd piece it all together down to every detail.

When I told Father Ardley the news, I aimed the words and threw them at him one by one like darts. But his tone was not what I expected. He wasn't angry with me. "I suppose it was that summer boy you were seeing," he sighed, and he knew enough not to suggest the marriage he'd have insisted upon had Billy Tober been a Compton boy. Instead, he gave me the name of Brighton Adoption Agency.

For all of the nine months, I carried the child as if it were a sin beyond forgiveness and there was no forgetting or ignoring it. I felt my father's wrath in every room of the house, and I never visited his or my mother's graves, knowing the affront it would be. As if they had died again, I felt bereft. I was sure they wanted no part of me now and that I could never turn to them again.

Compton people were not so harsh. One hundred years ago they might have stoned me or run me out of town. Now, as much as they disapproved, they also pitied me. No one tried to deprive me of my job. Though there were some who would no longer speak to me, there were more whose pity moved them to be kinder than before. My humiliation was enough for them and lesson enough for their children. When they saw that my cross was sufficiently heavy, they approved. Even today, times when my heart is light and I'm tempted to laugh in public, I check myself. I know I'll always be on good behavior in Compton, and the more abject I appear the better off I'll be.

It is two o'clock, the last day of May, a Saturday, and all of the windows in the house are open for the first time this season. There is a cold breeze coming off the harbor, running through the rooms in currents which break against the walls and boil the curtains halfway to the ceiling. Every year it is the same, the day of opening the windows. The sea wind scours every corner of the house until its heavy atmosphere is broken. All of the memories which hang in odors are borne away until the rooms are only rooms and this woman, dreaming at a littered kitchen table, is just as relieved as if she'd just received communion, left all of her habits at the altar rail, and returned to her pew with no identity but her joy.

It is so quiet. The baby is asleep upstairs under a pink quilt. When he wakes, he will have roses in his cheeks. He is so blonde, his hair is nearly white. He bears no likeness to my family, and yet the night he was born I knew he was mine as surely as these arms or thoughts belong to me. After the pain of labor, as if I had been delivered of all shame, I asked to see the child. When I saw two waving arms, a tiny head, my heart rose up, amazed. And when they put him in my arms, it was love I held, all warmly wrapped, alive.

So many tired-looking mothers you see in Compton. They hardly seem to care how they appear. Wearing shabby clothes, herding their little broods across the streets, worried and snapping orders at them. But a Compton woman never shows her deepest feelings to the world. When Paul was first at home, I used to kiss his little face at least a hundred times a day. Who but an infant or God could stand so much affection? And all of those kisses were just the beginning of love, the first expression of my newly seeded heart which bloomed, expanded, and flowered with every kiss.

At five o'clock I'd pick the baby up from Mrs. Warren who cared for him the hours I worked. We'd ride home on a crowded bus of Compton women in their fifties, carefully dressed, who rested their heavy bodies behind a row of shopping bags. When they saw the child, their eyes grew soft and bright. "What a love," they'd say, all smiles, and they'd ask his name or age and touch the corner of his blanket so gingerly, with reverence, as if he were to them the fearful treasure he was to me, and they had forgotten all of the strain, the distraction, the heavy weight of care which had exalted them and only remembered how close they once had come to perfect love. I could see them in their kitchens years ago, bathing their babies in the little plastic tubs that Compton mothers use. I could imagine them, once so shy and bending to the will of the town, their fathers, and their husbands, becoming fierce and stubborn, demanding so much satisfaction, comfort, and such happiness for their little ones as they had never dreamed of for themselves.

By now I ought to have the kitchen clean, the wash brought in and folded, and the vegetables picked and washed. It is so rare I sit and dream that when I do the memories come fast and heavy as an avalanche. I've known some cynics who remember only pain and ugliness, as if the way a man remembers corresponds with what he hopes. When Paul was born, it changed my past as well as the future. Now, when I look back, I see beauty. The older the memory, the more beautiful it has become. Even moments of great pain or disappointment have been transformed, given an importance and a dignity they never had at the time, as if whatever happens and wherever I have failed may one day be redeemed in the far future. I pray it will be so.

🔥 🔥 🔥

THE CARIBBEAN WRITER AND EXILE

by JAN CAREW

from CALIBAN

nominated by CALIBAN

THERE WAS a traditional format in the classical Akan theatre around which all drama—comedy, tragedy, farce—evolved. The important features of this drama were these: there was an archetypal middle-man and on either side of him were powerful spirits opposing one another. The figure in the middle often stood between malevolent and benign spirits of the ancestral dead, and a host of other spirits that were urbane or demonic, creative or destructive, compassionate or cruel, surrogates of the living or the dead, ethereal or earthy, part saint, part trickster. These spirits were involved in eternal conflicts which could only be resolved if the human being periodically renewed contact with communal wellsprings of rhythm, creation and life.

The Caribbean writer today is a creature balanced between limbo and nothingness, exile abroad and homelessness at home, between the people on the one hand and the creole and the colonizer on the other. Exile can be voluntary or it can be imposed by stress of circumstances; it can be a punishment or a pleasure. The exile can leave home for a short time or he can be expelled forever. The colonizing zeal of the European made indigenous peoples exiles in their own countries—Prospero made Caliban an exile in his. The Caribbean writer by going abroad is, in fact, searching for an end to exile.

This, at first, appears to be a contradiction until one lays bare some of the truths of Caribbean life. The Caribbean person is subject to successive waves of cultural alienation from birth—a process that has its origins embedded in a mosaic of cultural fragments—Amerindian, African, European, Asian. The European fragment is brought into sharper focus than the others, but it remains a fragment. Hiding behind the screen of this European cultural fragment the Caribbean writer oscillates in and out of sunlight and shadows, exile abroad and homelessness at home. At home, he is what C. L. R. James described very aptly as a "twentieth century man living in a seventeenth century economy," (1972) while abroad he is a performer in a circus of civilization.

There are times when he claims that he is a nomad, but this is one of his clever evasions. The irony of it all is that he can only become a nomad when his place in the sun, the speck on the globe that is his home is freed from the economic, psychological and political clutches of usurpers, who had seized it since the beginning of the Columbian era. The spaces that the nomad's imagination encompass exist within a circumference of seasons, and national borders have no meaning for him.

For the Caribbean writer, therefore, to become a true nomad his feet must traverse a territory that his imagination encompasses without let or hindrance. In his country, however, the land, the air-space, the water, the minerals under the earth are owned from abroad and administered by local surrogates; the rights of passage are overtly or covertly restricted. Every new trespass, therefore, is a kind of reckless lurch into a wider indifference. The term Caribbean in this essay describes the island archipelago, the countries on the Caribbean littoral and Guyana, Surinam and Cayenne. Cuba is the exception that proves the rule. Cuba belongs to the Cubans. In Cuba, the northeastern sheet anchor of the Caribbean archipelago, the pre-revolutionary economic relationship between expatriate owners, local surrogates and the majority of people, no longer exists. Cuba is, therefore, a point of reference for us, a living example of how in less than two decades, age-old problems of economic and cultural alienation, race and color, caste, class and identity, can be looked at afresh and in many instances successfully dealt with.

In order to deal with our heritage of exile today, one must return to the beginnings of the Columbian era. Marx had said that history always repeats itself, the first time is tragedy and the next time farce, and in the Caribbean we often appear to be like sleepwalkers reliving the history and repeating the farce.

The early accounts written by European colonizers, about their apocalyptic intrusion into the Amerindian domains, are characterized, with few exceptions, by romantic evasions of truth and voluminous omissions. Have we ever really examined the images that these historical fictions have created of us? If we do so empirically, then we can begin to understand this question of exile abroad and homelessness at home, of the writer.

After Columbus and his sailors were discovered by the Arawakian Lucayos on their beaches in 1492, the Americas of the colonizer came into being as part of both a literary exercise and one of the most appalling acts of ethnocide in recorded history. First, there were Columbus's diaries (the first literary offering of the interlopers), which told us more about the man himself than about the islands he had stumbled upon; and the man revealed to us was a schizoid being, a Janus astride two worlds, one medieval the other of the Renaissance. These diaries are a blend of fantasies fed by writings from the Middle Ages; obsessive ramblings about a new crusade to recapture Jerusalem from the infidel Turks; special pleadings to the sovereigns of Castile; a precise sailor's log and useful scientific observations about the flora, fauna and topography of the lands visited. His writings about the people he met are contradictory, inaccurate, biased and in the midst of pious declarations about converting "natives" to Christianity, sprinkled with asides of racial arrogance and a lust for gold.

Columbus led an early life that was very similar to the one that future Caribbean artists, vagabonds, sailors, writers and immigrants would lead centuries later. In his journey from a nameless street in Genoa to the Portuguese and Spanish courts, he had to cross two centuries. Son of a wool carder, he began his trespass into the fifteenth and sixteenth centuries with little more than great expectations, and his whole life, in fact, was to become a journey to new illusions. He had had to cross not only distances in time and space, but the almost immeasureable gulf between the lower middle class and the nobility. Having made this impossible leap he carried with him a multitude of insecurities and a persistent fear of looking back and acknowledging his lowly beginnings.

On his first journey across the Atlantic, Columbus became prey to the medieval fantasies nurtured like fungus on his narrow Genonese street with its gloomy doorways yawning like entrances to minotaur caves, its shuttered windows and its persistent odours of decay which the sea breezes even now do not seem to dispel completely. As he became more and more convinced that he would survive the Atlantic Crossing, his mind was filled with dreams of golden-roofed palaces on the one-hand, and on the other, a bestiary inhabited by gryphons and by other fabulous creatures, some of which ate human flesh, had human bodies and the snouts of dogs. When he did not find the monsters that medieval writers had dreamed up, Columbus invented a monstrous racial slander: he declared that the Caribs were cannibals.

What we can prove about the Caribs is that they fought with surpassing courage and skill against the European intruders, and that this became the basis for a new kind of ideological arrangement. Those who welcomed the colonizers were praised, enslaved and exterminated, and those who resisted were damned. The contumely heaped upon the heads of the Caribs by Columbus led to interesting lexical and literary aberrations—from Carib, derived the word cannibal and from cannibal Shakespeare gave us Caliban. The institutionalization of racism and colonialism begins with the Carib, cannibal, Caliban slander, one that has persisted for five centuries. In the Caribbean, school children are still being taught from texts, some of which have ostensibly been written by eminent Caribbean historians, that the Caribs ate human flesh. Richard Moore, the Barbadian historian (1972) refuted this calumny in a brilliant booklet, and a very well researched one entitled *Caribs, "Cannibals" and Human Relations*. Both the Carib cannibal, and the African and the other Third World species, are fruit from the same tree of racism. Everytime a Caribbean child reads about the ancestral cannibal it becomes an unconscious act of psychological self-mutilation. "Do we not know", Jose Martí has written, "that the same blow that paralyzes the Indian, cripples us." (Retamar, 1974) But our children neither read the works of Martí nor know who he is. They are still taught to idolize the colonizer and in so doing hate themselves.

On his second voyage, Columbus found human bones, relics of ancestor worship, in Carib huts in Dominica. He used this as evidence to prove his racial slander. Had a group of Caribs "discovered" Rome and visited the catacombs, they too would have found certain Catholic Orders preserving human bones, and by the same curious logic that Columbus used, could have assumed that the Pope and his followers were cannibals.

If the Admiral of the Ocean Sea had stayed on in Genoa he would most likely have remained a part time sailor and a worker in wool. His family had for generations been clothmakers. They took sheep's wool, spun it into thread and wove the thread into cloth which they finally sold. Since ancient times, the Genoese youth, particularly those from the lower middle class, had gone to sea in search of fame and fortune. For, if they were ambitious, it would be clear as bells of the Angelus that for them their society was one of many dogs and few bones. So the urge to seasons of adventure was not entirely a romantic one. During the Renaissance the challenge of conquering the seemingly infinite spaces of the Atlantic beyond the Pillars of Hercules began to excite the imaginations of those young Genoese as it had never done before. Many of them migrated to Portugal, the foremost centre of the nautical sciences in fifteenth century Europe. There were so many Genoese in Portugal, that the Cortes in 1481 petitioned the King to exclude them from his dominions.

Columbus arrived in Portugal when he was about thirty years old. He is a man with whom we should be well acquainted, for he had heaped so much suffering upon our ancestors that we would be betraying their dreams of freedom for all mankind, if we did not mark him well. We should know not only the mythical Columbus, but also the real one. And, since knowing is not just an abstract concept for us, we should be able to divine clearly what he looked like. His son Ferdinand said of him:

The Admiral was a well built man of more than medium

structure, long visaged with cheeks somewhat high, but
neither fat nor thin. He had an aquiline nose and his eyes
were light in color; his complexion too was light, but
kindling to a vivid red. In youth his hair was blond, but
when he came to his thirtieth year it all turned white.
(Morison, 1942a:62).

Bartolomé de Las Casas, the Dominican monk, amplifies this
description telling us that:

He was more than middling tall; face long and giving an
air of authority; aquiline nose, blue eyes, complexion
light and tending to bright red; beard and hair bright red
when young but very soon turned gray from his
labours. . .(Morison,1942a:62-63).

While Ferdinand, the Admiral's son was writing his father's biography, he was receiving the revenue from four hundred African
slaves in Hispaniola. It would be interesting to discover how many
generations of the Columbus family subsequently rode on the
backs of sweating and anonymous Africans.

But, let us return to the impoverished Columbus setting himself
up in Portugal. He did not remain in penury for long, because he
soon married a noble, wealthy and well-connected lady, Beatriz
Enríquez de Harana, and he was eventually able to plead for royal
sponsorship of what he himself described as *La empresa de las
Indias*, the Enterprise of the Indies.

The King of Portugal turned him down, but nine years later
Ferdinand and Isabella, the Rulers of Castile, became his patrons.
Certain that he could sail to India and China via the Western Seas,
he surprised the Indians on their island beaches in the Bahamas;
believing for a while that these islands were in the Bay of Bengal.

Alberigo Vespucci, and I deliberately use his authentic Christian
name, a Florentine dilettante and rascal, corrected Columbus's
error, if error it really was, because Columbus and Vespucci
remained on very close and friendly terms until the former's death
in 1506. Vespucci, having sailed to the American mainland declared that what Columbus had indeed stumbled upon was a New
World—a surprising declaration about twin continents which had
already been inhabited for over two hundred milleniums! Having

returned from his travels, Vespucci wrote a number of letters to the Duc de Medici in Paris, using a lively and entertaining prose style, and causing a great stir when these letters were published.

Columbus's writings are intense, humourless, turgid, occasionally poetic. The intensity of his passions seemed to burn through the dense prose and illuminate it for moments, until once again it becomes uneven, repetitive and dense—the culminative effect of what is left of his writing (most of the originals have been lost), is like fists drumming against one's brain.

Vespucci, on the other hand, composing his *Quatuor Navigationes* (c. 1504-1505) (Marcou, 1888a:12) in Portugal, did not write in the white heat of his experiences. He gave us an elegant, retrospective and very persuasive view, and he was never averse to plagiarism if the accounts of other people's voyages could enhance his own. Vespucci invented a colonizer's America, and the reality that is ours never recovered from this literary assault and the distortions he inflicted upon it. The fiction of a "virgin land" inhabited by savages, at once a racist one and a contradiction, remains with us to this day. Amerigo was undoubtedly a Florentine dilettante, but he was also an extraordinarily clever one. Why would he otherwise have changed his Christian name after his voyages to the Americas?

There is a mountain range in Nicaragua called the Sierra Amerrique, and a group of Indians called Los Amerriques. These mountains stretch between Juigalpa and Libertad in the province of Chontales, and they separate Lake Nicaragua from the Mosquito Coast. The Amerriques had, since pre-Columbian times, always been in contact with the area around Cape Gracia a Dios, and the whole length of the Mosquito Coast (Marcou, 1888b:8). In 1502, Columbus visited this coast at Carriai and Carambaru. In 1497, Vespucci landed at Cape Gracia a Dios, and, in 1505, sailed along the Mosquito Coast. Both navigators must certainly have heard the word "Amerrique" from the Indians over and over again during those voyages.

After the initial greetings and the limping exchange of pleasantries, it was a tradition with explorers like Columbus and Vespucci, they confirm this repeatedly in their writings, to ask the Indians where gold could be found. For, as Cortez confessed, they all suffered from a disease that only gold could cure. The alluvial gravels of the Sierra Amerrique had yielded gold for the Indians from time immemorial. They used gold, the sun's sweat, to create objects of surpassing beauty. It was a good metal for sculpture. Beyond that it had little value in itself until it was touched by man's creative genius. By capturing light on the burnished surfaces that metal workers and sculptors created through the use of fire, gold could link people to the sun, moon and stars, and both the act of creative labour and the object created became touched by magic, mystery and beauty. Sometimes they indented pieces of raw gold, and putting them in a sack full of sand, allowed the sea or a running stream to sculpt and polish them, and so through these processes the objects, man, Nature and the gods could become one.

For the colonizer gold meant money, personal and national aggradizement and power over others. In their burgeoning capitalist system, gold could buy a place in the very Throne Room of the Kingdom of Heaven for the most despicable sinner. And in particular, once this sinner made the right propitiatory noises to the Almighty and gave generously to the Church, he could be assured of absolution from any crime committed against the colonized. "I came for gold, not to till the land," Cortez had declared. He was noted for his occasional outbursts of brutal frankness about himself and his countrymen. Their lust for gold was such that the Indians declared that the colonizer would even rape the sun to rob it of its miraculous sweat.

For Columbus and Vespucci, therefore, the words "Amerrique" and "gold" have become synonymous. After his visits to the Mosquito Coast, he made the last one in 1505, Vespucci changed his Christian name from Alberico to Amerigo. In the archives of Toledo, a letter from Vespucci to the Cardinal dated December 9, 1508, is signed Amerrigo with the double 'r' as in the Indian Amerrique (Marcou, 1888c:79). And between 1508 and 1512, the year in which Vespucci died, at least two other signatures with the Christian name Amerrigo were recorded.

Robbing peoples and countries of their indigenous names was one of the cruel games that colonizers played with the colonized. Names are like magic markers in the long and labyrinthine streams of racial memory, for racial memories are rivers leading to the sea where the memory of mankind is stored. To rob people or countries of their name is to set in motion a psychic disturbance which can in turn create a permanent crisis of identity. As if to underline this fact, the theft of an important place-name from the heartland of the Americas and the claim that it was a dilettante's Christian name robs the original name of its elemental meaning. Dr. A. Le Plongeon, a 19th century scholar from Mérida (Yucatan), in a letter to the French Professor Jules Marcou dated December 10th, 1881, wrote:

> The name AMERICA or AMERRIQUE in the Mayan language means, a country of perpetually strong wind, or the Land of the Wind, and sometimes the suffix "-ique", "-ik" and "-ika" can mean not only wind or air but also a spirit that breathes, life itself (Marcou, 1888d:6).

We must, therefore, reclaim the name of our America and give it once again its primordial meaning, land of the wind, the fountainhead of life and movement.

In the Mayan genesis myth, the Popol Vuh, Wind stands at the centre of creation. As the story unfolds, we are told that it was manifested to the gods:

> That at dawn man should appear. So they decided on the creation and the growth of trees and bees and the birth of life and the creation of man. This was resolved in the darkness and in the night by the Heart of Heaven called Hurricane (Paz 1972a).

On the rocky eastern slopes of the Sierra Amerrique the wind pounds like giant fists upon the gates of time demanding to be recognized.

Asturias's novel, *Strong Wind* (1968), resurrects this symbol of the wind in a Guatemalan setting that is near to the Sierra Amerrique. In this novel, Hurricane, the Heart of Heaven, the Mayan and Carib god, unleashed its avenging wrath upon the huge banana plantations owned by an overseas concern that was remarkably like the United Fruit Company. Other Caribbean writers, English speaking ones, have written about hurricanes. There are John Hearne (1960) and Edgar Mittelholzer (1954); but their hurricanes have no roots in America's mythological archetypes, the British did not encourage this kind of thing in their stultified colonial educational systems. Hearne can be excused. The Jamaican indigenous connection was absolutely severed by

ethnocide, but Mittleholzer came from a country where the
Amerindian still lives in the forests of the Guyana hinterland and in
the forests of our flesh and blood. In *Strong Wind* (1968), Asturias
reunites myth, magic, man, creative labor and the elements. His
American characters with the exception of Stoner, the hero, are
slightly unreal; and Stoner is real because he became indigenized.
He fought with and for the people and in the process became their
brother and no longer their master. So, by the time Stoner and his
wife were killed, it was a death outside the pale of the Judaeo-
Christian tradition; rather it was one that the god Hurricane
demanded so that an act of expiation could be immortalized.

Hearne and Mittleholzer's hurricanes are depicted with a kind of
clinical detachment. Their strong wind seems anglicized when
compared to Asturias's Amerindian-ized one.

The similarity between Columbus's life and that of the colonials
he ultimately helped to bring into being, ends the moment he
himself became a colonizer. The Atlantic crossing created profound
psychological changes in those who made it. If all the cultural
baggage dumped in the Middle Passage during the five centuries of
the Columbian era were to be dredged up, it would need a new
planet to house it.

Having survived the crossing, Columbus and his sailors announced to their Indian hosts that they had come "from Heaven."
(Morison, 1942c:371). It was something of a contradiction, Las
Casas remarked cryptically, to have come from Heaven and to be
so overcome with a lust for gold. As a dying Cuban cacique was to
reveal, the colonizer gave Heaven a bad name in the eyes of the
colonized. In 1509, the self-proclaimed "men from Heaven" had
turned their attention to the beautiful island of Cuba. One of the
principal caciques there, hearing in advance of their coming,
carried out a propitiatory ceremony of drowning all the gold he and
his subjects possessed. He was convinced that since gold was the
only real god the Spanish worshipped, if this god was thrown away,
perhaps he and his people would be spared. The invaders incensed
by this act of sacrilege had the cacique burnt alive. When he was in
the midst of the flames a Franciscan Friar of great piety, holding a
cross before him, promised the cacique eternal life if he would
embrace the Christian faith and hell and damnation if he didn't.
With the fire burning slowly to prolong the torture, the Friar, as
best as he could, tried to explain some half a hundred doctrines of

the Christian faith. The cacique, in the midst of his discomfort, enquired if Heaven was open to all Spaniards:

> "Some who were good can hope to be admitted there," the Friar replied. "Then", declared the cacique, "since I would prefer not to share Heaven with such cruel company, if you'd swear that none of your people will go to hell, hell would be the perfect place for me." (Thatcher, 1903a:128).

We are, in fact, re-examining the roots of our Columbian exile because as an Amerindian proverb says, those who forget the past will re-live it again and again. If we neglect to complete this task of re-examination, then the contradictions between our psychological and actual exile, an induced state of intellectual amnesia and a conscious awareness of what was, what is, and what is to be done, is liable to lead us into a labyrinth of metaphysics. For our intention must be not merely to analyse the world, our world, but to change it. Only by changing our world can we inherit it, and only by inheriting it can we end our internal and external exile.

The first European settlement in the Americas was established in Marien, one of the five Kingdoms on the island of Bohio which the Spaniards renamed Hispaniola. The settlement was called La Navidad. Guacanagari, the ruler of Marien had treated the Spaniards with great hospitality on their arrival. When the Santa María was wrecked on Christmas Day 1492, because Juan de la Costa and a group of Basque shipmates had disobeyed Columbus's orders and tried to save their own skins, the Admiral himself wrote that at sunrise on December 26, this same Guacanagari came abroad the Niña:

> and said that he would give him all that he had, and that he had given the Christians who were ashore two very big houses, and would give more if necessary . . . "To such extent" says the Admiral, "are they loyal and without greed for the property of others, and that King was virtuous above all" (Thatcher, 1903b:125).

Las Casa revealed the fate that befell Guananagari barely a decade later:

The Spaniards pursued this Chief with peculiar bitterness and forced him to abandon his Kingdom . . . he died of fatigue and sorrow. Those of his people who were not fortunate enough to be killed suffered countless pains in slavery (Morison, 1942e:390-391).

After a warm and hospitable reception, Columbus repaid his Amerindian hosts by enslaving them hardly a year later. The Atlantic Slave Trade began when under Columbus's sponsorship, a shipload of five hundred Indians was dispatched to Spain in 1493.

The Absence of greed for the property of others is definitely not a quality that has surfaced in the hearts of colonizers during the five centuries of the Columbian era.

After the five Kingdoms of Hispaniola and their estimated three million inhabitants were erased, the peoples of Jamaica and Puerto Rico were next in line for their journey to oblivion. By 1540, these two islands which between them had a population of six hundred thousand, could boast of having hardly 200 of their original inhabitants alive. The population figures are those of Las Casa and, naturally, apologists for the colonizer have often warned us that his figures should be doubted. But who should be believed, the initiators, sponsors and apologists of ethnocide, or one who fought for its victims for sixty-eight of his ninety-two years? The silences and the empty spaces which remained in the wake of this early example of a final solution bore eloquent testimony to the enormity of the crime. Even if the figures are incorrect we might well ask where then are the indigenous peoples of the Caribbean today? Why don't they come forward and speak for themselves? I have penetrated into those profound silences which remain in the aftermath of ethnocide, for it is not only a crime of past centuries, it lives on today. In vast areas of the Guyana highlands west of the Pakaraimas and south of the Akarai, the Amerindian peoples are still being exterminated and their land is still being violated by usurpers. There are islands of silence in those vast spaces which leave a more terrible impression on the mind than screams of the dying. In those profound silences, the Mayan Popol Vuh is no longer a genesis myth, but a prophecy, for it began like this:

This is the story of how everything was in suspense, everything becalmed, wrapped in silence, everything

immobile, silent and empty in the vastness of the sky.
(Paz, 1972b).

As one penetrates into those brooding spaces, one feels the pain
and suffering of the dead Amerindian hosts, and at that moment
one begins to realize that the real dead are the sowers of death, not
its victims; at that moment one understands the unwritten histories
of the victims intuitively and enters into the heart of their suffering. One feels their anguish in the same way that an amputee feels
a persistent ache in the limb he has lost; and at that moment one
also becomes the inheritor of the dauntless courage and the
humanity of the victims, and at that moment suffering is no longer
suffering and death is no longer death. Perhaps it is at that moment
too, that one sees the beginning of the end of exile. But before one
deals with the cure one must diagnose the ailment. The history of
our exile is a dismal one of ethnocide, slavery, indentured labor,
racism, colonialism and more recently neo-colonialism.
Everywhere that we touch the earth in this hemisphere and seek to
establish roots, the roots are bound to invade the graves of the
innocent dead. For, after the Indian was sent on his journey to
oblivion, the colonizer established new colonies of the dead—
slaves from Africa, indentured labor from India, China, Java,
Madiera and once again Africa, and along with these the permanent human flotsam in Capitalism's Kingdom of Chance, the
unemployed, the hungry, the sick who belong to no special race,
color or creed, they are numbers in statistical tables, raw material
for academics to pontificate upon. To define this situation today in
simplistic clichés about black, brown or white power is to induce a
kind of intellectual euphoria in which the mind becomes anes-
thetized with half-truths. One has to excavate the answers from the
abyss of one's self and one's mutilated society.

I had pointed out earlier that the Caribbean writer was,
poisoned between limbo and nothingness, like the middle man in
Akan classical drama; but we, in fact, Caribbean-ized the role and
became not so much a figure in the middle of Furies and benign
spirits, but an honorary marginal person. The writer is, therefore,
islanded in the midst of marginal tides of sorrow, despair, hope,
whirlpools of anxiety, cataracts of rage. He is the most articulate
member of the marginal class, articulate, that is, with the written
word. There are others of his class who speak to the mind's ear with

music—the calypso, reggae, the folk-song—and who speak with immediacy and a sensuous ease to a much vaster audience. The marginal class is a creation of the "system" in the Caribbean. The system sustained itself for centuries, by ensuring that at all times there would be a large reservoir of cheap labor. Expatriate manipulators, while controlling vast acreages of land, brought only a fraction of what they controlled into productive use; they also exercised absolute controls over all other important means of production, distribution and exchange by an economic and cosmetic sleight-of-hand, which makes it appear as if the local surrogates were the real bosses, which they never were, and, under the present system, will never become. The economic base of the marginal class is, therefore, like mud on the Guyana coast. The tides carpet beaches with this mud for a season and then roll it up and move it elsewhere.

After centuries in the wilderness the first law of the marginals is that of survival. To the middle class, which has only recently left the shiftless and insecure world of marginality, the marginal class appears to be truly menacing, a breeding ground for symbols of terror.

The middle class, and particularly the most recent recruits to its ranks, haunted by the spectre of the marginal class, tries almost in a fury to shut itself behind ramparts of philistinism and iron bars. A regular job, a bicycle and a collar and tie used to be the symbols of emancipation from the marginals, but now the symbols have become more expensive and they are a shirtjack, a car, and the third symbol which is optional, is what Andrew Salkey (1976) described as "a wagon-wheel Afro." When the Black Power gesticulation promised to be safe, social and definitely not socialist, the most unlikely people began to decorate themselves with its exotic accoutrements. But, as soon as it began to crystallize into a class struggle, the middle class abandoned it and hitched their wagon-wheels once more to old tried-and-true neo-colonialist symbols. One of our distinguished literary colleagues made the profound pontifical declaration that it lacked intellectual content. But the Caribbean writer, whether he likes it or not, is an honorary marginal person, and it is from the constantly shifting islands of marginality that he makes his sallies into the world, into the wider indifference of Britain, the United States, Canada, France or wherever the rumor-gram noises it abroad, that the pastures are greener.

When the colonizers exterminated the indigenous inhabitants in many regions of the Americas, they severed connections with a vast network of secret tributaries that led into the mainstream of the memory of mankind. The total reservoir of memory was seriously impoverished by this loss. The colonizer, reaching into the cultural reserves he believed he had brought with him, discovered that these were soon exhausted, leaving him with psychic voids that could not be filled. The cultural baggage he had dumped in the Middle Passage could not be salvaged. In any event, it was mostly the culturally deprived who immigrated to the Americas, so that from the start they had set out with depleted stocks. Of all the major groups that came to the Americas during the initial three hundred years of the Columbian era, the African alone understood the profound need to create a fusion of his culture with that of his Indian host:

> The African brought with him, regardless of the mosaic of cultural groups from which he derived, a built-in ethic which bound him first, as a stranger in a strange land, to study and respect the host culture before he established elements of his own. This gave the children of the African diaspora a means of surviving anywhere in the human world and they did not need guns and superior weapons in order to do this. When the African arrived in the New World, he knew that the colonizer who had brought him there was a usurper who had seized the land of the Indians, desecrated the graves and the altars of their ancestors, and sent countless of the ones who had welcomed them to the Forest of the Long Night. It was clear to the slave from Africa, that in order to escape the terrible retribution that was certain to overtake their masters, they had to make peace with both the living and the dead in this new land . . . The African had to recreate his vision of himself in the universe often being violently uprooted . . . to have seen himself only through his master's eyes and to have even appeared to be an accomplice in his obnoxious deeds, would have left him

with a permanent heritage of self-hatred, distorted self images and guilt. In order to reconstruct his ontological system, the African was compelled by the logic of his own cultural past, to establish relations with his Indian host independent of the white man. (Carew, 1974).

It was fortunate for us all in this hemisphere that the African began once more to make his appearance in the New World from around 1502. It was also a matter of profound cultural significance that Africans had come to the Americas in pre-Columbian times. But within two decades of his arrival in the Columbian era, there were rebellions in Hispaniola, Puerto Rico, Cuba, Jamaica and Mexico, in which Africans and Indians joined forces against a common enemy.

Herrera tells us that the Wolofs of San Juan de Puerto Rico "walked rebelliously through the land," (Wiener, 1920a:158) and that no sooner had they set foot in the Indies, than they "began to disaffect the Indians." (Wiener, 1920b:158). The Wolofs could, thereafter, only move from one island to another with special permission from the Viceroy.

The humane and civilized African example of cultural accomodation which runs counter to the bigotry of the white settler mentality, has largely been ignored by both our historians and the colonizers. And yet in dealing with questions of cultural roots, alienation and identity in the Americas, it is an example that cannot be overlooked.

At a time when independence, that is, an anthem, a flag and a color on the map, brings into sharper focus questions of national identity and liberation, the Caribbean writer is faced with harsh choices. The end of his marginal status is now in sight. As an honorary member of the marginal class he has both consciously and unconsciously internalized the mounting chaos that is pushing this class inexorably, not into revolution but revolutionary situations. Their ranks have been swelled by unemployed graduates from high-schools and universities, by preachers of cults and fads, by crooks, pushers, choke-and-rob practitioners, political louts and bouncers, by instant prophets and trans-Atlantic Gurus; their dress, their speech, their music, the mumbo-jumbo they invent and discard seasonally are all imaginative forms of protest; they are often unsure of what they are for, but are absolutely certain of what they're against; the corrupt, bullying, pompous, dishonest, cruel, incompetent and often mindless regimes under which they live.

Elements from the marginal class have taken to the streets again and again during the past decade. Their most dramatic street scenes were acted out in Trinidad in 1969. "The revolution has started!," some of the more naive cried out. But these street demonstrations could best be described by two lines from a Robert Burns poem—for they were "like the Borealis race, that flits e'er you can point its place . . ."

Yet, one should not dismiss the street demonstrations of the marginals lightly. In every instance they attracted elements from the working class and a minority of the intelligensia. These elements went back to bear the brunt of the repression that followed, to become more politicized and to move the struggle to a higher level.

The Caribbean writer, during this period, played the role of the middleman in the Akan Classical theatre to such perfection that scholars researching African survivals would have been delighted.

Some went into hiding, others wore the gaudy costumes and transformed the slogans into academic canons. If occasionally their denunciations of white imperialism sounded too emotional, they ended by declaring that Marx was irrelevant, long live Fanon. Others played a cunning counterrevolutionary role. The honorary marginal is a supreme mimic and in addition to this quality can perform a literary ventriloquism. He can imitate his colonial master so perfectly that the master hears himself speaking through the servant. This servant has a phonal apparatus inside his head that those who behold it marvel at its sensitivity.

The colonial intellectual passes through three stages—at the first stage, he is an imitator, devoted to the idea of showing the colonizer that he has learnt all his cultural catechisms well and is ready to be accepted as an honorary white man. He is a creature who lives as though he were constantly under the scrutiny of a disapproving colonizer's eye. He is even careful about the way in which he talks in his sleep. At the second stage, our colonial has grown bold enough to be disgruntled. He has grown cunning enough to understand that Uncle Tomming from the heart is no longer in fashion; he therefore assumes postures of protest. The language that he has come to know better than the colonizer himself is used like a stick to beat the man, but the beating is handed out guardedly. The intention is more to make noise than to inflict pain. It is, in essence, a protest inspired by petulance, a signal to the colonizer, a plea for recognition, a cry from the emptiness of the creole soul which says: accept me as an honorary white man and I will commit new and unspeakable treacheries against my own.

The third stage is one of unequivocal adherence to the cause of liberation, one that challenges the Caribbean writer to take sides with the sufferers and not their exploiters, local and expatriate, with the have-nots, not the have-gots, with the scorned and rejected, not those lapping the fat of the years. Once the writer has made the choice he is on the road to the end of exile, the road to hope, the Freedom road, the road to the new day where:

> with morning bursting
> like pale lightnings from our eyes
> together side by side
> we'll burst asunder
> pale ramparts of Heaven
> with bare hands and bare feet
> to pluck wild orchids
> of ultimate release (Carew, 1956).

The Caribbean writer is a person from the sun. "Sun's in my blood today" (1952) Seymour writes in his very fine poem, unconsciously entering into regions of African myth which tells of how Nyankopon, the Sky-God, shoots a particle of the sun's fire into the bloodstream of the child, thus bringing the blood to life. In the Caribbean world-view, the sun is a dialectical entity: it is creative and destructive, it gives life and takes it away. Anancy, the West African folk archetype in whose name all fables were told, is shaped like a gadwal, a sun-wheel, a mathematically perfect calendar. Anancy was also the victim of an encounter with the Wax Girl. The story goes that Anancy lost his perfect shape after this encounter.

Among the Hausas, the rainbow was called the spider's bow. This shows how close Anancy was to the divinities from heaven. And, his bow which had the shape of a snake was called the god of rains and storms.

In the Caribbean, Anancy lost his contacts with divinities and is known exclusively as a trickster.

The European, settling in the tropical world in the Columbian era brought Medieval fantasies with him, of the equatorial region being a land of fire, and when this turned out to be untrue, he invented the myth that only dark-skinned peoples could do strenuous manual labor in the sun. White workers in Cuba, and those thousands of miles away in tropical Australia, and white peasants in the Caribbean have proved this to be the fiction that it is, but the myth persists; and the myth is now embraced not only by its originators but also by its victims. The creoles will still declare unblushingly that their constitutions are too delicate for them to attempt strenuous manual labor in the sun; that only blacks or coolies are fit for that kind of thing. Exile from the sun, therefore, begins in the creole mind. It is the result of a plot hatched by parents who are mesmerized by colonial fantasies of class and color escape. These parents begin telling children as soon as the amniotic fluid is washed from their eyes, that the only hope for them is to go abroad, away from the sun. The sun must, in this sick creole imagination, always be kept at a distance. The sun darkens the complexion and threatens to hurl the creole back into the ranks of the blacks and coolies which he had only recently abandoned.

The title of Sam Selvon's novel *A Brighter Sun* (1954) suggests an unconscious desire to move closer to his peasant origins, not to the distant lands of pale sunlight, but to the regions where it is brightest. Going away from the tropics, one loses one's place in the sun. What follows is a psychic unbalance from which one seldom recovers.

But creating distances between oneself and the tropical sun was not only a question of removing one's physical presence from an equatorial to a temperate region, the colonized could also do it as part of a conditioned/psychological reflex. The colonial person rooted in the parasitical economic relationships and the schizoid cultural ones he had had with the mother country, could in his imagination be at home and overseas, in the furnace heat of his brighter sun and in pale winter sunshine at the same time. The arch colonial still locks himself up in warm, heavy clothing in the equatorial sun and will swear that he feels no discomfort; on certain ceremonial occasions, the neo-colonial ladies and gentlemen even wear gloves. But the creole, from the beginning of his emergence as a middle-man in the Columbian era, the word creole originally meant "bred in the house" so that the creole stood between the field slave and the master, has been forever trying to sever his connections with the dark hinterlands under the sun. His journeys have been outward bound ones, towards the "superior" culture of the colonizer and away from the "inferior" one of the colonized. The very communication networks that vein neocolonial territories are like tracings from the creole mind and the psyche of the colonized—all roads lead outwards towards overseas cultural and spiritual meccas. The situation, though, remains a dialectical one at its core. There have always been important, living cultural and spiritual bases outside the ethos of the creole's facile borrowings and spurious imitations. Both urban and rural groups, who were rejected by the colonizer and the creole alike, incorporated rich and enduring cultural survivals into the fabric of their daily life, transforming them and keeping them alive at the same time.

The Caribbean writer and artist, if he must end his exile, is compelled by the exigencies of history to move back and forth from the heart of those cultural survivals and others into whatever regions of the twentieth century the island, the continent or the cosmos his imagination encompasses; and, in roaming across the ages of man in this bloodstained hemisphere, he must penetrate into the unfathomable silences where a part of the Amerindian past is entombed, he must gnaw at the bones of universal griefs, and the reservoir of compassion in his heart for the dispossessed must be limitless.

An Acewayo droger once told me of the journeys he took in and out of the regions of his mind. The band across his forehead, and the harness strapped under his armpits distributed the hundred and twenty-five pounds he carried in his wareshi so that by thrusting his head forward he could walk at a steady, rhythmic, shuffle from day-clean to sunset. We were averaging twenty-five miles a day in the mountainous Potaro district.

"How do you manage?" I asked, thinking of the thirty pounds I was carrying and the way it seemed to double itself after every ten miles. After a long pause he replied, "It's like this, skipper, most of the time you see me walking here, carrying this big load, I'm not here at all . . . is only a shadow here, the substance is back home in Aquero, hunting agouti or deer or labba, playing with my children, catching a gaff, listening to the Old Ones speak, talking to the Ancestors or to God. You can ask me then how come I can be two places at the same time, I will tell you the secret: the pressure of this wareshi on my brain makes it easy for me to send my mind away . . . At the start I feel like a drunken man, there's a singing inside my head, my body feels heavy and the wareshi feels like a mountain on my back. Then all of a sudden everything gets lighter and lighter until I feel like a silk-cotton blossom floating on wind. Once I reach this stage, I can walk from here to the Forst of the Long Night without feeling any weariness."

The Acewayo droger had remained for most of his life outside the awful grinding inevitability of linear time that the Columbian era had imposed upon his people. The Amerindian induction into the remorseless cycles of time on the European calendar had been traumatic. In 1493, Columbus ordered that every able-bodied Amerindian in Marien, one of the five Kingdoms of Hispaniola, should, within a specified time, pay the Spanish Crown a tribute of a hawk's bell full of gold. Those who failed were enslaved, mutilated or put to death. This was also the Amerindian's introduction to a cruel system in which forced labor of the colonized would produce wealth for the colonizer. Labor and the colonizer's time-clock became the totems heralding a new age for the Amerindian and the African. For both of these peoples, time had been something one felt like a pulse or a heartbeat. Time for them was finite. In their cosmologies, past time went back as far as the genesis of their races; it was a link between the living and their ancestors; present time merely spanned the seasons of each day, while future time covered the shortest span of all, it was restricted to the inevitable future and little else. This was how it had always been with the black and brown Men of Corn—one could live in the midst of infinities of stasis, of no time—and when one chose, one could then generate new time. In order to turn the Men of Corn into Natives of Capitalism the colonizer committed unspeakable atrocities of ethnocide and the enslavement of millions. He then attempted to remove all traces of his crime. He did it with the same cunning the authorities had used after the massacre of workers in the public square in Marquez's novel *A Hundred Years of Solitude* (1970). In the ghoulish silence and the emptiness that came in the wake of the massacre, even the stones could not speak after they were washed clean of the bloodstains.

308CALIBAN

Having shattered forever the Afro-Amerindian concepts of time, the colonizer created a new time which he chained inexorably to his own future expectations, and time became money.

In order to illuminate the dialectic of pre-Columbian time and time in the Columbian era a few Caribbean writers had to unlock secrets of lost centuries. They used rivers as the symbol of their journeys into the past.

In *Black Midas,* Aron Smart had said about his grandparents that, "they felt time like a river in their blood." (Carew, 1958a:10).

An early Wilson Harris poem had described the journey of one of his mythical characters:

> Down Rivers of his Night
> Where he must drown to banish fear (1952).

This orphic journey was re-enacted later in the search for the *Palace of the Peacock* (Harris, a 1960).

In Alejo Carpentier's *The Lost Steps* (1956), the hero travels into primordial hinterlands up one of the great rivers of South America, traversing milleniums in his orphic journey. Carpentier went far afield from his island home to find a setting for his hero's wanderings. He needed a continent.

Edouard Glissant chose a river in Martinque as the symbol of his search for roots and a genuine identity in his novel *La Lézarde,* (1959).

What was interesting about the droger's psychological escape route is that it led inwards. It never occurred to him to move beyond the frontiers of home and the forest. Glissant's river "la lézarde" however, takes us inland to its source and from the secret spring where it rises to the sea. For on an island your cosmos of the imagination begins with the sea.

In the search for an identity, one of the major themes in Caribbean writing, the impulse is either to move inwards towards some undiscovered heartland as in Carpentier's *The Lost Steps* (1956), Glissant's *La Lézarde* (1959), Reid's *Newday* (1970), Asturias's *Hombres De Maíz* (1957), Harris's *Palace of the Peacock* (1960), my own *Black Midas* (1958): or outwards towards the meccas of the colonizer as in Lamming's *The Emigrants* (1955), *Natives of My Person* (1972), Clarke's *Survivors of the Crossing (1965), The Meeting Point* (1967). These novels are works I have chosen from what has now become an impressive array. They are, therefore, by no means the only ones that illustrate the dichotomy of the inward and the outward vision in Caribbean writing.

Salkey's *Come Home, Malcolm Heartland* (1976) is a novel about a Caribbean exile preparing to return home. Having explored the outward vision to its utmost limits, the hero is escaping the wide indifference of decades abroad to return to a spiritual Sleepy Hollow.

The hero of Carpentier's *The Lost Steps* (1956) is a Euro-American musicologist and composer. In his search for an identity, he first goes to Europe but does not find the illusory Europe that his father had brought him up to revere. His disillusionment is complete when he realizes that a psychic uprootment had taken place when his ancestors abandoned the Old Country. But in America as a white settler, he also had to seek out and find the inner sanctuaries of a spiritual heartland that racist fantasies, a strident and spurious nationalism, and a spate of colonizer's myths had unconsciously prevented him from exploring. But he was also an artist surrounded by dilettantes and colonial cultists of art with a capital 'A'. After a chance encounter with the curator of a museum, he sets out from New York on an expedition to find the first musical instruments that man created in the Americas. He is delayed for a while in a South American city where, from the relative safety of a tourist hotel, he watched a palace revolt flare up only to be extinguished. His journey continues over mountains as close to heaven as a man can hope to be without leaving the earth. A steep descent brings him to tropical lowlands, the main setting of his search for an American and a human identity. In a few weeks he journeys to the upper reaches of the great river, and, in the milleniums he traverses during this small span of time, his journey becomes one of self-discovery—the discovery of a new American self which was hidden in primodial rainforest fastnesses; the roots of the Amerindian psyche and the Amerindian person; the inner spiritual sanctum of the Men of Corn; the point from which they began their migrations outwards. In this remote world where linear time as he knew it had become meaningless, the hero is, he believes at first, reborn. But this was a romantic illusion. He goes back to the world of the twentieth century, his spirit refurbished, the scales scraped away from his eyes; when he tries to return to the Eden he thought he had rediscovered, the steps are lost. Yet, he had gathered unto himself an immense creative power in that trespass into pre-history and back. He returned to the sisyphian tasks of the artist, chastened and reformed, knowing that he had to cross not only past centuries but to venture into future ones. In Glissant's *La Lézarde* (1959) the search for an identity follows the course of a river to its source, and the spring from which it rises is enclosed by an old colonial stone house. The river takes us into the heartland of a country. Glissant, introduces us to a journey of discovery with a poem:

> "What is this country?" he asked.
> And the answer was:
> "First weigh every word,
> make the acquaintance of every sorrow." (1959a).

The author's Lézarde is really a river of life which runs through both a physical and spiritual landscape. As the river makes its way to the sea, one can feel the people stirring, the land awakening and the people, the land, the river, the sky coming together in a miraculous unity. And during the long season of a people's consciousness ripening, the author poses a question that goes to the heart of the dream to end the feeling of homelessness at home. "Can we," he asks, "give a name to any parcel of earth before the man and woman who inhabits it has arisen? (Glissant, 1959b: 18).

La Lézarde (1959) illuminates the psychological landscape it traverses like flashes of lightning. Its symbols are revealed to us like the vast array of different species of flora and fauna secreted away in a rain forest. The river brings clarity to the apparent chaos; it is linked to geological time; it existed before man did; it flows into an expectation of countless seasons. It is like Alegría's *The Golden Serpent* (1947), a Peruvian river that threads its way through the life of a people and one that becomes a timeless symbol of a people's fight for freedom. The river is a perfect symbol of man's seminal connection with life and being. The interior landscapes of Harris's novels are veined with dreaming rivers of life, death and seasons of eternity.

Pia and Makunaima, the Children of the Sun, are the oldest and most universal culture heroes in this hemisphere. From Patagonia to the edge of the Canadian Barens, the same story was told by the Amerindians from time immemorial. It is the story of how these twins were born and how their two greatest feats were to bring fire to man, and to tame the rivers by placing gigantic rocks and boulders across them. An Amerindian poem sings about:

> The white sun
> raping dark rivers
> the white sun
> biting like a Vaquero's ship
> the white sun singing, singing
> singing the songs of the dead
> the white sun
> a burning requiem
> but the cool night must come (Carew, 1952).

In this song-poem the seminal anthropomorphic symbols—the sun, the dark interior river, the songs of the dead, the night are united. The river rises in hinterlands of silence and flows to the clamorous sea and on the way its tributaries reach into the flesh of the land like so many capillaries. The river can be the symbol of the exile journeying outwards or the exile coming home.

"All men return to the hills finally" (1949) the Roger Mais poem had declared. His hills, both real and symbolical, were an oasis where the writer and artist went to gather strength, to heal the wounds inflicted by the philistines at home and racists abroad. From the hills one moves outwards, towards the sea. Both the consciousness of the sea and the absence of this consciousness is an interesting psychological phenomenon in the Caribbean. The dream that emerges in Caribbean writing is one of crossing the sea or of contemplating its moods, never of conquering it. The Caribs and the Europeans were conquerors of the sea, creators of sagas; their imaginations were forever encompassing new horizons of turbulent water. But for the new Caribbean man the sea was a capricious and often dangerous moat between stepping stones of islands and continents. The sea, which Lamming describes in great detail in *Natives of My Person* (1972) is perceived as though from a great distance; it is something, not only separating continents and islands, but suspended between them. It is a weightless, static sea, like the one described in the Mayan genesis myth, the Popol Vuh, rather than a heaving, turbulent reality.

In an earlier novel, Lamming's emigrants cross the Atlantic and

are barely aware of this ocean's existence. But in their conversations it is clear that they're carrying enduring memories of the
smell of their earth and the dreams of their people with them. The
journey by sea is an interlude between home and the Caribbean
communities islanded abroad. Clarke's *Survivors of the Crossing*
(1965) also erase the reality of the ocean they crossed from their
minds. In *The Meeting Point*, (1967) the emigrants have moved to
air travel and are more at ease. Perhaps, we all carry deep in our
unconscious minds the traumatic memory of the ancestral crossing
in the Columbian and slave era. In Salkey's *Come Home, Malcolm
Heartland* (1976), the Caribbean Janus, astride two worlds, is
about to abandon one of the two and return home regardless of the
philistines, the areas of mindlessness that he must invade and
conquer, the malice waiting to ambush him and the deep awareness that a part of him had died during the decades abroad in the
emptiness, the racial scorn, the endless encounters with real and
imagined acts of discrimination he had had to endure. Malcolm
Heartland also knows that the home to which he is returning is
innocent of many social and political resonances for which he had
developed an inner ear. Heartland dies both a real and symbolical
death before he takes the plunge. But there are Heartlands at
home who survived both crossings, the one to the meccas of the
colonizer and the other home to the secret heartlands where the
waters of the River of Life began their flow. Perhaps the finest
evocation of this return home to slowly awakening Sleepy Hollows
perched on top of a people's volcanic discontents can be found in
Mervyn Morris's poetry. This poetry is uncompromisingly honest,
sensitive and it penetrates the heart of the discontents that centuries of exile and cultural alienation gave birth to.

"All people have a right to share the waters of the River of Life
and to drink with their own cups, but our cups have been broken"
laments the Carib poem-hymn. The writer, artist, musician, is
directly involved in the creative process of reshaping the broken
cups. But as an Asian writer had said from a Republic perched on
the Roof of the World in the Soviet Far east, "Art and Literature
are like lightning, and lightning can never be timid." Therefore,
while we shape exquisite new cups, we must side by side with the
disinherited millions of the Third World, confront those who would
deny us our fair share of the Waters of the River of Life, for it was at

the source of those waters that the exile of the Caribbean writer began and it is there that his exile will end.

References

ALEGRIA, C. (1947) *The Golden Serpent*. N.Y.: Farrar & Rinehart, Inc.
ASTURIAS, M. (1957) *Hombres de Maiz*. (The Men of Corn)
———(1968) *Strong Wind*. New York: Laurel Edition, Dell Publishing Co.
CAREW, J. (1952) Unpublished poem.
———(1956) poem.
———(1958) *Black Midas*. London: Secker & Warburg Ltd.
———(1974) "The Fusions of African and Amerindian Cultures", an unpublished work.
———(1976) "Exile", poem.
CARPENTER, A. (1956) *The Lost Steps*. New York: Alfred A. Knopf, Inc.
CLARKE, A. (1965) *Survivors of the Crossing*. Toronto: McClelland & Stewart
———(1967) *The Meeting Point*. Boston: Little, Brown & Co.
GLISSANT, E. (1959) *La L´ezarde*. (The Ripening). New York: George Braziller, Inc.
———(1959a) *La L´ezarde*. (The Ripening). New York: George Braziller Inc. frontispiece.
———(1959b) *La L´ezarde*. (The Ripening). New York: George Braziller Inc.
HARRIS, W. (1952) "Rivers of His Night". Guyana: *Kyk-over-al*.
———(1960) *Palace of the Peacock*. London: Faber & Faber.
HEARNE, J. (1960) *Autumn Equinox*. London: Faber & Faber.
JAMES, C. L. R. (1972) From a talk given at Princeton University.
LAMMING, G. (1955) *The Emigrants*. New York: Holt, Rinehart & Winston Co.
———(1972) *Natives of My Person*. New York: Holt, Rinehart & Winston Co.
MAIS, R. (1949) Unpublished poem.
MARCOU, J. (1888a) "L'Origine du Nom d'Amérique". Paris: *Bulletin of the American Geographical Society*, No. 4.
———(1888b) "L'Origine du Nom d'Amérique". Paris: *Bulletin of the American Geographical Society*, No. 4.
———(1888c) "L'Origine du Nom d'Amérique". Paris: *Bulletin of the American Geographical Society*, No. 4.
———(1888d) "L'Origine du Nom d'Amérique". Paris: *Bulletin of the American Geographical Society*, No. 4.
GARCIA MARQUEZ, G. (1970) *A Hundred Years of Solitude*. London: Jonathan Cape Ltd.
MITTELHOLZER, E. (1954) *Of Trees and the Sea*. London: Secker & Warburg.
MOORE, R. (1972) *Caribs, "Cannibals", and Human Relations*. New York: Afro-American Institute, Pathway Publishers.
MORISON, S. E. (1942a) *Admiral of the Ocean Sea*, vol. 1. Boston: Little, Brown & Co.
———(1942b) *Admiral of the Ocean Sea*, vol. 1. Boston: Little, Brown & Co.
———(1942c) *Admiral of the Ocean Sea*, vol. 1. Boston: Little, Brown & Co.
———(1942d) *Admiral of the Ocean Sea*, vol. 1. Boston: Little, Brown & Co.
———(1942e) *Admiral of the Ocean Sea*, vol. 1. Boston: Little, Brown & Co.
PAZ, S. (1972a) "Popol Vuh". An unpublished translation.
———(1972b) "Popol Vuh". An unpublished translation.

REID, V. (1970) *Newday*. Jamaica: Sangster's Book Stores Ltd. in association with Heinemann Educational Books.

RETAMAR, R. (1974) "Caliban". Amherst: *The Massachusetts Review*, vol. XV, Nos, 1 & 2.

SALKEY, A. (1976) *Come Home, Malcolm Heartland*. London: Hutchison & Co. Ltd.

SELVON, S. (1954) *A Brighter Sun*. London: MacGibbon & Kee Ltd.

SEYMOUR, A. (1952) "The Sun's In My Blood". Guyana: *Kyk-over-al*.

THATCHER, J. (1903a). *Christopher Columbus*, vol. 1. New York: G. P. Putnam & Sons.

———(1903b) *Christopher Columbus*, vol. 1. New York: G. P. Putnam & Sons.

WIENER, L. (1902a) *Africa and the Discovery of America*, vol. 1. Philadelphia: Innes & Sons.

———(1920b) *Africa and the Discovery of America*, vol. 1. Philadelphia: Innes & Sons.

PORTRAIT OF

THE ARTIST WITH LI PO

by CHARLES WRIGHT

from DURAK: AN INTERNATIONAL MAGAZINE OF POETRY

nominated by DURAK: AN INTERNATIONAL MAGAZINE OF POETRY,
Joyce Carol Oates and David St. John

The "high heavenly priest of the White Lake" is now
A small mound in an endless plain of grass,
His pendants clicking and pearls shading his eyes.
He never said anything about the life after death,
Whose body is clothed in a blue rust and the smoke of dew.

He liked flowers and water most.
Everyone knows the true story of how he would write his verses
    and float them,
Like paper boats, downstream
           just to watch them drift away.
Death never entered his poems, but rowed, with its hair down,
    far out on the lake,
Laughing and looking up at the sky.

Over a 1000 years later, I write out one of his lines in a notebook,
The peach blossom follows the moving water,
And watch the October darkness gather against the hills.
All night long the river of heaven will move westward while no
    one notices.
The distance between the dead and the living
        is more than a heart beat and a breath.

I WAS TAUGHT THREE

by JORIE GRAHAM

from PLOUGHSHARES

nominated by PLOUGHSHARES, *Dave Smith and R. C. Day*

names for the tree facing my window
almost within reach, elastic

with squirrels, memory banks, homes.
Castagno took itself to heart, its pods

like urchins clung to where they landed
claiming every bit of shadow

at the hem. *Chassagne,* on windier days,
nervous in taffeta gowns.

whispering, on the verge of being
anarchic, though well bred.

And then *chestnut,* whipped pale and clean
by all the inner reservoirs

called upon to do their even share of work.
It was not the kind of tree

got at by default—imagine that—not one
in which the only remaining leaf

was loyal. No, this
was all first person, and I

was the stem, holding within myself the whole
bouquet of three

at once given and received: smallest roadmaps
of coincidence. What is the idea

that governs blossoming? The human tree
clothed with its nouns, or this one

just outside my window promising more firmly
than can be

that it will reach my sill eventually, the leaves
silent as suppressed desires, and I

a name among them.

AMSTERDAM STREET SCENE, 1972

by RAPHAEL RUDNIK

from OPEN PLACES

nominated by Grace Schulman

The cupid-faced hooligan standing on tip-
toe with his tin cup comes down

on the beat of the roar on the floor of glittering cement while turning the white wheel

of his music-truck, clapping coins in the cup
(a gull banks invisible to the eye to avoid a wall.)

And with strange, charming deadness
puppets moved by wires drawn through their foreheads

move around a frail keyboard of bones, surrounded by
emblems and treasures, impaled on spikes (a great beast
    branded by

a Scarlet Woman, candlesticks, whips, wands, skulls, chalices,
a fox with a bird on a billhook, the lid of a tomb

flying off) all done in fond, dreamy pastels.
(Light drifting down like a bright brass puff,

lands on the rim of a cup like a halo) but no one gives.
People huddle by in ones and twos, smiling.

And as (no one hears it, now) the music runs down,
the wheel stops with a glad, eager grunt—

locking the puppets into the very dumbness
of each last gesture—he smiles once fast at them

eyes as clear gray as the invisible eyes of glass
he gets behind, driving off—into the city's secret heart.

🔥 🔥 🔥

THE GIRL
WHO LOVED HORSES

fiction by ELIZABETH SPENCER

from THE ONTARIO REVIEW

nominated by THE ONTARIO REVIEW, *Maxine Kumin, Robert Phillips and Joyce Carol Oates*

I

SHE HAD DRAWN BACK from throwing a pan of bird scraps out the door because she heard what was coming, the two-part pounding of a full gallop, not the graceful triple notes of a canter. They were mounting the drive now, turning into the stretch along the side of the house; once before someone appearing at the screen door had made the horse shy, so that, barely held beneath the rider, barely restrained, he had plunged off into the flower beds. So she stepped back from the door and saw the two of them shoot past, rounding a final corner, heading for the straight run of drive into the cattle gate and the barn lot back of it.

She flung out the scraps, then walked to the other side of the kitchen and peered through the window, raised for spring, toward the barn lot. The horse had slowed, out of habit, knowing what came next. And the white shirt that had passed hugged so low as to seem some strange part of the animal's trappings, or as though he had run under a low line of drying laundry and caught something to an otherwise empty saddle and bare withers, now rose up, angling to an upright posture. A gloved hand extended to pat the lathered neck.

"Lord have mercy," the woman said. The young woman riding the horse was her daughter, but she was speaking also for her son-in-law who went in for even more reckless behavior in the jumping ring the two of them had set up. What she meant by it was that they were going to kill themselves before they ever had any children, or if they did have children safely they'd bring up the children to be just as foolish about horses and careless of life and limb as they were themselves.

The young woman's booted heel struck the back steps. The screen door banged.

"You ought not to bring him in hot like that," the mother said. "I do know that much."

"Cottrell is out there," she said.

"It's still March, even if it has got warm."

"Cottrell knows what to do."

She ran water at the sink, and cupping her hand drank primitive fashion out of it, bending to the tap, then wet her hands in the running water and thrust her fingers into the dusty, sweat-damp roots of her sand-colored hair. It had been a good ride.

"I hope he doesn't take up too much time," the mother said. "My beds need working."

She spoke mildly but it was always part of the same quarrel they were in like a stream that was now a trickle, now a still pool, but sometimes after a freshet could turn into a torrent. Such as: "Y'all are just crazy. Y'all are wasting everything on those things. And what are they? I know they're pretty and all that, but they're not a thing in the world but animals. Cows are animals. You can make a lot more money in cattle, than carting those things around over two states and three counties."

She could work herself up too much to eat, leaving the two of them at the table, but would see them just the same in her mind's eye, just as if she'd stayed. There were the sandy-haired young woman, already thirty—married four years and still apparently with no intention of producing a family (she was an only child and the estate, though small, was a fine piece of land)—and across from her the dark spare still young man she had married.

She knew how they would sit there alone and not even look at one another or discuss what she'd said or talk against her; they would just sit there and maybe pass each other some food or one of them would get up for the coffee pot. The fanatics of a strange cult would do the same, she often thought, loosening her long hair upstairs, brushing the gray and brown together to a colorless patina, putting on one of her long cotton gowns with the rouched neck, crawling in between white cotton sheets. She was a widow and if she didn't want to sit up and try to talk to the family after a hard day, she didn't have to. Reading was a joy, life-long. She found her place in *Middlemarch,* one of her favorites.

But during the day not even reading (if she'd had the time) could shut out the sounds from back of the privet hedge, plainly to be heard from the house. The trudging of the trot, the pause, the low directive, the thud of hooves, the heave and shout, and sometimes the ring of struck wood as a bar came down. And every jump a risk of life and limb. One dislocated shoulder—Clyde's, thank heaven, not Deedee's—a taping, a sling, a contraption of boards, and pain "like a hot knife," he had said. A hot knife. Wouldn't that hurt anybody enough to make him quit risking life and limb with those two blood horses, quit at least talking about getting still another one while swallowing down painkiller he said he hated to be sissy enough to take?

"Uh-huh," the mother said. "But it'll be Deborah next. You thought about that?"

"Aw, now, Miss Emma," he'd lean back to say, charming her through his warrior's haze of pain. "Deedee and me—that's what we're hooked on. Think of us without it, Mama. You really want to kill us. We couldn't live."

He was speaking to his mother-in-law but smiling at his wife. And she, Deborah, was smiling back.

Her name was Deborah Dale, but they'd always, of course, being from LaGrange, Tennessee, right over the Mississippi border, that is to say, real South, had had a hundred nicknames for her. Deedee, her father had named her, and "Deeds" her funny cousins said—"Hey, Deeds, how ya' doin'?" Being on this property in a town of pretty properties, though theirs was a little way out, a little bit larger than most, she was always out romping, swimming in forbidden creeks, climbing forbidden fences, going barefoot too soon in the spring, the last one in at recess, the first one to turn in an exam paper. ("Are you quite sure that you have finished, Deborah?" "Yes, ma'am.")

When she graduated from ponies to that sturdy calico her uncle gave her, bringing it in from his farm because he had an eye for a good match, there was almost no finding her. "I always know she's somewhere on the place," her mother said. "We just can't see it all at once," said her father. He was ailing even back then but he undertook walks. Once when the leaves had all but gone from the trees, on a warm November afternoon, from a slight rise, he saw her down in a little-used pasture with a straight open stretch among some oaks. The ground was spongy and clotted with damp and a child ought not to have tried to run there. But there went the calico with Deedee clinging low, going like the wind, and knowing furthermore out of what couldn't be anything but long practice, where to turn, where to veer, where to stop.

"One fine afternoon," he said to himself, suspecting even then (they hadn't told him yet) what his illness was, "and Emma's going to be left with nobody." He remarked on this privately, not without anguish and not without humor.

They stopped her riding, at least like that, by sending her off to boarding school, where a watchful ringmaster took "those girls interested in equitation" out on leafy trails, "at the walk, at the trot, and at the canter." They also, with that depth of consideration which must flourish even among those Southerners unlucky enough to wind up in the lower reaches of hell, kept her young spirit out of the worst of the dying. She just got a call from the housemother one night. Her father had "passed away."

After college she forgot it, she gave it up. It was too expensive, it took a lot of time and devotion, she was interested in boys. Some boys were interested in her. She worked in Memphis, drove home to her mother every night. In winter she had to eat breakfast in the dark. On some evenings the phone rang; on some it was silent. Her mother treated both kinds of evenings just the same.

To Emma Tyler it always seemed that Clyde Mecklin materialized out of nowhere. She ran straight into him when opening the front door one evening to get the paper off the porch, he being just about to turn the bell or knock. There he stood, dark and straight in the late light that comes after first dark and is so clear. He was clear as anything in it, clear as the first stamp of a young man ever cast.

"Is Deb'rah here?" At least no Yankee. But not Miss Tyler or Miss Deborah Tyler, or Miss Deborah. No, he was city all right.

She did not answer at first.

"What's the matter, scare you? I was just about to knock."

She still said nothing.

"Maybe this is the wrong place," he said.

"No, it's the right place," Emma Tyler finally said. She stepped back and held the door wider. "Come on in."

"Scared the life out of me," she told Deborah when she finally came down to breakfast the next day, Clyde's car having been heard to depart by Emma Tyler in her upstairs bedroom at an hour she did not care to verify. "Why didn't you tell me you were expecting him? I just opened the door and there he was."

"I liked him so much," said Deborah with grave honesty. "I guess I was scared he wouldn't come. That would have hurt."

"Do you still like him?" her mother ventured, after this confidence.

"He's all for outdoors," said Deborah, as dreamy over coffee as any mother had ever beheld. "Everybody is so indoors. He likes hunting, going fishing, farms."

"Has he got one?"

"He'd like to have. All he's got's this job. He's coming back next weekend. You can talk to him. He's interested in horses."

"But does he know we don't keep horses anymore?"

"That was just my thumbnail sketch," said Deborah. "We don't have to run out and buy any."

"No, I don't imagine so," said her mother, but Deborah hardly remarked the peculiar turn of tone, the dryness. She was letting coast through her head the scene: her mother (whom she now loved better than she ever had in her life) opening the door just before Clyde knocked, so seeing unexpectedly for the first time, that face, that head, that being. . . . When he had kissed her her ears drummed, and it came back to her once more, not thought of in years, the drumming hooves of the calico, and the ghosting father, behind, invisible, observant, off on the bare distant November rise.

It was after she married that Deborah got beautiful. All La-Grange noticed it. "I declare," they said to her mother or sometimes right out to her face, "I always said she was nice looking but I never thought anything like that."

II

Emma first saw the boy in the parking lot. He was new.

In former days she'd parked in front of nearly any place she wanted to go—hardware, or drugstore, or courthouse: change for the meter was her biggest problem. But so many streets were one-way now and what with the increased numbers of cars, the growth of the town, those days were gone; she used a parking lot back of a cafe, near the newspaper office. The entrance to the lot was a bottleneck of a narrow drive between the two brick buildings; once in, it was hard sometimes to park.

That day the boy offered to help. He was an expert driver, she noted, whereas Emma was inclined to perspire, crane and fret, fearful of scraping a fender or grazing a door. He spun the wheel with one hand; a glance told him all he had to know; he as good as sat the car in place, as skillful (she reluctantly thought) as her children on their horses. When she returned an hour later, the cars were denser still; he helped her again. She wondered whether to tip him. This happened twice more.

"You've been so nice to me," she said, the last time. "They're lucky to have you."

"It's not much of a job," he said. "Just all I can get for the moment. Being new and all."

"I might need some help," she said. "You can call up at the Tyler place if you want to work. It's in the book. Right now I'm in a hurry."

On the warm June day, Deborah sat the horse comfortably in the side yard and watched her mother and the young man (whose name was Willett? Williams?), who, having worked the beds and straightened a fence post, was now replacing warped fence boards with new ones.

"Who is he?" she asked her mother, not quite low enough, and meaning what a Southern woman invariably means by that question, not what is his name but where did he come from, is he anybody we know? What excuse, in other words, does he have for even being born?

"One thing, he's a good worker," her mother said, preening a little. Did they think she couldn't manage if she had to? "Now don't you make him feel bad."

"Feel bad!" But once again, if only to spite her mother, who was in a way criticizing her and Clyde by hiring anybody at all to do work that Clyde or the Negro help would have been able to do if only it weren't for those horses—once again Deborah had spoken too loudly.

If she ever had freely to admit things, even to herself, Deborah would have to say she knew she not only looked good that June day, she looked sexy as hell. Her light hair, tousled from a ride in the fields, had grown longer in the last year; it had slipped its pins on one side and lay in a sensuous lock along her cheek. A breeze stirred it, then passed by. Her soft poplin shirt was loose at the throat, the two top buttons open, the cuffs turned back to her elbows. The new horse, the third, was gentle, too much so (this worried them); she sat it easily, one leg up, crossed lazily over the flat English pommel, while the horse, head stretched down, cropped at the tender grass. In the silence between their voices, the tearing of the grass was the only sound except for a shrill jay's cry.

"Make him feel bad!" she repeated.

The boy looked up. The horse, seeking grass, had moved forward; she was closer than before, eyes looking down on him above the rise of her breasts and throat; she saw the closeness go through him, saw her presence register as strongly as if the earth's accidental shifting had slammed them physically together. For a minute there was nothing but the two of them. The jay was silent; even the horse, sensing something, had raised his head.

Stepping back, the boy stumbled over the pile of lumber, then fell in it. Deborah laughed. Nothing, that day, could have stopped her laughter. She was beautifully, languidly, atop a fine horse on the year's choice day at the peak of her life.

"You know what?" Deborah said at supper, when they were

discussing her mother's helper. "I thought who he looks like. He looks like Clyde."

"The poor guy," Clyde said. "Was that the best you could do?"

Emma sat still. Now that she thought of it, he did look like Clyde. She stopped eating, to think it over. What difference did it make if he did? She returned to her plate.

Deborah ate lustily, her table manners unrestrained. She swobbed bread into the empty salad bowl, drenched it with dressing, bit it in hunks.

"The poor woman's Clyde, that's what you hired," she said. She looked up.

The screen door had just softly closed in the kitchen behind them. Emma's hired man had come in for his money.

It was the next day that the boy, whose name was Willett or Williams, broke the riding mower by running it full speed into a rock pile overgrown with weeds but clearly visible, and left without asking for pay but evidently taking with him in his car a number of selected items from barn, garage, and tack room, along with a transistor radio that Clyde kept in the kitchen for getting news with his early coffee.

Emma Tyler, vexed for a number of reasons she did not care to sort out (prime among them was the very peaceful and good time she had been having with the boy the day before in the yard before Deborah had chosen to ride over and join them), telephoned the police and reported the whole matter. But boy, car, and stolen articles vanished into the nowhere. That was all, for what they took to be forever.

III

Three years later, aged 33, Deborah Mecklin was carrying her fine head higher than ever uptown in LaGrange. She drove herself on errands back and forth in car or station wagon, not looking to left or right, not speaking so much as before. She was trying not to hear from the outside what they were now saying about Clyde, how well he'd done with the horses, that place was as good as a stud farm now that he kept ten or a dozen, advertised and traded, as well as showed. And the money was coming in hard and fast. But, they would add, he moved with a fast set, and there was also the occasional gossip item, too often, in Clyde's case, with someone ready to report first hand; look how quick, now you thought of it, he'd taken up with Deborah, and how she'd snapped him up too soon to hear what his reputation was, even back then. It would be a cold day in August before any one woman would be enough for him. And his father before him? And his father before him. So the voices said.

Deborah, too, was trying not to hear what was still sounding from inside her head after her fall in the last big horse show:

The doctor: You barely escaped concussion, young lady.

Clyde: I just never saw your timing go off like that. I can't get over it.

Emma: You'd better let it go for a while, honey. There're other things, so many other things.

Back home, she later said to Emma: "Oh, Mama, I know you're right sometimes, and sometimes I'm sick of it all, but Clyde depends on me, he always has, and now look—"

"Yes, and 'Now look' is right, he has to be out with it to keep it all running. You got your wish, is all I can say."

Emma was frequently over at her sister-in-law Marian's farm these days. The ladies were aging, Marian especially down in the back, and those twilights in the house alone were more and more all that Deedee had to keep herself company with. Sometimes the phone rang and there'd be Clyde on it, to say he'd be late again. Or there'd be no call at all. And once she (of all people) pressed some curtains and hung them, and once hunted for old photographs, and once, standing in the middle of the little-used parlor among the walnut Victorian furniture upholstered in gold and blue and rose, she had said "Daddy?" right out loud, like he might have been there to answer, really been there. It had surprised her, the word falling out like that as though a thought took reality all by itself and made a word on its own.

And once there came a knock at the door.

All she thought, though she hadn't heard the car, was that it was Clyde and that he'd forgotten his key, or seeing her there, his arms loaded maybe, was asking her to let him in. It was past dark. Though times were a little more chancy now, LaGrange was a safe place. People nearer to town used to brag that if they went off for any length of time less than a weekend and locked the doors, the neighbors would get their feelings hurt; and if the Tylers lived further out and "locked up," the feeling for it was ritual mainly, a precaution.

She glanced through the sidelight, saw what she took for Clyde and opened the door. There were cedars in the front yard, not too near the house, but dense enough to block out whatever gathering of light there might have been from the long slope of property beyond the front gate. There was no moon.

The man she took for Clyde, instead of stepping through the door or up to the threshold to greet her, withdrew a step and leaned down and to one side, turning outward as though to pick up something. It was she who stepped forward, to greet, help, inquire; for deep within was the idea her mother had seen to it was firmly and forever planted: that one day one of them was going to get too badly hurt by "those things" ever to be patched up.

So it was in outer dark, three paces from the safe threshold and to the left of the area where the light was falling outward, a dim single sidelight near the mantlepiece having been all she had switched on, too faint to penetrate the sheer gathered curtains of the sidelight, that the man at the door rose up, that he tried to take her. The first she knew of it, his face was in hers, not Clyde's but something like it and at Clyde's exact height, so that for the moment she thought that some joke was on, and then the strange hand caught the parting of her blouse, a new mouth fell hard on her own, one knee thrust her legs apart, the free hand diving in to clutch and press against the thin nylon between her thighs. She recoiled at the same time that she felt, touched in the quick, the painful glory of desire brought on too fast—looking back on that instant's two-edged meaning, she would never hear about rape without the lightning quiver of ambivalence within the word. However, at the time no meditation stopped her knee from coming up into the nameless groin and nothing stopped her from tearing back her mouth slathered with spit so suddenly smeared into it as to drag it into the shape of a scream she was unable yet to find voice for. Her good right arm struck like a hard backhand against a line-smoking tennis serve. Then from the driveway came the stream of twin headlights thrusting through the cedars.

"Bitch!" The word, distorted and low, was like a groan; she had hurt him, freed herself for a moment, but the struggle would have just begun except for the lights, and the screams that were just trying to get out of her. "You fucking bitch." He saw the car lights, wavered, then turned. His leap into the shrubbery was bent, like a hunchback's. She stopped screaming suddenly. Hurt where he lived, she thought. The animal motion, wounded, drew her curiosity for a second. Saved, she saw the car sweep round the drive, but watched the bushes shake, put up her hand to touch but not to close the torn halves of the blouse, which was ripped open to her waist.

Inside, she stood looking down at herself in the dim light. There was a nail scratch near the left nipple, two teeth marks between elbow and wrist where she'd smashed into his mouth. She wiped her own mouth on the back of her hand, gagging at the taste of cigarette smoke, bitterly staled. Animals! She'd always had a special feeling for them, a helpless tenderness. In her memory the bushes, shaking to a crippled flight, shook forever.

She went upstairs, stood trembling in her mother's room (Emma was away), combed her hair with her mother's comb. Then, hearing Clyde's voice calling her below, she stripped off her ravaged blouse and hastened across to their own rooms to hide it in a drawer, change into a fresh one, come downstairs. She had made her decision already. Who was this man? A nothing . . . an unknown. She hated women who shouted Rape! Rape! It was an incident, but once she told it everyone would know, along with the police, and would add to it: they'd say she'd been violated. It was an incident, but Clyde, once he knew, would trace him down. Clyde would kill him.

"Did you know the door was wide open?" He was standing in the livingroom.

"I know. I must have opened it when I heard the car. I thought you were stopping in the front."

"Well, I hardly ever do."

"Sometimes you do."

"Deedee, have you been drinking?"

"Drinking. . .? Me?" She squinted at him, joking in her own way; it was a standing quarrel now that alone she sometimes poured one or two.

He would check her breath but not her marked body. Lust with him was mole-dark now, not desire in the soft increase of morning light, or on slowly westering afternoons or by the nightlight's glow. He would kill for her because she was his wife. . . .

"Who was that man?"

Uptown one winter afternoon late, she had seen him again. He had been coming out of the hamburger place and looking back, seeing her through the streetlights, he had turned quickly into an alley. She had hurried to catch up, to see. But only a form was hastening there, deeper into the unlit slit between brick walls, down toward a street and a section nobody went into without good reason.

"That man," she repeated to the owner (also the proprietor and cook) in the hamburger place. "He was in here just now."

"I don't know him. He hangs around. Wondered myself. You know him?"

"I think he used to work for us once, two or three years ago. I just wondered."

"I thought I seen him somewhere myself."

"He looks a little bit like Clyde."

"Maybe so. Now you mention it." He wiped the counter with a wet rag. "Get you anything, Miss Deborah?"

"I got to get home."

"Y'all got yourselves some prizes, huh?"

"Aw, just some good luck." She was gone.

Prizes, yes. Two trophies at the Shelby County Fair, one in Brownsville where she'd almost lost control again, and Clyde not worrying about her so much as scolding her. His recent theory was that she was out to spite him. He would think it if he was guilty about the women, and she didn't doubt any more that he was. But worse than spite was what had got to her, hating as she did to admit it.

It was fear.

She'd never known it before. When it first started she hadn't even known what the name of it was.

Over two years ago, Clyde had started buying colts not broken yet from a stud farm south of Nashville, bringing them home for him and Deborah to get in shape together. It saved a pile of money to do it that way. She'd been thrown in consequence three times, trampled once, a terrifying moment as the double reins had caught up her outstretched arm so she couldn't fall free. Now when she closed her eyes at night, steel hooves sometimes hung through the dark above them, and she felt hard ground beneath her head, smelt smeared grass on cheek and elbow. To Clyde she murmured in the dark: "I'm not good at it any more." "Why, Deeds, you were always good. It's temporary, honey. That was a bad luck day."

A great couple. That's what Clyde thought of them. But more than half their name had been made by her, by the sight of her, Deborah Mecklin, out in full dress, black broadcloth and white satin stock with hair drawn trimly back beneath the smooth rise of the hat, entering the show ring. She looked damned good back of the glossy neck's steep arch, the pointed ears and lacquered hooves which hardly touched earth before springing upward, as though in the instant before actual flight. There was always the stillness, then the murmur, the rustle of the crowd. At top form she could even get applause. A fame for a time spread round them. The Mecklins. Great riders. "Ridgewood Stables. Blood horses trained. Saddle and Show." He'd had it put up in wrought iron, with a sign as well, old English style, of a horseman spurring.

("Well, you got to make money," said Miss Emma to her son-in-law. "And don't I know it," she said. "But I just hate to think how many times I kept those historical people from putting up a marker on this place. And now all I do is worry one of y'all's going to break your neck. If it wasn't for Marian needing me and all . . . I just can't sleep a wink over here."

("You like to be over there anyway, Mama," Deborah said. "You know we want you here."

("Sure, we want you here," said Clyde. "As for the property, we talked it all out beforehand. I don't think I've damaged it any way."

("I just never saw it as a horse farm. But it's you all I worry about. It's the danger.")

Deborah drove home.

When the working man her mother had hired three years before had stolen things and left, he had left too on the garage wall inside, a long pair of crossing diagonal lines, brown, in mud, she thought, until she smelled what it was, and there were the blood-stained menstrual pads she later came across in the driveway, dug up out of the garbage, strewed out into the yard.

She told Clyde about the first but not the second discovery. "Some critters are mean," he'd shrugged it off. "Some critters are just mean."

They'd been dancing, out at the club. And so in love back then, he'd turned and turned her, far apart, then close, talking into her ear, making her laugh and answer, but finally he said: "Are you a mean critter, Deedee? Some critters are mean." And she'd remembered what she didn't tell.

But in those days Clyde was passionate and fun, both marvellously together, and the devil appearing at midnight in the bend of a country road would not have scared her. Nothing would have. It was the day of her life when they bought the first two horses.

"I thought I seen him somewhere myself."

"He looks a little bit like Clyde."

And dusk again, a third and final time.

The parking lot where she'd come after a movie was empty except for a few cars. The small office was unlighted, but a man she took for the attendant was bending to the door on the far side of a long cream-colored sedan near the back fence. "Want my ticket?" she called. The man straightened, head rising above the body frame, and she knew him. Had he been about to steal a car, or was he breaking in for whatever he could find, or was it her coming all alone that he was waiting for? However it was, he knew her as instantly as she knew him. Each other was what they had, by whatever design or absence of it, found. Deborah did not cry out or stir.

Who knew how many lines life had cut away from him down through the years till the moment when an arrogant woman on a horse had ridden him down with lust and laughter? He wasn't bad looking; his eyes were beautiful; he was the kind to whom nothing good could happen. From that bright day to this chilly dusk, it had probably just been the same old story.

Deborah waited. Someway or other, what was coming, threading through the cars like an animal lost for years catching the scent of a former owner, was her own.

("You're losing nerve, Deedee." Clyde had told her recently. "That's what's really bothering me. You're scared, aren't you?")

The bitter-stale smell of cigarette breath, though not so near as before, not forced against her mouth, was still unmistakably familiar. But the prod of a gun's nuzzle just under the rise of her breast was not. It had never happened to her before. She shuddered at the touch with a chill spring-like start of something like life, which was also something like death.

"Get inside," he said.

"Are you the same one?" she asked. "Just tell me that. Three years ago, Mama hired somebody. Was that you?"

"Get in the car."

She opened the door, slid over to the driver's seat, found him beside her. The gun, thrust under his crossed arm, resumed its place against her.

"Drive."

"Was it you the other night at the door?" Her voice trembled as the motor started, the gear caught.

"He left me with the lot; ain't nobody coming."

The car eased into an empty street.

"Go out of town. The Memphis road."

She was driving past familiar, cared-for lawns and houses, trees and intersections. Someone waved from a car at a stoplight, taking them for her and Clyde. She was frightened and accepting fear which come to think of it was all she'd been doing for months, working with those horses. ("Don't let him bluff you, Deedee. It's you or him. He'll do it if he can.")

"What do you want with me? What is it you want?"

He spoke straight outward, only his mouth moving, watching the road, never turning his head to her. "You're going out on that Memphis road and you're going up a side road with me. There's some woods I know. When I'm through with you you ain't never going to have nothing to ask nobody about me because you're going to know it all and it ain't going to make you laugh none, I guarantee."

Deborah cleared the town and swinging into the highway wondered at herself. Did she want him? She had waited when she might have run. Did she want, trembling, pleading, degraded, finally to let him have every single thing his own way?

(Do you see steel hooves above you over and over because you want them one day to smash into your brain?

("Daddy, Daddy," she had murmured long ago when the old unshaven tramp had come up into the lawn, bleary-eyed, face blood-burst with years of drink and weather, frightening as the boogeyman, "raw head and bloody bones," like the Negro women scared her with. That day the sky streamed with end-of-the-world fire. But she hadn't called so loudly as she might have, she'd let him come closer, to look at him better, until the threatening voice of her father behind her, just on the door's slamming, had cried:

"What do you want in this yard? What you think you want here? Deborah! You come in this house this minute!" But the mystery still lay dark within her, forgotten for years, then stirring to life again: When I said "Daddy, Daddy?" was I calling to the tramp or to the house? Did I think the tramp was him in some sort of joke or dream or trick? If not, why did I say it? Why?

("Why do you ride a horse so fast, Deedee? Why do you like to do that?" *I'm going where the sky breaks open.* "I just like to." "Why do you like to drive so fast?" "I don't know.")

Suppose he kills me, too, thought Deborah, striking the straight stretch on the Memphis road, the beginning of the long rolling run through farms and woods. She stole a glance to her right. He looked like Clyde, all right. What right did he have to look like Clyde?

("It's you or him, Deedee." All her life they'd said that to her from the time her first pony, scared at something, didn't want to cross a bridge. "Don't let him get away with it. It's you or him.")

Righting the big car into the road ahead, she understood what was demanded of her. She pressed the accelerator gradually downward toward the floor.

"And by the time he realized," she said, sitting straight in her chair at supper between Clyde and Emma, who by chance were there that night together; "—by the time he knew, we were hitting above seventy-five, and he said, 'What you speeding for?' and I said, 'I want to get it over with.' And he said, 'Okay, but that's too fast.' By that time we were touching eighty and he said, 'What the fucking hell—' Excuse me, Mama, '—you think you're doing? You slow this thing down.' So I said, 'I tell you what I'm doing. This is a rolling road with high banks and trees and lots of curves. If you try to take the wheel away from me, I'm going to wreck us both. If you try to sit there with that gun in my side I'm going to go faster and faster and sooner or later something will happen, like a curve too sharpe to take or a car too many to pass with a big truck coming and we're both going to get smashed up at the very least. It won't do any good to shoot me when it's more than likely both of us will die. You want that?'

"He grabbed at the wheel but I put on another spurt of speed and when he pulled at the wheel we side-rolled, skidded back and another car coming almost didn't get out of the way. I said, 'You see what you're doing, I guess.' And he said, 'Jesus God.' Then I knew I had him, had whipped him down.

"But it was another two or three miles like that before he said, 'Okay, okay, so I quit. Just slow down and let's forget it.' And I said, 'You give me that gun. The mood I'm in, I can drive with one hand or no hands at all, and don't think I won't do it.' But he wanted his gun at least, I could tell. He didn't give in till a truck was ahead and we passed but barely missed a car that was coming (it had to run off the concrete), and he put it down, in my lap."

(Like a dog, she could have said, but didn't. And I felt sorry for him, she could have added, because it was his glory's end.)

"So I said, 'Get over, way over,' and he did, and I coasted from fast to slow. I turned the gun around on him and let him out on an empty stretch of road, by a rise with a wood and a country side road rambling off, real pretty, and I thought, maybe that's where he was talking about, where he meant to screw hell—Excuse me, Mama—out of me. I held the gun till he closed the door and went down in the ditch a little way, then I put the safety catch on and threw it at him. It hit his shoulder then fell in the weeds. I saw it fall, driving off."

"Oh, my poor baby," said Emma. "Oh, my precious child."

It was Clyde who rose, came round the table to her, drew her to her feet, held her close. "That's nerve," he said. "That's class." He let her go and she sat down again. "Why didn't you shoot him?"

"I don't know."

"He was that one we hired that time," Emma said. "I'd be willing to bet you anything."

"No, it wasn't," said Deborah quickly. "This one was blond and short, red-nosed from too much drinking, I guess. Awful like Mickey Rooney, gone and gotten old. Like the boogeyman, I guess."

"The poor woman's Mickey Rooney. You women find yourselves the damnedest men."

"She's not right about that," said Emma. "What do you want to tell that for? I know it was him. I feel like it was."

"Why'd you throw the gun away?" Clyde asked. "We could trace that."

"It's what I felt like doing," she said. She had seen it strike, how his shoulder, struck, went back a little.

Clyde Mecklin sat watching his wife. She had scarcely touched her food and now, pale, distracted, she had risen to wander toward the windows, look out at the empty lawn, the shrubs and flowers, the stretch of white painted fence, ghostly by moonlight.

"It's the last horse I'll ever break," she said, more to herself than not, but Clyde heard and stood up and was coming to her.

"Now, Deedee—"

"When you know you know," she said, and turned, her face set against him: her anger, her victory, held up like a blade against his stubborn willfulness. "I want my children now," she said.

At the mention of children, Emma's presence with them became multiple and vague; it trembled with thanksgiving, it spiralled on wings of joy.

Deborah turned again, back to the window. Whenever she looked away, the eyes by the road were there below her: they were worthless, nothing, but infinite, never finishing—the surface there was no touching bottom of—taking to them, into themselves, the self that was hers no longer.

CODEX

WHITE BLIZZARD

by ED SANDERS

from MONTEMORA

nominated by MONTEMORA *and Ron Silliman*

EDITOR'S NOTE: This essay was one of several in an issue of *Montemora* devoted to "The current poetry pandemic"

The following decisions on the Question of the WHITE BLIZ-ZARD have been promulgated by the Sacred Council of the Bards.

> Thus came the day of the WHITE BLIZZARD. At any given moment in time, the United States Postal System had in its custody over 5,000,000 units of the publication known as the WHITE BLIZZARD: poetry magazines, often grant-funded, often hastily photo-offset or stapled 8½ × 11 mimeo'd models with two-color covers.

> Thus came the day of the Grants Junkie: mammals caught in the desperate cycle: publish—get the grants; get the grants—publish; publish—get the grants . . .

> Thus came the day of the "Enormous Organized Cowardice." The Great Fear of offending Government Literary Executives. Thus an endless alleyway of blandness.

Thus the following decisions:

1. The FERN HILL Rule. No final version of any poem may

henceforth be published without at least 50 draft versions placed on file for public verification at the Library of Congress.

2. The "VOG*" Rule. Poets may not, at any time, rely on the Rilkean Synapse in order to write. Dictation from any Numinal Entity, Deity, and in fact any automatic writing based on information supplied by any putative extrasensory apparatus is forbidden.

3. The writing of more than 75 poems in any fiscal year will be punishable by a fine of $500 per ten additional poems.

4. Any person with a collected output of verse over 900 poems in length, especially if the person is under 24, will be ineligible for further government grants for a period of seven years. One year will be removed for each certified destruction of all copies of each 100 poems.

5. GRANTS IN LIEU OF VERSE. The keep-th'-farmers-from-planting-corn-by-paying-them-for-not-plowing principle. A Grant of $5000 (to come from surplus in the Dept. of Defense) for any poet who agrees not to write for one year.

6. OPERATION EPIC. Prolific poets are to be encouraged to write book-length poems. The definition of a book-length poem shall be:

   A. Must be metrically scored (see the PINDAR Rule below)

   B. May not contain less than 750 single-spaced pages

   C. May not be completed before 17 complete initial drafts are are on file at the Library of Congress

   D. Must require no less than 5 (five) years of exclusive labor

   E. Sonnets, lyrics, and any form of philosophic ode may not be written by the bard during period of composition of the Epic

7. Enforced "OTHERISM." The Capital "I" Rule. Any poet found in his or her collected works to have struck the Capital I

more than 27,500 times shall have the said Capital I key on any and all typewriters in his or her possession removed and melted down for a period of 11 years.

8. The Scare-off Tactic. Every member of any High School or College creative writing class shall, on penalty of fine, receive and read the following book: *Lives of the Poets from the Point of View of Starvation*, with emphasis on such cases as the penurious suicide of Thomas Chatterton, and the possible death by starvation of Edmund Spenser.

9. Encouragment of Dithyrambs, Dirges, and Public Choral Poesy: The Pindar Principle. The development in modern times of the ancient tradition of the κύκλιος χορός, the circular poetic choir of 50 singers/chanters who perform poetry for public or national events. Such Pindaric Choruses would provide employment for tens of thousands of bards-in-training.

It could follow the Greek route

Tragedy
(the electronic
poem-opera)

The Bifurcated
Dithyramb
Tradition

The Chanted
"Metrically Scored"
Pindaric
Athletic
Commentary (say,
Pro Basketball
play-offs)

Choral
Military-Industrial
National Events
"Flatterer of
Tyrants" verse

The Gibberish
Dithyramb, "The
verse of the dithy-
ramb became proverb-
ial for lack of sense"

The Sho-Sto-Po
(Short Story Poem)
Dithyramb

10. The Encouragement of Poetic Vaudeville. While of a less lofty inspiration than the Pindaric Choral Verse principle, Poetic Vaudeville would supply many of the needs of the bard. First, it would establish a national circuit of places to perform.

Many poets want to be SEEN, to be FAMOUS, to be a ★ to be a SKY ★, a ★ among ★'s, a ★'s ★. Therefore, why not emphasize the POET PERFORMING? We could see the development of P-PITS, Performance Poetry in the Schools.

11. Creation of a NATIONAL POETIC GRID: The Stake-out Principle. Let us postulate, for this occasion, the existence of 10,000 poets in the United States. With a population of 300,000,000 humans, that's one poet for every 30,000 citizens.

    Therefore, be it resolved by the Sacred Council of Bards, that each poet forthwith stake out his or her 30,000 citizens to service with verse, lyrics, epics, epithalamia, dirges, and poesy for all occasions, public and private. Once a poet has staked out his or her turf, it shall henceforth be illegal for any other poet to encroach or to otherwise horn in on said poet's home turf.

    The game is then a cinch, o bards; for all a poet has then to do per year is to find a way to obtain circa one dollar from each person in his or her 30,000-person service unit.

And thus a method to escape the perilous

OUROBOREAN WHEEL OF VERSE:

and an aid to overcome the dire

OUROBOREAN WHEEL OF POV:

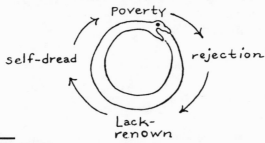

---

*VOG. Voice of God.

BREATH

by HEATHER McHUGH

from ASPEN ANTHOLOGY

nominated by ASPEN ANTHOLOGY

What I want from God, feared to be
unlovable, is none
of the body's business, nasty
lunches of blood and host, and none

of the yes-man networks,
neural, capillary or electric.
No little histories recited
in the temple, in the neck and wrist.
I want the heavy air,
unhymned, uncyclical,
and a deep kiss: absence's.
I want to be rid of men

who seem friendly, but die,
and rid of my studies
wired for sound.
I want the space in which all names
for worship sink away,
and earth recedes
to silver vanishing, the point
at which we can forget
our history of longing, and become

his great blue breath,
his ghost and only song.

GIANT STEPS

by JOHN TAGGART

from CHICAGO REVIEW

nominated by CHICAGO REVIEW *and Ron Silliman*

1

To want to be a saint to want to be a saint to want to
to want to be a saint to be the snake-tailed one to want to
be snake-tailed with wings to be a snake-tailed saint with wings to
want to be a saint to want to awaken men wake men from
    nightmare.

To go down to raise to go down to raise to go to go down the
ladder to go down as taught as dance steps taught by the master
    as
taught to dance to step-dance to dance with giant steps to go to
    dance to
step-dance to dance with giant steps as taught by the master to
dance to go down the ladder to go down to raise men from
    nightmare.

2

To want to be a saint to want to be a saint to want to
to be snake-tailed with wings to be a snake-tailed saint with
wings to leap upon the horse-headed woman the blue-eyed
    woman
who chokes the throat to want to be a saint to wake men from
    nightmare.

To go down to raise to go down to raise to go to go down the
ladder to go down as taught by the master as taught to dance to

343

step-dance to dance with giant steps to dance with giant steps
down the ladder to dance down as taught by the master to dance
    down the
ladder to obtain possession to go down to raise men from
    nightmare.

3

To want to be a saint to want to be a saint to want to
to want to be a snake-tailed saint with wings to leap upon the
    horse-
headed woman the blue-eyed woman the woman with the little
    moon
who chokes the throat to want to be a saint to wake men from
    nightmare.

To go down to raise to go down to raise to go to go down the
ladder to go to dance as taught by the master to dance to
    step-dance to
dance with giant steps to dance with giant steps to dance down
    the
ladder as taught by the master to obtain possession to dance down
    to
raise men with a horn to go down to raise men from nightmare.

4

To want to be a saint to want to be a saint to want to
be a snake-tailed saint with wings to leap upon the horse-headed
    the
blue-eyed woman with the little moon the woman with nine
    shadows
who chokes the throat to want to be a saint to wake men from
    nightmare.

To go down to raise to go down to raise to go to go down the
ladder to dance as taught by the master to step-dance to dance
    with

giant steps to dance with giant steps to dance down as taught by
   the
master to obtain possession to dance down to raise men with a
   horn a
tenor horn to go to go down to raise men from nightmare.

MICHAEL AT SIXTEEN MONTHS

by AL YOUNG

from CALAFIA (Y'Bird Books)

nominated by Y'BIRD BOOKS

Ball	His whole world revolves around light dark
Bird	things sailing thru the air around chairs
Dog	the mystery of rising & falling & getting
Cheese	up again in the morning at night/scratching
Shoes	at windows to get our bananas oranges a
Cat	step/stepping down stepping up/keep the music
Juice	going/TV theme songs/walks on stones, dancing
Baby	on manhole covers, anything circular, objects
Daddy	that hang & flap in the breeze/the wind as
Mama	it foams into a room making the skin cool
Boat	puffing out curtains/baths/water/legs/kiss
Mama	Here we go into the rain turning sunlight
	Here we go down the slide into sandpiles
Mommy	Here we go clapping our hands as blocks fall
	Here we go running from Mama Mommy Mimi baby
No	crashing into Daddy dozing on the floor, a
	world is shooting out of rubber tree leaves
Nose	The window is a magic mirror/sad to see time
	flowing throwing itself thru flesh electric
Hot	that hard months ago was only a flash in
	a sea of possibility/the suffering afloat
Car	The meanness he will have to endure is only
	life ungathered in the eye of no world/is light
Book	pure & not so simple after all is living life
	alive alive O!

346

MY VEGETABLE LOVE

fiction by BARBARA GROSSMAN

from THE PARIS REVIEW

nominated by THE PARIS REVIEW *and Gordon Lish*

M‍Y BROTHER is a horticulturist. From where nobody knows. We are a family of merchants, shopkeepers, purveyors of service; none of us is concerned with growth. But, my brother keeps two hundred healthy plants on our porch, and they respond to his tending as if he'd come from farmers. On that porch, in heavy clay pots stacked so close as to become walls, hanging in curtains from glinting hooks screwed into the ceiling, on shelves and windowsills and perched upon the edges of upturned orange crates, grow plants with names enough to provide an entire generation identity.

I too have had some small success with growing things. A sensible variety of cacti grow along my south window; not lovely,

347

but strong, stubborn plants, requiring little care, going dormant during cold months. I cannot share my brother's enthusiasm for quantity. Certainly plants are decorative and it is pleasing to see them grow, to observe a change in shape or be surprised by a bloom. I therefore keep a few beneath my window to enjoy. My brother's skill with his collection, his ability to nurture magnificent specimens of so many varieties, is too much related to his desire to possess so many. There has not been a week in the past four years when he's not come breathing up our front steps with a tenderly wrapped addition in his arms. I have dreams about their weight causing the floors to fall in.

Not long ago I discovered, buried under a boy's stamp, coin and stone collections, two grade school notebooks with marble designed covers. Amused, that after so many purges, these had survived on my brother's closet floor I opened one. There were no spelling lists or addition problems, rather a journal; his diary. The entries were not dated and his style was graphic, detailed, highly descriptive. Whole pages were devoted to the record of a single event. It was compulsive, it was overwritten. I found it sordid.

Excess was his trait from the beginning. So corpulent a newborn our pediatrician steadily reduced his ration of formula from what the others in his glassy nursery were allowed. He slept such terrifying, long hours, that Mother would awaken at those hours she was accustomed to feeding me and drop books on the linoleum to get him up, crying for food. She tells us that he was an inordinately good baby and this frightened her.

I was her careful child. Athletic, sturdy, having muscles adults pinched with surprised winks of pleasure, I never so much as cut myself enough to require suturing. To this day I've had no broken bones, no loosened tendons or slippery joints. Injury is something I never meet. My teeth resist decay and disalignment with a tenacity that makes dentists marvel. I don't remember being especially careful—but there it is.

My brother was known by his first name at County General. Embedded fish hooks were his trademark, but a split skull and femur, poisoning, unstoppable bleeding and a first degree burn were his as well. He swallowed two ounces of india ink, a bottle of flavored aspirin, random cleaning preparations and a bit of ammonia during his early years and was pumped clean of all these liquids by stern interns. Never do I recall seeing him make it to first base without twisting an ankle. When he climbed the stairlike pines in the arboretum he fell. Puddles he could not avoid, and though this trait is common to children he was the only one of us to fall unconscious into one from his bike, inhaling nearly a pint before a panicked friend yanked him out. Once frightened by the approach of a nasty janitor, while shoving his head between the bars of a steel banister, he pulled out too fast and put a gash into his forehead that ran four inches north from his left eye and vanished into his hairline. The jokes of the emergency room played upon his seemingly endless supply of blood and method. My parents worried that the numbers of insurance claims made would provoke suspicion. I think I must have feared him.

When I see him at work in the startling glare of the porch I am galled by the awful redness of his hands. I am still shocked by his body, the concavity of belly and buttock. There is no way to pinpoint the time he became angled like this—it is as if it occurred when I turned away. It is like another accident. Not that he is unattractive; he is manly and draws the eyes of women on the street. Perhaps I never expected him to succeed to maturity.

I observe him with his plants. He stands with tools slung around his hips, dripping filtered water from a can, poking holes near roots with a copper spade, snipping dry leaves and spindly stems off plants he names for me in a low drone, an incantation of his concern. The Latin is comfortable in his mouth. I am not used to seeing him this calm and at ease; it confuses me. The light there, the moist air, the unexpected touch of a branch against my cheek make me too alert. I leave to take a walk. On the front steps I find the palms are stained brown as if I'd touched his potting soil. I never do, though.

Most of his injuries are self-inflicted, yet I admit to responsibility for some of his trips to County General. All of us finally hurt him. In a neighborhood playground during a hot vacation afternoon, father moved to break my brother's swift decent on a sliding board and cracked the youngster's forearm just above the wrist. While retrieving him from off the refrigerator top, mother fell with him in her grip and smacked a knot into the ridge above his nose that subsided after a month to become a strawberry colored scar. Helping him to untangle his hand from the mouth of our in-sink disposal, an uncle dislocated my brother's shoulder. And my grandmother, in her attempt to push the boy away from the

white-hot element of an electric range, knocked a pot of but-
terscotch pudding across the cuffs of his pajama bottoms and onto
his naked feet.

From me he suffered the normal quantities of bumps and
bruises. We fought with pleasure, tumbling back-to-belly across
the lawn, screaming into the grass. Indians, Marines, wrestlers;
there are rough games. We made violent mistakes.

One spring a thunderstorm tore the shingles off the roof and
scattered them, along with the dead refuse of unpruned trees,
woody rose branches and the heads of flowers, over the yard. My
brother and I watched the excited weather from the dry cave of the
awning father had erected over the patio. Water caught in pools
above. We prodded the ballooning canvas with broomsticks and
sent cascades of rain off the braided cotton fringe at the awning's
hem. When the rain broke we moved out onto the grass. The sky
was green. Familiar trees had changed shape. A willow had fallen
across the wheelbarrow. We grabbed hold of two rain-black
branches and whirled them above our heads, yelling into the air,
turning faster on our toes than we wanted. My branch caught my
brother on his back. He took this as a challenge and when I saw that
he did I made it one. Running after me he found his weapon too
clumsy and exchanged it for a heavily tarred shingle. It glinted wet
in his fist. I ran from him, he followed at terrific, sprinter's speed
and threw the shingle in my direction. The trajectory of the falling
shingle coincided not with my head, but his own, dropping edge
earthward, velocity times mass. A rush of colored blood burst up
from his skull what seemed feet into the air.

He was awake during the ride to County General. I remember
he looked almost regal, infinitely dignified. I was infuriated by his
clumsiness, hilarious with its result. There I learned irony.

I think that when I dream about dogs I am dreaming about my
brother. Swaddled miniatures are carried through rooms by nurses
with a sense of urgency. We owned a dog; a small collie all fur and
dusty eyes. I trained her. Our parents enjoyed her warm friendli-
ness, my brother loved her, but every night I filled her bowl with
dry food and she became mine. When at last she was sent, crippled
by arthritis, to be gassed, there was in the quality of our mourning
both a sadness for her death and a pity at my loss. Perhaps her
being dead gives me these sweaty dreams. I am not sensitive and
am bewildered by so strong a reaction. When I look for reasons I

find my brother, though my route there is skeletal and the destination unnerving.

None of us knows what to make of him. He will not choose a profession. Father offered to take him into the business. Mother produced a secret saving account that might purchase the stock and pay a year's rent for a small flower shop. I have nothing to offer but my schooling. My brother refuses all we suggest. He is not charmed by finance, commercial considerations would kill his joy in horticulture, the academy he finds deadening. He will not identify his calling. To us his life is too solitary—we worry about futures. He claims contentment and argues the present.

I don't know how to understand his silence because I leap to speech and detest shyness. His solitude has not always been so strong. When young he had friends, although he chose for his companions the unusual children in the neighborhood: a boy with sun-white hair and glasses thick as his fingers; a set of twins so freckled as to be disfigured in summer; that violent little girl across the street who I found once sitting on my brother's head and screaming like a loosened fanbelt. I ran to them and pulled so hard on that creature's hair that some tore loose. She ran home. My brother took the tangle from my hand and we went into the house. I had never done anything like that before. I still doubt the memory.

Father keeps portraits of us on his office walls. They are ordinary photographs. Mother is smiling over a holiday table. I am seen twisted three-quarters profile into the lens of a yearbook photographer's camera. Only my brother appears in action. He is walking toward the frame from a pier that extends into a flat ocean. His jeans push up his knees in folds that are alive and his T-shirt stretches across a chest that's a year's growth too large for it. From one arm falls a string of blank-eyed fish. His elbow bends with their weight to rest on his waist and push out his hip in a gesture that is slatternly. He views his catch; a smile drags toward his ear. It is not an extraordinary picture—it is an extraordinary smile. Not another photograph exists in which he smiles, for he rarely responds with humor, just a benign seriousness that makes us wonder at the texture of his thoughts.

The diaries I've found confirm his humorlessness. All that he writes there is done so without regard for the jokes in his life. When I discovered these notes I thought them to be intentionally written for me, toward some shared and secret understanding. But he is too ruthless in his disclosures, too graphic and droll to mean the contents to be anything more than a private record. I was embarrassed at his candor. I do not regret finding those notebooks, I wish only that he had not written them. They invade my privacy.

Lately he eats poorly. Mother tempts him with former favorites but he abstains. He leaves the table as if relieved of the chore of chewing and goes directly to his porch. I follow him and find my brother gulping air over his pots, nauseated.

Once, everything within his reach passed eventually into his mouth. He was sent from classrooms to stand fugitive in the corridor for his too generous consumption of mucilage and rubber eraser. He'd devour jars of white paste in an afternoon. A pencil lasted a week before it was taken from him looking as if some rodent had made a meal of it. Father's tiny saccarin pills disappeared with a rapidity that aroused suspicion. I came upon him one evening after supper as he hunched elbows to knees in the yard, licking the silver specs of mica out of a handful of earth.

This diet disturbed his digestion. His times on the toilet were infrequent and troubled, bad times when all of us suffered the closed grunts echoing off the tiled walls. Nightly he ingested patent medicines, bland and sticky concoctions impossible to swallow— nothing relieved him. Sometimes three weeks would pass without action. Questions were whispered after meals, after hot baths. The answer continued in the negative. A doctor's advice would be sought and mechanical means counseled against. Finally my brother would be deposited upon the toilet with instructions not to . leave his post until the desired effect was produced. His feces were black and hard as hamster pellets, musical in their fall. Always he flushed too late and father was dispatched with plunger and snake to clear the pipes for our more daily use. My brother called me to witness a miracle in that bathroom. Sparkling under water was a half-exposed copper indian head. An unremembered snack.

His odd habits brought down a regular assignment of punish- ments. Neither father nor mother could strike us and so were forced to imagine and enact deprivations appropriate to the mis- demeanor. This was most difficult. For strange swallowings my brother was made to spend meal hours in the guest room, a lap-tray on his knees. This bedroom was as dull as a bed and an empty closet. We'd hear him humming in there, humming without tune two long notes that varied not in pitch but only duration. This worked so as to antagonize my ulcerous father, who, to protect his delicate stomach, would end my brother's captivity early. Nothing discouraged him. His allowance was so often cut off it was no allowance. Gifts were retrieved like fish lures. He ate.

And he retaliated. He poured varnish over mother's dress watch. He placed a can of aerosol air freshener on the shelf where mother habitually kept her hairspray. Mother spent an evening at the theatre stinking of pine forests. He rigged rugs to vases; I opened doors, porceline shattered. Our toothbrushes were regularly rubbed in antiseptic soap. Mornings we gagged and foamed. His most ingenious trick was to shave redwood into father's pipe tobacco. None of these acts endeared him to us.

He came home recently with a succulent. He gave it to me, he held the fleshy plant out at the ends of his arms and made his presentation muttering a phrase I recognized from his diaries. It was a mistake. To express my thanks I rose early the next morning and washed his plants with the spray gun he normally employs for that purpose. My brother arrived on the porch when I was high on a stool reaching up to a fern. Water dripped into my armpits. I lowered the spray gun and repeated to him the phrase he'd used unconsciously. He screwed the faucet shut, helped me off the stool. I repeated the phrase. He opened the front door and faced the neighborhood. Again I began to speak but he turned to me midsentence, his expression so disinterested that I swallowed my spit and left the porch.

I have remembered a game we played. Bedtimes were not welcome during the long summer evenings. We were sent up to bathe and dress for bed while it was still light and the sounds of older children rose to the open windows. Unable to sleep we developed a system of communication composed of knocks. We shared a wall—his bed and mine lined either side of a thin plaster partition. One knock meant come in. Two knocks meant stay out. Three knocks indicated danger, parent in the corridor.

I was the initiator—knock. Came my brother's reply—knock knock knock. We waited. Knock. He'd creep into my room and stand at the foot of my bed awaiting my signal to join me there. I took the space close to the wall. As a precautionary measure we

locked legs at our knees. Now no parent could part us in our sleep
without a fuss. Close as shoes tucked one in one we exchanged
back-tickling while chanting a song:

We're going on a treasure hunt,
X marks the spot,
Three big circles and one big dot.
Go up, go down,
Follow the dotted line,
Take three big steps and stop.

Each line had an accompanying gesture, a design we traced across
each other's spine. The light going blue in the windows we would
stroke ourselves to sleep. We never awoke together for sometime
in the night mother would find us linked there and remove my
brother to his own bed on the other side of the partition.

I should mention that he was a bed-wetter. I should say that
every night before our parents turned out their lights a cry would
go down the corridor that connected our bedrooms: Have you
urinated? Then father'd trundle brother to the bathroom. This
process did not insure a dry night, somehow my brother found
reserves with which to soak his sheets. We covered his mattress
with rubber. It rotted away in a month. His tinkling looked like an
ancient map of Europe. Devices were purchased. A moisture
responsive alarm ran copper wires through a plastic sheet that lay
beneath his cotton contour. When the suggestion of liquid con-
tacted metal an alarm startled the entire family from its sleep. My
brother waited till the buzzer ran itself down and then relieved
himself without discovery until morning. We instituted a system of
all-night walks to the toilet. He learned to intuit our approach and
timed himself thirty minutes before and after so that the parent
scheduled would find him damp and sweetly odiferous and give it
up. I think he enjoyed the warmth of his urine.

Three times I've left his notebooks in some place other than
where I found them. I have ruffled pages, laid down black thumb
prints. I tear corners and remove entire pages. Nothing makes him
respond. Rehearsed endlessly in my mind is a small speech intended to make clear to him my knowledge of these diaries. I
cannot deliver it. I think of writing notes, slipping them between
the leaves, notes to assert my participation. He will not answer. I
am quickly running out of method. I fear that my intrusion will

make him abandon writing. I also fear that he may continue too long. I do not know everything; this is some comfort.

Yesterday white fly invaded his porch. Enraged he announced the predator's presence during breakfast. His appetite was astounding. I offered assistance, we cleared the table and entered the humid room. In the dark my brother mixed chemicals as I examined leaves for damage and picked at the white bits of fur this insect wraps about itself. Working with a flashlight we laboriously sponged each green surface with the solution he'd prepared. I understood that these ministrations contained an element of danger, that the slightest miscalculation in the proportion of acid to base might halt photosynthesis entirely. We washed our hands and left. All day he has been in his room reading from a large blue botany manual.

I cannot sleep. The house grows shadows around me as I settle and resettle into the snaking bedclothes. I want to knock on the partition. I have gone so far as to raise my fist to do so. It occurs to me that his plants are all that keep him with us here.

𝈓 𝈓 𝈓

THE SHARK
AND THE BUREAUCRAT

fiction by VLADA BULATOVIC-VIB

from MODERN YUGLOSLAV SATIRE (Cross-Cultural Communications)

nominated by Cross-Cultural Communications

ONE DAY, FISHING ON THE SEASHORE, the Bureaucrat saw the Shark. He said to it:

"I marvel at you, Shark!"

"And I marvel at you, Bureaucrat!"

"You swim wonderfully."

"So do you."

"You are strong, Shark."

"It is nothing compared to your strength."

"I wanted to ask you: How do you manage to keep going in so much water?"

"Quite simply, When it gets cold, I go under; when it gets warm, I come up. That's why I swim only in my own circle."

"You are a big fish, but now it's no longer fashionable to say: 'Big fish eat little ones.' How do you feed yourself under the new conditions?"

"I fight for equality. For example, I say to the whitebait: 'Do you want us to be equal?' 'Yes,' it says. 'Then, go ahead, swallow me,' I say. It tries and can't. Then I try and can."

"How do you teach the whitebait to obey?"

"I take up a pedagogical position."

"What did you say: demagogical?"

"I said: pedagogical. I say to the whitebait: 'You ought to be ashamed of yourselves. How can you swim in different directions?' They are ashamed and swim in my direction. I open my mouth to greet them with enthusiastic welcome, but they are impulsive and rush to my throat by mistake."

"When people start to criticize you, Shark, what do you do?"

"I turn over onto my back and swim lazily like a corpse. Then I allow the whitebait to spread and nibble at me."

"How does a shark make a career?"

"I don't understand."

"For example, first you are a shark in one town, then in a larger field, in a district; then you swim further and further."

"We don't have any of that. The sea is not divided, and climbing upwards is limited. You can only go as far as the surface."

"I shouldn't want much more. I, too, would like to swim up to the surface."

"Just be a bit more cunning. When whales notice your tendency to swim to the surface, you admit that your tail smells and renounce it. And don't worry, a new and better tail will grow."

"What is your position, Shark?"

"Normal. Head down, tail up, fins at the side."

"I don't mean that. I was thinking of your function."

"Oh, that. With us the fish that swims fastest succeeds."

"You lucky fish."

The Shark proffered its fins as a sign of parting. The Bureaucrat in shaking hands, leaned too far forward and fell into the sea. Some time later, the Bureaucrat came out of the water with the Shark in his teeth.

Translated by Nada Ćurčija-Prodanović

STONES

by MICHAEL BLUMENTHAL

from THE POET UPSTAIRS (Washington Writers' Publishing House)

nominated by Washington Writers Publishing House

"A man in terror of impotence
or infertility, not knowing the difference . . ."
Adrienne Rich

We live in dread of something:

Need, perhaps. Tears,
the air inside a woman's dress,
the deep breath of non-ambition.

In a valley of stone,
men had to carry stones.
In a sea of fertility,
women could drown
in the wake of conceptions.

We no longer build in stone—
houses of rice paper, beds
of feather. Manhood
is the one stone we still
insist on, lifting it

From abandoned quarries,
carrying it on our backs
even when we make love,
until the woman beneath us
calls passion a kind of

Suffocation, surfaces for air
like a young child whose head
has been pushed beneath the water,
a way to learn swimming.

Did you come?, we ask,
her head bobbing above the brine
that pours from us. Applause
is what we want now,

The sound of her wet hands
clapping in the last wind
before she sinks again,
before she holds us again
so tight we both plunge
like a cry for help
into the water,

Before we fall to the bottom—

Stones
not even the fish
will pause to tell apart.

🔥 🔥 🔥

THE INFINITE PASSION
OF EXPECTATION

fiction by GINA BERRIAULT

from Ploughshares

nominated by PLOUGHSHARES

THE GIRL AND THE ELDERLY MAN descended the steep stairs to the channel's narrow beach and walked along by the water's edge. Several small fishing boats were moving out to sea, passing a freighter entering the bay, booms raised, a foreign name at her bow. His sturdy hiking boots came down flatly on the firm sand, the same way they came down on the trails of the mountain that he climbed, staff in hand, every Sunday. Up in his elegant neighborhood, on the cliff above the channel, he stamped along the sidewalks in the same way, his long, stiff legs attempting ease and flair. He appeared to feel no differences in terrain. The day was cold, and every time the little transparent fans of water swept in and drew back, the wet sand mirrored a clear sky and the sun on its way down. He wore an overcoat, a cap, and a thick muffler, and, with his head high, his large, arched nose set into the currents of air from off the ocean, he described for her his fantasy of their honeymoon in Mexico.

He was jovial, he laughed his English laugh that was like a bird's hooting, like a very sincere imitation of a laugh. If she married him, he said, she, so many years younger, could take a young lover and he would not protest. The psychologist was seventy-nine, but he allowed himself great expectations of love and other pleasures, and advised her to do the same. She always mocked herself for dreams, because to dream was to delude herself. She was a waitress and lived in a neighborhood of littered streets, where rusting cars stood unmoved for months. She brought him ten dollars each visit, sometimes more, sometimes less; he asked of her only a fee she could afford. Since she always looked downward in her own surroundings, avoiding the scene that might be all there was to her future, she could not look upward in his surroundings, resisting its dazzling diminishment of her. But out on these walks with him she tried looking up. It was what she had come to see him for—that he might reveal to her how to look up and around.

On their other walks and now, he told her about his life. She had only to ask, and he was off into memory, and memory took on a prophetic sound. His life seemed like a life expected and not yet lived, and it sounded that way because, within the overcoat, was a youth, someone always looking forward. The girl wondered if he were outstripping time, with his long stride and emphatic soles, and if his expectation of love and other pleasures served the same purpose. He was born in Pontefract, in England, a Roman name, meaning broken bridge. He had been a sick child, suffering from rheumatic fever. In his twenties he was a rector, and he and his first wife, emancipated from their time, each had a lover, and some very modern nights went on in the rectory. They traveled to Vienna to see what psycho-analysis was all about. Freud was ill and referred them to Rank, and as soon as introductions were over, his wife and Rank were lovers. "She divorced me," he said, "and had a child by that fellow. But since he wasn't the marrying kind, I gave his son my family name, and they came with me to America. She hallucinates her Otto," he told her. "Otto guides her to wise decisions."

The wife of his youth lived in a small town across the bay, and he often went over to work in her garden. Once, the girl passed her on the path, and the woman, going hastily to her car, stepped shyly aside like a country schoolteacher afraid of a student; and the girl, too, stepped sideways shyly, knowing, without ever having seen her, who she was, even though the woman—tall, broad-hipped, freckled, a gray braid fuzzed with amber wound around her head—failed to answer the description in the girl's imagination. Some days after, the girl encountered her again, in a dream, as she was years ago: a very slender young woman in a long white skirt, her amber hair to her waist, her pale eyes coal-black with ardor.

On the way home through his neighborhood, he took her hand and tucked it into the crook of his arm, and this gesture, by drawing her up against him, hindered her step and his and slowed them down. His house was Spanish style, common to that vanward section of San Francisco. Inside, everything was heavily antique—carven furniture and cloisonné vases and thin and dusty Oriental carpets. With him lived the family that was to inherit his estate—friends who had moved in with him when his second wife died; but the atmosphere the family provided seemed, to the girl, a turnabout one, as if he were an adventurous uncle, long away and now come home to them at last, cheerily grateful, bearing a fortune. He had no children, he had no brother, and his only sister, older than he and unmarried, lived in a village in England and was in no need of an inheritance. For several months after the family moved in, the husband, who was an organist in the Episcopal Church, gave piano lessons at home, and the innocent banality of repeated notes sounded from a far room while the psychologist sat in the study with his clients. A month ago the husband left, and everthing grew quiet. Occasionally, the son was seen about the house—a high school track star, small and blond like his mother, impassive like his father, his legs usually bare.

The psychologist took off his overcoat and cap, left on his muffler, and went into his study. The girl was offered tea by the mother, and they sat down at the dining table, by sunstruck windows. The woman pushed her sewing aside, and they sat in tete-a-tete position at a corner of the table.

The woman's face was too close. Now that the girl was a companion on his walks, the woman expected a womanly intimacy with her. They were going away for a week, she and her son, and would the girl please stay with the old man and take care of him? He couldn't even boil an egg or make a pot of tea, and two months ago he'd had a spell, he had fainted as he was climbing the stairs to bed. They were going to visit her sister in Kansas. She had composed a song about the loss of her husband's love, and she was taking the song to her sister. Her sister, she said, had a beautiful voice.

The sun over the woman's shoulder was like an accomplice's face, striking down the girl's resistance. And she heard herself confiding—"He asked me to marry him"—knowing that she would not and knowing why she had told the woman. Because to specu-late about the possibility was to accept his esteem of her. At times it was necessary to grant the name of love to something less than love.

On the day the woman and her son left, the girl came half-an-hour before their departure. The woman, already wearing a coat and hat, led the way upstairs and opened, first, the door to the psychologist's bedroom. It seemed a trespass, entering that very small room, its space taken up by a mirrorless bureau and a bed of bird's-eye maple that appeared higher than most and was covered by a faded red quilt. On the bureau was a doilie, a tin box of watercolors, a nautilus shell, and a shallow drawer from a cabinet, in which lay, under glass, several tiny bird's-eggs of delicate tints. And pinned to the wallpaper were pages cut from magazines of another decade—the faces of young and wholesome beauties, girls with short, marcelled hair, cherry-red lips, plump cheeks, and little white collars. She had expected the faces of the mentors of his spirit, of Thoreau, of Gandhi, of the other great men whose words he quoted for her like passwords into the realm of wisdom.

The woman led the way across the hall and into the master bedroom. It was the woman's room and would be the girl's. A large, almost empty room, with a double bed no longer shared by her husband, a spindly dresser, a fireplace never used. It was as if a servant, or someone awaiting a more prosperous time, had moved into a room whose call for elegance she could not yet answer. The woman stood with her back to the narrow glass doors that led onto a balcony, her eyes the same cold blue of the winter sky in the row of panes.

"This house is ours," the woman said. "What's his is ours."

There was a cringe in the woman's body, so slight a cringe it

would have gone unnoticed by the girl, but the open coat seemed
hung upon a sudden emptiness. The girl was being told that the old
man's fantasies were shaking the foundation of the house, of the
son's future, and of the woman's own fantasies of an affluent old
age. It was an accusation, and she chose not to answer it and not to
ease the woman's fears. If she were to assure the woman that her
desires had no bearing on anyone living in that house, her denial
would seem untrue and go unheard, because the woman saw her
now as the man saw her: a figure fortified by her youth and by her
appeal and by her future, a time when all that she would want of
life might come about.

Alone, she set her suitcase on a chair, refusing the drawer the
woman had emptied and left open. The woman and her son were
gone, after a flurry of banging doors and goodbyes. Faintly, up
through the floor, came the murmur of the two men down in the
study. A burst of emotion—the client's voice raised in anger or
anguish and the psychologist's voice rising in order to calm. Silence
again, the silence of the substantiality of the house and of the
triumph of reason.

"We're both so thin," he said when he embraced her and they
were alone, by the table set for supper. The remark was a jocular
hint of intimacy to come. He poured a sweet blackberry wine, and
was sipping the last of his second glass when she began to sip her
first glass. "She offered herself to me," he said. "She came into my
room not long after her husband left her. She had only her kimono
on and it was open to her naval. She said she just wanted to say
goodnight, but I knew what was on her mind. But she doesn't
attract me. No." How lightly he told it. She felt shame, hearing
about the woman's secret dismissal.

After supper he went into his study with a client, and she left a
note on the table, telling him she had gone to pick up something
she had forgotten to bring. Roaming out into the night to avoid as
long as possible the confrontation with the unknown person within
his familiar person, she rode a streetcar that went toward the ocean
and, at the end of the line, remained in her seat while the
motorman drank coffee from a thermos and read a newspaper.
From over the sand dunes came the sound of heavy breakers. She
gazed out into the dark, avoiding the reflection of her face in the
glass, but after a time she turned toward it, because, half-dark and

obscure her face seemed to be enticing into itself a future of love and wisdom, like a future beauty.

By the time she returned to his neighborhood the lights were out in most of the houses. The leaves of the birch in his yard shone like gold in the light from his living room window; either he had left the lamps on for her and was upstairs, asleep, or he was in the living room, waiting for the turn of her key. He was lying on the sofa.

He sat up, very erect, curving his long, bony, graceful hands one upon the other on his crossed knees. "Now I know you," he said. "You are cold. You may never be able to love anyone and so you will never be loved."

In terror, trembling, she sat down in a chair distant from him. She believed that he had perceived a fatal flaw, at last. The present moment seemed a lifetime later, and all that she had wanted of herself, of life, had never come about, because of that fatal flaw.

"You can change, however," he said. "There's time enough to change. That's why I prefer to work with the young."

She went up the stairs and into her room, closing the door. She sat on the bed, unable to stop the trembling that became even more severe in the large, humble bedroom, unable to believe that he would resort to trickery, this man who had spent so many years revealing to others the trickery of their minds. She heard him in the hallway and in his room, fussing sounds, discordant with his familiar presence. He knocked, waited a moment, and opened the door.

He had removed his shirt, and the lamp shone on the smooth flesh of his long chest, on flesh made slack by the downward pull of age. He stood in the doorway, silent, awkward, as if preoccupied with more important matters than this muddled seduction.

"We ought at least to say goodnight," he said, and when she complied he remained where he was, and she knew that he wanted her to glance up again at his naked chest to see how young it appeared and how yearning. "My door remains open," he said, and left hers open.

She closed the door, undressed, and lay down, and in the dark the call within herself to respond to him flared up. She imagined herself leaving her bed and lying down beside him. But, lying alone, observing through the narrow panes the clusters of lights atop the dark mountains across the channel, she knew that the

longing was not for him but for a life of love and wisdom. There was
another way to prove him wrong about her. There was another way
to prove that she was a loving woman, that there was no fatal flaw,
that she was filled with love, and the other way was to give herself
over to expectation, as to a passion.

Rising early, she found a note under her door. His handwriting
was of many peaks, the aspiring style of a century ago. He likened
her behavior to that of his first wife, way back before they were
married, when she had tantalized him so frequently and always
fled. It was a humorous, forgiving note, changing her into that
other girl of sixty years ago. The weather was fair, he wrote, and he
was off by early bus to his mountain across the bay, there to climb
his trails, staff in hand and knapsack on his back. *And I still love
you.*

That evening he was jovial again. He drank his blackberry wine
at supper; sat with her on the sofa and read aloud from his collected
essays, *Religion and Science in the Light of Psychoanalysis,* often
closing the small, red leather book to repudiate the theories of his
youth; gave her, as gifts, Kierkegaard's *Purity of Heart* and three
novels of Conrad in leather bindings; and appeared again, briefly,
at her door, his chest bare.

She went out again, a few nights later, to visit a friend, and he
escorted her graciously to the door. "Come back any time you need
to see me," he called after her. Puzzled, she turned on the path.
The light from within the house shone around his dark figure in the
rectangle of the open door. "But I live here for now," she called
back, flapping her coat out on both sides to make herself more
evident to him. "Of course! Of course! I forgot!" he laughed,
stamping his foot, dismayed with himself. And she knew that her
presence was not so intense a presence as they thought. It would
not matter to him as the days went by, as the years left to him went
by, that she had not come into his bed.

On the last night, before they went upstairs and after switching
off the lamps, he stood at a distance from her, gazing down. "I am
senile now, I think," he said. "I see signs of it. Landslides go on in
there." The declaration in the dark, the shifting feet, the gazing
down, all were disclosures of his fear that she might, on this last
night, come to him at last.

The girl left the house early, before the woman and her son

appeared. She looked for him through the house and found him at a window downstairs, almost obscured at first sight by the swath of morning light in which he stood. With shaving brush in hand and a white linen handtowel around his neck, he was watching a flock of birds in branches close to the pane, birds so tiny she mistook them for fluttering leaves. He told her their name, speaking in a whisper toward the birds, his profile entranced as if by his whole life.

The girl never entered the house again, and she did not see him for a year. In that year she got along by remembering his words of wisdom, lifting her head again and again above deep waters to hear his voice. When she could not hear him anymore, she phoned him and they arranged to meet on the beach below his house. The only difference she could see, watching him from below, was that he descended the long stairs with more care, as if time were now underfoot. Other than that, he seemed the same. But as they talked, seated side by side on a rock, she saw that he had drawn back unto himself his life's expectations. They were way inside, and they required, now, no other person for their fulfilling.

🔥 🔥 🔥

HOW ST. PETER
GOT BALD

fiction by ROMULUS LINNEY

from ST. ANDREWS REVIEW

nominated by ST. ANDREWS REVIEW *and Len Fulton*

This was in the days when the Lord
and his great friend Saint Peter
made their tour of the world.
–Les Litteratures Populaires
 de Toutes les Nations.
 Paris 1881

Saint Peter loved Jesus, said the Basque Country Spaniard
but he didn't always understand him.

One time they were traveling here in Spain. They walked up and
down the roads, the dust spreading out from their heels, naming
towns, founding churches, baptizing babies, and doing good.

Early one morning, they passed a farmer on the road. His wagon
had hit something and tipped over on its side. His vegetables, his
wheat, his wine kegs, cheese gourds, everything, lay spilled out
over the road and into the ditch.

It was a mess.

But this farmer, he was calm about it. He was a big, fat fellow, who just wasn't getting himself upset like his wagon was. No, instead he was down on his knees, in a very relaxed way. His hands were clasped together. His eyes were closed.

He was praying.

"Lord Jesus," he was saying, not very loud. He certainly couldn't see Jesus and Saint Peter coming up behind him, or know that they were there. "This is just what I deserve. I am a careless, miserable sinner. I could have seen that big rock in the middle of the road but I wasn't watching. But I'm not going to feel bad about it. I'm going to be grateful for all the good things that have happened to me. Praise God."

Saint Peter was impressed.

"What a healthy, humble attitude," he said to the Lord. "Let's give him a hand, and get all his goods back in his wagon."

Jesus looked straight ahead.

"Keep walking," he said.

"But Lord," said Saint Peter.

"Hush," said Jesus.

They walked right past this unfortunate man, and right on down the road. Saint Peter kept looking back until Jesus told him stop it.

They didn't get very far until they came upon the same sight all over again. Another wagon was in a ditch. This time a whole side of the wagon was smashed in. There was a big load of hay and wood, thrown every which way.

This farmer was on his knees, too, but he wasn't praying. He was swearing. He had one bony shoulder jammed under one side of his wagon-bed, trying to rock the wagon up out of the ditch. He was sweating and straining and swearing, and he couldn't do it.

This was a tough, stringy fellow. Scars on his face and hands. A long, crooked nose, all squashed and damaged looking. And that swearing.

Saint Peter was dismayed. The man was sending one evil curse after another out upon the innocent world. They didn't even make sense, thought Saint Peter, being about highroads that ate manure, and haywagons that slept with their mothers.

But it put Saint Peter off.

"Don't stop," he whispered to Jesus.

Jesus stopped.

"Lord, we better leave this man alone."

Jesus stood right by him, looking down.

"What are you doing?"

The farmer sat back on his heels, scowling. He wiped sweat out of his eyes.

"The hell you mean, what am I doing? What does it look like?"

"In trouble, eh?"

That farmer got up slowly. Lean and stringy, but big and mean.

"If I am, I don't need you to tell me. Get moving!"

And he cursed Jesus roundly.

Saint Peter didn't believe what he saw.

Jesus socked the farmer. He hauled off and belted him. Knocked him flat.

The Lord Jesus Christ did that.

Saint Peter knew it couldn't happen. If Jesus said it once, he said it a thousand times. Don't hit other people. Just don't.

But here he laid this farmer out cold.

Saint Peter put a hand over his face, and shook his head.

When he looked again, he saw Jesus down on one knee. He was fitting one end of his little walking stick under the wagon bed. Jesus glanced at the knocked out farmer, and chuckled. He stood up, pulling on his little stick.

The wagon rocked up out of the ditch. It rolled out onto the road, and stopped. It stood right side up, axles straight. There wasn't a mark on the side that was smashed. All the wood and hay was back where it had been.

"There," said Jesus.

He walked off down the road.

Saint Peter stared at the Wagon, and the sleeping farmer. He ran after Jesus.

Who didn't want to talk about it.

Now, Saint Peter was a good man. But he had to be certain in his mind about every little thing, or he worried. He was brave as a lion, when he knew what the trouble was. When he wasn't sure, he got nervous.

I mean, if someone anywhere near him acted cold, he worried. If they seemed disappointed, he worried. And if he saw somebody laughing, and couldn't figure out why, he always thought it was him.

And he came unstrung, and got uncertain, and started making excuses for himself for no reason.

This is what Jesus enjoyed about Saint Peter. He loved kidding him about that, and never got tired of it.

Take the first time Saint Peter took Jesus fishing. He figured it out where the big schools of fish would run in the Sea of Galilee that day. He had Jesus up and into his boat before dawn.

They were first out of the harbour. Saint Peter stood up in his boat and called to the other fishermen.

"Follow me!" he shouted. He was out to show Jesus how professional fishermen operated.

Away they sailed, the other boats following. They sailed way out there to the middle of the Sea of Galilee. They couldn't see anything but water, all around.

Saint Peter slacked his sail. He sniffed the air. He slid one hand quietly into the water. He tasted a finger.

In their boats, gliding silently around them, the other fishermen waited.

Saint Peter pointed about a hundred feet to his left.

"There," he said softly.

The nets went out, easily. They weren't thrown. Jesus watched with interest.

"Why don't we throw the nets?" he whispered.

"Because there are so many fish down there, we don't want to scare them."

It was true. They were there.

"Oh," said Jesus.

He peered down into the water. He tapped the edge of the boat with his walking stick.

More fish than anybody can count dived straight to the bottom of the Sea of Galilee.

The nets were pulled through the water. They were pulled and pulled, and they came up empty.

Not one fish.

Saint Peter sat there dumbfounded. His boat was soon surrounded by other boats, when several throws brought up nothing, full of angry professionals. They called Saint Peter, in no uncertain terms, a damn blockhead. They swore about his wasting half a day for them. They sailed off.

Saint Peter rubbed his head. He went over his calculations. He'd never been that wrong before. He inspected his nets. Not a hole anywhere. He couldn't understand what happened.

Jesus remarked that fishing surely was an interesting profession. That made Saint Peter feel very queer.

Which is just the way he felt, running after Jesus down the road, after Jesus knocked out that mean farmer, and then fixed his wagon.

And didn't want to talk about it.

It had Saint Peter all confused. Finally, he just stopped, in the middle of the road.

"Lord, wait a minute!," he shouted.

Jesus turned around and came back to him.

"Well?"

Saint Peter counted it off on his fingers.

"One farmer in a ditch prays to you. You pass him by. Another farmer in a ditch swears at you. You do to him what you plainly tell every Christian never do to anybody, and then you save his neck by pulling his wagon out of the ditch."

"Well?"

"I don't understand. What was so bad about the first farmer? What was so good about the second farmer? If something was so good about the second farmer, and not about the first farmer, why hit the second farmer before helping him? I can't find the sense in it."

"Try," said Jesus.

It was getting close to noon, and hot. Jesus saw a good shade tree a few yards off. He laid himself down beneath its branches, ate a pear from his pack, and took a nap.

While Saint Peter tried. He figured things this way, and he figured them that. He paced about in circles, drew lines and arrows in the dirt, put one stone over here and another over there and lined them up in different ways, rubbed his head and knocked his fist against his palm. He thought about it from every side, top and bottom.

When Jesus woke, Saint Peter was ready for him.

"Lord, I understand."

"Good," said Jesus. He yawned.

"A decent man's curse is better than a shifty man's prayer."

Jesus seemed impressed.

"That's it. Isn't it?"

Jesus complimented Saint Peter on his powers of deduction. Saint Peter blushed with pride and pleasure.

Jesus yawned again.

A spasm of doubt hit Saint Peter.

"But if the second farmer was so decent, and the first farmer wasn't, why hit the first farmer and not the second farmer?"

Jesus stretched, and shook himself awake.

"Because if the second farmer was too proud to be helped, which is possible, and had to be put to sleep so you could help him, which is reasonable, then why was he worth helping in the first place, being proud? And if the first farmer—"

But Jesus was off down the road again. His step was light and bouncy. He was feeling good about the pleasant afternoon, and wasn't going to say any more about it.

Saint Peter felt queer again.

He ran down the road after Jesus, thinking as he ran. He rubbed his head, and scratched his head, and rubbed his head, and scratched it.

That is how Saint Peter got so bald so young.

THE CHICAGO ODYSSEY

by JIM BARNES

from SHANTIH

nominated by SHANTIH

Looking north you try to break through the sky
with your bad eyes. You want to map the town.
The lake and leaden sky are one, a blank
canvas on which you'd like to sketch a face.
The artist in you tells you to wait for dream.
You wait and nothing comes. You try museums,
their rigid worth, view mummies and other
wonders hardly half as strange as this place,
this time. A gauze of snow spirals up your spine.
You tell yourself the ice age now begins
and you alone must escape to tell the tale:
the horror of his and hers fleshed in frost,
the scream caught suddenly in mid-flight,
the running child quick-frozen in the park,
towers icicled in reverse, the el turned
easy slope for otters.
                                    All as the world turns
the other way. You turn and traffic whirs.
The astronomy is wrong: there are no stars,
moon breaks crystaline, the only zodiac
is flake on flake, a kaleidoscope of air.
You swore you'd know this town and now you don't.
Something has tipped the day and up is down;
you're trying your best to leave while there's still
a time. From each corner comes a siren's song.
Every street's a cliff you tack away from,
cotton in your ears against the damning wind

you never thought could be so cold, so insistent
on its icy trade, that barter would mean
the loss of teeth. You'll suck your eyes back in
your head, lean hard into the coming night,
lie always, go native, and by god survive.

ƀ ƀ ƀ

THE TORTOISE

by IRVING FELDMAN

from CANTO

nominated by Cynthia Ozick

SURELY HE DEEMED himself swiftness personified, muttering as he went, My name is Diligence, I am Alacrity: I leap to serve. Yet while one or another blazing messenger came and left a thousand times, the tortoise on the vestibule floor—at each flitting shadow, at the trembling of flagstones under the skimming feet, at the little buffets of air—paused a thousand times to rehearse his ancient repertoire of discretions. As if all this coming and going were aimed against him or against the word he bore most carefully within.

Comic or pathetic he may seem to those of us who measure his miles as inches, who at every stride hurdle a hundred diapasons— yet the throne room shall greet the tortoise with unstinted glory and the new message entrusted him shall be no less urgent, no less momentous.

Then see the majesty of his slow turning, his smile of wisdom too wise to smile, see how high his foot is lifted!

ON THE BIG WIND

fiction by DAVID MADDEN

from NEW LETTERS

nominated by NEW LETTERS, *Carolyn Forché and James B. Hall*

"Cousin, you touch that dial and I'll never speak to you again. Right *here's* where you'll hear the best, the latest, and greatest country music, on good ol' WFTZ in Huddersfield, Kentucky, where those two great rivers, the Mississippi and the O-hio, crash into each other, and the greatest people in the world make their home. And you just make yourself at home on WFTZ with ol' Big Bob until, oh, seven o'clock—that about right, Toby?

"Toby Mayfield over yonder, nodding his head. Toby Mayfield, your good neighbor and mine, from birth to balding middle-age, a man you can trust today and still track down with no sweat tomorrow, none other than the manager of Colonial Mobile

Homes, right *here* in the Tri-State area, one of one thousand Colonial Mobile Homes lots in the U.S. of A. You'll find them all *up* and *down* and *across* this great land of ours, cousins.

"And as I said before we broke for network news, we're broadcasting on this cloudy, sultry Saturday afternoon out of a tent, set up here at Toby Mayfield's Colonial Mobile Homes, between the Huddersfield city limits and the Indian mounds. That's what you keep your eyes out for—the Indian mounds, and you'll know you're not far from a place that will welcome you with open arms.

"And the doors of these magnificent trailers are open too, for your inspection. And Odell, our chef here, has free hot dogs and frosty Coca-Colas, waiting for you and the entire family here under the big tent, *at* the *curve* of the *road.* And what else will the folks find when they come to see us this afternoon, Toby?"

"Well, Big Bob, we want the folks to just enjoy themselves, looking over our lot here, at the—We got the latest model mobile homes you'll find anywhere in the country, cause like you say, Big Bob, we're all over, with one thousand lots, coast to coast, with the best, the latest—a complete line of new-model mobile homes. We got Executives, Wide Worlds, Free Spirits, New American Clippers, Fleetwoods, with every convenience you can want, features that just make it a—well, what you call a castle on wheels."

"Well, I'll buy that, Toby. I've been browsing around myself, a little, when I'm not on the big wind, and I can testify *in court* to what Toby's saying. And they *are* on sale, every sweet rolling one of them. A special July clearance before the new fall line comes rolling across the country. You can't miss us, cousins. Ten miles off, north, south, east, and west, you can see our billboards—showing Toby as a giant, dragging your own mobile home unit to the plot of your choice.

"And while you're on your way down here, I want you to enjoy listening to Tammy Wynette, singing her latest hit, number ten on the big ten chart, 'Southern California,' where she's living in one of Toby's New American Clippers . . ."

Big Bob Travis turns the main mike pot down, lets number 2 turntable roll, turns up number 2 pot, and dashes past Odell's steamtable, out from under the tent into the office trailer and shudders at the shock of refrigerated air.

"Like a swamp out yonder, like a morgue in here," he says to Toby, who has dropped his pants. "What the hell are *you* doing?"

he asks, dropping his own pants, picking, as Toby is, at his undershorts that sweat sticks to his waist and crotch.

"Both of us catching our death of cold, if you ask me," says Toby, "dashing in and out of this ol' iceberg."

"Better'n slow death." Big Bob sneezes violently, feels the trailer rock, slightly. "Must be one hundred degrees under that tent."

"Well, I better git back out yonder and hustle 'em."

"Hustle who? All *I* see is fifty trailers, radiating heat."

"*Mobile homes!* The manual underlines Mobile Homes. Don't say 'trailers' on the air, Lord God, I'll catch hell from the home office."

Toby goes out, letting in a furnace blast of luminous air. In the cramped toilet, Big Bob takes a leak, dashes back out under the tent, reaching for the main mike pot, noticing a middle-aged man in a lime linen business suit get out of his LTD and head for the trailers as if for an oasis.

"I love that woman, don't you? Cousins, if the angels sing that sweet, I can't get my wings soon enough to suit me. Hey, cousins, be sure to listen to my regular program, Big Bob's Night Owl Show every week night. What you're listening to now is a special Saturday event. And we're all having a great time out here, cousins—at the famous sign of the Colonial Mansion on wheels, under a big o' tent. Can't miss that red tent, if you ever skated under it over in Barlow. And listen, whether you're local folks, just out riding around, or out-of-staters passing through, you *are* welcome to come by and visit with Toby Mayfield and all the good ol' boys at Colonial Mobile Homes." He remembers Toby sent all the salesmen home for lack of customers. "So, if you're traveling South from Cape Girardeau or Cairo, or West from Paducah," Big Bob breaks into sing-song, "keep on truckin' till you get here, can't miss it, right on the curve, between the Indian mounds and Huddersfield city limits, *in* the Tri-State area, *by* the Mississippi River—and you just heard why I got nowhere as a Nashville singer. Now, we're looking for you, so come on, cousins. No obligation to buy or even look. Just step out of the sun, get out of that hot car, and—enjoy a hot dog from Blue Ribbon Meat Market, on a bun from Dayfresh Bakery, complimented with a thirst-quenching *Co*-ca Cola, from our own local brewery—bottling plant. They're waiting for you, and you—and even you, yes, you."

Big Bob takes a swig of Coke spiked with white lightnin.'

"Tell them not to worry about no heat, Big Bob, for I've turned *on* the air conditioners in all the trailers—mobile homes! on the lot!"

"With Toby's lungs, who needs radio? . . . Say, listen, don't forget the drawing, here at Colonial Mobile Homes."

Toby sees a wholesome couple with three kids step out of an expandable, and Big Bob watches him hustle to accompany them on their tour, the only family prospect on the lot.

"Well, where you all *been?*" asks Toby. "We been lookin' for you all day long," a softener that makes folks smile shyly.

"Prizes galore. Milk shakes for two at the Dairy Queen . . ." Big Bob watches a rusty car pull up at the curve, park right on the highway in the line of fire of a raving tractor trailer that swerves to miss the car and its cargo of out-of-the-hills white trash, kids, old folks, and a woman whose husband is probably driving. ". . . a steak dinner for the entire family at Bubbers. . . ." Forty-nine Olds, patch painted, fenders smashed. Skinny as a rail, out slithers the driver, smoking, Big Bob sees against the eyeball aching sun, something he rolled, and maybe grew, himself. "It's on the radio they's a Klan meetin' here'bouts!"

Odell's been watching the arrival of the relic of the Forties and just outside the tent, yells, "Keep on this road—"

One hand smothering the mike, Big Bob puts a finger to his lips. "Shhhh. On the big wind, Odell!"

"—the way you going," Odell yells, coming down a notch, "on into Huddersfield, neighbor!"

"One of Toby's faithful customers, cousins, eager for information about the give-aways. Well, we got a CB unit up too, a pair of panty hose for the missus . . ."

Big Bob remembers now, hearing public service announcements on the rival station, of a Ku Klux Klan rally for this evening, called because up in Paducah somebody shot at the Wizard. ". . . and fishing lures for all you good ol' boys . . ." Hotshot Hank Harris has probably been plugging away at his listeners on WLLL right along with Big Bob, offering the inducement of free hot dogs and Pepsis, and it is Hank this tribe has heard and heeded.

"*And* the grand prize—a shotgun from Kyle's Gun Shop."

Sure enough, she's gonna hit that Olds: a van, painted up like a dragon, tearing around a curve, trees obscuring the driver's vision.

"And—so you—don't want—to miss—"

On the split-second, the van swerves, swoops up the drive toward the tent, eyes and fangs over the grill, scales on the sides, fire breathing through the nostrils.

"—this opportunity—to drop your ticket *in* the box and come *up* a winner."

Goodness gracious, I want you to look! Odell turns to look, too. Got to be a rock band. In 1977, hippies are history, and only costumed rock bands keep the memory sharp.

"Tell 'em Odell sent you!" yells Odell, too quick for Big Bob to cover the mike, the driver of the Olds down on the highway getting back in behind the wheel. "I can't help it, I got to work!"

"Let's give a listen now to one of my favorite golden oldies . . . Hank Williams—'I'm So Lonesome I Could Cry.' "

A neater set of wheels you never saw. The driver and passengers climb out, rear facing the tent, and sides. Two girls and two boys. No, three girls and one boy. No, three boys and one girl. Big Bob kids them, silently, gagging on his own pretentiousness. All boys? All girls?

The Olds pulls out in front of a Mayflower moving van that swerves, brakes squealing, and lurches perilously up along the opposite bank, tipping pulling back over in front of the spastically chugging Oldsmobile, which wiggles to avoid hitting the truck's back end, for the brakes apparently don't apply.

The four kids out of the dragon van, half-smiling, their bodies nodding in appreciation, watch the Oldsmobile weave out of sight, going into Huddersfield, where the Ku Klux Klan rally in the high school football stadium is offering free hot dogs and Pepsis.

Big Bob lights a Real, to which he switched when he saw billboards announcing "The Natural Cigarette Is Here!" preferring *rusty* coffin nails. Glad to see the invasion of the wandering band, as if their very presence can make ruins of the gleaming, factory-fresh mobile homes by sundown. They stand under the umbrella of Hank Williams's voice, piped out, like his own, over the lot, over the highway. He resists an impulse to wave them in under the tent, up to the steamtable.

Well, children, the love generation went thataway, and this is as good a watering hole *on* the way as any. But do be careful how you walk and talk. Be humble. But be thou not scared-looking, or the bugger-man will get you.

Mr. Manson, would you care to say a few words to all the folks out there in radioland, the shut-ins and the travelers, the transistors a-walkin', the CBers a-squawkin'? Don't be shy. Spit it out.

They'll mix well with the middle-aged respectable-looking gentleman in lime stepping out of a double-wide mobile home, the air-conditioned LTD awaiting his departure.

The tribe hovers around the van. To get a fix on an escape route in case this far-out food stop becomes a bummer?

Suddenly aware of the silence, Big Bob jolts into action. "Hank Williams. One in a million, cousins. We shall never see his likes again" sticks in his throat. "A great favorite of everybody's, 'I'm So Lonesome I Could Cry.' Coming to you courtesy of Colonial Mobile Homes, and if you don't recognize who this is talking to you, you'll hurt Big Bob's feelings

"This is WFTZ, *where country folks feel at home*, coming to you remote, from the red tent outside Huddersfield—the coolest spot in town today, I tell you, neighbors. Currently, it's a cloudy 97 degrees at 6:30 Central Standard Time.

"In the headlines today, the North Koreans return the bodies of 3 U.S. airmen shot down over Korea." Big Bob reads from the afternoon Nashville *Banner*. "An army of parasites are destroying soybean crops in Missouri and Illinois. And updated reports on the effects of the New York City blackout say the looting and burning have slowed down. . . . One feature, cousins, of our mobile homes here is that they all carry auxiliary battery units in case all America goes dark."

He smells rain on the air. Another tornado brewing? A flash flood? "Air-conditioned mobile homes *on* display. No obligation. The hot dogs are free of charge, and I tell you a good cold Coke tastes mighty good today."

And don't those rockers *know* it? A small, struggling band, just starting out, adrift without bread, following Big Bob's dulcet tones down the open highway.

All right, no harm in trying. Step under the tent and see what happens.

"Cousins, don't forget now, we also have a few travel trailers here on the Colonial Homes lot for your inspection. You can take your pick from Taurus, King's Highway, Kountry Aire, Argosy, Holiday Rambler, Open Road, Prowler, and one acid nightmare

van—No, I'm just kiddin', cousins. Whether you see a travel trailer
or a mobile home in your future, before you invest, check *us*
out—*our* future is *your* future, at Colonial Mobile Homes, and just
ask for Toby Mayfield or one of his equally friendly salesmen and
they'll give you a guided tour of the homes on the lot." Friendly
salesmen sitting home, by God, drinking beer, listening to me and
laughing, or boiling in the sun at the Klan rally.

"Right now, cousins, when Johnny Rodriguez tells you 'Practice
Makes Perfect,' you better believe it."

Big Bob takes a swig from the sweating Coke bottle, watches two
of them, shoulder to shoulder, step up to the steamtable, pretending to search their pockets for money, the other two hanging
back—their old ladies? Yes, the curve of breasts under the billowy
blouse of one, a nipple nub under another. The two dudes expecting, waiting for the man behind the steamtable to wave away their
offer of money, ready to nod "far out." But under his tall, puffed,
chef's hat, Odell doesn't move, looking away, sucking his teeth,
like he sees something down the highway that hasn't been there in
the fifty years he's been watching it. The invisible generation? Big
Bob squashes a cigarette, lights another.

When the four kids turn, Big Bob watches with them as Toby
steps out of a trailer behind the wholesome family, leaves them to
look at other units alone, as if he knows when to quit, watches him
wander among the other trailers.

"Thank you there, Johnny, for that little lesson. "If Practice
Makes Perfect.' Never worked for me, but. . . If it's perfection you
insist on, cousins, the mobile homes at Colonial meet the highest
standards, Skylines, Redmans, Midas, Cobra, Pace Arrow, Mobile
Scouts, Vaqueros, and on down the line of famous names. And
Colonial Mobile Homes offers free delivery and set up. We'll pour
your concret slab and runners for you, and we'll anchor her against
the strongest winds, cyclones, tornados the Midwest can stir up,
and if you elect to go for the optional extras, we'll install your
garage or carport, your cabana or ramada or patio, your awnings,
flower boxes, your screened-in front and/or back porch, your
smoke detector, and even your TV antenna. I think you'll agree
with Big Bob, if you come down and take a look at them, that it's
really worth spending your Saturday afternoon.

"And here's somebody to make your Saturday afternoon more

enjoyable—Waylon Jennings, singing 'Honky Tonk Heroes,' while you make up your mind whether to come see us now or a little later in the evening."

The wholesome family leaving one trailer, entering another behind his back, Toby sees the four kids at the steamtable, stops in the sun between the mobile homes and the tent to look them over, then at the van, and when Odell catches his eye, Toby shakes his head like he's told these kids ten times before it's, as he'd put it, no dice.

The kids don't seem to see this sign language, but Big Bob knows they feel the vibrations in the air. They don't hassle Odell. They turn and lope on the balls of their feet out from under the scorching canvas, slow-motion, their loose clothes flowing in a breeze only they can feel, and start an inspection of the mobile homes with one of the double-wide jobs.

"Waylon Jennings, 'Honky Tonk Heroes.' I reckon I *had* some heroes, but I can't remember who they were.

"Cousins, new mobile homes are our specialty here at Colonial, but we do have a few used, rebuilt, repossessed units on the lot. Toby, how much is that repainted blue job going for?"

"I tell you, Big Bob, I'm willing to turn loose of that pretty little gal for—Well, foot-fire, let it go for $3,999."

"Thank you, cousin. Toby has to go now. Take care of the folks coming onto the lot, while Odell deals out the Cokes and hot dogs, here at Colonial Mobile Homes—*the home of stretched deals.* I mean, whatever your pocketbook cries out for, your good neighbor Toby Mayfield can arrange it. Escape from apartment living and high rents into your own homestead, cousins." You don't hear Hank Harris ad-libbing that smoothly.

"You're listening to WFTZ—*where country folks feel at home.* And here's homely—*homey* ol' Nat Stuckey with number 7 on the big ten—stay in there with us, cousins, and we'll be to number 1 before you can say Colonial Mobile Homes—'Buddy, I Lied.' Who said that?"

Big Bob watches a crow flap up out of a tree on the cliff. In the trees, the sunlight is bright, on the jagged cliff-face shadows are darkening.

"Should I run them off," Toby says to Odell, "or should I try to put them *in* one?" To show he's up to either task, he dry spits.

"If you've got one that looks like the front of a freakhouse at the

carnival. . . ." Odell, turning the weenies, says. "But if it was
me. . . ."

"Yeah. . . . Well. . . ."

"Why don't you sic Big Bob on them? With that hair of his, he
ort to be able to speak that orangutan language."

"Just because that G.I. haircut they give you at Camp Chaffee in
1942 ain't growed out yet. . . ." Big Bob tries to keep his footing
with them, sensing Odell's hostility isn't entirely feigned.

"Maybe I'll just tell them to hit the damnedbygod road."

"Would if it was *me*. . . ." says Odell, sucking his teeth, his eyes
blank.

Big Bob resists an impulse to leave "Buddy, I Lied" spinning and
jump in the dragon van and hit the highway himself, south to
Jackson, Tennessee, then east to Nashville. Where he left the
wreckage of his marriage and his career, a man might best make a
fresh start. Huddersfield isn't much better than Mt. Galilee,
Tennessee where he was a night shift announcer before Huddersfield. And that he'd taken fewer sips of spiked Coke than on
most days proves he's getting a grip on his life. But he wonders
what makes his life worth the effort.

He watches Toby follow the kids as they circle the trailer. Well,
they may be free to roam far beyond Huddersfield, wherever
impulse leads them, but they rode in *here* on my voice.

"Nat Stuckey, number 7, 'Buddy, I Lied,' moving right up the
Nashville charts, towards number one. Cousins, the only way you
gonna catch *me* in a lie today is if you make a smart right turn, or
left turn, or u-turn, right there in the street or the superhighway,
and head down highway 51 toward the Indian mounds outside
Huddersfield where the mighty Mississippi and the Ohio Rivers
come together. See for yourself, the cold Cokes and the hot dogs
are waiting for you on the steamtable right by my turntables—good
food, good music that you can still hear when you leave your car
and roam among the mobile homes here at Colonial—the Vogues,
the Hiltons, the Blue Birds, the Winnebago Chieftains, the
Champions—we got them all, and seeing is believing." His vocal
cords feel taut, as if his voice is pulling them toward the red tent.

"Here's to all you losers—deal *me* in. Dottsy says, 'Play "Born to
Lose" Again.' Okay, honey, for *you*, anything."

Not sure whether he smells or imagines the scent of grass. Big
Bob feels an urge to stroll over to the van and take a look, see if

they're hauling electric guitars and sound systems. He regrets he never picked up on the spirit of rock, doubts he could make a fresh start even as a country rock jockey.

A visitation from the last of the hippies, the humidity, the sickening smell of hot dogs and mustard . . . he feels his energy draining, watches one of the kids come around the corner of the expandable mobile home, rolling his eyes, Toby right behind, the others following, their gliding, dipping walk, their drooping posture, the sudden but languid toss of hair away from eyes lucidly expressing their contempt for these manifestations of a life-style so close to their own and yet poles apart.

Their manner seems to have challenged, animated the super, quota-striving salesman in Toby. Big Bob enjoys watching the contrast between Toby's country boy, city-slicker learned gestures and their slow shrugs, slow, palms-up raising of arms. A dance, two styles, clashing, each differently choreographed, separately over-rehearsed.

Speaking again, he feels his voice is a third element. "Dottsy, singing, 'Play "Born to Lose" Again,' number 6, creeping up on the big uno.

"On your way, are you cousins, to Colonial Mobile Homes? Well, I tell you one thing, if it's mobile homes you're thinking about, you won't want to miss this opportunity to see the finest line shown anywhere in the country. Let Toby Mayfield put you *in* one of the five million mobile homes"—and pray you don't get one of the fire hazards—"that provide luxury living here in America. You can become one of the ten million Americans *living* in mobile homes, from sea to shining sea. They're safe, durable, comfortable, convenient, and easily financed. Choose from a range that goes from mini motor homes to luxury units, from two to four-ton jobs, each one with frames of steel, cousins. Colonial Homes offers complete mobile home, factory-authorized service. It's living in the grand manner.

"And here's singing in the grand manner—Mr. Johnny Cash, the man in black himself, 'Ring of Fire.' "

And I got to take the pause that refreshes. Big Bob snuffs his cigarette, races into Toby's office trailer, almost faints in the freezing air as he takes a leak, dashes back out, takes a swig, lights another Real, watches Toby trying to impress the kids, perhaps persuade them, at least control them, and, a little recklessly, lead them into one unit after another, pointing out salient features.

Toby entices the tribe into a repossessed unit that tips as they all bunch in the doorway, and he has to reach out and shut the door behind them to encourage them to move on inside.

Toby doesn't see the one family on the lot finally leave, feeling neglected, casting back looks of scorn as they climb into their bright new blue pick-up truck, American flag decal above the dash, shotgun in the rack behind their heads.

"You folks come back," says Odell, weakly, unheard.

Come out of there, wherever you are, Big Bob says to the middle-aged man who has been inspecting the green Fleetwood quite a while now. He wants to see what will happen if his path crosses with the nomads. Will Toby, disgusted for having let himself get sidetracked, dash after the man, or has the heat so softened his brain, he won't let go of the kids, pride of profession and hatred of difference pushing and pulling at him?

Big Bob wishes he could force his voice and his wit to pull in other cars and trucks, add to the mix, produce something interesting to watch. Too hot. Threat of thunderstorms too obvious. Klan rally competing. Hank Harris pulling them in. Big Bob feels his power fading like a tube in the back of his grandmother's old Philco. Yeah? Well, goddamn it, listen to *this*.

"Thank you, John. Johnny Cash, 'Ring of Fire.'

"You know, you don't have to join a country club to enjoy country club living. With a mobile home from Colonial you can park your castle on wheels right there at Country Club Mobile Homes Park, enjoy a carefree life-style, with country club recreation facilities and atmosphere. *More money—More home for less money*, cousins, at Colonial.

"The music's free, though, right on till the end of the day and here's Vern Gosdin with number 5 on the charts, 'Till the End,' at 6:45, under cloudy skies, on WFTZ, where *country folks feel at home*."

Stepping out of a medium-sized trailer behind the kids, Toby sees the gentleman in lime linen for the first time, coming out of the green Fleetwood. Unable to cope with the kids, he skips after the man.

"If it was me," said Odell, his blank eyes having watched every movement, distance muting Toby's and the man's voice, "I wouldn't have wasted three seconds of my precious life on them."

"How about two?" Big Bob knows he's made a mistake.

"How 'bout kissing my rusty?"

"That was the end of 'Till the End' . . . Vern Gosdin, singing. . . . Where in the world did all these new kids come from? Ever wonder what happened to ol' Red Foley, Ernest Tubb, Goldie Hill, Eddie Arnold, Webb Pierce, Jean Shepard, and them?

"Well, I'll tell you what's happening out here between the Indian mounds and Huddersfield at the sign of the Colonial Mansion on wheels, under Barlow's old roller rink's red tent—It's good eatin', hot dogs and cold Cokes to wash 'em down. And Toby Mayfield getting himself a good tan, showing folks the dreams he has on display, dreams you ain't even dreamed yet."

The middle-aged man in the lime linen business suit shakes his head but takes the brochure Toby offers, and starts for his LTD. I know that look. That's a look of guilt. The one that goes with a minor crime. He peels off, as if fleeing the scene.

Toby looks over at the tent, where Odell, arms crossed, sweat streaking down his face and neck from under the chef's hat, shakes his head slowly, as if he's told Toby a hundred times not to give those kids an inch.

"Talking about dreams and where have the good old singers gone, here's one of the best, Miss Kitty Wells, the queen of country music herself, singing that unforgettable classic, 'It Wasn't God Who Made Honky Tonk Angels.' "

To Big Bob, Toby mouths, "You—on the—big wind?"

"Not right now!"

"Well, goddamn it! Pull me some people in here! Air time is cold cash wasting, get on it, by God, or get off the pot!"

"Aw, they wouldn't listen to the voice of God!"

"Well, that's what I thought I was paying good money fer!"

"Naw, I'm just a chip off the old block, Toby."

"You think you ort to be talking like that about Jesus?" asks Odell.

Toby turns, the hippies have disappeared, he yells back at Odell and Big Bob, "Just watch me!"

"Think I'll *give* 'em their damned hot dogs." Odell forks one, two, three, four, crams five, six, seven, and trots out to the van.

He unscrews the gas cap and scrapes the fork against the lip of the tank neck, making the weenies flop out of sight, sending up smoke that makes Odell stumble backwards, ask, "Did you see that?" as Big Bob turns up the main mike pot.

"That voice goes all through you, don't it? Gives me chills even in this heat, it's so beautiful, so—Well, she sings like she means it.

"And *I* mean, ladies, if you're sick of cleaning those big ol' houses or those rambling ranch styles, or the crooks and corners of those apartments, come on out and take a look at a mobile home here on Toby's Colonial Homes lot. Mobile homes are easy to clean, they have plenty of storage space, and, listen, men, they are practically maintenance free.

"Larry Gatlin probably bought him a Free Spirit mobile home because he says, 'I Don't Want to Cry'—"

Toby dashes out of the green Fleetwood, screams over to the tent, "You all see where they went?"

Big Bob mutes the mike with his hand. "Watch it, Toby! I'm on the wind!"

"Who gives a damn! They all shit in the toilet, and it don't flush!"

"Cousins, Gatlin must have taken one look at the mess you get in a big house and bought him a Free Spirit mobile home. It's number 4, cousins, on the chart, and moving up. And *we'll* move up to number 1, directly." Weak, weak, weak, Big Bob. He takes a swig, hoping boss Lester isn't listening.

He imagines the man in the lime linen business suit sick on the hot dog, thankful for the hippie distraction, using the john in the Fleetwood, and now he's heading South to the superhighway, feeling much better, mile by mile.

Out in the furnace blast, Odell stands, immobile, staring at the van's gas tank. Is the painted reptile, stimulated by Odell's fear and awe, rousing itself to life? Tune in tomorrow, sports fans. Ah, shit . . . Big Bob is interested in the pattern taking shape but his own responses to it nauseate him.

Toby is racing, risking heat stroke, from trailer to trailer, yelling into each, "Get your dirty asses out of there, you dopefiends!"

The rocking motion of a Holiday Rambler travel trailer, not much fatter than the dragon van, catches Big Bob's attention as he riffles through the records, hot to the touch, imagining the sex smell the kids are stirring up.

"I Don't Want to Cry" runs out, Big Bob still hasn't chosen the next record, his intent to improvise another commercial sticks in his throat, he chats with the man going south in the LTD, "If you've already passed us by and you're heading east to Nashville on U.S. 40, you don't know what you're missing. A rain dance? The frug? No, that one's on the ash heap. The watusi? That one, too. What the latest? Punk Rock? Assault with intent to love? You should have stuck around, mister. Nashville can wait. What's happening in that Holiday Rambler's probably a once-in-a-lifetime episode on the road of life. . . . That's an oldie, 'the road of life,' play it only on graduation night, remember? Anyway, it's happening right here on highway 51 between Huddersfield and the Indian mounds and whatever it is, free hot dogs and Co-Colas go with it, cousins, so what you doing sitting at home, or over yonder in Stinnit Stadium at the Klan rally, when you could be here with me, watching and wondering? What's ol' Toby Mayfield going to do when he opens the door to that little trailer at the back of the lot? If you've got a transistor radio dialing across the band, you have just snagged onto WFTZ. Forget them Pepsis, we got Co-Colas over here—the pause that refreshes. You ain't the Pepsi generation, are you? The Pepsi generation is a generation of vipers, my Bible tells me so.

"Ut! There's Toby, coming around the bend, his legs and arms working like choo-choo train pistons, and he's huffing and puffing, and about to blow the house down. Four little pigs in there—doing what? Trailer rocking like a cradle, like a cattle truck on a washboard road. Look at it, folks, look at it. And there he goes, Toby's twisting that handle like wringing a chicken's neck, but it don't give, it's stuck, it's stubborn, it don't want to open, is it locked? He's pounding on the door, he's dancing, he's so hopping mad. You would be too. But they ain't letting him in." Meanwhile, let Hotshot Hank Harris drone on about the Klan rally he can't even see, couped up in the control room.

"Until now Odell's been hypnotized by the dragon that brought the hippies in here, but now he's about to get in the act. He's hesitating, 'cause he knows what a temper he has—and you all know it, too, if you've ever crossed him when he's chugged down a few too many at Hoot's Waterhole. Giving me a look that would turn a Sunday shirt black, cause what I tell you goes out over the p. a. system. Will he ride to Toby's rescue?"

Big Bob's instinct for the dramatic is to spin a record to keep the suspense high. He takes one at random from the oldie rack, slaps it on turntable 2, turns it loose—spits on it, shocked at his own impulsiveness, wondering what made him do that.

No, the door was only stuck, it shooshes in, Toby loses balance, cracks his chin on the steel threshold of the trailer, looks up as one of the hippies, airborne, holding his pants up, lands outside between Odell as he comes close to the trailer and Toby as he rises. Exploding through the narrow door, manes of hair flying, come a girl, bare-assed, the other boy, unzipped, the other girl, bare-breasted. A moil and scramble of bodies—

"A scramble of bodies, cousins," says Big Bob, cutting in over Jimmie Rodgers singing 'Mother, Queen of My Heart,' "as the hippies and Toby and Odell mix it up on the scorched grass between the trailers. Toby just caught the whole pack of them, doing what used to come naturally, you know, you're in a hayloft, and there you are, and you can't help it, and years later, you beat your kids if they even look like they might do what you did back yonder in the good ol' days," aching with nostalgia for the Southern Ohio poor white trash squalor he was raised in and fled when he was 16, a precocious radio announcer, Big Bob knows he's rambling, "but don't get me to preachin', even if they is a moral to all this, and that is, that if you'd just done what I've been telling you all day long out here in this smothering heat, come down to look over the mobile homes Toby Mayfield has on display down here at Colonial, at the curve of the highway, between Huddersfield and the Indian mounds, you'd see it all for yourself, because no telling what they'll think of next, and so on and so on and so on.

"Like right now, they're all on their feet and—" Big Bob sees three pickup trucks caravan up the highway from Huddersfield— "the hippies cut out like greased lightnin' and Toby and Odell get in each other's way trying to strike out after them."

Tires squeal in rapid succession as the three trucks cut sharp onto the gravel drive, roar up to the apron in front of the tent, catching the van as if in a pincher, and Big Bob feels his blood leap.

"Well, I see some of you out there in radioland are listening to Big Bob. Nothing looks better than to see company coming down the road, does it? And here comes some more."

Cars and pick-ups covered with back roads dust coming up from the south and down from the north, exhaust fumes shimmering in the hot air, the smell so strong Big Bob tastes it.

"What this needs is background music," says Big Bob, looking for, quickly finding, putting on turntable number one Merle Haggard singing "Okie from Muskogee" that he'd played earlier, sometime back there in the eye of the heat-throbbing calm before the kids arrived, wanting to get the picture before fulfilling his obligation to give the public the news "when it happens as it happens," as he used to say on the Nashville station two decades ago.

Their colors flash between the trailers as the hippies elude Odell and Toby.

The instantaneousness with which the six men in the pickup trucks thrust themselves into the action, showing an even better instinct than Toby for where the kids would pop up next among the mobile homes, startles Big Bob. One of them, type-cast heavy, doubles back to the cab to snatch his rifle off the rack above his seat.

The crowd at the live concert cheers Merle Haggard's put-down of draft card burners. Oh, Jesus, he'd forgotten that part of it. He stands up, looks around, as if looking will conjure up some stabilizing force. He takes a swig, lights another lung duster, hacks. Jesus, got to piss *again!*

Maybe the man in the LTD will return to explain. Get the kids off the hook. "Hook" bothers him. Believing in the magic of words, he rephrases, aloud, "Out of trouble."

Watching the kids leap into one of the standard units, Big Bob panics, cornered, caught, but is relieved when he sees Hobart Crowley, his postman in Huddersfield, try the door, fail to open it.

The men gather outside the door and Toby yells at the kids inside. Big Bob wipes his brow with his shirt sleeve, gets a whiff of his underarms.

Then the men break away and begin walking around the trailer, cursing, taunting, slapping the metal sides.

"I know you're dying to hear number 3, so that'll put you closer to number 1, so here, without further ado, is Mo Bandy singing 'Cowboys Ain't Supposed To Cry.' "

The hot dogs Odell left on the grill are black, starting to smoke. Let them. To hell with Odell and all the rest of them. Let them eat ashes. Big Bob gives in to the impulse to bump a precariously leaning tower of bun boxes. He wishes he had a punk rock record to shake the local yokels out of their slowly boiling Klan rage.

As more cars come in, from both directions, but mostly from

Huddersfield, people ask Big Bob what's going on. Begrudgingly, he tells them. To make himself look less accessible, he puts on his headphones. In the tree tops on the cliff, the twilight is fading.

"Number 3 on the chart, Mo Bandy, 'Cowboys Ain't Supposed to Cry,' and because you all were real quiet while he sang that one for you, your reward is to hear Tom T. Hall singing 'Old Children— Old Dogs, Children, and Watermelon Wine'—from the red tent on the Colonial Mobile Homes lot where a July sale *is* going on. Tom T., sing it!"

Among the cars climbing the gravel drive, he recognizes Lester's Cadillac. Leaping over to the tent, his boss yells, "What the hell's going on, Bob?"

"Sorry, Lester, it's this heat, the pressure in the air's got to me, I guess, and what came out stirred all this up."

"I know, my sister heard it driving home from Memphis and got me on the CB, and I tuned you in."

"Yeah, hell, everybody else is related to each other, too, and they got a CB network that makes radio obsolete."

"Yeah, well, what I want to know is what the hell's that music doing end to end, when you got something hot going for us here? We out to capture Hank Harris's listeners or not?" Lester routinely *sniffs* the Coke, frowns.

"When you see what's really going on here, Lester, I think you'll change your tune. Take a look down there. See those—"

Big Bob notices the pick-up arm wavering, turns down the pot, Frisbee tosses the Tom T. Hall record over his shoulder, slaps a record on, turns up the turntable number 1 pot, swivels in his chair to face Lester. "You see them down there?"

"They're just having a little fun. And what I want you to do is pull in everybody within our puny thirty-mile radius to share in it before we get rained out."

"They're only working up to something rougher, Lester. That's not bee-bee guns in those racks and that's not fun gleaming in those beady eyes. And it looks like word's reached the Klan meeting because here comes Giles Monroe and Buddy Kotcher, without whom there ain't no Klan in these parts."

"You damned right. Now, report the news like I pay you to, Bob."

"Toby's already got a better crowd than any million dollar ad could draw. A few more thrill-seekers and he'll have a riot."

"*You* said it, not *me*. Now, cut off that shit-kickin' music and report the news—eyebygod*witness* news, the way the public has a right to hear it."

Lester stands over him as Big Bob fades out Tanya Tucker singing "Would You Lay With Me In a Field of Stone," turns up the main mike pot. "You're listening to WFTZ, Huddersfield, Kentucky . . . at 7 o'clock under stormy skies, 99 degrees.

"If you're just tuning in, in the local news, there's been some trouble here at Colonial Mobile Homes, involving four hippies who arrived here from nowhere in a psychedelic van and became involved in an altercation with the manager, Mr. Toby Mayfield."

Big Bob catches Lester sneering at his dampered diction and cool delivery.

"And, cousins, I tell you, it's a sight: This is local news in the making, reported exclusively from WFTZ by your first cousin, Big Bob."

He reaches for the Coke bottle that Lester pushes within his grasp. Hot Coke and white lightnin' fire-ball into his empty stomach and by a phantom circuit reach his head where something shatters, spangles.

Lester gives Big Bob a victory sign, leaves the tent, and breaks through the spectators, probably so he can become Big Bob's eyes and ears now that the cars and crowds obstruct his vision.

Big Bob sees only the top of the hippie-occupied trailer and by its movements judges the shifting mood of the aggressive ones in the crowd. They no longer punctuate their curses with slaps on the side of the trailer, they are rocking it violently, and Big Bob narrates as if he has a total picture. He smells rain on the air.

But hearing a shot, he cannot infer from his fragmented vision what provoked it.

Men in the first group that arrived break through the passive spectators and wrench open the doors of their cabs and take their rifles and shotguns back down to the trailer.

"Hey, hey, hey! Come on now, gentlemen!" yells Big Bob, sensing the feeble effect of his nonairborne voice.

Big Bob knows he cannot be heard over the air above the rifle and shotgun fire, the racket of bullets ripping into the sides of Toby's New American Clipper. He selects a Mother Maybelle and Carter Family album, 1930's broadcast re-recorded, and without an intro, sends it off on the big wind, hoping to pacify the crowd with "Heaven's Radio," "That Meeting in the Air," and "Will the

Circle Be Unbroken," expecting Lester to run up to the tent with a description. But he imagines Lester is too enthralled by what he sees and hears to remember his self-interest. Well, those kids were asking for it, coming in here like kamikazes.

The gunfire over the radio and over the humidity-muffled air has reached the sheriff, who is forced to park on the highway and climb the clay bank. His car is drenched in rain from Huddersfield.

Without breaking his stride, he walks toward the crowd, pointing his finger at Big Bob, "One more word out of *you*. . . !"

Me? I only work here, man, like, man, I only work here. Yeah. Far out. Yeah. Shit.

The top of the trailer tips over. The crash vibrating in his feet makes Big Bob stand up. The Coke bottle is empty. He lights his last cigarette. He leaves the tent to look.

People let him through, "Here comes Big Bob," "Don't I know him?" "He's Big Bob that plays the records on WFTZ," "Yeah, that's him." In the flesh, cousins. He feels like a phantom wandering among real folks.

The trailer, bullet-riddled, lies on its side, buckled inward by the impact. The whole crowd seems to be involved in what has happened and is about to happen but a few say, "That's no way to act!" "Leave them alone," "They're only passing through," "That's pure meanness." Encouraged, Big Bob says, "Hey! Come on! Do Big Bob a favor, will you! and cut it out!"

Seeing a window slide open on the side, near the top, Big Bob stifles an impulse to blurt, *There* they are!

They are out and down and running in the midst of the crowd before even the men with guns can react, one of the kids bumps into the sheriff, who is reprimanding the gunmen, Big Bob thinks he hears the kid say, "Excuse me," and the people by the road are so nonplussed, they step aside to let them through, and Big Bob, on his feet full of Coke and lightnin' too suddenly, leans against a car, feels a cool draft as the hair flaps and the skirts and the shirts balloon past him, and bless the Lord, here it comes, the rain, and theatrical thunder, by God.

The kids are in the van, the driver swiftly maneuvering in a cramped space, before the crowd recovers and starts toward them. Down the bank! Big Bob urges them, staggering toward the van, his vision blurred by the rain and blowing mist and the Coke and white lightnin' and eye fatigue, It's the only way!

As if on cue, down the bank they go and impact the dragon's scales on the sheriff's front bumper, an enormous coal truck bears down on them, diesel smoke shooting up black at the clouds that move faster over the treetops on the cliff, brakes screeching, horn bleating like a factory whistle, the tribe making their getaway around the curve into, good God, Huddersfield, where the black clouds at last have rained out those in the rally the kids' own drama did not lure away. They'll get trapped in the traffic jam.

As everyone runs to the cars and they begin to creep down the drive, the deluge is so thick, Big Bob staggers back to the console under the tent and wonders how long the needle's been hissing at the end of the Carter Family.

SONG: SO OFTEN, SO LONG I HAVE THOUGHT

by HAYDEN CARRUTH

from THE OCONEE REVIEW

nominated by H. L. Van Brunt

So often, so long I have thought of death
That the fear has softened. It has worn away.
Strange. Here in autumn again, late October,
I am late too, my woodshed still half empty.
Hurriedly I split these blocks in the rain,
Maple and beech. And south three hundred miles
My mother lies sterile and white in the room
Of her great age and pain, while I myself
Have come to the edge of the "vale." Strange.
Hurrying to our ends, the generations almost
Collide, pushing one another. And in twilight
The October raindrops thicken and turn to snow.

Cindy stacks while I split, here where I once
Worked alone, my helper now younger than I
By more years than I am younger than my mother—
Cindy, fresh as the snow petals forming on this old
Goldenrod. It was war then. In my work I wondered
Obsessively about those unarmed Orientals swarming
Uphill into the machine guns, or those earlier
Who had gone smiling to be roasted in their bronze
Cauldrons, or the Cappadocian children strewn—oh,
Strewn, strewn, and my horror uncomprehending. Were they
People, killers and killed, real people? In twilight
The October raindrops thickened and turned to snow.

I understand now. Not thoughtfully, never;
But feeling this old strange personal unconcern,
How my mother, I, even Cindy might vanish
And still the twilight fall. Something has made me
A man of the soil at last, like those old
Death-takers. And has consciousness, once so dear,
Worn down like theirs, to run in the dim
Seasonal continuance? Year by year my hands
Grow to the axe. Is there a comfort now
In this? Or shall I still, and ultimately, rebel,
As I had resolved to do? I look at Cindy. Twilight.
In her hair the thick October raindrops turn to snow.

Ϙ Ϙ Ϙ

STORY

fiction by PATRICIA ZELVER

from THE OHIO REVIEW

nominated by Raymond Carver

IT WAS EARLY NOVEMBER, past the tourist season, and cold for this place. Around seven o'clock, a new black Chrysler New Yorker drove up. A man got out, an older man, middle-aged. He was wearing a tweed jacket and a green wool tie and flannel trousers.

"You can fill it up and just get the front windshield," the man said. "Everything else is okay." His voice was friendly. He had a nice, friendly manner. He stood around as if he would like to help, but couldn't, because of the way he was dressed.

Then the front door on the passenger side opened and a woman hopped out. She was a tiny middle-aged woman, with grey hair and dainty features; she had the kind of face that probably had been pretty once when she was young. She was dressed in a long plaid skirt and high-heel shoes and a short, furry jacket. She still had a good figure. She was spry, too; she moved like a young girl. She skipped around the station, rubbing her little hands to keep them warm.

"You ought to have my jacket," she said to the attendant, while he put the nozzle in the gas tank. Her voice was girlish and friendly. She followed him around while he attended to the windshield. "It's so cold," she said. "It's so cold, it could snow. Does it ever snow down here?"

"It did once," the attendant said. "A long time ago, when I was little."

399

"How little?" said the woman. She sounded interested.

"Five. I was five years old, I guess."

"I bet you really remember that day," the woman said.

The attendant had the squeegee in his hand and was starting back toward the pump, where the man was still standing, but the woman maneuvered around in front of him, so he had to stop. She looked up at him with big violet-colored eyes and smiled. She had a friendly smile. She was a friendly little old lady, the attendant thought.

"Sure do," he said. "It hasn't snowed down here since."

The man was holding out his credit card. The attendant went to take it, with the woman hopping along after him.

"Ask him directions," the woman said. "Ask him how to get to the yacht harbor. We're going to visit our son," she said. "He's living on a boat, and we're going to take him out to dinner. We've been there at least a thousand times, but this fellow always gets lost." She laughed cheerfully.

"I don't always get lost," said the man, giving the attendant the card.

"I'd like to know the day he didn't get lost," said the woman. "He gets lost going around the block at home."

"It's easy to find the harbor," the attendant said, while he punched the card. He handed the slip to the man to sign. "You just go straight down this street to the first light and turn left."

"I'm listening even if he isn't," said the woman.

"I'm listening," said the man as he signed.

"You go one block, turn left, and then keep on going. You'll run right into it. You can't miss it."

"He could," said the woman, with her cheerful laugh. "He could miss anything. He always has to consult a map, but he still misses everything. I'd hate to go into the woods with him. You'd read about us in the papers. They'd find our skeletons!"

The man said, "Her instincts are not reliable. She doesn't take one-way streets or off-ramps into account. She can get you good and lost listening to her instincts. 'Straight down this street to the first light,' " he said, repeating the attendant's directions, " 'then turn left and you run right into it.' "

"He'll probably run right into the harbor," the woman said. She seemed overcome with amusement at the thought. "But it's all right, because I'll be on the lookout. I have an excellent memory for landmarks."

"She may have an excellent memory for landmarks, but it's hard to tell," said the man. "She pulls the sun-visor down, so I can't see the street signs. She doesn't look for landmarks, she looks at herself in the mirror. We're going to have a wreck one of these days if she keeps this up. I'm considering having the mirror taken out." He took the receipt and credit card from the attendant. "I don't know what she's looking at, anyhow," the man said.

"If he has the mirror taken out, I'll get another one put in," the woman said. "He likes to make a big fuss over nothing. He likes to have everything—just so. His way, if you know what I mean. I'm not the only one who thinks so. My son—the one we're going to visit—has suggested he just relax. Do you relax?" she said.

The attendant said he'd never tried it, but maybe he would someday.

"You ought to start now, before it's too late," the woman said. "It's hard to get an old dog to change his spots."

"She means it's hard to get a leopard to change his spots," the man said. "She gets everything mixed up like that. You can see what I mean by relying on her instincts. My son—the one she just referred to—has had certain suggestions for her, too. Courtesy prevents me from mentioning them."

The woman giggled. "I'd like to know when courtesy prevented anything. He has a tendency to be overcritical. He's used to bossing people around, so he has the idea he can act that way with me. You've probably seen people like that in your line of work. I imagine you see lots of people who drive in here and order you about like you're some sort of slave."

"I try not to notice," the attendant said.

"It must get on your nerves, though. You must want to pour oil in their gas tank, or vice versa. It must rankle. That's what I mean about him. But I don't let him get away with it. I speak up."

"You know what she does?" said the man. "If you don't jump at her beck-and-call, she takes revenge. Once, in Spain, she threw one of my shoes out of the hotel window. She has a violent streak in her. And she's filled with ancient grievances. They're bottled up inside of her. She suffers from gastritis as a result."

The man held the door open for the woman. He did it in an

old-fashioned, courtly way. The woman stepped in, daintily. She turned and smiled at the attendant.

"You ought to have a nice warm jacket on a night like this," she said.

The man closed her door and got in on his side.

"I remember the directions. Ten to one he doesn't," the woman said through the window.

"Her gastritis takes the form of diarrhea," the man said. "She has diarrhea almost everyday."

He started up the engine. "Once, in Hawaii, it got so bad, she went in her pants," he said as the car rolled away from the pumps.

The woman stuck her head out of the window. "Guess what?" she called out from the moving car. "For the last two years, he's been practically impotent. He tries to get it up, but he can't! It's because he has his nose to the grindstone and can't relax! All he cares about is his work!"

The man stopped the car at the curb. He stuck his head out of his window. "That's a lie! And she knows it!" he shouted. "She'll say anything! She has no scruples, whatsoever!" He edged the car out into the street, and it picked up speed.

She was leaning halfway out of her window, yelling at the top of her voice as the car moved away. "That isn't the half of it!" she yelled. She still sounded cheerful and friendly. "There's plenty more I could tell you! But he's rushing off, so I won't!—But I could tell you things that would make your hair curl!"

The Chrysler moved away into the night. The attendant watched it go. The man was driving in the slow, relaxed, leisurely fashion older folks drive. They appeared to be chatting in a relaxed, leisurely, middle-aged-couple way.

JOSEFA KANKOVSKA

by BARBARA WATKINS

from 13th MOON

nominated by 13th MOON

It is a photograph of my grandmother, very young,
perhaps fifteen, standing with her family:
father, stepmother, half sisters, her brother,

standing in their country before it became
Czechoslovakia, before the photographs
were carried to America.
                    Their faces are stern
as if the parents knew they would take their children
to another continent and leave them, sailing the boat back
alone, as if the children knew.
                    There are other photographs:
an Atlantic City beach, 1916. Her husband
lounges on the sand, her arms around his neck.
Their faces are full of sun. They are laughing.

Later came their son, and then
his father died, 1926, the day before Christmas.
Their son was only nine and could barely remember
how his mother tried to detach the radiator
from the wall, carry it out to the cemetery.
It was so cold.

It could have started then, the ice
that formed in her eyes, the distrust of people
because they disappear on ships that leave no tracks—
because they die.

          For ten years in old age
she lived with us, carrying her closed face like a fist
but a few times in dim rooms in summer
she spoke of Europe.
                    And when in the heat of July
her body finally loosened, we found these photographs
carried for years like a map.

from THE DEATH OF LOVE:

A SATANIC ESSAY

IN MÖBIUS FORM

by RICHARD VINE

from THE GEORGIA REVIEW

nominated by THE GEORGIA REVIEW, *Ellen Gilchrist and Charles Moles-worth*

> "I tell you, Madame, if one gave birth to a heart on a plate, it would say 'Love' and twitch like the lopped leg of a frog."
> —Djuna Barnes, *Nightwood*

> Now you can understand me: if I love order, it's not—as with so many others—the mark of a character subjected to an inner discipline, a repression of instincts. In me the idea of an absolutely regular world, symmetrical and methodical, is associated with that first impulse and burgeoning of nature, that amorous tension—what you call eros—while the rest of your images, those that according to you associate passion with disorder, love with intemperate over-flow—river fire whirlpool volcano—for me are memories of nothingness and listlessness and boredom.
> —Italo Calvino, "Crystals"

The excerpt that follows constitutes the first chapter of a book-length meditation entitled The
Death of Love: A Satanic Essay in Möbius Form, *which is itself part of an encompassing
fiction called* Notes Toward a Final Testament. *As the adjectives indicate, the speaker here is
a man whose sanity, indeed whose very existence, is in question. He may or may not at any
given moment correspond to myself.*

WORDS IN THE DESERT
An Overture

THE RENUNCIATION of love is not difficult; it merely requires that
one learn to live without a certain unreasonable joy. The fact that
this exhilaration has for centuries been considered the summit of
human existence need detain us no more. There have been other
illusions. Yahweh, we recall, was once Lord of the cosmos and
men. Today we are free: the heavens are desolate, and so are our
hearts.

The sacrifice demanded of us at this hour, though painful, is
more apparent than real. In a sense we have made it before. Long
ago a voice from the shadows hissed in our ear that beneath the
shimmering surfaces of the quotidian two darker revelations
awaited. Like twin corpses in the basement of a busy house, these
truths greeted us when we were forced to grasp a light and
descend. In that gloom, their eyes fixed us, saying: Were love
possible for us now, it would not be worth its price. But no matter.
For those who wish to live in consonance with their nature and the
times love is at any rate an unacceptable option. All lovers are
already dead. The age if not yet the myth of love is defunct.

Value is commonly, and sensibly, regarded as a net function: the
worth of any thing is determined not by the splendor of its
constituents, but by the difference, positive or negative, between
the strength it provides us and the strength it takes away. By this
standard, love swindles us, defrauding and exhausting our souls,
while we, like the marks of an intricate con game, obstinately
cherish the very process that debilitates us. We can save ourselves
only by recognizing in time that the destitution we deplore even-
tuates from a system of ruination we enjoy. Love is the disease of

which we are dying. In the still center of night, alone with only music and drugs, we must acknowledge that our misery results not from solitude—which is our first, last, and most natural state—but from the error of once, in the arms of another, having yielded to the delusion that we were and could always be otherwise.

The lowest cruelty is, of course, to inspire an unfounded hope. We recognize as unspeakably base those magazine ads which promise a cure of the victims of cancer. Yet this is the crime in which all advocates of love find themselves sooner or later enmeshed. A miraculous restoration of life to the doomed—this is the promise. The actualization, we learn, is something quite different: a disillusionment more crushing than the original need. For if we were called upon to define love to the Socrates in our hearts, would we not have to say that its essence is to attempt the utmost and to fail? None who has loved, therefore, can be guiltless; and none who would be guiltless can love. A gruesome pattern persists. The hope we posit as an antidote to the world's noxious sway proves, after a brief heady period of illusory health, to be the most damaging poison of all.

Such is our plague, as history will testify. The chronicle of the last three thousand years contains an account of the gradual apotheosis and precipitous fall of this noble ideal. No more than three years after its full inception, man's most exquisite fantasy, the incarnation of a boundless unreasoning love, suffered its first defeat on the Cross. And for twenty centuries Christ has never for one instant ceased dying. The evidence of our continuing inadequacy is expressed directly in the catalogue of our slaughters and indirectly in the record of our negligences. Verdun, Guernica, Auschwitz, Dresden, My Lai—such names may serve as a catechism for our collective mortification. But we have little need, finally, for recourse to public annals when the individual heart yearns to confess. We have all known love, and that is horror enough. In affairs of the flesh, as in affairs of the world, we have each lived our Calvary and our Buchenwald, each been by turns victim and executioner, Nazi and Jew.

The absence of empirical evidence for the existence of love has not, as one would rationally expect, led many to question its reality. No one has *personally* known love to succeed, but everyone assumes that it can. The most pragmatic man, when he loves, is magically converted to a Platonist: his Idea is in no way diminished by the imperfections of its terrestrial manifestations. The consideration that, as a relationship between two living beings, love cannot exist except in the actual motives and deeds of lovers, seems to trouble its advocates less than it should. Given the pains of a life—any life—this reluctance to doubt is perhaps understandable, if not excusable. There can be no question that something *like* love exists, and that approximation deceives us. Instead of examining this unnamed attachment as a thing in itself, we have treated it as an intimation of something much greater abiding just slightly beyond. Beyond what? Beyond anything you and I now—or will ever—know.

The problem lies neither in ourselves nor in our dream, but in the incommensurateness of the two—in our inherent inability to live and to be what we envision. The imagination, though it preserves and exalts us, is also our severest woe. If we believed in a Creator, we might forgive him everything except the agony inflicted by this capacity to imagine ourselves better than we are or can ever become. It is not earnestness we lack, but consistency. Who has not embraced one woman in his own bed in the morning and another in a strange room that night? To each, no doubt, we vowed ardent and exclusive devotion; and to each we were telling the truth. Much more than a little distance and time intervened; into this minute breach our very self inserted its forlorn principle. Of necessity we are, in our deepest selves, creatures of paradox, preceiving and desiring all and one, longing to be simultaneously connected and free. We did not choose our nature or our state, but we must live them. Intuiting that in some ultimate sense the world is multiplicity and unity at once, we yearn to merge our own duality with it. The name we once gave to our hunger was love.

A grand irony presides over our yearning. To merge perfectly with the world or another would render us singular again—once more hungering and alone. We cannot escape what we are: such is the meaning of fate. But mercifully we are preserved from this supreme solitude by another. We do not, and cannot, merge—at least not in life. For a man, to live is to be separate, and to know that an endless nostalgia is the emblem of humanness. Hence, by contrast, death's subtle allure for the lover. As a result of our living separateness certain lapses occur. A door opens unexpectedly in a long corridor. A woman instantly and unaccountably familiar steps out. Our faces animate briefly in greeting, then close. It is enough.

A peculiar curving of the cheek, a darkness in the glance, a slow turning away of the head have unsettled us, and the remainder of the day is tinged with a question. Only weeks later, while speaking to a friend or walking to a cafe alone or reading the *Aeneid* at midnight, do we suddenly and out of nowhere recall that the lean body passed like a stranger's in the hall is one we once tasted and caressed. Into those somber eyes we once swore an undying fidelity. The forgotten woman was, in short, one we had loved—in the truest sense of the word.

The pain we inflict is not only that of our indiscretions, for love defeats itself, and us, even as it succeeds. Its victories are those of an insidious murder, and insidious suicide. While appearing to offer an incomparable fullness, it in fact slowly and surreptitiously depletes us by imposing the most rigorous conditions on the only true liberty we ever possess. Both lover and beloved must barter away their once ennobling disdain. Jealousy, that most human of all emotions, blossoms forth in the sick rose of desire. To love, one must deal with the determinate—that is, the debased. The lover openly avows that his intention is to cultivate, to discover and nurture the best in himself and the other. In other words (which he dare not utter even to himself), he wishes to exploit. Here we enter the garden, that oldest and most apposite of love's metaphors. The grasses shine around us and the trees drip with fruit. This monitored, circumscribed space seems to tender a calm rapture of beauty, sustenance, ease. Could this be at last the land of full increase and peace? The answer is as obvious as the order that first tempted us. The garden exists for the sake of the gardener: this Adam and Eve learned when they made the error of thinking themselves truly free. (Opposed to the garden is, always, the wilderness, where voices cry and the tempter awaits—the Redeemer's first stop. There alone can genuine selfhood begin.) Even God gardens for profit, for a more than compensatory return on His labor. So one loves. Such affection amounts to a capitalism of the soul. Those of us who survive this ravishment are often, like many victims of rape, reluctant to admit our desolation even to those we know share it. We assume our suffering betokens some inscrutable guilt and so—out of shame, out of fear—perpetuate the legend of love's benevolent glory, paying to a hollow idol the tribute of our half-sincere perjury.

And if for once we were to refuse the metaphor and the lie? What image could we give to correspond more closely to the facts? There is no need for melodrama; that, after all, is the legitimate domain of romance. Let us simply sketch the portrait of a man who is loved. A lawyer argues before the bench in the morning, lunches with his partners at twelve, spends the afternoon preparing a brief. Such is the ordinary rhythm of his day. At four o'clock he telephones his wife. He wishes to remain in the city beyond the accustomed hour. In the face of her silence, he attempts to explain why he wants to confer over drinks with a stockbroker friend; and, for the first time, he stammers. Finally she tells him that of course he must stay—her *love* for him would not permit her to do otherwise—but her tone implies inconvenience, resentment, suspicion. He searches for the real meaning of her words. He has become a cryptographer.

Such incidents should make us wary of a naïve acceptance of love's rhetoric. The lover espouses mutual growth, but the surface of these statements must be broken through and the inner nuances assayed. Our gullibility is potentially immense. It is perhaps no coincidence that in an age so enthralled with professions of love our most charismatic leaders have been fascists who posed as deliverers.

Actions, according to the maxim, speak more loudly than words. We have only to watch two lovers parting from each other on a street corner to feel afresh, and sickeningly, the eloquence of their gestures. They instill us with ignominy. We cannot look upon those doleful eyes, those lingering hands, those kissing lips without a quick spasm of disgust. We avert our eyes, wishing that these pettings and deep gazes and whisperings had been carried out *elsewhere*, feeling for ourselves and for the lovers a kind of disgrace. We have glimpsed man at his weakest. All that is most distasteful in love—its flightiness, its dependency, its desperation—arises out of man's awareness of his precariousness, out of his fear. Love is the sublimation of cowardice, sanctioning our urge to immobilize a happiness that in reality cannot be transfixed.

Death surrounds us, and felicity shifts in our very clutches like Proteus. This is the source of our terror; too easily we forget that it is also at present the only reliable source of our pleasure. Love tempts us to violate the fundamental terms of our contract with life:

it makes us unwilling to lose. This craving for safety is contrary to all that is vital. Living itself is a risk, and the man who will not hazard a loss is one in the process of dying; the thing he fears most is already upon him. The executive who goes stale, the writer who blocks, the lover who clings—these are the unfortunates who having once succeeded live now in a constantly escalating dread of defeat. No existence is more unreal or more vulnerable than that of the first-time winner. Only those who have lost and know how to lose are no longer susceptible. The future holds for them no prizes to be distributed, no points to be gained. Their minds and their credo are clear. Life comes to us, and one day it ends: that is all. There is no compromise. In order to be born into living, we must first die to love.

Even when we resolve to speak scrupulously of love, to analyze and evaluate it like any other phenomenon, we tend to hedge. We sense that we are transgressing a mystery, and accordingly segment the subject in order to diminish our awe. We fret endlessly over the categories of love, distinguishing *eros* from *agape*, comparing courtly love to the divine, wondering how affection directed toward a sister differs from that addressed to a wife, tracing the history of such permutations from Genesis to Robbe-Grillet. To an extent, this is fruitful, but if persisted in, it merely allows us to disperse our attention (and any possible retribution) and avoid the essential. This is the manner of Schoolmen, or Pharisees.

But sooner or later comes a prophet—one wearing a camel's skin or one fresh from the carpenter's shop—who reminds us, with the air of a madman, that there is only one indispensable question: *What will you do?* The old distinctions are inadequate precisely because they permit us to answer only in part. One cannot, however, commit half an act. Whatever we do, no matter how seemingly incomplete, is the whole of what we do; and on that we are destined to fall or rise. There may be partial programs, but there are no partial lives. Moreover, conceptual divisions, when properly employed, are never more than temporary and instrumental. They point us back to the one. If a single term applies to so many disparate experiences, that term, if it is meaningful, must ultimately correspond to some constant, some *arché*, immanent in each and all. What is it in the relationship between Heloise and Abelard, between Priam and Hector, between St. Francis and his birds, that we recognize as the same? This question implies a methodology but no system. Given our topic, this is probably for the best. Our aim here is unificational but otherwise modest. We intend nothing more than to observe a number of commonly acknowledged examples of love, and to draw the consequences.

To accurately distinguish our phenomenon we need first to identify the background against which it surges up as distinct. Most of existence, as Camus has so memorably remarked, is mundane. Day after day we rise, eat, labor, amuse ourselves briefly, and sleep. Hour bleeds into hour, day into day, season into season, year into year. From time to time we awake long enough to notice that we have passed another stage: we are no longer young; we are at the height of our career; we are old. Such realizations change nothing. Only when the dread they occasion is coupled with a potentiality does exhilaration ensue. Potentiality, or more rigorously the illusion of potentiality, is the contribution of love. Belief may suddenly shake even the most desiccated soul, inciting and renewing like Eliot's unmerciful spring. Again we see the world primordially, as an infinite array of chances not already expended, not already conditioned by previous choice. There arises within us a new hope—the conviction that we can accomplish labors infused with a sharp happiness. We are full of the world and its vistas.

Despite this, the cravings expressed in our appetite prove, when examined, to be directed not toward this life, but beyond it. Lovers may retreat from the world and create their own, or they may plunge desperately into contingency in pursuit of a triumph over it; but in either case the world of brute existence or the others is nothing more than a means; it is never an end. The drama of King Edward VIII is hardly unique. Every lover would sacrifice his kingdom for his love; every lover, so long as he loves, in fact does. He passes through the world as through the resistance of water, propelling himself by rejection. Time and again, to the verge of monotony, we witness loves which seem like a passion for the world and the fullness of life culminating in the tender nihilism of a shared desire for death. This is no contradiction. Love yearns for something beyond life and death, something for which the worldly plenitude embodied in the beloved is no more than a symbol. Men have designated this great void the Divine.

So it is that loss, for all its anguish, at least has the virtue of restoring us to the world of mankind and ourselves. Love set us apart. The diminishment of love draws us back to the earth in its indifference and beauty, and to the community of mortals who struggle there. This is Ithaca. Responsibility in its most conscious and enduring aspect begins only after love has expired.

Such knowing is not tantamount to action; divorced from the will, it is futile. Most men love compulsively and nothing, it seems, will restrain them. Ironically, there is a liberation and a comfort even in this bitterest of thoughts. Since all are condemned to love and all love is condemned to fail, one has only to wait. With the aid of a few suggestions, lucidity may dawn even upon the obsessed. For the moment, the anti-lover can concede everything and step away. Time will vindicate his detachment. What is more, because he is temporarily defeated in advance, he may dare all with serenity. The loss of love is sometimes a tragedy, but the loss of the capacity to love—what Dostoyevsky sentimentally defines as hell—is always a release: the soul, once the early trauma is past, stands free and views the display of its loves like a spectator no longer moved by the sight of repetitive slaughters. The loveless man rejects as absurd any sense of election. He knows he has not been singled out for special punishment by the gods or denied a fulfillment that other men are permitted to have. He is normal, the only difference being that he is aware. With impervious disinterest, he observes himself as the most curious fauna.

Thus we re-engage history. We are not undertaking a solely personal exile; we are merely individualizing and making conscious the primary emotional transformation of our age. That modern man is perplexed all would agree: our arts as well as our crimes testify to our bafflement. Few, however, have been willing to admit that this estrangement stems in part from our insistence upon a *kind* of answer totally inappropriate to the problem we face. This phantom solution is to a large extent an exacerbation, or a cause, of our pain. Our philosophers, perhaps remembering the fate of their brethren in the centuries of faith, leave the issue essentially untouched. They have abandoned the field to the poets. They do well, for love is never so unmistakably love as when it asserts itself in defiance of logic. Faced with this outrage, one must either lyricize or else forego the contention that man has, or is capable of, an orderly mind. This leaves the logician no alternative. He has, after all, trained himself to detect what eludes the systems of other men; yet

he knows that in his own he must ignore—often with great
ingenuity—what he cannot account for or refute. We are presented, consequently, with countless songs of love, but no established rationale. Fortunately, music too has a structure. In order to
probe it, we must first steel ourselves against rapture. Here is the
mast; let us bind ourselves to it. The song of love is far more
seductive—and lethal—than that of the Sirens, but it too must be
heard and known to be overcome.

It is easy to sing, but it is difficult to explain. Possibly this is why
the objective study of love has yielded so many traitors. One must
be hard. We are in the position of a pathologist about to perform an
autopsy on his own wife. The anatomy we are here to dissect is the
one we have cherished most, and with good reason. Myths embody
their truths; that is what makes them compelling. But there are
many truths and each of us lives, at any given moment, with only a
few. Yes, whatever the apparent contradictions, all truths can and
must, like the gods, coexist; nonetheless, an age as well as an
individual of necessity makes characteristic selections. One com-
pound does not supersede another, but significant change may
result from a shift in attention. The Greek pantheon and the
Hebrew Jehovah each constituted a major incarnation of the Western genius. The historical displacement of the former by the latter
bespoke a transfer of emphasis, not a gladiatorial triumph. The
conversion is not necessarily permanent, or even complete. To
resist the rising and falling of myths is to invite stultification and
death. Each era must live its collective preoccupations, and ours
has been love. For generations men common and great have
expended themselves in its service until it looms now before us like
an idol still worshiped but more feared than adored. The time has
come to knock it aside, to stand up in the sanctuary and announce
in a clear voice what love is and has always been—a passing and
quaint superstition.

Heretics, too, must have a strategy. If they are not to be derided
into silence, they must know the articles of faith better than those
who defend them. More than sheer will and sheer strength are
required; our liberations must also be cunningly plotted. If in fact,
as Sartre once maintained, we have no determining nature, there is
nothing to bind us to love against our wishes; we may free
ourselves out of freedom. Experience, however, cautions us that

extrication will not be so simple. We do not live in a pure state, but caught in the meshes of our own commitments and the expectations of others. The believers in love will fight to hold us, as will our own remorse. We will discover distilled within ourselves—so distilled as to seem innate—a desire to be pious, a desire to reaffirm that we are indeed inherently the subjects of love. This is the bondage to which we are accustomed. We will need to examine our hearts and our history with inordinate candor to establish whether the facts support or confute the necessity of our reliance upon this purportedly enhancing emotion.

Matthew Arnold alleged that Jesus had a "secret." So do we all. We are bored. At the core of our lives, beneath the disguises of action, lurks an exasperating and potentially fatal ennui. Everything springs out of our ambivalence toward this state. We do not wish to be troubled, and we do not wish to be static: hence in any job, including the job of living, the only bane worse than having too much to do is that of having too little. Boredom is the presence of death *within* our lives, and we at once fear and desire it. I make my coffee in the morning, nod to the mirror, and sit down at my table to work; and all the while death is inside me like a worm. My life is the tension between two voids. Occasionally a great weariness invites me to sit still, to let the world transpire as it will, to care little, to accept. This the aged, those of them who have lost their determination with their force, actually do. We see them in their wheelchairs and rockers, in dark sitting rooms, in hotel lobbies, in homes, and our sympathy wrestles with our fear. We apprehend in them our own despair. We, too, sit in the dark waiting for a final transformation, the eruption of magic into our tedious lives.

And sooner or later, because we await it, it comes. My imitation of death is not death. No matter how quiescent I become, I cannot divest myself of the awareness of my quiescence, either current or past. (The mystic who attained a true annihilation of self would, of necessity, be unable to know or remember that event. Thus, contrary to the usual argument, only those who have *not* achieved union with the One can, with consistency, attest that such an experience is real.) To remain at rest requires the sustaining of a negative resolve. Far from being liberated from all volition, I must continuously choose not to act, not to think. This is itself, of course, an act and a thought: my very lethargy derives from an effort. It also wearies me. A moment comes when I find it easier to respond than to resist. This first stirring is the beginning of affection. Once one positive action is taken, an acceleration sets in; like Orpheus, we rise at an ever quickening rate from the depths. From each new response comes a new rush of energy. There is gratification in decision, even when erroneous, and in movement, even when blind. Each act feeds the next in a forceful hungering surge until, like the insomniac, we can rest content with nothing: we are haunted, voracious; we yearn to consume the world without pause. We are ready to love; we cast a lurid eye about for an object.

All or nothing. Suspended in flame between these poles of desire, we dangle over eternity, aching to devour the world in our fire or to drown that fire in an oblivious peace. Moderation, could we accomplish it, would be our most admirable feat. But the times are against us. We are the heirs of Romanticism, which has convinced us that the man apart and the man of deep feeling are one. Thus progress routinely contributes to our disease. Modernity has already snatched us away from the tribe and revealed once more our aloneness. Immersed in the most elaborate social matrix ever conceived, we live, in effect, lives of solitude. Human interdependencies—in communication, in commerce, in government, in learning, in art—have never been greater, but the impression they create for the individual is one of virtual self-sufficiency. All places, all times, all things *seem* accessible. The jet, the auto, the television, the credit card now produce that sense of perpetual abundance which, however false then or now, was once the definitive boon of love. A man today stands bewildered. Love was once the best means he had for seizing the dazzling richness of life. Now everything is at hand, but in his breast is a vacuum. So profusely gifted, he is tormented by the conviction that he ought somehow to be able to love. He is in debt. Desperately, he fastens upon some object—a person, an institution, a cause—and tries to love deeply, sincerely, lastingly. He fails. The cycle repeats many times. There is, it seems, something wrong with himself or the world.

The most blatant and most painful working out of this curse occurs in contemporary sexual practices. We act freely and feel enslaved; the continual substitution of new partners does little to alleviate the grip of a tyrannical pattern. Those who thought their actions constituted a sexual revolution are disturbed when cultural history informs them that practices have not in fact greatly changed. How much more alarming that reality sounds: we are not liberating sex; we are, more importantly, discrediting love. This is a much harder and more valuable task. Evolution has thrust us to the verge of a new paganism: deprived of a doctrine, of a fold, and of a hope, we are challenged once again to be men.

Man is doubtlessly a social animal, but we must not be overly simplistic in our enumeration of the ways one may participate in the human community. Even the convict in solitary confinement participates—by virtue of his punishment. In the future we may all come to more closely resemble those recluses—mystics, monks, philosophers, criminals—who open out to the world by drawing closer to themselves. Already the average man knows a degree of privacy and repose his grandfather could only have fantasized. Does he presently fritter those endowments? Give him time. One must learn to use leisure as one learns to use wealth; the first few generations are apt to be crass. What is essential now is to acknowledge that this solitude is of value. The view of a city from a far mountaintop is as valid and as revealing as the view from the corner of a principal street. In a balanced life, each of these perspectives has its time, as the biographies of Socrates and Jesus confirm. Success, from the most elementary survival to the most sublime accomplishment, depends upon sensing what is right for the moment. Today our circumstances dictate the abandonment of a vestigial belief grown clumsy and hazardous. Love, once the best means to the most life, now diminishes the being it once maximized. The times are no longer propitious for love. The old notion lingers now like a residue in the mind, inducing, like an ancestor's diary, vague melancholy for a world and a past we would not in fact choose to live in if we could. We have surrendered the assurances of fidelity and slow time and depth; we have gained the world in its fluid immediacy.

We shall not pull loose without reluctance or the pain of a terrible rending. Locked in our genetic code there must be still the memory of our chattering company in the trees, of our desperate bands of the savannas and caves. All but the last few decades of our fully human existence we have spent as essentially tribal creatures, defining ourselves in a network of generations and gods. Love, our past comfort, endorsed the belief that we could not find fulfillment alone. If this is true, modern man is condemned out of hand. It behooves us, therefore, to reconsider the nature of solitude and of pleasure.

When Thoreau went to Walden, he went of his own very deliberate choice. Today we are all more or less in the woods whether we like it or not. Our wilderness is likely to be dense with neon and faces rather than trees, but the separation from our kind even while in their midst is much the same. Once a martyr could retreat to his pillar in the sands because his intention was simple: he merely wished to be holy. A humanist does not get off so lightly. Thoreau wanted the essential: to find it, he had to train himself both to exclude *and* to see, to discover the full self upon which any authentic life must be based. The full self and with it the full world: one implies the other as surely as blood implies the heart. And the full world can mean nothing other than the deep world, not its shifting surfaces and diurnal turmoils. From this marriage of the deep self with the deep world comes the imperative to propagate. Solitude that is to be a function neither of cowardice nor of madness nor of conceit must eventually carry us back to the others. The beauty of Plato's parable is not so much that one man escaped as that he immediately returned to those still enchained in the cave. They derided him, it is true; but this does not attenuate the morality of his act, or the reality of his truth.

If few of us follow Thoreau's steps into conscious retreat, into being, fewer still duplicate his return. This is an omission yet more unfortunate than the first, for one loses thereby the benefit both of ebb and of flow. True solitude is fulfilled in the presence of others, nurtured like the wisdom it makes possible on the tension of paradox. So it is, to speak in the most physical terms, that autoeroticism seems so pointless: it pleases, but it accomplishes nothing. The high sentimentalists, meanwhile, having tasted the paradoxical aloneness of bilateral sex, confuse their fleeting en-counter with a permanent breakthrough and wish to enshrine it in marriage or romance. This clutching at constancy exposes their lack of real solitude. For an authentic seeker, he who carries his holiness calmly within, such encounters are no more than chapel niches on the way to the altar. One does well to stop at each, but not to linger. The sanctuary encompasses and surpasses its parts. At center, the mystery of the many and one is reconfirmed: the sacraments, those most penetratingly personal of transports, are received in a place and for a purpose dramatically public. One may pray in one's closet, one may meditate in one's tower: all that is good, but it is mere preparation. Plato speaks of a ripening into manhood, into that time that is at last auspicious for a giving birth to the things of the soul; Jesus, we know, prepared thirty years. So long as the labor remains hidden, unavowed, it is no more than a practice—the admirable but incomplete discipline of an athlete or musician alone. The full consummation can occur only in public, before the eyes of angels and men, as a species of performance. Such was the Academe, such was Golgotha. Out of the world in all its multiplicity, before the world in all its doubt, these heroes affirmed a progenitive solitude that, ignoring nothing, transcended everything, including themselves.

To go beyond one's going beyond, to go so far one returns—this vision of infinity's curve is shared by the formulator of relativity and the author of the *Odyssey*. If our arts today lack decorum, they at least provide the possibility of attempting in a new way this necessary fusion of contraries. To perform sex on stage is a start, but the more difficult undertaking lies ahead: to move our intercourse to the altar, or to sanctify the theater where it currently takes place. (This, beneath the trappings of commerce and sentiment, is what the traditional marriage ritual signifies to the subconscious mind. Hence the sniggerings of uncles and the mothers' inevitable tears.) All intense striving partakes of this urge to express the deepest collective desire in a supremely personal act. The moment has come, then, to assert our devotion to a complex and legitimate quest, to proclaim ourselves the willing and natural heirs of the divine orgiasts and Don Juan.

There will be those, no doubt, who object that we are discussing something other than love in its fully realized state, discussing indeed its failures and perversions. To them we must reply that, regrettably, these are the only forms in which men have been permitted to know it. The impulse which motivates love's apologists is commendable, but our sympathy for their intentions must not lull us into a neglect of the facts. Love, like gravity or like God, *is* nothing other than its actual effects. A more ideal version is conceivable, but, being an ideal, it concerns us only by virtue of the contrast it creates to the day-to-day reality enacted in its name. The idealists remind us of those convinced ideologists who attribute any progress made in the Soviet Union to the inherent superiority of the socialist system, while assigning the deprivations and injustices found there to corruptions which are transitory and merely "human." Likewise many Christians insist upon viewing the charity of the churches as a natural manifestation of the true faith, while regarding the mystifications and abuses of those institutions as the result of mortal frailty. Such arguments cannot be refuted in theory—or substantiated in flesh. Some ideas appear perfect, and men are unquestionably fallible. Very well. It may be that, in theory, socialism is devoid of exploitation and Christianity is identical with grace. Unfortunately, we are not angels in a heaven of forms; we are men. When we shake off our daydreams, we know that all that is meaningful for us, all that is real, is what actually occurs, what actually *can* occur. If socialism or Christianity or love fails in this world, in the lives of real men, that in itself is the most devastating criticism one can level against it. Of what use to us, except as a flagellum, is any end—however noble, however beautiful—which cannot be reified? The essence of the problem, which the idealists neatly avoid, is to find a solution that takes into account the fallibility of men, that is derived from and compatible with what they are. In this sense, it is correct to say that we are repudiating only false dreams and failures. We seek an answer not that we can adore, but that we can live.

There is a rather ungrateful stubbornness in this attitude which signals its evolutionary function. The process of becoming civilized beings has been, as the *Oresteia* and the New Testament signify, a process of learning to surrender crude gratifications for those of a more refined and therefore less immediately enthralling impact. We relinquish the pleasures of rapine for pleasure of order, the pleasure of totalitarianism for the pleasures of justice. Even the most primitive form of sexual conquest, entailing as it did a parrying of desires and a grudging adversarial respect, was an advance over mindless procreation, a step away from the caves in the direction of the stars. Love was the stage beyond conquest, a dignification, through disguise, of the combatants' desires. Now that the tenure of love has expired, now that the needs and possibilities of men have altered once again, we should lament its passing no more than the atrophy of our primordial tails.

We are called to an inglorious heroism. Our predecessors in this century have demonstrated—in its mines and factories to say nothing of its wars—that heroism consists of doing unhesitatingly and precisely what the situation demands. So, too, the most celebrated instances of classical grandeur reveal themselves, beneath their bravado, as acts of an unflinchingly assumed obligation. Achilles rouses and fights, finally and irrepressibly, because the laws of friendship cry out for retribution against the killers of Patroclus. Aeneas forsakes Dido because the weight of a heavier calling has been laid on his life. Heroism, for these champions and for us, is the attempt to fulfill both the highest dictates of our nature and the most stringent demands of the situation at hand. Hence no one escapes. None can perfectly ordain the conditions into which he will arrive, but it is the duty of each man to be a hero in his own circumstance. For us, this means accepting the onus of deposing a tyrannical love. Our act of disavowal is no less momentous than Achilles' act of revenge. In effect, it *is* a revenge.

To succeed, we will need to evoke in ourselves an iron philanthropy. The cruelty we undertake springs, like the surgeon's, from its own contradiction. We must butcher in order to heal. The Resistance taught us once more that men must sometimes act without mercy for the sake of a larger compassion. Some will undoubtedly find the disinterestedness we espouse a pathological code, a robot's Pentateuch. Our only defense is that it arises from a contrary desire—the wish to confront squarely the realities of human interaction and to elaborate, out of a profound sympathy for those mutilated in the clash between our inhuman ideas and our too human selves, a response that will allow us to live as long and as sanely as possible.

Our subject, by its very nature, appears to us first and most forcefully in terms of its errors. Here a few images speak. From them, in the very throes of crisis, are cast off the seeds of a new dispensation.

IDOLATRY

by CAROL MUSKE

from AMERICAN POETRY REVIEW

nominated by DeWitt Henry and John Love

for Delmira Augustini (1880-1914)

You wrote: "better than holding God's head
in your hands." That was before you knew
God wore a horse-trader's suit
and came strutting through Pocitos,
looking over the shoulders of the locals:

the dimsighted, the skittish,
the dray-nag in tandem with the graveyard plug.
The world, in his image, bored him
till he heard you talking. Every groan
or curse surfaced to him as prayer

and even the makeshift heresy of language
meant less to him than gesture, the gold
in the trough raised to power.
That little doll you carried—he figured
you worshipped it—though you worshipped just

its invention: nails and hint of teeth,
its wheeze of puppet lust. Idolatry
was that small—but you could pray
to the prayer itself, word after word
on the rolling pedestals. Dear Jesus,

the curtains don't live up to it,
the china pitcher, the mantilla,
the rosary nor candles lit to the dead—
don't live up. When you crossed your heart
and put your head down, you saw the veins

bulge in the studded livery,
his glove full of blood on your body
and on this very night he begged you to love him,
he begged you, already counting your ribs
and the proud occipital bones.

He was God, a horse-trader, and he didn't think
it would take but a month
to break you.

PRETEND DINNERS

fiction by W. P. KINSELLA

from CRAZY HORSE

nominated by Joe Ashby Porter

For Barbara Kostynyk

It was Oscar Stick she married. The thing that surprise me most about Oscar and Bonnie getting together is that Oscar be a man who don't really like women, and Bonnie seem to me a woman who need more love than anybody I ever knowed.

She was Bonnie Brightfeathers to start with and a girl who always been into this here Women's Lib stuff. She been three years older than me for as long as I can remember. That age make quite a difference at times. When she was eighteen she don't even talk to a kid like me, but now that she's 23 and I'm 20, it don't seem to make any difference at all.

Bonnie Brightfeathers graduate the grade twelve class at the Residential School with really good report cards. She hold her head up, walk with long steps like she going someplace, and she don't chase around with guys or drink a lot. Her and Bedelia Coyote is friends and they always say they don't need men for nothing.

"A woman without a man be like a fish without a bicycle," Bedelia say all the time. She read that in one of these MS Magazines that she subscribe to, and she like to say it to my girlfriend Sadie One-wound when she see us walk along the road have our arms around each other.

After high school Bonnie get a job with one of these night patrol and security companies in Wetaskiwin. Northwest Security and Investigations is the right name. She wear a light brown uniform and carry on her hip in a holster what everybody say is a real gun. She move away from her parents who got more kids than anything else except maybe beer bottles what been throwed through the broke front window of their cabin and lay in the yard like cow chips. She move from the reserve to Wetaskiwin after her first pay cheque. Pretty soon she got her own little yellow car and an apartment in a new building at the end of 51st avenue.

All this before she was even nineteen. It was almost a year later that I got to know her good. A Government looking letter come to the reserve for her and her father ask me to take it up to Wetaskiwin the next time I go. That same night I went in Blind Louis Coyote's pickup truck and Bonnie invite me up to her apartment after I buzzed the talk-back machine in the lobby.

It be an apartment where the living room/bed room be all one. The kitchen is about as big as most closets but she got the whole place fixed up cheerful: soft cushions all over the place, lamps with colored bulbs, and pretty dishes. She got too a record player and a glass coffee table with chrome legs. The kitchen table be so new that it still smell like the inside of a new car. There are plants too, hang on a wool rope from the ceiling and brush my shoulder when I cross the room to sit on her sofa. Whole apartment ain't big enough to swing a cat in, but it is a soft, warm place to be, like the inside of a sleeping bag.

Bonnie is a real pretty person remind me some of my sister Illianna. She got long hair tied in kind of a pony-tail on each side of her head and dark eyes just a little too big for her face. Her skin is a browny-yellow color like furniture I seen in an antique store

window. She is a lot taller than most Indian girls and real slim. She
wear cut off jeans and a scarlet blouse the night I come to see her.

She give me a beer in a tall glass. I don't even get to see the
bottle except when she take it out of the fridge. She put out for us
some peanuts in a sky-blue colored dish the shape of a heart while
she talk to me about how happy she is.

This is about the time that I write down my first stories for Mr.
Nichols. Being able to do something that I want to do sit way off in
the future like a bird so high in the sky that it be just a speck, but I
can understand how proud Bonnie feel to see her life turning out
good.

"Someday, Silas, I'm going to have me a whole big house. I
babysit one time for people in Wetaskiwin who got a living room
bigger than this whole apartment." She pour herself a beer and
come sit down beside me.

"You know what they teached us at the Home Economics class in
high school? About something called gracious living. Old Miss
Lupus, she show us how to set a table for a dinner party of eight.
She show us what forks to put where and learned us what kind of
wine to serve with what dish."

Bonnie got at the end of her room the top half of a cupboard with
doors that are like mirrored sunglasses, all moonlight colored and
you can sort of see yourself in them. When she tell me the cupboard
is called a hutch I make jokes about how•nany rabbits she could
keep in there.

"I remember Bedelia Coyote saying, 'Hell, we have a dinner
party for fifteen every night, but we only got eleven plates so the
late ones get to wait for a second setting, if the food don't run out
first.' "

After a while Bonnie show me the inside of the cupboard. She
got two dinner plates be real white and heavy, two sets of silver
knives, spoon, and fat and thin forks, two wine glasses with stems
must be six inches long, and four or five bottles of wine and liquor.
The bottles be all different colors and shapes.

"Most everybody make fun of that stuff Miss Lupus teach us, but
I remember it all good and I'm gonna use it someday. One time
Sharon Fence-post asked, 'What kind of wine do you serve with
Kraft Dinner?' and Miss Lupus try to give her a straight answer,
but everybody laugh so hard we can't hear what she say."

Bonnie take down the bottles from the cabinet to show me. "I buy them because they look pretty. See, I never even crack the seals," and she take out a tall bottle of what could be lemon pop except the label say, *Galliano*. She got too a bottle of dark green with a neck over a foot long and it have a funny name that I have to write down on the back of a match book, *Valpolicella*.

"We put on pretend dinners up there at the school. They got real fancy wine glasses, look like a frosted window, and real wine bottles except they got in them only water and food coloring. We joke about how Miss Lupus and Mr. Gortner, the principal, drink up all the real wine before they fill up the bottles for us to pretend with. Vicki Crowchild took a slug out of one of them bottles, then spit it clean across the room and say, 'This wine tastes like shit.' Miss Lupus suspended her for two weeks for that.

"See this one," Bonnie say, and show me a bottle that be both a bottle and a basket, all made of glass and filled with white wine. "Rich people do that," she say, "put out wine bottles in little wood baskets. They sit it up on the table just like a baby lay in a crib."

There is a stone crock of blue and white got funny birds fly around on it, and one that be stocky and square like a bottle of Brute Shaving Lotion, and be full of a bright green drink called *Sciarda*. I'd sure like to taste me that one sometime.

It is like we been friends, Bonnie and me, for a long time, or better than friends, maybe a brother and sister. Bonnie got in her lamp soft colored light bulbs that make the room kind of golden. She put Merle Haggard on the record player and we talk for a long time. Later on, my friends Frank and Rufus give me a bad time 'cause I stay there maybe three hours and leave them wait in the truck. They tease me about what we maybe done up there, but I know we are just friends and what anybody else think don't matter.

"Sit up to the table here, Silas, and I make for you a pretend dinner," Bonnie say. She put that heavy plate, white as new snow, in front of me, and she arrange the knife and other tools in the special way she been taught.

"Put your beer way off to the side there. Beer got no place at pretend dinners," and she set out the tall wine glasses and take the glass bottle and basket and make believe she fill up our glasses. "Know what we having for dinner?"

"Roast moose," I say.

Bonnie laugh pretty at that, but tell me we having chicken or maybe fish 'cause when you having white wine you got to serve only certain things like that with it.

"I remember that, the next time we have a bottle in the bushes outside Blue Quills Hall on Saturday night," I tell her.

Bonnie make me a whole pretend dinner, right from things she say is appetizers to the roast chicken stuffed with rice. "What do you want for dessert?" she ask me. When I say chocolate pudding, she say I should have a fancy one like strawberry shortcake or peaches with brandy. "Might as well have the best when you making believe."

I stick with chocolate pudding. I like the kind that come in a can what is painted white inside.

"Some of this here stuff is meant to be drunk after dinner," Bonnie say, waving the tall yellow bottle that got the picture of an old fashioned soldier on the label. "I ain't got the right glasses for this yet. Supposed to use tiny ones no bigger than the cap off a whiskey bottle. This time you got to pretend both the bottle and glass. Miss Lupus tell us that people take their after dinner drinks to the living room, have their cigarette there and relax their stomach after a big meal."

I light up Bonnie's cigarette for her and we pretend to relax our stomachs.

"I'm gonna really do all this oneday, Silas. I'm gonna get me a man who likes to share real things with me, but one who can make believe too."

"Thought you and Bedelia don't like men?"

"Bedelia's different from me. She really believe what she say, and she's strong enough to follow it through. I believe women should have a choice of what they do, but that other stuff, about hating men, and liking to live all alone, for me at least that just be a front that is all pretend like these here dinners."

She say something awful nice to me then. We talking in Cree and it be a hard language to say beautiful things in. What Bonnie say to me come up because we carried on talking about love. I say I figure most everybody find someone to love at least once or twice.

"How many people you know who is happy in their marriage?" Bonnie say.

"Maybe only one or two," I tell her.

"I don't want no marriage like I seen around here. For me it got to be more. I want somebody to twine my nights and days around, the way roses grow up a wire fence."

When I tell her how pretty I figure that is her face break open in a great smile and the dimples on each side of her mouth wink at me. I wish her luck and tell her how much I enjoy that pretend dinner of hers. Bonnie got a good heart. I hope she find the kind of man she looking for.

That's why it be such a surprise when she marry Oscar Stick.

Oscar is about 25. He is short and stocky with bowed legs. He walk rough, drink hard, and fist-fight anybody who happen to meet his eye. He like to stand on the step of the Hobbema General Store with his thumbs in his belt loops. Oscar can roll a cigarette with only one hand and he always wear a black felt hat that make him look most a foot taller than he really is. He rodeo all summer and do not much in the winter.

Oscar be one of these mean, rough dudes who like to see how many women he can get and then he brag to everybody and tell all about what he done with each one.

"A woman is just a fuck. The quicker you let her know that the better off everybody is." Oscar say that to us guys one night at the pool hall. He is giving me and my friend Frank Fence-post a bad time 'cause we try to be mostly nice to our girlfriends.

"Always let a woman know all you want to do is screw her and get to hell away from her. It turns them on to think you're like that. And everyone thinks they is the one gonna change your mind. You should see how hard they try, and the only way a woman know to change you is to fuck you better. . ." and he laugh, wink at us guys, and light up a cigarette by crack a blue-headed match with his thumbnail.

Guess Bonnie must of thought she could change him.

"Bedelia's never once said 'I told you so' to me. She been a good friend." It is last week already and it is Bonnie Stick talking to me.

Not long after that time three years ago when her and Oscar married, her folks got one of them new houses that the Indian Affairs Department build up on the ridge. After things start going bad for Oscar and Bonnie they move into Brightfeathers' old cabin on the reserve.

"It was Bedelia who got the Welfare for me when Oscar went off to rodeo last summer and never sent home no money."

I met Bonnie just about dusk walking back to her cabin from

Hobbema. She carrying a package of tea bags, couple of Kraft Dinner, and a red package of DuMaurier cigarettes. She invite me to her place for tea.

We've seen each other to say hello to once in a while but we never have another good visit like we did in Wetaskiwin. I am just a little bit shy to talk to her 'cause I know about her dreams and I only have to look at her to tell that things turned out pretty bad so far.

She still wear the tan colored pants from her uniform but by now they is faded, got spots all over them, and one back pocket been ripped off. Bonnie got a tooth gone on her right side top and it make her smile kind of crooked. She got three babies and look like maybe she all set for a fourth by the way her belly bulge. I remember Oscar standing on the steps of the store saying, "A woman's like a rifle: should be kept loaded up and in a corner."

She boil up the tea in a tin pan on the stove. We load it up with canned milk and sugar. Bonnie look over at the babies spread out like dolls been tossed on the bed. The biggest one lay on her stomach with her bum way up in the air. "We got caught the first time we ever done it, Oscar and me," and she make a little laugh as she light up a cigarette. "This here coal-oil lamp ain't as fancy as what I had in the apartment, eh?"

We talk for a while about that apartment.

"I really thought it would be alright with Oscar. I could of stayed working if it weren't for the babies. They took back the car and all my furniture 'cause I couldn't pay for it. At first Oscar loved me so good, again and again, so's I didn't mind living in here like this," and she wave her hand around the dark cabin with the black woodstove and a few pieces of broke furniture. "Then he stopped. He go off to the rodeo for all summer, and when he is around he only hold me when he's drunk and then only long enough to make himself happy.

"I shouldn't be talking to you like this, Silas. Seems like every time I see you I tell you my secrets."

I remind her about those pretty words she said to me about twining around someone. She make a sad laugh. "You can only pretend about things like that. . .they don't really happen," and she make that sad laugh again. "Sometimes I turn away from him first just to show I don't give a care for him either. And sometimes I feel like I'm as empty inside as a meadow all blue with moonlight, and that I'm gonna die if I don't get held. . ."

Bonnie come up to me and put her arms around me then. She fit herself up close and put her head on my chest. She hang on to me so tight, like she was going to fall a long way if she was to let go. I feel my body get interested in her and I guess she can too 'cause we be so close together. I wonder if she is going to raise her face up to me and maybe fit her mouth inside mine the ways girls like to do.

But she don't raise her face up. "It ain't like you think," she say into my chest. "I know you got a woman and I got my old man, wherever he is. It's just that sometimes. . ." and her voice trail off.

I kind of rub my lips against the top of her head. Her arms been holding me so long that they started to tremble. "I charge up my batteries with you, Silas. Then I can go along for another while and pretend that everything is going to be okay. Hey, remember the time that I made up the pretend dinner for you? I still got the stuff," she say, and take her arms from around me. From under the bed she bring out a cardboard box say Hoover Vacuum Cleaner on the side, and take out that tall wine bottle, and the heavy white plates, only one been broke and glued back together so it got a scar clean across it.

She clear off a space on the table and set out the plates and wine glasses. One glass got a part broken out of it, a V shape, like the beak of a bird. The wine bottles is dusty and been empty for a long time.

"Oscar drink them up when he first moved in with me, go to sleep with his head on the fancy table of mine," Bonnie say as she tip up the tall bottle. She laugh a little and the dimples show on each side of her mouth.

"I'll take the broke glass," she say, "though I guess it not make much difference if we don't have no wine. If you're hungry, Silas, I make some more tea and there's buscuits and syrup on the counter."

"No thanks," I say. "We don't want to spoil these here pretend dinners by having no food."

🔥 🔥 🔥

selections from
THE POETS'
ENCYCLOPEDIA
by ANDREI CODRESCU and MARVIN BELL

from UNMUZZLED OX

nominated by UNMUZZLED OX *and Walter Abish*

EDITOR'S NOTE: these selections appeared in a special issue of Unmuzzled Ox titled *The Poets' Encyclopedia* and billed as "The World's Basic Knowledge Transformed by 225 Poets, Artists, Musicians and Novelists."

ANESTHETIC

An anesthetic, which comes at times as Gas, at times as Liquid but always as a Drug, is the very opposite of an esthetic which comes solely as choice and is always an acknowledgement of pain. The anesthetic and the esthetic have battled for time immemorial for domination of the mind. The anesthetic has always come at the time of an excess of esthetic and has always produced new reasons for the next esthetic.

The greatest anesthetic ever assembled is the United States of America. Its political, social and economic structures are at the service of an anesthetic impulse: the elimination of pain at all cost, the so-called "pursuit of happiness." This Nation-Drug has produced a human mutation here, a person who is individually ruthless and tribally dedicated to the art of abstraction, to the annihilation of particulars. The rituals of this society consist in a squeezing upward of energy toward an obscure repository of spirituality *which never overflows* thereby giving rise to the perfectly plausible assumption that this energy *feeds something or someone up there*. American culture is a commentary on a future inspiration which *hasn't paid a red cent yet*. America has no present, it is a huge investment in a Future nothing is known about except that it is *exact*, like a machine. Under the sanction of exactitude, it has stamped out its imagination. North America is the most structurally oriented society in the world and it has found myriad ways to instantly comprehend form. Forms are grasped at once, while content and its attending mysteries does not exist except as a commentary on the capture of form, for which a computerized hunt is waged day and night. For a nation, an experience composed entirely in the act of capturing form, is an enormous spiritual drain, it is indeed a shameless exhibit of the rape of biology by mechanical models. This rape and its pain are the modern esthetic of America.

The anesthetic required by this esthetic cannot be produced communally, it can be found in one place only: in the imaginations of people who can populate the world with Imaginary Beings (*q.v.*).

Fortunately, these people are omni-present. Conventionally, there aren't many of them. But if counted with their Creations, the statistics skyrocket. These people, in disguises, under cover, pro personae, are to be found at *every capture of form*. In fact, their presence slowly permeates the essence of the hunt until the hunt comes to a standstill. The Century Insurance Man, with his rifle pointed dreamily in the air, is a statue. He cannot move. America is going through the motions. It is at this moment, when the world is at a standstill, that we have a paradoxical commitment of faith to an esthetic which propagandises the anesthetic. But the moment passes, and the underbelly of the wheel shows up.

—ANDREI CODRESCU

FIVE-AND-TEN
A kind of American store, found now only in small towns considered "backward." Real Five-and-Tens have wooden floors and fixtures, carry a little of everything common but nothing rare or expensive, do not sell medicine or groceries do not advertise or cut prices, and were largely run out of business by the loss-leaders of

large American corporations with the blessing of the American government, which has a parasitic relationship to large business. The Five-and-Ten made its money selling thread, socks and drinking glasses. The register was always at the front and the word *stealing* had not yet been changed to the word *shrinkage*. The store's profits rested on inventory and goodwill. If a store's shelves revealed empty spaces where small items had not been replaced when sold, you could be certain that the store would fail. The name of a failed Five-and-Ten was soon torn down to give a better businessman a chance, but the name of a good store was money-in-the-bank and a new owner would have to pay extra for the "goodwill." A man's father, after several heart attacks, sold his Five-and-Ten and retired, but he couldn't stand it because in those days the Five-and-Ten meant service and the friendship of one's customers as well as personal success. It couldn't have happened in Russia, so the immigrant Five-and-Ten owners often came out of retirement to die in their stores. One owner knew no songs but sang all the time. A dog who was run over by an automobile got well in the back room. The Five-and-Ten, for those who knew it, is like a coloring book on a rainy day, when toy sales boomed. Because the Five-and-Ten sold little things—thimbles, rulers, birthday candles—the distinctions between things still seem important (one might say, primary) to one who grew up handling them. It is possible, therefore, for such a one to believe that language begins in the (mathematical) concept of entity and separation, and that poetry is a way of using meaning (for which the ordinary dictionary is the final arbiter) to apprehend Meaning (for which experience is the source and this kind of Dictionary/ Encyclopedia the testimony) and make it known. Notions, "fancy goods," and trinkets. Less is more. Everyone knows what a thimble is. The General Store was friendly. The Five-and-Ten was *personal*.

—MARVIN BELL

♨ ♨ ♨

THE PEARS

by PAMELA STEWART

from CASCADES (L'Epervier Press)

nominated by L'Epervier Press

> *And the pears were useless and soft*
> *Like used hopes, under the starlight's*
> *Small knowledge . . .*
> — Delmore Schwartz

At noon the wasps clink and whir
Under the pear tree like bits
Of brown and yellow fruit rising sharply
Back into the leaves; they
Dive again where the soft pears
Flatten in the grass. It's late September

And the whole garden is giving up
To a grey collapse while I cut the last
Green tomatoes with their rust spots; they join
The garlic, celery and dill in clear jars
I fill with vinegar. Our father

Is dead, having sickened faster than the small
Plot of vegetables I raised in this gritty
New England soil. A sudden
Wing drooped from his body while the three
Of you stood by, believing in his death
As your private shadow. He never told you

He married a girl from Boston at nineteen
Who he didn't see again after
She had given birth
To me one winter morning.
But I grew up knowing of you, your faces
Nearly Asian like your mother's,
And wondering
If just one of our features
Were the same, perhaps his unmistakable
Eyebrows. I can smell

The fallen pears from the window,
Even stronger in the evening now, damp
And sweet like a fresh cake.
The wasps are sleeping
In the eaves. It's cooler and in just
Weeks those clouds of grosbeaks
Will start descending, morning and night,
To feed in the yard, in the broken sticks
Of the garden. The pears

Will have melted by the roots of the tree
Like they never existed, even in the memory
Of chilly wasps, fat and dying,
In their grey paper nests. You have buried
Our father out where it's always summer,
Near a garden of keyaki, pink lotus and jasmine. Perhaps,
You've finally learned of me, the facts of death
Not included in his life. You might think of me, then,
As a blonde working in a dress-store—as impossible

As halves of a pear—left out
To be shared
By an odd number of difficult children.

ﬖ ﬖ ﬖ

SCENES FROM THE HOMEFRONT

fiction by SARA VOGAN

from ANTAEUS

nominated by Raymond Carver and Barbara Grossman

O<small>N THE DAY</small> my father was born Kaiser Wilhelm the Second was planning the invasion of Belgium although he would not declare war for another six weeks. In Shenandoah, Pennsylvania, coal dust drifted through the cracks in the windows where my grandmother, a girl of seventeen, was in labor. My grandfather, fifty years old and probably wearing his usual white suit, paced in the living room and awaited the birth of his first child.

It was a breech birth and, as was common at the time, the doctor had to break both my father's arms during delivery. The baby was healthy except for the muscles of his right eye. Many children are born like my father, with tight muscles in their eyes. Doctors still cut those muscles so they will grow back the proper length and the eye will look forward, not inward to the side of the nose as my father's did. But the doctor who delivered my father cut a little too deep. He snipped the optic nerve and blinded my father permanently in his right eye.

My grandfather was too old to serve in World War I. By the time his first child was ten, my grandfather was senile. He lived to be ninety-three, seeing the First World War, the Spanish Civil War, World War II, and the Korean Conflict. But in the last part of his life my grandfather lived mostly in the Civil War. He had been named Ulysses Simpson Grant Vogan, presumably after the general and president, who was perhaps a relative, although we never knew for sure. U.G., or Grant as my mother called him, seemed to have Southern sympathies. From the middle 1920s until he died in 1957, Ulysses Simpson Grant Vogan believed himself to be Robert E. Lee and sometimes Clarence Darrow. By the time I knew him no one bothered to correct him anymore. He told me about the Monkey Trial and John Scopes. He told me about his surrender at Appomattox. Talking about the Monkey Trial made him sweat and swear and smile. "Never charged that fellow a penny," he always said. "You can't buy the truth." When he talked about Appomattox he sometimes wet himself, the yellow stain creeping down the front of his white linen suit.

My grandfather believed his daughter, Annie, died in North Carolina in 1862 after the Second Bull Run. "I was a soldier then," he always said. "I couldn't let the men see my tears."

One night as my mother tucked me into bed she said, "You can't believe everything Grant tells you. He's confused a lot of the time."

"Because he was a soldier?"

"No. Not that." She fussed with my blankets. "Your Aunt Ann died back in the twenties. From mumps."

"How do you know?" At that age anything was possible, like the swelling of my mother before my baby brother was born.

"Your father told me. Now go to sleep."

I thought she had violated some grown-up law that had to do with what parents couldn't say "in front of the children." Listening at night to the whispered sounds from their bedroom next door, I assumed they told stories they couldn't tell me. My father never spoke of Ann, but then he seldom talked about his family, not even about his younger brother Robert. All I knew then about my Uncle Robert was that he joined the U.S. Army in 1940 at the beginning of American involvement in World War II.

My father could not join the service; not one branch would take him because of his bad eye. He looked perfectly normal, both of his hazel eyes seeming to draw in all the light from the room. But with his vision limited to only one eye he had no peripheral vision and no depth perception. I always imagined he must see the world flattened out like an Egyptian hieroglyphic or perhaps the way Mondrian might have painted a landscape.

If my father could not fight he would not sit behind a desk and record the fighting of others. When he met my mother in 1943 he was in private business, repossessing used cars.

They did not have a family right away. "It wouldn't have seemed right, with the war on," my father told me once. But when the war was won my father decided the time was right and I was born shortly thereafter. I should have been a boy; the birth certificate was all filled out, an act of my father's as he paced in the hospital waiting room. They renamed me after my mother.

My Uncle Robert had married a Canadian woman he had met in Trenton before he shipped out for the European theater. Uncle Robert's last letter came in 1942, congratulating his wife on the birth of their boy. She had no letters from him after that, nor had my father or his parents. The Army investigation could only report he picked up his last pay parcel in October 1942. There was no more news of him, no confirmation he had died or deserted, no record of his capture. I remember his homecoming in 1953. I do not know where he had been all those years and neither does my father. I imagine Robert became a spy, or perhaps took a lover and lived in Paris. I wonder what his wife, my aunt, felt during all those years. I wonder if she knew he would come back to her.

On a June morning in 1953 Robert walked into the living room of his wife's house in Trenton. He was wearing his Army uniform. "I bet you don't know who I am," he said to my cousin, ten at the time. "I am your father. Is your mother at home?"

They came to see us, Uncle Robert still wearing his Army uniform but without any medals, no color on the drab green except for the yellow U.S. Army insignia on his shoulder.

I didn't know him and had heard almost nothing about him. But

I knew what to say. "Where were you?" I asked, parroting the questions of my parents. He sat me on his lap and ran his hand over my head, down my back. He stroked my legs.

"All over," he said. "Do you know Vogan is a Prussian name?"

I shook my head.

"The only good thing about being Prussian is that Prussia doesn't exist anymore," he said.

I nodded solemnly, not sure I understood what he was telling me.

"Remember that when you get married," he said. "Don't marry a man with a German name."

"Why?"

"Any don't marry any foreigners. In China and Japan they use the same word for woman and dustpan."

My grandfather was angry when he saw my uncle. His voice was measured. "I'm glad you're safe," he said. "But the men are all lost. All of them trapped. Damn minié balls!" My grandfather shook his head sadly. "Did you get the message through? Are the reinforcements coming?"

They left abruptly one morning and I never saw my Uncle Robert or his family again. Later I was told they had moved away. Robert and my father had quarreled, about my grandfather, I suppose. About the war, maybe. We never saw them after that and received no cards at Christmas.

The war was important to my father. For him it never ended. Each year we had a Victory Garden. My mother, my brother and I would hoe, plant, pull weeds and build scarecrows. My mother canned and made me help her while my brother picked and washed the fresh vegetables. In the late fifties we stopped eating the home-canned beans and peas. Instead my father made us store them in the basement along with 55-gallon drums of distilled water. We had the first fallout shelter on our block. My brother and I had wanted a swimming pool.

In his pine-paneled den my father kept a memorial to the war, a wall full of books on the campaigns, biographies of the generals, memoirs of the survivors. There was a closet full of magazines from the forties, dog-eared and yellowed with age. When my father tucked my brother and me in for the night he would bring along an old *Life* or *Saturday Evening Post*, sometimes *Colliers*. Often he keyed the magazines to the day. "On this very day, eleven years ago the Allied Forces. . ." We would sit on the bed and look at pictures of the dead, the pyrotechnics of bursting bombs and burning ships. He showed us pictures of Africa and the Aleutians, of gutted towns in Sicily and Japan. He made us identify airplanes and ships by letter and number. My brother loved the machines, the Green Dragons, Alligator Tanks, Amphibious Ducks. "You can't understand peace if you don't realize the nature of war," my father would say. "All these people will have died in vain if you won't look at them."

He helped us with our homework. Math and spelling were his favorite subjects. My brother, three years younger than I, worked the same problems I did, tutored by my father through a year of sixth-grade math when my brother was only in the third grade.

"Okay," my father would say. "If a tank is traveling at thirty miles an hour along a well-defended road toward a beach and a cargo carrier is offshore sailing along at forty-two miles an hour, first, let's figure how fast the ship is going in knots. That's how they measure a ship's speed, in knots."

"But what about the two trains going to Chicago?" I would ask.

"It's the same. See, one train at thirty, one train at forty-two. I'm just making it more interesting."

"You are not," I would say. "You are just making it harder."

My father would laugh. "I bet your brother can do it, can't you, Doug?" And my brother would smile because he knew my father would help him if he only looked puzzled and tried.

"Let's do spelling," my father would say. I handed him my list and went to stand in line next to my brother. "Campaign," my father would say.

"That's not on the list. The first word is sincerely."

"Is it going to hurt you to learn to spell campaign?"

"It won't do any good. I have to learn to spell sincerely."

"I bet Doug can do it. Want to try campaign? It's a C word, not a K."

We had a swing set behind the garden. Kicking my legs harder and harder, I pushed the swing in its half-arc above the rows of tomato plants, the long green leaves of the onions. The tomatoes became trees, the onions hedgerows, and if I squinted my eyes I could make the neat rows my mother set out go askew and a small village would form. Sometimes I would place rocks in the garden and swing as fast as I could. The rocks became houses. I was flying.

"I'm Sky King!" I would yell, pumping with my legs as the rusted swing chains screamed. "I'm flying!"

My brother threw a rock at me. It hit me on the foot. "You are not," he said. "I'm Sky King."

I wobbled down from my flying arc, the swing swaying back and forth, up and down, losing momentum. "I am too Sky King," I said, "I can go higher than you."

"You're just a girl. You have to be Penny."

"I'll beat you up." I began to limp across the yard toward my brother, who retreated, throwing rocks.

"I'll tell Dad."

"I'll break your mouth so you can't talk." I heaved a rock from my village at him.

"I'm Sky King!" he hollered, running away from me now. "I'm the Red Baron! Lucky Lindy!"

I could hear my brother laugh as he disappeared around the corner. "You," he called, hidden by the house. "Florence Nightingale. Betsy Ross. I Love Lucy." He took off running up the road. "And they can't fly!"

I was crying because my foot hurt and knelt to see where the bruise would form. Behind me the swing hung motionless in the hot air. I could get right back on. I could put the rocks back in my village, hop on my swing, and fly bombing missions over Germany, Japan. Instead I pulled out all my mother's tomato plants, crying as I cut down the trees in my village.

In school we had World History every three years and I don't remember getting past the Invasion of Poland. The next year we would start again with American History and finish the Civil War by Christmas. My grandfather would complain. He once burned my *American History for Junior Scholars,* saying it was a piece of "Yankee propaganda crap." He took it to his room and burned each offending page separately with a match over the wastebasket, no one paying any attention to him until he asked my mother for a third pack of matches.

"They never get it right," he said. "They never tell our side."

Spring semester took us through World War I and we generally got to the Great Depression, but it would be time for summer vacation before we could start the New Deal. The next fall would be a Current Events year and we would begin with the Cold War. I once figured if we went to school year round like children in Europe we would be at Pearl Harbor on the Fourth of July.

My father filled our summers with facts from World War II. Unlike other children our age, my brother and I learned early never to say "There's nothing to do." Out would come the magazines, the hard-bound books, and we would sit in the den and read or stare at the pictures. I looked at the dead men in my father's collection, their twisted arms and mud-covered faces. Men die with their mouths open; some look like they are smiling. Only the living men look somber, their eyes growing larger as the war goes on. The men in the German camps are nothing but eyes, dark rags for clothes, mouths clamped shut, then the eyes, like matching bullet holes in their heads.

"The only suitable occupation for a gentleman is a soldier," my grandfather would say. "In times of peace he fights for freedom with his mind, not his arms." Shortly before he died my grandfather's two fantasies became integrated. He believed that as a young man he had run his wife's plantation at Arlington in Virginia, treating their Negroes kindly because Negroes could not take care of themselves. After his surrender at Appomattox he took up law again and practiced the Scopes case year after year. "You fight for the truth," he always said. "That young Scopes, he knows. Faith in the truth, that's the ticket."

He wanted to die a soldier and be buried beneath his Confederate flag. Sometimes he searched the house, trying to remember where he had mislaid it. Other days he remembered giving it to Grant at the Surrender and would walk into town saying "Steady, Traveller." Somewhere in the heart of our city my grandfather believed there was a flag maker who would make him a new flag and blow holes in it to simulate one taken from the field. "The men won't mind," he always said. "So much was lost during the War."

When my grandfather died in 1957 Uncle Robert and his family sent a wreath, a horseshoe wreath that would have looked better draped over the sweating neck of a Derby winner. There was no card.

"When you were little," I asked my mother, "what did you want to be?" She was washing dishes and I was drying. Even at that age I knew dish drying for what it actually was—a waste of time. The dishes would dry in the rack without my help. But I dried them for her anyway. It was what we did after dinner.

"I wanted to marry your father," she said.

"Did you know him then?"

"Oh no. Not until much later."

"How did you know it was him?"

My mother smiled at me. "You don't need to know all this now." She stuck her hands back in the dishwater.

I persisted. "But didn't you want to be anything just for yourself?"

"Oh I guess." She placed another dish in the rack. "For a long time I wanted to be like Eleanor Roosevelt. I always saw her as the power behind the throne."

I picked up a dish and dried it, thinking of Eleanor Roosevelt. My images of the President's wife must have been much different from my mother's. Mrs. Roosevelt looked like my grandmother, gone big in the bones so her weight seemed to rest in her hips and shoulders, not on the balls of her feet the way my mother's did. The face was pouchy, which I assumed happened because F. D. R. had died. That was what happened to women when their husbands died. It had happened to my grandmother. It would happen to my mother. Perhaps it came from too much crying.

In my father's magazines there was one picture of Eleanor Roosevelt with her hands folded in her lap. The fingers seemed blunted, and ropes of veins curled up her arms. She wasn't smiling. I didn't believe my mother wanted to be like Eleanor Roosevelt.

"Didn't you want to be anything else?"

She put another dish in the rack. "Before I met your father I thought a lot about Amelia Earhart. During the war I wanted to join the Air Force. WAFs. But it would have hurt your father's feelings." She turned and dried her hands on my towel. "And then I would have missed you." She smiled as if that sealed it. For my twelfth birthday my father bought me a book of photographs by Margaret Bourke-White. I expected to see all the old famous pictures, the ones that were repeated in different magazines. London schoolchildren huddled in a ditch staring with large eyes at the planes fighting overhead. Hitler mounting the steps flanked by his storm troopers and a corridor of swastikas. The blind Australian in Buna helped down the road by an aborigine. But these were new pictures. We sat on the couch and looked at them together, leafing over the text my father told me I should read later. These were all pictures of Russians. Women holding rakes over their shoulders. Women in kerchiefs kneeling in church. The lighted paths of the bombs falling on the Kremlin at night. Joseph Stalin with a cigarette in his hand.

"A very important lady," my father said. "Her pictures made people see."

That year for Christmas I got a camera I was not allowed to touch because I was too young. My father would set the exposure, focus the lens, and stand behind me as I released the shutter. "You can be like Margaret Bourke-White when you grow up," my father said. "She took pictures of a lot of important things. Battles. Bomb sites. The way the women worked for the war." He set all the dials and lenses on the camera and placed it in my hands. "You have to have steady hands for a job like this," he said as he settled himself into his favorite chair, posing for his photograph. "And chemistry. Be sure to take chemistry in school." He smiled. "Okay. Shoot. Cheese."

In school we learned that Swastika originally meant good luck in light, life and love, a combination of the four L's. Swastikas have been found in excavations of ancient Rome, on Chinese coins, and in the sites of the Mound Builders in Mexico. We learned American Indians believed photographs would steal their souls.

"Don't marry a small man," my father said. "They have problems you can never imagine." Only tall boys were allowed to take me to basketball games and high-school dances. Although only of medium height myself, my father had evolved some theory about personality and height. "Hitler was a small man," he always said. "A small country too. Germany isn't as big as Pennsylvania. Tojo and Japan. Look at Japan." He told me small men and countries start wars to prove they are big enough to be bullies. He explained the guns-and-butter theory of economics. Germany needed copper and coal. "And Japan. Lord knows what they thought they needed." Over the years my father decided it was merely prestige Japan wanted, with China, such a big country, lying over their shoulders across the Sea of Japan.

"Look at Ike and MacArthur, at least six feet, each of them." And

ANTAEUS

then he gave me the heights of the enemy personnel. Club-footed Goebbels was only five foot two.

Over iced drinks in the dark of a summer evening, the fireflies and our cigarettes the only light against a cloudy sky, my father and I talked about History. History with a capital H, just as he always said War with a capital W. The History of the War 1939-1945. I was careful not to mention him at all. My father had aged, but perhaps that evening was the first time I noticed. In the last few years I had looked only at my own body, worrying about the fat on my hips, the budding of my breasts, or I had been watching others looking at my body, analyzing it, fantasizing about it. But in the dying light of the evening I could see the sag of his profile, the softness of his chin, the weight under his eyes. I asked him about the war. Not my war, but his.

"I used to think it was Hitler's fault," he said. "But then my Dad thought the Civil War was started by Harriet Beecher Stowe." He rattled the ice in his glass and I knew if I did not say something the moment would pass and he would rise, ask me if I would like another drink, and retreat into the house. When he returned we would talk of different things, the new car he had his eye on, his plans for retirement.

"Was it the same?" I asked. "The same as this one?"

His cigarette glowed. Fathers have a way of being fathers forever. Their children, though grown with lives of their own, are always children to their fathers. It was a child's question, the timing too slow, the voice too timid.

"I was a young man then," he said. "Things seem very important to young men. We believed we were fighting the last war. The War to End All Wars. Of course," he laughed, "we were wrong. Maybe all young men are wrong."

"Why aren't you against this war?" the child again.

He said, "The problem with you peaceniks is that you are too young to understand love. The kind of love that causes wars, or at any rate keeps them going. Love of our country, our way of life. The Germans were fighting for that too."

I didn't understand then, maybe not now. "Where's the love in blowing babies to bits? Bombing rice paddies and bamboo huts?"

"The love is here," he said as he tapped his chest. "And here." He swept his arm across the darkening yard. "I'll tell you something corny, then maybe you'll understand. When I was trying to join the service I was looking for this mental picture. All those months from office to office I kept my eyes open for a picture I could take with me overseas. And one day I saw it. I concentrated on it so it would be mine. I can still see it.

"It is a girl, a young woman. It is summer and she is wearing a lime-green dress and white shoes. Her hair is blonde and curly, down to her shoulders. Soft. And she is standing under a cotton-wood tree, patterned by the shade. There is a creek and she is casting crumbs to some ducks. Behind her, up the hill, is a white farmhouse."

He was quiet for a moment. "I'd go for that. I'd fight for that. I'd burn babies, as you say. Drop bombs. For you. For your mother. But maybe you have to be older to understand why."

"I don't think age will change my mind about this war," I said, and I felt guilty as if I had deliberately misunderstood.

He shifted in his chair, cleared his throat. "Do you know the mystery writer Dashiell Hammett? You're a bright college girl, you ought to know about him."

"What's that got to do with anything?" He wasn't going to let me grow up; I would be trapped in his summer-green photograph forever.

"He was an interesting fellow. Had TB. Signed up for the war anyhow. Served in the Aleutians. And when McCarthy was on his tail he still wanted to fight. Even with a lot of the country against him. It's that kind of love."

He rose, rattling his glass loudly and I silently held out mine. "I'd have gone," he said as he moved toward the door. "If they had let me."

In college I took photography and forged student identification cards. They were easy, the hard part was stealing the special paper from the university supply house. We would make up names and Social Security numbers and I took mug shots of men I would claim to have married. We bought a damaged carton of marriage certificates at a fire sale and two gold-plated wedding bands.

The rides to the border were at night, the three of us, the guide, myself the bride, and the boy, all sitting in the front seat staring at the road revealed through the yellow headlights. Our talk was quiet; we were part of the resistance and felt this was something important and dangerous. Our guide seldom spoke after he gave us the instructions and any piece of news we might need.

I took the ride nine times and now some of the boys seem to run together. One cried and asked if I would hold him and I did, feeling no warmth or excitement, only his pain and fear. A few years ago I heard that one had committed suicide in Sweden, but I couldn't remember his face. Just last year one of the boys, a man now with a wife and child, stopped me in a shopping mall in Ohio.

We left the guide in our safe house, put New York license plates on the car. The boy and I checked into a motel, a different one each time.

In the morning, the boy and I would pretend to be newlyweds and would wander hand in hand through the sights on the American side of Niagara Falls. We would look in expensive souvenir shops, eat lunch in fancy restaurants, kiss each other in public, especially in front of policemen. We would lean over the guard rails and look into the foaming gorge. At three o'clock I would look at my husband for the day and tell him it was time. Some of them laughed. All of them wanted to delay it, to get drunk or stoned, to go over the bridge under the cover of darkness.

With a throng of tourists, we went over to Canada, presenting our forged identification papers to the border guards and assuring them we were only sightseers visiting for the day. We were never stopped. I've been told we were lucky; other couples had tried it and failed.

We looked at the Floral Clock, more gift shops, gave a last backward glance at the falls before making our way to a side street and a small quiet bar where all the signs were printed in French and English. Two men would be sitting at a table in the back playing dominoes. We would join them, have a drink, swap rings and the extra IDs. None of the boys changed their minds, but one got very drunk before the Canadian could lead him out of the bar. One boy kissed me, thanking me for my help. They each left, some to Toronto, some as far away as Winnipeg or Halifax. My husband for the day would begin his new life, his new identity, as a deserter from the Vietnam War.

The other domino player would go back across the border with me. Sometimes we would kiss. We always came back after dark.

In 1968 my father flew to Oklahoma for Uncle Robert's funeral.

When he returned a week later my father told us his brother had committed suicide. With tears in his eyes my father said Robert gassed himself in a sealed room. Then he began to sob in my mother's arms, his tears rolling down her neck and making pale spots on the shoulders of her blouse. My brother left the room, motioning for me to follow. But I stayed, watching my father cry and the way my mother rocked him in her arms.

Later, when he had more control, my father told us we had four new cousins, mostly grown now, the sons and daughters of my Uncle Robert that were born after his return from the war. My eldest cousin has two children of his own, boys. My eldest cousin is a lieutenant in the Air Force.

My father was not political except when it came to Eisenhower. In my father's mind The General could make no mistakes and his Presidency was perfect. Ike was his man and Richard Nixon was his second favorite. "Democrats start wars," he always said. "They leave it to the Republicans to finish them." He would laugh then. "And we have never lost a war."

In high school my brother was a wrestler, tall and very thin. My father thought he should play basketball but approved of wrestling when he decided the West Point basketball team was of not much account. My brother could go to West Point when he graduated, or to the Air Force Academy if he wished. My brother didn't even apply to West Point and lied to my father about the forms he never filled out. With the memory of the pictures in the worn magazines, and with the TV news covering the Vietnam War every evening, my brother decided he wanted to be a television cameraman and go to the journalism school at Northwestern. My brother's lottery number was thirteen—very high in the scale—and my father was pleased. "This time thirteen is a lucky number," my father told his friends.

My brother was six foot four and wrestled in the 180 class. Most wrestlers in that class are brawny, but my brother was wiry and quick. He had a metabolism like mercury, adjustable to any change. The United States Army will take a six-foot-four male if he is over 140 pounds and under 248. For his first Army physical my brother weighed in at 136.

"Jesus Christ God Damn It!" my father shouted, pounding his fist on the table when he heard the news.

My brother laughed at him. "You know, I was nine years old before I realized that wasn't my real name. Jesus Christ God Damn It."

"A goddamned subversive, that's what you are."

My mother and I picked carefully at our food. I could tell by the look on her face, set tight and unblinking, that she would let them fight. She had defended my brother when he didn't go to West Point, soothed my father's disappointment, covered my brother's lies. But she would be quiet tonight.

My brother looked across the dinner table and over my shoulder. Walter Cronkite was reporting the number of Vietnamese dead for that day. "I don't want to fight," he said.

"And why the hell not?"

"This war is a mistake."

"A mistake? Says who? You? You know so goddamned much you can decide this country's foreign policy? You don't even have to shave every day."

My brother was calm, listing his answers as if this were a test. "I know we are overextended. I know it is none of our business. I know people on both sides are dying for nothing."

"It is your duty," my father said, making the words sound as if they were in capital, three dimensional letters. "It is as inevitable as the fact your sister will have children. Able-bodied men have a moral duty to defend their country."

"No one is attacking us. We are doing the attacking."

My father took a deep, shaky breath. His eyes were black pits, rimmed with the red of his shame and frustration. "You are a coward. I have raised a coward."

"I'm not going," my brother said again. "If this weight thing doesn't work I'll go to Canada."

"You are not my son," my father said. "You are a coward piece of trash. A no-talent, lying cheat. A dog has more loyalty than you."

"What do you want from me? My body in a pine box? Dog tags hanging over the mantel?"

"Yes!" my father shouted, rising from the table. "I want a son I can be proud of."

"All you want is another number on the TV news. Do you think anyone is going to notice if Douglas MacArthur Vogan is killed in action? Name any of the dead ones, American, Vietnamese. One soldier on either side you can name and remember." My brother rose slowly and pushed back his chair as if squaring off for fight. "I don't believe this is even happening. The bodies don't look human. Melted flesh. Pairs of ears strung on wires. It's a TV movie. They march the recruits into the ovens just like at Dachau. Vietnam doesn't exist."

I could see the lie of that statement in my brother's face. After school and in the summers my brother worked at a small manufacturing Company, Hannah's Orthopedic Devices, where they made prostheses. Mr. Hannah, who used to play checkers with my grandfather, was expanding. The war brought new orders from the VA hospital for feet, legs, arms, mechanical hands. My brother delivered them, brought them back if they didn't fit.

My father sat down again, leaving my brother standing alone in the room above the rest of us. I watched my brother staring down at my father, his eyes sunk deep in his face, the bones just visible beneath the skin.

"That's your trouble," my father said. "You have no faith. Faith is everything. Even the Germans and Japanese believed in their countries."

"The Germans believed in gassing Jews. Some faith."

"In the long run maybe what those men did was wrong. But you have to grant a certain admiration to those kamikaze pilots. They kissed their wives and children good-bye and flew their planes out over the ocean. An amazing act of faith."

I looked at my mother, who was still studying her food. "It's not the same," I said.

"You stay out of this," my father said. My mother put her hand on my arm. "Women and children don't fight," he said. "This is none of your business."

"He's my brother."

"Cool it," my brother told me. "I'm not going to Nam. I'll fight here."

"You just don't understand," my father said, his voice almost pleading this time.

My brother looked him dead in the eye.

"No," my father said. "You fight this war for the good of your country. It's what makes us what we are today."

"Terrific," my brother said. "You want me to fight for a country

that has made it possible to blow up the entire world. It's like
Hitler recruiting Jew-gassers."

"You were born in a hospital," my father said with tears in his
eyes. "You are strong and healthy. When I was a kid children still
died of mumps. Polio. You fight for science. Your health. Your
education. The freedom you have to make this decision to abandon
the principles that made you what you are. If you won't defend
those ideals you are no son of mine."

"You want me to go because you couldn't."

My father rose to leave the table. "Children are only the dreams
of their parents."

Just recently my father retired and took my mother on a trip
around the world. They visited battlefields. I can see my father
standing by the sea, his arm sweeping across the horizon as he
points out to my mother where the ships must have moored, how
the landing craft pulled up to Omaha Beach as the Germans fired
from the safety of their bunkers. Behind them stand acres of white
crosses, the names of the dead facing the sea. My parents stand
beside a concrete sphere, remnant of the Maginot Line that was
supposed to defend France. They walk through Dachau to stare at
the showers, pick through the rubble of Cassino to see the stones of
the monastery.

They send postcards to me and my brother, brightly colored
pictures in contrast to the severe photographs of our childhood. My
brother laughed when I talked to him on the phone. "When I was a
kid I thought America was the only country in color. The rest of the
world was in black and white," he said.

We get postcards of smiling Dutch girls, children playing in a
fountain in Rome. Europe disappointed my father. Most of the
scars were hidden, he said. "Europe is a lie," he wrote on the back
of a card from Ardennes. "Historical battles that changed the
course of the world have been fought here. Europeans try to hide
that. No one will talk about The War. A French wine merchant said
to me: Which one? There were so many."

My mother loved Hawaii; my father hated Pearl Harbor. He sent
me a postcard of the burning of the USS West Virginia, small boats
in the foreground spraying water across her decks, the flag of the
USS Arizona waving in the background. "Some of them have

forgotten," the card said. In my mother's hand across the bottom was a postscript: "It has ruined the whole time we have been here."

My father loved the Pacific Theater. The climate might have hidden the scars there, but at least the people hadn't. In New Guinea my father said you could look out over a field in a tropical forest and it would look as even as the back of your hand. But walking through it you went up and down through bomb craters, the plants in the depressions growing taller than the rest to give the appearance of evenness. They toured the tinier islands, my father explaining to my mother their strategic importance. He recounted for her the Battle of Boat 13, unlucky enough to have landed its troops in front of a Japanese pillbox. My mother knows the story, as do I. My father had read it to us out of an old *Life* magazine, a February issue saved from 1944.

Flying across the Pacific, my father wants to see buoys or plaques marking the surface of the ocean like white crosses placed beside roads. He wants billboards erected on the sea. "The USS *Wasp* was torpedoed here by a Japanese submarine while sailing in convoy to Guadalcanal. Ninety-two percent of her crew were lost although 23 Americans floated in a rubber raft for 18 days before being picked up off Port Moresby."

They were denied permission to go into Vietnam, but my father did not seem disappointed. "It wouldn't be safe for your mother," he wrote. "It probably looks just like the rest."

A few years before my grandfather died we took him to Gettysburg as part of our vacation. My father thought my brother and I should have a normal view of the Civil War, a view not colored by his father's fantasies. In the car my mother wanted me to play a card game with my brother, but I refused for no reason I could explain then. My attention was on my grandfather, the look on his face as he watched the countryside rolling by. We had to stop once because my grandfather had wet himself and the smell of his urine threatened to make my brother sick. My grandfather said nothing during the drive, and I watched his face, unable to read anything into the ninety-year-old features.

We stood on the battlefield and read the signs, listened to the guides and picked up handfuls of brochures. We saw where the

Union soldiers had built their reinforcements, the trenches now mortared together with cement to keep tourists from stealing the field stones. Guides with loudspeakers walked little groups of us around the site of the three-day battle, describing what happened at each spot.

My grandfather began to cry. We walked him over to the shade of a tree, away from the guide and the sound of his loudspeaker. "All those lives," he said through his tears, and my mother offered him her handkerchief. "Thousands of men, just farmers. Lost. All lost." He cried as he told us the story of his most bitter defeat, and my mother sat with her hand on his shoulder while my father turned his back and walked away.

"They had our plans, our dispatches, before we even crossed the river." He told us how J. E. B. Stuart left the Confederation troops with no reconnoitering force. He saw the deaths of men he could name, heard the roar of the cannons in the quiet Pennsylvania hills. I saw his dead men littered across the field. I heard the crack of his rifles.

I wait for my father's card from Japan, his reaction to Hiroshima. He could send the picture postcard of the building they left as a memorial, but he won't. Maybe it will be a picture of the way Hiroshima looked sometime before August 6, 1945, or a card of the watch that was found stopped at 8:16. My mother might send a picture of the shadows on the stones. When the bombs fell, the bodies of men and women who had been sitting on benches watching birds or the sunrise disintegrated from the heat of the blast, leaving only their shadows imprinted forever on the stone benches. For me, there is really only one picture of Hiroshima. In my father's magazines Hiroshima is the mushroom cloud billowing over the horizon.

I would like to get a picture of the Hiroshima maidens, the twelve or twenty women who were interviewed in a bombed-out hotel to see if they could be sent to New York for plastic surgery. I imagine them standing in line with their burned bodies, vying for a free trip to America where they could be reconstructed. I wonder what happened to the ones who were turned down. The Hiroshima maidens that came to New York lived in the homes of wealthy socialites while they waited for the bandages to be removed. When they returned to Japan they became models.

My father's card will be a picture of Hiroshima as it has been rebuilt. I will see new bars and hotels, modern office buildings. Pictures of progress and a denial that so much hatred can be loosed upon the world.

I wait and I imagine the postcard, but deep in my heart I hope he will not be able to write it. I hope he will not be able to put Hiroshima into words, place a foreign stamp on it and stuff it into a Japanese mailbox. It is only a hope, my last hope for my father.

FOR JOHANNES BOBROWSKI

by SANDRA McPHERSON

from CHICAGO REVIEW

nominated by CHICAGO REVIEW, *Kristine Batey, Michael Harper and George Venn*

1

The quiet snake
and what my friend did as soldier
make room for each other
in a meadow.
Target and air and knoll
are part of the world
that quiets the bullet
and rests and waves in the sun.
Wildflowers
rushing the clearing,
a pheasant flower breaks safe.
My look down the gunbarrel
accepts a place to the side
by the birch trees.
The sun turns over all
like a basket handle,
makes us closeness
as the cricket
who thinks me hidden in a tower
of grass begins near roots
his armor-crossing song.

2

The hunter comes home with his paper target.
The pattern of birdshot squares
with the layout of some city—European.
My eye put to its most wayward perforation
sees the skaters' pond
cleaned off in rings
like half the onion a drunk told me he eats
in his car at the first flashing light.
An officer. Two dead.
Then his terrible breath
says he's innocent.
In our village
everyplace is close—
he could walk the white line
and be halfway across town.
But try to walk in the snow:
you'll cut your tracks like the hunter,
settled in now for winter,
who cleans three quail on a roadmap
he won't be using.

🔥 🔥 🔥

SHOWDOWN

fiction by MICHAEL BRONDOLI

from SHENANDOAH

nominated by Carolyn Kizer and Reynolds Price

Nobody, helped. The night Cammie Lewis quit the Only Bar not a soul helped. Her boyfriend who wasn't supposed to be there swaggered in at 9:30, a day early but they had their six hundred bags of scallops. He wanted her to kiss him, wanted to show her his hundred-dollar bills, wanted to show everybody what he'd come home to, what he'd been calling on the radio every night.

The pay phone rang but whoever called hung up—probably wanted to talk to Tish, who looked over from the other end of the bar, her face hot with expectation.

Ange Buthrell, Tish's husband, owner of the place, signalled for another round at the back table, where he and his friends were

458

anteing for Nan Twiford to change blouses in front of them. She
was prolonging negotiations.

Dressed to kill, Tish was drinking and talking up a storm. In the
bar, and there alone, Ange let her go.

The Duke checked another half gallon of Beefeater's—this was
North Carolina, you checked your liquor—for him and Dallas
Alice, who was singing as loud as she could, which was loud. The
Nunemaker brothers borrowed Cammie's screwdriver to crank up
the jukebox. Already Conway Twitty sounded like soul music and
the buzz of the bass notes made the wineglasses tremble foot to
foot. Chas (the Razz) Rollins was weeping at the bar over getting in
early to find his woman gone, down fucking that wop in Drum.

Then Tish left, answered the phone herself this time, told
Cammie, "Take care of things a while," flashed a bright, tricky
smile and left. Usually Cammie could handle a weeknight but the
trawlboats were in and besides this was the dead of winter.

Nan changed, for fifty dollars, into an old blouse of Tish's from
the office. Ange ordered a round for the house and asked her to
travel to Bermuda with him, departure tonight. He asked Cammie
to turn the rheostat to zero, leaving in all the bulbs in the place
nineteen watts, and these negated by smoke. Nobody would have
given Cammie trouble. Anybody would have killed for her or tried
to. Still it would be a long night if Tish didn't return.

Cammie's boyfriend R. L. Caffrey, half heifer, half Popeye—he
needed his big shoulders to carry the chips—stood by the first
booth checking things out, checking her out, trying to get easy with
people. Cammie bore marks from his last trip in, a couple of which
might scar, temporarily anyway. At least with R.L. there Chas quit
asking her to wipe his tears with her lovely hands, gaze with her
eyes of wisdom and so forth.

"Let's go back to the office, catch a buzz," R.L. said as she
passed with two armloads.

"Yea, okay." She went to ask Ange to watch the bar, knowing full
well he would not, would simply let people take what they needed.
He justified his inability to accept money from people he knew as a
form of public relations. Tish on the other hand refused the
employee discount to her own sister.

"Hell, I missed you all the time," R.L. said in the office, a faint
chunky rhythm going in his body. He removed his cap; the yoke of

curly hair over his collar remained. "I almost caught my hand in the winch thinking about you." To his mind she was the prettiest woman on earth, the earth he'd seen, Water County, Cape May and Rhode Island. She might not have much of a figure but she carried herself with a nice cool style, good posture, knew how to dress—tonight she was wearing a corduroy skirt, a ruffly top, a thin silver necklace and dark stockings—and had these large eyes, the only part of her face she made up. And had this hair, so thick, so deep a red. When she tied it back for work it hung like grapes the size of eggs. Every time he saw her hair was as if somebody took a redwood log and split it open before his eyes.

"I really am getting varicose veins," she said, fingering a small bulge.

"That's not a varicose vein, that's muscle from carrying beer. My mother, now she's got some varicose veins." On Cammie the veins had nowhere to lie except close to the surface and the skin was so tight even her breasts felt like muscle.

"I hope you're right."

"I'm right. I've been at sea two weeks."

"R.L.," she said: a warning.

Sometimes, like now, she could look like an old maid on a farm. Other times, she could look warm, she could look cold, she could look innocent, she could look hard, she could look like a little girl who loved her daddy. "You want me to come back at one, help you clean?"

"R.L. We've been through this a million times. I've got to go back out front."

"Serve me another Bud."

She raised her eyebrows to show it didn't matter to her, it was his business, and lit a Marlboro from the desk drawer.

Sitting at the bar was a newcomer, a stranger to Cammie and whom nobody was talking to. In her judgment he seemed a tad too handsome and hip, might even be a narc. Then she wondered if she hadn't been seeing nothing but crabbers and carpenters for way too long.

Ange was on the phone, hurting. Not everyone could have detected his mood, since he kept his face calm under any conditions, his voice low, but Cammie recognized trouble in him quicker than in herself. He never forgot his courtesies. Trouble in him rose like a hungry fish, never quite to the surface but causing a disturbance if you knew how to look. He dialed another number.

R.L. deck-walked out the door, pulling his cap down his nose, pulling his black coat around to hide the beer in his hand. He walked out thinking of her shoulders still dark with freckles from summer.

The regulars at the table with Nan called for beer but Ange wanted her to stay and talk first. He leaned against the backbar, thin and quiet, let his arms hang, looked at the floor, mumbled, "Cammie, I guess it comes to my having to ask you—I apologize, but I have to ask where she went, if you know."

"I have no idea, Ange. Don't go jumping to conclusions though."

"The situation is such—I mean what other damn conclusion can I jump to?"

The Duke ordered gin and tonics, two-thirds and one-third in twelve-ounce mugs for himself, Alice and her cousin Cecelia Curles at the middle booth, and a pack of Winstons.

"I don't know, Ange. She said something earlier about Cloth Barn Road." Without having to think she pulled out three Schlitzes, two Blues, a Bud, a Miller Lite and a red Malt Duck.

"Right, visiting my mother. Cammie, don't try to—" He didn't finish. He appreciated the difficulty of her position and never would have faulted her for anything anyway. "I'm riding up there, carrying Warren to his grandmomma's, then riding up to Norfolk and I guess taking my gun. Just, you know, close whenever your opinion—no more food starting now, no barbecue buns or nothing."

She delivered the drinks and went back to the office. Ange had put on his sportcoat, was mixing a thermos of Blue Hawaiis, using rum somebody had checked and forgotten the night before. "I know you're upset but really you could be wrong." She didn't think he was wrong.

"Who's that guy at the bar wearing a necklace?"

"I was wondering."

"He looks like a narc, do you reckon?"

"Maybe he's an A.B.C. officer."

"I don't believe so."

"Anyway you should sort of clean up a little."

This he was already doing, slipping baggies out of the adding

machine, from behind the Busch Bavarian clock, from a case of
Collins mix, from the spiral of the Only Bar Halloween photograph
album. For all his skill at hiding his real self he was pathetically
inept at keeping his other self under wraps. His debts, his
schemes, his liking for a new drug became public overnight. A
five-year-old could have walked in and uncovered every bit of stash
in two minutes. He took a handful of ones from the cash box, put on
his sunglasses, a sure sign he meant to go. Day or night he wore
them whenever he left, sometimes in the bar, thinking they hid the
redness.

"Don't take the gun at least."

"It's kept in the car."

"Don't *leave.*" She ran to the front and pleaded with his closest
friend Slue Swain to talk Ange out of this desperation.

"Just right," Slue said, his voicebox full of sand. He tipped his
Blue Ribbon straight up. "Just right, he should have done this
two years ago. But no, kept letting it slide and letting it slide, that's
the way the man operates, tying himself in knots instead of hauling
in the slack on anybody else."

One of the Nunemakers, Acey, came up from behind, rested his
chin on Cammie's head. Booths and tables needed drinks. The
jukebox stuck on the chorus of a Kenny Rodgers song. "Talk to
him."

"Hell, I've tried to talk him into it for two years."

She waited.

"I'll talk."

He didn't have to leave the table. Ange was returning to make
the rounds, shake his friends' hands, tell them he'd see them
tomorrow and to give and take a look with each. "Riding up to
Norfolk to pick up our cruise boat tickets, first boat out," he said to
Nan Twiford.

"You take care of yourself," she said.

"Slue," Cammie said.

Slue nodded and followed his friend out the door. When he
came back he cried out, "Drinks for everybody and put it on my
goddamn tab and I don't care if my engine stays laid up for a
month!"

Cammie was out the door in time to see Ange's cream-color
Lincoln pull onto the causeway road, which led across the bridge to
the beach bypass to the upper bridge, which led back across the

sound and north. He didn't peel out, he eased out, a worse sign, the tires not popping but squeezing gravel.

With close timing Police Chief Omie Marr rolled into the lot from the other direction and parked in Ange's space. Accompanied by a man whose suit and metal-rimmed glasses announced State A.B.C. Board, he ambled toward the entrance. "Got anybody watching the inside?" he asked Cammie.

"Me."

"Well now Ange has installed remote control. Is that in the manual, remote control?" he asked the A.B.C. man, who didn't respond.

The wind had shifted to south-southwest and blowing up the sound and across the marsh and the road smelled of oyster mud, bad fishing and false spring. For the how manyeth time, Cammie wondered, am I wishing I had a boat lying off the breakwater? She stayed at the Only Bar only because of Tish and Ange, who couldn't run the place without her and were her best friends.

Ange's Lincoln always gave Cammie the impression of riding in a space capsule. The quiet and casualness of handling, particularly in comparison with her Dodge van, approached no gravity. The radio tuned itself, its little eye bopping from station to station, its speakers turning guitars to harps. When she had her house, she wanted a livingroom as cozy as the Lincoln, as ideal for getting stoned in. Nearly every night Ange would say, "Let's go for a ride-around." They'd crawl up and down the beach road, pull off back of a dune, roll down the windows with the touch of a button, light up, listen to the waves. Ford Motor Company sold a line of automobiles whose purpose was to provide the rich with mobile livingrooms to get stoned in.

"Yea they're stoned all the time," Ange had agreed. He was. It suited his physiology, his gait and manner, his hospitableness, his chalky voice. On alcohol he used to wreck cars. On dope he glided, miles below the speed limit. They'd smoke, he'd talk about Tish and Del Benoit because if there was anybody he let inside anymore it was Cammie.

He wasn't rich, he just lived rich, in constant danger of being gill-netted by criss-crossing lines of credit in and out of town. The Only Bar—he despised the name, a result of his own neglect—was so in fact in winter aside from the Ramada Inn on the beach. The amount of cash spilling through screened him when he walked into a bank. People tended to believe in him, weak voice included. He'd taken a decomposing crabhouse, doubled the size, made tables and booths out of hatchcovers and sawed-up church pews, paneled it with barnwood, framed old pictures in rope—redneck, but tasteful redneck.

He didn't worry about money thus he was rich. He worried about Tish. Even at nineteen he'd known he'd never feel the same for anyone else. He'd tried stray but found it impossible to go more than once, once at night after which he pretended to pass out, once in the morning pretending she was Tish or nothing in the morning if he could sidestep. With her the thing seemed spring-loaded no matter how she treated him.

He wasn't redneck. Time and again he'd cut her slack. He'd kept his mind years ahead of the standards of Water County, educated it by dragging it to this and that cosmopolitan spot, ski resorts, San Francisco, Bermuda. People have to believe in each other's best interests, he liked to tell Cammie, who understood, act in good faith, help each other in trouble, talk and deal straight.

But with Del, Tish had fucked with him way beyond any maximum. He sat with his friends in his bar knowing, *knowing* that at that moment she was laying up with Del. Then he felt like a living fish on the gutting board.

On the mainland side of the upper bridge, turning up N.C. 158, he capped the thermos and lit a joint. Omie Marr himself back when they drank together gave him the gun he reached under the seat and slid into his pocket. Though he continued to drive languidly a determination set in, from button-down collar to Hush Puppies, a cement that hardened from the inside out.

"Riding to Norfolk, riding to Norfolk."

"Now where do you suppose Ange's gotten to?" Omie Marr asked, directing his flashlight across the checked liquor bottles to make certain they were labeled with legal names, not Duke but Terrence H. Minton, not Chas or Razz but Charles O. Rollins.

"He went to buy plastic cups," Cammie said. She was keeping tabs on Timmy Spratt, a mean little scrapper whom Ange had barred a dozen times then put on probation a dozen. Omie and the A.B.C. man were going out of their way to avoid noticing the stranger. Normally Omie would have pumped the guy, offhand he thought, for some information about himself. Her worst nightmare was of having the bar closed down when she was on alone.

"Tell him I want to sit down with him," the Chief said.

"Oh, what for?" she asked, surprised at herself.

Omie appeared surprised too. It didn't take him long however to come up with, "Hallie across the road's complaining again about parking." Hallie Gaspar, who'd buried three full and several fractional husbands—among them Ange's daddy—had a fetish about parking, also about not using lights.

The A.B.C. man was fooling with a loose strip of paneling. Ange believed Omie, who held onto grudges tighter than the raffle tickets he preserved years past date of drawing, to be on a new tack. He'd never gotten an alcohol citation to stick, due to common sense and as everybody knew Del Benoit's political connections—no wonder Ange turned a blind eye, or put her up to her slutting. But there was no way a drug bust wouldn't stick.

Chas the Razz, having donned his Stetson and moved in on two women tellers from Planters Bank, was acting noticeably drunk, unusual for him, the noticeability. Omie cocked his head. "Girl, you know it's against the law to let anybody get drunk in a bar."

"I'll cut him off. Thanks. Did you gentlemen want anything to drink?

"Yes m'am," the Chief said, "two waters."

For these the A.B.C. man dropped fifty cents on the bar and he and Omie proceeded to the door, slow.

Slue's wife called, he refused to talk. Cammie gave him the message his dried-out chicken was going in the setter's bowl, a message intended to enrage him on the subject of a dog's esophagus and chicken bones. Cammie explained once again to Tobacco Ted how to spin quarters into the cigarette machine.

The Duke dragged Chas to the bar, told him to straighten out, right now and in general, ordered drinks and asked Chas if Cammie had ever described the special night they spent. "That was a real special night, wasn't it, darling? You never told Chas about that night, what went down, what kept on going down till the dawn's early light? Wasn't that one special night?"

"I guess it was."

"You know it was, darling, you know it was. Brother," he said to Chas, "brother, we got looned right on out, looned right on out to the *max*." He brought his large, elegant, ruined head, loaded with energy, close to hers. Something about looking at the Duke resembled looking at the jukebox from too close up.

Chas ducked from under the Duke's arm and said, "I don't like you talking that way to my lady, she's too fine for that. She understands." He drew out *understands* to twice its length. "From the moment she stepped off the bus, even when she took up with my raggedy-ass brother, I saw she understood, understood everything, all the towns and the oceans and the winds of the soul, all the hopes and sorrows of the heart."

"Tell it, brother, tell it."

"You cocksucking liar."

"You blind son of a bitch."

"Cammie," Chas said, taking a breath, exhaling smoke, shaking his head as he lifted his eyes to hers and lifted his eyebrows like a hound's or a believer's in church. "Cammie," he said, and had to stop. He reached for her hand, shut his eyes as he pressed it to his lips.

"I wish I understood a few things."

"Don't give me that bullshit." A native of East Lake, Chas pronounced it boolshit. "Don't try and put the bullshit over on me. You're real. Cammie, you're real." Every time he said her name he shut his eyes.

Loaded with indecision, Budweiser and low-tar nicotine Tish Buthrell was zooming north on N.C. 158 towards Norfolk, empty bottles volleying beneath the pedals. The breeze boosted the horsepower of her 1968 Chevy, although with two warnings on her provisional license, good to and from work, she tried to watch the towns. She slowed to forty through the north end of Grandy, too many shadows under trees. Entering Barco she slammed on the brakes so hard the wheels almost locked—she'd remembered her cousin Nibbie's getting stopped there, past the Sunoco station. Outside town she tapped the brake pedal for stoplights.

She wasn't fooling herself. She knew what she was risking. People accused her of a self-destructive impulse; well now they'd have something to go on. At twenty-nine you are too young to spend your life dreading consequences. She wasn't cut out to be the devoted wife and mother three hundred and sixty-five days a year. Every now and then the human organism—she used Del's phrase—needed a little Mardi Gras like in New Orleans and those people are Catholics. She was risking the house, two years old, the longest brick house in Water County, everything in it, a good living, maybe even Warren though she doubted that. Warren could take care of himself but Ange couldn't take care of Warren.

But it was a damn good living, even if she had to kiss a few asses. She would kiss, she would slobber over Omie *Marr's* behind if that's what it took to make a living. And it was ever her, ever her lips sent on these missions, never Ange's lily-white kisser. He preserved his for preaching the brotherhood of the world. She had to fawn, she had to act gracious, my heavens. She supplied every other form of manpower too seven days a week, eleven a.m. to one a.m., ever there, ever hustling while Ange cut out with his buddies and stayed smoked up all his conscious moments. He supplied the ideas. Great, just great if there wasn't somebody to carry them out, talk to carpenters, talk to salesmen, mop, order, straighten the walk-in, hire and fire in summer, cook pizzas in the eight-thousand degree oven, collect tabs, return broken bottles for credit, feed a family on the quarters from the jukebox and cigarette machines. Right, they went skiing a couple weekends. What about the vacations he took by himself while she handled the bar, her and Cammie? He never finished a thing. Even the sign, the fifteen-hundred dollar sign saying Causeway Inn had remained in the crate so long the customers named the bar. In a week Ange spent at the outside ninety minutes in the place when he wasn't blowed out. She and Cammie carried the load.

Married at nineteen and seventeen they were supposed to settle each other down, a laugh. Ange hadn't settled, he'd merely gotten slower and stopped punching cops.

She realized she was putting her guilt onto him but he messed around, he took money from the register to gawk at Nan Twiford's puny tits, just because she didn't know jealousy didn't change that fact. She couldn't give up Del, didn't understand why she had to. Ange complained Water was too small for *his* ideas. Every woman loved more than one man but didn't do anything about it or did once or twice on the sly. Why should she care what people who'd bad-mouthed her all her life said? Why should he? They'd bad-mouthed him. Ange the sick drunk, Ange the dopehead, Tish the wildwoman. They couldn't live to please those blowfish.

She was no good at giving up. She'd tried with cigarettes, with beer, Lord knows with Del, sometimes going for weeks. Lucky nobody ever gave her heroin.

Ange would go crazy, break furniture and china, bash in the color set, lock her out of the house forever, rip her clothes and throw the shreds out the window, which is why she kept her best things, including her new dress for the Shrine Club dance, in the trunk. But he'd never find strength to give her up. Your nipples are like stethoscopes reading my heart, he'd croaked to her once.

How many more opportunities would Water County present her with? Her body was filling out, catching up with her frame. Her complexion aged two years for every one in the cigarette smoke of the bar, that tannery.

She figured she'd stop at a filling station before Norfolk to comb her hair, as she drove with the windows wide open.

"Riding to Norfolk." Ange couldn't decide if he wanted to overtake her or not, a far-fetched notion to begin with considering the rate she drove unless she broke down, a more likely notion, a habit. He didn't know if he could trust his hands once he snatched her out. She'd be cussing, hitting at him, as a damn joke, squealing like he'd nabbed her in nothing more than hide-and-seek. I knew you'd chase after me, she'd say, I wanted you to, she'd say, and try to thrust her pelvis against his. I'm coming home, I was planning to turn around come home if you didn't catch up. She'd tilt her head, relax her mouth for him.

Staying laid on back was definitely the right idea. The little eye on the fuel gauge started blinking and while there was plenty to reach Norfolk he turned in at a Sav-Mor self-service filling station, one pump under one light in the middle of nowhere. Fallow tobacco fields all around, a creek to the west flagged by trees. The breeze rustled his flat hair, which hung in front of his face as he fed bills. Looking toward the creek he thought he saw flashlights moving between trees, coon hunters. He'd taken Warren duck-hunting, he and Del had a couple years back, but never to Stumpy Point after animal.

Steering with a wrist he passed the stores and early-to-bedder houses of Succutuck County. Reflecting his headlights in stale flashes they put him in mind of plywood tombstones.

His heart became a drum, a tub bass, a whole rhythm band of

injury. For long stretches he set his vision on automatic pilot, went blind to everything but his own separate life, him, alone, in a space capsule—as Cammie called it—free, white and thirty-one, money in his pocket, credit cards, dope under the dash, full tank of gas and no reason to stop short in Norfolk, no reason not to go on to D.C., N.Y.C., Montreal.

An old pickup passing him brought his attention back to the road. He was entering Grandy. He entered Grandy as a gentleman but free. No reason was the best reason with a gun.

Coasting out of the north end of town he saw a phone booth, one phone with one light in the middle of nowhere.

Cindy Spruill flew off the barstool.

"Chas!" Cammie said.

Chas threw his hands up like a basketball player showing he didn't foul. "I brushed her by accident, I swear. Cammie, you know I couldn't hurt her back, even a heartsick old man like me"—he was forty-two—"couldn't injure a little girl"—she twenty—"who doesn't even comprehend the damage she does laying up with another man while I'm out on the goddamn, god-fucking sea working to where my arms grip the air in *sleep*, who doesn't even know I can see right through her pretty eyes, right into her soul when she walks in tells me she's been faithful to me."

The phone rang, wouldn't stop ringing. The Duke, everywhere at once, picked it up and nodded the receiver towards Cammie.

"I've got news for you," Tobacco Ted was saying, wiping foam out of his beard at the same time he missed the ashtray. "Damn you're a fine-looking thing, aren't you? What was your name?"

"Ted, how many times have you been in here? Cammie."

"Cammie, I've got news for you."

"How could I be blaming a little girl for failure to comprehend the passion of a man?" Chas asked.

Cindy, accustomed to hearing herself discussed, settled back next to him, straightened the collar of her blouse. "I'd lost my balance."

Cammie took the receiver. "Cammie, this is Ange." He always identified himself over the phone. "I don't suppose—Tish hasn't shown up or anything, has she?"

She considered lying but he'd be able to tell and anyway she couldn't face him were he to return and no Tish. He wouldn't get angry with her, she just couldn't bear the thought. "Not yet but really you know she could be anywhere."

"That's exactly my assumption I'm operating on. I meant what I said about closing, you know, if it gets too busy, or hell if it doesn't."

"It's already kind of busy. I wish you were here."

"I have to stick to priorities, for once. I guess I'll be seeing you."

"Well all right, Ange."

"You can search the whole world over," Tobacco Ted, retired from the Merchant Marine, was saying. "You can search the whole world over, and you will never find, a man, as sorry, as old Tobacco Ted. I'm telling you truth, you can search the whole world over."

"Aw, you're not so bad."

"I don't blame nobody for not liking old Ted," said Ted. "I hate him myself. But you can search the whole world over, but I've got news for you."

Thirty seconds later Ange called again. "Cammie, this is Ange. I forgot to tell you she's fired. I've fired her. Cross her name off the schedule, you hear me?"

"All right, Ange."

"Hard night, huh?" commented the narc, who insisted on coming on despite her obvious indifference, and nervousness now that R.L. was back, leaning, cap tight, into a group of mates at the middle table, making gestures that fell short.

"Normal," she said. She didn't let him light her cigarette, lit it from a bar candle.

The Duke cleared mugs out of the way and lay across to whisper at the level a bear might whisper, "I've got a little something for you, sugar darling, help you through the evening, little bit of fisherman's friend." He and Ange had gone partners on a few buys.

"Just shut up, okay?" She backed off, because of R.L. and because the Duke was liable to just stuff it in her hand.

"Check it out, check it right on out," he urged. He caught up with her emptying ashtrays and no longer pretending to whisper said, "It's some fine toot. My teeth are buzzed."

"The guy at the bar's a narc. Now you take anything you've got out to your truck and you leave it."

"The day anybody gets the balls to bust me is the day the damn geese grow balls."

"I'm not worried about you, I'm worried about the bar."

"Let me know when you can slip out and join me over my picture of Jesus."

At the table with Slue, Cal Quinley—once one of Ange's close friends now his blood enemy over rental of the Tourist Office— started chuckling, wheezing through his teeth rather. All Ange's enemies drank at his bar; he wouldn't stand for their not. When Del Benoit came in, Ange paid for his soda mixes, sat down with him, took him back to the office to indulge in the main thing they shared besides Tish, love of bullshit.

Cal grabbed Cammie around the butt. "One's a fool, the other one's a pure fool and you love them both, don't you, girl?"

"I just want to keep the place open."

Del Benoit was sitting by the window on the fourteenth floor of the Holiday Inn, formerly the Triangle Hotel, his feet up on the air conditioning unit, a bottle of J&B in his crotch, a bucket of reamed ice cubes at hand. He looked down over the parking lots and church converted to a memorial for Douglas MacArthur and philosophized, which meant think about women—Woman, to be precise.

He maintained an apartment on the beach which nobody knew the whereabouts of, not his wife, not his men friends, not Tish. No telephone, only a CB transceiver. Two days a week in the off-season, or three, he holed up there, with a picture window out to sea, classical records, cases of J&B, two silk robes. Once he sent off for the complete Great Books for his hideaway. Twelve hours after their arrival, however, in the dead of night he'd packed the set in liquor boxes and dropped it at the county library without identification. "Bequest of the Delbert R. Benoit Memorial," read the endpapers, which pleased him, the librarian's knowing both his brand and his liver.

At age fifty he prided himself on having finished with the sex of life, the ins and outs of making money. He'd sweated blood to turn his brine-eaten frame inn into the landmark of what passed for hospitality. The middle class checked into the new brick places, eating fried oysters. The rich stayed in wood, dining on them raw. He'd knocked down walls, torn up floors, poured cement—him and the Duke—laid tile, added two wings in the old style. For fifteen years he'd given up liquor, gone stone dry from Memorial to

Labor Days inclusive. This season he could afford to stand pat, didn't need to sacrifice a thing, except Tish, and she was merely the goal of all philosophy, the illumination of all liquor, the harmony of the sex not of life but of sex.

The Norfolk Holiday was the hotel, this the room that had worked the cure for alcohol fifteen years straight.

His wife couldn't have cared about his philandering nor he about hers. She saw some guy from Elizabeth City, some travel agent or arts director—whatever, he always had a mouthful of Lifesavers, and a pocketful of Del's money, which also he could have cared about. Maybe if he concentrated on his waitress from Greensboro College, made a fool of himself, he could transfer his feelings for Tish, not to the girl but to the making of a fool of himself.

Granted he and Tish burned coal in bed. Granted she loved him for the unpredictability, the risk while loving Ange for real. In the beginning this had been his comfort. He'd preferred second fiddle, confirming as it did his theory that Woman is not basically polygamous but a fine tuner of monogamy.

Yet now. Yet now, occasionally, he and Tish would be ambushed in an embrace that sailed and sailed beyond every attempt at philosophy and he wondered if his life hadn't been a lie and if there had not been some moment when he didn't notice a face he was meant to stay very near the rest of his days.

Once or twice he'd tipped his hand, exposed his bleary dreams to the laser gun of hers. And she hadn't fired, she'd cried. Then fired.

He considered calling room service to remove his telephone but decided if he could keep liquor around to serve guests when he was on the wagon he could keep a damn phone in his room.

"Cammie, this is Ange."

"Where are you?"

"Coinjock. Sounds busy in there."

"Well I could use some help."

"What that means is she hasn't shown."

By now Cammie thought she could lie once, but never twice— when he asked to speak with Tish she'd have to tell him she was out buying ice at the Fishing Center or something, the ice maker had broken down again: making three lies. "Haven't seen her but I was hoping you'd take the hint. Everybody's in a hassling mood tonight, the Chief's on the prowl, Hallie's hot, Pook and Eljay waded in and I don't know about this narc."

"Seems to be a long way to Norfolk."

"Are you buzzed?"

"Like a bitch."

"You think you know what you're doing. I hope you don't end hating yourself."

"I'm neutral about myself."

"You're assuming."

"How about it."

Eljay raised two fingers, two three-quarter-inch dowels, for him and his partner Pook, captains out of Swann's Bay, hugh, gray, gabardined men who when drunk lost consciousness wide awake without dropping any of their guard. Loose, they became less than animal but more than ordinarily dangerous to other animals. They didn't stagger or slur; they rarely talked. In slow motion they raised Luckies to their lips and barely seemed to drag although the ash burned with amazing evenness. They were like juniper trunks washed up on the shore, with depth charges inside.

"We ain't looking for no trouble," Eljay said when Cammie set the Blue Ribbons down.

"Of course you aren't, Eljay." He hadn't been home as his crew for the most part had, still smelled.

His cigarette took a good ten seconds to describe a perfect arc to the ashtray. "We come in to have a good time."

"That's right, I know you did."

"No trouble."

"Why would there by any trouble?"

"You can search the whole world over, but I've got news for you. Nobody likes old Ted, and I don't blame them. He'll do anything in the world for you but nobody likes him. They know he's no damn good on the inside."

"Shut him up," Eljay said. "We don't want to."

"Ted," Cammie said, wiping around his ashtray, "could you cool it a little while? You're sort of getting on people's nerves."

"See what I tell you. Nobody likes Ted."

"Getting on somebody's nerves doesn't mean they don't like you. People in love get on each other's nerves."

"You can search the whole world over, and you will never find, a person, in love."

"Possibility of getting another Heineken down here?" called the narc.

"Slim."

In the darkness Cammie relied on a sort of radar to track troublespots, an installation in the back of her mind that was constantly scanning, lighting up corners and groupings of bad energy. Tonight the screen had been busy but the blips hadn't come with the timing and density that signalled alarm. With Pook and Eljay there they brightened, quickened. Ange's departure had left an uneasiness in the back. The first night ashore drew the worst out of fishermen. The Chief, the narc and R. L. added to the strain, hers anyhow, as did the Duke, who never looked for trouble but was careless. Sides wouldn't prove that important, simply the existence of an excuse.

"There's them in here don't like us," Eljay said, or Pook—she couldn't tell which—causing Ted to turn his head with interest. Eljay or Pook was referring to Slue and his crew. Pook had pistol-whipped Slue's fifteen-year-old son off Cape May, left him in such shape the mate had radioed a helicopter to carry the boy to the hospital. Cammie didn't think Slue, hot-headed as he was, would give Pook the chance to settle the matter outright—he'd bided his time for months—but tonight she couldn't tell.

"Everybody's got people who don't like them."

"Ain't looking to start no trouble. You keep trouble clear of us, hear?" She not only couldn't see a mouth move, she couldn't see eyes under the brims of their caps.

The runners on the righthand cooler were getting stickier and stickier. She reached under the register for Crisco.

"That your boyfriend just left?" the narc wanted to know.

"Sort of." She knew exactly why he'd left, so he could sneak back and catch her leaning on the bar talking to the narc or letting the Duke hang on her while he whispered in her ear.

"You ever go out with anybody else?"

She narrowed her suspicion to the guy's fastidiousness, his pressed workshirt with the cuffs rolled back twice, his gold watch, his long hair hanging just so, the way he wiped the condensation off the bar with his napkin. Then she knew his background. It was that air that stayed with a guy forever, that scent he can never bathe, drink or smoke off, the Lysol of the service. She figured Army intelligence. "I try not to go out with anybody."

"You know, that's a crushing damn disappointment. Literally. I was developing this crush on you."

"Anybody develops interest in me's asking for trouble."

"Do you mean you're a heartbreaker or do you mean your boyfriend's a hard customer?"

"I mean I'm fucked up from head to toe."

Startled he spread his arms, smiled, causing a pendant to swing into view on his chest, a little gold cross.

"Shouldn't you be wearing a pair of those?" Cammie asked. Most nights she possessed stamina to burn but R.L. sucked it out of her. She took a bottle of Visine from her pocketbook. On the job she chain-smoked herself but by eleven the smoke, combined with the effort of keeping her radar focused, put embers in her eyes.

The phone—Del's disguised voice, which he disguised by talking timidly and accenting the wrong syllables or words. "May I please speak to Tish Buthrell?"

"Del, look—" She was sniffling with the Visine.

"Cammie? Cammie, tell Tish I want to speak to her but tell her don't say a word, I can't take the sound of her voice."

"She's not here, she—"

Before she could explain he hung up actually moaning.

Taking off from a crossroads where all four directions looked identical, scruffy trees, bumpy pavement, everything a dead shade of blue-gray, Ange was pitying her for her limitations. Every direction was a reflection in the rear-view mirror until the one in front backed down, resumed three dimensions. He hadn't turned, he swore he hadn't. She didn't know how to insert a split-second of thought between the information and the response. Because she lacked concentration she worked five times as hard as necessary. She had two phases, laziness and craziness, nothing in between, the one as full of deceit as the other.

He pictured her lying across the bar exposing the tops of her squashed breasts, dying for customers, talking to some old drunk like Tabacco Ted, rambling as if falling asleep word by drowsy word. Then in a heartbeat up strongarming some two hundred and fifty pound sea captain out the door.

Through the years the thing he'd longed for was stretches of plain and lingering tenderness. The minute you believed you had one, were safe, it dawned on you she was laughing up her sleeve.

Was that what that lard-ass drunk was able to draw from her, patient attention?

He assumed she'd reached Norfolk by now, was rapping on the door, making some teasing remark. Del might put on a show of turning her away but he enjoyed his weaknesses too much to hold out, especially if he was drinking. No if about it. He'd see her face lit up with beer, he'd see that shiny dress, the highheels she changed into in the parking lot—she wore deck shoes to drive— he'd see those eyes making fun of the situation. They were laughing, guzzling booze, going to it. He didn't delude himself they were laughing specifically at him but they were letting out some kind of giggle that shriveled his balls.

Try a little tenderness—that's what he'd say as he popped them.

He lit another joint to maintain the cool the job required, the feeling of being just another part of the Lincoln, an interior power accessory registering neither wind nor road. He took an uphill curve, flew across a little bridge. The headlights picked out a pinto pony, a beautiful thing, standing against its shed by the fence. Goddamn, he thought, goddamn beautiful peaceful animal, full of wisdom. It doesn't matter to him, my popping them.

The trees thickened up, met over the road. Branches whipped closer and closer in the slipstream. Maybe he did turn wrong. This wasn't far from skiing, nearly out of control toward the top of one range then sort of waxing into the next speed, the higher the speed the truer the aim. He knew damn well the road lay level here but it seemed to be falling away. He was through the next crossroads before he saw it come, before the flash that lasted in the car for miles like red perfume. The tons of vehicle rode on a single blade, perfectly balanced.

He'd better slow down, he was thinking when he crested a hill and five full pints of blood shunted to his head.

R.L. loved to see her wash mugs, for although not a native or sturdy looking she knew how to work as well as anybody. He wanted to press his face to that spot on her shoulder, get a faceful of both shoulder and hair, the one spot of her she couldn't drain of heat no matter how she tried. "I mean, couldn't we get together after closing and sit down and talk? Here, even, here's fine."

"It would be the same conversation. It's not what we say to each other, it's the sameness that drives me up the wall."

One in each hand, onto the brushes, right, left, she could wash those mugs. "I did wrong last time, but when a man finds his woman—" With her wrist she brushed back a couple of reddish-copper hairs.

"We were *talking*. Damn it, this is what I mean. Never anything different, never the slightest thing changed. That's what'll drive me away from here, not what people do, the sameness of the doing."

"I bought some Thai sticks off Bud Loring. We could sit at the bar after we close."

"No!" She looked around the corner to the front, squinting out of the light over the sink. "You'll drive me right out of Water County."

"Cammie, I'm making a load of money. I'm saving three-fourths. I'll have enough for a downpayment, you know? Bud told me about this house on the soundside, you know, we might run by check out some time." His hands had caves in them where her hips were supposed to fit.

"I've got to get change."

Warren was lying on the office floor with sticks of wood, Eveready batteries, strips of bellwire around him, his head on a stack of placemats. He had Ange's straight black hair, Tish's wide mouth and eyes.

"Damn I thought I had a hard road," R.L. said. He spread his coat over him. Cammie admitted there was a sweetness to R.L.'s voice at times, to him, misplaced in this case.

When she shut the door to block out the jukebox, the high notes, Warren woke.

"What are you doing, boy?" R.L. asked.

"R.L., you like World War II?" He copied Ange's muffled tone.

"Yea."

"Look what Hammerhead gave me." He took a khaki tin of C-rations out of his jacket; he'd been sleeping on the thing. "Check this out."

"That's all right."

"Did you read it?"

"Yea, U.S. Army."

"I mean all of it."

"It says what's in it," Cammie put in.

"There's a chicken in here."

"Well not a whole chicken," R.L. said.

"There is."

"They took the bones out."

"Yea of course they took the *bones* out. Hell."

"That's really an all right thing to have."

"How much you give me? It's quite valuable, genuine World War II."

"A thirty-year-old chicken," Cammie said. "Thirty-one."

"It's still good."

"How much you asking?" R.L. said.

"Five dollars."

"Holy moses."

"Think how much a museum like in Norfolk'd give me."

"I think Hammerhead meant you to keep it for yourself," Cammie said. "He'd be upset if you sold it."

"I can do anything I want with it."

"He'd be upset."

"If he cared he wouldn't give it to me."

"Warren, I'm calling your grandmomma, see if she's home. R.L.'ll run you over there, all right?" She was asking R.L.

"I don't give a shit. I just hitchhiked from there."

"You got some mouth on you," R.L. said.

Warren cocked his head, bobbed it. "You got a ugly fucked-up mouth on you. Your mouth makes me sick to my stomach."

"Warren," Cammie said, "you ready to go back to your grand-momma's?"

"Yea, I'll sleep on the beach. I always sleep on the beach."

"You don't watch your mouth, boy, you'll be sleeping on the bottom of the sound. I'll pitch you out crossing the bridge."

"R.L., for God's sake."

"I like to see you pitch me out, you candyass, you old nerd."

"I better not see that new guy when I get back," R.L. told Cammie, his muscles betraying bad wiring. "I see him, his face is his ass."

"I've got to get back out front. I'll call from there."

At the bar she lit a Marlboro and pretended she didn't catch anybody gesturing or hear anybody call her name. She took partial consolation from Timmy Spratt's having left, unless he was in the john. Running out from the back, arms full, Warren asked, "You see any extra batteries around here?"

"Nope."

At the door R.L. transmitted a final message to assure her she wasn't putting anything over. At first she thought he was going to give her the finger; then she realized what dredged up wasn't anger but pain, so pure it shone.

Her mother had tried to help her father. A total drunk—Chas the Razz given ten years—visibly yellow, he used to grab her, and Cammie if handy, around the legs like timber after a shipwreck, convincing her mother he would kill himself if she divorced him.

At nineteen Cammie drove trucks for a construction company in Richmond. The practical fact was R.L. didn't do it for her anymore and knew this but couldn't understand the last remedy in the world was harder.

Tish, southbound on N.C. 158, experienced a close call passing a groggy farmer up a hill. It reminded her of the beach when all the waves stop at once and silence falls heavier than lying underneath surf. She skinned by, thanks to the farmer's diddling, her reflexes and the Lincoln's wallow at the last moment but the incident persuaded her virtue didn't pay either. It was over too fast to fix the color of the Lincoln, yellow, maybe cream. If Ange *had* pursued her, he wouldn't have gotten this far at his usual fifty.

She had turned around. She'd stopped at a closed filling station, combed her hair in pump chrome and without fully deciding when she pulled out, pulled out south. She couldn't give up the work she'd plowed into the bar, not for one night when Del might spring something like not let her in or let her in to see some naked prostitute with scotch dribbling off her tits.

From now on she'll be goody-goody for the most part. Three beers per night, no speed—it wasn't beer, it was those little doozies when they overshot. Once in a blue moon she'll see Del. He'll never quit. "Don't talk, just listen," he'd said this afternoon. "I'm not telling you where I am (as if everybody didn't know). I'm telling you it's got to be over. Next time we're friends, mutual friends of Ange. We're on his side. I don't mean to deny nothing, try to prove nothing. We're historical friends, a couple of damn philosophers." She'd taken a breath. "Don't be heartless, breathing."

Coming to the bridge north of Grandy her headlights scared piss out of a pony by the side of the road, made him toss and paw.

The spies will carry no tales. She'll keep her legs ever crossed, her laughter ever low, perch on her twenty-nine-year-old hips like they are forty-nine, finish cleaning rooms, serve meals of something other than pizzas heated over. With the costumers she'll let loose but stay this side of the line. No tight clothing. More time with Warren to prevent him from turning into another mumbling conniver. If only their skulls didn't have the same peanut shape.

She'll phone Cammie from the next booth. What would she do without that girl? She loved to see her driving her van, with not an expression on her face, not seeing anybody, not acknowledging a honk or wave, just sitting up there horsing the wheel, shifting gears, cutting corners, eyes miles down the road, just flying in that big blue van.

Omie Marr stalked minors, making sure nobody had gone to the bar, ordered mixed drinks and carried them to a table where a minor, just off a boat, sat with a warm beer sneaking hard liquor. Chas had sent Cindy home, sobbing, wailing out the door, which Cammie knew led to reconciliation, hopefully before the wop made the mistake of wandering in. Teresa Sawyer was waiting for her ex-husband to wander in with his girl from College Park, meanwhile staying near enough a man, any man, to cuddle and lick when he did. Slue, Quinley, the Nunemakers, Carl Peasley (County Dogcatcher, a political job thanks to Del) waited. Pook and Eljay, on their eighteenth Blue Ribbons—they raised their bottles slow but had to raise each only once or twice—were waiting and not waiting. Even the Duke seemed to have entered anticipation, letting his women talk to each other.

Deucey Nunemaker dragged a plastic trash bag of scallops to the bar; in his best ladies' man style, blond, woozy, and sharp-eyed, asked Cammie to cook.

"Everything's off," she said. She couldn't deny he made her think how pretty his arms must be, the armpits too, full of cords and knots. He could dance.

"I want to give some to everybody."

"I can set them in the walk-in till tomorrow."

"I give that little girl, my little neice, two thousand dollars for a car for school and she never come back. I don't blame her for not liking old Ted."

Cammie didn't have to make up her mind about trying to call

Del. He called; starting off sounding like a sick old chinaman, one of those you saw coming downstairs to Granby Street in Norfolk whom R.L. always wanted to ask for opium.

"God, Cammie." A native of Beaufort, he pronounced it Gawd. "You're good people, Cammie. Someday you'll turn into the lovely, heartful woman you're meant to be, I have faith you will. Just talk with me and don't put your bosslady on the line."

"Isn't she with you?"

"God no, our race is run. I've wanted to tell you how much I valued your putting up with us so long."

"She left here two hours ago."

"Don't tell me that. Don't tell me the black widow's still on the feed. Do you know why I call her the black widow?"

Her hearing went not long after her sight. She knelt behind the cooler, put a hand to her open ear. "You've told me." A thousand times.

"She doesn't know my room."

"Del, I want to tell you something but you have to give me a double promise. I mean promise for now and for when you're sober."

"I wish I could get drunk."

"You'll never say where you heard."

"If I wasn't true to anybody I'd be true to you. I don't need to promise to promise to you."

"Ange is on his way to the Holiday with his gun."

"Don't tell me that."

Cammie's radar picked up flashes so vivid she stood to look: Thad Scarborough strolling in with his new wife, a woman Slue Swain ran with prior to the marriage and Thad, the major buyer at the docks, was an associate of Pook and Eljay's—they and his daddy until his death last year welding high tackle made a trio—and why was Slue hanging around, why hadn't he gone home at his usual hour? Was all he was waiting for news of Ange?

"He's got his .32."

"Well that changes the lineup."

She knelt, caught a whiff of the sour beer that collected under the coolers, the marsh mice's swimming pool, the roaches' watering hole. She expected crabs to crawl out. "Del, get to another hotel. Now."

"I don't run scared."

"It's not scared," she began, then cussed herself for repeating that word with a drunk.

"In my life I've run blind, I've run ragged, I've run one-legged but I've never run scared. Does the mate of the black widow spider turn tail? He waits, fucking waits—excuse my French. That is his grace, and honor."

"I want to see you walking in here again."

"I carry a gun."

"Lord."

"I'd best get it out of my Dopp kit. You're good people, Cammie, damn solid people."

She went to wait on Thad and Ruelle although Thad, the perfect gentleman—to a point—when out with his wife, his prize, a woman his daddy would have taken to, always came to the bar to save her. She determined his and Slue's tables were ignoring each other, presenting backs and no glances. The Nunemakers showed the extra voltage more than anyone else. "When you going to cook scallops? We got butter," Slue said. "We want to share with our neighbors yonder."

"Call for you, sweetheart," the narc said at the bar.

"So how you doing," stated Tish over an excellent connection.

"Where are you, lady?"

"Oh I come over to see this girl who babysits, ask her to sit for Shriners."

"Warren needs a babysitter now?"

"Well I was sort of on the road to Norfolk. Damn it's dark outside this booth."

"Ange is driving up with his gun, Del's waiting with his."

"You're kidding me!" She attempted to drop to a somberer note. "When did he leave?"

"Half hour after you did."

"I'd better turn around."

"You'd better get here as fast as you can. If you show at the Holiday, Ange'll never believe why. Besides I can use some help."

"You don't imagine those two nerds'll do anything!"

"Hurry. Don't stop for beer."

"Where's a place *open?*"

"We'll call from here."

Two fingers from Eljay, one stub—the rest lost to a weeded screw—from Ted. The narc, pouring his third Heineken in two hours, was saying, "You know there's one thing I like as much as I like an attractive woman. You know what that is?"

"I don't care to."

"You'd never guess."

"I hope that's right."

He checked around. "Cocaine," he said. "Co, caine. And when I look at you I understand every toot I've taken had you in it. You know, I seem to come across a few passes on the old railroad."

"In your line of work you mean."

That gave him pause. "I've got a lot of lines of work."

The Duke, in full sail after a trip to the john, cut in and swung her away from the bar. "Won't you slip out with me for a minute, sugar darling? It breaks Jesus's heart not to share. Here, just to see you through the next couple hours, turn these ugly faces to angels, turn this bullshit into something you can listen to. Sneak on back to the office, sneak right on back, sugar. I'll handle all aspects out here."

She jammed it back in his pocket, which wasn't easy to locate under his Mexican shirt, his new and only style, comfortable on the belly. The narc was watching and R.L. was watching.

I suppose I've always been an extravagent man, Del Benoit thought, listening for her or his footsteps in the hall, fishing the last cubes from the water. He blamed alcohol, which as scientists claimed and he could substantiate destroyed braincells. What they hadn't discovered was alcohol didn't kill the sex cells of the brain but tumorized them, swelled them, pushed them out of every orifice.

Any one of those cars. . .footsteps; too far apart to be hers, with her center of gravity, too distinct for Ange. Intent on murder Ange would still shuffle.

He appreciated the effect of suspense of philosophy.

The candle on the back table melted a hole in Deucey's scallop bag and what seemed like gallons of milky juice ran on the floor, mixing with spilled beer, slippery as snot. Mop in hand, Cammie answered the pay phone.

"God, Cammie, how badly of me do you think for this?"

"If you're still at the Holiday not very highly."

"This is my bed and I'm laying in it, next to it to be precise, slipping shells in my little pistol, ready to frap if Ange noses in the door."

"Catching some long *dis*tance shit tonight, aren't you, darling?" the Duke wanted to know.

"Are you clean? I mean it, are you?"

"Everything but my head, and that's where it's all happening."

"I wish."

Slue rushed past, meaning to plug in the deep fat for scallops, unaware Cammie had thrown the circuit breaker.

"You heard us, did you?" Eljay said.

"Riding *in*to Norfolk, *in*to Norfolk"—by Ange's calculation the trip has lasted a half hour over. The drizzle continued as the Holiday Inn hove into sight. If there was any flaw to the Lincoln it was that the wipers had picked up a hum, which didn't disturb them in their sweeping, their near vacuuming of droplets but nettled him. In the way he sometimes became paralyzed on a vacation, he worried over action outside of Water County, where the checks and balances of private violence protected you. City laws, with ethnics to control, overlooked human rage and error, washed these into the gutters to keep the streets passable. His friend from boyhood Malcolm Sedgwick was the best lawyer in Water but what if he clutched in a city courtroom? Ange was looking at seven years before parole, seven years without so much as touching a woman.

There was only one woman for him anyway, and no reason to predict his lying down and dying after the act, not with D.C., N.Y.C. and Montreal calling his name, or alias.

He parked on yellow lines by the entrance. He took three or four tokes to clear the brain. With a hundred-dollar bill he took a toot of cocaine up each nostril to clear the muscles. A sort of electrical current dropped down his spine, electrical but liquid in that it pooled in his balls and sloshed as he got out and swung the door. In case he exited in a hurry he didn't lock. He didn't need to cut off the lights, which extinguished themselves after a passage of time. The night air, amazingly thin despite the rain, revealed seaweed and motor oil both in one sharp scent.

Across acres of thin carpet he approached and approached the desk, thinking midway that it stood too high, only his head would clear. He was aware he trailed disturbance. Suddenly he had to raise his hands to brake the forward motion. The desk hit belt level, covered the gun pocket. The dropped ceiling and angled wood converged on the blotchy, clever face of the night clerk, like faces Ange recalled from Las Vegas.

"How you doing this evening," Ange said. "Could you please—I'm here to see Del Benoit, friend of mine. What room's he in anyway?" He fingered the rolled-up bill while with his deportment dismissing any difference between monied caller and graveyard shift employee. They were twins, equal princes of night.

"Sir, I'm not permitted to give out the information."

"Shit I forgot to write it down, my own damn fault, as usual."

"We have instructions from the party."

He watched the clerk's hands as he notated cards and the clerk noticed he was watching his hands. They breathed each other, Ange through his iced nose breathing hairspray and a touch of Columbian, thinking the clerk breathed Lincoln heat and the same.

"You know who I'm talking about? Damn, I tell you, do they have freon running in this ceiling? I feel a draft."

"Sir, I understand this interior was stripped from an old wrecked rocketship discovered on Loft Mountain, in the Blue Ridge."

"I believe it. To tell you the truth I decorate with junk myself." He unrolled the bill.

"Please don't try that."

A few white flakes hit the blotter. "Squirrelly little sucker, legs like toothpicks, thick glasses, likes to mess with other men's wives."

The clerk twisted a turquoise ring on his fourth finger. "As I say, I can't give out the information. Obviously he forgot he asked a friend to call. You're free to look around, of course. Perhaps he'll be coming out of his room to go to an ice machine. There's one on the fourteenth floor for example. Perhaps luck will bring you together."

Ange understood he was to take his money back. He headed for the elevators, a lineup of the straightest faces he'd ever seen. Yessir, one said. "With you in a second," Ange said, having spotted the phone booths. Five times he got a busy signal before giving up on Cammie.

At the western end of the upper bridge, twenty miles shy of the

Only Bar, Tish vowed never take their records off. Ange hadn't changed records in so long anyway the new were sliding all over the office, cracking underfoot. Once in a blue moon Del'll mosey over and punch "Try As I Might" or "Leaving You's the Easiest Thing (Since Leaving Town)." She'll mosey back and select "Crazy" or "Torn Between Two Lovers" or "Let's Just Kiss and Say Goodbye." He'll drink another scotch, tell the crew he has business at the courthouse, wander down to the dock phone, which lacks a booth. She'll answer in the office—not in the first couple calls, Cammie can take those. She'll answer, speaking to the Sandler Foods man, asking time of delivery. She won't show. Next morning flowers will appear on the backbar. Next afternoon Del'll disappear to catch football practice at the school. She'll answer, whispering, hearing mostly wind from his end. With the wind and salt in the wires, these conversations amounted to reading lips over a crystal radio.

Ange was locating the door by intuition, strolling up and down the hall waiting for one to communicate. From sitting in blinds together he knew the man's life, breath and sweat (part Ivory soap, part J&B). He'd eliminated two legs of the triangle and the inner wall by assuming Del would choose a view but not the sea—he had one of those from his secret pad up the beach. A view of melancholy, the parking lots, the church. He played the kids' game, You're getting hotter, You're burning up. Sooner or later a door would change from wood to skin to oilskin.

It was probably, but didn't matter, Acey Nunemaker who started chucking scallops. It might have been Slue, but all in all he'd been sitting pretty quiet for him. Whoever, they aimed at selected targets at first, Tobacco Ted, the Duke, R.L. at the middle table, all of whom took it all right, even R.L. It was definitely Acey who dumped the bag, got everybody chucking, aiming they claimed for bottles, candles, caps, apologizing for misses. The radar lit up like Christmas. Still, tempers stayed unnaturally cool unnaturally long. The hit threw back, Acey and Slue back and forthed, people threw scallops, ate scallops raw, slipped and fell on scallops until the pile was exhausted and they had to pick them off the floor, which worsened by the second—juice, drinks, boot mud, rain under the door, the leak from the men's urinal—floated cigarette butts.

"You sorry sucker!" Chas yelled at nobody in particular. "I'll whip all your asses!"

It didn't matter who yelled. People heard what they wanted to from the mouth they wanted to.

"Shut your jellyfish, toadfish, all-mouth mouth!" the Duke yelled.

"Shut it, candy-ass!" Somebody else.

"Goddamn right, I'll shut it tighter than your asshole!" Somebody.

"Come get old Ted! Put Ted out of his misery!"

Cammie wasted no time turning the lights up and getting to the back before scallops hit Thad Scarborough's table and he and Slue were on their feet and primed.

"I've wanted a piece of you so long I can taste it." Thad's hair flung in fishbooks across his forehead.

"Just because you can't satisfy her after a real man, that's a hard road, ain't it boy?"

"Thad, please," Ruelle pleaded, cracking her rosy makeup with the effort.

"Ready to take this outside, you all?" Cammie said.

Sides chose up. Pook and Eljay, who'd taken time to finish their twenty-first beers, were moving.

"Watch yourself, Cam, watch yourself," R.L. kept saying. He tried to stand in front of her but she wouldn't let him. She thought her two scraps of authority—that she was a woman and had the power to bar a person from the only actual bar in the county— might save things yet. Too, she counted on Slue to ease back finally, since against these odds to do so would count more as judgment than cowardice among the opinions that mattered. Not a man in the bar could be provoked to go against a black man, for example.

"She made her choice."

"And been regretting it ever since ain't you, Ru? Ain't you, baby?"

The screen blipped the Duke slipping out the back. Teresa hung on Chas; he shook her off. R.L. shed his coat, rolled his sleeves.

Pook and Eljay moved with the force, the listlessness of naval cruisers on the sound. They flipped the tables, kicked the chairs to either side without fury, rather as a service, as if clearing for a dance.

Slue climbed up on his chair, Thad up on his upholstered pew, and the air between them transformed into hull steel.

"You been begging to have yourself mangled."

"Damn if that ain't so," said Eljay, whose statement carried as easily as over diesel engines.

Cammie put her left hand to Slue's beltbuckle, her right to Thad's. "Outside," she said. "Omie Marr's shut down every other, you want this bar shut too?"

"I reckon I had her more ways than you ever will," Slue said. Next his chair sloshed out from under, he collapsed, and although the motion was the reverse of attack it was motion itself that triggered Thad. The table see-sawed. Pitchers shattered into icicles. The jukebox swung out from the wall like a toy, smashed into something, a second later sprayed colored glass and choked dead on the music. Suddenly you could hear the women around the edges cuss. Cammie crawled from under R.L., who'd thrown himself on top her, and wedged between Thad and Slue. Neither one hit her—they froze at sight of her—but she went down, from a combination of Pook and Eljay's vanguard and the footing.

When she came up she stopped everything.

Blood ran from her nose and from a gash in her hand—pulsed, didn't gush. She knew she was fine. Her nose bled all the time; the cut was clean, maybe off a wineglass. But working at speed her mind told her she ought to play this up. She rocked her head back so the blood spread over the lower half of her face; she raised her drenched hand in the pose of a prophet or Indian. "I don't mean the damn parking lot neither! I mean off this property completely!"

"Look at her—shame!"

"I don't care who I start on," R.L. gave notice.

Cammie shoved Slue to the door, slapping his chest, printing her cut hand, knowing he couldn't honorably resist.

"Outside'll go," Eljay said.

"I'm *turning* you inside out." Thad reached over Cammie to swing. She turned and beat on *his* chest.

"I'm waiting on you all parakeet dicks!" Slue said. "I guess me and Ange both settle tonight."

"Other side of the bridge!" Cammie yelled. "Beach Police!"

This surprised her: that Slue, dragging one moment the next was hopping out the door, with Acey, Deucey, Peasley, Chas and them bulling their way after him.

"Run, I'm on your tail!"

"Shut up, take care of this girl you injured," Ruelle said.

A ring of black smoke two feet in diameter wobbled in the door, firecrackers went off, and suddenly everybody inside knew what was happening. The Duke had backed his pickup to the door, was peeling out with Slue and the crew aboard.

"God*damn!*"

"This here's a island," Eljay said. He and his partners were the only ones not to take off running for the fastest cars in the lot, Quinley's stoked-out Ranchero, Merle Leekins's Bonneville.

Cecelia, Teresa and Alice clustered Ruelle, her hair sobbing around her head on the table, her orlon sweater sobbing on her back.

"You all too," Cammie said. She didn't mind showing no mercy. "Party's done."

"You're lightheaded," Alice said.

"I'm riding her over to the clinic," R.L. said, with the same frustration at missing the scuffle as missing a fuck. The clinic, the only doctor, was in Grandy.

"You aren't riding me. Go to my house and wait."

"Cammie, damn, you are lightheaded with loss of blood."

"The blood's nearly clotted. I'll be at my house in fifteen minutes. Don't let the cat out. If you don't listen I'll be so long gone you won't ever see, you won't dream of me again."

"Your blouse is soaked red."

"I promise you I won't."

She just wanted to get the door locked and herself out of there before the Chief returned and before she discovered what had happened to the narc. She remembered to cut off the hot dog steamer. Adrenalin ceased filling in for the missing blood. Threading her way out in the dark, slop coming over the tops of her sneakers, she noticed a wooziness, which explained her feeling sorry for Tobacco Ted pissing at the edge of the road, raising steam.

"Come on in, Ange, door's unlocked."

"Evening, Del. Wait, I'm—" Positive before, when the door seemed to go concave at his touch, Ange now thought he'd entered the wrong room. The face kept eluding him, kept twisting out of perspective. The details were right, chinese brocade robe, hairless chest, grinning bifocals, the target pistol in the hand. But the man was too small and flat and distant. Ange pivoted, thinking what he was facing was a mirror but pivoted to a reproduction of boys driving geese through woods and stream. He turned back, his eyes undeceived him. They deceived him, he saw this salesman in town to work a stall at a bathroom fixtures show, hardly somebody who could threaten his very being, hardly somebody who bore the prick that gave a woman whatever he could not. "Who warned you, Cammie? Hell I don't blame her." He stood at a multiple angle to Del, the bed and the vanity mirror.

"You tell *me*," Del said.

He meant, You tell me if she's been here. If she'd been there Ange could have smelled her, sensed her the way when you're swimming a pocket of warmth will well up around your legs and chest. "She's in another room. I'll find her."

"Stop playing and give us the chance to prove ourselves."

If she'd set foot in that room the light from the polelamp would have changed. Ange gripped his gun so tight it turned waxy. He could scrape curls of metal off it with his thumbnail. "It don't make much difference she doesn't happen to be in here at the moment, or yet."

"You know what I'm thinking about with you ready to blow my head off? The riddle of the sphinx. What has four legs in the morning, two at noon, three in the evening."

"I've made up my mind, my mind's on ice. It's your prerogative to bullshit a while but why don't you work on what's real? You can goddamn empty that little twenty-two and not affect my aim."

Del placed the pistol on the air conditioning unit. "Would you take a drink with me?"

"I guess that's your prerogative. Glad to." He sat on the end of the bed, lifted the gun out and balanced it on his knee, accepted the bottle.

"Simplicity, that's what the goddamn riddle is about, the goddamn heartbreaking simplicity of the human organism. Did you ever have a dog that didn't want to romp and misbehave and eat and sleep and chase bitches? I ain't nothing but a hound dog. We ain't nothing but hound dogs."

"I never had a dog that married, raised a kid for ten years and built things. You never had a dog that bullshat."

"You never had a dog that didn't spend one night a week *howling* bullshit."

"You know what I'm thinking about after popping you? Riding to a brand new town, changing name and everything, finding people who deal straight and don't deceive and help each other live." He stood the bottle on the mattress in perfect balance.

"I appreciate your allowing me time."

"I'm waiting for a backfire."

After Cammie locked up, and loosened her hair, she headed straight for her van. When she was two strides from the door the narc, as she'd anticipated, walked out of the shed where they stored beer boxes.

"I've got a confession," he said, zipped up in his leather jacket.

"Make it to the seagulls. I don't enjoy standing in the rain."

"Two confessions. First, I'm a narcotics agent."

"Big surprise."

"Second confession, I want to spend some time with you, ride over to the beach, do a little coke, talk. Just talk. I won't try a single move."

"Let me pass." By the road Ted was warming his hands in his steam.

"Look, I can be heavy but I've got another side. Did you see the papers, five guys shot dead in Raleigh? That was my work in back of it. I'm out here mostly on a little r & r. The job doesn't have to be that important. We'll talk and I'll leave in the morning for Atlanta and that's it."

"Forget it."

"You sure you understand me? You're in the hotbox, baby."

She brushed past him, climbed in and pulled out of there. The narc, who was the one parked in front of Hallie's. pulled out behind her in his plain Plymouth without cutting his lights on.

She pushed to eighty, he stuck as if she was towing him across the bridge. Strut-strut-strut and boo-hoo-hoo, that was all for men, never a glimpse of middle ground and anytime you got beneath their talk all that really mattered was whether their woman fucked anybody else and would you fuck them. She mashed the accelerator, lit a Marlboro, planning her move a mile ahead. Her cut hand glued to the wheel.

The narc fell for it, drawing alongside and gesturing to the shoulder. Side by side they came up on Cuttlebone Junction, where the road split three ways, the bypass and beach road north, the cape road south, and there was a cement divider. She floored the gas then just as the divider appeared hit the brake. The narc peeled left but snaked past safely. At one second he was beside her, at two seconds he'd vanished, at three seconds he was in front jamming *his* brakes; his brake lights lit. But now she had steam and cut by him. He drew alongside, started tapping. She jockeyed from gas to brakes but he stuck, tapping, keeping the metal of the van in a shiver. Further up the bypass he began to bang, cinderblocks hitting, booming in the interior. Sand streamed across the road in a low fog, hissed underneath. Then a thunderclap—her right wheel jogged off the pavement and once into sand burrowed. The van knotted around the right front wheel.

She tossed her cigarette into the boxelders and stepped down, bringing the length of radiator hose R.L.'d intended to install. "You're really sick, man." She glanced back to appraise what damage she could in the backglow of the high-beams—some paint, a few dents, not too bad.

"You can't afford to stay nasty. We know the whole thing, the whirlybirds flying in from the trawlboats, landing in Ange's daddy's marshland."

"You're sick. That man can't organize the walk-in cooler. He can't decide where to stack Budweiser. You're out of your tree listening to Omie Marr. Ange dumped paint on his face on Water Street, that's the story if you're interested."

"We're doing us a job on Ange and Tish both if you don't reconsider. Come on, let's whiff a little, forget this."

"*Screw* yourself in the nose! You can all screw yourself in the noses!" Her hair, which sponged up the rain, puffed out as she whipped the big wire-wrapped hose so fast even he, with his experience, couldn't catch hold. He didn't lose his cool; he protected his face, stayed cool. "Baby, you just screwed your friends."

"I don't have friends."

Also, assuming the van started, she didn't have anywhere to run next—she'd rather face the narc than R.L.—except back to the Only Bar.

Ange told him, "Your bullshit comes out of your mouth like nickels and dimes out of a coin changer. Your mouth keeps shifting from here to here to here. You can't hit ducks, you sorry fool, you can't hit when you talk. They slither out and plop." He pictured him chucking himself all over her, tonguing the sweat she produced in pints. The room felt like a mausoleum already when the door yawned behind him, not a cop, not to release a cop but to give him space to move and fire in.

That the door was unlocked made Cammie wonder but she'd come to no conclusion by the time she was deep in the bar going for the phone, to call Del's room or the State Police, she didn't know anymore. She avoided overturned tables and chairs, she avoided bottles and pitchers, in the pitch blackness she avoided all obstacles until she ran full tilt into something: someone, flesh and arms so familiar yet scary she backed up her mind, retraced the last steps before deciding it was real and ought to be screamed at. Sweat, beer and perfume; rain, blood and shampoo—she and Tish collided, recoiled, collided and held on.

"Lord scare me to death," Tish said. Tugging Cammie's hair she clamped her closer.

"Don't."

"Where are you going? What happened? Why didn't you clean? What's all over this floor?"

"We have to call the Holiday Inn."

Bright blue bats winged one after another through the porthole in the door, followed by hammering.

"Open the damn door!" Omie Marr called.

"Fuck you it's open," Tish said. She cut the lights on.

Omie and the narc strode in like real jackboots, slack-jowled and oiled, wearing muscles off all the cops in the world, mouths stuffed with phrases of all the cops in the world. The narc carried an ax.

With them came Hallie Gaspar in her bathrobe, which her cats slept in. She looked her usual hurricane survivor warmed over, not that they'd yanked her from bed. She did two things in life and they were both walk, by day, by night, barefoot, August sun or winter moon. "That's the sleazy bitch right yonder!" she said, Tish.

"I reckon you won't be opening tomorrow," Omie said.

"I reckon I will. Show me a warrant."

He handed it over, a document whose creases perforated. "This lady has reason to believe your husband stole twenty-eight antique telephone insulators from her front room. We're going to have to tear the place apart unless you lead us to them. Or is our report true Ange's on his way to Norfolk to a collector?"

"Shall I start with the office?" the narc asked; asked Cammie.

"Who cares?"

"I care, so do you," Tish said. "You're not doing nothing till I get Malcolm Sedgwick on the phone."

"Don't listen to that thing!"

"Dry up! More! The wind tips your damn barricades, Hallie!"

"You can leave now, Hallie, we're grateful to you," Omie said.

"I'm not occupied." She regarded Cammie with a kind of sympathy, conveying she held no brief against the simply young or drunk but against those who failed to perceive terrors.

"This lady could've saved you trouble," the narc said, and headed back.

"What does he mean? What did you do?" Tish asked.

"I didn't do anything." Instead of taking her slicker off she buttoned it to the neck, and stuck her hand in her pocket.

"I'll follow this prick, you call Malcolm."

"Yea, right." She sat down at a booth where somehow a smudgy glass of chablis stood upright among spillage, breakage and napkin wads, tried not to let the words bother her. *What did you do?*

"You're staying patient," Omie instructed Tish. With two hundred pounds of body he blocked the way around the bar, with five pounds of right hand pinned the phone receiver.

"At eight in the morning you're out of a job. You'll go to California and not find a job, not security guard in K-Mart."

"I believe your influential boyfriend'll be hog-tied on this rig."

"Your name'll be shit."

"Better than being," Hallie said.

Tish's temper was nothing but bare brain on the fly, Cammie knew better than anyone. Yet when she tried to nudge the tonearm over it weighed too many tons. *What did you do? Why didn't you clean?* What had Tish and Ange done except for one thing let her paychecks fall five weeks in arrears through last Friday, less than they blew at Wintergreen, Virginia, on a weekend, not to mention bills out of her pocket like a hundred and forty dollars to the Miller man.

Furniture scuffed and screeched; drawers bounced on the floor; blows, chops reverbrated through the walls; wood splintered.

"He's wild in there. Your last fucking chance, Omie."

"Tell me about it."

"Cammie, will you run call *Malcolm*! Go to the dock phone, run call!"

More wood cracking—cedar shingles by the front as an automobile jumped the railroad-tie chock and hit the building, roared, died. R.L. walked in to the sight of Omie Marr and Tish Buthrell spitting at each other, smelly old Hallie twisting her toes in the muck, housewreckers ripping through the backbar and Cammie at a booth facing the door shaking in her coat.

Tish whirled. "R.L., praise Lord, run call Malcolm. We're staying all night, Cammie and I are staying in here all night."

Cammie reclined slightly, opened her eyes full, fluttered her lashes, shrugged, and sipped some wine.

Five times Del had tried to call Cammie without getting through. A quarter hour later he was dialing again when footsteps told him too late, partner, too damn late, the watch's done changed.

The room contracted. He felt something in his gullet or maybe solar plexus spring towards this man who entered hesitantly in shades and a stylish sportjacket that listed. He tasted situations in the back of his throat and this one tasted ripe and strange to think intellectual, intellectual in that it was scaly, clean and rang all the tastebuds at one lick.

He struggled to tell the truth but Ange, percolating like a porpoise, kept calling him down, forcing him to approach from every conceivable angle until he was picking through things he had no right to say to Tish's husband and any one of which might prove the triphammer. On the plane underneath this philosophy flew to pieces.

The creases in Ange's cheeks plumbed to the vertical. Del sensed the rise in velocity in the room. Mentally he strapped himself to his chair.

"She devours her mate after fucking," he said. "Were you aware of that? She fucks him, she eats him, every bristle of the poor bastard. He's had what he wanted, life goes on. She chomps him down, not giving a goddamn, stopping to test the web, test the breeze, make a few repairs. Climbs back finishes another leg— leaves one for him to hang with. Climbs back eats his ass. Doesn't occur to her, or him."

"You're telling me about disillusionment?"

"I'm telling you how simple life is."

Not solely as a result of the particular night, though it followed a long dry season, Cammie's reservoir had hit bottom. Tish and Ange irritated her sometimes but not being romantic she wasn't vengeful and would have given anything for it not to have run out tonight. At two a.m., at the instant R.L. appeared, she'd simply gurgled dry. The pouring rain outside turned into a sandstorm. The wine turned to dust on reaching her stomach. She regretted its happening tonight but there was nothing left to tap. Her hand hurt and she might as well leave.

She got up, told R.L., "I said I'd meet you at the house."

For the second time in their lives Tish put her hands on her. "You'll stay with me, won't you?"

"Tish, I don't know, it wouldn't do any good."

"Listen to the child!" Hallie said.

"You can't leave me in this mess."

"Well I sort of have to. R.L. and I are getting up early to househunt."

She avoided whatever expression R.L. flashed, probably one so direct it hurt him. "Yea, we got to get some rest. I haven't slept in two weeks," he said.

"R.L., let her stay tonight."

The narc presented Omie with a roach of marijuana out of the ladies' room and a small crumpled square of plastic.

"I'll come by in the morning, see how you're making out, okay?"

"God, you can't. I pledge we'll run this place really straight from here out."

"I know. I'll see you in the morning."

Outside, Cammie reiterated her demand that they meet at home but added he could wait in bed.

Ange wanted to parachute, horizontally, use the lobes of his brain in jellyfish propulsion over the lights of the city and on into the black across the sea and jet on.

"We have to learn from her," Del was saying.

Ange realized he'd let his attention wander plenty long enough for Del to have gone for his pistol. "Who do you mean," he asked, "Cammie?"

"Ange, I tell you."

It was the simplest thing, floats. Captain Del used cork or styrofoam floats or old Clorox containers that bobbed, dipped, generally rode high, painted black or orange or in the case of Clorox containers left white. Captain Ange favored glass like those Tish always looked for on the beach and which when Warren took swimming sank more than floated, rolled more than bobbed, swam, barely, in a saltwater the consistency of oil. Ange's lacked any excuse for visibility except what remained from reflecting the fast dead stars all night. He considered this room in the Holiday Inn to be the Atlantic, saw blown away floats running down waves in darkness, grouping, knocking, scattering when the next crest rose. Paying attention wave by wave he saw them knocking each other to less and less distance—somebody had put magnets in them, obvious in styrofoam, trickier in glass—the pause between knocks growing shorter, the rebounds closing to a matter of inches then fractions of an inch, the knocks becoming taps the speed of a telegraph key then quicker until they were no more than molecular palpitations. A last wave cleared, the magnets homed to each other, the floats galvanized into a clump, a litter.

The racheting of a heavy-gauge door stories below vibrated the entire building. A delivery van backfired. Del could have buried him.

At Cuttlebone Junction Cammie turned south on the cape road, drove the seven miles to the inlet, crossed the bridge and drove nine miles south of there despite the front end jittering and complaining. She eased onto a turnoff of hard sand which she'd tested before, back to a spot where scrub hid her from the road. She couldn't see the ocean, certainly didn't step out to. All she'd find at night was ghost crabs, fish heads and wind; all she found in the day was seaweed, fish heads and wind.

She cracked the window on the side away from the rain, took off her shoes, peeled off her blouse and put on a sweatshirt and after sliding into the sleeping bag in back undid her skirt. The rain hit in tacks. The breeze shook her, fell to a lipless whistle, like beer bottles with bad caps. For some reason she thought of Tish at the beach, never willing to lie flat, ready to leave as soon as they arrived—then wondering why she didn't tan—every minute looking around, peering over her shoulder into the dunes.

More often than in her bed Cammie slept at turnoffs. She did fine in the cold, didn't mind waking up to sleet on the windshield. Some nights she even had the thought it would be all right to marry R.L. if they slept in here. Not R.L., not breath in winter, nothing filled the van. Lying in the van made her feel suited to lying in herself, for this was what her heart was like, a metal box forty times the size of a human being and there was no one to help.

FARMING

by **HANDSOME LAKE** as transcribed by
JOSEPH BRUCHAC

from THE GOOD MESSAGE OF HANDSOME LAKE
(Unicorn Press)

nominated by Unicorn Press

editor's note: Handsome Lake was an early 18th Century Seneca prophet. This selection is
from a book of his visions and teachings transcribed by Joseph Bruchac

Three things done
by our younger brothers
are right to follow.

The white man works a tract of land
and harvests food for his family,
so if he should die
they have the ground for help.

If any of your people
have cultivated land
let them not be proud
on that account.

If one is proud,
there is sin within,
but without pride,
there is no sin.

The white man builds
a fine looking warm house
so if he dies
his family has the house for help.

Anyone who does this does right
if there is no pride.
If there is pride, there is evil,
without it all is well.

The white man keeps cattle and horses
and they are a help to his family
if he should die
his family has the stock for help.

No evil will follow
if the animals are fed well,
kindly treated
and not overworked.

Now all this is right
if there is no pride.

So they said and he said.
It was that way.

OUT-AND-DOWN PATTERN

by WILLIAM KLOEFKORN

from BROTHER SONGS (Holy Cow!), Windflower Press and *The Spirit That Moves Us*

nominated by Holy Cow! and *The Spirit That Moves Us*

My young son pushes a football into my stomach
and tells me that he is going to run
an out-and-down pattern,
and before I can check the signals
already he is half way across the front lawn,
approaching the year-old mountain ash,
and I turn the football slowly in my hands,
my fingers like tentacles
exploring the seams,
searching out the lacing,
and by the time I have the ball positioned
just so against the grain-tight leather,
he has made his cut downfield
and is now well beyond the mountain ash,
approaching the linden,
and I pump my arm once, then once again,
and let fire.

The ball in a high arc
rises up and out and over the linden,
up and out over the figure
that has now crossed the street,
that is now all the way to Leighton Avenue,

now far beyond,
the arms outstretched,
the head as I remember it
turned back, as I remember it
the small voice calling.

And the ball at the height of its high arc
begins now to drift,
to float as if weightless
atop the streetlights and the trees,
becoming at last that first bright star in the west.

Late into an early morning
I stand on the front porch,
looking into my hands.

My son is gone.

The berries on the mountain ash
are bursting red this year,
and on the linden
blossoms spread like children.

EIRON *EYES*

by WILLIAM HARMON

from PARNASSUS: POETRY IN REVIEW

nominated by PARNASSUS: POETRY IN REVIEW

IF THE HINDUS are right and the destiny of every creature in the universe is governed by an inescapably just Karma that dictates the types and durations of an indefinite succession of reincarnations inflexibly delivering rewards and punishments that match what one has done in previous existences, then Harriet Monroe (1860-1936), founder of *Poetry* magazine, will by now have undergone any number of rebirths, via the wombs of a crawling insect (for her pedestrian imagination), flying insect (capriciousness and inability to sit still), jellyfish (occasional spinelessness and tendency to sting the innocent), tortoise (taking too much time with some important chores), jay (hysteria plus silly litigiousness), third-world chur-

EDITOR'S NOTE: this essay was written in review of Louis Zukofsky's *A* published by the University of California Press, 826 pages, $16.95.

chmouse (to compensate for excessive wealth), and chairpersoness of the Greater Teaneck Arts Council and Begonia Guild (on general principles plus two counts of suffering Morton Dauwen Zabel gladly).

Any schoolchild today can look back at Ms. Monroe's errors in just the single year of 1915 and think, "Jesus! How could she have been such a ninny? She sat on 'Prufrock' for eight months before burying it in the back pages, all the while showcasing Arthur Davison Ficke and similar jive-turkeys. Deaf to the essential integrity of the original eight-stanza 'Sunday Morning,' she made Stevens omit three stanzas, so that he felt constrained to rearrange the remaining five. She was a poet of zero talent herself, and she so overrated Masters, Sandburg, and Robinson that she had insufficient I.Q. left when the time came to give Hart Crane the appreciation and sympathy that he frantically needed."

We—you and I—can be sure, can't we, that *we* would never be guilty of such mistakes; we'd have "Prufrock" right up there in the front of the magazine with no eight-month delay (if, that is, we had ever mustered the courage and resources to get a magazine going); we'd keep "Sunday Morning" intact all along without putting Stevens and his obviously brilliant poem through what must have been a humiliating and emasculating experience; if we had been calling the shots, Hart Crane would probably still be alive, surrounded by sycophants gaily helping to celebrate his eightieth birthday with a cake in the shape of a big Life Saver; and . . . and, well, and *everything*.

You bet.

My point is that, if the Hindus are right, Ms. Monroe ought to be about due for some release from her punishing passage through all those mortifying wombs, some recognition for the things she managed to do at least half-right. Death's first minister and chief of data processing, old Citragupta, will be on hand to recite evidence from his scrupulous printout that Ms. Monroe *did*, after all, found the magazine and run it vigorously for many years; she paid her contributors; she *did*, after all, print Eliot and Stevens and dozens of other first-rate poets; she *did* have the perspicacity to accept the advice of Ezra Pound when he was twenty-six (exactly half her age), even before he got so buddy-buddy with Yeats. And she *did*, early in 1924, publish a sonnet that had been written by a teenage prodigy in New York City:

"Spare us of dying beauty," cries out Youth,
"Of marble gods that moulder into dust—
Wide-eyed and pensive with an ancient truth
That even gods will go as old things must."
Where fading splendor grays to powdered earth,
And time's slow movement darkens quiet skies,
Youth weeps the old, yet gives her beauty birth
And molds again, though the old beauty dies.
Time plays an ancient dirge amid old places
Where ruins are a sign of passing strength,
As in the weariness of aged faces
A token of a beauty gone at length.
Yet youth will always come self-willed and gay—
A sun-god in a temple of decay.

("Of Dying Beauty")

You guessed it: Louis Zukofsky (1904-1978). And your verdict is correct: not bad—for a kid (he turned twenty in January 1924 but the poem was written earlier) not bad at all. He may have absorbed too much Santayana, he may have affected the dark-fantastic too much, but he was no damned ego-freak (no "I" mars the poem) and he knew how to write a good dignified sonnet.

Scarcely seven years later, Ms. Monroe turned her magazine over to the same prodigy for a special number (February 1931) devoted to "Objectivist" poetry along with some modest polemics that provoked from her in the next issue a few condescending but indulgent remarks about the arrogance of youth (she was seventy, her guest-editor twenty-seven). But she *did* let Zukofsky edit a whole issue, even though nobody had any very prismatic idea of what an "Objectivist" poem may be (years later Kenneth Rexroth summarized the contributors as "anybody who would say yes and didn't write sonnets," but some of Zukofsky's own offerings were sonnets; and the point was in no way cleared up by the publication of Zukofsky's An "Objectivists" Anthology in 1932). Here is a poem from the special issue of *Poetry:*

The moving masses of clouds, and the standing
Freights on the siding in the sun, alike induce in us
That despair which we, brother, know there is no
    withstanding. . . .

The note on the contributor of those lines says, by the way: "Whittaker Chambers, of Lynbrook, N.Y., was born in 1901. He has appeared in *The Nation, The New Masses,* and is a translator of note." Small world.

Zukofsky's own contribution to these "Objectivist" enterprises was a part of a long poem called "A" of which seven movements were finished by 1930. To approach a discussion of the whole poem, I want to start by looking at the original opening of the second movement:

> The clear music—
> Zoo-zoo-kaw-kaw-of-the-sky,
> Not mentioning names, says Kay,
> Poetry is not made of such things,
> Old music, itch according to its wonts,
> Snapped old cat-guts from Johann Sebastian,
> Society, traduction twice over.

The version, called "A"-2 in the eventual book form, shows some interesting adjustments:

> —Clear music—

> Not calling you names, says Kay,
> Poetry is not made of such things,
> Music, itch according to its wonts,
> Snapped old catguts of Johann Sebastian,
> Society, traduction twice over.

I want first to note that the poet had put his own name into the poem but in a mangled form, like the cries of beasts and birds: "Zoo-zoo-kaw-kaw-of-the-sky"; later he eliminated the name entirely, here and in other passages. Such a distortion of one's name followed by effacement of it impresses me as the gesture of a particular sort of personage, the *eiron* of antiquity who was both an ethical and a theatrical type.

Aristotle (*Nicomachean Ethics* 4) described the *eiron* and other such types so as to outfit a kind of Central Casting for life and literature. Zukofsky's generation, *Epigonoi* coming after a generation of giants like Stevens, Williams, Pound, and Eliot, may seem particularly rich in pure types: Charles Olson a *philosophus gloriosus et maximus,* Beckett a tragic clown. Rexroth a lordly pedant of incredible erudition in sixty-seven languages, and Zukofsky himself, in person and in print, the classic *eiron* described in Northrop Frye's *Anatomy of Criticism*: self-deprecating, seldom vulnerable, artful, given to understatement, modest or mock-modest, indirect, objective, dispassionate, unassertive, sophisticated, and maybe foreign (all of these terms apply to the *eiron* both as author and as character). The derivation of *eiron* from a Greek word meaning "to say" (and kin to "word," "verb," "verve," "Rhematic," and "rhetor") suggests that irony is chiefly a kind of speech and that the *eiron* is recognized chiefly by a manner of habit of speaking. He—whether Socrates, Swift, or Art Carney in the role of Ed Norton—says less than he means; now and then he says the reverse. He may be Prufrock, crying, "It is impossible to say just what I mean!" or Polonius, knowing how we "With windlasses and with assays of bias, / By indirections find directions out."

Now, from an objective or Objectivist point of view, epic contains history along with one or another measure of myth. The greater the measure of myth, the higher the status of the epic poet himself, so that Moses, Homer, and Vyāsa (who was said to have compiled the *Mahābhārata*) are themselves legendary, as, in modern times, such poets as Milton, Whitman, and Pound have become. So grand is the epic enterprise, indeed, that the author thereof threatens to turn into a boastful *alazon*, ordering the Muses around and organizing gods and devils in overweening patterns. Besides, these poets make up among themselves a kind of hermetic society of trade secrets and inside dope, a tradition of precursors, guides, and counsellors, each one becoming *"mio Virgilio"* for the next one, who becomes *"il miglior fabbro"* for his associate, and so on. Since 1700, we have seen a succession of secularized or individualized epics or mock-epics, all of them more or less inconsistent and turbulent (if they are not outright flops), and they test the possibility of a sustained poem without a sustaining body of supernatural lore. The question seems to have been: What, other than a system of myth-dignified ideological conflicts and resolutions, can keep a long poem going?

The obvious answer from the *eiron's* viewpoint: *Nothing.* A somewhat less obvious addendum from the viewpoint of the modern *eiron* would be: *But it doesn't make any difference.* There persists an article of faith that supposes that we have somehow lost a paradise, that Homer or Dante or Milton could write tremendous poems because the poet and his audience *in illo tempore,* in that spell of magic and an organic oral tradition, shared a whole complex of beliefs capable of organizing and running an epic poem. That's a crock. If Homer, Dante, and Milton have anything in common, it is that they seem, fitfully, to have entertained beliefs that nobody could share. A cursory look at the debates among their audiences and successors will show very quickly that their appeal was not based on any shared system of beliefs, opinions, or even historical data. Their appeal was and still is based on their extremely powerful presentation of artworks so compelling that they over-whelm our disbelief with enchantment, and we—if we believe anything short of suicidal nihilism—assent.

Nothing is lost, but things can change and centers can shift around among comedy, tragedy, romance, and irony. It looks as though the general drift since 1700 has been toward irony, maybe because of the rise of science and the spread of middle-class commerce. In any event, we have been privileged witnesses to a prolonged flowering of ironies, some very amusing and some very touching. The general environment is a diachronic matrix, so to speak, in which mythic meanings have fled from literature to music, and a modernist-ironist like Zukofsky can best orient his own most ambitious literary work by going back two centuries—from 1928 to 1729—pick up a moment of metamorphosis ("traduc-tion twice over," which means the two ironically contrasted mean-ings of "traduction"—from Old and New Testament to German to English—along with the transferral of energy from score to per-formance to repeated performance) and to chase that moment or movement as a fugue:

> A
> Round of fiddles playing Bach.
>   *Come. ye daughters. share my anguish—*
> Bare arms, black dresses,
>   *See Him! Whom?*
> Bediamond the passion of our Lord,
>   *See Him! How?*

. . . .
The Passion According to Matthew,
Composed seventeen twenty-nine,
Rendered at Carnegie Hall,
Nineteen twenty-eight,
Thursday evening, the fifth of April.
The autos parked, honking.

These lines of condensed polyphonic counterpoint enact the marriage of music and irony. For whatever reason (and reasons are legion), the *eiron's* art—irony—amounts to saying two or more things at one time, so that an auditor with 20/20 ears ought to hear an ironic utterance as a chord of sorts, one that displays its own meaning in its own sound as harmonies among *cord* and *chord*, *accord* and *a chord*, even *choral* and *coral*. (In the case of Zukofsky's introductory "Round," we are dealing with a fact. In 1928, Seder was Wednesday, 4 April, and Passover began the next day, which was also Maundy Thursday for Christians, and on that evening in Carnegie Hall there was a performance of Bach's St. Matthew Passion by the Detroit Symphony Orchestra and Choir, conducted by Ossip Gabrilowitsch. Olin Downes's enthusiastic review the next day noted that the conductor "had requested plain dark dress and a silent reception of the masterpiece.")

At times, the drawing together of many meanings in one word amounts to an ecstatic joining of ostensible opposites, as when Hopkins, in "The Windhover," uses "buckle" to mean, simultaneously, both "fall apart" and "come together." Freud, in a note based on some pretty unruly speculations of the linguist Karl Abel, explored the possible psychic meaning of the "antithetical sense of primal words," such as the English "let," "fast," and "still" (or those contrasting twin daughters of a single mother, "queen" and "quean"). The presence of such Siamese chords permits the approach of monophonic language to polyphonic music. Oddly, "fugue" itself is fugal, because it means both "a polyphonic musical style or form" and "a pathological amnesiac condition" (both meanings derive from the concept of "chase" or "flight"). Whether perfidious or merely economical, the capacity in language for such halvings and doublings will give a high rhetorical valence to such figures as zeugma and syllepsis (which don't mean *quite* the same thing) and such devices as parallel plots and contrast-rhymes ("hire"-"fire," "town"-"gown," "womb"-"tomb," and so forth).

What the solo modern prose voice at the beginning of "A" accomplishes is, then, to suggest both irony and fugue complexly: by talking about a piece of vocal-instrumental polyphony and by doing so in ways that are themselves fugal or quasi-fugal:

A
Round of fiddles playing Bach.

"A" equals air (aria) with different values in ancient and modern English, or in English and other European languages, or in English itself variable according to stress. Prefixed in this way or that, it means "with" and it means "without." It means "one" and "he" and "they" and "of." Here, right off the baton, it plays "around" against "a round," which is iridescent with musical, poetic, geometric, and mundane meanings. The part-for-whole figure of "fiddles" (for "fiddlers") plays against the whole-for-part figure of "Bach" (for "a work by Bach"), and "playing," as I have been leaking none too subtly, means everything that both "work" and "play" can mean, including the ideas of performance and impersonation and contest. (At about the same time, Yeats was scrutinizing near-by ranges of meaning in "play" and "labor" in another poem that has to do with time, memory, age, youth, and music: "Among School Children," which moves from an ironic "I walk" to an ecstatic "dance?").

Then, hundreds of pages later, in an interpolation in "A"-21 (p. 474), Zukofsky resumes the theme of roundness by means of a related word, "rote":

> there cannot be too much
> music R—O—T—E
> rote, fiddle
>
> like noise of surf . . .

Let me confess that I went for most of my life with only one meaning for "rote," one phrase ("learn by rote"), and one circumscribed connotation (bad). I took that verbal poverty with me to a study of Eliot's "The Dry Salvages" and appraised the line "The distant rote in the granite teeth" as a very effective figure of speech that rendered the sound of water against a rock as a lesson mechanically repeated (*rota:* circle). In fact, English "rote" has three meanings, of which Eliot, writing in 1942, used two and Zukofsky, in 1967, used all three. It also means "a medieval stringed instrument" and "the sound of surf breaking on the shore" (*American Heritage Dictionary*). (It could appear in the name of an enterprise called POTH, if that name be Greek.) The verbal chord may be tabulated:

rote				
	rote 1	routine	ME from Lat. *rota*, wheel	IE *ret*—to run, roll
	rote 2	surf	ON *rauta*, to roar	IE *reu*—to bellow
	rote 3	instrument	OF from Gmc.	IE *krut*—
				instrument

Such an etymological history of three words converging in a single sound—*rote*—may be seen as a model of Zukofsky's main themes and techniques in "A." No modern ironic poem of any length could possibly be self-standing, and Zukofsky's resembles those by Williams, Pound, and Eliot in including precursors and companions. A shrewd programmer should design a map that would show Pound appearing in Eliot's and Williams' poems (and, later, in Lowell's and Berryman's), Eliot and Williams in Pound's (and Lowell's and Berryman's), and so on, in a serial *agon* that is at the same time an old-boy network. As is noted in "A"-1, Zukofsky's poem gets going not long after the death of Thomas Hardy in January 1928. Some unconscious ironist says of the most conscious ironist of modern letters, "Poor Thomas Hardy he had to go so soon" (which is ironic because he had been born in 1840). But that note is enough to suggest that the long poem at hand will carry on the work of *The Dynasts*. Hardy's immense epic drama that could be called "The Convergence of the Twain," because it traces, in a somewhat fugal staggered form, the fate of two men born in 1769, Napoleon and Wellington, whose paths finally cross, or collide, at Waterloo. As Hardy is dying, the successors maintain the ironic dynasty, and Zukofsky launches his long poem by assimilating the techniques of Pound, Eliot, Williams, and Hardy. With Zukofsky, the focus is on technique and the fabric of the language itself, but the notion of tellingly ironic convergence remains as it had been in Hardy's poems.

Zukofsky begins his poem on a particular April evening in 1928, and for him—as for Whitman, Yeats, and Eliot before him—this paschal time of Passover and Passion, converging in the syncretism of Eos-East-Easter with its terrible beauty, furnishes an ideal prism for seeing the world clearly and for intelligently hearing its ironies and harmonies. (Of "When Lilacs Last in the Dooryard Bloom'd," "Easter 1916," *The Waste Land, Ulysses,* and *The Sound and the Fury* alike, one could say that the typical modern literary work begins and centers, on a particular day in spring. Oddly, for both Faulkner and Zukofsky, the focus happens to be the same few days in April 1928.) Given this matrix of ideal convergences, the *eiron's* eyes and ears can subject language to a detailed inquisition, though it hardly takes the full third degree to remove hide and hair from verbal surfaces. In a sixty-year career, Zukofsky experimented with every species of rhematic and thematic irony as ways of saying more than one thing at a time, and he devoted an inordinate amount of his genius to the transfiguration into English of various foreign texts. Since Zukofsky tried to preserve sound and sense alike—which is impossible— "translation" is not quite the correct word for this process. Pound's "creative translations" showed the path here, especially in versions of Old English and Latin (to which I shall come back in a few moments), but Pound is only one member of a large modern club that has trafficked in the Englishing and modernizing of many sorts of foreign and ancient texts. Some years ago, for instance, there was a black film version of "Carmen" called "Carmen Jones," in which Escamillo became "Husky Miller." Any number of modern characters, in their names if not otherwise, show this sort of metempsychosis: Shaw's John Tanner out of Don Juan Tenorio, O'Neill's Ezra Mannon out of Agamemnon, Eliot's Harcourt-Reilly out of Heracles, Faulkner's Joe Christmas out of Jesus Christ, Updike's Caldwell out of Chiron. Zukofsky's refinement, which may echo certain Talmudic or Cabalistic techniques of interpretation, has been to apply this principle of nomenclature to whole texts, typically ironic or comic-lyric, and to produce a complete *Catallus* by this method, as well as a version (appearing as "A"-21) of Plautus' *Rudens,* which is evidently a reworking of a lost Greek play by Diphilus.

One of those shipwreck-and-lost-daughter comedies, *Rudens* (i.e., *The Rope*) resembles Shakespeare's *Pericles* (although it is not, strictly speaking, the source of *Pericles,* as one critic has stated). At any rate, we may note here that Volume II of Zukofsky's *Bottom:*

On Shakespeare is a musical setting for *Pericles* by Zukofsky's wife, Celia. One may regard all of *Bottom* as a long poem that works as an appendix to "A." It is typically ironic of Zukofsky to see all of Shakespeare through the eyes of Nick Bottom, big-mouthed weaver and man of the theatre (not to mention part-time ass and boyfriend of the fairy queen).

Zukofsky's novel handling of Latin and other foreign languages has been duly admired by some, but I have to say that I think his Catullus and Plautus are dull distortions. Their purpose may be to breathe (literally) new breath through their consonants and vowels, but the result is a high-handed botch.

I am not qualified to discuss the fine points of this complicated problem of translation. It's just that sound and sense cannot be transferred from one language to another, and it may also be true that not even sense by itself can be moved. Now and then, as in the acoustic and semantic nearness of Hebrew *pāsaḥ*, Latin *passiō*, and English *pass*, there seems to be a linguistic kinship that resembles the connection among *Pesach*, *Passion*, and *Passover;* but such harmonies are rare. More commonly, even "cognates" from closely related languages may not be good translations for one another, especially in the realm of abstractions. *Stupor Mundi* just isn't "stupor of the world."

Consider these two lines from *Rudens*, in which Charmides (a *senex*) is needling his friend, the pimp Labrax, about a shipwreck:

> *Pol minime miror, navis si fractast tibi.*
> *scelus te et sceleste parta quae vexit bona.*

"Pol" is a faint oath that abridges something like "by Pollux." "Minime" is an adverb meaning "least" (or "not at all"). "Miror" (as some may recall from their high-school Latin version of "Twinkle, Twinkle, Little Star") is the present first-person singular declarative of a deponent verb (hence the passive form) meaning "I wonder." "Well, by God, I'm not a bit surprised," as you might say. The Loeb translation by Paul Nixon captures all of these meanings: "Gad! I don't wonder at all that your ship was wrecked, with a rascal like you and your rascally gains aboard." Zukofsky:

> Pole! minimal mirror! the ship
> fractured from your ill-begot goods.

Well: "Pole! minimal mirror!" does preserve the general sound pattern of "Pol minime miror," and it may preserve some of the sense (if calling one "Pole" and "minimal mirror" suggests that he doesn't do much reflecting). But at what price? This: the subordination of sense to sound, which is exactly what Imagists and Objectivists complain about in the verse of sonneteers and what Olson complained about in Pound's later Chinese translations. And this: the sacrifice of the character's personal style. Kept up doggedly for seventy pages, Zukofsky's Plautus 'Diphilus' *Rudens* is the most tiresome part of "A."

The next most tiresome part is "A"-24, which is another fugal experiment. "A"-21 amounts to a superposed transmogrifiation of the folk theme of the recovered daughter with Greco-Roman voices joined by synthetic English (a tricky sort of technique that Pound was intelligent enough, in Canto I, to limit to seventy-six lines and to carbonate, ad lib, with matter, rhythms, and "cross-lights" from sources other than his Greek-Latin-English triad). "A"-24, which was composed by Celia Zukofsky (with help from the Zukofsky's brilliant son, Paul) before Louis Zukofsky wrote "A"-22 and "A"-23, is not so much the real conclusion of "A" as a kind of addendum called *L. Z. Masque,* "a five-part score—music, thought, drama, story, poem." The score is presented contrapuntally with music in two staves (treble and bass) above four verbal lines in type of varying sizes. The music is Handel's, the words from Zukofsky's *Prepositions* (thought), *Arise, Arise* (drama), *It was* (story), and "A" itself (poem). The two acts are divided into nine scenes named for characters and musical forms (Cousin: Lesson, Nurse: Prelude & Allegro, Father: Suite, Girl: Fantasia, Attendants: Chaconne, Mother: Sonata, Doctor: Capriccio, Aunt: Passacaille, and Son: Fugues). The text is about 240 pages, with an indicated duration of about 70 minutes. Presumably, a harpsichord plays while four voices speak the words ("The words are NEVER SUNG to the music. . . . Each voice should come through clearly"). I have taken some pains to describe "A"-24, because I don't want to be judged indifferent or careless when I say that the thing is unreadable. I have done my best, line-by-line and also measure-by-measure, and in my cranial studio I get only the effect of five non-profit educational stations going at one time. I'll keep at it, but for the present I can't find anything to admire. In both "A"-21 and "A"-24 the fugue fails.

That failure is more than disappointing. It is heartbreaking. As the ironic poem progresses through its early and middle phases, its moments of greatest tenderness and beauty coincide with the moments of most concentrated attention on Zukofsky's marriage to Celia Thaew in 1939 and the birth, on 22 October 1943, of their son, the *Wunderkind* violinist Paul Zukofsky, whose childhood experiences contributed to Louis Zukofsky's novel called *Little*. *Baker's Biographical Dictionary of Musicians*, edited by Nicolas Slonimsky, praises Paul Zukofsky's sympathy for contemporary music and the "maximal celerity, dexterity, and alacrity" of his playing. Even so, the Plautus translation, which was probably done as the Catullus was—by Louis and Celia Zukofsky together—and the five part happening of "*A*"-24, in which all three Zukofskys had a part, subtract from the overall integrity and intensity of "*A*".

The remaining twenty-two sections add up to about five hundred pages of poetry that takes the initial fugal subjects and styles through a forty-five-year development, conditioned by external historical and personal events but never, I think, completely irrelevant to the promises potently implicit in

A
Round of fiddles playing Bach.

Earlier I suggested a number of the possible meanings, but I did not mention the chance that the fiddles are playing B A C H, which, in a peculiar German style of notation used at one time before the seven-note nomenclature was adopted, would sound as B-flat, A, C, B-natural. J. S. and C. P. E. Bach used this sequence as a musical subject, as did Schumann, Liszt, Rimsky-Korsakov, and a score (ha) of other composers. Zukofsky's use of this musical acrostic to organize the very long (135 pages) "*A*"-12—

Blest
Ardent
Celia
            unhurt and
Happy—

brings us back to the alphabet and its gifts and challenges to the ironic poet.

Bach's adding his "signature" to a piece of music is an uncommon
but not a unique phenomenon. It is recorded that Bach, who may
have written a four-note "cruciform" motif for the Crucifixion in
the St. Matthew Passion, once sketched out a canon formula for a
friend named Schmidt. Translating *Schmidt* into the Latin *faber*.
Bach then canonized his friend in the form of F A B E Repetatur,
then signed the formula with the tribute, *Bonae Artis Cultorem
Habeas*. It is said that the *paytanim,* composers of Hebrew liturgical poetry, "signed" their works by placing their names or ana-
grams thereof as an acrostic at the beginning of each line. It is also
said that certain Jewish names may have been formed as acronyms
drawn from devotional formulae, as "Atlas" from *akh tov leyisrael
selah* ("Truly God is good to Israel") and not from the Greek name
of the world-bearing Titan or the German word for "satin." That
may belong in the same uncertain category as the oddity of the
King James version of Psalm 46, written when Shakespeare was 46
years old: the forty-sixth word from the beginning is "shake," the
forty-sixth from the end "spear." It is certain, however, that writers
now and then have used their own names or initials to "sign" their
works internally, as it were, as well as on the title page. Shakespeare and Donne used "will" and "done" in poems as puns on
their own first or last names. Robert Browning used his initials for
The Ring and the Book, and T. S. Eliot may have had a variation of
the same policy in mind when he titled a play *The Elder States-
man.* J. D. Salinger once named a character Jean de Daumier-
Smith, and Martin Gardner's fascinating column in *Scientific
American* is called "Mathematical Games."* In modern prose's
grandest ironic epic, Mann's *Doktor Faustus,* the composer Lever-
kühn repeatedly uses certain notes, Bach-fashion, to trace non-
musical meanings over musical themes; and at the end of the book,
in the *Nachschrift,* the author's own names rises touchingly
through the prose of his rather foolish narrator, "Dr. phil. Serenus
Zeitblom": *"Es ist getan."* he says. He now writes as *"ein alter
Mann, gebengt. . . ."* Pound reversed the process once, in Canto
IV, when he alluded to Whitman's "Beat! beat! . . . whirr and
pound" but changed the wording to "Beat, beat, whirr, thud."
Later, though, he made up for this avoidance of his own name by
putting three archaic Chinese characters on the title page of
Thrones: pao en tê, pronounced, more or less, "Pound."

So what? So the work of art inherently resists being used for autobiography or any other kind of direct representation. Only by certain tricks can an artist register his own presence in a self-willed medium, especially if he is an *eiron* approaching that medium and its social environment from below or outside. The *eiron*'s infrastructural position resembles the alien's extra-structural condition. so that if one has to be both—a talented son, say, of Yiddish-speaking immigrants—then one's ears will, with luck, be attuned to speech as a foreign entity and, particularly, to American English as the native property of others. "Abcedminded," then, as it says in *Finnegans Wake*, verbal comedy leads ironic outsiders of various sorts to write *The Comedian as the Letter C* and an uproarious novel called *V.* and a long poem called "*A*" (just as Stephen Dedalus contemplated calling his novels by letters of the alphabet). This is elevated comedy, a plane of discourse where linguistic perspicuity and literally broken English are joined in rapturous wedlock. Here Gandhi, mindful of gentry's "plus fours," will describe his loincloth as "minus fours," and Vladimir Nabokov will notice how, on more than one level, "therapist" may equal "the rapist." The fine ear of Zukofsky's Wisconsin friend Lorine Niedecker will pick up and decoct the miraculous fission of language when it is forced through the double warp of music and translation:

> O Tannenbaum
> the children sing
> round and round
> one child sings out:
> atomic bomb

(This is, incidentally, part of a garland, *For Paul*, written for Zukofsky's son.) Poetry tests the language as language tests the world.

An ironic epic, accordingly, is going to be partly an ordeal for words themselves, starting, conventionally enough, with the virtually pure air of the first letter and first vowel, *a*. The purpose of the ordeal, from the viewpoint of ironic skepticism, will be to follow the contours of language without undue distortion, so that most of Zukofsky's prosody is a natural-seeming measure of syllables-per-line or words-per-line with no twisting, chipping, or padding to fit an imposed meter that may depend on an arbitrary Morse of

qualitative or quantitative dots and dashes given further shape by a
rhyme scheme. Once the measure by syllable-unit or word-unit is
established along with a modest devotion to short lines, however,
the purest music of consonant and vowel, stress and pitch, fancy
and plain can come through with an effect, usually, of delicacy,
eloquence, accuracy, and fidelity.

Such an idiom works best with its inherent data of ambiguity,
inquisition, and multiple irony. These data are most lucidly presented in fairly short poems (like Zukofsky's, and like those of Cid
Corman and Robert Creeley, both of whom owe much to
Zukofsky's example) in which the courtesy and modesty can balance the potentially injurious clarity of perception and memory.
The idiom does not work so well in longer flights, in which it tends
to become otiose or academic. ("A" comes equipped with an index,
but it quirkily omits some important items. Lorine Niedecker
seems to be in the poem—pp. 165 and 214-15, for example—but is
not in the index; neither is "A friend, a Z the 3rd letter of his (the
first of my) last name"—p. 193—who I think must be Charles
Reznikoff.) Yet another difficulty with this idiom is the way it
refreshingly insists on seeing everything anew, with unprejudiced
eyes; but that means the propagandist for the idiom, whether in
lyric or in critical writing, had better be sure he is original. Often,
however, Zukofsky seems merely derivative. His A Test of Poetry,
for instance, promises to chuck out academic biases but winds up as
little more than a replay of Pound's "How to Read" and A B C of
Reading, even to the extent of repeating Pound's dogmatic concentration on Book XI of the Odyssey. A teacher can get a funny
feeling when a bold student merely repeats the once-original
gestures of Creeley, say, and justifies them on principles that really
are "academic" in the worse sense: "I do this because Creeley
does, because Olson and Zukofsky told him, because they got it
from Pound, because Pound thought Fenollosa was right," etc. I
am not sure that originality is very important. I am not even sure it
is quite possible. But if you make a fuss about it, then you ought to
be able to do some other thing than imitate, echo, and repeat.

At his best, Zukofsky dissolves illusion and punches sham to
pieces. He breaks things up into particles and articles: under his
testing, for example, the ambiguity-loaded anathema is analyzed
into "an, a, the—" (p. 397). Once the alphabet has been taken
apart, though, the problem is how to put it back together with

honest energies and designs. Zukofsky's life must have confirmed some of his early ironic suspicions; after twenty years at a technical school, he retired as an associate professor, and for a long time he "was not well." The one time I met him, in June 1975, he was frowning through the sickliest-looking yellow-green complexion I think I have ever seen; but his voice was very youthful, his wit intact. On the whole, though, I think he found himself on the receiving end of an enjoyable destiny. He was brilliant, he loved his noble father, he found the perfect wife, his son appeared with the New Haven Symphony at the age of eight, and his work tended after all in the direction suggested by the title of a late poem: "Finally a valentine."

As "A"-24 is arranged, the whole book ends on a nicely cadenced C-minor chord in the harpsichord, the drama voice saying, "New gloves, mother?" and the poem voice repeating the end of "A"-20, "What is it, I wonder, that makes thee so loved." Finally, with "love" sounding simultaneously in "gloves" and "loved," a valentine, indeed.

Well, I must be churlish. I prefer consigning "A"-24 to the status of appendix of appendum, because I think the poem itself (if not the life of the poet) finds a more authentic and convincing conclusion in the end of "A"-23, which was the last part written by Zukofsky. It does not end, *Heldenleben*-style, with a survey and synthesis of the artist's life-in-work, but with a return to the alphabetical keynote that started "A"-1. What we have is a scrupulously measured twenty-six-line alphabet stretto:

> A living calendar, names inwreath'd
> Bach's innocence longing Handel's untouched.
> Cue in new-old quantities—'Don't
> bother me'—Bach quieted bothered;
> since Eden gardens labor, For
> series distributes harmonies, attraction Governs
> destinies. Histories dye the streets:
> intimate whispers magnanimity flourishes: doubts'
> passionate Judgment, passion the task.
> *Kalenderes enlumined* 21-2-3, *nigher . . . fire*—
> Land or—sea, air—gathered.
> Most art, object-the-mentor, donn'd one—
> smiles ray *immaterial Nimbus . . . Oes*

        sun-pinned to red threads—thrice-urged
        posato (poised) 'support from the
        source'—horn-note out of a
        string (Quest returns answer—'to
        rethink the Caprices') *sawhorses silver*
        all these fruit-tree tops: consonances
        and dissonances only of degree, never-
        Unfinished hairlike water of notes
        vital free as Itself—impossible's
        sort-of think-cramp work x: moonwort:
        music, thought, drama, story, poem
        parks' sunburst—animals, grace notes—
        z-sited path are but us.

This garland names names (Bach, Handel) and suggests others without quite pronouncing them outright (Landor, Mozart, maybe Anaximander, John Donne inwreathed, as is fitting, with Don Juan). It covers instruments, voices, plants, animals (including a goat inside "Caprices" and an A-shaped sawhorse that is a Wooden Horse too: a running theme through the poem, so to speak). I don't know what all is included in "z-sited," aside from the author's and alphabet's final monogram, but I suspect it may include a reminder that the early Semitic and Greek character for *zayinzeta* may be pronounced "eye" or "I," which is roughly what the Hebrew *zayin* still looks like—hence "eyesight." "Are but us" looks and sounds like a re-vision of "arbutus" with an adumbration of widespread (if not universal) identity, community, and harmony.

That hermetic hint is, I think, a more satisfying conclusion than an adventitious pun on "love." We have come too far through too many agonies and mazes at too much intellectual and emotional expense to accept at the end the weakly established assertion that love matters or some similar Hallmark sentiment. It's like the Calvin Coolidge whom one can imagine in Purgatory taking a look at Pound's sweet little Canto CXX. "What's it about, Cal?" "Forgiveness." "What's he say?" "He's for it."

One of these days a scholarly critic with time on his hands is going to discover or invent a tabular schema. In "A"-12 there is evidence that Zukofsky had the twenty-four-book plan in mind by 1950 and possibly somewhat earlier. There too (p. 258) there is a recognition that both of Homer's epics have been divided into twenty-four books by scholars, and it would not surprise me to learn that Zukofsky knew that Bach's St. Matthew Passion can be divided into twenty-four scenes: Schweitzer calculated it as "twelve smaller ones, indicated by chorales, and twelve larger ones, marked by arias." But Zukofsky's general design does not gracefully fall into twenty-four shapely parts. With or without the marginal "A"-21 *(Rudens)* and "A"-24 *(L. Z. Masque)*, the shape of the whole is asymmetrical. The contour may match that of a diary or revery, but there is no essential literary progression. Such development as may emerge is more along the lines of an experimental fugue and variations, with room along the way for one poem 135 pages long ("A"-12) and another four words ("A"-16). A-6 asks:

> *Can*
> The design
> Of the fugue
> Be transferred
> To poetry?

When the "plot" has to include a piece of history—such as the death of Williams or the assassination of President Kennedy—then the writing slackens, and the grief seems perfunctory. In other stretches, the author's vigor and sincerity seem to thin out and his wordplay ("Pith or gore has" for "Pythagoras") nosedives towards the asymptote of crossword puzzles and tricks like Henny Youngman's superseding "diamond pin" with "dime and pin."

The scholiasts have their work cut out for them. For all I know, the audience for poems like Zukofsky's may be nothing but scholiasts. I hate to think that world poetry today amounts to nothing more than a hundred people writing something for an audience of a hundred (probably the same hundred). The dismal situation would be no less dismal if that figure were a thousand or even a million, because the proportion is so small up against the whole human race. Maybe the University of California Press ought to keep a few copies of the full "A" available for specialists, and they may be wise to market it in an ugly Clearasil-pink dust jacket, to keep amateurs at arm's length. But maybe the publisher should also issue a 250-page volume of selections. I would suggest that 1–7, 9–11, 15–18, and 20 could be kept as wholes, 21 and 24 done without, and the rest given in generous selections. That sort of book would reach more people with a more concentrated representation of a fine poet's best work. Whatever is planned in the way of new editions, the Index should be re-done to provide a better key to main themes, motifs, and characters (including those in any number of alphabets).

*Two further examples: The Boy Scouts chose a motto with initials to match those of their founder, Lord Baden-Powell; and in the graphic arts, Al Hirschfeld always weaves the name of his daughter Nina into his caricatures, hidden there among wrinkles or ruffles or extravagant coiffures.

WHISPER SONG

by DAVID WAGONER

from THE MONTANA REVIEW

nominated by THE MONTANA REVIEW, *James B. Hall and George Venn*

Listening and listening
Closely, you may hear
(After its other
Incredibly clear song)
The one the winter wren
Sings in the thinnest of whispers
More quietly than soft rain
Proclaiming almost nothing
To itself and to you,
And you must be
Only a step away
To hear it even faintly
(No one knows why
It will sing so softly),
Its tiny claws
Braced for arpeggios,
Its dark eyes
Gleaming with a small
Astonishing promise,
Its beak held open
For its hushed throat,
Whispering to itself
From its mysterious heart.

🔥 🔥 🔥

TWO LIVES

fiction by H. E. Francis

from KANSAS QUARTERLY

nominated by KANSAS QUARTERLY, *Maxine Kumin, Anne Tyler
and Max Zimmer*

I WAS RIGHT to come home, Martha. Mother and Dad are getting old—I didn't realize how old; and—forgive me this—it's good to be alone. Up to a point. I mean—I watch. That's what I tried to write you last night (not mailed): I find myself watching—with a stillness I never had before. Not because they don't move the way they used to, Dad especially; they're running down, like planets that will stop. There. You see how I think? I can't get away from it—distance. When we're sitting still, I study their faces, wrinkles and poor scrawny necks, sinks, watery eyes, hear the dry flicks of their lashes, chafing hands, stare at the raised freckles on their skin, like worlds themselves, and think everything's just earth like the fields my father and grandfather and great-grandfather plowed into Long Island potatoes and corn and cauliflower and that turned up emptied after the harvest and changed color and filled with dry twigs. I know they're dying, we all are, our sons too, everything; and I think my space flight, all space flights to come, are plunges up to break out of some great skin that's dying, to find a way out so life will go on. Something yearns for more than the minds does. That's what I was talking about—distance. Mom and Dad could be planets 240,000 miles away, like earth from the moon. I can't get *to* them—I see them, but *know* how far away they are, like earthshine from up there. This morning at breakfast I was struck by their happiness in having me home—not simply for their place in things, the neighbors (though my visit is secret), and maybe the little edge against dying that a name can have in papers and books all over the world; they seem sure, as they always were anyway, that I am something—in all the nothing, something. For an instant it did me good to see their happy eyes feeding on me—Dad has incipient cataracts now, which he can't have removed until they're more grown; mother babies him, like having me again, I think, time removed for her—back. Something comes into both of them— love, of course, pride, and consolation, I expect, for a long life they see in me, but mostly in the photos of the boys. They can't wait for spring and school to be out so Greg and David will be here the whole summer long with them. What will you do then, my darling? I hope you'll spend the summer here too. They'll love that, and I'd want it. Every time I think of the kids in the silo, standing under the corn pouring down on them—wonderful but hazardous—I think it's me, years back—and climbing fences, riding Blackguard, dodging cow turds, swimming. But when I try to connect all that with the bodies beside me, and my own, I feel a distance—not merely between now and that time on the moon, but sight dis- tance, emotional distance. I see across an infinite ravine, but *I* can't cross it—something inside me stays stationary. Distance. I've discovered space, Martha, and new time. I feel outside them. I know I'm not, but I can't move through, connect.—More eggs, Kyle? my mother said, me thinking, What's the use of eating? Yet I *wanted* to eat—voraciously. I got up abruptly. Till then I'd been so careful; it's the first time I startled them. I felt apologetic but couldn't apologize, knowing the apology would be *for* something and make them worry more. I wanted to, wanted to speak, but I saw them suddenly as objects, as isolated as a dish, the frying pan, the wagon wheel Dad had propped on the lawn. I went outside. I ended up in the barn. I sat in the dim light like a child huddled with my forehead hard against my knees and shut my eyes, but I couldn't shut out all that: endless space. Nothing, going on and on: as if I'd missed the zone and couldn't re-enter earth's gravity. Martha, *nothing* got into my head—How could I tell you that?— cut me off from my place, from you, Greg and David, neighbors . . . The near sight of things is the only way I can hold them; but the minute I close my eyes, my head is emptied of them. I find myself staring unblinking at the earth, stubble dead, brown twigs, hard clumps, the pines, Mill Pond, not daring to raise my eyes to the cliffs and the Sound, the sky, and beyond—too far. I wanted to hold my mother's face, Dad's, and the boys' and yours, hold them *in* me, real. I left the barn. I crossed the fields. And do you know what I did, Martha? I went down on my knees and grabbed dirt. I had all I could do to keep from stuffing it in my mouth—because maybe they were watching. Now I've said too much. I can't write this. I want to, but I won't. Not yet.

(Ubeda, Spain. December, 1591: Hear, O Lord, the prayers of your servant, John of the Cross. Let my words fly up, for my body is heavy with this world, it dies. My foot rots and ulcers eat my back and gall my shoulder blades. My flesh stinks. Let me have the pain. May the soul that first startled me in Medina del Campo—over twenty years ago—flower sweet from this putrid flesh and ascend. I was fourteen when my patron, Don Antonio Alvarez de Toledo, took me to that rich city to train for Orders at the charity hospital. If him you chose to lead me, it was the inmates began me on the holy war—me no stranger to disease and death, for we were poor. My father early died, leaving three boys for whom my mother worked, weaving. Poverty laid my way. But that moment when I entered the courtyard of the Hospital, the sight smote me dumb: lepers everywhere, con- sumptives, syphilitics, bodies ridden by plague. Herds of them. Their rags were the color of earth; pustules and buboes covered their flesh. Some were moaning and weeping, some cried out in epileptic fits, jerking. But the rest—they were too still. They stared. Even in the unceasing blow of dust, their eyes stood, cataleptic, with terrible endurance. But what beauty cried out to me in their stillness? Was this the lot of man? I walked among

them. Whom could I ask? Their eyes fixed on distances. And when I went close to them, those orbs, each one, held infinite deeps, perilous and beautiful, tiny islands as still and strange as the archipelagoes the cartographers have set down on the maps they call the New World. Each was on his journey. Could no one enter? I was terrified. I had never felt so alone. Was my own within me? My heart beat, fearful. I see their faces yet. I have seen them all my days. They were my duty. Each afternoon after my two hours of Latin, I begged in the streets for them. I tended them six years.)

My mother still has our toys, mine and Jerry's. There's a big green metal grasshopper with a hollow back that opens like a lid. I'd hide things in it. One summer when my brother came home from Gram's, he looked at it with such longing—I was so glad to see him, I wanted to make friends all over again, so I pushed it over to him. I've never forgotten the look of wonder—such wonder—in his face.—It'll carry us in its back, Jerry said. He'd hop it clump clump clump with his hand. That toy made the boys and you come back, sitting on the living room floor the day after I got out of quarantine, with those thousands of messages from all over the world, the President's too, seeing the letters like meaningless galaxies— maybe that was the first time the discomfort came . . . Now, this instant, why do I feel I've never been so close to a human being since Jerry? Have I grown so cruel that I can tell you this when I love you and the boys? I see him and me graduating from that grasshopper to model planes and boats, model gasoline engines all going at once in the cellar, then military planes, jets, and me finally to spaceships, vehicles that would carry us to some kind of destiny we couldn't avoid that confirmed our choices. But I know better. Who could believe in destiny these days? I think more and more about Jerry. I'd like to know what my brother'd think. Maybe if he were alive he'd be the one person so much the same we could be one feeling for the two of us, we'd break through something—Last night, thinking of him, I got so excited I wanted to talk to Jerry, and him dead, my mind going faster than seven miles a second, any minute I'd break through some kind of gravity farther than any planet's, I'd cross the threshold into a new atmosphere. Alice and the mirror, I thought, yes—My father saw how upset I was.—Kyle and I're going for a walk along the beach awhile, he said.—You? she said.—Well, he hasn't been along the Sound yet, Dad said. It was full moon. The beach was white and powdery looking and the cliffs fell away like the edge of craters in the Sea of Tranquillity. I almost felt I'd have to pivot on my weight and lean in the direction I wanted to go. My father saved me—he talked government control, tons of potatoes dumped wasted in the Sound, the starving world, the bridge from the Connecticut mainland to the Island. And I was ashamed, because he was trying to keep me from being ashamed, understanding a thing he didn't even have to know, that *I* didn't know, like a deed I did against somebody and couldn't figure out. It haunts me. I'm here to find it out. And now Mother knows—though both know I'm here for rest and more reasons than love of them—because she knows Dad. The walk did it. She's worried. I understand her helplessness. She's reached that invisible barrier too, awful to reach limits you can't break through. I tell the thing inside me that: What's true of space is true of us. Then we can break from some personal gravity, leap through, if only we can get enough . . .?

(Do I smell tallow? My candle burning low? There. Brother Jerónimo comes and leaves me gruel. He does not understand I want no food; I will my passage to Thee. Jerónimo—I think I see my brother Francisco in his face?—is young in Your service, young as I was when Mother Teresa came to Medina del Campo. O great day! I had not long since left the University and celebrated my first mass. It was You again, in her: She kept me from joining the cloistered life of the silent Carthusians, so I went back to Salamanca to ponder if I would follow her. I gave her one year to get us a beginning. Surely kind old Don Alonso forgave me the day I refused the Chaplaincy and left the Hospital after my six years with him. I could give no reasons, but knew: I saw the Way. But those sick and putrefying bodies— what strength they gave me, how they made me look to God: All things pass but not God passes. They—in my eyes still. We— beggars all, before God, for the eye of the needle. Listen! Bells. Vespers, is it? Ah, they sound me back to that day our beloved Teresa came with the news of our first hermitage in the hamlet of Duruelo, our broken farmhouse, but for me and Mother Teresa and all the Discalced Carmelites the beginning of a whole new world. She kept her word; we had our monastery. Three of us there were: Prior Antonio, Jesús, and I, but how we loved labor and rejoiced in hardships. The hermitage roof was too low to

stand under, we set out crosses and skulls to keep death ever near, one broken pitcher and two gourds to eat our lentils from, we used stones for pillows, straw for bed. No life but Yours. We preached and taught in the villages. Five clocks—five!—the Prior set out, not to miss our prayers and duties. All was rock, dust, and the merciless cold of our Castille. Snow drove through cracks, covered our habits when we contemplated in the Chapel and while we slept. Fevers came, chilblains and swellings which have never left me. Pain kept me close to You, as now closer this rotting body does, my God. Soon we were seven, my mother came to cook for us, and Francisco and his wife to aid in our labors. Fast we grew, and through Your mercy that rich man gave us new quarters in Mancera. Through all my high posts after, my heart has never forsaken those hardships. But most I bowed down humbled in joy when one day our great mother kneeled before me, small and thin, all bony, her hands clutched white and strong, her lids sunk and the flesh gone almost to bone on her face, but a light everlasting in her eyes, bright and hard, filled with fast fire.—Confess me, Father, she said. Almost— God forgive!—I could not bear that joy: Me she'd chosen to lead the nuns back to the simple way. I confessed her and all the nuns. We could not know then Your enemies would strike to try to break our reforms, make us recant, strike at Teresa and all the Discalced Carmelites through me. Christmas was coming. The Carmelites of the Observance seized me at night. They took me to Toledo as their prisoner. December third it was.)

Rain. The Sound has come right up gray and endless to the windows. I feel enclosed. A day for instruments. Chess with Dad all afternoon. She is knitting a blue sweater for Greg's Christmas. David's will be green. The land is dead, cold, and raw. I get my raincoat.—For heaven's sake, she says, you'll drown out!—I thought I'd see the pumpkins, I say.—Well, they *are* clean, and pretty as suns all over the place. I feel like a child chided by her common sense, take off my coat. Suns. I see sun after sun—and after that, and after that, what? She smiles.—You're never too old to be my boy. You'll be gone soon. I have to enjoy you while you're here. Days now she's talked out my life, old times. I feel Jerry back sometimes, sure if I look in mirrors I'll *be* a sandy-haired kid again with big blue eyes for the world, and suddenly everything will be future again: West Point and orbital mechanics, Korea, rocks and lunar landing training, space walk, the moon, but mostly you, Martha, you and the boys. And I'm struck by the speed it all can come and go, because some speed inside me outstrips mind, memory—to new time? I want to press memory back, back, farther than I can remember, get into—into what? I am afraid to look up, afraid, Martha: nothing, endless nothing. Where does nothing go? Where? And I want to grab one of those pumpkins in my hands and know *this* can hold back tomorrow. Why am I driven home? I ask me, him, in the mirror. A current sucks. Go with it, something says. It presses close—in the gray rain, the air, the one hundred percent humidity that makes a sea over a sea. Gray. I can see nothing. Somewhere's the moon. I swear I've crossed over to it once in a dream, hallucination. But no—solid: If I don't trust memory, I have a rock in my pocket. I carry a piece of the moon with me. I left something up there. Does that mean I'm more or less? the moon more or less? I look at Mom and Dad's faces, as I did yours and every face I've seen since I came back to earth—I feel *far,* I see them *far.* I belong but don't. Somehow I'm always *there;* standing here I'm *there.* I close my eyes, but earth moves over my eyeballs—there . . . I am no longer an earthbound creature. I'm just beginning to learn what that means. I know I'm the smallest step toward something, but the horror is I can't wait, I want to push out, want to *know* if, when this world is dead, destroyed, exploded, we'll have penetrated some invisible wall into another kind of universe. I feel we're on the verge of a new threshold and I don't want to die before we leap into it. I can't wait in another person in fifty or a hundred years from now; *I've* been, *I've* seen, and I can't stop traveling, I can't, I'm afraid. And I can't hold what's in me. *Stop it. Read.* I go up to my room. But words have no more meaning. I masturbate. I masturbate three and four times a day now. It's because I think of Martha, I say, but it isn't. I never did before, I held off when I wasn't with you because it cheated by denying us the most complete experience. No, it's . . . I feel alive then; something dies, things I forget, and I can go out, struggle up over . . . break my own gravity? I don't know, but for one instant, just one . . . Then I'm back in my room, lying on Aunt Marilda's patchwork quilt, red roses in the wallpaper, the twin gabled windows, the marble-topped dresser, Gram's glass hurricane lamps on the little shelf. Caught. Wanting to be here, but wanting— In me *he* fights my gravity. Let go, I say. But he pulls back. Death we won't escape, he says. Must we die to escape death? I think. And the thought besieges me at such strange times: In the barn I masturbate among the cows (luckily, the farmhands aren't around, or the two dogs); on the beach, lying in the cold under the scrub oak; in the attic after poring over old trunks, after mother'd gone down. When I go downstairs again, I look at them, so tranquil: at her, knitting, my father watching TV, the figures on the screen. I watch her hands, the needles, such precision, speed. The screens leap in my father's eyes. *Father*—I want to tell him what I see, what I feel, but I don't know what it is.

(All things begin in black of night, and so it was with me. In dark they seized me and took me to the monastery at Toledo, their prisoner. Prisoner! As if in this flesh I had not always been. They took me before Father Tostado, that extraordinary man learned in the ways of the Order, a brilliant casuist. Filled with energy, his hands, never still, drove his words. Candles glittered in his eyes. He was firm. Forgive him, Lord. He believed—thus, must attack in me Mother Teresa and the Order. —You, John, he said, know that the General Chapter outlawed all advocates of Reform in Piacenza two years ago—two!—and yet you persist in challenging the entire Order. Is it your vanity holds forth against our unity? Lord, I answered him—How could I not do so?—of our desire to make pure, bare ourselves to poverty and the nothing we are, seeking the exclusive ways of the soul, sheep with the sheep and shepherd to the flock. —As the soul is pure in a body corruptible and temporary, so must ours be. My faith swears me to that one purpose that should bring nothing but harmony to our communities. —Renounce, I beg of you, John, he said. I have no recourse left me, if you do not, but force. You and the Reform are regarded—you are—rebels, the most dangerous of innovators, eating a cancer in our soul. I give this choice: Compel all your Reform to rejoin the Carmelites of the Mitigated Observance or go to the dungeon. —Ah, Father Tostado, that would be to renounce Mother Teresa, all our Order, and my God. Surely never would you ask such betrayal of yourself. As I spoke, his rage grew. —You are obstinate and disobedient and malicious. John! he cried. —Rot with your convictions. Take him to the cell.

What would it do, Lord, not to be immovable as a rock, if your Church be founded on such as we?

I came to love my prison. It was nearly perpetual dark, one dim high opening I read my breviary by, damp, and wet walls, little air. The cell was the length of a man wide and perhaps ten feet long, but so low even I, short as I am, could not stand erect. I sat and lay in dark. Juan de Santa María, my guard, let me into the hall for bread and water and my wastes each day. Kind he was. Bless him, Lord. Once a week, thinking my faith would waste with my body, Tostado sent for me. —Recant. Renounce the Reform. Recant? Never. In turn, each brother in the circle lashed me for my silence. How could they know my joy, tortured for love of You? Back in my cell, I lay in dark, where my eyes saw nothing of this world, nine months of dark, and no friend knew and no relation where I was hidden. My body wasted. The old swellings, sores, chilblains and fevers day and night returned. I prayed to be despised, counted for nothing. I surrendered and embraced my sufferings:

In dark, love, I burned,
burning feverish in love of you,
and secretly I stole my way
over mountain reaches in pursuit of you
and through a black and nothing sea.
My love made the black sea burn.
Sick in a faint and agony I called to you,
'Why do you hide? I open to your love.'
Close at my ear your sweet voice whispered, 'Here.'
And—O love!—that sea burst into a living light
and your flames ravished me.

Never before had I such plenitude of supernatural light and consolation, and O how I prayed for my great benefactors my enemies, Father Tostado and all the Mitigated Observance, who gave me this dark wherein I made the secret journey and my soul began to sing the true Way, following Thee in total surrender, which turns suffering ecstasy, death life, and all darkness light.

But it was Your will, and so mine, that I escape and write my songs and give the Way through the passive night of the soul. I watched and listened. All my body heard: footsteps, rats, roaches, dampness moving in the stones, vermin over my skin; knew the silences when no one moved, the soundless hours far above, the activities, when they prayed, when worked. To find a way—You would guide me—to escape that prison. With my plate day after day I began to loosen the screws on the heavy lock.)

Martha, I've grown secretive—I don't mean because we've kept my visit here quiet, but I didn't tell them I called you this afternoon while they were in town shopping, rain or no. It won't let up. Despite our big house I feel encapsuled—that made me call you; but you were just an echo in me I remembered; you could have been standing by the barbecue pit, talking across the salad, Greg and David getting burgers ready, moving the picnic table, as if I'd gone through a wall onto our lawn with your peonies, bleeding heart, and roses behind. But: I was watching me— him, watching him *there* with you and watching him *here* talking over the phone. Who is he listening to me? For seconds I heard his voice talking about me; yours went and then came back, why he kept saying—Keep talking, Martha, let me hear your voice, lying on the floor with the phone propped and clutching himself—Keep talking, Martha, and jacking off to your voice, trying to bring you close.—Tell me about the boys, I'm glad Greg got to play at least once on the first team, David's virus isn't bad, is it? Yes, back for Thanksgiving . . . And then he turned the receiver; your voice went far; he came; he couldn't breathe into it. —Is everything all right, Kyle darling? The long silence frightened you. You know his silences too well. He knew—knew—what you were thinking: *I'm going to him, I'll take a plane as soon as I can get the boys settled with somebody around. Or take them?* Maybe it's why he called—to get you here. He can't leave his self.—You're sure you're all right, Kyle? He couldn't answer. All right? Was that the signal to you, his silence—the same *no answer* technique to mean *I don't know* in a marriage that might be three hundred years old? When he hung up, his hand was wet with you; he stared at the ceiling, walls, the gray light outside, windows and rain pummeling from all that space. Shuttled back, he can't hold distances. In an instant he can be anywhere he's been, but why nowhere he hasn't been? Imagination couldn't take him past it. I want to imagine something beyond all the something, moon, planet, stars, I've seen out there—and can't, can't—His blood beat so hard, panicked, he broke into a sweat, his head near burst, and yes he choked, tears blinded him. He heard Dad's car in the drive. He got up and went into the bathroom.

(Friday, you say? The thirteenth? Ten o'clock? Ah, we had five

*clocks ticking then—how many years ago? No no, do not touch
my wounds. Your physician's work is done, Villarreal. I am to
die. You can no more. But, Doctor, before you leave, hand me
my little book of verses made in prison. Thank you. Go with
God. . . Let the pain grip. The soul grows large on suffering.
From the beginning You cursed my body, Lord, but for all my
thanks never cursed my flesh enough to let me show You my love,
never. Deny all comfort always was my aim, seek cold, hardship,
pain to make strong my spirit so to serve and come the lowest of
the low into Your sight. That day at the Hospital when in their
eyes I saw earths and seas I could not travel but alone—ever
since, I have been fearful, vigilant lest I miss each sign You sent.
Those signs led from prison to Prior and Rector until at Segovia I
was struck with all the joys of heavenly blindness when You
admitted me for one instant into the Grace of Union and left me
ravished and reborn into this life, dying because I do not die.
Always You gave my will strength and slow patience to move my
body. So at Toledo day after day I worked unscrewing the great
lock on my cell door, silently in dark all night working—my aim
that one window high in the hall gallery, the only hope of escape.
I measured out the strips torn carefully—my surcoat and two
blankets—and bound them each to each and that night stole past
the two bodies sleeping there—God help me!—and gained that
window, looked out, and saw: Your sky—O God, how my soul
soared!—the earth below, the river Tagus all shining moon and
flowing. The window wood was rotten, I feared the clatter, I
crept through carefully, prayed, leaped into dark, and clutched
that dry earth—safe! But there was a dog! My heart struck.
Quick I cast stones at it and prayed Don't bark. He fled, I
followed in his tracks, and reached the city. The nuns at the
Convent gave me shelter until Don Pedro González, bless him,
took me into the Hospital of the Holy Cross to heal. To all I was a
ghost come back, but most joy to our poor Teresa, who had
sought me everywhere, had written epistle after epistle—
unanswered—to King Philip. Ah, only You, Lord, know the
humiliation done to Teresa, but then the Superior General died,
the Pope placed us under the General Order, and though there
was no violence, none, silently we did not accept and kept to our
ascetic path. Now all my end became to write my guide for all the
nuns how to ascend Mount Carmel and journey the dark night of*

*the soul, and order all Teresa and I had worked for. Teresa! O
great thing of us! Blessed are you with God! Blessed too, before
you'd died, to know Pope Gregory's brief at last gave us independence and our own Provincial. Each day on Granada's soil at
Los Mártires, each orange blossom, each stone, all green leaves
bore your name, Teresa. From you our work sprang at God's
will and your own, out of your thin sick body, your eyes of
brown fire, from that thin coarse hand that could work as clean
and fast as your mind moved, and your tongue: Into our hearts
your words cut everlastingly. What would we do when you died?
More your death gave–sent in ecstasy our souls to follow you to
God. More, yes, All your will we assumed—and so it builds, our
ladder. Your end prepared us for this new beginning. For
enemies never rest. Each crest makes the trough lower. A new
wave cast me and the Order farther down, as if after founding
new chapters at Córdoba, Seville, Madrid, Manchuela,
Caravaca, we had forgotten poverty, discipline, the right way.
We fought—Reform against Reform. God chastises and reminds:
returns us to our place—down. Nothing we are. They cast me
out, elected Father Doria . . . Well, I welcome enemies: Tostado, Rubeo, Doria, and now Crisóstomo, Prior of this last
refuge on earth for me. Enemies drive me closer to Thee. Each
test is Thine. Through them You work your wondrous way, I
know: You never do betray as man betrays.*

*From Segovia I asked the Order to send me to New Spain—
there, yes, to undergo once more what new ordeal for Your
name's sake. The Order sent me to La Peñuela—to prepare
myself for the new world, so I thought. But since I had no elected
post—they had stripped me, I thanked you for the
punishment—it was to isolate me so they could defame me within
the Order and without, and to the king. I learned how they
collected declarations of defamation, testimonials of ill-repute,
of sins I never dreamed—made brothers and sisters sign, bribed,
taught them lies by suggestion, made them sin. Expel me? Never.
I would endure anything, obey. Long since, from my first
thinking day, I learned that: silence. Defend myself? I refused.
Let the burden grow; it comes from You, a test. May my soul
survive that test.*

*But, old man, who . . .? And you? That woman's eyes? Ah. . .
Alms for the love of God. I tended you, six years. Begged. Your*

faces never leave me. Begged too for that—to hold you in my
sight till the walls of this tiny room my body fall away. I thank
You, God. But who—in their midst—there? Father Crisóstomo
come again? How his eyes hate! He never speaks but to rail at
me. Forgive him, Lord, he knows not. . . A time will come. I
pray it come for him. Is Crisóstomo Your final test? For his hate
strengthens me. There, beyond him—What light is that? It
moves. Oh, God, once—day after day at Segovia—Your light
came: descended, covered me, took all my soul up into it. It
breathed, I fed, I grew.

　You, Father Crisóstomo, why do you stand there? Once, in
Segovia. . . Where is my candle? Aside, Crisóstomo, do not
blight the light.)

Dreams: I miss the angle of re-entry into earth's atmosphere—
doomed to circle everlastingly/ / / /I'm floating in space. You're
racing toward me, Martha, Greg, David, friends, relatives,
teachers, strangers, faces; my eyes burn with joy; but when you
reach, your arms split into ribbons, flutter up, away, past me; I
shout shout; you ignore me/ / / /Lunar morning. I am walking
between the Sea of Fertility and the Sea of Tranquillity. All is gray,
an ashen cast, cocoa-colored pits and shadows, caves. Pickering,
Messier, Maskelyne are like people to me now. But I cannot stay, I
cannot go back to earth: My blood heart demands *never back,* but
on up out. I will cast everything down to lie with the seismometer,
laser reflector, solar wind collector forever, yes. I toss down the
rãdio, free my pack, tear·at my helmet, yes, to get out, there must
be a way. My head bursts into flame, my body falls to ash, and he
rises long thin and beautiful with light, speeds outward toward the
stars/ / / /The cheers turn to jeering: *Send him back to the moon*
Isolate him. Quarantine him in his own place. I plead with them.
They're afraid of me. I'll infect them. What has changed? Can't
they see me behind flesh? live my mind waves? They turn away,
shudder, run/ / / /I look down at earth as if I had created it,
wandered among them as one, and then discovered I belong on the
moon, apart from my creations. If I could imagine anyone out there
above me, I could pity him. I would join him. We would sit
together and commiserate. Martha! I cry. Greg! David! Suddenly
you appear. But when you look at me your eyes blaze with what
you see: You bow your heads, bow to me, and kneel. Martha!/ / /
/Will I have to wait up here till one by one you join me from

earth—and then look out and move again, one by one, group by group? When we get there, will we meet ourselves? Is our self waiting for ourselves there? Is nothing ourselves?

I wake up. I hear my mother in the hall. Have I been talking in my sleep again?

Far, the waves are—or is it my blood?—beating on the shore.

I cannot wait much longer, I can't, Martha.

(Is it really you, Antonio, my first prior? Were you not old, dear friend, your visits would have me believe this tiny cell to be our first hermitage again. Listen! Do I hear . . . music? But it is denied me here. It may be I . . . Do I imagine even you, Antonio? Does the Devil so delude? For I was denied all visits until you came. At times Crisóstomo comes, but only to accuse—and so confirm my faith—and when he forbids the women bathe my wounds or wash my linen, forbids townsfolk to bring food, forbids music. I rejoice: It is my God who speaks as once that painting of Jesus Christ did speak to me:—What is your most desire? He asked.—The more deeply to beg persecution for so much loving You, I said. From Him, great Teresa, and my own dear mother Catalina—turned Mariá de la Incarnación, sweet nun—from them I learn to die. And from those inmates, all.

But it was you, Antonio, gave me this final choice. We choose, ever, tremblingly. Not to miss the appointed moment, to make right choice are ever the Grace of God. You were the agent, Antonio, for at La Peñuela was no medicine; and though I welcomed suffering, still there was the world's work to be done.—Send me elsewhere, I asked.—Baeza or Ubeda? you said. Baeza? Why would I go to friends, comfort, consolation when once I begged God let me die no prelate, die where I am unknown, die only after suffering all for His sake? All I suffer is His answer, I know: Renounce. Renounce. Thus, I chose Ubeda, where all were strangers to me.

So we made this journey, my little mule and I, long and slow, up, up the sierra, crags, rock, cold wind and smiting dust like my own Castille, the only warmth my mule's breath when his head turned back to me, poor creature. My bad leg hung, struck his side so painfully I could but hang too, or fall, and climb. I was burning all with fever. I could not see—I prayed for blindness—but my mule's slow feet God guided sure, right into night, and so we came high up to Ubeda and this cell and bed and crucifix.

Ah, that mule, had he a soul, would go to God.

Good you are, Antonio, to comfort me. You always did have instant charity. You'll come no more? So be it. Thank you, Antonio. Go with God . . .

All is God's law, this silence and this darkness here, my little candle blowing low, the blackened ceiling, this pain so great I move to make it worse, keep all my thoughts on You, who in an instant—which?—will make me the deepest journey, so far within, past time to where all memory begins, burst into it and live—forever. If You but grant me Grace. Yes, pain will kill breath at last. The light will glow, hover, descend and—O Christ!—make me bride eternally, as at Segovia once—

After, seven years I was at Granada, Prior to the Convent of Los Mártires. I smell the orange blossoms yet. The waters babble in the Morrish fountains. What great gift the Generalife gardens and that our great Alhambra so delicate and white with moon it seems a lace against the sky. The very air made you delirious, water struck tiles, moon glowed over everything, eternal music in the air. Where else is such profusion of beauty one thanks God momentarily? Yet it was too much, too soothing—when I lay down on stones at night, I saw that other beauty I longed for: my own Castille, barren and forlorn, all rock, sand, and dry shrubs, and endless wind that casts at you. Thank God there was no end to duties: convents founded and established, the running of Los Mártires, confessing our sisters, counseling, receiving laymen; to preach, teach, attend—and always my loyal brother—ah, Francisco, older—by my side: joyfully tired, both, but not to sleep long, never long: Mortify the flesh, renounce. What more for God?—Goodnight, Francisco. I watched him down the colonnade, opened my cell, then wrote, wrote at rule books and glosses to my poems to make clear the Way, wrote till the candle died, and then lay still in dark.

Where did I go?

Lying still, I left my body: I heard the fountain, one. I went out in dark to follow the sounding water: It led me into deeper dark. Loud it grew. Cool winds came from it and I ran, ran, until at last I fell exhausted, hearing the flowing fountain flow, strained till all my body heard. I could not move. All the waters rushed over and carried me. I drank the waters that carried me. And far I saw a flame grow and grow, spread through the waters. The dark burned with it. Light blinded and entered me, and all my body blazed and sang in sweet union with You, O living fountain.

Ayyyyyyyyyyyy . . .

Let all the waters come.

Who is that shadow? Antonio? No, no, he's gone. That . . . one? Not my faces, no. You, friars? But know you Father Crisóstomo will scold you. I am forbid. Your entry is prohibited.

Not? Crisóstomo lets you come?

What? He comes again himself?

You take my hand? You, Crisóstomo?

What act of grace is this, my enemy? No, not enemy—friend if enemy: for even this last consolation I fear, that comfort that my God does not love nor I. You let the brethren come, Crisóstomo? Ah, thanks to Antonio. Yes, yes, I understand. It is a grace I did not expect. It shames me I am so hard. Let God forgive. I thank you, Crisóstomo.

Brothers, friends, and ah . . . women from the village? And that—? No, no, no music yet—well, yes, let it be the mass. But come closer, gather round . . .)

I was wrong: You didn't come, Martha. Why do I call every night now? I am trying to make contact, my darling. But that man your husband, when I talk to you, who asks all the things you know he'll ask, watches himself so he won't say any of the things I feel. He won't help me: *He* slips farther off, watches. All the time I know that. How can I tell you? I try to summon up the man I once was. Who was it who made those missions over Korea? Who went into X-15s and stepped out of that lunar landing vehicle onto the moon? He was all adrenaline, every muscle charged. He was convinced the body—beautiful and disciplined—could do, make. But my body stops now, yet my head soars, hurls past moon, not of earth: Moon lives under my lids; Cape Venus and Bear Mountain, Boot Hill, Pickering, all the rills and scars make a permanent landscape in my head—and I can't break moon's gravity. Even closing my eyes cancels out re-entering earth's atmosphere, splashdown, quarantine—and home. Your voice sounds like a recording from down there. If I could find the way back, grip in, and be sure mind heart whatever would not rise again, never look up, never one time dare reach outward . . . But then the boys would go to school, you'd go shopping, and at work I'd begin to—

Would I do it all again?

What thing says Yes in me?

I'm the only man left of my training group: Rich shot himself, Doug disappeared in the Canadian woods, they say Everett's in some jungle, a missionary, if he *is* alive. Did *they* live *me?* I them? Men can't know what it means to be one of the only men not of earth. Something has been born that can't rest, wants to be fulfilled—something *in* me that uses me and will leave me *behind,* I *know,* not take me with it. I wake up sweaty and cold thinking it. Gone? He's left my body here. I want to leap. I want to imagine myself there where he's gone so I can *be* there. But I can imagine nothing. What has died in me?

This morning the sun came like summer, though it was crisp and cool out.—Great day for a row to the lighthouse, my father said, good for the muscles. We parked at the Point, then rowed toward the Orient light.—Don't go too close. We get in that undertow and sucked down, that'll be it. The Gut, where the tides meet, was churning in a boil, choppy with whitecaps and foam. Plum Island looked winterdead and brown—and the sea slate. I headed out, rowed, fire in my arms.—Son, he said, *son!* The boat sucked to the side. He was frightened at my absorption.—Keep it *moving,* keep right, he said.—Head in, there! he signaled. I said nothing, suddenly headed in with all my might, sleeked over the hard gray surface. If I angled the boat just right, at the right speed, could we enter the water and descend into the atmosphere, take moon under, escape into—*Stop it!* I stared at the Point coming closer. *Don't look under.* Dad talked a blue streak, shades of my old physical geography teacher, talking end moraines, the glacier moving and melting its thousands of years and depositing this island, silt, sand, rock, and those great boulders that littered the north shore.—I'd like to live to see those Hebrides, Bahamas, Galapagos, all the archipelagoes—travel like you. Must be a great thing. Standing on it, Long Island's big, a hundred or more miles end to end—wouldn't think it, all Brooklyn top-heavy on one end. *We* look like a pinpoint from out there, hey? Can't even imagine it. TV pictures sure can't be the same. We don't know, do we? Dad loves the island like people, give and take like lovers. Brown and cracked he even looks like the island now. We hit the shore, I jump out, drag the boat on a thrust of wave, and moor it.—There're beds of scallops hereabouts. We could get us a good mess, he said, your Ma loves them. You love them, he meant.—I wondered about the basket and boots and rakes in the car, I said. —A man's got to be ready for anything. He laughed. —You could go in barefoot, I said. —Mighty cold, that water. We put on boots; he tied the basket rope to his waist, and we dug around with the hand rakes. As a kid I followed the basket, digging down, coming up with scallops and chucking them into it. Proud, my father—and now too, with me a man. Under, the waves shimmered my arms like ribbons, my face vague in the surface. Crabs scooted deeper, seaweed and darks under. I stared: Everywhere was moving, all the time moving, water and minnows, seaweed, a razor crab closing . . .—You'll break your back staring, he said. Far down, beginnings . . .— Think you're a kid again? He laughed. I said, We'd better not stay in too long. You'll catch pneumonia. —You don't worry about me, he said. —Sides, we've not caught half a bushel. His voice warmed. He looked fulfilled. Ma was happy at the fresh scallops, opened them with gusto. Dark came early, like one sea over the other. —Ready, she said, supper steaming. The TV was on. An old man weeping with a girl in his arms said, Is this the promised end? —Turn to Channel 5, she said, I never could take those British voices. Come, Son. In the pane I saw my father—watching me.

(I am confessed. Now bring me the sweet blood and body of Our Lord. I thank you, Father.

And you, my brothers, do not be grieved. All fevers go, aches, plagues, sufferings, in the dark night and how many are the blessings the soul attains. Discipline yourselves to go the Way. Pray for that night. Ah, yes, read me my verses that take me upward—I thank God for that Toledo night and all my jail. Pray for my enemies. How well you read, Sister. The mark's on you. Your eyes . . . they are Teresa's eyes—pure, good and great she was, who sits now in that multifoliate rose, her destiny fulfilled, all in pure light with God.

No, no, don't move! It is my body shrieks, not I—earthly pain, no more, the soul half journeyed there, far from the bones we leave behind to lesson the living. Men should go to charnel houses to learn of God, that no thing lasts but God Himself and we in Him. Teach that word, but when at night you lie down . . .

how once Antonio, Jesús, and I woke mornings with snow fallen on our robes, feeling nothing, chilblained and raw; young we were with all before us: convents to found, works to write, and God to pursue in everything . . . yes, when at night you lie down, let darkness turn you inward, seek the longest journey, ever take the hardest way, my brothers.

Let those faces in. No, I do not wander, but gather into my sight those pilgrims I have seen in Beas and Toledo, Granada, Avila, Segovia, Baeza, and—ever there—our sick and dying from that old Hospital at Medina del Campo, eyes I traveled into once, a boy so struck my heart quavered. What caused such misery? Filled with fear, my soul leaped to God. By what necessity did it come? Yet something in them stood fast, held— against it all. All together, each alone—alone: that, then, a thought more hideous than any rotting flesh that we must travel through. Now I am one with them. He gave me will. Once He came down, made me His bride to all eternity.

You see, friars, sisters, no cause to grieve. I told you that. You with Teresa's eyes, recite that passage from St. Luke touching on the eye and light.

Done. You are inspired.

My brother often read to me, and to my mother.

I heard Mother Teresa once—to all the nuns: words so pure I could not keep the tears away. She blessed me after. I never can forget her touch. I trembled before God speaking through her hand: as close on earth as I could get to anyone. I yearn to join the light she shares.

Ah, Teresa!

Listen! It is the bells. Matins?

The moment comes. He calls. I know. Brethren, gather round and listen to sweet words of consolation:

Never doubt there is one way for each of us, and for each a path so fragrant, melodious, and light, you must go down into all suffering and pain and misery to gain the joy of dark of night, and at the threshold when dark turns light, all self cast off, you will rise, rise forever into the arms of light. Ah, brothers—

All pain we yearned for, suffer, die for—so loved we God.

Bless you.

But—ah—your promise: Care for that little mule that brought me here.)

Martha, I can't wait for you. I don't know how to say goodbye. I'm always at the bottom of a sea. Once *you* were my sea. I went into you, submerged, but lifted—something magnificent happened I could never put into words. When he came back from space, after the moon—It's cruel, *I'm* cruel, I don't want to be cruel but I can't deny wanting to talk about it, wanting to make clear what I don't even know, but not wanting to tell you either—his body had no use, wasn't *going* anywhere; sex, yours and mine, our lives, meant nothing. Inside you he felt: I'm not here, I'm not her husband, somebody's in my body, they're not my children though they came through me, I'm used, they're not my mother and father. Moments, the way Dad looks at me, I'm sure he knows what I'm feeling. *Don't tell your mother.* Ma goes on magnificently tied to each task, apple jelly, the green sweater, pumpkins for the freezer, the field mice slipping into the cellar, sopping the bacon grease off the eggs just so. When she looks at me with such love, in her eyes I see him that isn't—never was—her son I carry inside me waiting to be born.

Martha, listen: *He* talks to you, *I* listen; he tells you every single thing he remembers, all his life, me listening to my voice that's not mine; he reviews every minute up to now, can't get past now, comes to a blank wall, stops; I'm frantic, I go near mad, straight ahead it's nothing, all blank. Did your head eyes ever fill with absolute blank. Is nothing nothing? Do I have to die to find that out? Will death break nothing? I have a madness to conceive something out of blank, make make make, but out of nothing *his* voice comes, I'm trapped in *his* memory, waiting to be released with one long wail into what new world? Please, I tell him, there's no rest, let me go—

I sit at my grandfather's desk. I try to write to myself, to tell myself what's happening. When I read it, I know he's written it. I can't push any farther than *he* tells. It's madness, I even *know* it's madness, to reach that edge and want to push past. Words can't do it.

I can no longer imagine, Martha.

I must go through.

—Your life story? my father says.

—What?

—You writing your memoirs? He laughs.

—In a way. I look at him: that man my father. I feel no

conception. Him, an island. Her. Chair. TV. Vase. Picture. Window. Dead to me? I'm waiting. I'm watching me waiting. Let me go, I want to live, I say. I write it: Let me go, I want to live.

My father says, You don't have much time left.

—No, I say.

—Four days, he says.

But Martha's coming. She'll be here in the morning. I know she will. I could tell by her voice.

—We haven't been anywhere, it seems, my father says.

—No, I say.

—Look at the sunset, my mother says. Beautiful!

The sky is a last glow, blood orange, edged with a lime green tinge thinning into blue far off, and the sea swells reddening. The sun burns into the sea and the water beats. I can't take my eyes off that pulsing. If I open my mouth, it will flow in and take my breath, breathe me down down. I want to touch it. In the pane I see him get up. Yes, he says, to touch it. Your eyes mouth blood heart, he says. I close my eyes: Nothing comes, wide and endless dark. Into. into. Down, he says.

—I think I'll take a walk along the Sound to old Rick's lobster pots. I see he keeps them all year round, I say.

—A greedy old thing, my mothers says. —Your jacket, she cries.

Jacket? I put on my lumber jacket.

My father says nothing. His image is watching.

I close the door, hurry, nearly running—I'm afraid to shut my eyes—straight to the edge of the fields: down the cliff, steep, and strike the shore, the gulls are crying at the great boulders, the water is red dark, waves lapping laps, past Rick's rowboat, the sun goes down the water, under the cold dark, down he says let your *Forgive me, Martha, I must know* legs arms your *if nothing will end* mouth your *nothing* eyes

THE AIR BETWEEN TWO DESERTS

by MAREA GORDETT

from CINCINNATI POETRY REVIEW

nominated by CINCINNATI POETRY REVIEW

Never the howling of humdrum moon
reminds me of you, nor the calamity of Tonto.
Not the black humor of Nijinsky's feet,
not music, my sometimes friend, nor the spell
of birds flying over to me.

Not the crenellated stars
nor the sadness of ordinary devils,
not the meditators in bathtubs,
the patrons of flophouses, the hotels
in Chinatown raping poppy merchants.

Not the first time in Exaltata's car,
nor the last cruise on Paradise Flats,
not the amputated mailman home from the jungle
running on his hands,
not the lunatic runners high on Nirvana fumes.

Not the bisons bumping heads in the dark,
not the question walking out of bed
staring at computerized roses.
Not madness,
ridicule or shame.

But Beauty:
the kid leaning on a tractor in 1949,
not smiling, the angel poet.

THE STUDENTS OF SNOW

by JANE FLANDERS

from THE CHOWDER REVIEW

nominated by THE CHOWDER REVIEW

The students of snow will tell you few flakes
attain perfect symmetry.
There are many irregular forms, icy
spicules, frost-like sprigs,
forms due to twinning.

They may be needle-shaped, columnar,
three-sided or quadrilateral. Even the whiteness
is illusory. They can tell you
of red and green
snow, of the fabulous blue snow
that saved Nebraska.

The students of snow would never
say snowflakes are
unique. They would only admit they have never
seen two alike.
And no two students of snow are alike: Professor
Squinabol, Mrs. Chickering,
Herr Sigsun, and "Snowflake"
Bentley, the first microphotographer of snow,
bending almost invisibly
over his slide in a white smock.

Even in old age the students of snow
adore bad weather,
but they will tell you, the light
glinting off their spectacles, snow can fall
even from clear skies.
They say that true
crystals are not formed from clouds,
but from the unseen molecules within them.
And then they cease to speak, caught up
in the study of silence, transparency,
the radiant wedding of nebulae.

THE ONLY POEM

by ROBERT PENN WARREN

from AMERICAN POETRY REVIEW

nominated by Alicia Ostriker, Robert Phillips and Rhoda Schwartz

The only poem to write I now have in mind
Will not be written because in memory, or eyes,
The scene is too vivid, so tears, not words, I find.
If, perhaps, I forget, it might catch me then by surprise.

But the facts lie long back, and are certainly trivial,
Though I've waked in the night, as though at a voice at my ear,
Till a flash of the dying dream comes back, and I haul
Up a sheet to angrily wipe at an angry tear.

My mother was middle-aged, and only retained
A sweetness of face, not the beauty my father, years later,
Near death, would try speaking of, could not, then refrained.
But the facts: that day she took me to see the new daughter

Of my friends left with Grandma while they went East for careers;
So, for friendship, I warily handled the sweet-smelling
   squaw-fruit,
All golden and pink, kissed the fingers, blew in the ears.
Then suddenly was at a loss. So my mother seized it,

And I knew, all at once, that she would have waited all day,
Sitting there on the floor, with her feet drawn up like a girl,
So half-laughing, half-crying, arms stretched, she swung up her
   prey,
And the prey shrieked with joy at the giddy swoop and swirl.

Yes, that was all, except for the formal farewell,
And wordless we wandered the snow-dabbled street, and day,
With her hands both clutching my arm till I thought it would
    swell,
Then home, fumbling key, she said: "Shucks! Time gets away!"

We entered. She laid out my supper. My train left at eight
To go back to the world where all is always the same.
Success nor failure—neither can alleviate
The pang of unworthiness that is built into Time's name.

THE COLD IN MIDDLE LATITUDES

by JOHN ENGELS

from THE BLACK WARRIOR REVIEW

nominated by THE BLACK WARRIOR REVIEW *and Tess Gallagher*

1

On the first of April I stand
a little before sunrise
on the porch step and observe
to the north a sudden
discontinuity of sky. I see

the first lights come on
in the houses of North Williston.
The morning
witholds itself, there is much in it
of refusal. I note
how it is that the world in early spring
exhales the odor of damp cellars,

which fact I have always known,
and of which I have spoken,
nor is this the last of it

2

April, which is to say
by my measure some small
equivocal truth about how

everything takes place
at the wrong time:
The black

locusts seem dead, the maples
have come half-alive, and wait.
In my yard, in all the yards
of North Williston, the spring muds
steam—and for the moment,

though I permit it
only for the moment,
something like the sun
takes place. For the moment
all the doors stand open,
this house airing,
readying itself,
by evening the spring frogs
chirping from the ditches,
and one which must have been
hiding there all winter,
singing out from the cellar

3
a sullen, invisible cold
breathes from the floorboards.
Warm rain begins

at the exact instant that, in the west,
the sky clears, greens, flares overhead,
that everything becomes
as if I were to breathe at the green
fluent heart of the sea,

and looking up
into the vast mirror of the under-
surface, be
permitted to look back upon
myself; which would be to fail
in these imaginings

4
Perhaps I am in
the wrong place:
over North Williston
in the earliest of skies
the sun dwindles into the knot
and smother of its heart.
And my heart,

as it carries itself in me,
as I have known it to undertake to do
sings out in the seasonal
startlement from hiding, willing

and unwilling to become
nothing, but always
unequal to the one
or other
of it

5
as it turns out,
as I expected that it would,
the sky in this place is no more
than merely about to darken,
deepen, become snow
which will fall and deepen,

and I have in all this weather-lock not
come to understand how it can be
the body warms
to its own and slight
sea-bearing,

the body, as I
have knowledge of it, wishing
always to rise and to beat down
upon a green and upward-
beating shore; and this,

though I see by the blue
shine of the ice that rises
slowly in the east, though I see
by that true and signatory light

I have
not fully deserved
this knowledge, have
not used it well

CONTRIBUTORS
NOTES

MICHAEL ANANIA was an editor at Swallow Press, head of The Coordinating Council of Literary Magazines, and editor of *Audit/ Poetry*. He is the author of two volumes of poetry, and a work of non-fiction, *The Red Menace*, is forthcoming.

ASA BABER lives in Chicago and is the author of a novel, *The Land of A Million Elephants*.

BO BALL lives in Decatur, Georgia. He has published fiction in *Roanoke Review, Southern Humanities Review, Prarie Schooner* and elsewhere.

JIM BARNES is editor of *The Chariton Review*. His work has appeared in many literary magazines and also in the book *Carriers of the Dream Wheel: Contemporary Native American Poetry*.

MARVIN BELL lives in Iowa City, Iowa and has published in a long list of literary presses.

GINA BERRIAULT is the author of *The Mistress and Other Stories* (1965) and three novels. A fourth novel is due soon.

MICHAEL BLUMENTHAL's first book, *Sympathetic Magic*, won the Water Mark Press first book award for 1980.

DAVID BROMIGE is the author of *My Poetry* (The Figures), *Birds of the West* (Coach House Press) and *Tight Corners & What's Around Them* (Black Sparrow Press).

MICHAEL BRONDOLI lives in New York City and is the author of *The Love Letter Hack.* (Paycock Press) and *Smithsburg* (Treacle Press).

JOSEPH BRUCHAC is editor of *The Greenfield Review*.

VLADA BULATOVÍC-VIB is one of the most popular of modern Yugoslav satirists. He is the author of four satirical books and two plays. He works as a columnist in *Politika,* Yugoslavia's outstanding newspaper.

DAVID BOSWORTH's stories have appeared in the *Ohio Review, Ploughshares, Agni Review* and elsewhere. He is working on a novel.

KATHY CALLAWAY lives in New York City and is completing a book-length collection of poetry.

JAN CAREW, born in Guyana in 1925, is the author of several books of fiction, most recently *The Wild Coast.* His essays and short stories have appeared in journals and anthologies throughout the Americas.

HAYDEN CARRUTH is poetry editor of *Harpers,* advisory editor of *The Hudson Review* and runs The Crows Mark Press.

ANDREI CODRESCU lives in Baltimore, and according to *Unmuzzled Ox,* "is terrific."

JOHN ENGELS has published three books of poetry with The University of Pittsburgh Press. He lives in Vermont.

IRVING FELDMAN's most recent book is *New and Selected Poems* (Viking, 1979). He teaches at SUNY Buffalo.

JANE FLANDERS is a winner of the 1979 *The Nation*/YM-YWHA Discovery Award.

H. E. FRANCIS' "Two Lives" won the Kansas Quarterly Award. A new collection is due from The University of Illinois Press.

MAREA GORDETT is a winner of the 1979 *The Nation*/YM-YWHA Discovery Award. She lives in Cambridge, Massachusetts.

JORIE GRAHAM's book of poems is just out from Princeton University Press. Her poems have appeared in *Ironwood, Antaeus,* and *Paris Review.*

ALLEN GROSSMAN is author of *The Woman on the Bridge Over The Chicago River* (New Directions).

BARBARA GROSSMAN works in publishing in New York City.

WILLIAM HARMON is the editor of *The Oxford Book of American Light Verse,* the author of two books of poems and is Professor of English at the University of North Carolina, Chapel Hill.

SEAMUS HEANEY is the author of *Field Work* (Farrar, Straus and Giroux), and *North* (Oxford). He lives in Ireland.

GEORGE HITCHCOCK is the editor of *Kayak.* His collected poems have been published most recently by Cloud Marauder press and Copper Canyon press.

JOHN HOLLANDER's recent books include *Spectral Emanations* and *In Place.* He is Professor of English at Yale.

LEWIS HYDE is the editor of *A Longing for The Light: Selected Poems of Vincente Aleixandre* (Harper and Row). This essay is part of a longer work to be published by Houghton Mifflin.

JANET KAUFFMAN's poems have appeared in *The Nation* and *New Letters.* She grew up on a tobacco farm.

FRANK KERMODE is Regius Professor at King's College, Cambridge University. His many books include *The Sense of An Ending, Romantic Image,* and *The Classic.*

W. P. KINSELLA's most recent collections of short stories are *Shoeless Joe Jackson Comes to Iowa,* and *Born Indian* (spring, 1981). He was born in Edmonton and teaches at the University of Calgary.

WILLIAM KLOEFKORN's most recent poetry collection is *Not Such A Bad Place To Be* (Windflower Press).

ROMULUS LINNEY works in all the genres but is best known for his plays "The Sorrows of Frederick" and "The Love Suicide at Schofield Barracks."

DAVID MADDEN lives in Baton Rouge and is the author of two novels *Bijou* and *Cassandra Singing.*

THOMAS MCGRATH is the author of *Letter to An Imaginary Friend* and *The Movie at the End of the World* (Swallow) and *Waiting for the Angel* (Uzzano Press). He lives in Moorhead, Minnesota.

HEATHER MCHUGH's poetry has appeared in *The New Yorker, Antaeus, Atlantic* and other magazines. She lives in Binghamton, New York.

SANDRA MCPHERSON's latest poetry collection was *The Year of Our Birth,* a 1979 National Book Award nominee. She lives in Iowa City.

CAROL MUSKE's second book of poems, *Skylight,* will be published soon by Doubleday. She teaches at Columbia University.

CYNTHIA OZICK is author of the novel, *Trust,* and two collections of shorter fiction. A third collection will be published soon.

DAVID PERKINS is editor of *Chouteau Review.*

DAVID PLANTE is the author of *The Family* (Farrar, Straus and Giroux). His work has appeared in *The New Yorker* and elsewhere.

RAPHAEL RUDNIK lived in Amsterdam, Holland for many years, but now resides in New York City. She has published two books and has recently completed a third collection of poems.

ED SANDERS is the author of *20,000 A.D.* (North Atlantic Books) and numerous other works. He lives in Woodstock, New York.

SHEROD SANTOS is at work on a critical book on Elizabeth Bishop. His work has appeared in *Antaeus, The Paris Review* and elsewhere.

GERARD SHYNE's selection is part of his book *Under The Influence of Mae* (Inwood Press). See the introduction to this volume for more about Mr. Shyne.

CHARLES SIMIC is the author of three books of poetry and numerous translations of French, Russian and Yugoslav poetry. He co-edited with Mark Strand the book *Another Republic.*

ELIZABETH SPENCER's collection of stories will be published soon by Doubleday.

GERALD STERN is the author of *Lucky Life* (Houghton Mifflin) and is a winner of The Lamont Prize.

PAMELA STEWART's most recent book is *Cascades* (L'Epervier Press). She lives in Arizona.

JOHN TAGGART's latest book is *Peace on Earth* (1980, Turtle Island Foundation). He teaches at Shippensburg State College in Pennsylvania.

STEPHANIE VAUGHN has published fiction in *Redbook* and *The New Yorker*. She teaches at Stanford University.

RICHARD VINE teaches at Riyadh University in the Kingdom of Saudi Arabia. He claims no history.

SARA VOGAN lives in California and has published stories in the *Iowa Review, Carolina Quarterly* and elsewhere. A novel is to be published soon.

DAVID WAGONER edits *Poetry Northwest* and has published eleven books of poetry. A novel will be published soon.

ROBERT PENN WARREN received the Copernicus Award from The Academy of American Poets in 1976. His books and awards are numerous.

BARBARA WATKINS has an MFA from the University of Massachusetts and lives in New York City.

BRUCE WEIGL's first poetry collection, *A Romance*, was published in 1979 by the University of Pittsburgh Press.

ELLEN WILBUR lives in Cambridge, Massachusetts. Her work has appeared in *Ploughshares* and *New Letters*.

CHARLES WRIGHT is the author of four books of poetry and is professor of English at the University of California at Irvine, where he directs the Irvine Writing Program.

JAMES WRIGHT's *Collected Poems* won the 1972 Pulitzer Prize. His most recent book is *To A Blossoming Pear Tree*. Mr. Wright died in March, 1980 after a long illness.

AL YOUNG is an editor of Y'Bird. His works have appeared in many small press publications.

PATRICIA ZELVER is the author of two novels and a new book, *A Man of Middle Age and Twelve Stories*, recently published by Holt, Rhinehart and Winston. She lives in California.

OUTSTANDING WRITERS

(The editors also wish to mention the following important works published by small presses in 1979. Listing is alphabetical by author's last name.)

FICTION

The Axing of Leo White Hat—Raymond Abbott (Apple-Wood Press)
The Party-Givers—Alice Adams (Epoch)
Truth or Consequences—Alice Adams (Shenandoah)
selections from A Golden Story—Daisy Aldan (Folder Editions)
Idealism and Illusion—Bruce Andrews (Cinemanews)
to Real Estate—David Antin (New Directions)
The Blue Hangar: A Space Novel—Ascher/Straus (Interstate)
Flight—J. G. Ballard (Antaeus)
A Piece of Monologue—Samuel Beckett (Kenyon Review)
Loving The Albatross—Ted Bent (Massachusetts Review)
Hanging Tough—Carol Berge (Aspect)
Here to Learn—Paul Bowles (Antaeus)
I Dated Jane Austen—T. Coraghessan Boyle (Georgia Review)
The Love Letter Hack—Michael Brondoli (Paycock Press)
Family Circle—Frederick Busch (Mississippi Review)
Heart of A Horse—Denise M. Cassens (Northwest Review)
The Old Couple—Andrei Codrescu (Departures)
New Vintage—Florence C. Cohen (Story Press)
A Scene from *Night Studies*—Cyrus Colter (New Letters)
Bunco—Marilyn Jean Conner (Ploughshares)
Il Spendore Della Luce A Bologna—Guy Davenport (Glitch)
Breaking Windows—Albert Drake (White Ewe Press)
A Decision For The Judenrat—Leslie Epstein (Partisan Review)

The Voice In The Closet—Raymond Federman (Coda Press, Paris Review)

Captain Bennett's Folly—Berry Fleming (Cotton Lane Press)

Ballad of the Engineer Carl Feldmann—H. E. Francis (Michigan Quarterly)

Naming Things—H. E. Francis (Virginia Quarterly)

The Man Who'd Bounce The World—Jon Freedman (Turtle Island Press)

Design—Thomas Friedmann (Micah Publications)

The Women—Eugene Graber (Fairleigh Dickinson Literary Review)

Between The Kisses and the Wine—Douglas Glover (Apalachee Quarterly)

Telephones—Ivy Goodman (Sun&Moon)

from Circumspections From An Equestrian Statue—Jaimy Gordon (Burning Deck)

Arthur Bond—William Goyen (Palaemon Press)

What About Us Grils?—Richard Grayson (Gargoyle)

The Edge of the Web—Gregory Gwenn (InterMuse)

"The Man Who Wanted Things Nice"—Rolaine Hochstein (The Fiddlehead)

Ground—Lyn Hejinian (Roof)

Billie Loses Her Job—Robert Henson (Antioch Review)

Twins—Christine L. Hewitt (New Directions)

Spanish-walking in a Snowstorm—Allen Hoey (New Renaissance)

Poison Oak—David Huddle (New England Review)

Snow—Alyce Ingram (Eureka Review)

Inheritance—Elizabeth Inness-Brown (North American Review)

The Home Front—Sarah Irwin (Richmond Literature and History Quarterly)

Sound of Shadows—Josephine Jacobsen (New Letters)

Genius Loci—Jascha Kessler (Michigan Quarterly Review)

Proxopera—Benedict Kiely (TriQuarterly)

Momentum is Always The Weapon—William Kittredge (Portland Review)

selections from *Bump City*—John Krich (City Miner Books)

To Be of Use—Maxine Kumin (Virginia Quarterly Review)

The Face of Hate—Mary Lavin (Southern Review)

I Will Look At All the Beautiful Things and Then Drink Champagne—Julius Lester (Caliban)

I'm Wide—Gordon Lish (Plum)
Weight—Gordon Lish (Mississippi Review)
Blue Day—Arnost Lustig (TriQuarterly)
Disputed Territory—Grant Lyons (Confrontation)
Uncle Vinnie—Jane M. Maher (Hudson Review)
Paper Options—Peter Makuck (Greensboro Review)
The Powers of Ten—Denis Mathis (*Ohio Journal*)
Alfred Kinsey, Alone After An Interview, Dreams of Indiana—
    Michael Martone (Iowa Review)
The Eternal Mortgage—Jack Matthews (Southwest Review)
Ponce de Leon—Jack Matthews (Mississippi Valley Review)
Jameson, Wake—James McCourt (Boss)
Snow Shoes—Michael McMahon (White Ewe Press)
Big Mama and The Rolling Store Man—Birthalene Miller (Black
    Warrior)
A Small Cartoon—Barbara Milton (Paris Review)
Femmes Damnees—Cat Nilan (Aurora)
The Murderess—Joyce Carol Oates (Western Humanities Review)
White Trash Genesis—Donald O'Donovan (The Smith)
Oneba and the Neutrodynes—David Ohle (New Mexico
    Humanities Review)
Hotel Death—John Perreault (Sun & Moon)
Cora's Tree—Mary Peterson (North American Review)
Taking The Night Plane to Tulsa—Samuel Pickering (New England
    Review)
Sleep Tight—James Purdy (Antioch Review)
Beekeeper—Kurt Rheinheimer (Story Quarterly)
Witness—Mary Elsie Robertson (Kansas Quarterly)
The Grignetzian Theorem—T.N.R. Rogers (Shankpainter)
Chekov at Badenweiler—Henry Roth (North American Review)
Lives In Flight—Michael Rutherford (Oconee Review)
Eric—Gerard Shyne (Quarto)
Saving Graces—Shirley Sikes (Kansas Quarterly)
The Return of Captain Midnight—Stephen Solnick (Kansas Quar-
    terly)
The Twittering Machine—Peter Spielberg (Eureka Review)
A Length of Wire—Megan Staffel (Ploughshares)
Guerin and The Presidential Revue—Les Standiford (Pawn Re-
    view)
Shipping Out—Michael Stephens (Apple-wood Press)

Sacred Text—Daniel Stern (Confrontation)
Issac and The Undertaker's Daughter—Steve Stern (Epoch)
The Missouri River Mystery—Wayne Stubbs (Northwest Review)
Endless Short Story: Boxes—Ronald Sukenick (Fiction)
The Editor of A—Barry Targen (Georgia Review)
The Garden—Barry Targan (Salmagundi)
A Polish Joke—Alexander Theroux (Paris Review)
Something Monty Thought You Might Like—Lisa Thomas (Cimarron Review)
Night Baseball—William F. Van Wert (Northwest Review)
Macklin's Epigraphic Loss—Gordon Weaver (Iowa Review)
selection from *Homebase*—Shawn Wong (I. Reed Books)
Shahan—Bekir Yildiz (New Letters)

NONFICTION

"A Great Tug At the Heart"—Maggie Anderson, Irene McKinney, Jayne Anne Phillips (Trellis)
A Department Dies—Stephen Arkin (New England Review)
Xavier Speaking—Charles Baxter (Antioch Review)
Frank Stanford: After the Fact—John Biguenet (New Orleans Review)
On The Experience of Unteaching Poetry—Alice Bloom (Hudson Review)
When People Publish—Frederick Busch (Ohio Review)
TV's "Holocaust": A Sellout To Assimilation—Aviva Cantor (Lilith)
Where Samisdat Comes From—Meritt Clifton (Samisdat)
Late August Notebook Entry—Peter Cummings (Greenfield Review)
Floods of Painful Memories—Helene J. F. de Aguilar (Parnassus)
The New Hollywood: American Films of the 1970's—Morris Dickstein (Bennington Review)
The H.D. Book—Robert Duncan (Chicago Review)
Political Heroes and Political Education—Scott Edwards (North American Review)
Memory and Fiction—Seymour Epstein (Pulp)
Interview With Stanley Berne and Arlene Zekowski—Welch Everman (X, A Journal of the Arts)

Steps In No Direction At All—Ellen Ferber (Dustbooks)

Sparrows and Scholars: Literary Criticism and the Sanctification of Data—Harold Fromm (Georgia Review)

The Reason of Surrealism—Gene Frumkin (Chelsea)

Interview with John Gardner—Paris Review

Pasolini's Salient Swan Song—Dan Georgakas (Boss)

Tennessee Williams In Tangier—Mohamed Ghoukri (Cadmus Editions)

The End of All our Exploring—Laurence Goldstein (Michigan Quarterly)

The Poem as an Action of Field—William Harmon (Sewanee Review)

The Right Bread and The Left—Stratis Haviaras (Ploughshares)

Interview With Larry Eigner—(Stony Hills)

I Will Tell the Meaning of Barthelme—James Hiner (Denver Quarterly)

Album of Suicides—Stanley Kauffmann (American Scholar)

Through The Looking Glass—Mary Kinzie (Ploughshares)

The Transcendental Contemporary—Richard Kostelanetz (Michigan Quarterly Review)

Man, Nature and Mechanistic Systems—Sigmund Kvaloy (North American Review)

Isak Dinesen and Feminist Criticism—Florence Lewis (North American Review)

The Disappearance of Weldon Kees—Sharon M. Libera (Ploughshares)

selections from Red Spanish Notebook—Mary Low and Juan Brea (City Lights Books)

"Men in Dark Times": Three New British Poets—David Middleton (The Southern Review)

Notes Toward a Reading of Song of Myself—Edwin H. Miller (West Hill)

The Heart of A Boy—Henry Miller (Stroker)

Joey—Henry Miller (Capra)

Backward Into the Future—Carol Muske (Parnassus)

The Question of the Jews: A Study in Culture—Larry Nachman (Salmagundi)

Her Cargo: Adrienne Rich And The Common Language—Alicia Ostriker (American Poetry Review)

Rereading Creeley—Sherman Paul (Boundary 2)

R. W. Emerson, Tourist—Lois Rather (The Rather Press)

The Reconstruction of Genre as Entry into Conscious History—
    John Reilly (Black American Literature Forum)

In Consideration of Mathematical Poetry—Ernest Robson and Jet
    Wimp (Primary Press)

The Restoration of High Culture in Chile—Martha Rosler (Min-
    nesota Review)

A Talk on Wallace Stevens—Michael Ryan (Poetry)

Poetry, Community and Climax—Gary Snyder (Field)

A Mystery—Jim Solheim (New Letters)

Finders, Losers; Frank Stanford's Song of the South—Lorenzo
    Thomas (Sun & Moon)

The Gallery of Wild Ivory—Constantin Toiu (Spirit That Moves
    Us)

Georgia O'Keeffe: A Late Greeting—Charles Tomlinson (Hudson
    Review)

Lowell in the Classroom—Helen Vendler (Harvard Advocate)

Personism—Linda W. Wagner (Happiness Holding Tank)

In Praise of Waste—Kingsley Widmer (Partisan Review)

Longtime Californ'—Shawn Wong (Y'Bird)

from The Sudden Testimony—Arlene Zekowski (Delirium)

POETRY

Lines for Pancho Aguila. . .—Steve Abbott (Second Coming)

Antithesis—A. R. Ammons (Hampden-Sydney Poetry Review)

In Distrust of Poetry—Jack Anderson (Hanging Loose)

The Pleiades—Mary Barnard (Breitenbush Publications)

On The Bridge At Fourche Maline River—Jim Barnes (Long Pond
    Review)

The Circumcision of The Lord—Giuseppe Gioachino Belli (Chari-
    ton Review)

The Litany of Lies—Michael Benedikt (Kayak)

Eleven—Robert Bensen (Nocturnal Canary)

The Rind—Duane BigEagle (Workingman's Press)

All Too Little Pictures—Charles Black (Arizona Quarterly)

Before Sleep—Philip Booth (Poetry Northwest)

Out of the Ordinary—Philip Booth (Field)

Seconds Apart—Michael Brownstein (Bombay Gin)

Paiute Legs—Allan Burgis (Harpoon)
Treatment—Christopher Bursk (Xanadu)
Thought—Victor Contoski (New Rivers Press)
The Blue Anchor—Jane Cooper (Pequod)
The Silent Y—Henri Coulette (Gramercy Review)
Once The Sole Province—Douglas Crase (Nobodaddy Press)
Gerald Manley Hopkins Meets Walt Whitman In Heaven—Philip
    Dacey (Mickle Street)
Gold Ring Triad—Madeline DeFrees (Woman Poet)
Sobre Esta Praia—Jorge De Sena (Mudborn Press)
The General Mule Poems—Wayne Dodd (Georgia Review)
Where Is Gary?—Albert Drake (Centering)
It Was I Who Dreamt The Sailor—Stephen Dunn (Thunder
    Mountain Review)
Outfielder—Stephen Dunn (Bits Press)
Dreams of Ducks—Stephen Dunning (Croissant and Co.)
On Cognition—Nancy Esposito (Carolina Quarterly)
It's Not Only That A Person Is Born—Kate Farrell (Mississippi
    Review)
The Snake Hunters—Jane Flanders (Poet and Critic)
Monsters—Maria Flook (Antioch Review)
A World Rich In Anniversaries—Jean Follain (Grilled Flowers)
A Chimney Sweep's Remarks—Gunter Bruno Fuchs (Mundus
    Artium/Unicorn)
From Dread In The Eyes of Horses—Tess Gallagher (Ironwood)
1943—Marea Gordett (Chicago Review)
A Feather For Voltaire—Jorie Graham (Antaeus)
A Woman Is Talking To Death—Judy Grahn (American Poetry
    Review)
To Leave, Looking Over the Shoulder—Patrick Worth Gray
    (Annex)
Trakl: Seven Rosary Songs—Frank Graziano (Gravida)
The Painter's Model—Debra Greger (New Letters)
Sea Change—Debra Greger (American Poetry Review)
The Thrush Relinquished—Allen Grossman (Ploughshares)
Whose Heads Crowd Under Their Wings—Jan Haagenson (Racoon)
The Hermit—Daniel Halpern (American Poetry Review)
Running Home—Susan Hankla (Burning Deck)
Silences—Robert Hazel (Countryman Press)
The Deodand—Anthony Hecht (Kenyon Review)

Venetian Vespers—Anthony Hecht (Poetry)
All These Things—Judith Hemschemeyer (Hudson Review)
Common/Wealth—Fanny Howe (United Artists)
How Good It Is—David Ignatow (Ontario Review)
On Love—Lady Izumi (Montemora)
V—Marilyn Johnson (Field)
Childhood—Donald Justice (Antaeus)
Word Raid—Kenneth King (Paris Review)
Your Letter—Steve Kowit (Antenna)
The Invention of Winter—Ann Lauterbach (Poetry In Motion)
Work II—David Lenson (L'Epervier Press)
The Soothsayer—Denise Levertov (LA House)
Homage To James Joyce—John Logan (Modern Poetry Studies)
Poems For My Brother—John Logan (Holy Cow Press)
En Route—William Logan (New Letters)
Absolution—Susan Ludvigson (Epoch)
His Dying—Susan Ludvigson (Tinderbox Quarterly)
As You Stalk The Sleep of My Forgetting—Cleopatra Mathis
    (Pequod)
Journey In The Snow Season—Cleopatra Mathis (Columbia)
The Traveler—Cleopatra Mathis (Sheep Meadow Press)
A Month In The Country—J. D. McClatchy (Four Quarters)
Christmas Poem—Thomas McGrath (Kayak)
Uses of the Lost Poets—Thomas McGrath (Praxis)
Twilight—Samuel Menasche (Maxy's Journal)
Charles On Fire—James Merrill (Poets On)
Gingerbread Ladies—Judith Moffett (Shenandoah)
Century Poem—Frederick Morgan (Hudson Review)
Bruce Dern In A Film Playing Myself—Herbert Morris (Alembic
    Press)
How To Improve Your Personality—Herbert Morris (New Eng-
    land Review)
The Branch—Stanley Moss (Graham House)
The Spy—Royal Murdoch (Fag Rag)
The Fault—Carol Muske (Missouri Review)
Low Calvary—Gloria Oden (SCOP Publications)
Eggs—Sharon Olds (New England Review)
Nurse Whitman—Sharon Olds (Carleton Miscellany)
Nightpoem—Gregory Orr (New England Review)
Part of An Old Story—Greg Pape (Quarterly West)

The Ashes of Gramsci—Pier Paolo Pasolini (Paris Review)
Near The End of Good Weather—Hames Pendergast (Ruthra)
Reparation (Matthew 1:18–25)—Reynolds Price (Ontario Review)
Mendota State—Ruthellen Quillen (Sibyl-Child)
Twenty-Eight Years—Miklos Radnoti (Minnesota Review)
Marriage—David Ray (The Spirit That Moves Us)
A Woman Dead In Her Forties—Adrienne Rich (13th Moon)
Embers—Richard Bonan (USI Workshop)
Winter Love Poem To the Memory of Keats—Gibbons Ruark
    (Graham House)
Frank 207—Raphel Rudnik (Open Places)
Her Horse In A Circle of Flowers—Mary Ruefle (Porch)
All The Time—Michael Ryan (Ploughshares)
The Avenues—David St. John (Poetry)
Lunch—David St. John (Paris Review)
Accidental Weather—Sherod Santos (Missouri Review)
W.C.W.'s Moment of Suspense—Sherod Santos (Iowa Review)
Cutting Out A Dress—Dennis Schmitz (Field)
We Are Just Kinda That Way—Ntozake Shange (Beloit Poetry
    Journal)
The Counter-Example—David Shapiro (New York Arts Journal)
Where I Live—Richard Shelton (Beyond Baroque)
The Re-Purchase—Paul Shiplett (Broken Whisker Studio)
Gazetteer—Jon Sisson (Antaeus)
The Actual Weight of Light—Dave Smith (Thunder Mountain
    Review)
Abscences—William Stafford (Field)
Thinking In The All-Nighter—William Stafford (Silverfish Review)
Returning The Evidence—Sue Standing (Ohio Review)
Alternatives In Costa Rica—Robert Steck (Aspect)
Seoul—Michael Stephens (# Magazine)
Joseph Pockets—Gerald Stern (Northwest Review)
Knowing—Sidney Sulkin (Southwest Review)
Primal Scene—Brian Swann (Southwest Review)
Spider Woman—Brian Swann (Antioch Review)
Night Visits With The Family—May Swenson (Shenandoah)
In The Realm of the Ignition—James Tate (Antaeus)
To Raphael, Angel of Happy Meeting—Jean Valentine (Barat
    Review)
Cheeseburger Serenade—Paul Violi (Hard Press)

To An Impoverished God—Renee Vivien (Naiad Press)

The Gymnast—Ellen Voigt (Ploughshares)

Your Fortune: A Cold Reading—David Wagoner (Kayak)

Function of Blizzard—Robert Penn Warren (Antaeus)

Swimming In The Pacific—Robert Penn Warren (American Poetry Review)

Sharing Our Dreams—Dara Wier (New Virginia Review)

My Life On The Road With Bread and Water—Nancy Willard (Kayak)

Form and Theory of Poetry—Miller Williams (Cimarron Review)

Bernini's Proserpine—A. Williamson (Ploughshares)

Elegy: Noah's Crow—John Witte (Iowa Review)

Childhood's Body—Charles Wright (Crazyhorse)

Homage To Paul Cezanne—Charles Wright (Grilled Flowers Press)

For Steve Royal—Bill Zavatsky (Marxist Perspective)

🔥 🔥 🔥

OUTSTANDING SMALL PRESSES

(These presses made or received nominations for the 1980–81 edition of *The Pushcart Prize*. See the *International Directory of Little Magazines and Small Presses*, Dustbooks, Box 1056, Paradise, CA 95969, for subscription rates, manuscript requirements and a complete international listing of small presses.)

The Agni Review, P. O. Box 329, Cambridge, MA 02138
Ahsahta Press, Dept. of English, Boise State Univ., Boise, ID 83725
Akiba Press, Box 13086, Oakland, CA 94611
Akwesasne Notes—Mohawk Nation, Rooseveltown, NY 13683
Alcatraz, 354 Hoover Rd., Santa Cruz, CA 95065
Aldebaran, Roger Williams College, Bristol, RI 02809
Aldebaran Review, 2209 California, Berkeley, CA 94703
Alembic, 1744 Slaterville Rd., Ithaca, NY 14850
Aleph Magazine, 7319 Willow Ave., Takoma Park, MD 20012
Alleghany Press, 111 North 10 St., Olean, NY 14780
The Altadena Review, P. O. Box 212, Altadena, CA 91001
The Alternative Press, Grindstone City, MI 48467
American-Canadian Publishers Inc., Drawer 2078, Portales, NM 88130
American Scholar, 1811 Q St., NW, Wasington, D.C. 20009
American Studies Press, Inc., 13511 Palmwood Ln., Tampa, FL 33624
Annex 21, Univ. of Nebraska at Omaha, 60th and Dodge St., Omaha, NB 68182
Another Chicago Magazine—Thunder's Mouth Press, 1152 S. East St., Oak Park, IL 60304
The Antares Foundation, Box 14051, San Francisco, CA 94114
Antaeus, 1 West 30th St., New York, NY 10001
Antenna, 5014 Narragansett #6, San Diego, CA 92107
Anthropos Theophoros, P. O. Box 3379, San Francisco, CA 94119
The Antioch Review, P. O. Box 148, Yellow Springs, OH 45387

Apalachee Quarterly, P. O. Box 20106, Tallahassee, FL 32304

Appearances, c/o Wite, 165 W. 26th St., New York, NY 10001

Apple Zaba Press, 333 Orizaba, Long Beach, CA 90814

Apple-wood Press, Box 2870, Cambridge, MA 02139

American Poetry Review, 1616 Walnut St., Philadelphia, PA 19103

Arete Press, 3527 North Mills, Claremont, CA 91711

Ark River Review, c/o Sobin, Box 14 WSU, Wichita, KS 67208

Arizona Quarterly, Univ. of Arizona, Tucson, AZ 85721

The Ark, Box 322 Times Square Station, New York, NY 10036

Charles Aronson, RR1 11520 Bixby Hill Rd., Arcade, NY 14009

Artful Dodge, 640 E. New York St., Indianapolis, IN 46202

Artichoke Press, 3274 Parkhurst, Rancho Palos Verdes, CA 90274

Arts. End Books, P. O. Box 162, Newton, MA 02168

As Is, 6302 Owen Pl., Bethesda, MD 20034

Ashford Press, RR1, Box 128, Ashford, CT 06278

Aspect, 13 Robinson St., Somerville, MA 02145

Aspen Anthology, P. O. Box 3185, Aspen, CO 81611

Assembling, P. O. Box 1967, Brooklyn, NY 11202

Associated Creative Writers, 9231 Molly Woods Ave., La Mesa, CA 92041

Astro Black Roots, Box 46, Sioux Falls, SD 57101

Attention Please, 708 Inglewood Dr., Broderick, CA 95605

Auriga, c/o Niles, Box F, Candlelight Ct., Clifton Park, NY 12065

Author! Author! 210 E. 58th St., New York, NY 10022

Back Bay View, c/o 33 Kaven Dr., Randolph, MA 02368

Back Door, P. O. Box 481, Athens, OH 45701

Baltic Ave. Press, 1045 Fulton Ave. SW, Birmingham, AL 35211

Barat Review, Barat College, Lake Forest, IL 60045

Bard Press, 799 Greenwich St., New York, NY 10014

The Barnwood Press, RR#2, Box 11-C, Daleville, IN 47334

William L. Bauhan, Dublin, NH 03444

The Bellingham Review, 412 N. State St., Bellingham, WA 98225

Beloit Poetry Journal, P. O. Box 2, Beloit, WI 53511

Bennington Review, Bennington College, Bennington, VT 05281

Berkeley Poets Cooperative, P. O. Box 459, Berkeley, CA 94701

Bertrand Russell Today, P. O. Box 431, Jerome Sta., Bronx, NY 10468

beyond baroque foundation, 681 Venice Blvd., Old Venice City Hall, P. O. Box 806, Venice, CA 90291

Bicentennial Era Enterprises, P. O. Box 1148, Scappoose, OR 97056

Billy Goat, c/o R. Hill, Clemson Univ., Clemson, SC 29631

Bits Press, Dept. of English, Case Western Reserve, Cleveland, OH 44106

Black American Literature Forum, Parsons Hall 237, Indiana State Univ., Terre Haute, IN 47809

Black Buzzard Press, c/o Strahan, 2213 Shorefield Rd., Apt. 631, Wheaton, MD 20902

Black Hole School of Poethnics, Long Island Campus, Box 555, Port Jefferson, NY 11777

Black Maria, 815 W. Wrightwood, Chicago, IL 60614

The Black Warrior Review, P. O. Box 2936, University, AL 35486

Blacksburg, Box 186, Brunswick, ME 04011

Blind Beggar Press, Inc., 163 W. 125th St., New York, NY

Bloodroot, Inc., P. O. Box 891, Grand Forks, ND 58201

Blue Building, 2800 Rutland, Des Moines, IA 50311

Blue Horse, 391 Balencia St., Suite 303, San Francisco, CA 94103

Blue Moon Press, Dept. of English, Univ. of Arizona, Tucson, AZ 85721

The Blue Ridge Review, P. O. Box 1425, Charlottesville, VA 22902

Blue Unicorn, 22 Avon Rd., Kensington, CA 94707

Boardwell-Kloner Press, 323 S. Franklin, Room 804 (B-69) Chicago, IL 60606

Bombay Gin, Naropa Inst., 1111 Pearl St., Boulder, CO 80302

Boss, Box 370, Madison Square Station, New York, NY 10010

Boundary, Dept. English, Suny, Binghampton, NY 13903

Box 749 Magazine, Box 749 Old Chelsea Station, New York, NY 10011

Brasch & Brasch, Publishers, Inc., c/o M. Essex, 220A West B St., Ontario, CA 91762

Breitenbush Books, P. O. Box 02137, Portland, OR 97207

Broken Whisker Studio, 4225 Seeley, P. O. Box 54, Downers Grove, IL 60515

Buckle, Dept. of English, State Univ. College, 1300 Elmwood Ave., Buffalo, NY 14222

Buffalo books, c/o Thaballa, 34 Sonora Way, Corte Madera, CA 94925

Burning Deck, 71 Elmgrove Ave., Providence, RI 02906

Cadmus Editions, P. O. Box 4725, Santa Barbara, CA 93103

Cafe Solo, 750 N. Pomo St., San Luis Obispo, CA 93401

Calamus Books, Box 689 Cooper Station, New York, NY 10003

Caliban, Box 797, Amhurst, MA 01002

California Free Poetry, 2480 Escalonia Ct., San Jose, CA 95121

Callaloo, Dept. of English, Univ. of Kentucky, Lexington, KY 40506

Calyx, Route 2, Box 118, Corvallis, OR 97330

The Cambric Press, 912 Strowbridge Dr., Huron, OH 44839

Camera Obscura, P. O. Box 4517, Berkeley, CA

Canto, 9 Bartlett St., Andover, MA 01810

The Cape Rock, Southeast Missouri State Univ., Cape Girardeau, MI 63701

Capra Press, P. O. Box 2068, Santa Barbara, CA 93120

Carleton Miscellany, Carleton College, Northfield, MN 55059

Carpenter Press, Route 4, Pomeroy, OH 45769

Carolina Quarterly, Univ. of N. Carolina, Chapel Hill, NC 27514

Cedar Rock, 1121 Madeline, New Braunfels, TX 78130

Celestial Gifts, P. O. Box 33, Estes Park, CO 80517

Celestial Otter Press, c/o J. Sennett, P. O. Box 152, Mount Prospect, IL 60056

Center, P. O. Box 7494, Old Albuquerque Station, Albuquerque, NM 87194

Center for the Art of Living, 2203 N. Sheffield, Chicago, IL 60614

Center for Southern Folklore, 1216 Peabody Ave., P. O. Box 40105, Memphis, TN 38104

Center for Study of Multiple Gestation, Suite 463-5, 333 E. Superior St., Chicago, IL 60611

Centering, c/o F. R. Thomas, Dept. of American Thought and Language, Michigan State Univ., East Lansing, MI 48824

Chandler & Sharp Publishers, Inc., 11A Commercial Blvd., Novato, CA 94947

Charisma Press, St. Francis Seminary, P. O. Box 263, Andover, MA 01810

Chariton Review, Northeast Missouri State Univ., Kirksville, MO 63501

Chelsea, P. O. Box 5880 Grand Central Station, New York, NY 10017

Chicago Review, Univ. of Chicago, Faculty Exchange, Box C, Chicago, IL 60637

Choomia, P. O. Box 40322, Tucson, AZ 85719

Chouteau Review, Box 10016, Kansas City, MO 64111

The Chowder Review, P. O. Box 33, Wollaston, MA 02170

Christophers Books, P. O. Box 2457, Santa Barbara, CA 93120

Cimarron Review, 208 Life Science East, Oklahoma State Univ., Stillwater, OK 74074

Cincinneti Poetry Review, 248 McMacker Hall, Univ. Cincinnati, Cincinnati, OH 45221

City Lights Press, 261 Columbus Ave., San Francisco, CA 94701

City Miner Mag., P. O. Box 176, Berkeley, CA 94705

Clarence House Publishers, 1820 Union St., Suite 136, San Francisco, CA 94123

Cliff Catton, P. O. Box 341, Cairo, NY 12413

Coast to Coast Books, 2934 NE 16th Ave., Portland, OR 97212

Coffee Break, P. O. Box 103, Burley, WV 98322

Coker Books, 3530 Timmons, Box 395, Houston, TX 77027

Earl M. Coleman Enterprises, Inc. Publishers, P. O. Box 143, Pine Plains, NJ 12567

Colorado Quarterly, Univ. Colorado, Boulder, CO 80309

Columbia, 404 Dodge, Columbia Univ., New York, NY 10027

The Combined Asian-American Resources Project, Inc., P. O. Box 18621, Seattle, WA 98118

Community Writer's Workshop, The Univ. of Nebraska, Box 688, Omaha, NE 68101

Communication Creativity, 5644 La Jolla Blvd., La Jolla, CA 92037

Confrontation, Dept. of English, Long Island Univ., Brooklyn, NY 11201

The Connecticut Quarterly, P. O. Box 68, Enfield, CT 06082

Contact II, P. O. Box 451, Bowling Green Sta., New York, NY 10004

Contraband Press, P. O. Box 4073 Sta. A., Portland, ME 04101

Copper Canyon Press, P. O. Box 271, Port Townsend, WA 98368

The Cotton Lane Press, 2 Cotton Lane, Augusta, GA 30902

Cottonwood Review Press, Box J Student Union, Lawrence, KS 66045

The Countryman Press, Taftsville, VT 05073

Crawl Out Your Window Magazine, 704 Nob Ave., Del Mar, CA 92014

Crazy Horse, Dept. English, Murray State Univ., Murray, KY 42071

Cream City Review, Univ. of Wisconsin—Milwaukee, Dept. of
English, P. O. Box 413, Milwaukee, WI 53201

Creative Music Foundation, Box 671, Woodstock, NY 12498

Croissant & Company, Route 1, Box 51, Athens, OH 45701

Cross Country, P. O. Box 21081, Woodhaven, NY 11421

Cross Country Press Ltd., 3553 Aylmer St., Apt. 6, Montreal,
Canada H2X209

Cross-Cultural Communications, 239 Wynsum Ave., Merrick, NY
11566

Crosscut Saw Press, c/o Book People, 2940 7th St., Berkeley, CA
94710

Croton Review—Croton Council on the Arts, Inc., P. O. Box 277,
Corton-On-Hudson, NY 10520

Crowfoot Press, P. O. Box 7631 Liberty Station, Ann Arbor, MI
48107

Cultural Custodial Service, 505 N. Maple Ln., Prospect Hts., IL
60070

Cultural Watchdog Newsletter, 6 Winslow Rd., White Plains, NY
10606

Curbstone Press, 321 Jackson St., Willimantic, CT 06226

Cutbank, Dept. English, Univ. Montana, Missoula, MT 59812

Dacotah Territory, P. O. Box 775, Moorhead, MN 56560

Dark Horse, 28 School St., Somerville, MA 02143

Dawn Valley Press, Box 58, New Wilmington, PA 16142

Delirium—Libra Press, Box 341, Wataga, IL 61488

Denver Quarterly, Univ. Denver, Denver, CO 80208

Departures, Box 1436, Boulder, CO 80306

Descant, Texas Christian Univ., Fort Worth, TX 76129

The Devil's Millhopper, Box 178, Lacrosse, FL 32658

Dialogue, Bard College, Annendale-On-Hudson, NY 12504

Downtown Poets, G.P.O. Box 1720, Brooklyn, NY 11217

Dryad Press, Presidio P. O. Box 29161, San Francisco, CA 94129

Duende Press/Tooth of Time Press, Box 571, Placitas, NM 87043

Durak, 166 S. Sycamore St., Los Angeles, CA 90036

Dustbooks, Box 100, Paradise, CA 95969

East River Anthology, 75 Gates Ave., Montclair, NJ 07042

Eleven, 340 Calkins Hall, Hofstra Univ., Hempstead, NY 11550

En Passant/Poetry, 1906 Brant Rd., Wilmington, DE 19810

Epoch, 245 Goldwin Smith Hall, Cornell Univ., Ithaca, NY 14850
Eureka Review Dept. English, Univ. Cincinnati, Cincinnati, OH
    45221
The Evener, Putney, VT 05346
Executive Sweet Enterprises, P. O. Box 445, Pasadena, CA 91102
Exit, c/o F. Judge, RD #1, Box 339, Glenmont, NY 12077
Expedition Press, 420 Davis, Kalamazoo, MI 49007

Fag Rag, Box 331 Kenmore Station, Boston, MA 02215
Fallen Angel Press, 1913 W. McNichols #C-6, Highland Park, MI
    48203
Feminist Studies, c/o Women's Studies Program, Univ. of Mary-
    land, College Park, MD 20902
FDU Press, Fairleigh Dickinson Univ., Madison, NJ 07940
Fiction International, St. Lawrence Univ., Canton, NY 13617
Field, Rice Hall, Oberlin College, Oberlin, OH 44074
Fifth Sun, 1134-B Chelsea Ave., Santa Monica, CA 90403
Figment, c/o J. Bloom, 34 Andrew St., Newton, MA 02161
Firelands Art Review, Firelands Campus, Huron, OH 44839
W. D. Firestone Press, 1313 S. Jefferson Ave., Springfield, MO
    65807
Floating Island Publications, P. O. Box 516, Pt. Reyes Station, CA
    94956
Florida Arts Gazette, P. O. Box 397, Ft. Lauderdale, FL 33302
Flying Buttress Publications, P. O. Box 254, Endicott, NY 13760
Format Magazine, 405 S. 7th St., St. Charles, IL 60174
4 Zoas Press, RFD Ware, MA 01082
Free Passage, 670 Main Ave., Fargo, ND 58103
Frontiers, Univ. of Colorado, Boulder, CO 80309
Fulcourte Press, P. O. Box 1961, Decatur, GA 30031
Full Fathom Five, 40 Yorkshire Dr., Oakland, CA 94618

Galaxy of Verse, 200 S. Chandler St., Fort Worth, TX 76111
Gamma Books, 307 Willow Ave., Ithaca, NY 14850
The Gardyloo Press, 736 University Ave., Madison, WI 53706
Gargoyle, 40 St. John St., Jamaica Plain, MA 02130
Gargoyle, P. O. Box 57206, Washington, DC 20037
Gay Community News, 22 Bromfield St., Boston, MA 02108
Georgia Review, Univ. of Georgia, Athens, GA 30602
Gilbert, P. O. Box 120841 Acklen Station, Nashville, TN 37212

Glitch, 515 Lamar, Apt. 271, Arlington, TX 76011

Gondwana Books, P. O. Box 407, Calistoga, CA 94515

Graham House Review, Bishop North, Phillips Academy, Andover, MA 01810

C. P. Graham Press, P. O. Box 5, Keswick, VA 22947

The Gramercy Review, P. O. Box 15362, Los Angeles, CA 90015

Grass-Hooper Press, 4030 Connecticut St., St. Louis, MO 63116

Gravida, Box 118, Bayville, NY 11709

Great Lakes Publishing, P. O. Box 461, Hudson, OH 44236

Great River Review, 59 Seymour Ave SE, Minneapolis, MN 55414

The Greenfield Review, Greenfield Center, NY 12833

Greenhouse Review, 126 Escalona Dr., Santa Cruz, CA 95060

Greens Magazine, Box 313, Detroit, MI 48231

Greensboro Review, Dept. of English, Univ. of North Carolina, Greensboro, NC 27412

Griffon House Publications, The Bagehot Council, P. O. Box 81, Whitestone, NY 11357

Grilled Flowers Press, P. O. Box 809, Iowa City, IA 52240

Grito Del Sol, 2150 Shattuck Ave., Berkeley, CA 94704

Grub Street, P. O. Box 1, Winterhill Branch, Somerville, MA 02145

Guest #, c/o B. Breger, 86 E. 3rd St., New York, NY 10003

Gusto Press, 2960 Philip Ave., Bronx, NY 10465

The Hampden-Sydney Poetry Review, P. O. Box 126, Hampden-Sydney, VA 23943

Hand Book, 50 Spring St., New York, NY 10012

Hanging Loose Press, 231 Wyckoff St., Brooklyn, NY 11217

Happiness Holding Tank, 1790 Grand River, Okemos, MI 48864

Hard Press, 340 E. 11th St., New York, NY 10003

Harian Creative Press, 47 Hyde Blvd., Ballston Spa, NY 12020

Harpoon, P. O. Box 2581, Anchorage, AK 99510

Hawk-Wind, Box 379, Mareksan, WI 53946

Heperidian Press, 105 Riverside Dr., New York, NY 10024

Ira Herman, 915 W. 4 St., Huntington, WV 25701

Hidden People Press, P. O. Box 243, Narragansett, RI 02882

High Performance, 240 S. Broadway, Los Angeles, CA 90012

Hiram Poetry Review, P. O. Box 162, Hiram, OH 44234

Holy Cow, P. O. Box 618, Minneapolis, MN 55440

Home Planet News, P. O. Box 415 Stuyvesant Station, New York NY 10009
Hudson-Browning Printery, 431 Abbott #6, East Lansing, MI 48823
Hudson Review, 65 E. 55th St., New York, NY 10022
Huerfano, 5730 N. Via Elena, Tucson, AZ 85718

I. Reed Books, 285 E. 3rd St., New York, NY 10009
Illuminations, 1321-L Dwight Way, Berkeley, CA 94702
Image Magazine, P. O. Box 28048, St. Louis, MO 63119
Images, Dept of English, Wright State Univ., Dayton, OH 45435
In A Nutshell/Hibiscus Press, Box 22248, Sacramento, CA 95822
In Between Books, P. O. Drawer T, Sausalito, CA 94965
In Business, Box 323, Emmaus, PA 18049
Indian Publications, 1869 2nd Ave., New York, NY 10029
Indiana Writes, 110 Morgan Hall, Indiana Univ., Bloomington, IN 47401
Inlet, Virginia Wesleyan College, Wesleyan Dr., Norfolk, VA 23502
Intermedia, P. O. Box 31-464, San Francisco, CA 94131
Intermuse, 1412 Roxburgh, East Lansing, MI 48823
International Galleries, 233 N. Pleasant St., P. O. Box 657, Amherst, MA 01002
Interstate, P. O. Box 7068, U.T. Sta., Austin, TX 78712
Introduction to Statistics, Univ. Statistical Tracts, 75-19 171st St., Flushing, NY 11366
Inwood Press, c/o Teachers and Writers Collabrative, 84 Fifth Ave., New York, NY 10011
Iowa Review, 308 EPB, The Univ. of Iowa, Iowa City, IA 52240
Ironwood, P. O. Box 40907, Tucson, AZ 85717
Ithaca House, 108 N. Plain St., Ithaca, NY 14850

Jack Green, Box 3, New York, NY 10003
Jam To-Day, P. O. Box 249, Northfield, VT 05663
Alice James Books, 138 Mt. Auburn St., Cambridge, MA 02138
Jazz Press, 2316 Glendon Ave., Los Angeles, CA 90064
JC/DC Cartoons Ink, 5536 Fruitland Rd. NE, Salem, OR 97301
Jelm Mountain Publications, 304 S. 3rd St., Laramie, WY 82070
A Journal of the Arts, P. O. Box 2648, Harrisburg, PA 17105

Jump River Review, 819 Single Ave., Wausau, WI 54401

Kaldron, 441 North 6th St., Grover City, CA 93433
Kansas Quarterly, Denison Hall, Kansas State Univ., Manhattan,
    KS 66506
Kayak, 325 Ocean View, Santa Crux, Santa Cruz, CA 95064
Kelsey St. Press, 2824 Kelsey St., Berkeley, CA 94705
Kent Publications, 18301 Halsted St., Northridge, CA 91324
The Kenyon Review, Kenyon College, Gambier, OH 43022
King Publications, P. O. Box 19332, Washington, DC 20036
Kitchen Harvest Press, 3N681 Bittersweet Dr., St. Charles, IL
    60174
Konglomerati Press, P. O. Box 5001, Gulfport, FL 33737
Kosmos, 258 Polk St., San Francisco, CA 94109

La Confluencia, P. O. Box 409, Albuquerque, NM 87103
La House, P. O. Box 41110, Los Angeles, CA 90041
Lake Street Review, c/o CD/DM Books, Box 488 Powderhorn
    Station, Minneapolis, NY 55407
Lame Johnny Press, Box 66, Hermosa, SD 57744
Landscape, P. O. Box 7107, Berkeley, CA 94707
L-A-N-G-U-A-G-E, c/o Bernstein, 464 Amsterdam Ave., New
    York, NY 10024
Lapis Educational Assoc. Inc., Box 1416, Homewood, IL 60430
Laurel Review, West Virginia Wesleyan College, Buckhannon,
    WV 26201
Stuart Lavin, RFD Campbell Rd., Ware, MA 01082
Lawton Press, 673 Pelham Rd., New Rochelle, NY 10801
L'Èpervier Press, 762 Hayes #15, Seattle, WA 98109
The Lightning Tree, P. O. Box 1837, Sante Fe, NM 87501
Lilith, 250 W. 57th, #1328, New York, NY 10019
Lintel Press, Box 34, St. George, Staten Island, NY 10301
L.I.P.C. Inc., P. O. Box 773, Huntington, NY 11743
The Literary Monitor, 1070 Noriega #7, Sunnyvale, CA 94086
Little River Press, 10 Lowell Ave., Westfield, MA 01085
Long Measure Press, P. O. Box 1618, Meraux, LA 70075
Long Pond Review, Dept. of English, Suffolk Community College,
    Selden, NY 11784
Lore Publications, Box 9, Prospect Hill, NC 27314

Lost Roads Publishing Co., P. O. Box 210, Fayetteville, AR

The Louisville Review, Univ. of Louisville, Louisville, KY 40208

Lowlands Review, 6048 Perrier, New Orleans, CA 70118

Luna Bisonte Prods, 137 Leland Ave., Columbus, OH 43214

Lynx House Press, P. O. Box 800, Amherst, MA 01002

Machete, Box 4225 St. Anthony Falls Station, Minneapolis, MN 55414

Maelstrom Review, P. O. Box 8087, Long Beach, CA 90808

Mag City, 437 East 12 St., #26, New York, NY 10009

Magic Change, 1923 Finchley Ct., Schaumburg, IL 60194

Main Trend—A.I.C.U., Box 344 Cooper Station, New York, NY 10003

Malahat Review, P. O. Box 1700, Victoria, B.C. Canada V8W272

The Massachusetts Review, Memorial Hall, Univ. of Massachusetts, Amherst, MA 01002

MATI, c/o E. Mihopoulos, 5548 N. Sawyer Ave., Chicago, IL 60625

Maxys Journal, 216 W. Academy St., Lonoke, AK 72086

MD Writers Council, 1110 St. Paul St., Baltimore, MD 21202

Merging Media, c/o R. Du Bois, 59 Sandra Ci. A-3, Westfield, NJ 07090

Merlin Papers, P. O. Box 5602, San Jose, CA 95150

Mesevydale Publishing Co., P. O. Box 558, Provo, UT 84601

Metis Press, 815 W. Wrightwood, Chicago, IL 60614

Micah Publications, 255 Humphrey St., Marblehead, MA 01945

The Michigan Quarterly Review, The Univ. of Michigan, Ann Arbor, MI 48106

The Mickle Street Review, 330 Mickle St., Camden, NJ 08102

Micronesia, c/o Erin St. Mawr, Box 356, Randolph, VT 05060

The Minnesota Review, Box 211, Bloomington, IN 47401

Mississippi Mud, 3125 SE Van Water St., Portland, OR 97222

Mississippi Review, Univ. of Southern Mississippi, Southern Station, Box 5144, Hattiesburg, MS 39401

Mississippi Valley Review, Dept. of English, Western Illinois Univ., Macomb, IL 61455

The Missouri Review, Dept. of English, 231 Arts and Sciences, Univ. of Missouri, Columbia, MO 65211

Minted Breed, Box 42, Delray Beach, FL 33444

MJG Company, P. O. Box 7743, Midland, TX 79703

M. N. Publishers, Route 2, Box 55, Bonnerdale, AR 71933

Modern Poetry Studies, 207 Delaware Ave., Buffalo, NY 19202

Modus Operandi, 14332 Howard Rd., Dayton, MD 21036

Momentum Press, 512 Hill St. #4, Santa Monica, CA 90405

Monday Books, Box 543, Cotati, CA 94928

Montana Review c/o Ives 520 South Second St., Missoula, MT 59801

The Montemora Foundation, Inc., Box 336 Cooper Station, New York, NY 10003

Mouth of The Dragon, 242 E. 15th St., New York, NY 10003

Mt. Alverno Press, Box 5143, Santa Monica, CA 90405

Mudborn Press, 209 W. De la Guerra, Santa Barbara, CA 93101

M. F. Murphy Pub., Co., 2770 W. Placita Del Santo, Tucson, AZ 85704

Mundus Artium, P. O. Box 688, Richardson, TX 75080

Magazine, c/o Berger, 86 East 3 St. #3A, New York, NY 10003

Naiad Press, Inc. 7800 Westside Dr., Weatherby Lake, MO 65152

Naturegraph Publishers, Inc., P. O. Box 1075, Happy Camp, CA 97034

Nethula Publishing House, Inc., P. O. Box 50368, Washington, DC 20004

New Boston Review, Boston Critic, Inc., 77 Sacramento St., Somerville, MA 02143

New England Review, Box 170, Hanover, NH 03755

New Hearer c/o M. Wentworth, 3035 Courts Isle, Flint, MI 48504

New Letters, 5346 Charlotte, Univ. of Missouri, Kansas City, Kansas City, MO 64110

New Magazine, P. O. Box 12, Boyes Hot Springs, CA 95416

New Mexico Humanities Review, Humanities Dept., New Mexico Tech., Cocorro, NM 87801

New Orleans Review, Loyola Univ., P. O. Box 195, New Orleans, LA 70118

New Poets Series, 541 Picadilly Rd., Baltimore, MD 21204

New Renaissance, 9 Heath Rd., Arlington, MA 02174

New Rivers Press, 1602 Selby Ave., St. Paul, MN 55104

New York Literary Press, New York Literary Society, 417 W. 56th St., New York, NY 10019

New York Quarterly, P. O. Box 2415 G. Central Sta., New York, NY 10017

New York State Waterways Project, Ten Penny Players, Inc., 799 Greenwich St., New York, NY 10014

Newscribes, 1223 Newkirk Ave., Brooklyn, NY 11230

Newsletter, Allentown Community Center, 111 Elmwood Ave., Buffalo, NY 14201

The Niagara Magazine, 195 Hicks St., Brooklyn, NY 11201

Nickel Review, Box 1066, Clinton Sq. Sta., Syracuse, NY 13201

No Deadlines Publisher, 241 Bonita, Portola Valley, CA 94025

Nobadaddy Press, 100 College Hill Rd., Clinton, NY 13323

Nocturnal Canary Press, 6 8th St., Oneonta, NY

The North American Review, Univ. of Northern Iowa, Cedar Falls, IA 50613

Northwest Review, Univ. of Oregon, Eugene, OR 97403

Northwoods Journal, c/o Paul Hodges, Route 5, Box 34, Mt. Airy, NC 27030

The Not Guilty Press, P. O. Box 2563, Grand Central Station, New York, NY 10017

Noumenon/Interstate, P. O. Box 7068, Austin, TX 78712

NRG, 228 SE 26th ST., Portland, OR 97214

O Press, c/o M. Lally, 190 A. Duane St., New York, NY 10013

Oconee Review, P. O. Box 6232, Athens, GA 30604

The Ohio Journal, 164 W. 17 Ave., Columbus, OH 43210

The Ohio Review, Ellis Hall, Ohio Univ., Athens, OH 45701

Only Prose, c/o J. Weinstein, 54 E. 17 St., New York, NY 10003

Ontario Review, 9 Honey Brook Dr., Princeton, N.J. 08540

Open Places, Box 2085 Stephens College, Columbia, MO 65201

ORFDA Press, 838 A Wisconsin St., Oshkosh, WI 54901

Osiris, Box 297, Deerfield, MA 01342

Out There Press, 5-W 156 W. 27th St., New York, NY 10001

Outerbridge, Dept. of English, College of Staten Island, 715 Ocean Terrace, Staten Island, NY 10301

Owl Creek Press, 520 S. Second W., Missoula, MT 59801

Ox Head Press, 414 N. 6th St., Marshall, MN 56258

Oyster Press, 103 S. Soledad St., Santa Barbara, CA 93103

Pacific Poetry and Fiction Review, Dept. of English and Comparative Literature, San Diego State Univ., San Diego, CA 92182

Palaemon Press LTD, P. O. Box 7527 Renolda Station, Winston-Salem, NC 27109

Paper Air Magazine, 825 Morris Rd., Blue Bell, PA 19422

Paragraph—The Antares Foundation, Box 14051, San Francisco, CA 94114

Paranoid Publications, 3928 N. St. Louis, Chicago, IL 60618

Paris Review, 541 E. 72nd St., New York, NY 10021

Parnassus: Poetry In Review, 205 W. 89th St., New York, NY 10024

Partisan Review, 128 Bay State Rd., Boston, NJ 02215

Parthenon Press, 7450 Bellfort #40, Houston, TX 77087

The Pawn Review, P. O. Box 5255, Overland, Park, KS 66204

Paycock Press, P. O. Box 57206, Washington, DC 00037

Pembroke Magazine, Box 60 PSU, Pembroke, NC 28372

Penmaen Press, Ltd., Old Sudbury Rd., Lincoln, MA 01773

Pentagram Press, Box 379, Markesan, WI 53946

Penumbra, Box 794, Portsmouth, NH 03901

The Penumbra Press, Route 1, Lisbon, IA 52253

People & Energy, 2408 18 St. NW, Washington, DC 20009

The Perishable Press Limited, P. O. Box 7, Mt. Horeb, WI 53272

Perivale Press, 13830 Erwin St., Van Nuys, CA 91401

Permafrost, Univ. of Alaska, Fairbanks, AK 99701

Petrarch Press, c/o D. Friedman, 22 Grove St., New York, NY 10014

Phantasm, P. O. Box 3606, Chico, CA 95927

Phoebe, 4400 University Dr., Fairfax, VA 22030

Phone-A-Poem, Box 193, Cambridge, MA 02141

Phosophene Magazine, P. O. Box 66842, Houston, TX 77006

Pig Iron Press, P. O. Box 237, Youngston, OH 44501

Pikestaff Publications, Inc., P. O. Box 127, Normal, IL 61761

Plainsong, P. O. Box 0245 College Heights, Bowling Green, KY 42101

Ploughshares, P. O. Box 529, Cambridge, MA 02129

Plucked Chicken, P. O. Box 5941, Chicago, IL 60680

Plum Magazine, 549 W. 113 St., #12, New York, NY 10025

Plumbers Ink, P. O. Box 2565, Taos, NM 87571

Poet and Critic, 203 Ross Hall, Iowa State Univ., Ames IA 50011

Poetry, P. O. Box 4348, Chicago, IL 60680

Poetry Forum, 77 Lakewood Pl., Highland Park, IL 60035

Poetry Northwest, 4045 Brooklyn NE, Univ. Washington, Seattle, WA 98195

Poetry Now, 3118 K St., Eureka, CA 95501

Poetry Project Newsletter, St. Mark's Church, 10th St. and 2nd Ave., New York, NY 10003

Poets On, Box 255, Chaplin, CT 00235

Porch, Dept. of English, Arizona State Univ., Tempe, AZ 85281

Portland Review, P. O. Box 751, Portland, OR 97207

Positively Prince Street, 777 Duke St., Alexandria, VA 22314

Samuel Powell Publishing Co., 2125½ I St., Sacramento, CA 95816

Prarie Schooner, 201 Andrews, Univ. of Nebraska, Lincoln, NE 68588

Praxis, P. O. Box 1280, Santa Monica, CA 90406

Prescott Street Press, 407 Postal Bldg., Portland, OR 97204

Press Pacifica, P. O. Box 47, Kailua, HI 96734

Primary Press, P. O. Box 105-A, Parker Ford, PA 19457

Primavera, Univ. of Chicago, 1212 E. 59 St., Chicago, IL 60637

Printed Editions, P. O. Box 26, West Glover, VT 05875

Prison, P. O. Box 12334, Portland, OR 97212

Ptolemy, 455-1 Seneca Trail, Rt. 4, Browns Mills, NJ 08015

Pulp, c/o H. Sage, 720 Greenwich St., New York, NY 10014

Quarterly Review of Literature, 26 Haslet Ave., Princeton, NJ 08540

Quarterly West, Univ. of Utah, Salt Lake City, UT 84112

Quarto, Columbia University, New York, NY 10028

Racoon, 323 Hodges St., Memphis, TN 38111

Rainy Day Books, 2812 W. 53rd St., Fairway, KS 66205

The Rather Press, 3200 Guido St., Oakland, CA 94602

Read Street, 80 E. San Francisco, Suite # 10, Santa Fe, NM 87501

Realities Library, 2480 Escalonia Ct., San Jose, CA 95121

Red Cedar Review, 325 Morril Hall, Dept. of English, Michigan State Univ., East Lansing, MI 48824

Red Earth Press, P. O. Box 26641, Albuquerque, NM 87125

Red Herring Press, 1209 W. Oregon, Urbana, IL 61801

Release Press, 411 Clinton St., Brooklyn, NY 11231

Richmond Literature and Historical Quarterly, P. O. Box 12263, Richmond, VA 23241

Rocky Ledge, 723 19th St., Boulder, CO 80302

Roof, c/o Sherry, 300 Bowery, New York, NY 10012
Ruhtra, P. O. Box 12, Boyes Hot Springs, CA 95416

S & S Press, P. O. Box 5931, Austin, TX 78763
Sackbut Review, 2510 E. Webster Pl., Milwaukee, WI 53211
St. Andrews Review and St. Andrews Press, Laurinburg, NC 28352
Salthouse Mining Company, 1562 Jones Dr., Ann Arbor, MI 48105
San Francisco Arts and Letters, P. O. Box 99894, San Francisco, CA 94109
Sands, 7170 Briar Cove Dr., Dallas, TX 75240
San Francisco Review of Books, 2140 Vallejo St., San Francisco, CA 94123
Scarf Press, 58 E. 83rd St., New York, NY 10028
Thomas Schmidt, 3238 Hewitt Ave., Aspen Hill, MD 20906
SCOP Publications, 5821 Swarthmore Dr., College Park, ND 20740
Sea Horse Press, 307 W. 11th St., New York, NY 10014
Second Coming Press, P. O. Box 31249, San Francisco, CA 94131
Second Wave, 75 Kneeland St., Boston, MA 02111
Seems, c/o K. Elder, Lakeland College, Sheboygan, WI 53081
Seneca Review, Hobart & William Smith College, Geneva, NY 14416
Seven Buffalos Press (Proud Harvest), Box 214, Big Timber, MT 59011
Sewanee Review, Univ. of The South. Sewanee, TN 37375
Shankpainter—Fine Arts Work Center, 24 Pearl St., Box 565, Provincetown, MA 02657
The Sheep Meadow Press, 145 Central Park W., New York, NY 10023
Sheba Review Literary Magazine for the Arts, 86 Loose Creek, MO 65054
Shenandoah, P. O. Box 722, Lexington, VA 24450
Sibyl-Child Press, P. O. Box 1773, Hyattsville, MD 20788
Silverfish Review, P. O. Box 3541, Eugene, OR 97403
Sing Heavenly Muse, P. O. Box 14027, Minneapolis, MN 55414
Skullpolish, c/o American School of Tangier, 149 Rue Christophe Clomb Tanger, Maroc
Skywriting 9—Blue Mt. Press, 511 Campbell St., Kalamazoo, MI 49007

Slough Press, Box 370, Edgewood, TX 75117

Slow Loris Press, 923 Highview St., Pittsburg, PA 15206

The Small Pond Magazine, 10 Overland Dr., Stratford, CT 06497

The Small Press, Box 236, Ellsworth, IA 50075

The Smith—The Generalist Association, Inc., 5 Beekman St., New York, NY 10038

Snapdragon, College of Letters and Science, Univ. of Idaho, Moscow, ID 83843

Snow Press, P. O. Box 427, Morton Grove, IL 60053

So & So, 1730 Carleton, Berkeley, CA 94703

Solo Press, 750 Nipomo, San Luis Obispo, CA 93401

Some, 309 W. 104th St., #9D, New York, NY 10025

Some Other Magazine, 47 Hazen Ct., Wayne, NJ 07470

Soundings/East, Salem State College, Salem, MA 01970

South Carolina Review, Dept. of English, Clemson Univ., Clemson, SC 29631

South Dakota Review, P. O. Box 11, Univ. Exchange, Vermillion, SD 57069

Southern Exposure, P. O. Box 230, Chapel Hill, NC 27514

Southern Libertarian Messenger, P. O. Box 1245, Florence, SC 29503

Southern Poetry Review, Dept. of English, Univ. of North Carolina, Charlotte, NC 28223

Southwest Review Southern Methodist Univ., Dallas, TX 75275

Southwestern Review, P. O. Box 44691, Lafayette, LA 70504

Sparrow Press/Vagrom Chap Books, 103 Waldron St., West Lafayette, IN 47514

Spectrum, Univ. of California, Santa Barbara, CA 93106

The Spirit That Moves Us Press, P. O. Box 1585, Iowa City, IA 52240

The Spoon River Quarterly, P. O. Box 1443, Peoria, IL 61655

Sproing, 1150 St. Paul St., Denver, CO 80206

The Stone, 3978 26th St., San Francisco, CA 94131

Stone Country, 20 Lorraine Rd., Madison, NJ 07040

Stony Hills, Box 715, Newburyport, MA 01950

Story Press, 7370 South Shore Dr., Chicago, IL 60649

Story Quarterly, 820 Ridge Rd., Highland Park, IL 60035

Street Press, Box 555, Port Jefferson, NY 11777

Stroker Magazine, 110 St. Marks Place #8, New York, NY 10009

The Sun, 412 West Rosemary St., Chapel Hill, NC 27514

Sun & Moon Press, 5440 Hartwick Rd., #418, College Park, MD 20740

Sun Dog, Dept. of English, FSU, 330 Williams St., Tallahassee, FL 32306

Sunbury, Box 274 Jerome Ave. Station, Bronx, NY 10468

Sun-Scape Publications, P. O. Box 42725, Tucson, AZ 85733

The Sunstone Press, P. O. Box 2321, Sante Fe, NM 87501

Suntracks, Dept. of English, Univ. of Arizona, Tucson, AZ 85721

Swift River, Box 264, Leverett, MA 01054

Tamarack, c/o A. Hoey, 909 Westcott St., Syracuse, NY 13210

Tamarisk, c/o D. Barone, 188 Forest Ave., Ramsey, NJ 07446

Tar River Poetry, Dept. of English, East Carolina Univ., Greenville, NC 27834

Tell Us c/o L. Bunch 1005 Rhode Island, Lawrence, KS 66044

Tendril Magazine, Box 512, Green Harbor, MA 02041

That New Publishing Company, 1525 Eielson St., Fairbanks, AK 99701

13th Moon, Inc., Box 3, Inwood Station, New York, NY 10034

THIS, c/o B. Watten, 1004 Hampshire St., San Francisco, CA 94110

Thunder Mountain Review, P. O. Box 11126, Birmingham, AL 35202

Time Capsule Magazine, G.P.O. Box 1185, New York, NY 10001

Tinderbox, 334 Molasses Lane, Mt. Pleasant, SC 29464

Toothpaste Press, P. O. Box 546, Westbranch, IA 52358

Total Abandon, P. O. Box 1207, Ashland, OR 97520

Touchstone, P. O. Drawer 42331, Houston, TX 77042

Toyon, Dept. of English, Humboldt State Univ., Arcata, CA

Trans-Traffic Corporation, 666 Washington Rd., Pittsburgh, PA 15228

Treacle Press, 437 Springtown Rd., New Paltz, NY 12561

Tree Line Books, P. O. Box 1062, Radio City Station, New York, NY 10019

Trek-Cir Publications, Box 898, Valley Forge, PA 19481

Trellis, P. O. Box 656, Morgantown, WV 26505

Trempealeau Press, 800 Hillcrest Dr., Santa Fe, NM 87501

Tri Quarterly, Northwestern Univ., Evanston, IL 60201

Truly Fine Press, P. O. Box 891, Bemidji, MN 56601

Tuumba Press, 2639 Russell St., Berkeley, CA 94705

Two Hands News, 1125 W. Webster, Chicago, IL 60614

Unicorn Foundation, P. O. Box 3307, Greensboro, NC 27402
United Artists, Flanders Rd., Henniker, NH 03242
Univ. of Colorado Publications Service, 364 Willard Administrative Center, Univ. of Colorado, Boulder, CO 80309
Unmuzzled Ox, 105 Hudson St., New York, NY 10013
USI Worksheets, Farm Lane, Roosevelt, NJ 08555

D. J. Valenti—Media Services, P. O. Box 2056, Wilkes-Barre, PA 18703
Van Dyk Publications, 10216 Takilma Rd., Cave Junction, OR 97523
Vega Magazine, 252 N. 16 St., Bloomfield, NJ 07003
Vile, 1183 Church St., San Francisco, CA 94114
Vintage, c/o Lucille Cyphers, 111 Lincoln Pl., Boulder, CO 80302
The Virginia Quarterly Review, Univ. of Virginia, Charlottesville, VA
Volcano Gazette, P. O. Box 189, Volcano, Hawaii 96785
The Volcano Review, P. O. Box 142, Volcano, CA 95689

The Walrus Said, P. O. Box 5904, St. Louis, MO 63134
Washington Review, Box 50132, Washington, DC 20004
Washington Writers' Publishing House, P. O. Box 50068, Washington, DC 20004
Waves, Rm. 357 Stong College, York Univ., 4700 Keele St., Downsview, Ont., M3J IP3 Canada
Webster Review, Webster College, Webster Groves, MO 63119
West Branch, Dept. of English, Bucknell Univ., Lewisburg, PA 17837
West Coast Poetry Review, 1335 Dartmouth Dr., Reno, NV 89509
West Hills Review: Walt Whitman Journal, 246 Walt Whitman Rd., Huntington Station, NY 11746
Western Humanities Review, Univ. of Utah, Salt Lake City, UT 84112
Westwind Press, Route 1, Box 208, Farmington, WV 26571
Whimsy Press, 1822 Northview Dr., Arnold, MO 63010
White Ewe Press, P. O. Box 996, Adelphi, MD 20783
Whatever Publishing, Box 3073, Berkeley, CA 94703
Willow Springs Magazine, P. O. Box 1063, Cheney, WA 99004

Wind/Literary Journal, RFD 1, Box 809K, Pikeville, KY 41501

The Windless Orchard, Purdue Dept. of English, Ft. Wayne, IN 46805

Wings Press, R2 Box 325, Belfast, ME 04915

Wisconsin Review, Dempsey Hall, Univ. of Wisconsin, Oshkosh, WI 54901

Wisdom House, 4030 Raleigh Ave., S., Minneapolis, MN 55416

Wolfsong Publications, 6930 Washington Ave., Racine, WI 53406

Woman's Choice, P. O. Box 480, Berkeley, CA 94701

Women Talking/Women Listening, P. O. Box 2414, Dublin, CA 94566

Woolmer/Brotherson LTD Pubs., Revere, PA 18953

The Word Shop, 3737 5 Ave., Suite 203, San Diego, CA 92103

The Word Works, Inc., P. O. Box 4054, Washington, DC 20015

The Workingmans Press, P. O. Box 12486, Seattle, WA 98111

Workspace Loft, Inc., 4 Elm St., Albany, NY 12202

The Wormwood Review, P. O. Box 8840, Stockton, CA 95204

Writers West Books, Dept. of English, Univ. of Colorado, Colorado Springs, CO 80907

X; A Journal of The Arts, Box 2648, Harrisburg, PA 17105

The Yale Review, 1902A Yale Station, New Haven, CT 06520

Y'Bird, 2140 Shattuck Ave., Berkeley, CA 94704

Yellow Press, 2394 Blue Island, Chicago, IL 60608

Yellow Umbrella Press, 2 Chelmsford St., Chelmsford, MA 01824

Z Press, Calais, VT 05648

Zahir Magazine, P. O. Box 75, Newburyport, MA 01950

Zirkus, Calhoun College, 189 Elm St., New Haven, CT 06502

🔥 🔥 🔥

INDEX

TO THE FIRST FIVE

PUSHCART PRIZE VOLUMES

The following is a listing in alphabetical order by author's last name of works reprinted in the first five *Pushcart Prize* editions.

PARTING SHOT
 Walter Abish   III, 261

ICE
 Al   IV, 81

THE WALTZ
 Vicente Aleixandre   III, 106

THE DEATH OF YURY GALANSKOV
 Amnesty International   I, 22

OF LIVING BELFRY AND RAMPART: ON AMERICAN LITERARY
MAGAZINES SINCE 1950
 Michael Anania   V, 138

CITY JOYS
 Jack Anderson   I, 374

LIVES OF THE SAINTS, PART I
 Jon Anderson   II, 73

KEY LARGO
 Bruce Andrews   III, 510

EVEN AFTER A MACHINE IS DISMANTLED, IT
CONTINUES TO OPERATE, WITH OR WITHOUT PURPOSE
 Ascher/Straus Collective   III, 402

ALL KINDS OF CARESSES
 John Ashbery   II, 257

THE MAN FROM MARS
 Margaret Atwood   III, 490

TRANQUILLITY BASE
    Asa Baber   V, 227

LATE TRACK
    Jane Bailey   I, 274

DOING GOOD
    John Balaban   III, 445

WISH BOOK
    Bo Ball   V, 124

THE CHICAGO ODYSSEY
    Jim Barnes   V, 374

LOT'S WIFE
    Kristine Batey   IV, 129

AUTUMN EVENING
    John H. Beauvais   I, 352

FIVE AND TEN
    Marvin Bell   V, 432

SOME QUESTIONS AND ANSWERS
    Saul Bellow   I, 295

BEAUTIFUL PEOPLE
    John Bennett   I, 403

VARIATIONS ON *THE MOUND OF CORPSES IN THE SNOW*
    Stephen Berg   I, 144

THE INFINITE PASSION OF EXPECTATION
    Gina Berriault   V, 360

DON'T YOU EVER SEE THE BUTTERFLIES
    Ana Blandiana   II, 256

STONES
    Michael Blumenthal   V, 358

BROKEN PORTRAITURE
    Bruce Boston   I, 346

THE LITERATURE OF AWE
    David Bosworth   V, 244

THE IRON TABLE
    Jane Bowles   III, 512

THE STONECUTTER'S HORSES
    Robert Bringhurst   IV, 495

INTRO
    Harold Brodkey   I, 419

ONE SPRING
    David Bromige   V, 156

SHOWDOWN
  Michael Brondoli   V, 458
BAD POEMS
  Michael Dennis Browne   I, 324
"TALK TO ME BABY"
  Michael Dennis Browne   III, 222
GETTING FREEDOM HIGH
  Wesley Brown   III, 87
THE SHARK AND THE BUREAUCRAT
  Vlada Bulatovic-Vib   V, 356
LOVERS
  Jerry Bumpus   II, 358
SOME RECOGNITION OF THE JOSHUA LIZARD
  Robert Burlingame   III, 356
THE ESSENTIAL ELLISON
  Steve Cannon (with Ishmael Reed and Quincy Troupe   III, 465
HEART OF THE GARFISH
  Kathy Callaway   V, 219
THE NAME, THE NOSE
  Italo Calvino   II, 321
THE CARIBBEAN WRITER AND EXILE
  Jan Carew   V, 287
MENDING THE ADOBE
  Hayden Carruth   II, 505
SONG: SO OFTEN, SO LONG I HAVE THOUGHT
  Hayden Carruth   V, 397
SO MUCH WATER SO CLOSE TO HOME
  Raymond Carver   I, 50
POOR GOD
  Carolyn Cassady   III, 386
MEETING MESCALITO AT OAK HILL CEMETERY
  Lorna Dee Cervantes   IV, 183
VETERAN'S HEAD
  Diane Chapman   I, 305
WHERE THE WINGED HORSES TAKE OFF
INTO THE WILD BLUE YONDER FROM
  Kelly Cherry   II, 164
THE BREAKER
  Naomi Clark   III, 167
ANESTHETIC
  Andrei Codrescu   V, 432

PRICKSONG
    Marilyn Coffey   I, 49
THE HUMAN TABLE
    Marvin Cohen   I, 210
STEPPING BACK
    Kathleen Collins   III, 418
CRASH
    David Cope   II, 500
CONVERSATION BY THE BODY'S LIGHT
    Jane Cooper   III, 352
THREE DAY NEW YORK BLUES
    Jayne Cortez   II, 471
CUYLERVILLE
    Douglas Crase   II, 51
WHORES
    James Crumley   III, 427
LIKE A GOOD UNKNOWN POET
    Art Cuelho   I, 334
THE SLEEP
    Philip Dacey   II, 369
KOYUKON RIDDLE-POEMS
    Richard Dauenhauer   III, 308
MOTHERS
    Lydia Davis   III, 443
FOR PAPA (AND MARCUS GARVEY)
    Thadious M. Davis   IV, 289
ANOTHER MARGOT CHAPTER
    R. C. Day   IV, 332
SOME CARRY AROUND THIS
    Susan Strayer Deal   IV, 493
THE ELEPHANT
    Carlos Drummond De Andrade   I, 342
CIVILIZATION AND ISOLATION
    Vine Deloria   IV, 389
FICTION HOT AND KOOL: DILEMMAS OF THE
EXPERIMENTAL WRITER
    Morris Dickstein   I, 309
MILK IS VERY GOOD FOR YOU
    Stephen Dixon   II, 179
MONSTERFEST
    "H. Bustos Domecq"   III, 152

THE MAN WHOSE BLOOD TILTED THE EARTH
  M. R. Doty   IV, 313
THERE IS A DREAM DREAMING US
  Norman Dubie   III, 164
THE FAT GIRL
  Andre Dubus   III, 357
THE DEATH OF SUN
  William Eastlake   I, 175
THE NEIGHBORHOOD DOG
  Russell Edson   II, 308
A PUDDLE
  Larry Eigner   III, 398
THE COLD IN MIDDLE LATITUDES
  John Engels   V, 550
THE MAN WHO INVENTED
THE AUTOMATIC JUMPING BEAN
  "El Huitlacoche"   II, 371
UNTITLED
  Loris Essary   III, 487
THE BUICKSPECIAL
  Raymond Federman   II, 402
LOWGHOST TO LOWGHOST
  Ross Feld   II, 430
THE TORTOISE
  Irving Feldman   V, 376
THE SAGE OF APPLE VALLEY ON LOVE
  Edward Field   II, 241
MIENTRAS DURE VIDA, SOBRA EL TIEMPO
  Carolyn Forché   II, 209
THE FLOWERING CACTI
  Gene Fowler   I, 97
THE STUDENTS OF SNOW
  Jane Flanders   V, 546
THE JUGGLER
  Siv Cedering Fox   II, 459
A CHRONICLE OF LOVE
  H. E. Francis   I, 31
TWO LIVES
  H. E. Francis   V, 524
BLACK MONEY
  Tess Gallagher   I, 276

THE RITUAL OF MEMORIES
  Tess Gallagher   IV, 178
EVERYONE KNOWS WHOM THE SAVED ENVY
  James Galvin   III, 249
THE LOVER
  Eugene K. Garber   II, 288
MORAL FICTION
  John Gardner   III, 52
I WISH YOU WOULDN'T
  William Gass   I, 98
RICH
  Ellen Gilchrist   IV, 502
AT DAWN IN WINTER
  John Glowney   I, 216
THE DREAM OF MOURNING
  Louise Glück   III, 169
THOUGH IT LOOKS LIKE A THROAT IT IS NOT
  Patricia Goedicke   II, 91
THE TENNIS-GAME
  Paul Goodman   II, 387
I WAS TAUGHT THREE
  Jorie Graham   V, 316
I COME HOME LATE AT NIGHT
  Patrick Worth Gray   I, 214
HORST WESSEL
  C. W. Gusewelle   III, 228
LETTER FOR A DAUGHTER
  Lorrie Goldensohn   III, 220
NOW I AM MARRIED
  Mary Gordon   I, 227
THE AIR BETWEEN TWO DESERTS
  Marea Gordett   V, 545
THE POLITICS OF ANTI-REALISM
  Gerald Graff   IV, 203
BY THE POOL
  Allen Grossman   V, 221
MY VEGETABLE LOVE
  Barbara Grossman   V, 347
MY WORK IN CALIFORNIA
  James B. Hall   IV, 267

FARMING
    Handsome Lake, transcribed by Joseph Bruchac   V, 499

EIRON *EYES*
    William Harmon   V, 503

MADE CONNECTIONS
    Michael Harper   IV, 352

CHINATOWN SONATA
    Yuki Hartman   III, 354

THE PARTY
    James Hashim   II, 258

LOWELL'S GRAVEYARD
    Robert Hass   III, 332

SWEENEY ASTRAY
    Seamus Heaney   III, 251

THE OTTER
    Seamus Heaney   V, 84

MORAL CAKE
    Don Hendrie Jr.   III, 76

SNAKE
    Anne Herbert   III, 281

THE DAISY DOLLS
    Felisberto Hernández   IV, 88

THE BIG STORE
    Alan V. Hewat   II, 95

ANONYMOUS COURTESAN IN A JADE SHROUD
    Brenda Hillman   IV, 354

MARATHON OF MARMALADE
    George Hitchcock   V, 154

SILENCE
    Michael Hogan   I, 273

SPRING
    Michael Hogan   I, 30

BLUE WINE
    John Hollander   V, 222

PROTEUS
    Judith Hoover   IV, 368

MEDICINE BOW
    Richard Hugo   II, 145

THE WU GENERAL WRITES FROM FAR AWAY
    Christopher Howell   III, 85

ALCOHOL AND POETRY: JOHN BERRYMAN AND
THE BOOZE TALKING
    Lewis Hyde   I, 71

SOME FOOD WE COULD NOT EAT: GIFT EXCHANGE
AND THE IMAGINATION
    Lewis Hyde   V, 165

WHERE THE RECORD PLAYS
    Gyula Illyés   III, 304

THE PENSION GRILLPARZER
    John Irving   II, 25

THE CROW IS MISCHIEF
    Laura Jensen   III, 459

MENNONITE FARM WIFE
    Janet Kauffman   V, 155

LAWRENCE AT TAOS
    Shirley Kaufman   IV, 316

LIVING WITH ANIMALS
    Margaret Kent   IV, 547

INSTITUTIONAL CONTROL OF INTERPRETATION
    Frank Kermode   V, 107

PRETEND DINNERS
    W. P. Kinsella   V, 424

RUNNING AWAY FROM HOME
    Carolyn Kizer   IV, 435

OUT-AND-DOWN PATTERN
    William Kloefkorn   V, 501

WE FREE SINGERS BE
    Etheridge Knight   II, 93

MY MOTHER'S LIST OF NAMES
    Bill Knott   III, 460

FROM "THE DUPLICATIONS"
    Kenneth Koch   II, 382

CLOE MORGAN
    Karl Kopp   I, 325

IN IOWA
    Cinda Kornblum   II, 503

OLYMPIAN PROGRESS
    Richard Kostelanetz   V, 456

ANOTHER FORM OF MARRIAGE
    Maxine Kumin   II, 347

QUINNAPOXET
  Stanley Kunitz   IV, 378
CORDIALS
  David Kranes   I, 3
HOW IT WILL BE
  Mary Lane   II, 368
THE FAMILY AS A HAVEN IN A
HEARTLESS WORLD
  Christopher Lasch   II, 194
IN ANOTHER COUNTRY
  James Laughlin   IV, 83
THE PILOT
  Naomi Lazard   I, 307
THE BEST RIDE TO NEW YORK
  Bob Levin   II, 115
THE STATION
  Miriam Levine   II, 427
A WOMAN WAKING
  Philip Levine   II, 457
THE OWNERSHIP OF THE NIGHT
  Larry Lewis   IV, 284
THEODORE ROETHKE
  James Lewisohn   II, 501
HOW ST. PETER GOT BALD
  Romulus Linney   V, 368
THE LAST ROMANTIC
  Gerald Locklin   II, 461
ODE TO SENILITY
  Phillip Lopate   II, 131
A VISION EXPRESSED BY
A SERIES OF FALSE STATEMENTS
  John Love   IV, 291
A WOMAN IN LOVE WITH A BOTTLE
  Barbara Lovell   IV, 356
BARRETT & BROWNING
  Thomas Lux   II, 463
ON THE BIG WIND
  David Madden   V, 377
FUNERAL
  Clarence Major   I, 275

A LETTER HOME
        Adrianne Marcus   II, 498
WHITMAN'S SONG OF MYSELF:
HOMOSEXUAL DREAM AND VISION
        Robert K. Martin   I, 379
THE SURVIVORS
        Dan Masterson   III, 69
HIM & ME
        Susan MacDonald   II, 212
MESSINGHAUSEN, 1945
        Ian Macmillan   II, 464
IS DON JUAN ALIVE AND WELL?
        Arnold J. Mandell M.D.   I, 199
GRANDMOTHER (1895–1928)
        Cleopatra Mathis   IV, 500
NUMBER SEVENTEEN
        George Mattingly   I, 209
CARLTON FISK IS MY IDEAL
        Bernadette Mayer   III, 485
WHAT LIGHT THERE IS
        Mekeel McBride   III, 399
DAVID
        David McCann   III, 260
THE GRIOTS WHO KNEW BRER FOX
        Colleen J. McElroy   I, 19
TRINC: PRAISES II
        Thomas McGrath   V, 268
BREATH
        Heather McHugh   V, 342
RETARDED CHILDREN IN THE SNOW
        Michael McMahon   I, 400
FOR JOHANNES BOBROWSKI
        Sandra McPherson   V, 456
THE WEEK THE DIRIGIBLE CAME
        Jay Meek   II, 470
THE HAT IN THE SWAMP
        Paul Metcalf   IV, 472
JIMMY PASTA
        Henry Miller   II, 243

HEY, IS ANYONE LISTENING?
    Stephen Minot   III, 239

CONTEMPORARY POETRY AND
THE METAPHORS FOR THE POEM
    Charles Molesworth   IV, 319

SHORT STORIES
    Howard Moss   II, 354

LECTURING MY DAUGHTER IN HER FIRST FALL RAIN
    Tom Montag   I, 69

XENIA
    Eugenio Montale   I, 439 (cloth ed. only)

THE END OF SCIENCE FICTION
    Lisel Mueller   II, 49

THE RED CROSS NIGHT
    Victor Muravin   II, 78

IDOLATRY
    Carol Muske   V, 422

A RENEWAL OF THE WORD
    Barbara Myerhoff   IV, 48

THE U.S. CHINESE IMMIGRANT'S BOOK
OF THE ART OF SEX
    Opal Nations   II, 310

JOHNNY APPLESEED
    Susan Schaefer Neville   IV, 486

SONG OF THE SOAPSTONE CARVER
    Sheila Nickerson   I, 399

WASTE OF TIMELESSNESS
    Anaïs Nin   III, 312

THE HALLUCINATION
    Joyce Carol Oates   I, 404

GOING AFTER CACCIATO
    Tim O'Brien   II, 53

THE BOY SCOUT
    David Ohle   II, 464

WINTER SLEEP
    Mary Oliver   IV, 232

ENCOUNTERS WITH EZRA POUND
    Charles Olson   I, 353

PREPARING TO SLEEP
    Gregory Orr   II, 504

THE NERVES OF A MIDWIFE:
CONTEMPORARY AMERICAN WOMEN'S POETRY
    Alicia Ostriker   IV, 45

PLOWING WITH ELEPHANTS
    Lon Otto   IV, 181

A LIBERAL'S AUSCHWITZ
    Cynthia Ozick   I, 149

LEVITATION
    Cynthia Ozick   V, 29

STEELMILL BLUES
    Steve Packard   I, 278

WOLFBANE FANE
    George Payerle   III, 318

HURRY
    Octavio Paz   I, 95

LAUGHTER AND PENITENCE
    Octavio Paz   II, 146

WRAPPED MINDS
    David Perkins   V, 212

UNTITLED
    Laura Pershin   I, 271

MAKING A NAME FOR MYSELF
    Joyce Peseroff   III, 400

TO DANCE
    Mary Peterson   III, 143

SWEETHEARTS
    Jayne Anne Phillips   II, 317

HOME
    Jayne Anne Phillips   IV, 29

LECHERY
    Jayne Anne Phillips   IV, 381

THE STONE CRAB: A LOVE POEM
    Robert Phillips   IV, 131

MY MOTHER'S NOVEL
    Marge Piercy   III, 488

TURTLE
    John Pilcrow   III, 458

JEAN RHYS: A REMEMBRANCE
    David Plante   V, 43

LIVING ON THE LOWER EAST SIDE . . .
    Allen Planz   II, 336

WILDFLOWER
    Stanley Plumly   IV, 233

POPOCATÉPETL   I, 174

SWEETNESS, A THINKING MACHINE
    Joe Ashby Porter   IV, 306

KING'S DAY
    T. E. Porter   II, 214

FROM *KISS OF THE SPIDER WOMAN*
    Manuel Puig   IV, 400

FATHER OF THE BRIDE
    Jack Pulaski   I, 218

EXPERIMENTAL LANGUAGE
    Tony Quagliano   I, 333

WEST VIRGINIA SLEEP SONG
    Ruthellen Quillen   III, 108

RABBIT TRANCE
    Jarold Ramsey   II, 191

TAKE ME BACK TO TULSA
    David Ray   I, 197

FIVE BLACK POETS: HISTORY, CONSCIOUSNESS,
LOVE AND HARSHNESS
    Eugene B. Redmond   I, 154

THE ESSENTIAL ELLISON
    Ishmael Reed (with Steve Cannon and Quincy Troupe)   III, 465

AMERICAN POETRY: LOOKING FOR A CENTER
    Ishmael Reed   IV, 524

THE BIOGRAPHY MAN
    Gary Reilly   IV, 441

THE DOG
    Avrom Reyzen   I, 115

POWER
    Adrienne Rich   I, 438

VESUVIUS AT HOME: THE POWER OF EMILY DICKINSON
    Adrienne Rich   III, 170

MEETING COOT
    William Pitt Root   III, 227

"ARMED FOR WAR": NOTES ON THE ANTITHETICAL
CRITICISM OF HAROLD BLOOM
    Alvin Rosenfeld   III, 372

AMSTERDAM STREET SCENE, 1972
    Raphael Rudnick   V, 318
PIG 311
    Margaret Ryan   IV, 522
THE PURE LONELINESS
    Michael Ryan   II, 144
LITERATURE AND ECOLOGY:
AN EXPERIMENT IN ECOCRITICISM
    William Rueckert   IV, 142
FROM A JOURNEY THROUGH THE LAND OF ISRAEL
    Pinchas Sadeh   III, 110
THE DEPORTATION OF SOLZHENITSYN
    Russian *samizdat* underground   II, 339
THE TRIAL OF ROZHDESTVOV
    Russian samizdat underground   IV, 549
CODEX WHITE BLIZZARD
    Ed Sanders   V, 338
THE MOTHER-IN-LAW
    Ed Sanders   I, 248
THEY SAID
    Reg Saner   II, 395
THE FIRE AT THE CATHOLIC CHURCH
    John Sanford   II, 473
MELANCHOLY DIVORCEE
    Sherod Santos   V, 86
THE MONK'S CHIMERA
    Teo Savory   II, 396
EARLY WINTER
    Max Schott   IV, 239
THE BANK ROBBERY
    Steve Schutzman   II, 464
SONG
    James Schuyler   II, 429
"ALL DRESSED UP BUT NO PLACE TO GO":
THE BLACK WRITER AND HIS AUDIENCE DURING
THE HARLEM RENAISSANCE
    Charles Scruggs   III, 283
THESE WOMEN
    Christine Schutt   IV, 473
ROUGH STRIFE
    Lynne Sharon Schwartz   III, 29

NOTHING VERY MUCH HAS HAPPENED HERE
    Rhoda Schwartz   I, 147

THE DAY OF THE NIGHT
    James Scully   I, 377

THE ANGEL AND THE MERMAID
    Ricardo da Silveira Lobo Sternberg   III, 307

THE PEARS
    Pamela Stewart   V, 435

ELEGY
    David St. John   IV, 176

THE MONSTER
    Ronald Sukenick   I, 255

THE GARMENT OF SADNESS
    Barbara Szerlip   II, 400

EMBARKMENT
    Hugh Seidman   III, 425

TOUSSAINT
    Ntozake Shange   II, 332

BONS
    Beth Tashery Shannon   III, 73

MUSICAL SHUTTLE
    Harvey Shapiro   I, 417

I SHOW THE DAFFODILS TO THE RETARDED KIDS
    Constance Sharp   IV, 545

COLUMN BEDA
    Gerard Shyne   V, 89

DEER DANCE/FOR YOUR RETURN
    Leslie Marmon Silko   III, 49

SITTING UP, STANDING, TAKING STEPS
    Ron Silliman   IV, 346

A COMFORT SPELL
    Maxine Silverman   III, 423

A SUITCASE STRAPPED WITH A ROPE
    Charles Simic   V, 198

JEFFREY, BELIEVE ME
    Jane Smiley   IV, 299

SNOW OWL
    Dave Smith   IV, 127

FROM LAUGHING WITH ONE EYE
    Gjertrud Schnackenberg Smyth   IV, 43

THE GIRL WHO LOVED HORSES
    Elizabeth Spencer   V, 320

A POSTSCRIPT TO THE BERKELEY RENAISSANCE
    Jack Spicer   I, 436

A SACRIFICE OF DOGS
    William Sprunt   III, 84

THINGS THAT HAPPEN WHERE
THERE AREN'T ANY PEOPLE
    William Stafford   IV, 380

RETURN OF THE GENERAL
    Jerry Stahl   II, 485

BATHROOM WALLS
    Maura Stanton   III, 421

THE NEW CONSCIOUSNESS,
THE NEA AND POETRY TODAY
    Felix Stefanile   V, 491

VESTIGES
    Meredith Steinbach   II, 133

PEACE IN THE NEAR EAST
    Gerald Stern   I, 146

I REMEMBER GALILEO
    Gerald Stern   V, 88

GIANT STEPS
    John Taggart   V,

GHOSTS LIKE THEM
    Shirley Ann Taggart   IV, 161

TO MY DAUGHTER
    Kathryn Terrill   II, 162

LYNDA VAN CATS
    Alexander Theroux   I, 139

THE ESSENTIAL ELLISON
    Quincy Troupe (with Steve Cannon and Ishmael Reed)   III, 465

THE ARTIFICIAL FAMILY
    Anne Tyler   I, 11

TO ED SISSMAN
    John Updike   IV, 311

THE SPANISH IMAGE OF DEATH
    Cesar Vallejo   IV, 287

THE SPRING
    H. L. Van Brunt   I, 195

LETTERS FROM A FATHER
 Mona Van Duyn   IV, 235
ARIZONA MOVIES
 Michael Van Walleghen   II, 279
SWEET TALK
 Stephanie Vaughn   V, 201
FORGIVE US . . .
 George Venn   IV, 470
FROM THE DEATH OF LOVE: A SATANIC ESSAY IN
MÖBIUS FORM
 Richard Vine   V, 405
THE LIFE THAT DISAPPEARED
 Roman Vishniac   III, 512
             (cloth only)
SCENES FROM THE HOMEFRONT
 Sara Vogan   V, 437
STYLE THREE and STYLE FIVE
 William Wantling   I, 328
THE ONLY POEM
 Robert Penn Warren   V, 548
JOSEFA KANKOVSKA
 Barbara Watkins   V, 403
MISSING THE TRAIL
 David Wagoner   I, 10
WHISPER SONG
 David Wagoner   V, 823
TWO STRANGE STORIES
 Robert Walser   III, 441
VICKIE LOANS-ARROW, FORT YATES, NO. DAK, 1970
 Marnie Walsh   II, 284
LOST COLONY
 Marvin Weaver   I, 376
TEMPLE NEAR QUANG TRI, NOT ON THE MAP
 Bruce Weigl   V, 199
A JEAN-MARIE COOKBOOK
 Jeff Weinstein   IV, 185
FALLING TOWARD THANKSGIVING
 David Weissmann   I, 401
SCIENCE AND THE COMPULSIVE PROGRAMMER
 Joseph Weizenbaum   I, 122

NIGHT FLIGHT TO STOCKHOLM
 Dallas Wiebe   IV, 133
FAITH
 Ellen Wilbur   V, 275
HOW THE HEN SOLD HER EGGS TO THE STINGY PRIEST
 Nancy Willard   III, 306
DREAM
 John Willson   IV, 546
THE UNITED STATES
 Robley Wilson, Jr.   III, 197
STATIONERY, CARDS, NOTIONS, BOOKS
 Harold Witt   I, 418
THE OTHER FACE OF BREAD
 "The Workers University"   III, 208
PORTRAIT OF THE ARTIST WITH LI PO
 Charles Wright   V, 315
YOUNG WOMEN AT CHARTRES
 James Wright   V, 136
AFRIKAAN BOTTLES
 G. K. Wuori   I, 336
MICHAEL AT SIXTEEN MONTHS
 Al Young   V, 346
THE TEARING OF THE SKIN
 Yvonne   III, 464
WITH THE REST OF MY BODY
 Christine Zawadiwsky   II, 192
STORY
 Patricia Zelver   V, 399
UTAH DIED FOR YOUR SINS
 Max Zimmer   III, 135
ZIMMER DRUNK AND ALONE, DREAMING OF
OLD FOOTBALL GAMES
 Paul Zimmer   II, 72
GRANDPARENTS
 Howard Zimmon   I, 245